THE CHINA CARD

IS A

"A young lawyer [...] Nixon's White House [...] working as Chou En-lai's man in Washington. Once Nixon shocks the world by flying to China, both the president and the premier regard the lawyer as dispensable. But the lawyer has his own China card to play.

"That's not a bad plot for a political thriller, especially when the author throws in a beautiful aide to Chou and a shoot-'em-up escapade in which the lawyer gets caught in the crossfire of Mao's Cultural Revolution.

"But what makes *The China Card* irresistible is author John Ehrlichman's close-up look at real-life characters . . . Ehrlichman's portrayal of a Nixon who can't figure out how to work a ballpoint pen, of a Kissinger obsessed with vanity, of a Haig who actually says at one point, 'I'm in charge here.'"

—*St. Louis Post-Dispatch*

*　　　*　　　*

"The plot is great in this book, the look at power devastating."

—*Houston Chronicle*

*　　　*　　　*

Please turn this page for more praise from the press and other authors for *The China Card*.

BOOKS BY JOHN EHRLICHMAN

THE CHINA CARD*
WITNESS TO POWER: The Nixon Years
THE WHOLE TRUTH
THE COMPANY

*Published by
WARNER BOOKS

THE CHINA CARD

A novel

JOHN EHRLICHMAN

WARNER BOOKS

A Warner Communications Company

WARNER BOOKS EDITION

The author is grateful for permission to reprint the poem "Theory" by Wallace Stevens, copyright 1923 and renewed 1951 by Wallace Stevens. Reprinted from *The Collected Poems of Wallace Stevens*, by permission of Alfred A. Knopf, Inc.

This Warner Books Edition is published by arrangement with Simon & Schuster, A Division of Simon & Schuster, Inc., Simon & Schuster Building, Rockefeller Center, 1230 Avenue of the Americas, New York, N.Y. 10020

Cover design by Jackie Merri Meyer
Cover Illustration by Paul Bacon

Warner Books, Inc.
666 Fifth Avenue
New York, N.Y. 10103

 A Warner Communications Company

Printed in the United States of America

First Warner Books Printing: August, 1987

10 9 8 7 6 5 4 3 2 1

FOR LILLIAN CATHERINE DANIELSON EHRLICHMAN
WITH MY LOVE.

Author's Note

This novel rests upon a foundation of fact: China's Cultural Revolution and the *rapprochement* between the United States and China, for example, are important events which are depicted within. These events, the leaders and Administration officials of the United States and China who were involved in them, and the political climate generally are the factual scenery before which this fictional drama is played. It is, however, a novel—the story of Matthew Thompson and what happened to him during those events. Matthew Thompson is a fictional character. Thus, his conversations with real persons—Richard Nixon, Chou En-lai, and Henry Kissinger, for example—are wholly fictional. What happened to Matthew Thompson is fictional. What real people said to or about him, did or threatened to do to or about him, is the product of my imagination. Glenna Harrison and Matt's other friends, lovers, and family are also fictional. The outcome of the novel and all related events are also imaginary, as are the conversations, thoughts, and actions (but for the widely known, historically documented actions) of Henry Kissinger, Alexander Haig, Chou En-lai, Richard Nixon, and the other real people. These fictional conversations, thoughts and actions are the product of my imagination, created for the sake of the novel's atmosphere and plot.

THEORY

I am what is around me.
Women understand this.
One is not a duchess
A hundred yards from a carriage.

These, then are portraits:
A black vestibule;
A high bed sheltered by curtains.

These are merely instances.
                    —WALLACE STEVENS

PROLOGUE

The White House

• FALL, 1974 •

"We did some very good things, Henry. I wonder if anyone will remember them."

"Of course they will, Mr. President. Within a historical perspective you will be seen as a strong President who brought the nation through difficult times."

"I wonder; people seem to recall only the worst about a President. Look at what they did to Wilson. Won't the historians dump me in with Harding and Grant? Do you think they will?"

"How can they, sir? There is SALT and China and an honorable end to the Viet Nam war. Achievements like that will not be overlooked."

"Perhaps you're right, Henry. China is the big one that can't be taken away from us, isn't it? We did that, didn't we? From now on the world is changed because the American President holds the China card in his hand. They have to give us credit for that, don't they, Henry?"

Henry Kissinger nodded slowly. It was idle, Kissinger reflected, to be concerned with history's ultimate judgment at the moment when the White House was about to collapse around their heads. "To a great extent history will be what we make it, Mr. President," Kissinger replied. "You will write. I will write. Our colleagues will write. We can do much to direct the historians' vision."

"That's true, isn't it?" the President said. "We must be very certain that our friends are encouraged to be among the first to write. What can we do about the others, though? What can we do about Thompson?"

"Not much, Mr. President, beyond what we have done. Thompson is gone. Wherever he is, he fears the Chinese, I am sure. I doubt that he will write a book."

"Good. It's people like Thompson who could badly confuse historians about the way we opened up China."

"Yes, Mr. President, he could," Henry Kissinger agreed. "He could indeed. But I think the risk is small."

PART
ONE

One

"This"—the young woman pointed—"must be filled out completely, Mr. Thompson. Every blank. And do try to be neat. Make it so I can read it. Your biography form becomes a permanent part of your personnel file. Remember that."

Matthew Thompson wondered if anyone really liked Miss Jamison. Maybe she was charming to the partners and revealed her true self only when she was talking to secretaries and young lawyers.

Thompson nodded. The light in his cubicle was not good. Miss Jamison was peering at the papers she had brought.

"I don't care if you fill out this one or not." Suzanne Jamison sniffed. "They have some athletic teams here and someone wants to know what games you play. I don't."

Thompson smiled. "I played softball when I was interning here, summer before last," he said. "We didn't do very well."

Miss Jamison tried harder to show that she didn't care. "My office will need all of this before you see Mr. Murphy at two thirty P.M.," she ordered. "You are assigned to . . ." She looked for a name on the front of the

3

file folder. "You are assigned to Eldon Carnahay; do you know him? He'll help you get settled if you need it."

"He wasn't here when I interned," Matt Thompson replied. "Is he on this floor?"

"He's in 2407, at the far end." She pointed in that direction. "My secretary is Miss Cohen. We are down in 2019. Your completion of these forms by two thirty P.M. is essential, Mr. Thompson." Suzanne Jamison tapped the papers on the metal desk top, first the short side, then the long side. She arranged them in the file folder, placed it directly in front of Thompson, stood, and curtly nodded her farewell. Thompson wasn't sure whether to stand up or not. The lady was not a lawyer, much less a partner. But a new, young lawyer has a whole universe of bosses, and Miss Jamison might be one of them. Thompson stood.

His summer boss at Nixon, Mudge, Rose, Guthrie and Alexander hadn't been a partner either. Milton Tsarsis was only a senior associate, but he'd been with the firm for about twenty years and was the Intern Supervisor. He never would be a partner, it was rumored, and no one seemed to know why; but he didn't behave as if it worried him. Matt Thompson always stood for Mr. Tsarsis, but that was because he was older and Matt respected him. Matt did not respect Miss Jamison.

When he returned from delivering the completed forms to a browbeaten Miss Cohen in 2019, Matt found a stranger slouched in the one side chair in his cubicle, a tall, redheaded man with an overcoat and hat on his lap.

"Thompson? I'm Carnahay," the redhead said, extending his hand without getting up. "I had this hole for a while, but I'd forgotten how dark it is in here. Care to run out for a little lunch? I hear it's stopped snowing."

The lunchtime crowd jostled and dodged in the narrow streets of the financial district of Manhattan, and the melting snow soaked their shoes and pant cuffs. Carnahay led Matt to a small sandwich shop around the corner from 20 Broad Street. As they waited for a table, Carnahay cursed the weather and brushed his cuffs with a paper napkin.

"You'll find that Al Murphy cares a lot how you look," Carnahay warned. "I'm supposed to usher you in this afternoon, and he'll chew my ass for your benefit if he can see anything wrong with me. Wet cuffs will be all he needs."

"Is Murphy hard to work for?" Matt asked.

"He's young and uptight." Carnahay smiled. "They've got him spread so thin that he's lost his sense of humor, but he's not bad. He handles about ten multinationals, so he's in the London and Paris offices as much as he's in New York, and he keeps five or six associates busy in each of the offices. He's a real money-maker for them. It's a good unit to be in."

"Who's 'them'?"

"Oh"—Carnahay laughed—"the Big Two—Guthrie and Alexander. Didn't you get the big picture when you interned?"

"I worked on a probate problem for Ridley all summer. I didn't really meet many people."

"I'm sure you didn't meet Guthrie or Alexander." Carnahay grinned. "They don't speak to many associates, let alone interns. God, we'd better order or we'll be late for Murphy."

As they ate, standing against the wall, Carnahay described the principal partners of Nixon, Mudge with broad strokes. "Len Garment runs the litigation department, but he's too damn nice to last. John Mitchell is new; they bought his firm. All he does is bond work—you know what that is?"

"Not really," Matt admitted. "Just what they gave us in law school."

"When cities or states borrow money by selling bonds, the big bond houses want an opinion by counsel that the procedures have all been followed and the bonds are enforceable. So Mitchell has a bunch of young guys who do nothing but flyspeck the procedures—was there proper notice of the Highway Commission meeting and all that stuff."

"Can the firm make money on that work?"

"Oh, hell, so much money! We get paid a percentage of the total bond issue. Mitchell lines up the work with the investment bankers and the local politicians, and keeps them happy, and that's about all he does. He's real tight with Nelson Rockefeller and the Albany boys, I know. I doubt that he's much of a lawyer—he went to Fordham or St. John's or one of those Catholic trade schools—but he doesn't need to be."

"What about Ridley?" Matt asked.

"There are about forty partners like Ridley—the workhorses. Good journeyman lawyers who do the things that keep the clients happy. Actually, we've got some damn good lawyers around there, believe it or not. Jesus, we've got to get back. It's nearly two, and you need to shine your shoes before you go in to see Murphy."

As they approached 20 Broad Street in the slush, Matt recalled the first time he'd seen the massive building on a humid June day in 1964, after his first year at Harvard Law School. He'd been summoned for an interview with Mr. Tsarsis and a young partner named Carpenter. He'd never seen Carpenter again. That first day, the receptionist on the twenty-fourth floor in that grass-clothed waiting room had been very kind to him. She sat at a desk beneath a Williamsburg Reproduction chandelier which was centered in a half-dome of gold leaf about the size of her desk. She could tell that he was nervous. One of Richard Nixon's secretaries had even come out to say hello. Nixon had arranged Matt's interview with Tsarsis because Thompson's father had written Nixon to ask the favor.

It surprised Matt that someone like Nixon remembered his father, but Whittier College is a small school. Matt wondered if Nixon remembered all of his teachers. The interview with Tsarsis and Carpenter had gone well enough, and almost at once he'd been asked to intern with Nixon, Mudge at the end of his second year of law school.

They'd liked him. Ridley had been easy to work for and Matt's third-year grades were good, so they'd hired him with no question at about the time he graduated from Harvard. The New York bar exam was not as difficult as he'd expected; and now here he was, a duly licensed and sworn-in lawyer—a Wall Street Lawyer, no less—about to receive his first assignment.

"Sit down, gentlemen, and I'll be with you shortly," Albert Murphy said. Murphy seemed smaller than Matt Thompson remembered. He was always impeccably groomed and expensively clothed. His dark hair was styled, perhaps in Paris. Murphy's nose was big and sharp, his eyebrows straight and slanted, his mouth too small for the rest of his face. Without looking up from the stack of letters he was signing, Murphy said: "Fall in a mud puddle, Carnahay?"

"No, sir. The snow is melting, sir."

"You're a mess. Seeing any clients today?"

"No, sir."

"That's a blessing. You worked for Ridley last summer, Thompson. He speaks well of you. Know any languages?"

"Yes, sir." Matt cleared his throat. "I speak some French, Spanish—and Chinese."

Murphy looked at Thompson sharply. "Chinese?"

"Yes, sir. My father was a teacher at a university there when he was young. He and my mother spoke Chinese at home."

Murphy nodded. "That won't hurt you around here. I don't have time to visit today, but sometime I'll talk to you about the Orient. I want you to work on PepsiCo's wine project now; here's my memorandum. I'll need something on it quickly; I think seven days is reasonable. Carnahay will help you get started and show you how to keep your time record. There is no excuse for a failure to keep accurate time records, Mr. Thompson. I insist upon our work being profitable."

Murphy finished signing the last of his mail and looked up, widening his eyes as if he were surprised that Matt and Carnahay were still with him. He raised his eyebrows as he regarded Matt, handed him a short memorandum on plain white paper, and looked him over thoroughly.

"Wait in the hall, please, Carnahay," Murphy said, almost absently.

When Carnahay had closed his door, Murphy folded his

hands. "You are a reasonably good-looking young man, Thompson. But you do not favor yourself by wearing clothing of that kind. This isn't Compton, California. Please go out and buy two decent blue suits with vests, some white shirts, some light blue shirts, and some quiet neckties. I will arrange for you to have a five-hundred-dollar advance for that purpose. Where do you get your hair cut?"

"I don't know a barber here."

"Here's a card for a good one. Ask for Jerry and put yourself in his hands. Let's try to get you in shape to be in touch with the clients. Are you wearing contact lenses?"

"No, sir. I don't wear glasses."

"Good. Are you married? Have a girl?"

"Not really."

"All right. I'd suggest you put the work first for a while. You'll have time for a social life later." Murphy nodded Matt's dismissal.

Eldon Carnahay was waiting in Matt's cubicle. "What was that all about?" he asked, smiling.

"He doesn't like my clothes and my haircut, I guess. And I got a little sermon about putting work ahead of my social life."

"Oho—he's sized you up as a California playboy because your jacket and pants don't match. You'll be ten years living that down. What's your assignment?"

"Something about French restrictions on U.S. investment in their wineries and vineyards. Have you run into that?"

"Nope. Come on down to my office when you've read the memo and I'll show you how to find out if anyone here has done any work on that. We've got an index. Then we'll explore the mysteries of the secretarial pool. To get any typing done here requires extended negotiation with a large lady named Sophie. You'll love her."

At 6:45 P.M. Matt Thompson was the only passenger in the elevator until the fourteenth floor. There a young blond woman got on, looked Matt over thoroughly, smiled, and turned to face the doors. All his college days Matt had been in love with tall blond women. It was, as they say in law school, a rebuttable presumption that he loved any blonde he saw, especially if she was tan and well built. This one, in the soft camel's-hair coat and brown boots, had a beautiful face, too. A high forehead, straight nose, gorgeous eyes, great teeth. No tan, of course, but in summer she'd be tanned. Maybe she worked on the four-teenth floor. She must have a good job—the coat looked as if it had cost a fortune.

The elevator doors opened and he followed her through the empty lobby and out the Broad Street doors. He watched as she got into a waiting limousine and was driven away.

He felt a stab of loneliness, as if his true love had just left him.

Two

• NOVEMBER, 1966 •

In more ways than most journalists and historians will admit, a campaign for President of the United States is a war. It demands enormous quantities of money, much of which is wasted, and the need for fresh manpower is infinite.

Between wars a campaign is more like an organism which can live for years in the national ganglion hidden from sight, its vital signs discernible only to the most sensitive of political diagnosticians.

On the twenty-fourth floor, amidst the five floors leased by Nixon, Mudge, Rose, Guthrie and Alexander at 20

Broad Street, in a back corner close by the door to Richard
Nixon's office, there incubated the incipient virus of a
Presidential political campaign. In 1966 it was slowly
thawing from a cryogenic storage that had begun after
Richard Nixon's defeat in the California gubernatorial
election in 1962. No larger than the total of six people and
a few filing cabinets, typewriters, and telephones, the
embryonic campaign fed on the ambition of Richard Nixon,
the money of several wealthy political speculators, and the
optimistic loyalty of a few people who admired Nixon.

Rose Mary Woods sat at the center of a warren of little
offices burrowed into the standard space allocated to a
senior partner by the management committee of Nixon,
Mudge. Miss Woods had been Richard Nixon's secretary
for nearly twenty years, from the time he was a congress-
man. She had been the Vice President's secretary, with an
office in the United States Capitol itself. She knew President Dwight D. Eisenhower and Nelson Rockefeller and J.
Edgar Hoover personally; and even more important, she
knew their secretaries.

As soon as Matt's telephone was installed in the
MacDougal Street apartment he had found, he telephoned
his father.

"Have you thanked Mr. Nixon for his help?" Professor
Thompson asked.

"No, Dad; I've really been busy tracking down French
investment regulations. I haven't had time."

"I'm going to be embarrassed if you don't do that soon,
Matt. After all, he went out of his way for you."

"I know, Dad. I'll do it tomorrow."

And so it was that Matt went to the far-back-left corner
of the twenty-fourth floor, behind the reception area,
where Richard Nixon had a large office with no view. A
receptionist had told Matt how to find Rose Mary Woods;
as he approached the maze of partitions and piles of
cardboard boxes, he sensed an atmosphere and tempo
completely different from the rest of the Nixon, Mudge

office. Three typewriters mounted on a rough pine tabletop were automatically and noisily producing form letters behind a low partition. On the hall floor nearby, piles of correspondence sagged against a wall. Telephones burred insistently.

Thompson looked into three small offices, all of which contained desks, chairs, and no people. Behind a partitioned area in the hallway he found Rose Mary woods seated at a secretary's desk which was buried in papers, a monadnock of a typewriter emerging a few inches above the drifts. Miss Woods was talking on the telephone while reaching athletically into a file cabinet behind her for a schedule she needed. As her eyes passed Matt Thompson, her recruiter's instinct recorded a positive entry. She nodded toward a side chair on which six boxes of typing paper were piled. Matt put the boxes on temporary, unpainted shelves that had been built against the wall and he sat to await Miss Woods.

"Mr. Nixon simply cannot be in Portland, Oregon, on May first, but he could arrive there on May third," she said. "Believe me, the Oregon primary is vitally important to us." Miss Woods raised her eyebrows in despair and grimaced at Matt. "He very much wanted to attend your Farm Bureau convention. But the May one date is out of the question. I am just certain. The third? Yes, I will be glad to confirm May three by letter." She made quick shorthand notes and expressed appropriate thanks.

Miss Woods smiled at Matt as she hung up. Someone, perhaps Elizabeth Arden, had done a good job on her, Matt thought. Her hair and eyes had been styled; without that she probably would have seemed pretty plain. Her voice had a surprisingly low pitch, a nasal timbre, and a Midwestern flavor.

"You are Matthew Thompson," she said. "I heard you started to work last week."

"Right," he nodded. "I work for Albert Murphy. I came by to thank Mr. Nixon for arranging everything for me." He looked at the closed door to the corner office.

"That's nice of you. I'll tell him. He's not here today. He's up in Boston to do a television show."

"Well, if you'll tell him, that will be fine."

"Have you ever done anything in politics, Matt? You went to Harvard?"

He nodded. "Dartmouth College and Harvard Law. No, I was active in a World Affairs Council but not in politics. Mr. Nixon was running for Governor in California ·the year I worked out there after Dartmouth, but I didn't get involved much. I went to hear him when he came to Whittier, and he was very good."

"Do you have any interest now? We're always looking for help."

"I guess. What kinds of things would I do?"

Before Miss Woods could answer, they were joined by a tall, sturdy woman about forty-five years of age with short black hair, wide black eyebrows, and a prominent nose.

"Matt, this is Nancy Mellor, Mr. Nixon's foreign affairs assistant. She's from Out West too. Eugene, Oregon. Matt Thompson is one of the new lawyers here, Nancy. His father was one of The Boss's professors at Whittier."

Nancy Mellor nodded curtly, her black bangs jiggling, then half-turned away from Matt. She wore a brown tweed outfit which emphasized her girth. "Rose, here is an article The Boss should read soon. I've marked the key paragraphs." Her voice came from somewhere above and behind her nose.

"Nancy, could you spend a few minutes with Matt? I know he's interested in international affairs. Maybe you could tell him a little about the foreign policy group?"

Miss Mellor looked imposed upon, but not surprised. "Sure, I guess so. Come in, Mr. . . . ."

"Thompson," Matt said to her back. She led him into one of the small offices he'd glanced into earlier. It was unadorned except for a *NATIONAL GEOGRAPHIC* map of the world pinned to one wall. The small window looked into an air shaft.

"So, what are your interests, Mr. Thompson?" Nancy Mellor folded her large hands on top of a pile of papers on her desk and leaned forward. Her thin, reedy voice didn't harmonize with her square jaw and wide brow.

"Well, at the moment I'm working on a French trade problem, but my real interest is in the Pacific rim," he replied. "My folks and grandparents lived in China as missionaries and my dad grew up there, so I'm strongly attracted to that part of the world."

Nancy Mellor grunted, looked at the wall map, as if to remind herself of China's whereabouts, and shook her head. "We are committed to Formosa," she said flatly. "Chiang Kai-shek has hosted The Boss in Taipei and he is a good ally of the United States. We can never forget what the Red Chinese did in Korea. They killed thousands of Americans."

Matt Thompson nodded.

"Your parents," Nancy Mellor continued, "were they driven out of China by the Communists during the Revolution?"

"No, we were finally run out by the Japanese. We left in 1943."

"Well, after that, of course, George Marshall sold Chiang out to the Communists. Harry Truman should have let Douglas MacArthur loose against the Red Chinese in Korea, too. We've made a great many mistakes with respect to Red China over the years. Now the bleeding hearts would like us to dump Chiang and just hand Formosa to the Communists. Well, that's one of the reasons I'm so strong for The Boss; he won't stand for that kind of betrayal."

Thompson nodded. "How do you and he see future relations with Japan, Mrs. Mellor?"

"Miss. I'm not married. Japan is the Marshall Plan all over again. We've made the Germans into formidable competitors and they are taking bread right away from American workers. We've been so helpful to the Japanese that they are now doing the same thing. Japanese cars flood into this country. The Boss is a quota man. He's not a free-trader who would let anyone and everyone compete in our American markets. They've got to be restrained.

The Boss would shake up things at the State Department and begin to put up some barriers to protect our workers and industries."

Matt wondered if this hard-line lady really reflected Nixon's points of view. Nancy Mellor was searching for something in a side drawer of her desk. She emerged with a sheaf of papers which she turned with a moistened forefinger. "This is a position paper on the Formosa question I prepared last year when I worked on the minority staff of the Senate Foreign Relations Committee. I'll make you a copy."

"Thanks, Miss Mellor. I guess I'd better get back to work."

Nancy Mellor thrust herself to her feet and extended her hand. "I enjoyed our talk," she piped, her little mouth arranged in an awkward smile. "I'll have a copy of this put on your desk."

Rose Mary Woods was not at her desk when Matt passed it. He was glad no one was there to ask him "How did you get along with Nancy Mellor?"

Three

• DECEMBER, 1966 •

"Carnahay, I need some advice," Matt Thompson announced as he slumped into his mentor's only chair. Carnahay looked up distractedly, put a finger at a place in the footnote he was reading, and took off his glasses.

"Are you still trying to figure out the Italian adoption laws, Matthew, me boy?" Carnahay rubbed his eyes slowly.

"As a matter of fact I am, but this is yet a new subject. I just got a call from the law clerk to one of the federal judges—Mendelsohn—and they've assigned me a criminal defendant.''

"Oh, shit. That's always trouble around here. You'll have to get out of it if you can. Murphy doesn't like his people giving away their billable time. How soon does it come up?''

"I'm really not sure. I'm supposed to go up to Foley Square tomorrow to sign up.''

"You'd better talk to Murphy right away. Tell him you don't think it's fair to the firm. Maybe he can get Garment or one of the other litigation boys to call Mendelsohn for you.''

"I really don't want to get out of it, Carnahay. I'd like to try a few criminal cases for the experience.''

"Bad attitude, man. Suppress the thought.''

"Sometimes I think I work at the wrong law firm.''

"Sure, don't we all?''

"Do any of the partners let their people take assignments?''

"Garment lets the litigation people do it, but he makes a career out of getting along with the judges. He serves on all their little judicial committees and all that crap.''

"Maybe I should talk to Garment.''

"Look, Matthew, you are Murphy's creature and only his. You'd better catch him today while he's in town. He's going to Paris tonight.''

Matt Thompson put both hands on Carnahay's old desk, palms down, and looked at his friend. "How do you think Al Murphy would like a small ultimatum?'' Thompson asked evenly.

"I'm just guessing, but I don't think he responds well to threats.''

"I'm in a mood to find out. There are plenty of other law firms.''

"There are plenty of young lawyers who would bust their asses to work for Murphy, too, and he knows it.''

"Yeah. Well, we'll see.''

Matt was able to see Albert Murphy just before the regular 1 P.M. partners' lunch. Murphy was clearing off his desk as the young man came in. "Yes, Thompson, an emergency?"

"Not exactly, Mr. Murphy. Judge Seth Mendelsohn's law clerk called me this morning. I'm to go to Foley Square tomorrow to take a criminal-defense assignment."

Murphy looked up from the side drawer where he was stacking "documents to be reviewed." "You didn't accept the assignment, did you?"

"Yes, sir."

"Without asking my permission?"

"I understand I have a professional obligation to take some indigent criminal assignments."

Murphy flushed. "You have only one professional obligation, young man, and that is to this firm and particularly to me. I decide how you will devote your time, and only I, morning, night, and Sundays. Is that clear?"

Thompson cleared his throat.

"Is that clear?" Murphy repeated loudly.

"I don't agree with that, Mr. Murphy; just because I work here doesn't vitiate my professional responsibilities."

"Mr. Thompson," Murphy said tightly, "I will discuss this with my colleagues at lunch. I will also talk with the judge. I'll see you again at three P.M."

"I want to take this assignment, Mr. Murphy. I'm sure it won't get in the way of my work for you, and I want the experience. Please don't tell the judge I'm too busy or not interested."

Murphy stood, his face flushed. "I'll tell the judge what I like, Thompson."

"If I have to make a choice between taking the assignment and working here, I'll leave, Mr. Murphy."

"Fine, I'll keep that in mind. Be here at three P.M. sharp. And meantime, get a shoeshine. You look like you herd cows every morning before you come to work."

At 3 P.M. Albert Murphy's secretary greeted Matt Thompson in place of her employer. Mr. Murphy had left for Europe early, she said. She read Matt a neatly typed message, in lieu of further discussion. It said:

> Thompson:
>   Hereafter you will accept no assignments from anyone (judges, other partners, clients) except me. You may tell such other assignors to talk with me. There will be no exceptions.
>   You may accept Judge Mendelsohn's assignment. I make this allowance because we had not thoroughly discussed this requirement in advance.
>
>   A.M.

Ron D'Amico qualified for a court-appointed attorney by filing an affidavit of poverty as required by the Federal Rules of Criminal Procedure. But by the time Matt Thompson got up to Foley Square to sign on as D'Amico's lawyer, a bail bondsman had posted a $50,000 bond, and Ron D'Amico had been released.

Matt Thompson read the clerk's file which contained very little other than the grand jury's indictment. Then he went downstairs to spend twenty minutes with Mary Finn, a redheaded Assistant United States Attorney who appeared able and very confident that she would convict Mr. D'Amico of Conspiracy to Defraud, Fraud, and dozens of counts of Forgery.

Mary Finn was bright as hell, and very pleasant. Matt liked the way she looked and handled herself. She gave him a telephone number for his client and wished him good luck without adding "You'll need it," and he liked that too.

Since Matt did not consider it politic to meet with his indigent client in the offices of Nixon, Mudge, his first interview with Ron D'Amico was at a small Long Island "California ranch house" in a residential quarter of Queens where D'Amico's sister and three nephews lived among plastic toys, unironed laundry, and a half-filled beer glass.

Matt and Ron D'Amico sat on a couch—the only furniture in the living room not overflowing with some item of personal property. A chair held coats, hats, and mufflers. A love seat was full of schoolbooks and lunch boxes, folded laundry, and a bag of groceries. The three boys, nine, seven, and six, were watching an afternoon action film on a very large television set. Automobiles driven by law officers in wide-brimmed hats kept running into each other, into stores, and off bridges into rivers, while good ol' boys and girls riding in Corvettes laughed and drank beer and successfully evaded the law.

Ron D'Amico was of quite ordinary appearance, about thirty-five, balding, neither tall nor short, unmemorable. Unmemorability was, in fact, his principal professional attribute. D'Amico, using the name Everett Gluck, could appear at a counter, apply for unemployment compensation, receive a check, cash a check, or make a bank deposit without interfering with a counter clerk's daydreams. As someone named Sam Henry, he could come back the following week and no teller would remember him as Mr. Gluck.

"I know I got a problem," D'Amico shouted earnestly over a car crash. "I need you to make me the best deal you can. They are loaded with evidence."

"Can we go somewhere?" Matt asked loudly. "I can't hear you."

"Goddamn kids," said D'Amico. "You got a car? We'll go get coffee."

"I know I got problems," D'Amico repeated quietly over coffee in the Jamaica Eats Shop.

"How did you get out of jail?" Matt asked.

D'Amico looked at him as if to say: How come you don't know that—you're a lawyer, ain't you? "A friend posted collateral with a bondsman. It don't affect my poverty, you know."

Matt nodded, as if to say: That's what I thought; I know all about this stuff. "What evidence do they have?"

"About forty-five identity kits I was getting ready to use. Birth certificates, Social Security cards, driver's licenses, credit cards. Good kits. I paid about six hundred dollars apiece for them."

"Did the FBI have a warrant?"

"Yeah. I saw it."

"Had you actually received any unemployment money?"

"Yeah, some. I'd been working Long Island and Connecticut some. New Jersey a little."

"How did you go about it?"

"This is privileged, right? No one hears what I tell you?"

"Correct. I'll take some notes, but no one else sees them."

"Okay. I set up some corporations in New York, Jersey, and Connecticut, and these little companies filed and paid premiums for unemployment insurance on their employees."

"Were there real employees?"

"Not actually. Then I began laying off some of them and they went in and began drawing their checks."

"How much money?"

"I'm not sure. Is that important?"

"I think so. If you're big-time it will be more difficult to bargain a light sentence."

"Listen, the FBI wants to know how I worked it. They told my other lawyer. Maybe we can work a trade."

"How many employees did you lay off?"

"I'm not sure."

"Did you have an identity kit for each one?"

"Sure. You got to prove who you are when you get your check."

"Where did you get the identity kits, Ron?"

"All over. The first ones I put together myself. But when I got help I needed professional kits."

"Help?"

"Sure. Women. Other men. I couldn't cover three states by myself, of course."

"I didn't realize you had a staff. How many?"

"Not a staff. They came and went. I'm not sure how many."

"How many the day you were arrested?"

"Four, plus Mindy, the girl they followed."

"Is that how they found you?"

"Yeah. The first rule is: Don't fraternize. You know? but this Mindy was too much—smart, and a great body. A good plain face, which is what you need, but really a beautiful woman. So we got together and when they began following her she led them right to me. She didn't mean to, I'm sure. We broke the first rule, goddammit."

"Did you ask for a lawyer when you were arrested?"

"I had one, but I fired him."

"Why?"

"The creep had represented my sister's ex-husband and I didn't know it until the arraignment. My sis saw him then and told me."

"Are you going to tell me how many runners you used?"

"I'm not sure."

"Then I'm going to assume the Government will prove that you are the mastermind of a huge welfare-fraud gang. If so, they are going to want you put away for a long time."

"Not huge. Small."

"Forty-five kits on hand. That's a lot."

"They maybe should think I'd decided to sell kits on the side. There's a big demand for those things."

"Where's the money?"

"Spent, most of it. High expenses and high living." D'Amico smiled.

"How much did you gross?"

"I'm not sure. I didn't keep records."

"Do you pay income tax?"

"No. That's a problem, right?"

"Right. I'll see what I can do, but they'll probably want taxes on everything."

"Like I told the judge, I'm broke. They got my bank-books. They cleaned me out."

Matt nodded. "I'll see what I can do."

*   *   *

Mary Finn had made it a rule never to go out with lawyers. In law school she had almost married a young man in her class; in the summer between their second and third years she had come to realize that he was much more interested in the law than he was in her, and she had broken the engagement. From then on she had socialized with boys from the Biz school.

Since graduation she had been seeing an orthopedic resident and a couple of businessmen. But Matthew Thompson looked like someone she might break the rule for, if he asked her out. He was tall and rugged-looking like the men she liked. He was probably a good lawyer and cared a lot about the law, but he didn't appear to be consumed by it.

Mary and Matt invented some good reasons to be together during that time. They had three meetings just to talk about Ron D'Amico. Matt explained to her that he could work on D'Amico's case only during the odd hours and off days when the partners at Nixon, Mudge did not require his services. Miss Finn's redheaded, freckled freshness never seemed to wilt, even on Saturday afternoons. He liked her looks, even though she wasn't a blonde.

They met for lunch once when they were arranging for D'Amico's interview with FBI agents. They had dinner together right after that interview, to talk about a plea bargain. Mary Finn demanded that the dinner check be split, Dutch treat. A few times Matt had been tempted to hold her hand or invite her to MacDougal Street for drinks, but she made it pretty clear—without ever flatly saying so—that socializing should wait until Ron D'Amico was disposed of.

The day D'Amico appeared before Judge Mendelsohn and was sentenced to four to eight years in prison, D'Amico handed Matt a sealed envelope when he thanked him for his help.

"You did a good job, kid. To be honest, I thought it would be worse. Now I should be out in two and a half. Read this letter when you get home tonight. Thanks for everything." The U.S. marshal took D'Amico by his left arm above the elbow. "I'll see you," said Matt's first criminal client. He was taken to a door beside the judge's bench which led to a prison elevator.

Mary Finn was talking with Mendelsohn's law clerk, a stocky young man with heavy glasses. Matt waited for her at the counsel table.

"Your Mr. D'Amico is going to Allenwood Prison Camp, not Danbury," she told Matt as she packed papers into her briefcase. "The probation officer recommended minimum security to the Bureau of Prisons."

"That's in Pennsylvania?"

"Right. It's not a bad place. I was there once to see an inmate."

"Listen, Mary, are you free for lunch? I'd like to take you somewhere nice, this time on me. You've been really good to work with."

"I'd love to, Matt, but I can't today. There's an office meeting I dare not miss. How about another day? I don't want to lose track of you."

"I'll call you. Maybe we could have dinner and go dancing."

"I'd like that."

Back at his office, emptying out his briefcase, Matt discovered Ron D'Amico's letter, opened it, and read:

> Dear Matt,
>   You did a good job on my case and I want to show my thanks.
>   Here is a telephone number. Memorize it and flush this letter down the can. If you ever need help call it. I have arranged that you should have one free one. You never know when you may need someone taken care of.
>   305-555-9283
>   Just tell the man who you are.
>
>   Good luck,
>   Ron

Matt's first instinct was to destroy the letter immediately, as he would a poisonous insect. Then he wanted to share the letter with someone—Carnahay, or Mary Finn—but no, for God's sake, not with Mary. With Eldon Carnahay, then. No, not with anyone. It was too hot.

The implication was crystal clear. Matt had a gift certificate for a hit, if he ever needed it. The phone number was probably that of a mobster or a contact for mobsters. Perhaps, he thought, he should copy the number into D'Amico's file, so that there would be a record of it. He wrote the telephone number on the lower margin of a copy of the indictment.

He couldn't imagine ever needing it.

A week later he called Mary Finn at her office. He had called two days before and left his number, but she hadn't called him back. It was close to Christmas and everyone was out of the office.

A secretary asked him to hold the line. In about four minutes Mary Finn picked up her phone: "Matthew Thompson, I'm glad you called."

"I tried the other day . . ."

"You may have a problem, bucko. I hope you aren't in too deep."

"What problem?"

"We'd better talk face to face. Can you come up here?"

"Sure. What is it, Mary? What problem?"

"I'll tell you then. How about an hour?"

"Sure."

Mary Finn was not alone. "Matt, this is my boss, Seymour Millbarger. He's senior attorney in my part of the office here in the Southern District. And this is Agent Jack Miller of the FBI."

Matt shook hands with Mary's friends.

The thin Mr. Millbarger, tall, bald, glasses, vest, said: "Mr. Thompson, we need to ask you some questions

about your client Mr. D'Amico. At the same time, I must
tell you that you are a target of our investigation."

Matt's back-of-the-neck hairs bristled.

"You have a right to remain silent. . . ."

Millbarger was reading him his rights, for God's sake.
He'd come up here thinking he'd romance Mary Finn, and
all of a sudden he's a criminal target! Mary Finn was
looking out the window, obviously upset. This was beyond
the point of being merely serious.

Millbarger finished his memorized Miranda ritual and
said that Agent Miller would ask the questions. Matt began
to think about phoning for Carnahay or Garment or Richard
Nixon to come to look out for him. Or even Albert
Murphy.

"Mr. Thompson, do you know that Ron D'Amico has
escaped from prison?"

"My God, no? When? How?"

"He walked in one door at Allenwood and walked out
another," Mary Finn said wryly. "They don't have fences
down there; he was there less than twenty-four hours."

Millbarger's look told Miss Finn to shut up.

"Do you have any idea where he is?" Millbarger asked.

Matt thought of D'Amico's Florida telephone number.
"No," he said.

"Were you aware of his bank accounts?"

"I was there when he told the FBI about them. I saw the
savings passbooks the FBI agents had. Ron D'Amico
identified them for you. I knew about them," Matt replied, a little defensively.

"Were you with him the day before he was sentenced?"

"Let's see; that would be a week ago Wednesday,
right?"

Miller nodded.

"I don't think so. I had my secretary phone and leave a
message for him that day, to be sure he wouldn't miss
court, but I didn't see or talk to him."

"Where were you?"

"At the office, all day. Why? What happened?" He

knew Miller wouldn't tell him, so he asked the question of Seymour Millbarger.

"Your client evidently knew that he didn't need the passbooks to withdraw money from these accounts," Millbarger began. "He went from one savings bank to the next, all day last Wednesday, and looted those accounts."

"There must have been twenty passbooks in that pile they showed him," Matt said with surprise. "He hit every one?"

"There were twenty-nine accounts," Mary Finn said. "He hit every single one."

"How much was in there? How much did he get?"

Millbarger picked up a piece of adding-machine tape; "$581,355.51," he said hollowly.

"All in cash?"

"He bought a big brown suitcase at a shop next door to the fourth savings institution he visited. It was all in unmarked bills of modest denomination."

Matt couldn't suppress a smile. "Can I ask a question? How come the FBI and the United States Attorney in and for the Southern District of the State of New York left all that money in those accounts? I'll bet you thought as long as the FBI had the passbooks no one could take the dough out but you, right?"

"Right," said Mary Finn. "Did you know different?"

"Nope. That's what I've always thought. Did he have to show some identification to make the withdrawals?"

"Yeah," Miller contributed. "But for him that is never a problem."

"Mr. Thompson," Millbarger began, "have you accepted money or anything of value from D'Amico?"

Matt thought again of the telephone number. "No," he answered. "You people must be pretty embarrassed, losing all that money that way."

"We'll apprehend him sooner or later, be certain of that," said Agent Miller of the Federal Bureau of Investigation formally.

"Yeah, embarrassed," said Mary Finn forlornly.

Matt felt very sorry for her. Seymour Millbarger obviously had put the intraoffice onus on her. "Did you think to put the money in a safe place, Mr. Millbarger?" Matt asked. "Did *you* know he could get it out without a passbook?"

Millbarger thought quite a while about whether to answer that question and, if so, how. Mary smiled just a little.

"It was not my case, sir. I had no occasion to consider its complexities. I supervise twenty-one assistants and hundreds of such files. I will not accept responsibility for every subsidiary decision in every file."

Matt grinned. "Five hundred and eighty-one thousand dollars isn't too subsidiary around my place. But then, everything is relative, isn't it? I'll tell you what: If I hear from Ron D'Amico, I'll let Mary know. How will that be?"

Millbarger nodded.

"Thanks, Matt," Mary Finn said. "I'll walk you to the door."

They stepped out into the grimy courthouse hallway.

"Under the circumstances, I don't think we can socialize for a while," Mary Finn said solemnly. "I hope they don't believe that you had anything to do with the money or the escape, but everyone is supertouchy about it. Millbarger would love to put all the blame on me or the FBI, or anyone but himself. I'm really on the spot."

"Listen, Mary, I'm sorry. I'll help any way I can. And I really do want to take you out. I want to show you my place; it's just about all fixed up now. But D'Amico won't be caught, I'd guess. He's an expert. He's got a new name by now, and all that money. He's long gone."

Mary put the back of her right hand on Matt's cheek. Her hand was very warm. "I'm really sorry too. When this blows over we'll do something, okay? I'll call you."

PART

TWO

Four

Teng Shan-li had saved one good jacket, dark blue, sewn in Shanghai in the early 1960s by a tailor who was said to have once made clothes for Chairman Mao. Teng had kept the jacket tightly rolled and tied with string in the bottom of his canvas bag all through his disgrace. Even at the farm of Chang Fong-yu, where he slept with the hogs, Teng had believed he would return to a position in life in which he would once again dress well, attend banquets, and participate in China's vital affairs. Someday, somehow, he had known he would find his way out of the green mountains of Szechwan, back to the northern plains. He would need his fine jacket again, perhaps soon, when China emerged from this madness and anarchy.

On the northbound train, Teng Shan-li took the jacket from his old bag, carefully untied the string, and rolled it out. Only steam and a hot iron could restore its shape; but if he wore it under his heavy quilted coat for the days and nights he was on the train, perhaps it would need less pressing when he arrived in Peking. The People's Liberation Army officer escorting him smiled, and two of the young people in the compartment laughed out loud

29

when with great difficulty Teng turned the coat right-side
out.

In the days before his disgrace Teng had taken a measure of pride in his attainments and in his appearance. The
sleeve ends were turned and hand-sewn, superbly tailored
to touch both his hands at precisely the same level, in spite
of a slight spinal curve which made one hand a little lower
than the other. Everyone in the government wore jackets in
the style of Sun Yat-sen and Chairman Mao, some gray and
some blue, but in the old days a glance at Teng Shan-li had
told the most casual onlooker that Ambassador Teng was a
man of substance.

Teng Shan-li had lost weight on the farm. When he
worked at the Foreign Ministry he had weighed about 180
pounds. He had been robust then, thick in the shoulders
and around the waist. His hair had thinned on the farm,
too, but he was not yet bald. Actually, he thought, the hard
work had improved his appearance some. He was still
fairly handsome. His features were regular, his body slim,
his head of gray hair rather distinguished.

The Army officer who was his "escort" either did not
know or would not say why he had been sent to Chang's
farm to move Teng to another place. But the man had a
high standing in the Army, notwithstanding the abolition of
grades and ranks. That was clear from the cut of his jacket
and overcoat and from the way the Production Brigade
officials had deferred to him. Teng was not permitted to
see the transfer papers which were shown to the Brigade
manager, but he knew he was on the train to Peking.

The railroad station in Chungking had been jammed
with young men and women, packs on their backs, little
red books in their hands, the red armbands on their
uniforms blazoned with the legend RED GUARD. They all
wanted to go to Peking too. Some were as young as eleven
or twelve, some were of college age, but most were from
the intermediate schools. There were dozens of homemade
red flags on poles scattered above the compressed crowd,
identifying groups of the young people; on several of them

Teng read THE LONG MARCH and PILGRIMAGE TO CHAIR-
MAN MAO.

Teng's escort had the help of four soldiers in wedging
Teng through the crowd of Red Guards. Most of the
students had tied bedrolls to their backs, and many had
apparently walked long distances to reach Chungking. As
the soldiers pushed past them, the young people made
friendly remarks to one another about the Army and tried
to move out of the way. Some smiled at Teng, assuming
that he was a Party official entitled to an Army escort.

The station walls were plastered with hand-lettered posters on white, yellow, and red paper. Clusters of the Red
Guards jostled and shoved their way from poster to poster,
pointing and reading aloud. The large station was filled,
wall to wall, with this tide of young people which swirled
and flowed within the room. It appeared that no one was
merely standing still and waiting.

The noise the crowd made was staggering. The cacophony was punctuated by a few of the Red Guards who had
loudspeakers with which they constantly harangued the
people around them. Everyone was talking, and everyone
had to shout to be heard by those nearest. The public-
address system in the depot had been turned to its full
power, but its announcements merely added to the din
without being intelligible.

The Army officer had explained to Teng that rail travel
was free for Red Guards who wished to travel, and
hundreds of thousands of young people were leaving home
for the first time to go to Peking to see Chairman Mao and
engage in the *Ch'ian-lien*—the exchange experience.

Teng Shan-li and his escort were muscled to a railroad-
car compartment being held for them by three People's
Liberation Army soldiers. One guarded the outside door,
another held the door to the interior passageway, and the
third sat on one of the cushioned seats, prepared to eject
any trespasser. Once Teng and his officer were seated, the
soldiers allowed some of the pressing crowd of Red Guards
in from the hallway to fill the rest of the "soft pillow"
seats. Teng watched the young people stow their bedrolls,

open their packs and examine the fixtures in the compartment with great curiosity. Teng felt a mixture of amusement and fear. Seven months before, the Red Guards had burst into Teng's home, burned his books and papers and marched him through the streets with a paper dunce cap on his head. These in the railroad car were from a Szechwanese village south of Chungking, but they were hot with the same Maoist fever as the kids who had driven Teng and his wife from their home in Peking. They called to their friends out the window, while two young women struggled in and out of the door, trying to tape a poster to the outside of their railroad car. Teng could not read it all as they unrolled it, but it appeared to be a denunciation of Liu Shao-chi, China's President, as "... the greatest corrupter of the true line of popular thought."

At last the train began to move, at first only a few inches; then, as the station crowd ebbed a little and began to shout, the engineer ventured more speed. It required several minutes for the train to creep through the red-speckled crowd, all turned toward their departing comrades, shouting unheard slogans and waving hands, little red books and crude flags.

Once before Teng had been on this train track. Then he was crammed into a boxcar with a hundred others and hauled south to be "rusticated" in the fields of Szechwan Province. The train of boxcars had gone south and west and south again on this same route.

Total passivity had pulled him through. Teng Shan-li had been forced out of the Ministry and his home, into the bitterly cold farm mud, hungry and degraded, but he had attempted to bear everything with a blank stoicism. He had forbidden himself to think of his wife or daughter. He read nothing—there were only the posters, a bulletin board plastered with ideological broadsides, and once in a rare while, a newspaper that was published in the county seat forty miles away. He read none of it. He only tended hogs. Twice he and Chang the farmer trussed the hogs' feet and carried the huge brutes a mile to the Brigade Office to be weighed and trucked to Chungking for slaughter. The rest of the time he stayed on the land Chang and his family were assigned to work.

The jacket was streaked where fine yellow dust had seeped into the canvas bag and onto one of the arms. Teng took his jacket through the crowded companionway to the galvanized water can at the forward end of the swaying railroad car. The dust was too deeply ingrained to be washed away. But the longer he wore the warped and wrinkled garment, the fainter the dust lines became. By the time the train reached Peking's outskirts, Teng appeared only a little more wrinkled than most of the other passengers who had slept four nights upright in the cold, overcrowded railroad car all the way from Chungking through Hsiang-fan and Chang-chou.

Teng disembarked in Peking with his Army-officer escort prepared for anything—more punishment, a show trial, extended interrogation, some menial job in the city, even another parade through the Square in a dunce cap. Whatever came, he would bear it without emotion. A younger soldier led them through the crowds of arriving Red Guards to a side door of the Peking railroad station where a gleaming new Red Flag limousine waited. The escort officer saluted a good-looking young man whose athletic build could not be concealed by his heavy padded coat.

"I am Yang Te-chong," the man said. "Please be seated in the car, Comrade Teng Shan-li."

It had been nearly a year since Teng had ridden in any kind of automobile, much less a Red Flag. This one was newer and more comfortable than the Foreign Minister's car, he thought. As they drove away from the station, he wished he dared pull the curtains aside so that he could see Peking.

During the short walk from the train to this automobile he had tasted and felt Peking. The biting wind of the northern plains carried its coal smoke and the smells of its cooking, the warm odor of manure, and the residual

flavors of ten centuries of compacted life, all so different
from the near-tropical tastes of Szechwan. Peking was all
grays and dull whites, a flat and inward place. Yet there
had always been an excitement about it for Teng—Peking
was the capital, and here the great issues were decided.
Here had rested for centuries the power and wisdom of
nearly a half-billion people, in the hands of an emperor.
Now the power lay in the hands of Chairman Mao, and in
the sinister hands of his wife, Chiang Ch'ing, and the
others who had fomented the Cultural Revolution.

The Peking railroad depot was plastered with red banners and handmade posters bearing slogans as strident as
any he had seen. ANGRILY ATTACK THE REVISIONIST
BLOODSUCKERS WHO OPPOSE THE PEOPLE'S GREAT CUL-
TURAL REVOLUTION, said one. OPEN FIRE ON BACKSLID-
ING REGIONALISM, said another, which had been crudely
lettered on a string of small pages glued together. DENOUNCE
TIME WASTING IN THE OPERATION OF THE PEOPLE'S
RAILWAYS, said the headline of a third poster, which listed
a dozen of the rail workers' grievances against a manager
of maintenance.

Teng reflected that he was being transported in some
splendor. He'd prepared himself for a tumbril ride. Now he
dared not speculate upon this apparent change in his
fortunes; he would ride this curious circumstance like a
feather too, and abide its outcome.

The Red Flag limousine was blessedly silent as it glided
north and then west from the Peking Station. But at Chang
'An Avenue and Wangfujing Street, a crowd was gathered
at the northeast corner and a blaring loudspeaker was
describing the wrongdoings of some hapless administrator
of the Capital Hospital, a couple of hundred meters north
of the corner, "A capitalist-roader, unrepentant and
vicious . . ."

From that intersection on, it seemed, every compound
and street corner had its loudspeaker, and every wall,
house side and gate was covered with layers of posters.
Crowds of Red Guards, pack-laden visitors like those on
the train, were moving from poster to poster, along with

the people of Peking, some wheeling bicycles as they read, others carrying children, shopping bags and packages. It appeared that everyone in the city was out in the streets, talking, listening and reading posters. It was like the Sundays in Peking Teng remembered, but it was still the middle of the week.

As they passed the Peking Hotel, Teng saw that armed Army sentries kept the street crowds at a distance there. Wires strung from tree to tree along Chang 'An Avenue held more posters which hung to the ground, obscuring the sidewalk and storefronts, like a fluttering paper wall. They were approaching Tien'anmen Square, which was festooned with red slogan banners. The Forbidden City lay behind the looming bulk of Tien'anmen Gate on their right. Several hundred yards west, just past Chongshan Park, the car slowed and turned right into a narrow entrance in a wall, guarded by sentries. It was, he realized, Hsin Hua Gate.

Chungnanhai! Teng's practiced passivity gave way to shock; they were entering the compound of the State Central Committee. He was being delivered to some very high official. The sentries saluted stiffly as their car approached. Yang, in the front seat, rather casually returned the salutes.

Teng perched forward on the soft seat, raising himself to see all that the windshield view could offer him. He had been inside the walls of Chungnanhai only twice in all of his career, many years before.

Inside the compound, the narrow street wound among gardens and passed low, walled buildings overhung with massive trees. Several two- and three-storied office buildings, screened by foliage, could be seen ahead to the left near the lake called Nanhai. The whole compound was bound by a wall nearly as high as the red walls of the Forbidden City. Through breaks in the trees he could occasionally see the compound's wall, made of gray brick. Where the two lakes joined, the car crossed a concrete bridge designed in the old Chinese style. They stopped in the porte cochere of a small European house that sat squarely in lush, old gardens which bordered the other

lake, Chunghai. A houseman came out quickly to open
Teng Shan-li's door and lead him into the house. Yang
followed them through the wide entry and into a small
library at the south side of the house.

"You are the guest of Premier Chou En-lai in this
house," Yang said. "It is he who has sent for you, Teng
Shan-li. The Premier will join you when he can. Do you
wish tea while you wait?"

"Thank you, yes, sir." Teng felt a tremor run through
his body. "Perhaps the tea will wash away my confusion,
Comrade Yang. I am a keeper of hogs in a faraway place. I
cannot conceive of a reason for Premier Chou to send for
me."

"He will explain his reason if he wishes to do so. I will
send you tea. There is a toilet across the hall," Yang said
pointedly as he left the room, closing the door behind him.

Teng had been in groups that met with Chou En-lai, but
he had never had a personal conversation with him. Chou
had been China's *de facto* Minister of Foreign Affairs ever
since creation of the Republic in 1949, and Teng Shan-li
had spent much of his adult life as one of the executors of
Chou's foreign policy, but Chou's decisions had always
come to him secondhand. For many years Chou had
permitted others to carry the title of Foreign Minister, but
everyone knew that Chou set the policy. Teng knew, too,
that much of the written work he had done in the late
1950s, as Deputy Minister of Foreign Affairs, had been
studied by Chou, particularly the political reviews of the
United States during the Eisenhower years.

Teng thought of how he would appear to Premier Chou.
Whenever Teng had seen him, the Premier was always
perfectly groomed and impeccably dressed. Teng went
across the hall to the lavatory, washed his hands and face,
and carefully dressed his thinning gray hair with the plastic
comb he found on the counter. His clothes were in shambles, his fine old jacket wrinkled and streaked. He looked
like the pig farmer he had become. He was deeply ashamed
of the appearance he would present to Premier Chou
En-lai.

Back in the library, Teng tried to overcome his nervousness by looking at the books on the shelves. There were several volumes from the United States which he recognized. He'd had no occasion to read English for nearly a year.

The Premier and a young woman came into the library behind Yang. Teng closed the book he was reading with a snap and bowed stiffly to Chou. The woman and Yang were virtually invisible to Teng Shan-li; Chou seemed to fill the room with his presence. Teng could not straighten up or look at the Premier; he was emotionally overcome as never before in his life. "Comrade Teng Shan-li, welcome back," Chou said quietly. "Please come and sit and have tea."

"Thank you, sir," Teng mumbled. He thought he should apologize for his disheveled appearance. But as he began to sit in a straight chair near the window, Chou waved him to an overstuffed lounge chair with a smile. "No, sit here by me, Teng Shan-li. We have much to talk about. I'm sure you are wondering why I have sent for you, and so first I will tell you my reason. Then we must talk about your family. I will tell you now that your wife is well and she is on her way back from Shanghai, where she has been working in a hospital. Your daughter is also well. She lives in Peking."

"Thank you, Comrade Premier," Teng said, his eyes stinging. "Thank you."

"Yang, here, is my secretary," Chou continued. "He does everything for me. Wang Li-fa assists him and interprets English and Japanese when I need it. I trust them both implicitly. They have arranged for your return because I am deeply concerned about some of the human beings who are vitally important to China's future. As I can, I am attempting to call back a few of our most valuable comrades, our precious human resource."

Chou's heavy eyebrows and deeply lined cheeks barely moved as he spoke, but his dark brown eyes were so vital, so active that Teng Shan-li had the impression of lively animation. Chou was neither tall nor robust, but he expressed great power—great personal strength. Teng knew the En-

glish word *charisma*, and perhaps some of Chou's exter-
nalized energy was charisma, he thought, but much more
of it was the force of an intellect.

"China is in some difficulty," Chou continued, "and
certain people question how much longer she can afford
the luxury of proletarian purity. Chairman Mao knows,
better than I, what is required to govern this huge and
diverse people successfully, and I am confident that he will
bring us safely out of the storm at the correct time."

Teng nodded, but he wondered how much of the Mao
thought was Chou's true belief and how much of it was
said because Chou didn't completely trust Teng. Chou had
been Chairman Mao's partner since the early days of the
Revolution. Perhaps no other living man knew Mao so
well as Chou. He must have a highly articulated sense of
Mao's weaknesses and strengths. Teng wondered if Mao
and his wife knew that Chou En-lai was rescuing bureaucrats and intellectuals from the Cultural Revolution. Would
Chou dare to do so without Mao's acquiescence?

"Unfortunately, we are not yet in the calm waters of the
harbor, but the tides of world affairs cannot be made to
wait for us," Chou said, lighting a cigarette. "We will
work with the conditions as we find them, of course, as we
always have. Comrade Teng, I want you to stay away from
the Foreign Ministry for the time being. At the moment it
is populated by fools, with no training or experience in the
external world. You would not find the company congenial."

Chou smiled broadly, stubbed out his cigarette, and
stretched his legs to full length. "I want you to work for
me at your home, beginning as soon as you are rested. I
regret the hardships you have undergone, and I hope you
will find it interesting and worthwhile to return to the work
of China's foreign relations."

Teng recognized the subtle question of his disillusionment
in Chou's statement. "Premier Chou," Teng began tentatively, "on Monday of this week I was slopping my hogs
on the farm of Production Brigade Five. A hog tender in
Szechwan knows nothing of the world. In fact, he knows
nothing of what is occurring in Chengtu or even Chungking.

I am sure much has happened in China and in the world since last year. I suspect I am without value to you.''

Chou smiled. ''I have asked Wang Li-fa to send for some books and magazines for you from the shops of Hong Kong. She has even obtained last Sunday's *New York Times*. Your old home is waiting for you. Go there and read Li-fa's bibliography, and then let us talk again. It appears that you also have some accumulated mail from the United States which may bring you in touch with recent events. When you are ready I should like you to write me your view of the current political situation in the United States.''

Teng folded his hands in his lap and looked from Wang Li-fa and Yang to the Premier. ''I am deeply grateful for this opportunity to be of service, sir. I cannot express how I feel. I have learned not to have feelings about what was happening to me, but now I am overwhelmed with joy at the prospect of resuming my work, in the company of my wife, in our old home. I am finding it difficult to maintain my composure.'' Teng felt tears rising in his eyes. ''I will do my best to serve you well.''

''I am sure you will, Teng Shan-li,'' Chou said, standing. ''You will be paid the stipend of a Deputy Foreign Minister, because you must eat, of course. Wang Li-fa will receive your analysis when it is prepared and I will look forward to studying it. You must be very circumspect, however. You must live as if you were in hiding. Please tell absolutely no one what you are doing or for whom. I am glad that you have returned.''

Chou and Yang Te-chong left the library before Teng could reply.

''I have your reading materials in boxes in the front hall,'' Wang Li-fa said to Teng.

For the first time Teng took a good look at her. She was tall for a Chinese woman, broad at the shoulders, slim. She wore her black hair short and was dressed in an unusual light blue jacket with a thin white decorative stripe round the high collar and a similar stripe along her shoulders and down the outsides of her arms. Had Teng encountered this young girl on a Szechwanese farm in the typical black pajamas of the farm women, he would have known her to be of extraordinary intelligence; it was apparent in her face and the way she moved.

"Here are your letters, Teng Shan-li," she said apologetically. "I'm afraid some of them were written a long time ago."

"I am grateful to have them."

"The car will take you to the Lane of the Crows now. I believe your wife is already there."

"Thank you," Teng said. She extended her hand, and he took it.

"I will come by to see if you need other readings, Comrade Teng. Perhaps I will come in three days. When you have writing to be typed I will arrange for that. Here is a paper on which I have written my name, an address where my office is in the Great Hall, and a telephone number. I am often here at this house, but you can leave a message."

Teng bowed slightly. "Thank you, Wang Li-fa. I shall look forward to your visit."

Teng's reunion with his wife, Hua Fan, was more like the reencounter of two old friends than a reunion of lovers. After an embrace at their open gate, Teng and Hua Fan had carried the five boxes of books and periodicals into the house. She seemed glad to see Teng, but remote. They had suffered different, divergent experiences, and it was as if they had lost their old intimacy in the process. They both felt the remoteness, he could see.

Fan explained to her husband that a large family had been living in the house for six months and she had not yet had time to put the place in proper order. When the boxes were stacked, they toured the four rooms and Fan pointed out the damage the old house had suffered. She would wash the ceilings, walls, and floors, then whitewash all the rooms, but there was a roof leak and the firebox of the stove in the kitchen was cracked.

They talked about their daughter and her new husband, a young man neither of them knew. Hua Fan had been working at a State Psychiatric Hospital in the outskirts of Shanghai during the time Teng was undergoing his rustification. Their daughter had been removed from the University and assigned to an electrical-construction group in Peking, where she had become a clerical worker. Her new husband was an electrical engineer in the same group.

Teng explained that he would require the use of the northwest room of the house as a workplace. He did not offer to tell Fan what his work would be or for whom he worked; she did not ask, but it seemed clear to her that Teng Shan-li was rehabilitated. She did not need to know more. She asked only if there was money for food.

The tied bundle of letters was an accumulation of the past seven months. Teng sat on a bench in the courtyard and leafed through them. A political-science professional association in England had invited Teng to be a guest speaker. Several foreign diplomats wrote that they would be visiting Peking and would like to see him.

Time had passed and most of the relevance of the letters had faded. He had an intuition that someone had carefully culled the collection. One letter was only ninety days old. It had been handwritten by Dr. Ezra Thompson and sent to Teng from a small place in California where Thompson was a college professor. Teng and Thompson had been boyhood friends in Tientsin, where Thompson's father had run the Methodist missionary school which Teng had attended for eight years.

The letter read:

Christmas, 1966

Dear Teng Shan-li—

I write to wish you the greetings of our holiday season and to inquire about your well-being. I hope this letter finds you in good health and happily pursuing your work.

Please give Madame Hua Fan my sincere best wishes too, and your daughter as well. I regret that I have never had an opportunity to come to know them.

I continue to teach here at Whittier College, in a growing suburb of Los Angeles. In a few years I will be eligible to retire on a small pension and so I've begun to think of how I might live a life of leisure. I'm not sure I will know how to do it.

My son, Matthew, has recently graduated from Harvard Law School. He chose to work in New York City, to my surprise, and has a position with a large law firm headed by a Whittier student of mine, former Vice President Richard Nixon. As a new, young lawyer, Matt does not have much personal contact with Nixon, of course, but the law firm offers some opportunity for experience in international law, the field of Matt's interest.

Nixon is spoken of as a possible Presidential candidate again, and he is showing up well in the early polling against President Johnson. I remember him as a rather shy and introverted student with a strong competitive streak and a good mind. It is hard to imagine this boy I knew becoming President, but stranger things have happened.

I suspect Matt would like to become involved in politics or government or both, but he says the partners of his law firm are discouraging him from such diversions. It is a very large firm with a substantial clientele and he can do very well for himself if he becomes a partner. Nixon was helpful in getting Matt the job, and I hope Matt will not allow Nixon to lure him into politics now.

I read everything I can about China and I hope you have survived these unsettled times. Perhaps it is no longer easy for you to write letters to

the United States. I guess it is over a year since
I have heard from you.

I value your friendship and will help you in
any way that I can. Just now I pray for your
well-being.

Sincerely,
Ezra

Five

• APRIL, 1967 •

"I am deeply apologetic, Comrade Premier, that I have
not yet completed the analysis you requested of me," Teng
Shan-li said after the formal greetings, the arrangement of
the chairs, and the first sip of tea.

Chou held up his hand. "I had not expected it this soon,
Comrade. Wang Li-fa tells me that you are making good
progress, so I am satisfied. I asked Comrade Li-fa to bring
you here only so that I could talk to you a little about
China. You have been on a farm with the peasants for—
how long? A year?"

"Seven months."

"In Szechwan."

"Yes, near the county seat of Kuang-an, north of
Chungking."

"Why were you sent there to that particular place? Do
you know?"

"I can only suspect; that is a very populous region, but
the level of education is poor. They certainly didn't need
another laborer there; there are great numbers of peasants.
But the city people they transported to that place could

read, write, and teach. That may have been the purpose of
sending us there.''

"And did you teach?''

"No. We were outcasts, rejected by everyone. We were
openly welcomed, but deeply resented. No one trusted us
to do anything but the most menial work. Most people
shunned me.''

"How did you pass the time?''

"I worked. I did manual labor from first light to dark,
every day of the week. I planted, cultivated, fertilized and
harvested. I fed hogs. I built walls. In Szechwan, when
there is nothing else to do you build walls and terraces so
crops may be planted on the mountainside. For a time I
was sent to a small coal mine, but I lacked the strength to
carry baskets of coal on my back down a mountain all day
long. So I was sent back to the hogs.''

"Did you live with a peasant family?''

"I was assigned to live with the family of a farmer
named Chang, but Chang's mangy dogs were better received than I. I slept in a small shed behind the house,
under a quilt that had been the mother's before she died. I
suspect she died of cold; her cover was very thin.'' Teng
smiled warmly. "I ate the last in the pot, just before the
dogs.''

"Were you a part of the life of the commune?''

"It was clear that the enemies of Chairman Mao had no
voice in the affairs of the Production Brigade or the
commune. Anyway, soon after I arrived at the Production
Brigade, the Red Guards created anarchy there too. There
there was no longer any real administration or management. All the old cadres who had run the commune were
driven out and a few were replaced. I suppose I could have
attended the mass meetings they held, but I knew I was not
welcome. At times I was required to go to rehabilitation
lectures in the evening. Traveling groups of the Red
Guards from Cheng-tu and faraway places came through to
lecture us every now and then, and twice informal cultural
troupes performed and my attendance was compulsory.''

Chou lit a cigarette and leaned back in his chair. He had

sent Wang Li-fa away as soon as Teng was seated beside him. Chou's office in the Great Hall of the People was large and elaborate, with a sixteen-foot ceiling. In the corner where they sat, away from the windows, four oversized easy chairs had been arranged facing each other, with small tables between. Teng sat so low in his chair that he could not lay his arms on the armrests. As Chou asked the next question a slim young woman entered from an anteroom to refill their teacups. No telephones rang; no sound came in from the busy street beneath the windows, nor could the unceasing noise of the Red Guards' loud-speakers be heard.

"Did you read there?"

"Almost nothing. I had no lamp in my shed so it was not possible at night, and the days were only work. Any extra time I had I used to repair my clothing or glean food. There are no books there; no one reads. I would guess the illiteracy rate is very high."

"I am told our illiteracy rate has been reduced to fifteen percent," Chou said with an ironic smile. "We reformed the education system three years ago, you know."

Teng shrugged. "They all went to school once, but no one goes now. The teachers are disapproved of, and they have been run out of the schools. Many village schools are used only for storerooms now. China is losing a whole generation, I fear. The children of the masses are always needed to work in the fields to fulfill the production quotas, even in good times, and they will not be schooled unless the parents are compelled to send them to school in the evenings. Just now the commune has no teachers because they are unreliable intellectuals. So there is no education."

"That does not bode well for our future," Chou said quietly. "I am thinking much of the future these days. We are like the farmer who eats his seed corn because he is hungry. We are serving the present need. We are preserving the Revolution. But what of the future?"

Teng felt that he dare not respond to the question; he knew too little of what was going on among those who

governed China. He could not guess whether Chou was
supporting Chairman Mao's Cultural Revolution or had
allied himself with Teng Hsiao-ping and the pragmatic
moderates who had sought a less radical path. It was time
for the exercise of caution. "A Szechwan pig tender has no
view of the nation or of the world. May I ask an ignorant
question?"

"Of course," Chou said, smiling.

"Will the Cultural Revolution be ended in the near
future?"

Chou's smile faded. Teng Shan-li was still something
of an unknown to him and the question was artfully
ambiguous. Teng obviously had not lost his talents; it was
a diplomat's question.

"I do not know when it will end," Chou replied.
"Chairman Mao will determine when these measures have
sufficiently destroyed outdated, counterrevolutionary symbols and values. I assume it will end when revolutionary
enthusiasm has in fact been rekindled."

Teng recognized the stylized phrases from some of the
banners in the public squares which quoted Chairman
Mao.

"May I ask, Premier—what of Russia? Do they just sit
by and watch?"

"They do not. They move more troops to our borders
every month, like a hyena smelling death. And our years
of isolation have left us without strong allies who might
protect our flank at a time like this. I do not know if we
have time to create alliances, but that is a subject you and I
will discuss at great length in the future.

"You have been harshly treated, Teng Shan-li," the
Premier continued, "and I wonder how you feel about
China now. What are your secret attitudes?"

"I am sixty years of age, Premier, and I have lived
through some bad times. China was ruled by an emperor
when I was born. As a young man I was a member of the
T'ung Meng Hui and a follower of Dr. Sun Yat-sen. I was
a Communist in Shanghai in the early days, and I fled to

Japan with Dr. Sun for a time. There was a price on my head then. This life has not been all sweet rice wine.

"I confess that it was very hard when I was singled out for ridicule and disgrace upon the ground that I lacked revolutionary fervor in my work at the Foreign Ministry. The Red Guards who took me were barely out of their slit trousers! None of them had fought the KMT or the Japanese, as I did. None had given their lives to the service of China as I have."

Chou En-lai lit another cigarette and drew deeply on it. "More tea, Comrade Teng? Please control your emotions; we have much to discuss."

Teng wiped his eyes with a handkerchief and drank some of his tea. "I am sorry, Comrade Premier. It seems that I always disgrace myself in your presence."

"I understand the emotions you feel. Do you blame Chairman Mao for what befell you?"

"I understand why he has upheld the left, sir. Our Revolution was hard won and must not be pissed away. In my heart I confessed my vanity, my deviations, and my improper desire for bourgeois comforts. I may serve China better as a result of my disgrace. But"—Teng's voice caught slightly—"it was very hard. I wish it had not been necessary for me and for my wife and daughter to endure the disgrace."

"Where were you posted during your diplomatic career?" Chou asked.

Surely he has read my dossier, Teng thought. Why does he ask questions which are easily answered by the written record? "Before the Revolution I was two years in Washington, D.C., in Chiang Kai-shek's delegation, as an interpreter. During that time I was Dr. Sun's agent and worked against the KMT. I guess you would say that I was a spy. During your days in Yenan I was in our embassy in Moscow. Then I helped open the embassy to the People's Democratic Republic of Germany. Between tours here in the Foreign Ministry I was two years in India, as Minister Counselor in the embassy there."

Chou nodded. "Did you know Comrade Chiang Ch-ing when you were in the Soviet Union?" he asked.

Teng instantly realized why Premier Chou was taking him in this conversational direction. Could it be? Had Mao's wife had him banished to the pig farm? Was she his hidden enemy and persecutor? If it was she, he had much to fear. "Only slightly," he replied. "Chairman Mao's wife was undergoing treatment part of the time I was in Moscow. On two occasions I visited her at a sanitarium to deliver mail and messages and to inquire about her health."

"She remains very much displeased with the people who were in our Moscow embassy in those days, you know," Chou said. "The man who was then our Ambassador is in detention, I understand."

Teng nodded slowly. "Could it be that everyone who was posted to the embassy then has been driven out of the Foreign Ministry?"

"I don't know," the Premier replied. "But stranger things have happened. People who were in motion-picture work in Shanghai in the thirties are in fear for their lives, I hear. Comrade Chiang is said to have a very long memory— and a long arm."

Teng rubbed his chin. "I am beginning to understand what happened to me, although it is bewildering. I cannot believe that the lady remembers me, or has any reason to feel that I wronged her in Moscow thirty years ago."

Chou smiled brightly. "Would you like me to ask Comrade Chiang if she has a grievance against you, Comrade?"

"Oh, please do not!" Teng protested in mock horror. "I think it will be best if Chiang Ch'ing believes that I fell into the pigs' mud and was drowned."

Chou nodded. "I think you are correct. You should make every effort to become invisible to that lady and her cohort. Now let me ask you another question. You have been posted to both Russia and the United States, and you understand something of their motivations. Who, in your opinion, is our greater enemy for the future, Russia or the United States?"

"Beyond question, Russia, Comrade Premier. The Americans would like us to govern ourselves exactly as they do, but I think they are no real threat to us. As time passes their link to Taiwan will erode, the Viet Nam War will end, and their businessmen will wish to sell razor blades to the citizens of Wu-han. The law of economic gravity will push the United States closer to us in the fullness of time."

Chou shook his head in disagreement. "Twice they have sent soldiers to our borders—in Korea and in Viet Nam. Their airplanes have bombed and strafed China. In Viet Nam they are opposing our ally. Shall we overlook all of that?"

"Yes, Comrade Premier. In spite of those incidents I think we will come to see that China's future interest lies on a path which leads to full relations with America. Russia will continue to be a greater threat to us. There are strong economic and strategic reasons for the Russians to covet our Pacific ports. They have always considered Manchuria theirs. And we are an ideological thorn in their side. They cannot let us alone."

"How do your Szechwan peasant friends view Russia and the United States?"

"They don't think about world affairs much, sir. The county radio and the mass meetings tell them only a little. I don't think I talked to anyone about the United States the whole time I was in Szechwan. Most people express a fear of Russia, if they talk about Russia at all."

"Let me caution you, Teng Shan-li, that there are elements of China's leadership which are very close to Russia. Your view of the future is not shared by our Minister of Defense, for example. I have heard him say that our soldiers even now should be in Viet Nam killing the imperialist Americans who threaten our borders. If Minister Lin Piao heard you talking as you have here today, you would be lucky to find yourself back with your pigs. Do not misunderstand: I wish for you to say openly to me the opinions you hold. But you must speak to no one else, no friend or relative or anyone, as you have here today. These are fluid and perilous times. I intend to study the question of China's foreign policy with your help, and I will attempt to chart the best course. But we must be realistic about the obstacles that exist. The Soviet Union will do almost anything—*anything*—to control China, and the Russian bear has its friends among us. Sooner or later we must deal with that reality.''

"I understand, Comrade Premier. I will be discreet.''

When the Premier dismissed him, Wang Li-fa led Teng to a south exit from the massive complex called the Great Hall of the People, along monumental, high-ceilinged hallways and through a narrow private passage. She used a ring of large keys to open several doors along the confined corridor.

"You are not from Peking?'' Teng asked.

"Canton,'' she said, "and Hong Kong before that.''

"Evidently you made an outstanding record at the language institute. You have a very important assignment.''

"I was raised in an English-speaking environment. I was fortunate. My father was a teacher.''

"Does he teach here?''

"He is dead. My mother repatriated us to Canton when he was killed in an accident.''

"I am very sorry,'' Teng said. "What does your husband do?''

The girl looked at him intently, as if to warn him that he was near to trespassing. "I am unmarried, Comrade,'' she said levelly.

"I am surprised. I am sure you have many suitors, though. Is there a favorite?''

Li-fa compressed her lips in annoyance.

Teng pressed on. "Are you a good cook?''

"No, very bad. I live in the Central Committee dormitory, so I never cook. I assume from all these questions, Comrade, that you have an unmarried son?''

Teng laughed. "No, no. No son at all; only one daughter, and she is married. No, I am just a curious old man who asks too many questions. I hope you will forgive me, Comrade Wang.''

"Here is your exit door,'' she said.

"Do you have any books in English I might borrow?" Teng asked. "My library is no more, and I miss it."

"I am sorry. Before the Cultural Revolution I did, but now I do not waste my time with antirevolutionary material."

"I am sure that is good advice," Teng said, shaking the young woman's hand.

When Teng arrived at home, via the crowded sidewalk of T'ien-t'an Pei-men Street, he found his wife standing on a box painting the big double gate that opened from the Lane of the Crows into their modest compound.

"That is a pleasing gray color, Wife," Teng greeted Hua Fan. "Where did you find that paint?" She climbed down, put her brush on the paint can, and followed him into the courtyard.

"It came from our new son-in-law, Husband. He drove here in a small truck this morning and brought us several treasures including a soft chair for you to read in. We have paint, some lumber, nails, and an electric lamp which can be turned in every direction. That boy is better than I thought. Did it go well at the Square for you?"

"Yes. There are huge crowds gathered there. Much noise. But you must not ask me to tell you about my work. Our safety depends upon my silence and your indifference to what I am doing."

"Forget that I did you the courtesy of asking," she said, offended. "I have no real interest in what you do, anyway. I am much more intrigued with the quality of the vegetables now offered in the market at the end of the lane. Perhaps after you die I will know how you have spent your life. I will read about it in a newspaper."

Teng shook his head in resignation. "I should send you back to Shanghai, I think. You belong in a hospital for nagging wives."

They walked across the stone courtyard to the rooms at the north side of their U-shaped house. To the right, on the east side of the yard, was the kitchen room where Hua Fan cooked and where they sat to eat. To the left was the west room, their bedroom, with the toilet in a shed behind. Ahead were two rooms which, like the others, opened onto the courtyard, but these two were joined by an interior door. Their daughter had been raised in the left-hand room and now it was Teng's workroom, smelling of fresh paint, furnished with the open boxes of books and magazines Li-fa had collected.

The right-hand room would serve as a living room, storage area, and catchall until Hua Fan finished her painting and cleaning. Then she intended to sew there, and they would sit in that room when they had guests.

Teng's room and the living room faced south; like the rooms in most northern Chinese houses, theirs had been built with a solid wall to the north, to block the bitterly cold winter winds. Windows opened to the southern sun.

Teng looked at the large black plastic easy chair his daughter's husband had placed in his workroom. He sat in it and found it comfortable, but he could see that it had known some hard use. Beside the chair was a pedestal lamp which Teng plugged in and turned on. Its light was brighter than anything else in the house. Suddenly the light went dark, and Teng twirled the switch fruitlessly. He walked out to the gate where his wife was finishing her painting.

"I turned on the new lamp and it was very bright for a short time; then it turned itself off. I fear it is broken."

"Perhaps not, useless scholar," she said sharply. "Have you tried the other lights? All the electricity often fails in this city now. I suspect the new, faithfully Red cadres in the powerhouses know too little about their machinery these days." She handed Teng her bucket and a rag. "I intend to paint the doors the same color as the gate, if we have enough paint. I will start with the kitchen door because it is the dirtiest. Pigs lived here while we were gone, I am sure. Human pigs."

Teng put the paint bucket near the kitchen door while his wife closed and bolted their heavy gate. She was putting on weight in Shanghai, he reflected, while I was losing twenty pounds. Where does a man's fat go when he loses it? To his spouse. An immutable law of the universe, perhaps.

Teng sat in his new easy chair, its back to the window. Hua Fan was right: The city electricity had failed; there were no lights in the house. Teng closed his eyes and thought about his conversation with Chou En-lai. Obviously, Chou was playing with the idea of a possible alliance with the United States. Teng was not surprised. Such an alliance made sense; China's economy was in a bad condition and Russia continually threatened its borders. Who else was strong enough to help? No European country, surely; and not Japan. The United States has become relatively weaker in the last decade—Viet Nam has bled her—and Russia has made herself stronger, but by a process of elimination, one is left with the United States as China's only choice.

Teng opened his eyes and reached for the small stack of *Newsweek* magazines Wang Li-fa had collected for him. The first copy offered a Presidential preference pool which had been taken by Lou Harris in November, 1966. George Romney was preferred to President Lyndon B. Johnson by 54 percent of American voters responding.

Among Richard Nixon, Nelson Rockefeller, George Romney, and Ronald Reagan, another poll showed Nixon as the choice of more Americans than the others. But if Nixon were to run against Johnson, Nixon would lose, especially if the splinter-party candidate George Wallace continued to seek voters. Wallace would attract some of the conservatives Nixon could get to vote for him if Wallace did not run.

Teng went across the small room to get his note pad. It felt marvelous to be working with a thick sheaf of paper again. His hands were clean (although some grime remained around his fingernails and in the cracks in his skin). He was using his mind.

Teng copied the *Newsweek* poll on his paper and browsed through the magazine, then picked up the next issue in sequence.

"I am like a warrior who has slept under a witch's curse

for a thousand years and now has been awakened by the touch of a beautiful maiden,'' he wrote at the top of a sheet of paper. "I am regaining parts of my life that were denied me for many months."

Teng resolved to keep a diary of his impressions as he went through this extraordinary process of awakening and reeducation. Someday, perhaps, he could share them with his grandson, if the gods smiled upon his daughter's marriage. At the least, his wife could read his diary someday and would know what he had been called upon to do by Premier Chou En-lai.

Six

• APRIL, 1967 •

Wang Li-fa smelled the fresh paint on Teng Shan-li's gate as she leaned her bicycle against the old wall. She looked up and down the lane at the weather-beaten gates and faded doors of the other compounds and houses on the short street.

Teng has been indiscreet, she thought. Uniquely, Teng has no *daiwan*, no workplace unit, she reflected, so his neighborhood street committee is his primary unit of identification. In a neighborhood like this the street committee probably consists of little old ladies who have lived here all their lives, know everyone, and know everyone's business. The auntie or granny who is the cadre on the Lane of the Crows probably watched every stroke of the paintbrush on this gate. Now she will be over here asking to see Teng's household-registration certificate, snooping into everything.

She will have plenty to tell the Neighborhood and

District Offices about this house. A large family has been removed by some authority, without even consulting the street committee, and the old couple who had been driven out in disgrace are mysteriously returned. The disgraced ones have such wealth that they buy *paint*! They flaunt their prosperity by painting their gate, when no one else on the Lane of the Crows can afford such amenities. Their rehabilitation from disgrace, which took place without participation of the street committee, is very irregular, even for these unsettled times. Everyone on the Lane remembers the old woman's family, the Family Hua, good merchant people who lived in this house at Number 8 for many years. Members of the street committee usually want no trouble; they might simply report the odd manner in which the change of occupants was effected. But it must be expected that posters will appear quickly, pasted to the beautiful gate, denouncing Teng for bourgeois tendencies and elitism, at the very least. If the street committee goes to the Red Guards, Teng could be in for another rough time, unless the Premier intervenes.

Wang Li-fa pounded on the closed gate. The gray paint was still a little sticky. Teng opened the gate and greeted her warmly. As she wheeled her bicycle into the small courtyard, Li-fa decided to say something to Teng about the panic; she did not wish to mention it to the Premier.

"Your gate looks very beautiful, Lau Teng. It is surely the richest-looking of any on the lane."

"Thank you. My wife . . ." he explained with a vague gesture.

"If I were a member of the street committee here I would rejoice that our newly returned neighbors had found wealth during their long absence in disgrace."

"Ah, I'm sure you would." Teng shook his head as he opened the door to his workroom. "Ostentation at a time when we should be discreetly invisible, eh? Unwise. Very imprudent."

Teng took Wang Li-fa's padded coat and gestured to his new chair. "Please sit here. My chair, along with the paint and the light, are gifts from our daughter's new husband. He is an engineer.''

"I prefer the straight chair, thank you. Perhaps your wife can tell one of the grannies on the street committee about the generosity of your daughter's new husband. Perhaps today?''

"Yes, I feel sure that can be done."

"Premier Chou En-lai asked me to come today to ask several questions."

Teng reached for his writing pad. "Will I respond to them now, or in a writing?''

"In a memorandum, please."

Teng settled into his new chair. The inside door opened, and Hua Fan came in carrying her two best covered teacups on a tray. She smiled a greeting to Wang Li-fa, who nodded respectfully. Teng did not introduce them.

When Teng's wife had left, Li-fa took a folded paper from her pocket. "The first question follows this explanation: There has been no diplomatic contact with the United States except the ambassadors' occasional talks in Warsaw, Poland. Those ambassadors of China and the United States have talked principally about Korea, very formally. What would be the best way to create a fruitful dialogue with the United States—in Warsaw, or by some other means?''

Teng made notes as Li-fa read from her paper.

"The second question relates to the same subject. China's economic resources continue to hemorrhage. Because our factories and farms now again have low productivity, it is necessary to spend China's scarce capital to import raw materials, arms, and essential manufactured products. It cannot be expected that productivity will rise until political stability is achieved, and that may require several years. Thus arises the question of the lapse of time: How soon might an alliance be achieved? Subsidiary is this question: In your opinion, Comrade Teng, when will the Viet Nam War end? Who will prevail? Will the United States withdraw? If our ally is defeated there, on what basis would it be possible for China to achieve a *rapprochement* with the United States?''

Teng mouthed the French word. "*Rapprochement*. I have not said that word for a long time.''

"You are further asked: Is it possible for China to borrow large sums of capital in the world money markets today? What are the nonideological arguments for and against doing so?''

"Nonideological?''

"That is, the Premier is well aware of the thoughts of Chairman Mao on the subject. Your response should state the considerations apart from that doctrine.''

"I understand.''

"Next, assume we arrive at the moment of our internal political equilibrium. What steps should immediately be taken with respect to foreign relations, import, export, the United Nations, Taiwan, the admission of foreigners, and the establishment of Chinese embassies abroad?''

Teng smiled. "A complex question. Please repeat it slowly.''

The young woman read it again, and added: "That is all I have brought you today. Your American-politics paper has been well received. The Premier will ask you to come to see him before long.''

"I'll be honored.''

Li-fa folded her paper. "Thank you for your hospitality, Lau Teng. I enjoyed the tea very much.''

"Thank you for mentioning the paint. You belong in our diplomatic corps, Li-fa.''

Wang Li-fa shrugged into her heavy coat. The girl smiled as she rolled her bicycle to the gate and waited for Teng to open it for her. "It will be wonderful to see the leaves on the trees again, won't it?'' she said.

"Some people in Peking prefer the autumn, but for me spring is the best time of the year,'' Teng answered. "Old men associate the autumn with the winter of death, I suppose. I read that somewhere. So it is natural that we rejoice at the resurgence of life, which is spring. You honor our house, Wang Li-fa. I hope you will visit us again.''

''Thank you, Lau Teng.''

Teng sat back in his chair, his eyes closed, and thought about Chou's questions. Viet Nam badly complicated the situation, of course. It would not be easy to accomplish an American accommodation, even if the war in Viet Nam did not exist. Taiwan remained an American client, armed and subsidized.

From a shelf Teng took a thick pile of heavy bond paper he had found in one of Wang Li-fa's boxes. He piled it neatly at the right of his desk and placed the top sheet in position in front of him. He savored its quality; it was an emperor's paper, almost too rich for an ordinary man to write upon.

''Memorandum Two,'' he wrote. His pen glided effortlessly.

Viet Nam.

China cannot abandon Hanoi for practical reasons:

1. Russia will immediately fill any vacuum created by such an abandonment. The U.S.S.R. covets warm-weather Asian ports. China would then face Russian forces to the south as well as the north.
2. A withdrawal of Chinese support for Hanoi would be mistrusted by the Cambodians, Koreans, and other Chinese clients.

The United States should be encouraged to withdraw from Viet Nam.

1. An American defeat there is unlikely. An American victory would bring American troops to China's border. Any subsequent accommodation to the Americans would be seen as a sign of China's fear or weakness.

2. The Viet Nam problem should be solved by the nations of the region, not by the U.S. or the U.S.S.R.
3. Substantial elements of the U.S. political society favor their withdrawal from Viet Nam. In 1968 candidates for U.S. President will be compelled to take a political position on that issue. China might secretly help those who favor withdrawal.
4. Rapprochement with the U.S. need not wait until all U.S. troops are out of Viet Nam but must only wait until their leaders have *decided* to withdraw and the process has begun. Then the Saigon government ceases to be an ally of the U.S. and becomes its pawn. The U.S. is then on the path of its own self-interest, and that path will lead it to China.

Taiwan

Similarly, the *frame of mind* of America's leaders regarding Taiwan is more important than what the U.S. actually does. Once leadership and popular thought accept the premise that Taiwan is not their ally but is our province, and that Taiwan is going through a transition (however slow) which inevitably will bring it to China, the battle is won.

China must begin to influence American *thought* in an organized, focused way. Business and political leaders . . .

"Now that you have a bright light, will you sit here all night, Husband?" Hua Fan asked as she opened the inner door.

Teng looked around. The light was gone from the sky; the windows were dark. "The time escaped me, Fan. Come and sit here with me for a moment and let me discuss something with you."

His wife sat uncomfortably on the straight wood chair where Li-fa had perched so lightly. "That is an interesting young girl," she said, "and I'm wondering why she comes to see you. Who is she?"

"She works for the Government."

"Just business of the Government brings you together?"

"Just business. She observed our beautiful gate, however, and I found it necessary to explain that our new son-in-law provided the paint. She suspected we had improperly obtained it."

"Everyone is suspicious these days."

"It made me think about the old people of the street committee and what they must be reporting to the District authorities. I think it would be a good idea for you to seek out that granny woman at the end of the lane who is on the committee. You may wish to hint to her several things, including a suggestion that I am doing secret work now which neither of us can discuss. I'd like those busybodies to be a little afraid of us. Tell her the paint came from our new son-in-law. Hint that he has influence."

"I'll think of something. I intend to complain about the loudspeakers, too. Those kids at the Institute yell all night long."

"Don't make up a big lie about us, Wife. Leave it mysterious. Just say it's so secret that you don't know what it is I'm doing, but it seems to you to be very important. And let us forget the Red Guards and their infernal loudspeakers. We don't want them coming around here again."

"At least the part about me not knowing will be no lie. Your supper is waiting for you, Husband. You had better come now. I will do as you suggest about the paint and the noisemakers. It was probably unwise to paint the gate, but as you know, I am a vain woman, given to many such frivolous decorations. My new spring dresses from Paris should be arriving tomorrow or the next day, and I intend to wear them to the market to buy cabbages. Your troubles are just beginning."

Teng smiled. The old woman was showing her wit once again. Perhaps she had really begun to put the disgrace behind her at last.

Seven

• APRIL, 1967 •

Whenever Matt Thompson rode an elevator at 20 Broad Street he looked for the blond young woman in the camel's-hair coat. But now that New York weather was warming he looked for her in a sleeveless dress, perhaps without stockings, with a narrow belt accenting her slim, firm waist. He had rehearsed what he would say to her, too, but he had no confidence that he would have the presence of mind to recall it if he encountered her.

Richard Nixon was equally elusive, if less ideal. Several times Matt had walked back to the Nixon corner of the twenty-fourth floor, hoping to meet and talk to his benefactor, but each time Matt inquired, Richard Nixon was out of town.

Eldon Carnahay told Matt about an office rumor that Nancy Mellor had told her boss, Nixon, that Matt was ideologically out of sympathy with Nixon. Carnahay was delighted with that bit of coffee-machine gossip. He confided to Matt that he'd feared that Matt might have lost his independence because Nixon had gotten him his job.

"My wife will cook you a big dinner now," Carnahay said happily. "Peg hates the idea that I'm even in the same building with Richard Nixon, not to mention in the same

firm. When I tell her the rumor about you she's going to
want to feed you."

"Look, Miss Mellor did all the talking," Matt protested.
"I couldn't get a word in. I didn't say anything to make
her think I opposed Nixon or his ideas. That really bothers
me. Hell, I am grateful to Nixon. He got me in here. I
don't want him to think I'm knocking him."

The next day, a Sunday, Matt called his father for their
weekly talk-in-lieu-of-a-letter. Matt expressed his dismay
at the office gossip: "This Mellor woman looks real tough
and I guess she didn't like me."

"Did you argue about China?"

"Nope. She gave me the standard Chiang Kai-shek
story and I just shut up. She asked me if you'd been run
out by the Communists and I said it had been the Japanese.
I'm sure I could have said a lot more than I did."

"I think you ought to talk to Rose, son. It's not good
for them to have the wrong impression of you."

"Right, Pop. That's what I'll do."

On Monday, Matt called Rose Mary Woods on the
interoffice telephone. "I need to talk to you privately, Miss
Woods. I have a problem."

When he arrived at the Nixon corner, he was shown into
Richard Nixon's office *by the blond girl from the elevator*!
He was totally thrown off stride. It was she; there could be
no question about it!

"Look," he said to her as she held the door to Nixon's
office for him, "don't go away, will you? We've got to
talk." She smiled, just as he remembered her smiling on
the elevator!

Rose Mary Woods was sitting in a cane-backed armchair
beside Richard Nixon's couch. The former Vice President's office was elaborately decorated with Oriental
mementos—a model Thai dragon boat, a large gold Japanese
wall screen, masks, a stringed musical instrument, several
framed ideographs. All the beige window curtains were
drawn closed. With the grass-cloth wall-covering and the
beige carpet it would have been a soporific room, but the
Oriental artifacts were spectacular.

"Who was that?" Matt blurted.

"Hello, Matt." Miss Woods smiled. "Who was who?"

"That blond girl."

"Which blonde? There are two of them out there. There is Shelly Skarney over in the corner and Glenna Harrison at the second desk. Which one do you mean?"

"The one in brown, right by the door."

"Oh, that's Glenna. She helps with the campaign chores. Do you want to meet her?"

"Yes, sure. Actually, we met before, but I didn't know her name."

"You have a problem?"

"Beg pardon?"

"You called me."

"Oh, right. I'm worried about you and Mr. Nixon getting the wrong impression of me."

"I don't know about him, but I have a very good impression, Matt. What's the question?"

"I hear that Miss Mellor believes I disapprove of Mr. Nixon and his foreign policy. I'd hate to have Mr. Nixon get that idea."

Rose Woods crossed her legs. "I think it's time you met Mr. Nixon, don't you?"

"Yes, I'd like that. I have a lot to thank him for, and I have a word for him from my father."

"Well, then, let's arrange it. He gets back from La Crosse tonight. I'll call you when I've cleared his schedule with him."

"I'd appreciate it, Miss Woods."

"Do you need an introduction to Glenna?" Rose Mary Woods smiled.

"I guess it wouldn't hurt. Thanks."

They stepped out into the confusion of piled boxes, partitions, and ringing phones. Glenna Harrison sat in a little fenced-off area next to Rose Woods's. Matt could see the top of her head above the partition. She was taller than he remembered her.

No preliminaries were necessary. After Rose Woods made the pro forma introductions and disappeared, it seemed very natural that Glenna would come to lunch with him. They both seemed to know that they needed to talk. As they rode down in the elevator, he said, "This is where I've been looking for you, going up and down. I thought you worked on fourteen. That's where you got on that night."

"I had left an envelope at an office there for Rose."

"Whose big car did you get into that night? Out front."

She looked puzzled, and he liked the way her eyebrows gathered in a little golden ridge above her eyes. "That's my dad's car. He picked me up for dinner."

"I guess I guessed that. Let's go uptown for lunch. There's no place quiet around here." He took her arm and it seemed exactly the right thing to do. He'd never felt so sure of his actions with a woman.

She smiled broadly. "How far uptown?"

"How about the Village?"

"Is this where I say 'My place or your place'?"

"Do you live in the Village too?"

"West Tenth."

"I live on MacDougal. Where do you like to eat around there?"

"Bigelow's."

"At the counter?"

She nodded. He hailed a cab and helped her in. Her dress had sleeves and no belt. He'd missed that.

"How about a place with tables?"

"Okay. Bigelow's can wait."

He told the cabdriver to take them to Sixth Avenue at Bleecker Street. Then he turned to face her and grinned. "Glenna," he said, "I'm just real glad to be with you."

"I'm glad to be with you too, Matt. I'm sorry we didn't talk in the elevator. I really wanted to, but my mommy always told me not to talk to strangers." She grinned broadly and squeezed his hand.

He talked his way into Puzzo's without a reservation. They sat at a small table against the wall and ordered from the blackboard. Matt knew the place was expensive, but he figured this was one of the few memorable occasions of his life, so what the hell? The Italian food was extraordinary, but he didn't taste the lunch, nor would he remember what he'd eaten. When they were seated their hands had touched on the table, parted in reaction, and come together again. He held her hand gently all through lunch, his thumb caressing her knuckles. He would remember how her skin felt.

She had graduated from Smith, where she'd known Julie Nixon; Julie had helped her get the job, Glenna said. For the past three weeks she'd been at Lyford Cay with her parents, water-skiing and loafing.

"You have a fantastic tan," he said. He looked at her face and the backs of her strong hands.

"Have you been to the Bahamas?" she asked.

"Nope. When I was at Dartmouth we went to St. Thomas once at spring break. Never the Bahamas."

"You went to Harvard too?"

"Harvard Law."

"Where are you from?" The way she looked directly into his eyes unnerved him.

"Whittier, in California."

"Why did you come east to school? Most Californians stay there, don't they?"

"I guess most do, but I really wanted to get away. My mother died when I was a senior in high school and my dad took it very hard. So I stayed home and worked a year. I had a real high draft number, so I knew I could go to school if I wanted. And my dad's a college professor, so I could get a little scholarship at Dartmouth. But I postponed it a year until Dad got adjusted to Mom being gone. When that time was up I was really ready for a change of scenery."

Glenna squeezed his hand. "That must have been hard. My father is so dependent on my mother to do everything for him."

"What does your dad do?"

"He's a stockbroker; he's in investment things. I'm not sure exactly what."

"Does your mother work?"

"God, no. I guess she did before she was married, but now she's the idle rich. The beautiful Marie goes out to lunch a lot. Did your mother work?"

Matt nodded. "She taught English at Whittier High for a long time. She kept winning the outstanding-teacher award."

"You must be smart," Glenna mused. "Any brothers or sisters?"

"No. How about you?"

"No. Girlfriends?"

"I went with a Cliffie for a couple of years, but she preferred doctors. I'll bet you've got a busy social life." It was true; he was sure she was engaged or living with someone. A stunning woman like Glenna must have men lined up down to the corner.

"I broke up with a fellow last year, just before graduation, and since then I haven't felt like getting involved. That breakup was pretty hard, and it still hurts a little." Glenna shook her head as if to shed the memories. "What do you do for fun?" she asked. "You look like you did sports. How tall are you?"

"Six foot two. Too tall?"

"Just right. Dartmouth crew?"

Matt nodded. "All four years. And I sculled for exercise at law school."

"The guy I went with rowed at Cornell."

"We beat them all three years I was varsity," Matt recalled. "What position did he row?"

"In the middle—one of those; I don't remember which one. Do you like the law firm?"

"Sure. I work for a tough taskmaster, but it's good. I'm on the international side. I'm surprised at how commercial everything is, though. Sometimes I think I might be happier at a firm that cared a little less about the bottom line."

"Aren't they all like that?"

"Maybe so. I don't know much about other offices, actually. My dad got Nixon to get me a summer job my second year of law school, so I didn't interview other firms. Maybe I should have." He shrugged. "Do you play tennis?"

"Sure. Squash and racquetball, too."

"Will you play with me.?"

"I'd like that."

"When I get my place fixed up, will you come for a Chinese dinner?"

"You cook?"

"Only Chinese. My mother taught me. We lived in China."

"What are you doing to your place?"

"It was in bad shape. I'm washing and painting everything and sanding the floors. I don't even have a decent bed yet."

"A good bed is important," Glenna said, their eyes meeting. "I don't cook very well, but I do have a good bed. It's big and firm," she said slowly.

Matt's throat tightened. "More iced tea?" he said irrelevantly.

Then the waiter brought Matt his check.

"Do you want part of the newspaper?" he asked her on the subway train as it lurched and roared southward toward the Battery.

She shook her head.

"Can I see you again, soon?" he asked, smiling.

She nodded and smiled. "I'd like that. I'm free most evenings."

He grinned.

Eight

"You sent for me, Comrade Premier?" Wang Li-fa asked as she came into the spacious west room of Chou En-lai's lakeside house.

"Comrade Wang, I have read both of Teng's papers now. Have you read them?"

"You handed me the first one to read, sir, and I did so. But not the second."

Chou nodded, lit a cigarette, and crossed his legs. He was seated in a blocky overstuffed chair, two large windows behind him. Li-fa could see People's Liberation Army workers cutting the lawn and cultivating the tree-shaded planting beds that sloped from the brown stucco house down to the lake. April bulbs were flowering along the borders. He was wearing an old blue jacket and light gray slacks; it appeared he planned to work at home.

"In the second paper, Comrade Teng proposed a very ambitious effort to persuade the Americans to pull out of Viet Nam. He reasons that unless they are committed to withdraw they will never come closer to China. It is a rather complicated argument. It is possible that he is correct, but it is perhaps a concept too sophisticated for my Politburo colleagues."

Li-fa stood at a respectful distance, her hands holding a small notebook in front of her. These conversations— just the Premier and her—were becoming more frequent, and they made her uncomfortable. He was confiding in her, saying things about his colleagues—even Chairman Mao—and about affairs of state which were indiscreet. He should not be saying them to her. He didn't know her well enough to talk to her in this manner. It imposed a heavy responsibility upon her; it delivered his life to her, in a sense.

All of this talk with Teng about the United States troubled her; she had no business knowing the things the Premier was allowing her to hear. It could be dangerous to know those things.

"Teng says," Chou continued, half to Li-fa, half to himself, "that we cannot hope for help from President Johnson, and I think he is right about that. Johnson obviously believes we are his irredeemable enemy in Viet Nam. Of those who may oppose Johnson at the next election, Richard Nixon and Nelson Rockefeller seem our best prospects. This Ronald Reagan, the movie actor, I cannot take seriously. He is a governor of a state, but he has no background; he knows nothing of China or the world. And Teng believes Reagan cannot be elected President. But one of the other two might beat Johnson, Teng says. He believes Rockefeller would have no trouble accepting our overtures; he is an internationalist of broad scope. But it occurs to me that Rockefeller might fear to do so; he might be criticized by his constituents for being too easy on Communists. That is always a problem for American politicians."

One of Chou's housekeepers came in quietly with tea. Chou pointed to the couch. "Sit there, Li-fa. I value your reaction to all of this. Will you have tea?"

"Thank you, Comrade Premier."

"Nixon is an interesting figure, you know," Chou continued. "I do not pretend to understand him. He made his career as an anti-Communist, as other American politicians have done. For some of them it has a nationalistic, almost jingoistic appeal. I think Nixon may be an insincere ideologue, however. He seems to be a practical person who will do what he must to gain a given objective."

Chou sipped his tea noisily. "Who will win the Americans' election, Comrade Wang?"

Wang Li-fa blushed a little. He is toying with me and will not take my response seriously, she thought. "I know nothing beyond what Comrade Teng has written for you, sir."

Reflectively, Chou touched the tips of his fingers as if praying. "I will see what can be done with Johnson, but I think my horse in this race must be Nixon. It is only when a horse is not expected to win that a bettor is given favorable odds, is it not so? It is then that one can make big winnings. What is the English idiom?"

Wang Li-fa supplied the English words: *"Long shot."*

"Long shot. Yes." And again in Chinese, Chou continued, "Please tell Yang I wish to see Comrade Teng in four or five days."

"Yes, sir. Comrade Premier, there was an occurrence of which I should tell you," Li-fa said apologetically. "When I went to Teng's house with your questions, I believe I was followed."

Chou's expression did not change, but he moved a little in his chair, one hand clenching. "Do you know who it was?"

"I saw them clearly but I did not recognize them. It was an older man and a woman. Teng lives in an old section of Ch'ung-wen District on a small lane, and I believe they followed me into the little street. When I came out of Teng's compound they were still there, at the end of the lane, and they followed me back. They were not very secretive about what they were doing. I don't think they were Red Guard."

Chou nodded slowly, his eyes half closed. "I want you to tell Yang Te-chong all about this. He will see that it does not occur again. I do not think you are in any danger, but it is troublesome. I would prefer that Teng be left to work in quiet. Thank you for being so alert."

Yang Te-chong was less sanguine about Wang Li-fa's story. He asked her many questions in his intense way, hunched forward in his chair. He made her think of a leopard, lithe, muscles bunched, claws working for a firm footing before it sprang onto its prey. He wanted to know everything.

Yang's quarters were near the front door of the Premier's lakeside house. When Chou was there Yang worked, ate, and slept in this office, leaving only when Chou left.

Wang Li-fa had never been in Yang's room before. There was very little of his personality in the shelves or on the tables except two handguns which he had been cleaning when she interrupted him. He offered her a chair, then went out to wash the oil from his hands. While he was gone she looked at the two books beside his cot, both classics written centuries ago.

Yang was said to have a family, but Wang Li-fa had

never heard Yang speak of them. Perhaps they were in Shanghai; she knew that Yang had come from there. There were no pictures of a wife or children in his room. Perhaps the story was untrue.

She had known since she was first assigned to be the Premier's staff interpreter that Yang desired her. Li-fa had not encouraged Yang in any way; she had long ago decided that nothing could be permitted to interfere with her work with the Premier. She found Yang very attractive, but he was probably a married man and it would be a scandal for them to have a romantic relationship. The Premier would never tolerate such a thing among his staff people, she was sure. And if there was a scandal, Chou would surely keep Yang and send her away.

Yang wanted a full description of the man and woman who had followed her, of their bicycles and their clothes. In a large city where people dress in two basic colors, ride the same kind of bicycles, and all have black hair, her descriptions were not very helpful, she was sure. But Yang took copious notes of Li-fa's answers.

"Were you frightened of them?" he asked solicitously.

"Not really. I was concerned that they might harm the Premier's work in some way. I did not wish to lead them back to him."

"Where did you go?"

"I came here to Chungnanhai instead of returning to our office. I reasoned that they might have the necessary credentials to gain entry to the Great Hall and could follow me to our office there, but very few people are permitted in the Chungnanhai Compound. They did not try to come in here. And I hoped that perhaps they would think I worked for one of the other officials in here and not the Premier."

Yang leaned forward to place his hand over Li-fa's where it rested on his desk. "Let me reassure you. I believe you did the right thing. You are a very intelligent young woman, very composed in a crisis."

Li-fa did not try to move her hand; she did not wish to appear to be rejecting Yang's touch. When she did not move, his hand embraced hers with a little more pressure. He looked into her eyes intently for some sign of encouragement, and she very nearly gave it to him. His contact was very pleasing and a little exciting. It wouldn't take much more for her to permit herself to become seriously involved with Yang.

The telephone on Yang's desk rang shrilly, startling them both out of the magnetic impulse which had held them. Yang slowly withdrew his hand and turned to the phone. Li-fa quickly rebuilt her defenses, rose, and went through the hallway and out the front door.

Li-fa took a deep breath, then another. She walked to the gray rack at the road's margin and pulled her bicycle out of the vertical bars which held its wheels. She slowly pedaled toward the gate, still shaken; the telephone bell had broken a sexual mood she hadn't experienced since her first year at the language school. She had been in love with a boy then; but she could not be in love with Yang, she vigorously told herself. It was a question of duty. She owed the Premier selfless devotion. There was no place in her life for a love affair. Of that she was very certain.

There had been an argument about the bed. Teng Shan-li and Hua Fan had enjoyed the bourgeois luxury of a Western bed for many years, until the night the Red Guards burst in on them. That same horror-filled night, Teng's library had been burned in the courtyard by a parade of chanting teen-aged ruffians, and all the family's Western clothes had been thrown on the fire. During the confusion Fan's beautiful innerspring mattress had disappeared.

The books and clothes were a cruel loss, but for Hua Fan the stolen bed became the recurrent, central recollection of that awful episode.

Shan-li and Fan had become addicted to Western beds in Germany in the time he was posted to the embassy there, thirteen years before. When they returned to Peking from Germany they had tried the customary Chinese bed, the felt pads laid on thin ropes which are strung from one side of the frame to the other. They had slept fitfully and quickly decided they were going to have to find a Western bed. In those days it was relatively easy for Teng to acquire the mattresses at no cost from the pliable chargé d'affaires of an embassy of one of the new African republics considered to be in the Chinese orbit. The chargé had been eager to accommodate an official of the Chinese Foreign Ministry, and he was able to conscientiously charge the disappearance of an embassy bed to "representation." The mattress had been made for export in France; its firm construction was precisely to Teng's liking.

The second night after his return to Peking from exile in Szechwan, Teng lay on his back on the rope bed that had been left behind by their dispossessed predecessors. He wistfully recalled the comfort of their former bed.

"What is the matter, husband?" Fan asked. "Do those radios keep you awake?"

"Loudspeakers, not radios. They are terrible, but I am sleepless because of this torture rack of a bed. I slept better on the ground among the pigs."

"We are lucky to have this narrow rack. You miss our French mattress, eh?"

"I do. That was the best bed in the world. I wonder who has it now."

"Those young vermin probably burned it. It wasn't Red enough for them, I suppose."

"I wonder if a good Western bed can be had in Peking these days. Perhaps from another embassy?"

"How could you afford to risk it? Isn't there still some danger from the Red Guards? Won't they be coming around and bursting in on us again?"

"I don't think they will, but I don't know. It is more likely that some in the neighborhood are watching us."

"How could you get a bed home? The streets are full of mobs of them; they would seize you. I heard of a woman in Western clothes being attacked the other day in broad daylight. The Red Guards who come to Peking from the countryside are harsher than those from Peking."

Teng nodded in the dark. "The Inner Kingdom has gone mad," he whispered. "They are pulling down the neon signs all over the city because they are not pure Chinese. I hear the big stone lions are gone from the entrance to the Foreign Ministry, too. They were too Western! And did you hear that the Guards have demanded that the traffic lights be changed? Red should be 'go,' they say. Crazy zealots!"

"One bunch," said Fan, "which comes from Harbin or somewhere up north, is going around Peking killing all the house pets they can find. It's bourgeois to have a bird or a cat, and besides, the pets eat food needed by our peasant comrades."

"They handed me a leaflet at the Square today which demands that everyone under thirty-five be prohibited from smoking or drinking alcohol. I guess they realized if they tried to stop older people there would be an even bigger revolution, eh? Well, what about a bed? What are we going to do?"

"Be sensible, husband! We are going to learn to sleep on this symbol of our solidarity with our peasant comrades; that's what we are going to do."

"Can we get some foam rubber or matting? I feel those ropes chewing into my back."

"Suppose we are caught with foam rubber?"

"Perhaps Dr. Fang would prescribe a mattress as a medical necessity."

"Dr. Fang is gone. I hear that most doctors have been forced to close their offices and go to clinics or hospitals. No one seems to know where he has been sent."

"So you will not permit me to have a decent bed? How will I sleep? I cannot sleep!"

"You have been sleeping on the ground for months. I think it is less the bed than all that noise which keeps you awake. Why not stuff some cloth in your ears to shut out those radios?"

"Can you hear that kid? Can you hear what he's shouting on his loudspeaker over there?"

Hua Fan listened closely. "He's saying 'Hung Ching,' isn't he? What is that?"

"That's what they want to call Peking. They are demanding that the name of the city be changed to Red Capital. That fool with the loudspeaker over at that Institute keeps chanting 'Hung Ching' over and over, and I guess he intends to shout it all night. Have you got something to put in my ears?"

Hua Fan got up and rummaged in a basket for bits of cloth, worked candle wax into the four pieces she found, and returned to bed.

"Listen to that vile rope creak!" Teng muttered.

"Put these in your ears and you won't hear it," Fan demanded. "There is nothing we can do about the bed and I am sick of hearing you complain about it. Now go to sleep!"

"I can't hear you," Teng said. "I have cloth in my ears, so I don't know what you are talking about. By the gods, this bed is uncomfortable!"

Nine

• APRIL, 1967 •

Chou En-lai did not tell his secretary and bodyguard, Yang Te-chong, precisely how to bring Teng to their next meeting; Chou was confident that Yang would make certain that no one followed Teng to him.

With a measure of irony Yang chose a religious landmark for his rendezvous with Teng; he calculated that its habitués would be no threat to Teng. And he guessed that Teng would know the place.

Teng Shan-li knew of the place, although he had never

worshiped there. He liked to tell people that he was a Christian by education, but a Communist by adherence and profession. For nine years, until he was sixteen years of age, Teng had attended the Methodists' mission school in Tientsin, the harbor city on the River Hai. It was there, in his last three years, that he had been befriended by Ezra Thompson, a classmate, the tall, thin son of two teachers from California, in the United States. Ezra Thompson was only a few months older than Teng and they had much in common. The American boy was broadly informed of what was going on in the world. Young Teng already had an acute, if elementary, sense of China's place and her destiny among the nations, and he had a thirst to know about foreigners and their countries.

Teng bombarded Ezra Thompson with questions about America. At the same time, Ezra Thompson was struggling to learn Chinese. He and Teng would sit talking for hours in the Thompsons' living room in the Methodist compound, Teng carrying on his half of the conversation in English and Ezra Thompson answering in Mandarin Chinese.

Teng had never been a Buddhist, as his mother was, but she had led him into temples when he was young to see the huge statues of Buddha. The Revolution had closed all churches and temples for more than ten years, but in 1960, in spite of Party doctrine, a few had been repaired by the Government and staffed with priests. The first to reopen in Peking was one of the oldest, the Yung-ho Temple in the East City District, close to the site of the old north wall of the inner city. Yung-ho became known as a place frequented by expatriate ethnics—Mongolians and Tibetans—in part because they were nearly all Buddhists. They also found the Yung-ho Temple congenial because many of the priests were ethnics too, and much of the ritual was provincial. In time it came to be called "the Tibetan temple" by the people in the District.

Yang sent Teng a terse note, delivered by a nondescript boy on a bicycle, summoning Teng to "the Tibetan temple." Teng rode his bicycle north on Tung-tan Street, almost due north from his house. When he crossed Ch'ang-an Avenue, where it becomes Chiang-kuo-mennei Avenue, he was unaware of those who were watching him: two men on bicycles, two men in a jeep a block behind the cyclists, and three men in a small white van fifty feet behind the jeep. The van appeared to be an ambulance.

Tung-tan Street was called Tung-si Street where it crossed Ch'ao-yang-mennei Street. A river of blue- and gray-clad pedestrians and bicyclists swirled through that urban cross-roads, all efficiently regulated by a white-uniformed po-liceman who gestured stiffly from a round wooden plat-form in the center. A few buses and trucks held to the centers of the intersecting streets, trying to keep away from the flowing mass of slow-moving bicycles.

At that crowded intersection the jeep and the van began to move up slowly in the stream of northbound traffic, sounding their horns and weaving among the bicycles. The two cyclists who were following Teng noticed the actions of others around them who turned to see the motor vehi-cles which were coming up behind them. The two men looked at each other in alarm and suddenly broke off their surveillance of Teng Shan-li. One man pedaled furiously to the right into a small side street which was too narrow and crowded to permit the jeep or van to follow. The other man dropped his bicycle at the curb and ran back south to the big intersection, crowded with a mass of gray- and blue-clad pedestrians crossing north and south. By the time the two men from the van had run to Ch'ao-yang-mennei Street on foot, they could not distinguish the cyclist from the rest of the bobbing, flowing crowd.

Teng was wholly unaware of any of this pursuit and escape behind him. The street ahead was crowded with bicycling people, some headed home to lunch, many on their way to a store or street market to do their daily shopping. Even the most experienced cyclist was obliged to be alert on Peking's major streets and to keep both hands on the handlebar, with a finger poised on the warning bell. At the corner called Andingmen, Teng turned right; there he rode along the site of the ancient city's north wall until he could see the tall, tiled roofs of the old Yung-ho Temple. Behind him, the jeep turned the corner and followed him slowly, its two occupants closely scrutinizing the bike riders between them and Teng Shan-li.

At the gate to the temple, which opened to a tree-lined side street, Teng put one foot on the ground, dismounted with some stiffness, and rolled his bicycle into a crowded rack beside the gate. As he straightened and looked at the tall red gate, Yang Te-chong walked to his side. "Good afternoon, Comrade Teng," the bodyguard said.

Teng had half-expected to be contacted in this fashion; he evidenced no surprise. He made a slight downward movement of his head, a fractional bow, and replied, "It's Comrade Yang, is it not?"

"Yes, Comrade. Will you join us in that small vehicle up the block? It will be cooler than riding your bicycle on such a warm day. I will have your bicycle returned to your home."

"Thank you. I am impressed with that accommodation and I am grateful."

Their destination was about a dozen blocks west, along the line of the old north wall, but the jeep driver crossed the north moat, passed Ditan Park, and turned west between the small lakes at Chiang-shi-kou. In the Huangsi neighborhood he turned south. Yang sat on the back seat, half-turned, watching the busy streets to their sides and rear.

At the Ku-lou intersection near the Drum Tower, the jeep driver turned the sharp angle to the northwest to drive along the northeast side of Shisha Lake. Charcoal dealers, stripped to the waist, were unloading a truckload of dusty black pellets on the bank of the lake. The white face masks over their noses and mouths were nearly black from the charcoal dust which had swirled into the air about them. Teng tasted the charcoal as the jeep drove by; then the air cleared as they passed under the great old willows that bordered the lake at its waist.

The jeep slowed as it reached the corner of a fourteen-foot-high gray brick wall that had been built some years before along the eastern edge of the lakeside roadway. At a large gate topped with a brown tiled pagoda roof, the jeep driver turned to his right and stopped. Two guards carrying Chinese-made submachine guns approached the jeep, one from each side of the red gate. Teng noticed the big doors of the gate and the red decorative poles on either side; unlike most gates in Peking, which were made of heavy timbers, these were of steel. The double gate slowly moved open, controlled by machinery which whirred somewhere inside the massive brick pilaster at the left of the red gate pole. Small trees in tubs were arranged along the exterior of the wall. The wall curved out of sight with the road's curve to the left of the gate. Teng could see no placard or sign outside the gate. Whoever lives behind this elaborate wall, Teng thought, must be of high rank and importance.

Immediately inside the gate the black-topped roadway forked; the jeep driver bore to the left, along the margin of a pond which separated them from a tall house. Both above them to the left (between their narrow roadway and the wall) and across the small lake there were dense groves of trees and a traditional, highly stylized Chinese rockery of oddly shaped, pocked boulders set in mortar. The lake was six or eight feet lower than the roadway; Teng saw that it was a kind of moat which seemed to meander through the woods to surround the house. In three hundred yards they came to a broad paved area just inside a second gate in the wall which they had been paralleling. There they turned right and crossed the moat on a thick concrete bridge.

A sturdy porte cochere sheltered the driveway at the front door. It was supported by eight square pillars, lacquered a deep green and bordered by more of the angular boulders and low plantings. Across the moat the woods were so dense that it was difficult to believe a wall and a teeming Peking neighborhood were three hundred yards away.

A uniformed guard in a dark green uniform—not a People's Liberation Army uniform—stood by the front door. His submachine gun was carried across his back on a leather strap. He watched impassively as Teng and Yang approached the door. A houseman in a white jacket opened the door and admitted them to a foyer bare of any furnishings. A long, high-ceilinged hallway ahead of them divided the big house into two parts. Plants in white pots sat upon tall, thin-legged tables at intervals along the hallway.

At the end of the passage the houseman opened a heavy door and they walked out into a courtyard, densely foliated with a profusion of plants and fruit trees set among small lawns and planting beds, each bordered with shin-high fences of open metalwork, painted white. In the center of the garden court, mounted on an elaborately carved white stone pedestal, was a rough stela of granite, evidently a very old and very important antiquity.

If the big house was faintly European, the courtyard was traditional Chinese. Three low, one-storied buildings formed the sides of the court, all of them trimmed in the bright green and red lacquers, fine wooden window details, and tapered pillars of the better old Chinese houses of the region.

Teng and Yang were led into the east house, which appeared to consist of one large room, hung with elaborate embroideries and furnished with many large rattan chairs and small tables.

Chou En-lai sat in a far corner talking with a large woman. Teng's eyes adjusted slowly to the dim light in the room. He could tell that when he entered the room their conversation stopped. When Premier Chou came to him Teng could see that his hand was outstretched. "Comrade, come in here and meet our hostess," Chou said with an overtone of enthusiasm.

As he walked closer, Teng recognized the woman; her picture was often in the Peking press, and he had met her once when he was a very young man. She had become very stout, her dark hair graying, but he knew her instantly. He was at once delighted and awestruck, and then somewhat impressed with his own recent attainment. Here he was in the company of the Premier of the People's Republic of China and the widow of his idol and leader,

Dr. Sun Yat-sen. Seeing Madame Soong vividly recalled for Teng those bitter days in Shanghai and in Tokyo when he and his friends had been so young and had believed so passionately in China's Revolution. He bowed deeply.

"Madame Soong, this is Comrade Teng Shan-li. I believe he too was a disciple of your husband," Chou said. "Sit here, Comrade."

"I am deeply honored to be a guest in your house," Teng said.

"You are welcome, Comrade Teng. I remember you. We were all in Japan together, eh?" She wore a loose-fitting caftan of some Middle Eastern style and ordinary black slippers over thick stockings which tightly bound her ample ankles. "The Premier has told me of your exile to Szechwan. I am sure it was difficult, and I am glad to see that you are restored to a situation of usefulness to China. There was a time this winter when I kept the gates closed and barred here, I don't mind telling you. My servants have all been with me for many years, so I had nothing to fear from them, but the Red Guards were very hard on our lovely old house in Shanghai. They looted it thoroughly. Occasionally one of them denounces me, so I think that one day the young people might be paying me a call here."

Chou chuckled. "Chairman Mao would not permit it. You are a national treasure."

"I'm not so sure," Madame Soong said.

"I have asked Comrade Teng to come today to talk to me about two very interesting papers he has written for me about the United States," Chou said.

"I lived there, you know," Madame Soong said, "many years ago. I've not been there for twenty years or more, but I liked the Americans as a people, very much."

Chou nodded.

"I am going to leave you, Comrades, to have your talk. If one of you will give me his hand, I will pull myself out of this accursed low chair and be on my way."

She shook Teng's hand back and forth several times. "I am glad to see you again, Teng Shan-li. My husband was very fond of you, you know. He would speak of your enthusiasm.''

"I am deeply honored, Madame Soong." Teng bowed.

The houseman who had brought Teng appeared at the door to take the old woman's thick arm. "Goodbye, Comrades. Stay as long as you like. This man will bring you tea, and later there will be supper if you are still here.'' Her slippers scuffed the rug as she moved slowly toward the door on the arm of her servant. When they had passed into the courtyard, Yang Te-chong and Wang Li-fa came in from the sunshine and stood awaiting Chou's instructions.

"You were not followed today?" Chou asked Yang, sitting back into his chair. He gestured for Teng to sit.

"Comrade Teng was followed by two men who disappeared when the guards tried to apprehend them,'' Yang replied tensely. "We were not followed to this place. I am sure of that.''

"Someone is watching Comrade Teng, then?''

"I believe they watch his house and follow him when he leaves.''

"Please determine who is doing this, Yang,'' the Premier said curtly. "Can you set a snare for them?''

"Yes, Premier. I will use some of the 8341 Guards and we will begin to watch the Lane of the Crows. We will apprehend them at the first opportunity.'' Yang spoke so intently that Teng felt sorry for whoever was following him.

"I hope you will determine their . . . ah . . . sponsors,'' Chou said.

"Yes, Comrade Premier.''

"Wang Li-fa, please stay here with us,'' Chou said. Yang Te-chong turned and walked to the door.

"I was unaware I was followed today,'' Teng said. "Perhaps I was careless.''

"It is probably better if you do not act suspicious.'' Chou shook his head. "It is deplorable that such a thing can occur, but it is a sign of the times. We are a badly divided nation, and our schisms weaken us. If we were united and strong, perhaps our need for external allies would be a minor consideration. But as things are, I consider it most vital. Tell me what you think of Richard Nixon.''

''I have read much about him,'' Teng began tentatively, ''and the authors disagree. I believe he is misunderstood by some of his biographers. I think it probable that he is singularly devoted to his public career, a very ambitious man whose natural inclination is toward the right. But to be elected he is perhaps willing to overcome his scruples.''

''Intelligent?''

''Yes, sir. But I suspect he is uninterested in most subjects. Politics, international affairs, and government take his attention to the exclusion of more mundane interests. I do not think he is a man who feeds his own horse.''

''If he is intelligent, how can he be a supporter of the KMT?''

''With many others of his faction in the U.S. Congress, he was effectively won over by the KMT and their American lackeys many years ago. Moreover, Nixon has made a career based on his public opposition to Communism. 'My enemy's enemy is my friend' is a doctrine that has caused Nixon to be friendly toward other reactionary regimes, too.''

''Why, then, is it reasonable to predict that Nixon will open relations with China if he becomes President?''

''Nixon today would not. But, I believe, if China were seen as a true counterweight to Soviet Russia, Nixon's international pragmatism would overcome his old loyalties. As President, his number one problem would be seen to be Russia. He is known to feel that President Johnson has allowed the Americans' European alliances to atrophy because he has been consumed with the war in Viet Nam. I believe Nixon could be brought to the frame of mind in which he would believe it necessary to pull out of Viet Nam—with or without a victory—and turn to solving his Russian problems. If he came to believe that an alliance with China would help him versus Russia, he would then seek it.''

"So his mind and the minds of the American people must be changed? How is that to be done?"

"I believe both have a chance to be successfully manipulated, Comrade Premier. I would propose that several agents be recruited to win Richard Nixon's mind. And the Russians and others are already hard at work to affect popular opinion in America concerning Viet Nam. We can help that effort.''

"Your plan is a chain of fragile links, Teng.'' Chou stubbed out his cigarette and lit another. "First, Nixon must defeat President Johnson in their 1968 election.''

"And we can help in that effort, with money and in our relations with Johnson.''

"Perhaps. Assuming Nixon wins, then his mind must be won. He is apparently tough and intelligent. There is no certainty that he will come to abandon old commitments and favor China.''

"That is so, but a young man who works with him is a friend of China and offers us a unique opportunity.''

"Who is this? Did you write to me of him?"

"No, sir. Discretion requires that only the three of us''—Teng looked at Wang Li-fa—"know of him. His name is Matthew Thompson, he works in Nixon's office in New York, and his father has been my friend since boyhood. He is about Comrade Wang's age, a lawyer, single, a supporter of Nixon's candidacy.''

"Will he do as we bid?"

"No one has asked his help yet. He must be skillfully recruited and managed.''

"Can he also help to defeat Lyndon Johnson?"

"No, sir. But our friends among America's *Genro* can help and advise in that effort. I feel that we can recruit other friends in America who can be of special assistance in planning for Johnson's downfall. They should be approached at once, and that effort should be undertaken independently of the recruitment of a Nixon adviser.''

"Why not simply persuade Johnson?"

"I think that is hopeless, sir. He sees Viet Nam as involving his personal honor. He sees China as his enemy there. He grossly underestimates the Russian threat. He is prideful, above all, and slow to listen to the advice of others. Our chance with Johnson was years ago, during his Senate years, and we did not take it."

Chou looked at Wang Li-fa. "Li-fa, what do you think of Comrade Teng's delicate chain of reasoning?"

Wang Li-fa blushed. "Sir, I am not informed."

"But you have heard what he says. Is it logical?"

The girl nodded. "It is logical, up to a certain point. The choice of Nixon is logical. But Nixon sounds like a difficult and complex old politician. Can a person of my age, such as this Thompson, influence such a man?"

"With deep respect"—Teng smiled—"the Premier of China is listening to a person of your age right now. It is not possible for me to say that he is being influenced, but clearly he is listening."

Chou grinned. "Comrade Teng has scored a point on you, Li-fa."

The girl smiled and nodded. "I confess it, but it has never seemed possible to me that the Premier truly gives heed to what I believe, nor is there any reason why he should do so."

The houseman came in with fresh hot tea in a large vacuum pitcher decorated with orange flowers. Chou asked him for sweet cakes.

"How would you recruit your friend's son?" the Premier asked Teng.

"I believe he should be invited to Hong Kong to meet with your envoy under some suitable and attractive pretext. Perhaps some law business?"

"Our rich friend in Hong Kong could offer him a brief, perhaps," Chou mused. "Whom can we send to recruit the American? His father's friend?"

"Or another in whom you repose confidence. You should decide, of course."

Chou pointed at Wang Li-fa with his cigarette. "What is

the name of our smart, rich friend in Hong Kong? The fat one who does a lot of business with America?''

"Mr. Hung. Hung Wai-lang."

Chou nodded. "Comrade Teng, let us cause Hung Wai-lang to invite your Mr. Thompson to come to talk with you in Hong Kong. You have never met the young man, eh?"

Teng shook his head. "No, Premier."

"Well, go down there and see what he is like. I will leave it up to you whether you enlist him or not. Before you leave here today perhaps you and Li-fa will draft the letter to Mr. Hung for me. She will cause it to be delivered in Hong Kong next week. Then Yang will see that you get home safely. You and he must discuss how to set a trap for those who watch you. I cannot have them following you to Hong Kong." Chou nodded. "Thank you for coming."

Teng stood and bowed slightly. "I am grateful for the confidence you repose in me, Comrade Premier. I am honored."

Chou nodded again.

Wang Li-fa led Teng across the courtyard in the twilight. The stela cast a long shadow up the side of the building in which Chou sat, wreathed in cigarette smoke, legs outstretched, his eyes half closed.

Yang's car waited beside the low Western building.

"Comrade Teng," Yang said as the crowded car backed slowly, "these men are from the 8341 Guard Unit, which looks after the Premier." Two young men in ill-fitting Mao jackets sat beside the driver. A third was jammed into the corner of the narrow back seat. Yang sat in the middle, his broad shoulders wedging Teng. "You will walk the last several blocks to your house, and they will be nearby. Do not think of yourself at that time."

The big red gates opened slowly. The fading western light reflected off Shisha Lake, silhouetting three men who were leaning on the iron fence at the lake's edge, smoking and talking.

"Those are our men too," Yang said. "We are determined to protect you, you have nothing to fear."

"I am comfortable, Comrade Yang, thank you. Your men look very competent."

Ten

Glenna Harrison's parents called it The Cottage, in the fashion of the old Newport social lions who took pleasure in such blithe understatement. The Harrisons' Rhode Island summer house was not actually in Newport, although some of their New York friends who had only heard of it had the clear impression that it was. In fact, the Harrisons' thirty acres looked across Sakonnet Bay to Newport Island, about a mile away.

It didn't really bother Marie and Joe Harrison that there wasn't a tree or bush on the whole thirty acres. As Marie would often explain, "We just aren't tree people, I guess." Joe liked the idea of the full summer sun's coming right down on them without the intervention of leaves and branches.

To prevent erosion, Joe Harrison had agreed that several hundred bushes should be planted around the house, but no trees. Down toward the beach and along the sides of the property the landscapers had been permitted to plant pines, at such a distance from the house that none would ever cast a shadow upon a terrace.

A high brick wall divided The Cottage from the county road. The Harrisons' steel-barred electric gate offered the passerby only a truncated view of a new black-paved driveway curving off to the left, the steep roofline and a timbered turret of the big Tudor house, and flashes of the bay beyond. Small cedar bushes bordered the driveway.

When they grew up, there would be no view at all from the road.

In May of 1967, Glenna had forewarned Matt Thompson about her parents and The Cottage, as most young women talk to young men who are about to meet a girl's parents for the first time.

"They will never let us sleep together there, because they are superstraight," she sighed. They were lying in her bed; it was Wednesday night, and he was trying to read a section of the *Times* he had not had time to read all day. Matt slipped his hand under the covers and between Glenna's legs, resting his arm along her naked torso.

"Why are we going, then?"

"Because I want them to meet you. I talk about you, and they are anxious to get to know you."

"Do they know we sleep together?"

"Of course not."

"Isn't it time they did?"

"I told you, they are superstraight. They think I'm a vestal virgin."

"Is it dress-up?" Matt turned the page with difficulty, withdrawing his hand from her body to crease the fold.

"Definitely. It always is. Do you have some white slacks?"

"Nope. How about if I wear Levi's?"

"Unh-unh. Could you get some? The uniform up there is slacks, Top-siders, blue blazers, and Lacoste shirts. The men wear ties at dinner."

"Jesus. I don't think I want to go. Why don't we go to Maine for the weekend? Tell them we have to."

"Look, I promised. If you don't come, I'll have to go up alone, by myself. I've got to show up."

"Okay. What do I talk to your dad about? The market?"

"That, and he's interested in politics and government."

"Does he read?"

"Are we on that again? Sure he reads. Just because I do

other things for pleasure, do you think my family is illiterate? My mother reads too."

"Touchy, touchy. What do I talk to her about?"

"Well, you can tell her," Glenna said, smiling, "what a lovely daughter she has. And I think her father went to Dartmouth, so you can talk about that, too."

"What do we do up there?"

"We have a boat, and—"

"Sailboat?"

"No, it has a big engine. It's a big cruiser. We'll probably go out on that for dinner one night."

"Fishing?"

"I guess so. We have a long dock and you can probably fish off that; but I don't think we have any fishing rods. There's a yardman; maybe he has one. We have a tennis court, a pool, croquet. There's plenty to do. Take your tennis racquet."

"Your folks are very social, right?"

"I guess. They entertain quite a lot. Oh, I forgot to tell you: there will be other people there for the weekend. Two couples from here who are old friends, and some reporter who is Swedish. They met him at dinner the other night and invited him up."

"Do your folks know Nixon?"

"Sure. How do you think I keep my job? Daddy has known him for years, and once he gave Nixon a lot of money; that was when Nixon ran against Kennedy. Daddy can't stand the Kennedys, not any of them. I first met Mr. Nixon when I was really young and he was Vice President. We all went to Washington for an inaugural ball and the next day he and Mrs. Nixon had us to their home for a reception. They are so nice. I'm really glad to be working for them—for him—well, I guess it's really for both of them. You can talk to Daddy about Mr. Nixon, because he's known him for a long time."

Matt dropped the newspaper to the floor beside the bed. "So I need swim trunks, tennis clothes, deck shoes and what else? What does one wear when one plays croquet?" he simpered.

"Just don't wear sharp heels on Daddy's croquet green, or he'll kill you."

"No cowboy boots?"

"You don't even have any cowboy boots."

"Hell, I don't have half this outfit you're talking about. I'm going to have to go out tomorrow and buy a bunch of stuff, just for the weekend."

"This isn't the last time we'll be going up there, Charlie."

Glass doors opened onto the pool terrace at the west side of the house, near the south end of the spacious flagstone terrace.

Glenna's father was talking to a short, blond Swede. The Swede wore chinos, tennis shoes and a red windbreaker which said TIME/LIFE BOOKS over his heart. Glenna interrupted their conversation to introduce Matt to her father.

Joe Harrison was a head shorter than Matt Thompson, about the same height as his only daughter. He had once been blond, too, but his hair had turned gray and was thinning in a band from front to back; as in all seasons, his high forehead was deeply tanned. He wore a 46 Short Stout now, to accommodate his broad shoulders and expansive belly; his tailor had done a good job of constructing a blue blazer that flattered his shape.

"Mr. Thompson, welcome," he growled. His voice was deep, and his words were somehow bent by a sideways movement of his jaw when he spoke. Matt found that he had to listen closely or he misunderstood the man.

"This is Mr. Bendixxon—Mr. Thompson." Joe Harrison waved them together like a fight referee. They shook hands. "Mr. Thompson is a fledgling lawyer in Wall Street. Mr. Bendixxon is a well-known Swedish journalist."

"And this is your daughter?" Bendixxon asked.

"Of course. Excuse me, dear. This is Glenna Harrison, who is Richard Nixon's secretary and girl Friday."

Glenna blushed. "How do you do, Mr. Bendixxon? I'm,

not really all that; I just help out his secretary and the others who work for him."

"How interesting to work for such a controversial person," the Swede said diplomatically. "Do you see him often?"

"Sure, every day that he's in the office. Matt works there too."

"You work for Nixon?"

"Not directly; I work for the law firm of which he's a partner."

"Does he really practice law?" Bendixxon asked.

Marie Harrison appeared in the open French door to announce lunch. "You didn't offer the children a drink," she chided her husband. "Perhaps Matt would have liked a Bloody Mary or something."

"No, thanks, I'm fine," Matt assured her.

A maid served shrimp salad and iced tea in the formal dining room. Joe Harrison received a special plate bearing a sirloin steak and a baked potato.

"Joe just can't eat shellfish," Marie Harrison explained apologetically to Sven Bendixxon. "It makes him very ill. But that's no reason for the rest of us to miss out on the fruits of the sea, is it? I just think that whenever we're here we should enjoy all the good things that the country has to offer us. Don't you agree, Matt? You look as if you were raised in the country—so rangy and tall."

"Not really. My dad is a college professor, and I grew up in a small town in Southern California."

"And in China," Glenna added.

"I have just come from China," Bendixxon said. His accent became more pronounced, as if his total concentration were on what he would say next. "Were you there recently?"

Matt shook his head. "I was very young; my father taught there, before it became the People's Republic."

"It gripes me when people call it that," Joe Harrison rumbled.

"That is its name," Bendixxon said, smiling.

"But it's a dictatorship," Harrison said. "The people don't own it; the place belongs to Mao."

"The people are in revolt," Bendixxon replied. "I have the impression that Chairman Mao and Chou En-lai and the other leaders have lost control in some important ways. Mao started this Cultural Revolution, but it has gotten out of hand."

"Will Chairman Mao be overthrown?" Matt asked.

"No, he still controls the Army, and just now that is the key to everything. But it is terrible to see what the Chinese are doing to themselves."

"I don't think it's terrible at all," Joe Harrison grated. "They are simply revolting against a Communist tyranny, and you can't blame them for that."

"Is that true, Mr. Bendixxon?" Matt asked quickly. "Or are the Red Guards and the others overthrowing leaders who aren't hewing close enough to the pure Maoist line?"

"Yes, that's it, I think," the journalist said. "I talked to some of the leaders of the Cultural Revolution who told me that Mao himself instigated much of what is going on."

"Why would he do that?" Glenna asked.

Bendixxon put down his fork. "Since they won the country in 1949, Mao and Chou and the others have been trying to learn to govern it, but there are eight hundred million people and the country is very diverse. It has rarely had a successful central government. It has never had a popularly elected government. China is a sick giant. They told me Chairman Mao saw that after less than twenty years, his Revolution was in danger of being lost because the Government, for very practical reasons, was drifting into moderate, pragmatic policies to solve its social and economic difficulties. Mao himself was being shunted aside, and he found himself listened to less and less by China's new leaders. So he turned the young people loose to restore the Revolution."

Joe Harrison had finished his steak and looked to his

wife for his dessert. She found the floor buzzer with her foot, and a maid appeared to begin clearing away dishes.

"What's become of the good Chinese people who have kept things going all these years?" Matt asked Bendixxon. Joe Harrison shot him a hard glance; Mr. Harrison didn't believe there were any good Chinese, obviously.

"Anyone who could be called an intellectual has been driven away from his work," Bendixxon said. "It is a society committing suicide."

"The same thing should happen to Russia," Joe Harrison growled.

"We know a great many Chinese, and they are wonderful people," Matt said defensively.

"You don't know any that are Communists, do you?" Glenna asked. She appeared a bit too obvious; she was asking the question to restore Matt to her father's side of the argument.

"Would self-determination work there?" Matt asked. "What would happen if everybody were suddenly given the vote?"

The journalist shook his head. "Anarchy. Chaos. You Americans will someday learn that your incredible freedom can't be exported everywhere like Coca-Cola. There are vast parts of the world where the people wouldn't know what to do with liberty if they were handed it on a silver platter."

"But couldn't they be taught to use it, and then wouldn't they be happier?" Marie Harrison suggested.

"I'm not sure they would." Bendixxon smiled. "Some women prefer a husband who runs their lives, eh? Tells them everything to do? Some peoples are like that, too."

Marie Harrison was flustered; she appeared to feel that the Swede was poking fun at her personally, and she didn't know what to say in reply. "What about tennis?" she suggested with a brave smile. "You play, don't you, Matt? Mr. Bendixxon does. How about mixed doubles?"

*   *   *

The weekend passed. Everyone ate, talked, slept, and ate again. Sunday morning a thick fog held over Sakonnet Bay until about ten thirty. Joe Harrison organized a compulsory croquet game in the fog. At three, Matt drove Glenna back to Manhattan in bright sunshine.

Someday The Cottage would belong to Glenna, Matt realized, and she and her husband would invite people there for the weekend. Glenna's husband. Matt saw that man beside her in tennis whites, greeting their guests. He was tall, well built, with broad shoulders, but he had no face. Matt pasted his face over the blank space and stood back to look at the scene.

He shook his head reflexively, negatively. Glenna's husband? Maybe. But not up there at The Cottage. Not there.

Eleven

• MAY, 1967 •

Exactly nine days passed from Teng Shan-li's meeting with the Premier in Madame Soong's house to Matthew Thompson's receipt of a letter from Mr. Hung Wai-lang of Hong Kong.

Mr. Hung had been very willing to have Thompson's draft letter typed on Hung and Company's finest bond paper. He was happy to sign the letter and send it to New York by air express. There was no question in his mind that the courier who brought him the draft had come straight from Chou En-lai himself. Mr. Hung felt deeply that it was an honor to be of service to Premier Chou. He also felt that it was good business to do the People's Republic of China a favor now and then. One hand must wash the other, as his Cantonese mother used to say.

When Albert Murphy telephoned him from New York, Mr. Hung was not too surprised at Murphy's respectful, solicitous manner. Since the previous February when *Fortune* magazine had published a long article about Hung and Company, its smiling proprietor, and his worldwide enterprises, Americans seemed to know who Hung Wai-lang had become.

"Mr. Hung, I am Albert Murphy, a partner in the law firm of Nixon, Mudge, Rose, Guthrie and Alexander, in New York."

Hung smiled at the secretary who was listening on the dead-key earphone, taking shorthand. "How may I help you, Mr. Murphy?" Hung asked.

"You have written a letter to our Mr. Matthew Thompson, sir, dated last week, May twenty-first."

"Yes, I did."

"As you may not know, Mr. Hung, our Mr. Thompson is a lawyer of somewhat limited experience. He is a young man."

"Yes, I know his father very well." Hung smiled again. It was a harmless pretext.

"Our partners are delighted to be of service to you, Mr. Hung. They have appointed me to contact you on behalf of the firm, and I will be happy to fly out to talk with you at your earliest convenience."

"And what has become of Mr. Thompson?" Hung grinned. He was enjoying this little game.

"Well, Mr. Thompson is here in our New York office, but we would hardly consider assigning him to a substantial client such as you until he'd gained a great deal more experience. I myself have—"

"Mr. Murphy," Hung interrupted, "did Mr. Thompson show you my letter?"

"Yes, Mr. Hung, and I have talked to my partners about it."

"Then you saw that I have selected him to come here and discuss my United States legal problems, did you?"

"Well, yes, Mr. Hung, but I assumed—"

"If I had selected you, Mr. Murphy, would I have sent the letter to Mr. Thompson?"

"I understand, Mr. Hung, but it's a question of competence. We must judge whether Mr. Thompson is best able to carry out your assignment. We have that responsibility."

"I can assume that burden, sir. I have selected Mr. Thompson. If he tells me he will not come, then I will select another lawyer. But I have no reason to select another lawyer from your office. I will go elsewhere."

"I see."

"I am prepared to pay Mr. Thompson a retainer of ten thousand dollars U.S., plus his expenses, to come here at once. I have substantial legal problems in the United States. Are you telling me he is not available to come?"

Al Murphy was silent. Hung Wai-lang assumed he was talking to someone else with his hand over the mouthpiece. Hung shrugged at his listening secretary and grinned. She smiled back.

"How soon will you want him there?" Murphy asked unhappily.

"Next week, please. Thursday will be fine."

"He will arrive in Hong Kong on Wednesday and he will call your office on that day," Murphy said.

"I prefer that you send no one with him," Hung added.

"It's been nice talking to you, Mr. Hung."

As soon as Murphy disconnected, Hung gave rapid-fire instructions to his secretary in Chinese. A courier must immediately deliver a letter to Wang Li-fa in Peking saying when Matthew Thompson would arrive in Hong Kong. Travel money must be cabled to Thompson. All appointments for Thursday must be changed to other days. Chen Yu-shen, the comptroller, must gather some American legal assignments to give Thompson when he comes. They should be of modest difficulty. After all, the young man is of limited experience.

"One can only speculate," he mused to his secretary, "why Peking is interested in a young American lawyer of modest attainments." He smiled broadly. "But I cannot think of a reason that can possibly hurt Hung and Company."

PART

THREE

PART

THREE

Twelve

It had been so hot in August in 1967 that few cooking fires were lit for the evening meals in the old neighborhoods near the Lane of the Crows; thus, the gentler August night winds carried a little less coal dust than usual. Still, even the most benign summer breeze brought with its cooling touch the faintest taste of coal.

As Teng Shan-li prepared to leave his house, dust and grit from the plains came on a freshet of the warm wind and stung the faces of the two young men who pressed their backs against the brick walls of the lane. Both were dressed in black short-sleeved shirts and black cotton pants; the younger of the two wore a black stocking cap. He was hidden by the deep shadow of an angle in the compound wall which fronted the third house.

It was very dark there; the man in the black hat had removed the gate light bulb and carefully placed it on top of the wall. The somewhat older man stood in a doorway of a house near the dogleg of the lane. He could not see Teng Shan-li's newly painted gate from where he stood. The faint light from the windows of the thirteenth house was sufficient, however, for the older man to see whoever walked in the lane east of Teng's gate.

Yang Te-chong had carefully chosen this night; it was the last moonless night before Teng's departure for Hong Kong. As usual, Teng had received a message from Yang delivered by a young boy on a bicycle. Teng was to walk from his gate exactly one hour before midnight, turn left, and walk in a normal fashion the length of the Lane of the Crows. At the marketplace at the corner of Tong-tan Street, Teng was to walk through the market and keep walking north on Tong-tan until Yang Te-chong approached him.

Teng wore a square-cut short-sleeved white shirt over his everyday black pants. He owned a couple of darker shirts, but if he must be a target he wanted to be a good one. The gate bar made a clattering noise when Teng opened it. The squeal of the hinges could be heard over the constant noise of the Red Guards' loudspeakers at the Institute six blocks away. Teng closed the gate behind him firmly and turned left toward the window light of the thirteenth house. He thought he heard someone in the lane behind him, but he had determined not to look back for any reason. He squared his shoulders and walked on. A dog barked in the compound behind the wall of the tenth house.

As he passed the small lighted window of the thirteenth house, which was the house of Chin, Teng looked in, but there were no people to be seen. The light came from a bare bulb hanging from a ceiling wire which was swinging gently back and forth. The warm, gusting wind at Teng's back was blowing inside the thirteenth house too, moving the light and making the blurred shadows of the window mullions slide up and down the lane at Teng's feet.

Teng expected to find the marketplace deserted so late at night, but there were still several vendors squatted by their piles of produce in the dim glow of Tong-tan's streetlights. Teng passed one old man in brown short pants and a dirty sleeveless undershirt, his arms resting on his bony knees; he was evidently the guardian of a huge pile of squash which towered over him as he sat on his heels at its margin. There were small green squashes around his sandaled feet, and among them were the butts of countless cigarettes.

As Teng walked by, he smelled the acrid smoke of the short cigarette in the man's mouth. The squash seller turned his head suddenly, and in spite of his resolve, Teng turned too, to look behind him. Where the Lane of the Crows opened into the market three men were silently struggling in and out of the shadow of an adjacent wall.

Teng was shocked by the extraordinary vigor with which the men went after each other. He had talked himself into the comfortable thought that whoever was watching him was a gentle, older person who was simply gathering information about where he went and whom he spoke to. If there was to be a nighttime encounter in the Lane of the Crows it might involve a hand on his elbow and no more than a hard shove in the small of his back.

But these were tough young men violently struggling in the corner of the marketplace, striking heavy blows, hurting each other, grunting with exertion and pain like young animals. It was terrifying to think that one or several of them might have attacked him that way.

The three wildly thrashing men fell across a pile of cabbages just as two more men in dark clothing ran from the Lane of the Crows. As they reached the sprawling, grappling trio there was a single gunshot and one man of the three stood for a moment and then fell heavily to the pavement. A second member of the trio sprang to his feet and ran south on Tong-tan Street. The two newcomers raced after him and disappeared from Teng's view.

Teng had not heard a gunshot for many years, but he was instantly aware that one of the strugglers had been shot. A crowd of pedestrians began to gather around the man who was lying on his back. Two jeeps pulled to the curb of Tong-tan, and six men in dark civilian clothes jumped out and roughly pushed their way through the onlookers. There was no mistaking their brusque technique; it was clear that officials had arrived.

Teng's first instinct was to go to where the man had fallen; he could explain to the authorities what he'd seen. But Yang's note had said, "Whatever happens, you will continue north on Tong-tan Street." Teng turned away as four of the officials carried the fallen man to one of the jeeps. Teng felt vulnerable. Perhaps the survivors of that fight were the people who were after him. He had no assurance that Yang had survived. Perhaps Yang Te-chong, the Premier's bodyguard, was the man who had been shot. As Teng walked hesitantly up Tong-tan he sensed that people behind him were looking at him, and he expected someone to begin chasing him. But no one did. He crossed several large intersecting streets and continued on, unapprehended, walking with the flow of the sidewalk crowd.

At the next corner a crowd had gathered to read hand-lettered posters that were fastened to a line of specially built wooden frames. Bare electric-light bulbs had been festooned above the frames, so the lettering was legible from a considerable distance. A young man in a blue Mao jacket stood in front of the posters, haranguing the crowd with the help of a small bullhorn.

"Beware!" he shouted. "This school has been seized by a faction which seeks only comfort and power. They are the People's enemies."

Teng stepped off the curb to detour around the listening crowd, which was so dense that it blocked his passage along the sidewalk. An olive-drab jeep going south came to an abrupt stop beside Teng. He found himself face to face with Yang Te-chong, who was sitting in the front passenger seat beside a husky young driver. The jeep had stopped so suddenly that several bicycle riders behind it nearly ran into its rear.

"Climb in, Comrade Teng," Yang said cheerfully. "You have had a long walk this evening." He gestured for the driver to start as soon as Teng had climbed behind Yang into the back seat. Teng's foot came down on an irregular object on the floor. He reached down to move it over and discovered that there were two submachine guns on the floor just behind the front seats. Teng straightened and moved his feet back out of contact with the guns. He found it necessary to brace himself by holding Yang's seat with both hands as the driver swerved around bicycles and turned west toward Chianmen.

Yang said nothing more to Teng for the ten minutes until the jeep turned into the Lane of the Crows. At Teng's gate, Yang turned and said, "We had some bad luck tonight, Comrade, and you must continue to be careful. There were two men here in the dark and both followed you. One shot himself with his own gun when we caught him. I think it was an accident; he meant to kill my men, not himself. He is in the hospital now. The other bastard escaped, I'm afraid. If the wounded man lives I will interrogate him, of course, and all this exercise will have been worthwhile.

"Meantime, you will fly to Hong Kong, but the Premier has arranged for a private airplane to take you as far as Canton. That will shake off any followers. Here is a card on which Comrade Wang has written your travel instructions. Until Tuesday, I suggest you stay in your house. Good night."

Teng climbed laboriously out of the jeep, and as he did he noticed that his gate was open about an inch. "Is it quite safe here now?" he asked Yang.

Yang smiled. "Yes, quite safe. The guard has patrolled this street and has even searched your house. There is no danger."

Teng nodded and walked toward his gate; it receded before him slowly to reveal Hua Fan. She was in a great state of excitement.

"Husband, there were big young men here, and a man was shot in the marketplace. What is happening? All the neighbors are awake, and they told me of a fight among men in the lane near the fourteenth house. Are you hurt?"

"I am fine," Teng said, shutting and barring the gate. "Let us go inside the house. Is there something to drink? Tea? I am suddenly very thirsty. I have heard men speak of a thirst for life. Perhaps that is what I now experience."

Thirteen

New York had been unusually pleasant the day Matt Thompson caught an early-morning flight to San Francisco. Glenna Harrison had insisted on driving him to the airport. Matt's instinct told him to decline her offer, but when he tried to tell her not to pick him up she looked as if she might cry. She was out in front of his apartment promptly at 5:30 A.M., motor idling, a small, fancy-wrapped package on the seat for him when he came down with his bags. "That goes in your briefcase now, and you are not to open it until you cross the international date line, darling. When is that, tomorrow or yesterday?" Glenna said with that early-morning cheer which is affected by tour guides, disk jockeys, and first-period teachers.

"I pick up a day; but I lose it coming back, of course."

Glenna gave Matt a wifely send-off at Pan Am's gate, and at that moment of parting he received and accepted some unpleasant realizations: The spouses, Glenna and Matt Thompson, part with a kiss; he flies off to serve the client and she walks out to the parking lot planning luncheons, shopping with the girls and her mother, and evenings alone. He feels pretty good about going, and about having some time without her. He returns and she meets him with the same kiss, the same car, and the news that her friends Peggy and Ann are pregnant. He doesn't know either one of them. He feels less good about returning than he did about leaving.

Glenna's package contained a gold travel alarm clock from Tiffany, engraved in two lines across the top in script:

"The years will seem like minutes. I love you, G." Matt
wound it, set it to New York time, and put it back in its
box somewhere over Kansas.

The trip to Hong Kong was a long and tiring flight for a
tall man in Pan American's coach seating, but over the
Pacific Thompson could not sleep, as tired as he was.
When he had read the *Fortune* article about Hung Wai-lang
again, he read the *Times* and a newsmagazine, then closed
his eyes, but his mind would not rest. His thoughts raced
over Hung's letter, Matt's last several talks with Albert
Murphy, and his first conversation with Richard Nixon.
Then, without volition, his thoughts rehearsed again what
he intended to say to Hung, then returned to Nixon.

Richard Nixon had been much less than Matt had
anticipated in their first meeting, and their encounter had been
so oddly flat that Matt found it troublesome. Whatever
Matt Thompson had been prepared to see—and hear—from
all his father had told him about Nixon and everything
he had read in the news and in biographies and in Nixon's
own autobiography, he was unprepared for lifelessness.
Perhaps he had come to it, Matt reflected, with an excess
of expectation.

To begin with, he'd expected to meet a much larger
man; Nixon was considerably shorter than Matt had thought.
Then, of course, there was the face. None of the photographs nor even the countless cartoons and caricatures had
prepared Matt Thompson for Nixon's face. That day Matt
had thought he was ready to see the face when Rose Mary
Woods telephoned at noon to ask him to come to talk to
Nixon at three o'clock that afternoon. In the intervening
hours he'd thought of what he wanted to say to Nixon: (1)
hello from his father, (2) thanks for the job, and (3) I don't
disagree with your foreign policy. During that rehearsal
he'd thought about Nixon's face. Matt sometimes had
trouble talking to ugly or disfigured people because a
person's physical appearance seemed to govern his reaction to that person. He knew that was unfair. He was
aware of his frailty in that respect, so he had prepared
himself to disregard Nixon's nose.

But when he walked into Richard Nixon's office and the man came around his desk to shake hands, Matt realized that in spite of his good intentions, he was fixated. Nixon's face held him. It was possible, Matt thought as he flew toward Hong Kong, that Nixon's conversation had been brilliant, but his physical appearance was so distracting that Matt had simply not heard or understood what the former Vice President was saying. They had briefly talked about Ezra Thompson, and when Matt said his father was still at Whittier College, Nixon asked how the Whittier football team had done this year. Matt didn't know. Nixon said he'd turned out for football at Whittier but had been too small to play much. He'd suited up for the games but spent most of his time on the bench. He said all that with an overlay of irony which barely kept the anecdote from being maudlin. The football coach at Whittier in Nixon's day was Chief Newman. Did Matt know him? Matt didn't. The Chief, Nixon went on—almost as if he couldn't stop this particular set piece of chitchat once he'd begun talking about Whittier College—Newman was a full-blood Indian and the boys called him Chief, although he was not really a tribal chief. He was perhaps the most inspiring man Nixon had ever known, and he'd known some of the world's leaders, of course.

Nixon finally came to the end of what he was compelled to say about Whittier and Chief Newman. He asked if Matt wanted coffee. Nixon sat deep in an overstuffed easy chair, his feet propped on a hassock, the top of his long stockings appearing from under his hiked-up pant legs. His upper shins were very pale and hairless, Matt noticed from where he sat on the couch. Nixon's black shoes were highly polished.

"So you're going to the Orient, Rose tells me." Nixon's voice dropped a tone as if his mind had moved from the Small Talk category to The Purpose of This Meeting.

"Yes, sir, a new client has asked me to come to Hong Kong. I guess he's a friend of Dad's."

"Good, good. That's a vital place, full of opportunities. I have an old Duke Law School classmate practicing law there—a Chinaman. I'd like you to look him up."

"Yes, sir." Matt was surprised.

"Just drop in and say hello for me. Might be good for the firm in the long run. We used to call him Willie at school, but that wasn't his Chinese name, of course. Rose has his name and address on this card for you." Nixon took a typed card from the table beside his chair.

Matt read aloud from the three-by-five card: "Lee Lung-fu, Q.C."

"Yes—hah! He's a Queen's Counsel now. They'll be knighting him before long, I suppose." Nixon's laugh had been an ironic bark, without humor. "Willie Lee, we called him. He was a bright little devil, but he kept to himself most of the time. He didn't have any close friends, I guess." Nixon pushed his nose to one side, as if to clear his left nostril. Matt could not recall having seen a more unpleasant displacement of a human face.

Did you have close friends? Matt wondered. Was your nose as big and rubbery then? Did it keep you out of Phi Alpha Delta at Duke Law? "I'll be glad to call on Mr. Lee," Matt said.

"When you return, I'd like to hear your impressions of Hong Kong," Nixon said, his tone higher, in transition. "Rose tells me you're interested in that part of the world."

"Yes, sir, I am."

"That's where the action's going to be." Nixon nodded solemnly. "I've been in that area for Pepsi-Cola a few times recently. Singapore. Manila. Tokyo. A lot of tough problems out there right now, for the United States." He sat thinking, staring at the curtained window, oblivious to Matt Thompson. "Well," he blurted suddenly, gathering his feet and struggling out of his chair, "have a good trip." He looked at Matt and held out his hand. "Stay away from those Chinese girlies and make a lot of money for the firm."

Flustered at Nixon's abrupt cast-iron jocularity, Matt shook his hand and said, "I'll give Mr. Lee your regards."

"You do that, Thompson. You do that."

Walking back to his twenty-fourth-floor cubicle, Matt realized he had not raised the Nancy Mellor problem with

Nixon. But now he could say something when he came back from Hong Kong. He'd see Nixon again to tell him about Mr. Lee, Q.C.

As he tried to sleep in his tight airplane seat Matt thought of his father, who had reacted oddly to this whole Hong Kong business when Matt called to tell him about it. The professor was obviously a little envious of his son, although he expressed his pride that Matt had been chosen to go.

"I think this Mr. Hung insisted that they send me," Matt explained.

"Hung? I don't place him."

"He's a Hong Kong business tycoon: Hung Wai-lang."

"Hung Wai-lang. Interesting name. Where will you stay, the Peninsula?"

"No, I'll be at the Hilton."

"That's on the island, eh?"

"On the Hong Kong side, it says. Queen's Road, Central."

"Well, that's right in the middle of things, as I recall. Of course, it's been decades since I've been there. You're a lucky boy. That's an exciting place. Hot this time of the year, though. And heavy rains."

"What can I bring back for you?"

"Jasmine tea. I can't find good jasmine here. That will be wonderful."

Glenna Harrison suggested Matt bring her some silk. Eldon Carnahay asked him to buy a small camera which Eldon could give Peg Carnahay for her birthday. Matt decided to look for some jade to give Mary Finn, too. Albert Murphy had suggested that Matt see about having some dress shirts and a suit made in Hong Kong to supplement his small, conservative wardrobe. All that shopping and a visit to Willie Lee would take time. Mr. Hung had first claim on him, of course, and Matt wondered if four days would be long enough in Hong Kong.

Somewhere just east of the Philippines, Matt Thompson finally fell asleep.

* * *

Matt was perspiring in the hot and humid Hong Kong night. His starched shirt collar was chafing, and he longed to loosen his necktie. That he did not take off his worsted jacket or his tie was solely to be credited to Albert Murphy's last-minute indoctrination: "Never forget, Thompson, that you are an associate of this firm, wherever you are, whatever you are doing. Never forget, you are my associate, Thompson. I expect you to think, act, and appear as if I were at your elbow, at all times moral, intelligent, and well dressed. If you are not, I shall hear of it, you may be sure, and I will hold you accountable. You assume a heavy responsibility by taking this trip on behalf of our firm." As he walked from the airplane toward the Hong Kong terminal, Matt could almost feel Mr. Murphy at his elbow.

Hong Kong Immigration bore the crisp, efficient imprint of the English civil service, although the people in the starched uniforms were Orientals. When his bag appeared on the luggage conveyor belt and he was waved through Customs, Thompson easily found the waiting air-conditioned bus that would deliver him to the Hilton, across the bay. He checked into the hotel at midnight and was handed a thick, square envelope with a small capital H embossed on the flap.

"Welcome to Hong Kong," the typewritten note began.

> Please call me tomorrow (Thursday) at
> 10 a.m. to confirm your appointment with Mr.
> Hung at 2 p.m.
> > Marianne Fu
> > Secretary to Mr. Hung Wai-lang

It was not until he walked through the lower floors of the hotel the next morning, after his American breakfast in the Hiltonesque coffee shop, that Thompson saw some real Hong Kong retailing. There, in the hotel "arcade," were Fenwick the suit maker, a custom shoe shop, an electronics and camera store, a shirt tailor, and countless little shops full of curios and tourists' gimcracks.

At the Fenwick shop he ordered two suits and a sport jacket made from bolts of woolen materials that were piled high on tables along the walls. The Chinese clerk who waited on him spoke English with a clipped British accent.

A wizened fitting tailor in a loose shirt shuffled out to measure Matt, and with surprise, the young American realized that he could understand a little of what the old tailor was saying in Chinese to the salesman. They were calling him the "large American" and were very business-like in recording his dimensions. When the salesman said, "He selected the better wool for one suit, although I tried to sell him the sheep dung, as I am instructed to do," Matt smiled in spite of himself. He had decided not to reveal his knowledge of Chinese to anyone. The salesman promised to have the clothing ready for a fitting at 4 P.M. that day and assured him that the finished garments would be boxed and in his room by noon on Saturday.

When Matt mentioned Richard Nixon's name it was not difficult to make an appointment to see Lee Lung-fu, Q.C., within an hour of his call.

Willie Lee was a short, thin, and superbly dressed Chinese with close-cropped gray hair, a broad nose, and lively, amused eyes. His English still held a trace of the North Carolina gentleness he'd affected during his seven years at Duke University. On a wall of his office he displayed a long photograph of his graduating class at Duke Law School, along with an impressive certificate from the Governor of Hong Kong designating him Queen's Counsel.

"Welcome, Mr. Thompson," said Lee. "Welcome to Hong Kong. Your first trip?"

"Thank you. Yes, sir. My first time."

"You are Dick Nixon's partner?"

"No, I work for his firm. He asked me to come by to pay his respects. He remembers you with great affection."

"I am glad. You care for tea? Coffee?"

"Tea, please."

Lee spoke to his secretary in Mandarin which Matt had no trouble understanding. Lee ordered tea and cookies and asked whether his morning's appointments had been successfully rearranged. The young woman reported that Mr. Chun at the bank had been a little upset.

Lee smiled at Matt. "How is my friend Dick Nixon?"

"He is well; he is running for President again, you know."

"I have read that. I intend to send him a little contribution, because I hope he succeeds. He has an understanding of this part of the world that is better than that of most Americans. We face some difficult problems here, and it would be very good to have a man like Dick in your White House."

"I'm sure he'll be grateful for your help."

"What brings you to Hong Kong, Mr. Thompson? Ai, here is our tea. Please eat a sweet with it."

"Thank you. I am here on the business of our firm. A client is here."

"Oh, I didn't know. Who is your client, if I may ask?"

"The Hung Company," Matt said. He wasn't sure he should be telling Lee that much about his firm's business.

"That is Mr. Hung Wai-lang?"

Matt nodded.

"Yes, I know him quite well. He is a substantial businessman. Our wives are distantly related, but Mr. Hung and I do not agree on the future fate of this colony and we are not social friends. He is a busy and wealthy man and would be a good client with many interests in the United States, I am sure."

"What do you see as Hong Kong's future, Mr. Lee?"

"Well, of course, the lease expires in 1997, about thirty years from now. I think it will be very bad for all of us if the British turn us over to the P.R.C., and I would like to see some independent status created for all of the New Territories and Hong Kong proper, perhaps guaranteed by the United Nations or by Japan and the United States. But at all costs we should keep the P.R.C. out of here."

"Is that realistic? Don't they have a strong legal claim?"

"The lease was made by a Chinese emperor, you know, and the Communists don't honor imperial bonds or the other old imperial undertakings. Peking seems to be very selective in what it seeks to enforce. I think the British have a strong argument that the lease was vitiated by the overthrow of the Emperor and that they hold this place in fee simple absolute, subject to no Chinese claims. Your client, Mr. Hung, and many other expatriate Chinese disagree, of course, and I guess they will welcome the Communists in 1997. Or even sooner if the British become much weaker."

"Can someone like Mr. Hung survive in a Communist-run economy?"

"He seems to think so; ask him about that. I personally believe the Communists would eventually take him over lock, stock, and barrel. You ask him how he intends to survive."

If I did, Murphy would kill me, Matt thought.

He looked at his watch. "Mr. Lee, it is getting late and I have imposed on you enough. I must keep my appointment with Mr. Hung soon. Thank you for seeing me."

Lee gave Matt a sealed enveloped addressed to Richard Nixon and ceremoniously said goodbye.

On the crowded sidewalk in front of the older building in which Lee had his office, Matt really felt, heard, and smelled the life of Hong Kong for the first time since he'd arrived. He'd only been in the cocoon of the hotel and the umbilical airport bus and taxicabs up to that moment. Now, at 11 A.M., it was oppressively hot and humid, and the heavy air carried the sounds and odors of the densely packed city with less diffusion than some lighter and cooler air does in cities in more temperate latitudes. Streetcars, trucks, and massive buses crowded the narrow street. Above the sidewalk level in the buildings that loomed over the street, a million people were jammed into tiny apartments where old parents sat on concrete floors doing piecework, making paper flowers, Christmas decorations, and electric fittings by the thousands. Cooking odors, urine, and the thick smell of decay mixed with automobile exhaust and harbor fumes, all overlaid by a unique Oriental flavor.

Matt had rather abruptly left Mr. Lee in order to have at least two hours to have lunch and locate Hung and Company. A pair of strolling constables informed him that the tall building in which Hung and Company had its offices was only four blocks away, so he decided to walk for a half-hour to the west, then return by another street. He hoped to find some lunch on the way.

A couple of blocks south he came upon Stanley Street, eight or ten feet wide, overhung with signs, balconies, and utility wires, full of hurrying Chinese. He peered through dusty windows to see small shops. In one he found dim sum and scalding-hot tea; then he crossed from side to side to look down intersecting lanes and mews. By way of cross streets he came upon Peel Street and turned north, toward the harbor. In the first block he found his father's jasmine tea and negotiated for it in halting Chinese. He could understand Chinese far better than he could express himself.

Matt Thompson arrived at the Hung Center exhilarated by his exposure to the vibrant life in Stanley and Peel streets. Hung Center was a column of steel and smoke-gray glass forty-seven stories high; it would have been dramatic even in New York or Chicago. In its first year of occupancy, Hung Center had become an international architectural landmark at the edge of Hong Kong's busy harbor, with the mountains of the Island rising behind it.

Thompson gave his name to an attendant in a white uniform at a reception desk in the lobby. It was evident that the entire building was occupied by the subsidiaries of Hung and Company. An attractive young Chinese woman in a white silk blouse and white slacks was waiting for him beside the reception area to escort him to Mr. Hung's private elevator.

As they ascended to the forty-fifth floor she smiled. "Is this your first time in Hong Kong, Mr. Thompson?"

"Yes, it is."

"I hope you will enjoy it."

The doors opened into a richly furnished room presided over by another, older white-clad woman who appeared to be Eurasian. She left the antique table which served as a desk and walked toward him.

"Mr. Thompson, I am Madame Lun. Mr. Hung asks that I bring you to his office as soon as you are refreshed. There is a washroom there. May we serve you tea?"

"No tea, thank you, Madame Lun. But I have been walking and it is hot outside. I'll just wash my face."

"May I take your parcel?"

"Yes, thanks. That's some tea for my father." He felt very much a part of the cultural ways he had seen in Stanley Street that morning. He was feeling that he could be very happy living in an Oriental environment with such cultural amenities. He would have been very comfortable telling this lady that the tea was for his honorable father.

Fourteen

Hung Wai-lang was standing behind his desk when his receptionist opened the office door for Matt Thompson. But before the American could focus on his host, Matt's attention was swept to his left and ahead, to the two sides of the square room which opened to the harbor. Those two walls consisted of clear sheets of glass, rising from the heavily carpeted floor to the low, dark-painted ceiling. The space contained only three chairs and Hung's glass-and-metal desk; it seemed that they were floating, five hundred feet above the junks, the freighters, and the Star Ferry which was cutting a narrow furrow in the deep blue water halfway to Kowloon.

"I am Hung Wai-lang, Mr. Thompson. Thank you for coming to see me."

Hung was short and stout, cylindrical in a white Philippine shirt which hung straight from his broad shoulders. His wide face was darker than most Chinese', his eyes even darker, his bald head glistening under recessed lights. His mouth was wide and fleshy over three layers of chins.

"Please sit down and I will tell you what I wish to do," Hung said, smiling. His teeth were yellow and crooked.

Matt Thompson sat in a chrome-and-reed chair, remembering to sit up straight as Albert Murphy would want him to do. The wall behind Hung's desk was made of highly polished exotic woods, inlaid to create a Mercator projection of the world. There were no pictures, plaques, or other adornments in the room. The two glass walls gave Hung all the light, color, and motion anyone could ask for in a work space.

"Mr. Thompson, I wish to retain you to do legal work for me," Hung began. His tenor voice carried a heavy Chinese accent. "But before we talk business, I will take you into the room next door to meet an old and dear friend of your honorable father. Do you recall him speaking of his boyhood classmate Teng Shan-li?"

"Yes, sir, I believe I do."

Hung smiled broadly. "Mr. Teng lives in Peking, and he comes here upon occasion. When he heard that you would be here today he wished to be introduced to you. You have no objection?"

"Of course not. My honorable father will be very pleased that I have been given this opportunity. I am grateful."

"Then come with me, please."

Hung led Matt behind his desk to a door built flush into the east wall where it met the huge window. The adjoining room was about a third the size of Hung's office, furnished with two overstuffed chairs, a couch, and three low tables. Teng Shan-li was standing, looking out the window next to the doorway, when they came in. Teng wore his best blue

Mao jacket and gray trousers. His black shoes needed a shoeshine.

"Teng Shan-li, may I introduce to you Matthew Thompson, son of Professor Ezra Thompson?" Hung said ceremoniously in English. Teng bowed slightly as they shook hands. "We will have tea," Hung announced. "Please sit in these chairs." Almost at once two young women in white dresses brought tea, cookies, and crackers.

"Your father wrote me a letter at Christmastime telling me about his life and his family," Teng said. "He is very proud of your professional success. Is his health good?"

"Yes, he is well, thank you. He teaches every day."

"Your mother died several years ago, is it not so?"

"Yes. And he is quite lonely, I fear. He misses her very much."

"When they came to China again during the Japanese war I met your mother. They had a small child then; was that you?"

"Yes, I am their only child."

"So you yourself have lived in China. How long?"

"Nearly three years when I was very young. But today as I walked about Hong Kong I felt as if I had returned to a beloved place. I guess it has always been in my blood."

Both Teng and Hung smiled appreciatively. Hung stood up. "You two should have a chance to visit. I will return to my work, and Mr. Thompson can join me later. If you wish more tea or anything, please press this signal. Do not hurry your conversation, please. I have plenty of time in which to discuss legal matters with Mr. Thompson. No, do not get up. I will be just next door."

When Hung had gone back to his office, Teng poured Matt and himself more tea. "Your grandmother was like a mother to me when I was a schoolboy, you know, Mr. Thompson."

"I hope you will call me Matt, Mr. Teng. I feel that you are a member of our family."

"I am honored that you feel that way, Matt. Yes, your grandmother and grandfather were like my parents for the years I was at school in Tientsin. Your grandmother helped me to learn English."

"You live in Peking now, Mr. Hung told me."

"Yes, I do. For many years I worked in the Foreign Ministry there. But in early 1966 the Ministry was drastically changed."

"The Cultural Revolution?"

"Yes. I was taken out. My wife and daughter were sent to different places. I was sent away to work on a farm. It is only recently that I have been rehabilitated and returned to Peking. It was then that I received your esteemed father's letter."

Matthew Thompson fully realized that this was no chance encounter or fortuitous meeting. He had no doubt that he had been lured to Hong Kong to talk to Teng Shan-li, not Mr. Hung. Teng was apparently a Communist. His Mao-jacket uniform was a jarring incongruity in this rich capitalist's glamorous office. In a few minutes Teng would tell him why they were talking, and Matt guessed he would be asked to help get Teng and his family into the United States as refugees from the Cultural Revolution.

"Conditions in China are very difficult just now," Teng continued. "There is much conflict and distrust, and Chairman Mao has undertaken a great effort to conserve our revolutionary values."

"How has that affected you, Mr. Teng? Are you no longer at the Foreign Ministry?"

"I was removed from the Ministry by some who believe that I was not sufficiently fervent. In fact, most Ministry officials have been replaced. But I have undergone a period of self-examination and self-correction which has been very good for me, and now I am once again making my contribution to my country. But enough about me. Your father wrote me that you are a New York lawyer in a powerful law firm. Do you find it to your liking?"

"Yes, because I have been assigned to the group handling international problems. That is the field of my strongest interest."

"Very good. Perhaps someday you will find yourself in

a position to help the Chinese people. It is very difficult just now because we have no ambassador in the United States, and no consulates. I am told that from time to time China needs a representative, a professional person in the United States to accept assignments.''

Matt Thompson was surprised at this turn in the conversation. Was China looking for a lawyer? He'd heard that some bondholders were demanding that the People's Republic of China pay off some old bonds which had been issued by the last Emperor, before 1911. Wouldn't that be a piece of work to bring back to the law firm! "I'd be very much interested in helping the Chinese people," Matt said, reaching for his teacup.

"There is really no reason for the estrangement between our countries," Teng continued. "Historically, your generals—Patrick Hurley and George Marshall—led your country to side with the KMT, and that is regrettable. Chairman Mao and Premier Chou were prepared to create amicable relations with the U.S. at that time. But as a result of Harry Truman's rebuffs we have had nearly twenty years with a wide gulf between us.''

"The Korean war made it worse, didn't it?''

"Yes, Matt, and the Chinese people do not understand why the United States Government sends soldiers to our borders with such disregard for our concerns. Imagine if Chinese soldiers were fighting in Nova Scotia or western Mexico; how would the American people feel about China? Your machines and men are in Viet Nam even now, a few miles from China. Your bombs have fallen inside China, you know.''

"No, I didn't know.''

"Yes. It is a documented fact. And, too, your battleships patrol our waters to protect the discredited Kuomintang faction in the Province of Taiwan. Your soldiers and airplanes are there on Taiwan, which has always been a part of China's territory since the earliest of times. These are difficult problems for China which can be solved only if our two nations have the will to do so in a spirit of mutual accommodation.''

"Yes, I see that."

"Occasionally, an opportunity comes to a man at a time in history when great changes can be made. Some men rise to the occasion and do wonderful things for mankind. Others shun the risk for their own reasons. Those opportunities are doors which stay open only briefly, and once they close, they can never be reopened. In the case of China, some doors can be passed through in only one direction."

"That is obscure to me, Mr. Teng. One direction?"

Teng smiled and cradled his teacup in his two hands, as if to warm them. He leaned forward slightly in his chair. "As your honorable father has perhaps explained to you, in China there is the matter of face."

Matt nodded.

"When I wished to offer marriage to my wife, Hua Fan, it was not possible for me to ask her the big question directly. Had I done so she or her father might have rejected me, with great personal loss of face for me and my family. That is one reason that marriages are arranged by the families, usually through a third person who can save both parties from any embarrassment. Often employment is sought through an intermediary, for much the same reason."

"Yes, I understand a little about the Chinese way," Matt said, wondering where all this was leading. For a moment he'd suspected Teng was going to try to recruit him to do espionage, and he had prepared himself to reject such a suggestion out of hand. Now it seemed that Teng was looking for a go-between, but it was certainly not clear. Matt had learned enough about the Chinese language from his father to understand that circumlocution was often a part of the rhetorical process. He resolved to sit back and let Teng Shan-li get to the point in his own way.

Matt was increasingly aware that he'd been brought to Hong Kong to listen to Teng, and that Hung and Company was just a go-between. Matt could not yet divine how Nixon, Mudge, Rose, Guthrie and Alexander, and most particularly Mr. Albert Murphy, could make any money out of serving Mr. Teng and the Chinese people, and that worried the young lawyer. He could imagine what Murphy would say if Matt came back with some *pro bono publico* assignment to better international relations. Murphy would kill him.

"Chairman Mao offered the hand of friendship to the United States and he was rebuffed," Teng was saying. In Geneva your John F. Dulles refused to shake the hand of Premier Chou En-lai, and this rejection was in public, seen by representatives of many nations. In the nature of men it is impossible for Chinese leaders to extend their hands again unless they first see that the United States Government leaders have extended their hands. Do you see?"

Matt nodded.

"China is a large and powerful nation today," Teng was saying. "We are nearly a fourth of all of the people of the world, and our People's Liberation Army is very large and modern. There is no need for China to beg for a position in the community of nations. Chairman Mao has made it clear that China stands alone but is interested in good relations with all nations. All nations."

"Including the United States?" Matt asked, hoping to move Teng toward his conclusion.

"Yes, certainly. If the United States came to us with hand outstretched, we would reciprocate."

"How could such an opening be arranged?" Matt asked.

"I think it requires the leadership of a courageous and farsighted American statesman," Teng said pensively. "His American countrymen are not now ready for a gesture toward China, of course, but surely they can be persuaded it is a good thing to do if such a leader believes in it."

Matt finally saw why Teng, his father's friend, had sent for Matthew Thompson. "And you believe that Richard Nixon is that leader, Mr. Teng?"

Teng smiled. "It is interesting that you would think of your law associate, Mr. Nixon, Matt. But I know that he has been considered a member of the KMT's China Lobby which is friendly toward Chiang Kai-shek. Do you estimate that Mr. Nixon nevertheless would agree with you and me that some friendly intercourse between China and the United States would greatly benefit both our peoples?"

"I've never talked to him about it, Mr. Teng. I suspect that he would agree with us, but I would also say that a Presidential candidate dares not say so in public these days. A Republican can't appear to be 'soft on Communism,' as the slogan goes."

Teng nodded. "So we have a situation in which Chairman Mao—in his heart—sees an opening as a desirable thing but cannot say so. And Richard Nixon also holds that realization in his heart—but dares not make an overt move *at this time*." Teng emphasized his last three words by tapping on the low table in front of him with his index finger.

Matt nodded.

"For many years now," Teng continued, "Mr. Nixon has said nothing about Chiang Kai-shek or Taiwan. He is like a fallow field where no corn has grown for six or seven years."

"But why Nixon?" Matt asked. "He may not be able to defeat Lyndon Johnson next November. He's not even a sure bet for the Republican nomination."

Teng spread his hands. "A farmer must farm the land he has been given, eh? When I look at those contending for President, your colleague seems to me to be the choice. It does no good to wish that the cornfield were on the other side of the mountain, you see."

"So you would gamble on Nixon?"

"I would. Let us suppose he said nothing now that would later prevent him—as President—from opening a new relationship with China. Suppose he encouraged some popular thought that was receptive to a better climate between our countries. Perhaps if the talks between our ambassadors resume in Warsaw, Nixon could say something approving."

Matt nodded. "Then if he is elected, he could do more. But if he's not, he has at least contributed to a bipartisan attitude which would make it easier for Johnson to do something. Is that it?"

"In general, yes. I feel that Lyndon Johnson will always see China as a military enemy as long as he is President. I doubt that he will ever extend his hand to Chairman Mao. But perhaps I misunderstand him."

"Mr. Teng," Matt countered, "I'm afraid my dad may have given you an exaggerated idea of my relationship with Mr. Nixon. I'm not at all close to him; in fact, I've only talked to him once since I went to work there last winter."

Teng nodded. "It is a question of how close you may become in the future, however. You are colleagues, is it not so?"

"He is a senior partner in the firm, and I am a new employee."

"Yes, and you yourself are involved with questions of international law."

"Well, that's true, but I work for a different partner, Albert Murphy. He is the international expert. I am a neophyte."

"I understand. What are your impressions of Mr. Nixon, Matt?"

"I'm not clear about that, to be honest. I've heard a lot about him from my father, and we had the one short visit, Nixon and I, but I'm not able to put it all together and give you an analytical answer. I'm sure Mr. Nixon is very intelligent, and he's certainly very interested in this part of the world. But I have the idea that there are a great many things that don't interest him at all and they go right by him. He was deep in thought during our talk and I might just as well have been on the moon; he paid no attention to what I was saying."

"You think he is interested in China?"

"I'm sure he is.

"But how about Taiwan?"

"How can China and the United States become reconciled as long as China demands Taiwan's return?"

"Taiwan has always been a part of China," Teng said flatly. "The KMT's occupation of our island province changes nothing. No Chinese leader, not even Chairman

Mao, could ever divorce Taiwan from China. But I can assure you, Taiwan will not prevent our two nations from joining hands when the time comes. Your friend Mr. Nixon realizes that, I wager. But as I was saying, I am curious about his work habits. I hear he works during the day. Chairman Mao prefers to read and write late at night, you know. Is Mr. Nixon studious?"

"I believe so. He recently spent three full days preparing for a court argument. I was told about it by a woman who works for him. He probably studies hard for specific events like that. I doubt that he sits around studying, abstractly, just for the sake of learning."

"Is his personality likable? Is he diplomatic and engaging?"

"I'd say not. His appearance is against him, for one thing. He has achieved a high office in our country in spite of his considerable physical ugliness. He's a master politician and a strong intellect, but he is shy and not particularly pleasant to talk to or be with. I did not especially enjoy my short visit with him."

"Is it your estimate that he would listen to what you told him about China?"

"He wants me to come back and tell him my impressions of Hong Kong. He said so. I'm sure he'd listen to whatever I had to say."

Teng stood and moved to the window. He looked at the crisscrossing wakes of the dozens of boats which were going in all directions. He turned back to Matt, folding his hands in front of his belly. "Are you willing to help reconcile our two peoples, Matt? I will say, frankly, that I'm not sure you and I can realize any results. I am only recently returned from a pig farm. You are very young and totally without experience. We are a couple of strange oxen to be yoked together, but in a way your honorable father, Ezra Thompson, has brought us to this shared moment, and that is a good omen. Your esteemed father has love for both our peoples. In his spirit, I ask you to help me."

"I'll do what I can, Mr. Teng, as long as you don't want

me to do espionage or become some kind of a foreign agent."

"Oh, no, of course not." Teng smiled and shook his head. "I seek only a messenger who has a chance of gaining Mr. Nixon's ear from time to time."

"I'll want to be very straight with him," Matt said seriously. "I'll want to tell him that you and I have talked."

"Of course you will," Teng replied. "A man who is seeking election to be President must receive much advice from those who want favors from him. If you are to be effective in planting a seed with this man, you must be a person in whom he has confidence. May I suggest that you offer to help him by working in his campaign?"

"I intend to do that."

"Good. I sense that he is one who will prefer to view this seed of an idea of reconciliation as his own, rather than as the brainchild of some other person. I encourage you to tell him of your father's old friend Teng, but to do so in a way that will not impeach the essential validity of the idea itself."

"You mean, I should not say that you are an emissary of the Chinese Government?"

"Ai, no, you cannot say that, for that would be most misleading and surely fatal to the idea! May I suggest that you recount to him how you encountered your esteemed father's old and true friend by chance? Then as we drank tea in the lobby of the Peninsula Hotel you were told of my loss of my lifetime employment at the Ministry and of my rustification in Szechwan Province. Your family friend is now an agent for a cotton-import-and-export corporation, and I come to Hong Kong quite often to facilitate international cotton trade. As a result of our conversation you can tell Mr. Nixon with some certainty of China's difficult isolation and economic weakness. If you invite his reaction to these circumstances, perhaps one can tell better whether a seed planted with him might grow well."

Matt shook his head in disagreement. "I'd rather just

tell him flat out that you were here at Mr. Hung's waiting for me."

Teng spread his arms, his palms up. "But you see, a seed must be allowed to grow. The farmer must provide it with the best of conditions. If it is not placed beneath a covering of good earth the sun will parch it and it will not germinate. Nor can it be forced to sprout before its time. It is the farmer's role to give it good conditions and to be patient."

"After I talk to Mr. Nixon when I get back, what else could I do?"

"Please write Mr. Hung what reaction Mr. Nixon evidences. From time to time Mr. Hung may send you suggestions or interesting reading material which may be helpful. By all means do not press for any particular reactions. Do not force things. If there is no overt response, that is enough to tell me."

"It would be best not to send materials or letters to me at the office. I'll write down my home address."

"Of course. And your telephone, too. I hope you will find it possible to work closely for and with Mr. Nixon in whatever campaign capacity he offers. You should miss no opportunity. To be an effective bridge between the nations you must have a strong footing upon each shore."

"I understand. But I can't believe that I can be very effective with him. He seems very tough-minded and pragmatic. Even suspicious."

"With such a person only subtlety and sensitivity can be effective. World peace is the prize, Matt, and it has been sought by great men all through time, without success. Perhaps it has fallen to two insignificants—you and me— to find the way that has eluded the others. Ai, what a turn of fate!"

Teng rose and walked to the sideboard behind the couch. "I have a small and unimportant gift for your honorable father," Teng said, handing Matt a cube about five inches in all dimensions, wrapped in white rice paper. "Can you deliver it to him for me?"

"Yes, of course. I'll see him on my way back to New York."

"Please also offer him my sincere regard and my hope that his health is good. This little box requires a soft pillow for its journey, Matt. Like our new, mutual undertaking, it is extremely fragile."

Matt accepted the box carefully.

"It will be for you to decide," Teng continued, "how much you should tell your esteemed father of our project. In matters of this kind some caution is often the best ingredient. But I think you can tell him that we have met through Mr. Hung's mutual friendship and that my business with Mr. Hung—my cotton business—brings me here often. I think my old friend Ezra Thompson will be happy to have some word of me through you."

"I'm sure he will, Mr. Teng. But I'm not very good at telling my father things that aren't true; he has always been able to see right through me."

Teng laughed at the idiom. "As I said, you must judge. Perhaps you should tell him everything, perhaps nothing. . . . Come, we should rejoin Mr. Hung. I know he has many things to discuss with you, and he must be jealous of the many minutes of your time I have taken."

Fifteen

"Mr. Thompson, I would not wish you to think I would bring you here under false pretenses," Hung Wai-lang said, smiling broadly. "I hope your visit with your old family friend was pleasant. Now please come back into my office and meet Mr. Chen Yu-shen, my comptroller and auditor.''

As he reentered Mr. Hung's extraordinary aerie, Matt was struck by the vitality of the scene beyond the enormous glass wall in front of him. Tankers and freighters lay at anchor to the right, gently moving up and down. In the foreground two Star Ferries were dashing in opposite directions, crammed with people. A large brown-and-ocher junk paralleled the near shore, moving with surprising speed for all its square ungainliness, the stained sail fanned out high above a thick wooden mast, the bamboo ribs of the sail silhouetted in the afternoon sun.

Chen, about fifty, thin and parchment-colored, stood by Hung's desk, his hand on top of a stack of files as if to keep them from flying away out over the harbor.

The glass walls momentarily made Matt Thompson feel as if he were floating high above the water, unfixed, and that he and the other men, the furniture, and other contents of Hung's office space were somehow suspended out over the great harbor, detached.

''Mr. Chen has made a copy of everything for you. I am having a hell of a time with New York real estate,'' Hung said with despair. ''Here are three leases I want you to look at. I think we should kick out all of these tenants, use the West Thirty-fourth Street building for our export company, and raise the rents on the other West Side building. Then maybe we should think about new management. I am not satisfied with the rental firm we are using. I want your recommendations.''

Matt took notes rapidly as Hung went through the files one by one with brisk, pessimistic efficiency. Mr. Chen explained a dispute they were having with a shipyard in Seattle. A Hung and Company ship had required emergency repairs there, and the ship's captain had certified work for payment. But the ship's purser reported that major items of repair listed on the invoice had not actually been done. The file needed further investigation, they agreed.

Mr. Chen, the comptroller, was coming to New York in three weeks to discuss a change in Hung's line of credit at

Manufacturers Hanover Bank. Hung asked Matt to go with Chen to talk to the bankers.

A Hung subsidiary would soon need a building in New Orleans. Another was going to buy a mill in Georgia. Mr. Hung would send Matt the details as soon as they came in, so that Matt could prepare the agreements involved.

"I am sorry I cannot dine with you this evening, Matt," Hung said. "Unfortunately, I am expected to go to the Governor's home for dinner. I hope you will forgive me."

"Of course, Mr. Hung."

"In fact, I must go now, and I will drop you at the Hilton on my way home to change. This package contains copies of Mr. Chen's files on the real estate and the repair problems. I have put in a copy of our annual report and some other background reading for you. This envelope contains your retainer, some additional payment for your expenses, and a small bonus in appreciation for your careful attention to the matters which are of concern to us all. Please give my secretary your home address and telephone." Hung stood and held out his hand. "It is my great pleasure to know that you are looking out for my interests."

Matt shook Hung's hand and put the envelopes into his attaché case. In the outer office he left his card with Hung's secretary, with his MacDougal Street home address and phone number written on it.

Later, in his room at the Hilton, Matt opened the smaller envelope to admire his retainer check. With it came five crisp and fresh U.S. one-thousand-dollar bills. A $1,000 check was marked EXPENSES. The retainer check, made payable to Nixon, Mudge, for $10,000 was precisely correct. The thousand-dollar bills were quite another matter.

Albert Murphy came to Matt's mind. What would Murphy say if the retainer check was stolen from Matt's room? Inexcusable stupidity? Worse; much worse. Matt took the currency and check to the Hilton's front desk and put them in a safe-deposit box.

At dinner, alone at a small table in the hotel dining room, he thought about the unexpected five thousand in cash. It really belonged to him, not the firm, he reasoned, and he could buy a new car with it if he wanted to. He'd never had that much money all in a pile; not ever before in his life. But it was troublesome. He needed to think through all the ramifications of keeping and spending that money.

He'd think about it the next day during his flight, Matt decided.

Sixteen

Matt was not surprised when Rose Mary Woods called at noon on Tuesday to ask him to come to visit with Richard Nixon. The night before, Glenna Harrison had told Matt that Rose would be calling. Glenna had also confided that the Nixon campaign would soon be hiring some additional help. H. R. Haldeman had been in New York while Matt was gone, and he was going to prepare a personnel plan for the campaign. In a few weeks the campaign might be moving out of Nixon, Mudge's Broad Street building into offices of its own, uptown. Glenna and Rose Woods would probably stay downtown with The Boss, but everyone else was going to move.

Glenna had been very glad to see Matt when he got off the flight from Los Angeles. She said she liked the peach-colored silk he'd found for her, and he thought it looked very good against her tanned skin.

As they rode to her apartment that evening from the airport he'd felt totally washed out, surfeited on airline food, groggy from too much reading while in motion, his body complaining of half a dozen functional irregularities.

She talked as she drove and he leaned back, his eyes closed, and let her monologue wash over him.

As a matter of office custom Matt was entitled to be late going to the office the next day. A lawyer back from a work trip was never expected before noon. But he didn't want to miss the Nixon summons when it came, and Glenna had assured him that it would come "first thing" Tuesday morning. So he rose and showered at seven.

Rose Mary Woods didn't call until noon. At ten Matt had been summoned by Albert Murphy and there was a small ceremony as Matt handed his supervising partner Mr. Hung's money—the check and the five one-thousand-dollar bills—and Al Murphy counted the currency and made a note of the amount on his calendar.

"Why did he give you this cash?" Murphy demanded.

"I'm not sure." Matt shrugged, and his new Hong Kong shirt rasped his neck. "Perhaps he thought I needed travel-expense cash."

"Odd. Very odd. When you first write to him to restate and acknowledge his assignments, be sure you acknowledge receipt of all these funds. Make a memo for Accounting on it. I will too. Cash is always troublesome. What advice did you give him?"

"Advice?"

"Advice. He did present legal problems, I assume," Murphy said ironically.

"Yes, sir."

"And he asked what to do?"

"Not really. He has all these problems and he asked me—the firm, of course—to help him; there's leasing, a dispute with a shipyard over repairs and his line of credit at the Hanover. But he knew what he wanted done in most cases. He said he would like advice on his real estate, but he implied that he'd like it later, so I didn't give him any on the spot. He's sending a Mr. Chen here soon and I figured I'd deliver it to him in writing."

"You gave him absolutely no advice?"

"Right."

"Be sure to make that clear in your first letter too. When is this Chen coming?"

"In two weeks."

"Speak English?"

"Yes, he speaks good English."

"I'll see him when he comes. We'll take him to lunch, you and I."

"Sure."

Murphy gave him neither criticism nor compliments during that first talk, and Matt Thompson felt disappointed as he crossed the hall to his office. He had come back with a damn good client for the firm and even Murphy the martinet should have said so.

Rose Woods called to say that it was her best guess that Mr. Nixon would return from his lunch about 2:30 P.M., so Matt should come to her desk then. He was there a few minutes early. Glenna was out running an errand and a young man wearing a Nixon button was sitting at her desk, typing. Since there was no place for a waiting visitor to sit, Matt went back to his own little office to wait for Nixon's return. At three ten Rose called to say that Nixon had returned but he had come back from lunch with a client, and they were talking in Nixon's office. Matt was to wait right where he was. At three thirty Rose called to say that the client was in the process of leaving. She talked in a very quiet tone so the client would not hear her and think he was being hurried along.

Matt arrived as Nixon was saying goodbye at his office door. His visitor was a large, portly man with a bald head and odd, wire-rimmed glasses with very thick lenses. When he turned his head the glasses distorted his eyes; with every movement his eyeballs seemed to scoot quickly across the lenses and off his head. Nixon noticed Matt waiting but gave no acknowledgment of his presence. The jowly visitor was excitedly describing a big party he intended to give—apparently for Nixon's benefit. Nixon was tiptoeing the narrow rhetorical line between concealed distaste and obligatory gratitude, answering in monosyllables, looking to Rose Woods occasionally as if he wanted her to provide him with an excuse to duck back into his office and lock the door.

The very large man eventually permitted Rose to guide him to the reception room and the elevators; he was effusively repeating his party plans to her as they went around the last corner.

"Well, how was Hong Kong?" Nixon asked Matt loudly. "Come in and tell me about it." Nixon followed Matt into the office, closed his door, and sank into his deep easy chair, propping both feet on the hassock. "Did you see Willie Lee?"

"Yes, sir. We had a good visit. Mr. Lee sends you his most cordial regards and gave me this letter for you." Matt was close enough to lay the envelope on Nixon's chairside table without getting up.

Nixon nodded one nod. He was wearing a hard-worsted gray wool suit and a dark necktie with small figures. His shoes were without a smear or blemish, but Matt noticed a grease spot the size of a dime on Nixon's left coat sleeve. Nixon did not reach for Lee's letter.

"And John Alexander tells me that you lined up a new client in Hong Kong. I for . . . I don't . . . who is it?"

"It's Hung and Company; Mr. Hung Wai-lang. He's a shipper, but he has many other interests."

Nixon looked at his wristwatch, then unstrapped it and held it in his hand. "What's your reading on Hong Kong, Mr. Thompson? Will it stay strong?"

"Mr. Lee is concerned that the P.R.C. will try to take it over from the British."

"Ah, the expiring land lease, eh? I'll bet that scares all the little Chinese capitalists shitless."

Matt was surprised that Nixon would use that word; he was supposed to be so straight-arrow. "It doesn't seem to worry Mr. Hung. He has a lot of business dealings with the People's Republic."

"Smart. He has it both ways. You can trade with the Chinese and the Russians and the other Communists, you see. They will do business when it is to their advantage, and they'll pay in gold if that's what it takes. They'll trade with democracies or the Hottentots if they have to. They don't care about your politics if you have something they need."

"I know the mainland Chinese are anxious to build their textile trade," Matt said quickly, seeing his opening. "I had an extraordinary chance meeting with one of Dad's old friends at Hung's office and he is one of their textile-export officials."

"A friend of your father's?"

"Yes, they went to the Tientsin mission school together, and they've always kept in touch ever since."

"And he's a Communist?"

Matt nodded. "He was an official in their Ministry of Foreign Affairs for years, but the Red Guards have kicked him out."

"Why?"

"I'm not sure. He said they humiliated him and shipped him off to a farm. Now he's rehabilitated, and he works for a government export corporation. I guess he wasn't leftist enough to work in the Foreign Ministry anymore."

"Mao is a clever son-of-a-bitch," Nixon said earnestly. "He's doing what we should do. Someone ought to make farmers out of those little shits down in our State Department. The bureaucracy has gotten so entrenched! I don't care if they're Chinese or American, the problem is the same. You need to have a housecleaning and pull some fresh ideas into those places. Fred Seaton was Eisenhower's Secretary of Interior, a newspaperman from Nebraska. Some reporter asked him why he was helping me to become President in 1960—what did he want out of it? He said, 'I want to be Secretary of State for three days— just long enough to clean the place out.'"

"Mr. Teng said Chairman Mao is winning back his revolution from the moderates."

"It must have been interesting to hear about this fellow's experiences."

"He wouldn't talk much about it. But he said quite a bit about China's need for outside contact. Since Russia pulled out in the fifties, China has been pretty isolationist,

I guess, and it has hurt them. They need trade and other foreign relations, he thinks.''

"I wonder if any Chinese leaders agree with him,'' Nixon mused. "They seem to be so unsettled internally that none of them is paying much attention to world affairs. Other than Viet Nam, of course. They are putting a lot of money into North Viet Nam, I am told.''

"Mr. Teng was very touchy about both Korea and Viet Nam. He says they deeply resent American troops being sent so close to China. He says, 'We have no troops in Mexico or Canada.' ''

"And they were upset about Taiwan, I'll bet,'' Nixon added. "Did he mention our troops there?''

"He did. I asked him about Taiwan specifically because that seems like an insurmountable obstacle to China and the United States ever getting together. Teng said it wasn't; he thinks it will take time and some negotiation, but he is optimistic that we could agree on some workable Taiwan settlement formula.''

"I doubt that his leaders would agree with him on that.'' Nixon was winding his wristwatch, staring at it intently. "I think their demand for Formosa is, as the Russians say, 'nonnegotiable.' But actually it may be time for the United States to rethink its position. Chiang is getting to be a very old man, and that son of his is a mean little bastard. We ought to be looking at the main chance, which is an improvement in relations with the mainland. It always comes down to a question of who has the most to offer, doesn't it?''

Matt nodded. He had quite a message to send Mr. Teng, he thought. Nixon was more open-minded than either of them had anticipated.

Nixon strapped on his wristwatch and crossed his legs. "You know, I have a left-handed invitation to go to China in the summer. It has come in over the transom, and I don't know whether to do it or not. The trouble is I'm asked to accompany two governors of Canadian provinces. On that kind of a trip I probably wouldn't get to talk with people at the highest levels. Governors get shunted off to some Deputy Minister of Foreign Affairs. And it would be awkward, too, because my visit to Communist China would be more newsworthy than the governors' and I'd probably be the center of attention. They wouldn't like that. I may turn it down."

"I'd love to see China again," Matt said.

"Yes, it's the great frontier of foreign affairs just now. China is potentially a great prize for the American leader with the courage to go after it. As you say, they are isolated, and that is bad for everyone—for China and for the rest of the world. Isolated countries do eccentric and harmful things sometimes. We need bridges of communication so trouble can be talked out and crises can be avoided."

Nixon stood slowly, walked to his desk, and picked up a file folder. Matt noticed with surprise that there was nothing on top of the elaborately carved wooden desk except that folder and a small typewritten card. No family pictures, no work in progress, not even a piece of etched glass or a Steuben eagle Given by a Grateful Nation for Eight Devoted Years of Public Service as Vice President of the United States. It was an absolutely clean desk.

"Here," Nixon said, returning to his easy chair, "is something that might interest you. Do you know *Foreign Affairs* magazine?"

"Yes, sir. The Council on Foreign Relations puts it out?"

"Right. Some of them in that crowd are nuts, but Allen Dulles and Al Gruenther and a few others balance them out. Anyway, they have asked me to do an article about Asia for a big anniversary edition they're getting out."

"Great."

"Instead of beating the dead horse of Viet Nam, I thought I'd write something about what the Asian problems are going to be after the war is over. I want to do a more farsighted piece than the usual crap about Viet Nam and Japan. This is a draft Nancy Mellor has helped me with. Would you like to read it?"

"Yes, sir. I sure would."

"Take it along, and write me a memo if you have any suggestions." Nixon handed Matt the folder. "It's due in a couple of weeks, so I'd need your ideas quickly. I don't mention Hong Kong in there, I don't think. You might want to write a paragraph about the lease problem. I tend to favor the creation of an international trade zone, but not under the U.N. That's as bad a bureaucracy as the State Department!"

"Yes, sir." Matt was elated. Imagine writing stuff for *Foreign Affairs*! "I'll be very interested to read it," he said.

"When I can get to it," Nixon added, "I'll be revising it. For one thing, I think it's too long. And as you'll see, I haven't said much about China or Taiwan, and I probably should. Maybe you could give me some ideas. Nancy is very good, but she is a charter member of the China Lobby. She hates the P.R.C. and she tends to be very tough on the subject. See what you can do with it."

Matt received the folder and held it in both hands in front of his knees.

Nixon looked up, and a smile quickly appeared and disappeared. "So what do you do now? Are you going back to Hong Kong?"

"Mr. Nixon, I'd like to help with your campaign if you think I could be of any help," Matt said earnestly.

"You're Ivy League, right?" Nixon asked.

Matt nodded. "Dartmouth College and Harvard Law. Dad arranged comity scholarships for me."

"But you're from California, and you come from good stock. Your father has his head screwed on straight," Nixon declared. "Maybe they didn't completely scramble your brains in those Ivy League schools. I'll tell you, we are just figuring out what people we are going to need to take aboard. I have Haldeman doing that now. Do you know him? No? He's from California. He is very buttoned-down for an advertising man, and he knows a lot about campaigns. He'll do a superb job on it. I'll have him call you, and the two of you can figure out what you should be

doing." Nixon laboriously lowered his feet from the hassock and stood.

Matt realized as he rose that Nixon's face had not
bothered him this time as it had on their first encounter.
Perhaps it had been swollen from hay fever or some
medicine the other time. Nixon surely was not handsome,
even this time, but the time before he had been—what?
—grotesque? Now he was merely a kind of businesslike-
ugly.

"Well, thanks for coming by, Mr. Thompson," Nixon
said, his hand on Matt's back.

"I'd be grateful if you'd call me Matt, sir. I feel as
though you are a good friend of the family."

"Sure." Nixon evidently didn't know how to respond
to that kind of familiarity. "Matt. Well, I'll see you
again." His voice seemed hesitant and strained.

"Yes, sir. Goodbye."

Nixon turned and hurried back into his office and
closed his door. Rose Mary Woods and Glenna were
looking at Matt inquisitively from their desks. They had
heard him invite Nixon to use his first name. Matt
thanked Rose Woods, winked at Glenna, and went back
to his office to compose a handwritten letter to Hung
Wai-lang.

Dear Mr. Hung,
    As an addition to the business letter I have
sent you, I wish you to know several things:
    First, that I thank you for your hospitality and
for your confidence in my ability to help your
company with its legal problems.
    Second, please tell our mutual friend that there
were reactions which I would call very favorable.
With regard to Taiwan, there is much less a
problem than I indicated. The reaction was very
pragmatic and realistic: "It probably is time for
the U.S. to rethink its position. Chiang is getting
old, and his son is a mean little bastard. We
should be looking for the main chance."

Third, I have volunteered and should know in
a few days if I am to work in the campaign.
   With thanks and deep respect,
                                    Matt Thompson

Two days later, Thursday morning, Rose Mary Woods
called Matthew Thompson, exactly as Glenna had predicted
Wednesday night that she would. Richard Nixon had flown
to California, but before he left he had asked that Matt be
invited to come to Harrisburg, Pennsylvania with him in
ten days as his "coatholder."

"You'll move around with him," Rose explained. "It's
your job to keep him on schedule and make sure he has
everything he needs—his speech notes, and that sort of
thing. Are you interested? We don't have any regular
advance men yet, so someone has to be with him every
minute to be sure everything goes the way it should."

Matt accepted enthusiastically. The law firm, Rose assured him, was willing to give him some time off, but
otherwise there would be no pay; the campaign reimbursed
for expenses, but that was all.

Matt sent his Hong Kong client another handwritten
letter:

   Dear Mr. Hung:
      I am accepted as a campaign worker and expect
   to begin as the candidate's personal assistant
   on a trip to Pennsylvania in ten days.
                                    Sincerely,
                                    Matt Thompson

   P.S. He says China should not exist in isolation.
   He doubts he will accept an invitation to the
   P.R.C. next summer with two Canadian governors
   because he would prefer talks at the highest level.
   The governors complicate things.
                                    M.T.

Seventeen

The trip began impressively: Nixon's limousine was waved through a guarded gate at LaGuardia Airport and a blue-and-yellow Port Authority Police car escorted it out onto the ramp at the Marine Air Terminal. Their airplane was a private, business-modified, high-winged, propeller-driven Fairchild. The plane was owned by a company that manufactured nuts, bolts, and screws. Nixon was permitted to borrow it for short campaign trips and he had used it several times, although it was not his favorite airplane. Rose Woods had warned Matt that the Fairchild was slow and very noisy. But it was free, and it always seemed to get to the destination on time; the hardware people had an excellent flying crew.

When Matt had finished supervising the transfer of Nixon's bags from the rented limousine to the plane, he discovered that there were to be two other passengers, middle-aged men in gray suits. The larger of the two was standing in the narrow aisle of the airplane, a drink in a plastic cup, leaning over an obviously unhappy Richard Nixon. Nixon was slumped into a large, first-class-size seat, his briefcase on his lap and his overcoat still on, as if he were seriously considering getting off the airplane and walking to Harrisburg, Pennsylvania.

"I'm Matt Thompson," Matt said to the man with the drink. The businessman evidently didn't hear him. He was earnestly talking to Nixon: ". . . and I don't think you ever actually met them, but they lived about eight or ten doors from your brother Don and his wife. We met your brother

139

at their house when we took the kids out there to Disneyland a couple of years ago.''

Nixon nodded glumly. Matt tapped the man on the shoulder and repeated his name. Turning, the man held out his free hand. "I'm Jerry Leffing, Vice President for Public Affairs. That's Lew Brown of our Washington office up there. We're glad to have you aboard.''

Matt shook his hand unenthusiastically. "We didn't know there would be anyone else aboard,'' Matt said.

"Oh, well, we were on our way to Harrisburg too, so the boss suggested that we fly along, to sort of host you. Does Mr. Nixon object?''

Matt looked at Nixon, who had pulled a yellow legal-size pad from his briefcase and was reading some notes. He had hunched deeper into his blue overcoat.

"No, I'm sure not,'' Matt said. "We don't want to kick you off your own airplane. But it is important that Mr. Nixon get some work done during this flight. I'll just sit here next to him.'' Matt slid into the adjoining seat and looked up at the hardware lobbyist. "Is there any chance that we could have some coffee?''

"Oh, sure,'' Jerry Leffing said. He turned and walked forward.

"Good work,'' Nixon muttered. "They've never done this to me before.''

Matt smiled. "Maybe all of a sudden they're optimistic about your chances.''

Nixon snorted.

After the thin lobbyist, Lew Brown, brought their coffee and introduced himself, the plane began to roll, lurching from side to side on the rough taxiway, making coffee drinking dangerous. Nixon put his pad back in his case and with Matt's help struggled out of his overcoat. Matt reminded Nixon about his seat belt and adjusted it for him.

As soon as they were airborne Nixon went to work again and said nothing to Matt for forty-five minutes. Matt read the Supreme Court advance sheets and reread Rose Mary Woods's Harrisburg memo and the schedule she had prepared.

As they were approaching Harrisburg to land, Nixon asked, "How much time?"

Matt looked at his watch. "We go straight to the hotel and have two hours before you need to go to the reception."

Nixon nodded. "How is your Hong Kong client?"

"Fine. I've been getting ready for his comptroller, who comes to New York in four days."

"You're working with Murphy?"

"Yes, sir."

"Murphy is a very impressive fellow."

The pilot made a smooth landing, and as soon as the plane stopped at the private-aircraft terminal, he and the copilot came back to say hello and goodbye to Nixon. With Leffing and Brown they crowded the aisle, waiting to shake hands with their celebrated passenger. Nixon was struggling into his coat, with Matt's help, but made appropriate small talk, thanked the lobbyists, and handed his briefcase to Matt.

A small delegation of Republicans from Cumberland, Perry, Dauphin, Lebanon, York, and Adams counties were gathered at the foot of the plane's steps to greet their Lincoln Day speaker. Matt watched Nixon shake hands and talk to them; at once Matt realized that Nixon was playing back the facts and figures he'd read in Rose Woods's memorandum about the Harrisburg area.

"I know you carried York County for us in '56 and '60," he was saying to a short, gray-haired man. "How does it look for the next time?" Nixon listened attentively as the county leader pessimistically explained the changing demographics of the area south of Harrisburg.

Miss Woods had admonished Matt that Nixon needed a full two hours in the hotel, so he allowed Nixon only about five minutes with the county leaders. During that time Matt thanked the pilots, double-checked that he had all the luggage in the limousine, verified with the uniformed driver that they were going direct to the hotel and that there were to be no other passengers in the car.

"I'm sorry, but Mr. Nixon has a very tight schedule," Matt said loudly as he worked his way into the group of county leaders. Nixon handed him a paper grocery bag and began shaking hands with those nearest him. "I'm sorry, I have to go," he said. "I'll see you all tonight."

In the limousine Nixon identified the woman who had given him the bag of preserves for his wife. "She's the Lebanon County chairman. You can get her name; make sure Pat writes her a thank-you note." Matt made notes on the back of his schedule. "And tell Rose about those jackasses on the plane. If they're going to do that to me, we just won't use their plane anymore. Let me explain, Matt. A trip like this demands my total concentration and it's very tiring. I just can't spend my energy backslapping idiots like that who really don't make any difference. Those county chairmen are another matter; those are the folks who produce the voters on election day, and we should spend the time with them. We must never forget who is important on these trips."

The manager of the Harrisburg Adelphi Hotel ushered them to the Presidential Suite, two bedrooms and a large living room with a dining alcove and pantry. Following Rose's instructions, Matt drew the curtains in Nixon's bedroom, unpacked his Valpak, and told him he could sleep for exactly sixty minutes. As Matt closed the bedroom door, Nixon was dutifully undressing.

Matt called the hotel operator and instructed that the bedroom telephone was not to be rung under any circumstances. He sent for the valet and gave him Nixon's tuxedo. The valet promised that it would be carefully pressed and returned on time, in not more than fifty minutes. Then Matt placed a Room Service order, had a long, hot shower, shaved, and dressed himself in the tuxedo Rose Woods had rented for him in New York.

At exactly 6 P.M. Matt turned on every light in the living room and knocked on Nixon's door. The candidate was deeply asleep, and it was necessary to open the door and call to him twice to wake him up. Once awake, Nixon quickly sat up, rubbing his eyes. He had slept in his underwear.

"Dinner will be here in fifteen minutes, sir," Matt said.

"They will come to get you in forty-five minutes for the head-table reception."

"Okay, okay, I'll be ready."

The damn valet hasn't brought his tux back, Matt thought with alarm. While Nixon showered and shaved, Matt phoned the valet, but no one answered. Frantically he called the manager and explained that he couldn't find the man who had the former Vice President's dress suit. The manager promised to find the tuxedo. In a few minutes he called to say that the valet had gone off duty at 6 P.M. The manager's secretary was trying to reach the man at home.

What the hell am I going to do? Matt wondered. He can't wear my tux; it's a foot too long for him.

The manager called back. "Mr. Thompson, there is no answer at the valet's house. My secretary has ransacked the valet shop and there is no tuxedo there. She wonders if it was dirty or spotted. Was there any reason for him to take it somewhere for special work?"

"No, all it needed was pressing," Matt said impatiently. What the hell was he going to do?

The manager promised to keep trying to find the valet.

Nixon called Matt from the bedroom. He was in his dress shirt and stocking feet, blue garters holding up his socks. "I can't get this cuff link to open up." Nixon pointed to his left cuff. Matt opened the link. On the unused twin bed Nixon had laid out his black bow tie, patent-leather shoes, and cummerbund; a dinner jacket and trousers hung on hangers from a wall sconce next to the desk.

"Thanks," said Nixon. "I can do the rest."

Matt walked over and inspected the hanging tuxedo. A tailor had done some fancy stitching on the inside coat pocket: VICE PRESIDENT RICHARD M. NIXON, it said.

Matt went back to the living room and called the manager. "The valet must have brought it and put it in Mr. Nixon's room while he was asleep and I was in the shower," Matt explained. "I'm really sorry to have gotten everyone all excited."

The manager assured him that no harm had been done and, at the same time, exacted his recompense: He would bring his mother by to meet Mr. Nixon in the morning. The old lady was Nixon's great admirer. They would only stay a minute.

Room service arrived on time with the meal Rose Woods had specified. Nixon stayed in his bedroom until the waiter left, then emerged in his shirt sleeves carrying his yellow pad. As Nixon ate his hamburger steak and a cottage cheese and fruit salad, Matt read to him from the briefing memo, in accordance with very firm instructions from Rose Woods. "Now, don't just hand it to him to read," she had said. "You've got to read it *to* him, word for word. Be sure you have his attention."

" 'The master of ceremonies is State Senator Henry Schellkopf,' " Matt read. " 'He was your county chairman here in 1960. You and President Eisenhower received him at the White House in 1953, 1956, and 1957. His wife, Enid, will be seated on your left. They live in Camp Hill, across the Susquehanna River. Book-of-the-Month has a big plant and is the big payroll in Camp Hill, Pennsylvania. They have six grown children. She gardens.' "

Nixon nodded impatiently. "I know them," he muttered, his mouth full.

Matt Thompson read Richard Nixon the rest of the briefing paper describing those who would be seated at the head table, the name of the high school band that would play, the glee club and soloists due to entertain, and the list of introducers and speakers. Nixon wrote the name of the high school band on his notes.

"Okay, is that all of it?" Nixon asked impatiently.

"Yes, sir."

"I need to review my notes." He stood, shoving his chair back from the table. "I'll be ready to go whenever you knock. Don't call me until it's time to go down." He went into his bedroom and closed the door firmly.

At 6:45 P.M. State Senator Schellkopf and his wife arrived to escort Nixon to the cocktail reception. According to the omniscient Miss Woods, those at the reception would be the head-table guests and about fifteen or twenty fat cats who had paid an extra thousand dollars apiece for the privilege of being able to say, the next day: "I was talking to Dick Nixon last night over at the Adelphi, and he told me—in some confidence—that he thinks we should be blockading Haiphong Harbor right now."

When Matt knocked on Nixon's door it opened immediately. Nixon appeared to have stepped from a bandbox; he was shaved, powdered, combed, and pressed, immaculate from head to toe.

The large Schellkopfs bracketed Nixon, one on each side, into and out of the elevator and to the Susquehanna Room, trailed by Matt Thompson. A large, tuxedoed off-duty policeman admitted the others with an obeisant smile, but stopped Matt.

"May I see your invitation, sir?"

"I'm Mr. Nixon's assistant," Matt protested.

"Your credentials?"

"My what? You think he issues some kind of certificate? We're in the same law firm, Nixon, Mudge, Rose—"

Senator Schellkopf had seen Matt stopped and came to his rescue, interjecting: "That's fine, Roy. Mr. Thompson is with Mr. Nixon."

"Sorry, Mr. Thompson," Officer Roy said unapologetically. "Just doing my job."

"Thanks, Senator," Matt said.

Schellkopf and his wife took Nixon around the small private dining room introducing him to the thirty-five or forty people. There was a bar in the corner and a table of hors d'oeuvre at one side, and Matt put himself in the corner between them, his back to the wall. After ten minutes of circulation, Nixon went to the side of the room and faced the group.

"Ladies and gentlemen," he said loudly, "I want to say that I'm glad for the opportunity to meet all of you. It's especially good to see Mommy and Hugh Scott, Mary and Bill Scranton and the Schellkopfs, and all my other old friends, and I just want to say to you all that I'm pleased to have a part in your Lincoln Day dinner this year, even if we did have to postpone it. As Hugh and the Governor know, these are busy days and sometimes scheduling is our biggest problem. I intend to talk tonight about some domestic problems which concern us all—crime, civil disorder, and civil rights; but I'll save the substance of those remarks for the speech.''

Schellkopf's secretary, a small, dark-haired woman in a long blue dress and an enormous orchid corsage, was starting to herd the head table into a line, referring to a seating chart, officiously checking off the people one by one as she placed them in her formation. When Nixon was efficiently sandwiched between the portly Senator Hugh Schott and Mrs. Schellkopf, Matt relaxed. Others would look after The Boss for a while.

Schellkopf's secretary stood by the door of the Susquehanna Room, ticking off the ragged line of dignitaries, then turned to the remaining guests and loudly ordered: "You should all be at your seats for the invocation. Hurry along now, please.''

Matt walked over to her slowly, giving some stray fat cats a chance to inquire of her first. "I'm Matthew Thompson, Mr. Nixon's assistant. Where would you like me to sit?''

The efficient lady had no idea where he should sit. "Do you have a ticket?'' she asked. "A reservation?''

"No, I don't think so.''

"Well, I don't see your name on the list. I don't have a seat for you. Perhaps you could sit at the press table. Those seats are first-come, first-served. Tables eleven and twenty-one, over on the side. That's the best''—she patted his arm—"you sit with the press.''

The Adelphi ballroom was large, and to Matt's surprise, it was full. There were perhaps two hundred round tables, laden with elaborate centerpieces featuring Abraham Lincoln's black stovepipe hat full of spring flowers, a placard bearing the table number in large red numerals, and an American flag. Huge souvenir programs stood at each place. Matt sat, rather tentatively, in one of three vacant chairs at the press table farthest from the dais. A brass band was playing a medley from *The Sound of Music*. The reporters did not seem to notice that a nonprofessional in a rented fancy dress suit had joined them. Matt wasn't sure whether he should introduce himself or not.

One of the men at Matt's table was a gray-haired veteran, but three of the other four looked surprisingly young. Two had long hair and open collars; the others wore ties. One of the longhairs asked his colleagues: "How come no text?"

The older man smiled the smile of experience. "Nixon outlines these things for himself, but he rarely releases a text. He'll get up there and extemporize. His office told us that tonight we'll hear about crime. That's all we get."

"If there was a text, I'd leave now," the young reporter said.

"He's been giving the same speech since '66," said a third, middle-aged journalist in an unpressed brown suit. Matt ate his salad and read the Lincoln Day Souvenir Program.

Everyone stood while a Lutheran minister gave the invocation. When they sat down, Senator Schellkopf briefly welcomed the crowd and introduced most of the head table. Then a swarm of waitresses began to deliver the roast beef and Duchess potatoes. The reporters talked local politics.

Schellkopf introduced Republicans who held city, county, and state offices; there were fourteen of them, and the reporters had something witty and sarcastic to say about each one.

Madame Bettina Feldschue sang Wagner, accompanied by a young pianist who played so loudly that Madame became visibly annoyed. A reporter flipped the pages of the Souvenir Program. "I can't find the name of the piano player," he complained, "and I sure as hell need his name for the story. Anybody know his name?"

"The way she's looking at him, you'll find him in the obits tomorrow."

Mayor Al Deutsch, the genial political leader of Harrisburg, announced the winners of nine door prizes, and the happy donees came forward to receive their bounty. All through this process, Matt noticed Richard Nixon was talking to Hugh Scott, the pipe-smoking Republican U.S. Senator from Pennsylvania. Occasionally, someone from the audience scuttled up to the head table to get Nixon to autograph a Souvenir Program, and both Nixon and Scott continued to talk as he signed his name for the people.

The Auditor of the Commonwealth of Pennsylvania was introduced to announce the winner of a Republican essay contest conducted in the high schools of the region. A girl about fifteen years old came forward to receive her check for $250 from the Auditor and to have her picture taken with Nixon and Senator Scott.

Miss Dauphin County Republican, a beauty queen, was asked to rise at table seven and was greeted with suitable applause.

At last, shortly after 10 P.M., Senator Hugh Scott was called upon to introduce the speaker of the evening. Unfortunately, as the older reporter noted, Scott was not in good form. A late-winter cold still plagued him, even after a prolonged stay in Florida. He stopped several times to cough and have drinks of water, wipe his mouth carefully with his handkerchief, and beg the pardon of the audience. Much of the introduction was a rambling reminiscence of the Eisenhower Administration's years in office. As Scott coughed and pontificated, Nixon sat impassively, looking out at the audience. A television crew arrived and noisily began setting up its camera and lights among the tables in the center of the audience.

Scott had arrived at the phrase "... a man who needs no introduction," but apparently he could not bring himself to think of Nixon as "the next President of the United States," so he ended his peroration rather abruptly, turned and pointed to Nixon, then stepped back as he said, "Vice President Richard M. Nixon."

Nixon stood quickly and walked to the rostrum while the audience stood and applauded. Matt was the only one at his table to stand or applaud; the others looked at him inquisitively. The younger men seemed to resent his interloping on the Fourth Estate's neutral territory.

Nixon's speech was well received by the long-suffering audience, if not by all the journalists. The television crew

turned on their hot, bright lights as soon as Scott surrendered
the podium and they filmed Nixon for about ten minutes.
Matt was startled when, in mid-sentence, the glaring lights
went off and the crew began to disassemble their tripod, pack
their lights and camera, and wind their cable. Matt could hear
a man at one of the tables near them admonishing the
television people to show some consideration for the folks
who wanted to hear the speech, but it did no visible good.

The partisan audience interrupted Nixon with applause
several times as he talked about Washington, D.C.'s ap-
palling crime rate, the need for stronger judges and for a
return to deterrent punishment. Attorneys General who
were soft on crime had no place in government, he
declared. It was time we began caring more for the victim
of crime than the criminal. There was much that a President could do to strengthen law enforcement at the local
level, Nixon assured the Pennsylvanians.

The reporters at Matt's table were skeptical. "What's he
saying—he wants federal street cops?"

"Maybe J. Edgar Hoover will run the Harrisburg police
department."

"Hoover couldn't do any worse."

"What's the lead? Nixon today proposed an increased
federal involvement in the war on crime?"

"Naw, the lead is his call for tougher judges."

"Or his attack on the A.G."

"I think I'll lead with the guy who won the TV set as a
door prize."

The crowd gave Nixon a standing ovation when he
finished. As Matt's table companions gathered their belongings and hurried to the side exit, Matt began to edge
his way around the tables to an aisle that would take him
to the end of the head table. Nixon was talking with some
people behind the table and a small crowd was gathering
below him in front of the rostrum, holding up programs
and asking for autographs.

"Did you get dinner?" Schellkopf's secretary asked
Matt when he encountered her at the end of the dais. He
assured her that he was well taken care of. "I thought the

speech was just wonderful," she enthused. "I'm glad we held out and postponed this thing twice so we could get Mr. Nixon to come. He's the only one we really wanted."

Matt nodded. Nixon stepped back from the table and caught Matt's eye; Matt walked over to him. "I'm going to have the Scotts and Scrantons and Schellkopfs up to the suite for drinks," Nixon said in a low voice. "Make sure there's a stocked bar up there, will you?"

"Yes, sir." Matt had seen some bottles behind the wet bar in the living room, but he wasn't sure about ice, mixer, and liqueurs. Rose Woods's memo hadn't warned him about cocktail parties. He saw a telephone behind the far end of the head table, walked quickly to it, and called Room Service for a bartender and a full bar.

By then Nixon and his friends were moving toward Matt, headed for the exit behind him, and Matt followed them to the elevators. When the elevator arrived it was barely large enough for Nixon's group of eight. At the suite the door was open and a bartender was already busy setting up his wares. Nixon headed directly for the bedroom, and in his absence Matt introduced himself to the guests, hung up coats, and took drink orders.

When Nixon returned to the living room it became clear to Matt from the conversation that the smaller man with the laconic, preppy style whose name was William Scranton was a former Governor of Pennsylvania. Matt had decided that Scranton's wife, Mary, was a bright and adroit woman. She reminded him of Mary Finn. The Scrantons talked Pennsylvania politics with Nixon, and as Matt looked after drink refills, the conversation turned to Lyndon Johnson and Viet Nam. Hugh Scott was of the opinion that most of the country deplored Johnson's escalation of the war. Mary Scranton rather aggressively said she disagreed, and Nixon asked her several questions about how she gauged public opinion about the war.

After nearly an hour of political shoptalk the Schellkopfs thanked Nixon elaborately for coming to their Lincoln Day Dinner and led the way to the door. Matt realized then that Hugh Scott's wife had said nothing but hello and goodbye.

It appeared that her silence was a demonstration of the fact that she had no use for Richard Nixon.

While Matt tipped the bartender and sent him away, Nixon went into his bedroom. Matt began to pick up glasses and turn off lights, then reached into his inside coat pocket for the Rose Woods schedule. He walked to Nixon's door and knocked softly.

Nixon was in his shirt sleeves, a drink in his hand, when he opened the door. "Well, what did you think of your first Lincoln Day Dinner?" he asked heartily.

"I couldn't believe all the preliminaries. Door prizes and all that. I thought your speech was great."

Nixon nodded diffidently. "Hugh Scott is a horse's ass. That was the worst introduction I've ever heard, I think. They should always be short, you know. And they should have some content, for God's sake. He went on and on and said absolutely nothing."

"We leave the hotel promptly at eight fifteen A.M.," Matt said. "We're flying commercial, and they take off at nine thirty. You'll be back at the office by noon. What would you like for breakfast?"

"I eat very little, as a rule. Juice and toast. Sometimes an egg." Nixon walked into the living room, sat in a big chair, and put his feet on the coffee table. "I'll eat just before we walk out. . . . They seemed to like it when I whacked LBJ's Attorney General, didn't they?"

He's really keyed up, Matt thought. Should I try to get him to go to sleep?

Nixon talked to Matt about the Supreme Court, about crime in Washington and about lawlessness in black neighborhoods.

"There is very little crime in China, I hear," Nixon said. "Russia has a big problem, but the People's Republic doesn't; why is that?"

"I'm not so sure that that's true," Matt said cautiously, unsure of the basis for Nixon's assertion. "These days, during the Cultural Revolution, law enforcement is left to the Army, according to a Swede I met who had just been there. Bands of kids roam around taking whatever they want, breaking into places, beating up people, even killing them, all in the name of Chairman Mao.''

"It sounds like anarchy.''

"That's just what this other fellow I told you about said—Teng Shan-li, my father's friend. He used the words 'intentional anarchy.' ''

"Meaning what?''

"Meaning that Mao Tse-tung is directing these destructive forces against his enemies, almost without regard to the cost of the country.''

"If it is a purge—an ideological catharsis—it's a remarkable historical event,'' Nixon observed. "And it's a courageous gamble. Those fellows like Mao who made the Long March are a tough bunch, aren't they?''

"Very tough, and single-minded. . . . Sir, it is now twelve thirty and you have to get up in about six hours. Do you want to turn in now?''

"You go ahead.'' Nixon nodded at Matt's bedroom door. "I'm not sleepy yet. I don't want to go in there and just lie and look at the ceiling and think about Hugh Scott's miserable performance tonight.'' Nixon walked across the room and poured more Scotch in his glass, dropped in some ice cubes and came back to his chair, stirring his drink with his index finger.

"Mr. Nixon, I read Nancy Mellor's draft of your article for *Foreign Affairs*,'' Matt said.

"What did you think?''

"Well, as you said, she doesn't really hit the China question constructively. She calls for an Asian alliance against Peking, backed by the United States, but she doesn't take the next step. What happens once her 'containment' is achieved? Does she really think the world can isolate a billion people forever?''

Nixon nodded. "You don't quarrel with her notion of an Asian collective-security organization to succeed SEATO?''

"No, she's right when she says that SEATO is dead. It was always too Western to succeed. Whatever collective is created has to be Oriental to be credible.''

"And you do agree," Nixon pressed, "that China is expansionist and a threat to the region?"

"Not right now. They have such internal problems that I don't think they could hurt anyone very much. They want friendly regimes on their borders, for sure, and so they will continue to try to dominate North Korea and North Viet Nam and all their neighbors. That's their policy. But I can't believe that China threatens Japan or India today."

"What about the problem of Formosa? Has she treated it well? I remember you saying you were concerned about that issue."

"First, I think the article should call it Taiwan. Whatever you write will be closely read in the People's Republic, and they care very much about what the island is called. Second, I think you will needlessly complicate the thesis of the article if you take a position of any kind on Taiwan. Not all the Asian countries in any new collective-security agreement are going to agree on the Taiwan issue. Every country is going to have to work it out with China, individually. And if you tell China in this article that she can never have Taiwan back, you may prejudice anything you may hope to accomplish with the P.R.C. in the future. If you were to say that, the Chinese will probably just write you off as a hopeless member of the China Lobby."

"Maybe so. What would you say about China's future in this piece?"

"I've written some paragraphs for you to look at, and I've made some changes in Miss Mellor's draft. I'll get them." Matt went into his bedroom and brought back a file folder. Nixon was looking at his drink. "Why don't you read me your paragraphs?" Nixon suggested.

"Sure. They go in sequence right after the section where she rejects the idea of a European anti-China alliance," Matt explained, reading:

" 'Our long-range aim should be to bring China back into the family of nations and so we must avoid even the appearance of ganging up on China. Our posture must be defensive and free of any taint of racism.' Then I'd tack this on the end of her next paragraph, which talks about an

Asian restraint on China, backed by the United States: 'As the nations of Asia become economically and politically strong and China's leaders demonstrate that they have turned their energies inward rather than outward, a dialogue with the People's Republic of China can and should begin.' "

Nixon looked at Matt sharply. "You want me to advocate negotiations with Communist China?"

"The way I've written it is very conditional. First, there must be regional collective security; then China must stop adventuring; and then, and only then, a dialogue."

Nixon extended his hand for the paper and sat reading it, then took out a fountain pen and began making changes in Matt's draft. "There are some other suggested paragraphs there, too." Matt pointed to his text.

"You write very well," Nixon said. "I don't think I can afford to be quite as easy on the Chinese as you suggest, but Nancy's first draft was way too tough. I like your analogy to the ghetto. That will grab the Council on Foreign Relations types who are always complaining that the cops are too tough on the poor little rock-throwing Negro kids who would cut their throats for a quarter. You equate them to the Chinese Army, and that's about right." Nixon grinned.

"You know how the papers will characterize this article, don't you? The headline will say: 'Nixon calls for Red Chinese dialogue.' You can make it as qualified and conditional as you want, but that's still how they will sensationalize it. We've got to be tougher on the Chinese in here. I'll work on it." Nixon put the pen cap in his mouth as he interlined his revisions with the rest of the pen. "You go ahead and sleep. I'm not sleepy."

Matt debated whether he should stay to argue for the language of his draft, and decided against it. Specific language wasn't as important as the formulation that would be the substance of the section on China. He'd be in a stronger position to resist Nancy Mellor's counterattack if the specific language actually were Nixon's and not Matt's. He bade Nixon good night and went into his bedroom.

Matt was very tired; it had been a day in which he had been alert and on edge every minute, thinking ahead to Nixon's next need and the demands of the schedule. The damn schedule! Half undressed, he unfolded the typewritten schedule and reviewed the next morning's events. He phoned a night telephone operator who promised to try to wake him up every ten minutes from 5:40 A.M. to 6:10. Room service contracted to appear at six thirty. He wondered if Nixon would remember to lock their front door.

Matt padded into the living room in bare feet and undershorts, expecting to find his restless candidate still at work in the big chair, but Nixon was gone. His bedroom door was closed. Every living-room light was still burning, so Matt went from one to the next turning them off. He locked the door—evidently great men couldn't be expected to think of such things.

In bed Matt thought about the China revisions to the *Foreign Affairs* manuscript. Nixon had taken the text into his room; Matt wondered if Nixon was awake in there, still working on it, at 2 A.M.

The morning's logistics were flawless; the wake-up, breakfast, even the limousine were exactly on time. But Richard Nixon looked as though he hadn't had much sleep; he appeared about seven twenty, ate a bite of toast and drank a little coffee, and scanned the morning paper.

The manager and his rail-thin mother arrived at the door of the Presidential Suite exactly at seven thirty, and Matt realized, too late, that he'd failed to warn Nixon of this little social engagement. He left the pin-striped host and his mama in the hall and closed the door.

"Sir"—he approached Nixon, who was deep in the sports section of *The New York Times*—"the hotel manager is here."

"Ummm," said Nixon.

"He would like to introduce his mother to you; she is a great supporter of yours."

Nixon looked up suddenly, confused. "Who?"

"The hotel manager's mother. She's out in the hall."

"What does she want?"

"To meet you."

"Now?"

"We leave in"—Matt looked at his watch—"four minutes."

"Wait. I'll put on my coat. I'll say hello to her on the way out. Why do they do this?" Nixon loped into his bedroom, and Matt heard his bathroom door close and lock.

Matt admitted the manager and Mrs. Martin the elder, who had brought with her a fat, pale yellow autograph book on the plastic cover of which the Japanese manufacturer had embossed the word MEMORIES. The Martins stood near the front door, hands folded in the fig-leaf position, saying nothing.

Nixon emerged from the bedroom dressed for a snowstorm in his overcoat, muffler, and black leather gloves.

"Well," he cried, "we're off!"

"Sir, this is Mrs. Martin, Mr. Martin's mother."

"Ah, yes, of course, how are you?"

"This is such a thrill," Mrs. Martin said softly. "I've admired you for so long. Since before you were Vice President."

"Well," Nixon replied, glancing around the room, "your son has taken very good care of us here. I'm sure you are very proud of him."

"Oh, yes. He's a good boy. Could I ask you for one favor, Mr. Nixon? I collect famous signatures for my granddaughter, and I was wondering if you would . . . ?" She opened the autograph book and held out a blank page.

"Do you have a pen?" Nixon asked.

"Frank?" She turned to her son.

The manager produced a ball-point pen from an inside pocket.

Nixon held the pen clumsily in his gloved hand, fumbled it, and tried to write his name. "It doesn't work," he declared in a tone which implied that his worst suspicions had been confirmed.

"You have to push in on the clasp," Martin said.

Nixon couldn't find the clasp with his bulky thumb. Both Martin and Matt reached to help him with the pen.

"I think I have one in my purse," Mrs. Martin volunteered. She put the book on a table in the foyer and opened her bag, which had been hanging on her arm. Matt pulled a felt-tip pen from his shirt pocket, opened it, and handed it to Nixon.

"Where's the book?" Nixon demanded. "What's your grandson's name?"

Mrs. Martin retrieved the book and held it out to him. "No, it's a girl, and her name is Lisa. She is Frank's niece. Lisa Mayer."

"How do you spell Lisa?" Nixon asked, pen poised.

"L-I-S-A. Mayer is spelled M-A-Y-E-R."

Nixon put the book on the foyer table and wrote busily, then closed the book with a snap and handed it to Frank Martin. "Well, we've got to run for an airplane," Nixon announced, turning to Matt. "Anything else? All set?"

"All set."

The airline preboarded Mr. Nixon and Matt Thompson, seating them in the last row of the first-class section with Matt on the aisle. Nixon busied himself with a book, not even glancing up when the other passengers were boarded. He had said goodbye to the hotel manager civilly, but once in the car it was evident that the little autograph session with Grandmother Martin had displeased him. He sat far into the corner of the back seat, looking at the passing traffic, and said nothing to Matt Thompson.

When the airport was in sight, Nixon said, "That was terrible."

"Sir?"

"That woman. With the kid's autograph book. We should always have a pen available at times like that. Everyone should carry pens. You might think about getting some inexpensive pens made up that have my name on them. You could give a woman like that a pen. It could be a cheap damn pen, but she would keep it and tell all of her friends about it.

"I worked on the *Foreign Affairs* article last night and I think it's going to be good. I'm tougher than you are on China, but I agree with you that there has to be dialogue. And I think you are right about Taiwan. I'll let you see it when I'm finished with it."

"Yes, sir."

Nixon said nothing more to Matt until they arrived at LaGuardia Airport. When the plane had landed and was taxiing toward its gate, a stewardess explained that she would hold the coach passengers back so Mr. Nixon could be the last of the first-class passengers to get off.

"I'm not going to the office," Nixon said to Matt. "I'm too sleepy."

"Fine. I'll have the car take you directly to the apartment."

"This is a book by George Kennan." Nixon dropped a thin volume on Matt's lap. "I wish you'd read it and see my notes in the margin. I'd like Nancy to rough out a speech for that World Affairs Council based on my notes. You tell her. And I'd like to know what you think of it."

"Sure," Matt said; "I'll be glad to."

"She's too hard-line, you know. She hates the idea of a détente with Russia and she does everything she can to position me that way. But I do believe we have to coexist with the Communist countries. We don't have to like them, but we have to live with them. That's the thing she doesn't seem to see. And I have to fight with her all the time to get things to come out the way I want them, rather than the way she wants them. I don't know how much longer I can put up with her."

Matt nodded with sympathy.

In his cab, headed for MacDougal Street, Matt thought of the letter he must send to Mr. Hung: I could hand it to Chen, the comptroller, to take back with him. It would be best not to tell them about the *Foreign Affairs* articles until I know what the final draft will say, I guess. Nancy Mellor is going to scream like a fat panther when she sees that China language, and she could well talk Nixon out of some or all of it. Nixon said on the plane that he intended to make it tougher, so I'd better wait and see, he thought.

But the Harrisburg trip went pretty well, and I could write and say that I am a part of the campaign now. Glenna Harrison will give me a reading on that; she will tell me what Nixon tells Rose Woods about this trip and how they intend to use me in the future, and I could write the Chinese that much. Then, when *Foreign Affairs* comes out, I can send them copies, if it's any good.

The Chinese should be pleased.

Eighteen

• OCTOBER, 1967 •

October 30, 1967

Mr. Hung Wai-lang
Hung and Company
Hung Building
Box 86
Hong Kong

Personal and Confidential

Dear Mr. Hung:

I enclose a copy of *Foreign Affairs* magazine, which is published by the Council on Foreign Relations every three months. It is considered to be very influential and is widely read by the people in and out of our government who shape this nation's foreign policy. I am sure you will find it interesting.

I also enclose a copy of a manuscript which I prepared, proposing certain amendments to the original draft of Mr. Nixon's article which is printed on page 111. A comparison will show that the author was willing to adopt both our ideas and some of Mr. Teng's specific language.

This article has been widely noticed and favorably commented upon. Mr. Nixon is now seen as advocating the resumption of a dialogue with the People's Republic of China (upon certain conditions which many believe were included in the article because Mr. Nixon is a candidate for high office and cannot take an unreasonably radical position at this time). In the press coverage there is very little focus on the author's proposed conditions precedent to a dialogue. I enclose articles from today's *New York Times* and *Washington Post*.

> Yours sincerely,
> Matthew Thompson

It was nearly midnight when Matt finished typing his letter and an address label to Mr. Hung. He sealed a large envelope containing two copies of the *Foreign Affairs* periodical, his manuscript and the clippings. He was certain the mail room on the nineteenth floor was locked, so he put the mailer in the lower tray of the mail rack on Al Murphy's secretary's desk. He looked at his watch; he felt like celebrating, but could think of no one in whom he could confide. He could call Glenna, but she would only insist that he come to her apartment for the night. And he could hardly tell her the China section of the Nixon article was mostly his. She would surely repeat his boasting to Rose Mary Woods. That kind of thing could get him kicked right out of the campaign.

Mary Finn would understand, and she could keep his secret, too. He reached for the telephone on the secretary's desk and dialed Mary Finn's home number. He had known it from memory for months. He felt rather daring calling a girl for a date in the middle of the night from a desk in the office hallway.

After four rings, a very sleepy woman answered: " 'Lo?"

"Mary? Mary Finn?"

"No. This is Carla; Mary is out. Who is this, any-way?"

"I'm just a friend of hers. Do you think she'll be home soon?"

"I don't even know what time it is. She's on a date. You woke me up. What time is it?"

"Twelve twenty."

"Jesus."

"Sorry to have disturbed you."

"Who *is* this?"

"Just a friend. Good night, Carla."

"Good night, you bastard."

Richard Nixon's November, 1967, speech to the San Francisco World Affairs Council staked out his campaign position on the Middle East, the centerpiece of which was a categorical commitment to Israel's future. A speech writer, Carl Markham, had been working with Nixon on the text for two weeks, and Markham went along to San Francisco to do some backgrounders with the newspaper reporters and columnists who were there to cover the speech. Nancy Mellor had spent some research time with three New York men known to be close to the Israeli Government, and she went to San Francisco too. Matt Thompson wondered why she had been asked to come along. At the same time, Matt wondered why he'd been included. Rose Mary Woods had recruited an advance man in California to make all the logistic arrangements and lead Nixon around once he got there. Nixon didn't need Matt Thompson to hold his coat.

But when H. R. Haldeman flew up from Los Angeles to see Nixon at the St. Francis Hotel, Nixon called in Nancy Mellor, Carl Markham, and Matt to meet him. The meeting was very short, barely more than a handshake and a Haldeman smile full of very white, straight teeth. Matt had the faint impression that the real reason they were all on the Coast was to get a look at Haldeman's teeth and to let Haldeman get a look at each of them.

Nixon, Haldeman, and the advance man, a near-invisible young man named Pete Wilson, went off to a reception at the end of the day. Neither Nancy Mellor nor Matt was invited to accompany Nixon, and it seemed taken for granted that Matt would know what to do with himself until he was needed again. Matt had been told by the advance man, almost offhandedly, that he would be going to the World Affairs lunch the next day, and must be in a car at the entrance precisely at 11 A.M. Matt had been given a nice enough room at the St. Francis, and he presumed that he was expected to stay near his telephone until someone needed him for something. He bought two newspapers and a paperback novel at the St. Francis newsstand and was walking toward his room on the fifth floor when Nancy Mellor came out of her room and called to him.

"Thompson! Have you eaten?"

Matt had successfully avoided Nancy Mellor in New York. Once they had ridden on the same elevator at 20 Broad Street, but he had ridden an extra floor after she got off to ensure that there was no occasion for conversation about the *Foreign Affairs* article. He'd made sure he sat with Carl Markham on the airplane from New York to San Francisco.

But there seemed to be no way to escape her dinner invitation gracefully. "I was hoping to get some time with Markham tonight," Matt finessed. "Have you seen him?"

"Yeah," Miss Mellor said curtly. "He's gone socializing with 'Frisco friends. I don't know if they are girls or boys; I've never really figured him out. But you won't see him tonight. I'm going down to the coffee shop now; come on along."

Matt shrugged. "I'll put this package in my room and meet you there."

"I'll wait right here," she said peremptorily.

When they'd settled into a booth in the coffee shop it became evident to Matt that Miss Mellor intended to interrogate him.

"Have you read the Middle East speech?" she opened.

"Carl showed it to me."

"What do you think of it?"

"It's good. I don't know much about the politics involved, and Carl tried to explain some of that to me; I guess it's a pretty important speech."

"Everything The Boss says these days is important," she corrected.

A waitress intervened to take their orders. "After you've been doing this for a while," Miss Mellor instructed, "you'll learn to eat the specialty of the location, wherever you are. One day it's Creole in New Orleans and the next day it's steak in Omaha."

"It seems that Mr. Nixon eats hamburger everywhere."

"The poor man has no palate, I'm afraid. He's brilliant, but you could feed him sawdust and he wouldn't notice. He just thinks about other things than food."

Matt nodded.

"That speech tomorrow will have the American Jews salivating, I promise you that. It's full of the things they care about. At the same time, it's a highly principled approach to a bundle of difficult problems. Did you write the *Foreign Affairs* article?" She shot the question like a quarrel from a crossbow.

"I thought you wrote the draft," Matt evaded.

"I wrote *a* draft, but it was a strong indictment of Communist China. He ended up throwing rose petals at them."

"I thought he was pretty tough."

"Shit!" Nancy Mellor exclaimed. People at a nearby table turned to look at her. She bisected an oyster and piled her fork high with egg and bivalve. As she specifically protested the content of the article, she waved her fork. She's going to spill all of that on the floor, Matt thought; she's really upset. He resolved to react with caution.

"That article puts The Boss squarely on Mao's side, and that's the way everyone is reading it. Tough, hell!" she exclaimed.

"Well, evidently he thinks that when the Viet Nam war ends the Orient will be a new ball game," Matt answered.

"What about old alliances and old friends?" she demanded, pointing her empty fork at him. "What about loyalty?" He wondered if she had eaten the load the fork had carried. He glanced at the floor but saw no oyster or egg.

"You are talking about Taiwan?"

"Taiwan; Formosa. Whatever you call it, those are our allies there. Red China intends to wipe them out. Don't we care about that?"

"Maybe we can mediate between them?"

"Horseshit!" The three older women at the next table turned again and stared. "Communists will say anything, but sooner or later they will go for the jugular. Did you ever read Lenin?"

"Some. But they are also realists. They have been known to pull back when they saw they couldn't win."

"Temporarily. Never permanently. They were twenty years driving the Nationalists out. Read your history! They said they wanted to be Chiang Kai-shek's ally when Japan invaded, but as soon as the Japs were defeated, Mao and the others went after Chiang again."

"They have a lot of internal problems now; they aren't much of a threat to anyone," Matt said.

Over apple pie and ice cream Nancy Mellor got around to saying what was on her mind: "You and I don't agree about Red China and Formosa, Thompson, and that is fine. There are a lot of people I disagree with and that doesn't bother me. But let me tell you what would bother me. It would bother the hell out of me if you gave The Boss a lot of information and he bought some of it."

"You needn't worry, Miss Mellor. I have no influence around here."

"I trust that's true. He can be President of the United States, you know, and he can do a vast amount of good for mankind, but he can't do any of that if he says and does a lot of crazy and unprincipled things like that goddamned *Foreign Affairs* piece."

"Why don't you tell him?"

"Ha! You have a few things to learn about working with Richard Nixon, my boy. One thing you never do, if you want to keep working for him, is you never tell him he's made a mistake.''

"Really?"

"Really. He'll cut you right out of his life if you make that error, believe me. Watch that Haldeman handle him; they've been political partners for ten or twelve years and Haldeman knows how to work Nixon. Five hundred times a day he says 'You're right' to Nixon, but he countermands Nixon's orders behind his back all the time. Rose Mary is the same. When they know The Boss has goofed they just fix it up without saying anything to him about it. He lets them do it and he says nothing to them about it either. They reinforce his ego or his psyche or whatever it is. Maybe he admits his mistakes to himself, but he's never confronted with them.''

"Is that good?"

"It's not a question of bad or good, my boy. It's simply how it is. So when I get a chance, I'll write him a speech kicking the shit out of the Communist Chinese and he'll deliver it somewhere and we'll get back on the right track again. I don't need to hit him over the head about it. We'll do it his way.''

The husky Miss Mellow gathered her purse and began to get up, then sat down firmly and picked up a spoon. She waved it at Matt forcefully as she delivered her coda: "If The Boss is going to beat Lyndon Johnson, he's got to push Johnson left and we've got to occupy the middle and the right. Everyone agrees on that. You don't keep to the right of L.B.J. by getting cozy with the Red Chinese, that's for sure. Johnson often calls the Chinese the enemy. The Boss's place on that issue is to say they are the enemy too, but to say it louder and better, and the *Foreign Affairs* essay didn't do that. It staked him out far to the left of Lyndon Johnson; and that was a bad mistake.'' The spoon jabbed at Matt slowly, then fell to the table with a clang. Nancy Mellor slid out of the banquette. "Get the check, will you?'' she demanded. "I'm so mad about the damn article I've got to go take a walk around the block.''

*   *   *

H. R. Haldeman came to New York a few days after
Richard Nixon returned from San Francisco and they
began to assemble a campaign staff, one by one. John
Mitchell agreed to leave the law firm to become the
campaign manager, the chief executive officer of the political enterprise. Dr. Arthur Burns was signed on as coordi-
nator of policy development, especially domestic policy
and economics. Maurice Stans became head of a large
fund-raising operation.

Three days after his return from San Francisco, Matt was
asked to visit H. R. Haldeman in his suite at the Essex House
Hotel. The call was not unexpected; Glenna Harrison had
told Matt when he would be called and that Haldeman would
offer him a full-time campaign job working on foreign policy
speeches and research. She was even able to tell Matt the
amount of salary Haldeman was going to offer to pay him.

But what Glenna had not warned him about was the
makeup of the rest of the foreign policy staff. As Haldeman
explained Matt's job, its impossibility became disappointingly
clear: Nancy Mellor would be designated Matt's boss.

"Look, Mr. Haldeman," Matt responded, "I want to do
whatever I can to help Mr. Nixon. I'm really happy to be
asked. But I can't work for Miss Mellor, and I'm sure
she'd be the first to tell you that."

"What's the problem?" Haldeman asked impatiently.

"From the time of our first conversation we haven't
gotten along. She's made it explicitly clear that she has no
use for me or my ideas, and I'm sure she considers me too
inexperienced to be of any value. Has anyone asked her
about this?"

"Not yet." Haldeman was annoyed. His tight schedule
contemplated short, perfunctory hiring conversations, not
troublesome interpersonal conflicts to be resolved. "Maybe I'd better talk to her first. After I do I'll call you."

Matt left the Essex House with the hollow sense that he
had just seen everything he had been counting on derailed,
and he wasn't sure how it had happened. Nor could he see

any way to get things back on the track. Someone wanted Nancy Mellor to head the foreign policy office—presumably, Nixon himself. It was really pretty simple: if Mellor was in, Thompson was out. Haldeman might know Mellor; perhaps he was her sponsor. Or Dr. Arthur Burns might have selected her and, since he was going to be the head man in the policy and research shop, he would surely get his way.

When Haldeman's call finally came, Matt would have to write Mr. Hung and explain that he would not be working in the campaign. That would be the end of the whole China adventure. That letter to Mr. Hung would be very difficult to write, Matt reflected.

It was Monday of the following week before Matt heard anything directly from the Nixon campaign. Indirectly, he was reassured by Glenna Harrison, who was certain she would have heard something if they had decided to drop Matt. Glenna did not like Nancy Mellor, and she was also certain that Nixon would prefer Matt if it came down to a choice between Mellor and him. It was unusual for Glenna to express a dislike for anyone; she had been raised to eat everything on her plate, to say Please and Thank you, and to emulate Thumper—or was it Bambi?—who would never say anything unless he could say something nice.

"I'm sorry, but she makes my flesh crawl," Glenna said. She and Matt were sprawled on her bed, late Saturday night, watching a movie on television. She knew that television movies helped her when she was "down in the dumps," as she described it. Matt was willing to do anything she suggested that night, and that was unusual too. Ordinarily, he wouldn't have been at all interested in a late-night British detective movie. Glenna had let him take off her jeans so he could run his hands up and down her legs, but he didn't become aroused, and that was unusual too. She was sure he was depressed because of Nancy Mellor and the campaign job.

"Are you going to just give up?" she challenged.

"Sure; if Nancy Mellor is the head of foreign policy, I'm sunk. What else can I do?"

"Maybe talk to The Boss and convince him that you're more valuable than she is."

"Fat chance. He'd have to explain to Arthur Burns why he didn't pick his protégée, and he couldn't do that. At least, he wouldn't want to." Matt doubled the pillow and leaned back against it.

"Maybe Rose could help. She'd help if I asked her to."

"What could she do? Can she get Nancy canned? She'd have to have an awfully good reason, and I don't know what that would be."

Glenna moved across the bed to him and put her hand on his upper arm. He rolled to his feet and walked to the bathroom. "I think I'm going home, Glenna," he said disconsolately. "I really don't feel like it tonight." He pushed the door closed and engaged the lock.

"I think you should stay here tonight, Matt," Glenna said, walking to the bathroom door. "I don't want you to be alone tonight. Can you hear me?"

"I can't, Glenna, I'm sorry. I need to be alone." He opened the door. "Where are my damn shoes?"

"Look in the living room where you were sitting," she said. She followed him, her bare feet making a brushing sound on the wood floor of her hallway. "Matt, please stay and talk to me."

"I really don't want to. This whole Nancy Mellor shit—all her high-powered influence and what she stands for and her ability to succeed and freeze me out—all that makes me sick. I don't need to talk about it. I just need to go home and be sick. I feel like I'm going to throw up."

"I want to help you."

"There is nothing you can do, Miss Harrison, and you know it and I know it." He stood and shrugged into his blue windbreaker. "So I'll call you." He left her standing there, tanned, a perfect female body, her hand outstretched toward him.

Monday morning Matt found a note from Glenna on his desk at work.

"I am so worried about you," she wrote. "Please call me as soon as you get here. I have something to tell you. I love you."

Matt didn't want to talk to anyone. He closed his door and instructed the switchboard to hold all his telephone calls until after lunch. He spent the morning trying to draft a letter to Hung explaining that he would not be working in the Nixon campaign. In one draft he elaborately described Nixon Mellor. In a later version he simply said he had been blocked from the foreign policy job by "internal political maneuvering" which had resulted from his success in influencing the *Foreign Affairs* text. By noon he was nearly finished with the final, handwritten letter as he intended to send it.

At a few minutes after twelve someone knocked on Matthew Thompson's door. His first thought was to holler "Go away," but it was obvious that he couldn't do that at Nixon, Mudge. That might be Albert Murphy out there, but more likely, it was Glenna.

A gray-haired woman in a gray blouse and skirt stood at his door. Even her shoes and stockings were gray. He was glad to see her, because he didn't know her.

"Mr. Thompson?" she asked. "I'm Mr. John Mitchell's secretary. He would like you to come to his office for a short meeting. Can you do that? I tried to telephone you several times but I couldn't get through."

"Oh, right. I've had it off; I'm doing some writing."

"Mr. Mitchell must go out of town in an hour, but he can see you now if you can come."

Matt rubbed his face, then turned to look for his coat. "Oh, sure. Just a minute and I'll go up with you. Let me get my jacket."

Although John N. Mitchell's corner office was adequately, even expensively furnished, Matt thought it somewhat austere. One wall, to Mitchell's right, was entirely bare except for a small black-and-white photograph of a young blond woman which had been hung a few feet from his desk at his eye level. A heavy file cabinet, conspicuously secured with a welded iron hasp and a large combination lock, sat in a corner, near the door.

Mitchell himself was expensively dressed in a dark blue suit and vest, white shirt, and small-figured dark tie. He lay back in his large desk chair, a pipe in his mouth, talking on the telephone when Matt was shown in by the lady in gray. Mitchell waved him into a chair that had been positioned directly at the center of the desk.

Mitchell was talking to someone named Jerry about Nixon campaign money. Matt had seen Mitchell around the office several times, but he'd never had a chance to look at him up close. From a distance of only six feet, Matt thought, the man looked very unhealthy. His large, curved nose was heavily veined; his eyes were bloodshot and danced rapidly side to side. Mitchell's hands trembled.

Mitchell put the telephone back on a small side table, swung his chair around full face, and put his elbows on his desk, hunching forward. "Matthew Thompson," he affirmed, "how do you do? I guess I've seen you around here, but this outfit is so big I have trouble keeping track of everyone."

"Yes, sir," Matt replied, "I don't think we've ever really met before."

"Well, I hear good things about you, both from the firm and from Richard Nixon. He's anxious to have you work in the campaign."

Matt nodded, moving forward in his chair. "I'd like that too, Mr. Mitchell, but I'm pretty sure Miss Mellor would blackball me."

Mitchell snorted, then relit his pipe with a chrome cylindrical lighter. "I don't think that's going to be a problem," he muttered around his pipe stem.

"Sir?"

"I say, I don't think you need to worry about Miss Mellor. She was being considered for several assignments, and we've pretty well decided on someone else to head up the foreign policy work. You know George Bothwell?"

"No, I don't."

"He's from Virginia. He says he's happy to work with you if you still want the job."

"Yes, sir," Matt said with a grin. "I sure do." He felt an adrenaline rush, and his mind raced. What had happened to Nancy Mellor?

"We'll pay you what the firm has been paying and they'll give you a leave of absence here. You can come back and work for Murphy after the campaign, if you want to."

"Good."

"We'll be moving up to Fifty-sixth and Park Avenue in about a week. Someone has given us an old building to use up there. It isn't very fancy, but it's a good location and the price is right. Can you leave here in a week?"

"I believe so. Yes, sir."

"A fellow named Cory Madison is handling personnel details. He'll call you. Then you should meet Bothwell when he comes up in a few days. Someone will let you know."

"Great."

Mitchell stood up and they shook hands. "Glad to have you aboard," Mitchell said.

Matt Thompson was euphorically disoriented, but he found Mitchell's door. He stood at the elevator for several minutes thinking. Now he could write Hung a different letter. Nancy Mellor was out, obviously. Had Nixon fired her because their philosophies were different? Now he could look after Nixon's China policy, assuming this George Bothwell was not a complete nut. But Bothwell was an unknown quantity; he would ask Glenna to find out all about him. Whatever Bothwell might be, he would certainly be a distinct improvement over Miss Nancy Mellor.

He thought about Glenna; he would have to make it up to her somehow, because he had given her a rough time the other night. She would probably be out at lunch until two, but he'd call her then. He would take her out to dinner by way of an apology.

First, however, he had to write a letter to China before he went to lunch.

Nineteen

A long-faced middle-aged woman in a light blue Main-bocher suit and pearls sat at a folding table in the ground-floor room at 450 Park Avenue. Like the other men and women in that bare space, piled with boxes, Mrs. John Eliott Garvey had volunteered to work at Nixon Campaign Headquarters. She had broken the pleasant routine of her life primarily because her husband was a bond trader and an old friend of John Mitchell's.

She had expected her volunteer assignment to be per-functory and brief—surely fully discharged by lunchtime—perhaps stuffing or addressing envelopes, as the TV news sometimes showed in its campaign stories. But when Mrs. Garvey arrived that morning, a young woman had led her to this table and had rather condescendingly shown her a dog-eared sheaf of papers on which was a long typewritten list of campaign workers with their telephone numbers, some names crossed out, many numbers changed, new names interlined in rough alphabetical order.

She was right next to the front door, where everyone would come in. The table was the first thing a visitor would notice. The tabletop was gouged, and some sort of food had caked in the declivities.

She was reaching for the telephone to send for a janitor to clean it up when a tall, good-looking young man in a blue suit came through the front door and rested his attaché case on her unsightly table.

"Good morning. I'm Matthew Thompson," he said. "Can you tell me where I belong?"

Mrs. Garvey reached for the staff list the young woman had given her. "I haven't the remotest notion where you belong, Mr. Thompson, but let's see if your name is here."

It wasn't. Nor was George Bothwell's name listed.

"What about Dr. Burns? Dr. Arthur Burns?" Matt asked.

"Yes! I have a number for him. Just let me dial."

A girl answered the Burns telephone number and gave the temporary receptionist a second number to dial, but it did not answer. Upon re-calling the first number, she was advised to try a third. At last, the third number was answered by a woman who suggested that Mr. Thompson be sent to the top floor. Mrs. Garvey triumphantly relayed that advice and pointed to an elevator which she had noticed nearly hidden behind a pile of cardboard boxes. Matt thanked the lady for her efforts and joined four other men who had been waiting for the lift for a long time.

At the fifth floor the door opened onto a narrow hallway, barely wide enough for two people to pass. Long before, the rooms on the fifth floor had been remodeled and enlarged at the expense of the hallway by the Bible publisher who owned the building, each room encroaching into the passage to a different depth, so the hallway narrowed and angled irregularly as it progressed. Across from the elevator, a door had been built on the bias where the hall wound around a particularly deep office. Wavy glass topped the partition for about fifteen feet. Matt could see distorted images moving around inside the room, but the door was closed. Down the dark hall to his right was an open door which seemed to invite his inquiry.

"Can you tell me where to find the policy research office?" he asked a stocky woman who was sorting papers at a filing cabinet in that room.

"Back beyond the elevator, I think," she said. "Ask for Angie. She works for them."

"Angie. Thanks," Matt replied. He backtracked and followed the passage beyond the elevator, then right and left to a door where the hallway turned right again. He opened the door and looked in; a young woman with black hair sat at a desk looking at him.

"Are you Angie?"

"Yeah. What can I do for you?"

"I'm Matt Thompson. I'm supposed to start work here—somewhere—today. Is this where I belong?"

"I don't know," the girl said. She reached for her copy of the staff directory and flipped the pages. "Thompson. No, I don't see you here. Who do you work for?" She had a faint Puerto Rican accent.

"I work for George Bothwell in foreign policy research," Matt said with a touch of annoyance.

"Well, this is his office, all right. But he's not here yet. He is due here today, but I don't know when. I haven't even met him yet. Do you want to wait for him? You can sit in his office if you want." Angie nodded toward an inner door through which Matt could see an old desk and several chairs.

Matt opened a gritty casement window which looked out into a brick light well. The air from the outside seemed to help the dismal office space a little. He sat at the desk and called to Angie. She came in hesitantly.

"Have you worked here long?" he asked.

"No, this is really my first full day. Friday I just filled out forms and left."

More questions got Angie talking. When he looked at her closely he thought of the word "sinew." She was thin, her face concave but not unattractive, her arms and legs spare but well shaped.

As she was beginning to tell Matt what she knew about the office, George Bothwell arrived carrying two large attaché cases.

"I had trouble finding this place," he announced with surprise. "I'm Dr. Bothwell."

"I'm Matt Thompson, and Angie is your secretary. I'm supposed to be your assistant."

Bothwell put his cases on the desk and shook Matt's hand. "Angie, can you get us some hot tea?" Bothwell asked. "Sit down, Mr. Thompson, and let's get acquainted. I've got about an hour and forty minutes before I'm due at the candidate's apartment over on Fifth Avenue."

* * *

After ten minutes, during which George Bothwell did most of the talking, Matt Thompson came to several tentative and random conclusions:

—As a foreign policy adviser to Richard Nixon, this fellow was out far beyond his depth.
—He appeared to be one of those ambitious, climbing young assistant professors one sees in the halls of political science departments at all the universities, conspicuously bright young men who are marking time teaching courses called "Patterns of Political Thought, 1931–1947" or "Labor Politics in the 1920s" to undergraduates and writing monographs entitled "The Matto Grosso Conflict and The Monroe Doctrine." All are looking for a way to break into the Big Time without jeopardizing their tenure.
—Bothwell was more hard-line on Russia than anyone Matt had ever run into.
—The self-important Dr. Bothwell had not the foggiest idea of how to go about organizing this campaign policy operation he had been appointed to lead.

In an imperfect world, Matt concluded, one works for imperfect people.

The foreign policy group had been allotted only the two rooms—Angie's little anteroom and Bothwell's office; there was no space for Matthew Thompson. The office manager's secretary advised Angie to put a desk in Bothwell's room for Matt. The office manager told Matt that space was very tight and he was sorry. John Mitchell told George Bothwell that he had nothing to do with the assignment of offices.

So Matt began to look for an office, and in two hours he found one, three doors down the crooked hallway from Angie and Bothwell, a spacious and well-lighted room at the front of the building, on the Park Avenue side. The office had been overlooked or forgotten when the campaign gods allocated office space; it belonged to no one. So when Matt found it the first day by going from one door to the next, turning the knobs and poking his head in, he quickly moved in. He furnished it with a desk which had been left down on the third floor, an extra desk chair which came from the first floor, and an excellent desk lamp that was found sitting on the floor in Angie's closet. That night Matt came back to his office after dinner carrying two large paper bags. By midnight he'd installed a strong lock on his door, painted his timeworn and dirty office walls the same off-white color as the ceiling of his apartment, washed the windows, and cleaned the old desk inside and out. During the next hour he roamed the empty building, acquiring two side chairs, a filing cabinet, and a large folding worktable. He needed a typewriter, but he decided to exhaust all legal means of acquiring one before lifting the blue IBM he'd seen in the personnel office on the second floor. He thought about installing a small carpet, but decided too much ostentation might breed jealousies which could call unwanted attention to his other basic comforts.

Matt knew no one in the building, but he saw that many of the people were old friends from one of Nixon's several previous campaigns in California and the big one in 1960 against John Kennedy. Matt quickly discovered that in the hierarchy of this political campaign the researchers, the policy experts, and most of the writers were considered quite unimportant. The money-raising people were important. In fact, they were so important that soon they were going to move out of the old building into real Park Avenue offices up the street. The media experts were important too. The tour people who scheduled the candidate, traveled the country setting up his arrangements, and moved with Nixon as he went about were the front-line, combat troops. As in every war, they had a tolerant contempt for the rear-echelon "paddle-feet" who stayed in New York, safe in their warm bunkers. "It's rough out there, but then, somebody has to stay back here and keep the supplies flowing" was their condescending mannerism.

The small group of policy people, among them Alan Greenspan, Agnes Waldron, Richard Allen, Arthur Burns, George Bothwell, and Matt Thompson, worked long and hard. They scoured the newspapers, analyzed what the other politicians were saying in attack or advocacy, met endlessly with speechwriters and media people, and wrote out reams of policy statements. They responded to dozens of questions every day from the candidate, the writers, and even the advance men, on every imaginable subject.

Matt and Angie worked together to cope with the flood of paper that poured into Bothwell's office. Angie had abilities which the Chemical Bank's secretarial pool had never discovered. Soon she was confidently dealing with the problems of George Bothwell's life, deflecting the unnecessary, coping with persistent newsmen, and routing work to Matt or to the writers or to those dealing with domestic issues, as she saw fit. Her instincts were good, and she rarely made a mistake; when she was in doubt, she brought her questions to Matt and they made a joint guess.

During the first ten days Angie and Matt found it necessary to work most evenings and all the weekend to tame the paper flow and produce the substantive work that was demanded by the speech writers. About the second day it had become clear to Matt that Dr. George Bothwell was both uninterested in and incapable of dealing with the daily grist that came to their mill. Bothwell leafed through his telephone messages and sipped a cup of tea when he arrived, about ten o'clock, each weekday morning. When Nixon was on the road campaigning, Bothwell spent his weekends with his family, a vast throng of children whose pictures soon occupied every level surface in his office.

Bothwell himself was a tall, angular person with thin, bony features and heavy glasses, about thirty-one or thirty-two years old. He had spent his last four years as a

functionary in the School of Government at the University
of Virginia, where he had made a small career of meeting
the correct people and becoming their friend. He adroitly
worked the names of the famous and powerful into every
conversation, leaving no doubt that he had been on the best
of terms with Dean Rusk, Clark Clifford, Dean Acheson,
Allen Dulles, Henry Steele Commager, and countless others.

When Bothwell had sorted the accumulated pink telephone-
call message slips, he would hand the bulk of the pile to
Matt and Angie to take care of. A few, notably the
television and print journalists' calls, Bothwell kept on his
desk, which was otherwise bereft of paper. The second
morning he explained to Matt that Mr. Nixon and Mr.
Mitchell were insistent that their foreign policy adviser
hold himself in constant readiness to fly to the candidate's
side in the event of some international crisis. Therefore, it
would be impossible for him to "fill his book" with a
schedule of ordinary work. Routinely, Bothwell spent his
late mornings reading *The New York Times* and *The Washington Post* and making a few telephone calls. At 1 P.M.
he was to be found at La Côte Basque lunching in the left
corner banquette in the back room, with a columnist,
commentator, or reporter of his selection. This drudgery,
he explained to Matt, was an essential part of "pumping
out the Nixon line" on foreign policy. But these long and
expensive luncheons were usually preceded by Bothwell's
frantic demands for information about some subject known
to be of particular interest to his guest for the day.

Afternoons were less of a problem because Dr. Bothwell
seldom found his way back to the confusion of the campaign until well after 3 P.M., and he usually tried to be
home in time to watch the evening television news cycle at
5 P.M.

When Richard Nixon was in town, however, Bothwell
put in long days by his office telephone, in readiness for
the call of summons. While waiting, he was willing to talk
to Matt about the work of their office, and although
Bothwell was young and of limited experience, he knew
something about the politics of foreign policy—surely

more than Matt did—and he knew Nixon, Mitchell, and the other campaign people.

Somehow, in the frantic disorganization of the place, Matt managed to prepare a work agenda and a rough calendar of foreign policy topics to be worked on. In the first week he assembled everything Richard Nixon had ever written or said about foreign affairs, and with the help of a couple of volunteers from Columbia University, Angie filed the material by subject so it was retrievable.

During that first month, Matt had no personal life. He worked fourteen or fifteen hours a day at the office, eating at his desk or on the run. During the first week he talked to Glenna on the telephone every day, but before long he was accumulating a pile of her messages without returning her calls. When she came by to see him in his new office, she brought a ceramic elephant to decorate his recently built bookshelves. She looked at him expectantly as he opened the fancy package.

"Hey, it's great," he said, lifting the fat ceramic animal out of its paper.

"Where are you going to put it?"

"Gee, I'm not sure. Can I decide later, Glen? I've got a really tight deadline on this material I'm working on." He began to stuff the wrapping in the scarred brown wastebasket at the corner of his desk.

"I was hoping we could have dinner together," she said.

"I really don't see how." Matt sat down and pulled his work toward him. "There is at least three more hours of stuff to do here." He looked up at her. "I'm sorry."

"Well, you've really got to eat something. How about if I go and get us some takeout? We can have a nice picnic right here on your desk."

"Look, *really*, darling, I've got to get this done. I have our secretary waiting for it; I can't keep her sitting there while we eat, can I? I'll eat when I get done, okay? I am glad you came up, and I do like my present, but I have all of this to do and I've just got to do it now."

"That's not a very nice way to treat a person, Matthew

Thompson," Glenna said, standing up. "I'm really sorry I got you this job, I think."

"Don't be mad, Glenna. We'll get together as soon as I can." He looked up at her sharply. "What did you mean by that?"

"By what?"

"That you got me this job?"

"Oh, you know. I put in a good word for you. I told Rose I liked you."

"And that got me this job? No, you said that like you meant it." He stood and walked around his desk to her. He gently took her bare arms in his hands and drew her close to him. "What's behind all this? Did you do something to Nancy Mellor?"

She raised her hands and held his head. Tears welled in her eyes. "I've missed you so much. I love you so much. I'd do anything for you."

"What did you do?"

"I guess I got her fired. You were so pathetic and depressed. I couldn't stand it."

"How did you get her fired?" His hands caressed her back familiarly. "What did you say?"

"I went to see Rose up at her apartment that Sunday and I told her that Nancy had made some passes at me." Glenna tightened her arms around Matt's neck.

"Passes? Had she? You never told me about that."

"Well, not really passes. She never threw me onto the floor or anything. But she was after me. A person can tell about something like that, you know."

"So you told Rose?"

"I said I thought it would be terrible if there was a scandal right in the middle of the campaign, and she agreed with me. She thanked me for having the courage to say something."

Matt held her tightly against his body. "You did that for me. You're quite a woman. Maybe I *could* just take some time for dinner. Angie would probably like to quit now, anyway. Will you come to dinner with me, Miss Harrison?"

Glenna backed away from him, wiping her eyes with the

back of her right hand. "It would be a pleasure, Mr. Thompson. I would have told you sooner, but I was a little ashamed of what I did. I thought you might be very angry with me."

"Right now I'm feeling very grateful to you, sweetheart. I guess I should have guessed you would do something, but I didn't know you were so good with the brass knuckles."

"Only where you're involved, Matt. You're my love. I'd probably kill someone who was being mean to you. That's the way I feel about you."

Deep in Matt's list of things to do was a comprehensive review of Sino-American relations. Once when he submitted a proposed outside work program to George Bothwell, Bothwell had returned it with the China study crossed out, but Matt had erased Bothwell's pencil line, restoring the China study to the list.

Seven foreign policy studies had been farmed out to experts at think tanks and universities who had volunteered to help in the Nixon campaign. Matt sent each volunteer a difficult research assignment with profuse gratitude but also with short and rigid deadlines. Several of the projects were historical catalogues, but from the others he solicited policy analysis and proposals for future policy. The China assignment had gone to a Republican professor who turned out to be a sympathizer with Chiang Kai-shek. Matt sent a duplicate request to Mr. Hung in Hong Kong with the reminder that all correspondence must go to his MacDougal Street apartment.

A week before the Johns Hopkins China expert submitted his policy paper, Matt received a long and analytical essay from Mr. Hung, with six paperback books and the little red book of Chairman Mao's writings. The box from Hong Kong bore a customs declaration describing the contents as "leases and other legal documents." Apparently, no one had opened the package to verify its contents.

The evening that Hung's box arrived, Matt sat at his

wooden table in the living room of his apartment and read
Hung's brief note, handwritten on plain, cheap paper:

> Dear American friend:
>   I am sending some writings about China which
> I hope you will find interesting.
>   If you would like some more please tell me.

The note was signed with one Chinese character which
Matt could not translate.

The monograph was in two parts. The first was a
chronology of the major events in the relationship between
the United States and the People's Republic of China since
the beginning of Communist rule in 1949. Part two was a
discussion of China's foreign policy toward the United
States, point by point. The section on China's claim to
Taiwan was a near-verbatim repetition of Teng Shan-li's
argument in the small conference room off Hung's office in
Hong Kong; it was so close in its language and the vigor
of its tone that Matt experienced a realization that he was
actually receiving a communication of thought from a
specific man in Peking, far away in another culture. It was
like picking up the distant voice of someone he knew on a
shortwave radio receiver, disembodied, only the words and
thoughts flowing.

Teng had also written short essays about Korea, Viet
Nam, India-Pakistan, Russian "hegemony," and SEATO
and other Asian collective security. Three separate pages
held a point-by-point reply to the China section of the
Nixon article in *Foreign Affairs* quarterly.

Matt laid aside the booklets and the red book of Mao's
sayings and writings. Rereading Mr. Teng's analysis of the
Foreign Affairs article, it appeared to Matt that Teng had
only one material disagreement with the thesis Nixon and
Matt had set out, and that related to whether or not some
new Asian collective-security organization would have to
be created to replace SEATO before China and the United
States could begin broad negotiations. Teng argued that

successful negotiations might well obviate such an organization.

So, Matt reflected, the Chinese are in a hurry to get going.

That night and over the next week Matt drafted a policy paper on China which softened Nixon's insistence on the creation of a collective-security organization as a condition precedent to talks with China. It called for a reexamination of American policy toward Taiwan, and proposed China's withdrawal of support for North Viet Nam as the only condition for the commencement of preliminary talks between the countries.

When Matt had typed a clean draft of the paper, he sealed it in a large envelope and locked it in his filing cabinet, along with the Johns Hopkins China expert's hard-line, and almost diametrically contrary, proposals.

Then Matthew Thompson turned to the development of a draft policy statement which would advocate a speedy withdrawal of all American troops from Viet Nam.

George Bothwell had told Matt that Nixon intended to attack Lyndon Johnson on Viet Nam only in the most general of terms in his everyday stump speeches. "It goes like this," Bothwell explained: "If the most powerful nation on earth has suffered x casualties and spent xx dollars and the situation in Viet Nam is still terrible, then it's time for new leadership." The Nixon campaign theme, cutting across the law-and-order issue, agricultural policy, civil rights, and the sad state of Russian relations, would be the same: "It's time for new leadership." But sooner or later, Nixon would be calling for the definitive speech on Viet Nam, to be delivered to some suitably somber audience; and he, George Bothwell, would like to be able to whip out of his pocket a ready-made outline for such a cornerstone declaration of policy.

"We want to be ready when R.N. asks for it, Matt," Bothwell said importantly, "and so I want you to get right on it as soon as you can. Send for the polls so we can attach them to the outline. Review everything R.N. has said before about the war, and don't forget to point out that it was Kennedy and Johnson who put us in there. Remember, we don't knuckle under to the Reds, and be sure to praise our gallant fighting men. See if you can get it done by Tuesday.''

When the Viet Nam polls arrived from David Derge, Nixon's polling expert, Matt read them with great care. In spite of all the controversy and a broad underlying popular yearning for their country to be at peace, the majority of Americans in 1967, the polls showed, generally supported Lyndon Johnson's attempt to keep the Communists from taking over South Viet Nam. ''Peace with honor'' was the bell ringer that one of Nixon's writers either had crafted or had stolen from somewhere. In Derge's polls it showed up as the result that almost everyone wanted in Viet Nam. No one was asked to explain just what ''honor'' meant in context, so that became the focus of Matt Thompson's policy outline. Richard Nixon would, he proposed, define the terms for a peace in Viet Nam and then declare them to be honorable.

Candidates for certain offices are told that the path to success winds through Ireland and Israel because of the potent ethnic content of their political constituencies. Those who would be mayor or governor or a senator in New York, and most Presidential aspirants, make the Irish/ Jewish pilgrimages a first order of business to show their concern for the interests of those segments of the political demography. The Irish care and the Jews care and so the politicians travel.

It was decided that the candidate should visit England, Scotland and the Republic of Ireland within a month, to make a speech in London and to create photo opportunities at his ancestral Irish home and in Glasgow. The schedulers hoped the photos would command every front page in the country. A trip to Israel had also been agreed to in the meeting, but only last night Nixon had personally disapproved that proposal as ''a waste of time.''

''It looks like the trip will be about mid-January,''

Bothwell said. "That's a terrible time to fly around England; it's bitter cold there then. But he can't go later, because the primaries begin in February and he'll have to be up in New Hampshire a lot. If the trip is set for around January fifteenth, I can't go, and I've told Mitchell that," Bothwell said flatly.

"Oh," Matt replied.

"I'm never away from my family in January, you see. My birthday is on January twenty-first and we always have a big traditional party then. My wife's birthday is on the ninth. Little George's is on the nineteenth and Maureen's is the twenty-fourth. We have all these birthdays in a row and the whole month is one big celebration around our house. All our relatives come, and our friends all know about it and they come, and there is just no way that I can be away then. So you will have to go."

Matt was nonplussed at Bothwell's arrangement of priorities; he could set aside Nixon's campaign just like that, to go to a birthday party! The man was even more self-centered than Matt had first guessed.

"Can you give me some idea of what I'm supposed to do on a trip like that?" Matt asked. He wondered if his disapproval of Bothwell showed, and he hoped that it did.

"Sure, I'll fill you in. Plenty of time. You'll need to prepare arrival statements for him to say to the cameras at every airport, of course. And he'll need toasts for each banquet. But you can do most of that here before you go. Do you own tails?"

"Tails?"

"A dress suit; you know, white tie, white vest, tails."

"No," Matt said curtly; he only wanted to hear more about the work he needed to do to get ready for the trip.

"Perhaps you'd better buy rather than rent," Bothwell said contemplatively. "If he's elected, you'll need them often. A good suit of tails is hard to rent."

"I'll think about it," said Matt.

Angie walked in with the day's correspondence, and Matt got up and moved toward the door. Over his shoulder

he said to Bothwell: "Remind me to ask you for the name
of your tailor."

Twenty

The bathtub at Claridge's Hotel was long enough to hold
Matthew Thompson at full length with a few inches to
spare; with his head back and his ears underwater, his toes
did not quite touch the end of the tub. That unusual
circumstance alone was enough to make his trip to London
memorable. Matt had rarely found a bathtub in which he
was comfortable, so he soaked late into the night, reading
the London papers and rereading several speeches and
toasts Richard Nixon would deliver over the following
three days in the British Isles.

At 1 A.M. the pearl-gray telephone in his bathroom rang
shrilly and insistently. In scrambling to answer it, Matt
sloshed water on the pile of newspapers on the floor next
to the tub.

"Thompson?" Matt recognized Richard Nixon's deep
nasal tones.

"Yes, sir."

"Asleep?"

"No, sir. Just doing some reading."

"Can you come in for a minute? I have a few things."

"Yes, sir. I'll be right there."

Matt dried his body quickly and brushed his hair. As he
unpacked fresh underwear and socks he wondered what he
was expected to wear to call upon the former Vice President in the middle of the night. Albert Murphy would have
prescribed a coat and tie, Matt was sure. He pulled a dark

green plaid shirt from its hanger and decided to defy The Code. In gray slacks and brown loafers, tieless, he made his way to Nixon's room at the end of the hallway. Nixon wore a blue bathrobe over his open white shirt and the knife-creased pants to the suit he'd worn that day. His black shoes were highly polished. Matt was glad he'd worn no tie.

"Come in," Nixon said. "I never can sleep the first night on one of these trips across the Atlantic. Jet leg seems to bother me more when I fly east than west. I can go out to Japan and sleep very well the first night. That's just the way things are. So we might as well work. Sit there." Someone had built a coal fire in the fireplace at one end of the sitting room where Nixon had been working. Matt recognized the final draft of the speech Nixon was to deliver the next day at lunch; it was spread out on the floor next to the chair. Evidently Nixon had taken the pages apart to emend it generously.

"Have you read this?" Nixon pointed to the pages.

"Is that the speech to the English-Speaking Union?"

"That's it. 'Hands Across the Atlantic.'"

"Yes, sir."

"Let me ask you, are these war-casualty figures correct? Did the British lose that many civilians?"

"They are correct. I checked them."

"What do you think of this idea for a technology exchange? Have they anything we want? Nothing over here seems to work very well."

"It isn't a bad idea. They are doing some very good work in ceramics, for instance. Their production is inferior, but the R and D is excellent. They are good in weapons and some electronics research, too. Britain is really concerned about the brain drain, so they would welcome this idea, I believe."

Nixon gathered up the sheets of paper and handed them to Matt. "Give these to Rose, will you? I've shortened it and changed some of the language, but the themes are the same. She'll need to type it on the machine with the big letters. How is your dad?"

Matt was taken by the abrupt change of subject. "Why, he is doing fine. He's beginning to think of retirement."

"Will that be soon? Is he that old? My God, I think of him as a young man."

"About another year. A year from June."

"Think of that! What will he do?"

"Oh, he wants to travel and perhaps write. He really wants to go back to China."

"Of course he does. Do you think he can get in?"

"I think so. He still has friends there, and our government will issue passports now for scholars and old China hands like him. He shouldn't have much trouble getting in. The cost of the trip is bothering him more than anything else."

"How much would it cost him?" Nixon asked alertly.

"About ten thousand dollars, he says."

"We could get that for him," Nixon said confidently. "That should be no problem. Remind me when the primaries are over—say, in July—and I'll make a few calls. He could be enormously useful to us if he were there, don't you think?"

Matt was hesitant to endorse his father for the role he'd claimed for himself. "He might be. I'm not sure how willing my father is to involve himself."

"Sure."

"What do you think a go-between might accomplish?" Matt asked.

"I'm not sure," Nixon admitted. "Perhaps someone could informally sound them out. They are saying some awfully bellicose things about the United States these days, and I can't help but feel that whatever they say about L.B.J., they might be friendlier toward a new President. It would be useful to know."

"Could a new president—like you—improve relations? Could you change our policy toward China, or do you need the Congress to go along too?"

"The old China Lobby might make some trouble with the Congress, but I think it would depend on how a President did it. If it were done with enough high drama, I don't think the Congress would dare to interfere. If a President went there and met with Mao and it was all televised, who could stand against that?" Nixon moved back and forth in his chair with enthusiasm. "All the press in the world would want to be there for that, eh? But we wouldn't let them all come; we'd have a little list, and when Scotty Reston begged to come to cover the story of the century, our press secretary would look at the list and say, 'Sorry, Scotty.' We'll take our friends and, of course, the television people. What's the time difference between Peking and Washington?"

"Twelve hours," Matt answered.

"Perfect," Nixon snapped. "The banquets can be live on all the morning shows. Imagine Mao lifting his glass to toast the President right in the middle of *The Today Show*! Perfect."

"Wouldn't they expect you to pay a pretty high price to get there?" Matt asked innocently.

"I don't think so. They need us as badly as we need them, right?"

"Perhaps. But it's my impression that they are very stiff-necked about Taiwan and about our troops near their borders in Viet Nam."

"Well"—Nixon sat back in the deep chair and reached up to snap off the old floor lamp next to it—"we couldn't promise them anything about Viet Nam except that we'll be out of there as soon as the situation is stable. In fact, they could help us there by persuading Ho to pull back beyond the DMZ. But Taiwan is a different matter. I think we could assure them that the future of Taiwan is an open question as far as the new Administration is concerned, couldn't we?"

Matt nodded.

"All those Nationalists who made it to the island would have to be protected, of course. Mao would like to cut off their heads, I suppose, but we couldn't allow that, could we?"

Matt shook his head in agreement. He was afraid to say

anything, lest he break Nixon's stream of thought. It was all just too good, he was thinking.

"No," Nixon continued, "we would need some kind of guarantee that any new Taiwan policy would protect the poor people on that miserable island. But with a guarantee like that, I'd have . . . there would be . . . um . . . I could go along with a change. Don't you agree?"

"I do," Matt replied. "Is this subject anything you want to talk about during the campaign?"

"Oh, God, no! All of this is political poison right now, don't you see? The right—George Murphy and Goldwater and the others—would do everything they could to keep me from being nominated if they thought I was even thinking about a new China policy. They would cut off my nuts! And I need those people, you know. I need their money, and they are the ones who get out and work. I didn't have them in California in '62, and we lost that one, of course. They are the true believers. We can't alienate them; never forget that."

"I understand."

"Let me make it very clear: we can't afford a leak about China. If I'm asked any questions I'll just waffle around some. If you are asked, just look dumb. We don't need to worry about Bothwell and the others. I'll say nothing to them and they will just be as hard-line as ever; we can be sure of that."

"I'll say nothing," Matt assured him.

"Right. When the election is all over we can talk about this again, and if we've won, it will be time enough to think about concrete action. In the meantime, you be thinking of what a President can do. Step one, do this. Step two, then do that. Step three, four, five. You be prepared to hand me a program then. I'll look to you on China. You'll be the only one in the organization on China, and I'll expect you to be ready to show me the way to go when the time comes. But until then we'll say nothing. I like to have one person I can look to on a subject rather than have it spread all over with everyone expecting the other fellow to be doing all the work. You're my one person on China from now on."

"Great. I'll be ready."

"Meanwhile, write me up some press-conference answers for China questions that will keep Goldwater happy but won't burn any bridges for later on. Can you do that? Fuzz it up so no one can understand it?"

Matt laughed. "I think I can do that."

"Use the *Foreign Affairs* article, but stress the hard-line parts of it. Keep me over on the right for now."

"Sure."

"Well, I guess I'll try some sleep now." Nixon stood. "Rose got me some sleeping pills, but I hate the damn things. When I take them I am so doped up in the morning that it takes me an hour to get going."

Nixon walked toward his bedroom carrying a glass he'd taken from a table. "Turn off the lights, will you? Remember, we don't talk about this subject until November, now. No more talk about it."

"Right," Matt said to Nixon's back.

"Good night," Nixon said as he closed his door.

Matt gathered up the manuscripts, turned off the lights, and stood looking at the light coming from under Nixon's door. "Good night," Matt Thompson muttered.

The next day Matt wrote a short letter to Hung Wai-lang on Claridge's stationery and handed the envelope to the concierge for posting to Hong Kong.

"Dear friend," the letter read:

> I am so looking forward to the harvest season
> in November. I am optimistic that the seeds which
> have been given me are planted in very fine,
> fertile soil and should produce an excellent crop
> in November if the fall growing conditions are
> as we all hope.
> Best wishes from London,
>   Matt Thompson

When Matt's letter was photographed by MI-5, the British Secret Service, a copy was sent to the British Foreign office as a matter of routine. There copies were filed under NIXON, RICHARD (UNITED STATES) and HUNG, WAI-LANG (HONG KONG). A new file was begun: THOMPSON, MATTHEW (UNITED STATES).

Twenty-one

• MARCH, 1968 •

"Mr. Thompson?"

Matt had picked up his bedside telephone automatically when it rang the first time, but he was having trouble understanding the faint voice that was calling him. He shook his head rapidly and rubbed his face with the palm of his hand. "Hello," he said thickly.

"Matthew Thompson?"

"Right." He was in bed in his own apartment, he knew, but it was dark and very late. He thought of his father and wondered if this was an emergency call. For several years he'd told himself that one of these days someone might call him to say that his father was ill or dead and that he must come to Whittier at once. He would call for an airline reservation and leave at once, he had rehearsed. As he groped for the light he wondered if he had any cash; he might have to wait for the bank to open.

"Right; I'm Matt Thompson."

"Please hold the line for Mr. Hung Wai-lang, calling from Hong Kong, sir."

Matt turned on the light, sat up, and jammed a pillow behind his head. He heard Hung's distinctive voice greet him faintly.

"Matthew Thompson? This is Hung Wai-lang. Are you well?"

"Hello, Mr. Hung," Matt said loudly. "Yes, I'm fine. But I'm barely awake."

"Yes, I apologize for calling at his hour but I have just received news which I must convey to you at once."

"Sure, that's okay."

"Okay? Fine. Do you know that President Lyndon Johnson and his government have placed a blockade on Haiphong and other northern ports in Viet Nam?"

"No, I didn't know that."

"It has just happened. Chinese ships are now prevented from sailing on the open seas to those ports with their supplies."

"I see."

"China will shortly announce a break-off of the Sino-American talks in Warsaw, in retaliation. Matters between the two countries have become very, very serious, Matthew."

"I understand. We—that is, I—didn't know about the blockade."

"If a Chinese ship should be attacked by the American blockaders there could be a very bad war. I think you should come here right away."

It was cold in the bedroom. Matt Thompson rubbed his chest, then scratched his shoulder. "Come where—Hong Kong?" Perhaps he should get up and close the window, he thought.

"Yes."

"I don't see how I can, Mr. Hung. We're in the middle of a very tough campaign." Matt swung his feet out of bed. The floor was ice-cold as he sprawled forward to reach his flannel shirt hanging on a chair. What did they expect him to do about a blockade? He put his feet back under the covers to get them warm as he struggled into the shirt, still holding the phone to his ear.

Hung's voice seemed to sharpen with insistence. "Your coming is not entirely my idea. I think you really should come very soon. I strongly advise you to do so."

"I don't see how it is possible, Mr. Hung. Nixon depends on me for all his foreign policy research work right now, and I just don't know who would do the work if I were gone."

"What about Mr. Bothwell?"

Matt Thompson blinked with surprise. He had never mentioned Bothwell to Hung; over in Hong Kong they knew more about the Nixon campaign than the information he provided them. "Bothwell is pretty useless, Mr. Hung. He can't do the work."

"I must strongly urge you to make any arrangements you must, Matthew. Plan to be away a week or so. This is not a casual request; please get on an airplane and come here! Cable your flight number and I will meet you."

The talk of blockade was a pretext; someone wanted to talk to him there—Teng perhaps. Matt looked at his watch. "It's almost four A.M. here, Mr. Hung. I won't be able to call you back for five or six hours at the soonest. I'll do my best, and I'll let you know."

"Things are very serious, Matthew. It is very important that you come."

After he'd hung up Matt turned out the bedside light and slid down under the quilt to get warm. His first thought was to go to Nixon's apartment immediately, in the middle of the night, to tell him about Hung's call. But any story he told Nixon couldn't stop there; he would have to explain who the people were for whom Hung was calling— or at least whom Matt guessed Hung was calling for. Surely his call had been ordered by the men Teng Shan-li worked for. Perhaps it was Mao himself. Matt quickly decided he couldn't go to Nixon with a story like that.

How could he get away to go to Hong Kong for a week? Maybe he could. He wanted to go; maybe they could do without him. Nixon would be leaving New York at noon to campaign during the coming week in the primary states, especially Wisconsin, Florida, and Illinois. There were no big foreign policy speeches scheduled for about ten days or two weeks. The Florida briefing book was already full of material about Israel and the Middle East.

But he couldn't tell Nixon and the others that he was flying to Hong Kong. If he went, he would have to construct some foolproof alibi for the time he was away. Perhaps he could say his father was very sick and needed him. No, Nixon would want to call and send flowers and tell his California friends to look in on the professor. So his father couldn't be sick; but Ezra Thompson might be a good alibi, if he said he absolutely needed Matt to be with him for a few days.

Matt reached for the telephone and dialed his father.

"Dad, it's Matt. I know it's the middle of the night out there and I'm sorry to wake you."

"Well, hello, son. As a matter of fact, I'm just sitting here reading. I've been thinking about going to bed, but I find Saint Augustine hard to put aside."

"Sure; me too. Listen, I need a very unusual favor from you, Dad. I can't really explain the reasons now, but it has to do with Mr. Nixon. Sometime in the future I will explain and I think you'll approve, but you'll have to commit an act of faith right now."

"Sounds mysterious. What am I supposed to do?"

"Just be my alibi for a week or so. I will tell people I'm visiting you. If anyone calls for me, just take a message as if I'll be right back."

"So, I'm to be a cover story, eh?"

"Right."

"Where will you actually be?"

"Well, I'm not supposed to tell anyone where I'll be. Those are my orders."

"It all sounds very cloak-and-dagger, son. Is it dangerous?"

"No, not at all, Dad. Very tame, but it's also very flattering that they repose that much trust in me. It's something I'd really like to do."

"Well, then, I guess I can help you. When are you supposedly going to get here?"

"In about twenty-four hours. You can say you know I'm en route but you're not sure when I'll arrive."

"All right. And you'll let me know when you're not here anymore?"

"Sure. Dad, I really appreciate this. I really do."

It had been impossible for Matt to talk with Nixon next morning, but Rose Mary Woods promised to explain to The Boss that Ezra Thompson needed his son for a few days. Matt assured Rose Woods that his father was not ill, but from time to time the professor's loneliness overcame him, and it was important for his only son to be with him at those times until the depression passed.

On his way to Kennedy International Airport, Matt Thompson left notes for John Mitchell and George Bothwell containing similar explanations. When he bought his tickets he sent Hung a cable giving his arrival time.

He had hurriedly packed at 5 A.M.; he discovered that his tweed jacket was not in his closet where he'd expected to find it. The Asian continent could be cold in March, even as far south as Hong Kong, so he stuffed a muffler, gloves, and a wool ski hat into the side pocket of his suitcase along with a heavy turtle-necked sweater. In a taxi on the way to Kennedy Airport, Matt remembered that his tweed jacket was at the cleaners over on Bleecker Street, but by then it was too late. Maybe, he thought, he'd have a new jacket made in Hong Kong.

Before boarding the afternoon Pan American plane which would take him to Tokyo by way of Anchorage, Matt thought of the people who might try to find him when he was gone. Only Glenna could be a problem, he decided. He would have to try to deflect her persistence somehow.

He wasn't sure if she and Rose Mary Woods confided in each other as much as they used to when their desks were jammed together at the Nixon, Mudge law office. Now Rose had a private office, and Glenna's desk was fifty feet away with two other secretaries outside the fancy office they'd set up for Richard Nixon in the modern office building across Park Avenue from the old Mitchell headquarters.

If Rose told Glenna that Matt was in California holding his father's hand, Glenna would certainly try to telephone him there. Matt had no doubt that she would try to make friends with his father, as surely as she'd tried to enlist Angie to make sure that Matt returned her calls at the office.

Glenna was not at the office, he was told when he called there. She had called in sick. So he rang her apartment and let the phone ring six times. Finally she answered thickly, sounding angry that someone had made her telephone ring so persistently.

"Glenna? This is Matt; are you okay?"

"Hi, Matt. I was asleep."

"Are you sick?"

"Not sick, just kind of depressed. I didn't feel like campaigning today so I called in. How come you're calling?"

"Listen, I'm going out of town for a while. I'm at the airport, but I didn't want to go without talking to you."

"Where are you going now? Wisconsin? Seems like everyone is up there now."

"No, California."

"Oh. When will you be back?"

"About a week or so."

"Will I see you? Will you call?"

"I'll call as soon as I'm back. I'm not too sure where I'll be out there. I'm going to try to take my dad for a little trip."

"Is he okay?"

"Not entirely. That's why I'm going out."

"I'm sorry. Can I call you at his house?"

"No. That's what I just said; I'm going to take him away for a while. We won't be at his place."

Glenna was disappointed. "Will you call me?"

"It depends on where we are. I will if I can. But you know I'll miss you, don't you?"

"Sure. I hope you'll get some rest out there, darling.

You've been working too hard. Stay away from the California primary; don't get involved in that.''

"Don't worry, beautiful. I'll call if I can, but don't count on it."

"I love you," she said.

"Goodbye, darling," he replied. "I'll miss you."

Mr. Hung Wai-lang himself was at Kai Tak Airport to welcome Matt to Hong Kong and to help him clear Customs and Immigration speedily and without questions. Hung wore a brown silk suit of generous cut, a yellow shirt, and a deep rose necktie. His straw fedora was banded in the same rose shade.

A chauffeur retrieved Matt's suitcase and brought it to Hung's Mercedes while the industrialist talked to his office on the car telephone. Matt was able to follow most of Hung's rapid Chinese conversation without indicating his understanding. Hung wanted to know if he'd received the message he'd been waiting for. Evidently his secretary read him a message, and Hung grinned and nodded as he listened.

"It's tomorrow? Are you sure of that?" he demanded. "All right, then we'll take him to the house for tonight. Tell Bill I want the airplane to take him to Canton at eight tomorrow morning. If the weather's bad he will take a ship up the Pearl River. In that case Mr. Lee will travel with him. Goodbye."

Hung turned toward Matt. "Are you very tired? I must return to my office, but I want you to stay at my house tonight and rest. The car will take you. When I come home we can talk."

"I feel pretty good," Matt said. "I don't need to sleep. Would you mind if I walked around the city while I wait for you?"

Hung's smile vanished. "Oh, that would not be too good, Matthew. It would be better if you rest at my house. It is a nice house and very comfortable, I think."

"I'm sure it is, Mr. Hung." Matt remembered how

Hung had steered him into the conference room to talk to Teng Shan-li the last time. Perhaps someone was waiting at Hung's house. Perhaps the message to Hung meant that he and some visitor—Teng Shan-li?—were intended to talk tonight and the Chinese person would be flown back to Canton in the morning. "I look forward to resting at your house," Matt said acquiescently.

The ride from the airport was without much conversation. Out of politeness Hung had asked about Matt's flight, but he was obviously preoccupied. As the Mercedes smoothly weaved through traffic, Hung looked out the window. Matt noticed that several times a deep frown lined Hung's usually carefree forehead. However, when Hung got out of the car in the basement of his office building he was suddenly filled with good humor again. His broad smile embraced Matt and the entire automobile. "My staff will be happy to bring you anything you need at home," he beamed. "Please eat when you wish to, Matthew. I will have eaten. My family is away, so you will be undisturbed."

"Thank you, Mr. Hung," Matt said.

Hung's home was starkly modern, a long glass box banded with stainless steel, built along and astride a ridge hundreds of feet above the harbor. The car pulled into a driveway hidden from the road by a high wall and dense landscaping. A thin Chinese in an alpaca jacket and cotton pants waited by the front door, one hand held out, palm up, in a kind of welcome.

"We are happy to have you at Sky House, Mr. Thompson," the man said. His English bore a heavy British accent. "I am Lee, Mr. Hung's house assistant. I am here to serve you."

Lee invited Matt to wash and rest, promised supper, and left him alone in a large, glassed guest room. Matt assumed that some Chinese visitor might be brought to him at any time, so he hastily washed, changed his shirt, and put his spare clothes on hangers in the empty closet. He noticed that the room was without a radio, a television set, or a telephone. As he buttoned his shirt he walked to his door, quietly turned the knob, and slowly pulled the door open. At least he wasn't locked in, he thought.

At once a young houseboy appeared at his door, inquiring if Matt needed anything. Matt asked for some fruit and drinking water, hastily improvising a request to mask his suspicious door testing.

Matt had no Chinese visitors. At dusk he abandoned his assumptions and walked to the huge living room, where hidden speakers eased soft music into the boxy glass space. He ate dinner alone, reading one of the day's English-language newspapers he'd found in the living room. The dining room was a spectacular glass cube cantilevered out away from the house above the lights of Hong Kong harbor. The table of heavy glass seemed almost invisible; the plates and silver appeared to levitate as the room space floated over the light-spattered, ever-moving water below. Matt's eyes were repeatedly drawn from the newspaper to the harbor until he laid it aside to look only at the remarkable city at his feet.

Hung did not come home until 10 P.M. He found Matthew still in the dining room, the lighting low, drinking tea and looking at the view. "I am sorry to be so late, Matthew. I hope you have rested," Hung said to announce his arrival. "I can now tell you your schedule."

"I'm fine, Mr. Hung. Yes, please tell me."

"Tomorrow at dawn my airplane will take you to Canton."

"Canton? I have no visa for China, Mr. Hung."

"Do not be concerned. That is all being cared for. In Canton my friends will meet you and take you to a meeting. They wish to learn more about the United States. When you are finished you will return here."

"I see. Who are your friends?"

"You have already met Mr. Teng. He will be very glad to see you again. He will introduce the others to you."

"That sounds very interesting. It will be exciting to return to China."

"Lee will wake you in the morning. While you eat he will pack your bag. You can dress informally, in the

Chinese manner, but do dress warmly. The weather threatens to be worse. I will bid you good night now.''

Matt returned to the guest room but found it impossible, in spite of his fatigue, to close his eyes and drop off to sleep. His father had often spoke of Canton, but Matt had never really believed he would see the old city his father called the Goat Castle. Matt couldn't remember his father's story about why the city bore that name. He would have done some reading about Canton had he known he was going there. He was actually going into Communist China! A very few Americans had been taken into the P.R.C. since the revolutionary government took over in 1949. And the irony of it all was that when he returned to New York he couldn't tell anyone where he'd been without jeopardizing his position with Nixon and the campaign. He wondered if he dared confide in his father. Surely there was no one else he could possibly tell.

Mr. Hung's Jet Star found a hole in the cloud cover west of Canton, circled over hilly farmland losing altitude, then swung to a northeasterly heading which afforded Matt a sweeping view of the broad, milky Pearl River and the city beyond. The white and gray buildings seemed tallest along the riverfront, descending in height back toward the lush green mountains that rose at the city's margins. Scows and a few powerboats moved up and down the river as the jet crossed, but there was far less boat traffic than in Hong Kong's harbor.

The surface of the river seemed unnaturally smooth, a lustrous gray liquid which appeared thicker than water as it moved slowly through the city that bordered its low banks. The airport, at the north margin of the city, also showed very little activity. Two transports of Russian manufacture with the logo of the Chinese Civil Airline stood near the terminal and one military truck drove slowly along the ramp, but nothing else moved until Hung's jet landed and taxied across the quiet runways toward a small building which sat low in the grass in a remote corner of the airfield. A small jet, painted khaki, the P.R.C.'s bright red star on its tail, was parked on a hardstand in front of the one-story building. A red flag flapped in the gusting wind at the top of a flagpole fastened to a back corner of the building. Matthew assumed he was being taken to a meeting in that building. His hosts had come in the small jet to meet him there.

Hung's copilot lowered the Jet Star's stairs and motioned for Matt to follow him out. Matt picked up his coat and made his way unsteadily down the steps. Then, looking up, he involuntarily lowered his head again when he felt the wind's full force against his face. He could sense the river in the wind; as gusty and strong as it was, it bore a softness unlike the razor winter wind off the Hudson in New York.

Matt was surprised at the quiet. There were no airport noises except the snapping of the red flag in the wind above the building.

Teng Shan-li walked to where Matt stood at the foot of the airplane steps putting on his coat. Teng wore a blue overcoat, buttoned at the neck, but he was hatless. The wind had disarranged his gray hair, standing some of it nearly on end. He smiled broadly, holding out his hand. Matt noticed Teng had a gold tooth at the left side of his mouth; he couldn't remember seeing that gold before.

"Welcome to China, Matthew Thompson," Teng said.

"Hello, Mr. Teng. It's good to see you."

The copilot was carrying Matt's suitcase to the khaki jet, where a Chinese in a blue uniform waited by the cargo door.

Teng saw Matt's look of surprise. "We are going on that aircraft in a few minutes," Teng explained. "I have asked them to look after your luggage. The wind is very strong; would you like to wait inside the building?"

"Where are we going? We aren't staying in Canton?"

"Oh, no. This is merely a convenient transfer place. Mr. Hung's airplane is not to be used beyond this point. We are going north to Peking."

"Peking? Is that where I'm to meet your friends?"

"Yes, it is. You will be our guest there for perhaps two days and then you will come back here to meet this airplane which brought you. Ah, I see that our pilot is ready; do you need a toilet or shall we board our flight? This is an aircraft of the Chinese Air Force."

The seats in the Air Force jet had been designed for the Chinese, a people both shorter and slimmer than Matthew Thompson. The plane's elliptical windows were badly scratched, making it difficult to clearly see some objects on the ground, but Matt, half-turned in his narrow seat, drank in every shape and color of China, however imperfectly seen. As they flew due north, China's landscape turned from lush green to an adobe brown, then back to green again.

Matt could see the pattern of life change, too. Small villages seemed to crowd the roads at every rural cross-roads, spilling back into the cultivated fields. Matt wondered why the Chinese located their houses on prime farmland instead of up on the ridges where growing would be more difficult. They crossed the great Yangtze River just east of the city of Wuhan and descended to refuel at a large Air Force field on the edge of the three cities which blended into a large metropolitan complex.

An Air Force officer led them into a two-story concrete building near the fueling area, and Matt was aware that he was the object of great attention. The men and women servicing the airplane stared at him from the moment he emerged to stretch beside the jet's door. A young Chinese man in uniform walked backward in order to keep watching him. Inside the operations building work came to a standstill when he was escorted in.

"People here have not seen many Caucasians," Teng observed. "They do not intend to be rude, but you are a great curiosity here. In Peking it will be better; there are diplomats and other foreigners there and the people are more accustomed."

Matt and Teng Shan-li were given an excellent lunch in

a small dining room in which they ate alone, served by two older women dressed in white jackets and pants. The central dish was a large fish, served whole in sauce and herbs. "Fish is the best food of Wuhan," Teng explained. "It may come from the Yangtze River, but I think this one was raised in the ponds of a fish farm near here. Their Wuchang fish are very famous. In fact, they are mentioned in one of Chairman Mao's poems, you know. He was here in Wuchang as head of the National Peasant Movement Institute back in the 1920s."

"The fish is delicious. What is this I'm eating?"

"A vegetable. I don't know the English word for it, but it is a little squash."

"Very good."

"Wuhan is really three cities. Now we are near Wuchang, the oldest of the three. It is a very strategic location, on the Yangtze, equidistant from Peking, Canton, Shanghai, and Chungking."

"So we're halfway to Peking?"

"Yes, and if you are finished with your lunch we'd better be on our way."

While he and Mr. Teng were eating, nearly a hundred uniformed curiosity seekers had gathered by the entrance to the operations building to get a look at Matt. As he passed them he could understand some of their comments, and he had to make an effort not to smile or laugh at what they were saying.

"He's a tall one, isn't he?"

"Look at those feet!"

"Is he Russian?"

"No, English, I think, from Hong Kong."

"He is a guest of some high official. That is a jet from the State Central Committee, the pilot says."

"They are taking him to Peking."

As the small jet rapidly flew up and away from Wuhan, Matt noted that the city and the surrounding farms were crisscrossed with canals and irrigation ditches. Within a few minutes, though, the terrain became dry and brown, and the villages appeared more austere. It seemed that the towns and villages were located closer together than they had been in the south, the rows of attached houses encroaching more and more into the cultivated land, the agriculture receding before the shelter needs of the rapidly growing Chinese population.

Spring had not yet come to the North China Plain by March 30. The six red flags over the military airfield at which they landed near Peking were held stiffly at the horizontal by a northeast wind which had buffeted the jet on its final approach to the wide landing strip.

"We are northwest of the center of the city," Teng said. "We have a forty-five-minute drive from here. Bundle up; it will be even colder in Peking."

A new but oddly unmodern automobile drove up to the jet, and a trim man wearing a long brown leather coat opened the back door and strode athletically to Teng.

"Any problems, Comrade Teng?"

"No, everything went very well, Comrade Yang. The young man is a little surprised to be here, but otherwise he is in good condition. He attracted many Air Force soldiers who stared at him in Wuhan, so his presence in China is no secret."

"No one knows who he is?"

"Of course not."

Teng turned to Matt, who had been standing with them waiting, his back to the wind. "Mr. Thompson, this is Mr. Yang Te-chong," he said in English. "Mr. Yang does not speak English, unfortunately, but he will be our escort during your stay in Peking."

Matt shook hands with Yang and took note of Yang's muscular hands and wrists. The jet's copilot put Matt's suitcase and a small black handbag into the trunk of the Red Flag limousine as Matt and his escorts walked toward it. About two hundred yards beyond the car a row of silver MIG fighters were tied down, their cockpits covered with canvas which vibrated in the wind. Matt counted twenty jets, carefully lined up at the edge of the camp, their ominous snouts in precise rank, brilliant Chinese red stars on their haunches.

"Mr. Yang says we must be going," Teng said, taking Matt's arm in his hand. "Please sit with me in the back of the limousine."

Matt and Teng were on either side of the rear seat and Yang sat in front with the driver. Sheer black curtains covered the side and rear windows, making the view out difficult. Matt could see the MIGs because they were bright silver, but the khaki jet was nearly invisible.

"I'm anxious to see Peking, Mr. Teng. Is it all right to open the curtains?" Matt asked.

"He wants the curtains open," Teng said to Yang in Chinese.

"Absolutely not," Yang replied with finality. "He must not be seen in Peking by anyone."

"I'm sorry," Teng said to Matt, "but Mr. Yang would prefer that we leave them closed. We are both sorry if this interferes with your view of Peking, but it is unavoidable. It is a rule."

The heavy car pulled away from the jet and drove between two square brown concrete buildings. Matt could see repair sheds dispersed in the rice and corn fields that bordered the runways. One MIG was nosed into a farm building made of wood and roofed with light blue tiles.

They passed dozens of people who were apparently hoeing the newly cultivated fields, readying them for planing. As the limousine approached, some laborers stood, shielding their eyes from the glare of the afternoon sun, watching the big car lumber by.

"When we go through the military gate we will be entering the city," Teng said. "Welcome to Peking, the Capital of the North."

Twenty-two

Yang Te-chong half-turned in the front seat and spoke in Chinese to Teng Shan-li: "Because of a couple of large Red Guards demonstrations planned for today, we have moved the meeting. All of the downtown area will probably be tied up."

"Where are we going?" Teng asked in response.

Matthew Thompson looked intently through the gauze side curtain, showing no sign of understanding their conversation. The view of the landscape had changed with surprising suddenness from a two-lane country road, bounded by farms, to a city street. Now all around them hundreds of men and women in padded jackets steadily pedaled black bicycles in a twilight haze. The street on which they were driving east was lined with four- and five-story apartment buildings. Young trees had been planted in rows, four deep, along both sides of the street; dozens of them were bunched in every open space around the buildings, and scores of saplings were ranked between the sidewalk and the apartments. Their wind-moved branches caught the light, then lost it, making tiny flashes of gold against the pale buildings. Matt first thought that the haze effect which blurred the buildings was the result of the car's gauze side curtains. But looking forward through the windshield, he saw that the cause was Peking's dust-suspended atmosphere; billions of particles were reflecting the setting sun, creating a luminescent, golden dry mist which swirled thousands of feet up into the sky.

On all sides, everywhere Matt looked, he saw the

hand-lettered posters of the Great Proletarian Cultural Revolution, plastered on walls and houses, flapping before the wind on wires strung between the trees, pasted on the traffic policeman's kiosk, even hung from the handlebars of a few bicycles. Crowds of pedestrians were gathered in front of some of the brightly colored broadsides, gesturing and talking.

The car swept by open markets, shops, and rows of small, tile-roofed houses which looked shabby and old. Everywhere chimneys and open braziers added their carbon particulate to the gusting air, the smoke quickly swept up and dispersed, adding a layer of motion to the amber light that pervaded the city.

There were few automobiles or trucks on the streets, but in the river of bicycles he saw horse-drawn wagons, with two or four wheels, piled high with boxes of produce, most carrying several passengers huddled against the chill wind.

The street life excited Matt Thompson in the same way he'd been captured in Hong Kong's vitality. New York's crowded avenues were busy too, but with a different feeling. All big cities are full of people and vehicles, but here in the Orient he sensed a quality of aliveness, and of being-about-to-become, that he did not feel in New York. Paradoxically, China was the ancient civilization; Peking had been a center of culture and government twenty centuries before there was a New York. Yet now that he lived there, Matt sensed that New York was decaying and declining, a city that had already seen its best days. What he seemed to see from the Red Flag limousine's windows, in contrast, was a society that was at its threshold.

"We are going to Ching-ling's," Yang said to Teng. "They have been ordered to let her alone, for whatever good that will do. Anyway, her walls are high, and our men are able to look after the place. You are to wait in the garden room until you are called. I will take the American."

Teng nodded. "Is it true that Guards attacked her Shanghai house and carried off her goods and her library?"

"It is true," Yang said. "The Premier was very angry."

They are talking about Premier Chou En-lai, Matt realized. Mr. Teng's superiors were near the top of the government apparatus.

"Where are we, Mr. Teng?" Matt asked.

"We have just passed the Capital Gymnasium and the zoo," Teng said. "This large building on our left up ahead is our Exhibition Center. We are in the northwest area of the city, in the West City District."

"It looks like the Russians designed the exhibition building."

"Yes, they built several of our public buildings about fifteen years ago. It doesn't look very Chinese, does it? We are near our destination now."

The limousine drove through a wide intersection into a narrow, winding, crowded street bordered with the old, dust-colored houses and walled compounds like some Matt had noticed in another neighborhood, north of the zoo. The street passed between two small lakes on an isthmus crowded with low-built houses and shops. When they came to a larger, tree-lined avenue, the car turned sharply right along the shore of the southern lake.

The twilight had lost its golden hue, and the remaining light was too dim to permit Matt to see much through the thin curtains. The driver had not turned on his headlights; through the windshield Matt could only see the lake as a dark mass on his right, reflecting what little fading light there was in the sky beyond to the west. The car turned left off the avenue and stopped before tall red gates. Two men with submachine guns materialized to look into the front windows of the car. One of them said, "Turn on the light so we may see," and the driver lit the overhead light. When the guards withdrew, the light was extinguished and Yang said, "Let's go. Drive directly to the main house." Matthew sensed the garden and foliage they passed through to reach the lighted porte cochere of the big house.

As he was led into the house and down the long central hall, Matt Thompson realized that he had no idea where he was and, moreover, that no one else knew where he was either. He had wholly disappeared from his world, and was at the mercy of these men; yet, oddly, he didn't believe he was in any physical danger. It was impossible for him to believe the Chinese would hurt him. Some Americans had been imprisoned by the Chinese for many years—a Catholic bishop named Walsh was one of them—but the Chinese had nothing to gain from locking him up, Matt assured himself.

What was troubling him was his disorientation. He continually wished he had a map of Peking and one of China; ever since he left Canton he had possessed only the sketchiest notion of where he was on the face of China. He knew he'd flown two thousand miles north from Canton, via Wuhan, to the airfield in the northwest suburbs of Peking, and then he'd been driven south, then east about twenty miles to this house. But the last two miles in the dusk, turning around the lakes and driving through the woods inside the gates, had turned him around. Ever since boyhood he had known which direction was north, wherever he was, because some inner gyro told him which way to turn to *feel* north. It was possible for him to get very confused and turned-around sometimes, especially in the dark. That mixed-up feeling had bothered him like a waking nightmare when he was a boy. As a grown man he found that total disorientation still made him very uncomfortable.

An element of his disorientation in the big house was the extreme *foreignness* of the whole place; he felt it in the dress of the people, the feel of the automobile he had ridden in, even in the textures and detail in the hall he was walking in at that moment. The very carpet under his feet felt alien and strange. The light switches were foreign to him; the wooden molding was wider than American trim, and it was a dimension that looked odd. The plaster was finished with a surface he had never seen before. The two hanging light fixtures gave a dim light, as if this foreign place lacked enough electricity to light the hallway in a proper, American fashion.

He had left no trail, and at the moment he had only an uncertain sense that he was walking south in a hallway that was deep within a house behind high walls. In hindsight, he thought it might have been smart to leave a note with

Angie or Carnahay or someone, just in case, because there were really no clues that would lead anyone to ask about him here in Peking. He was in *Peking*, for God's sake! In Communist China, walking down a hallway, led by a tough-looking Chinese man in a leather jacket, toward God knew what!

Yang led him through the last door on the left into a large living room, lit dimly by old-fashioned fringed floor lamps and a corner torchère. A young Chinese woman stood just inside the door waiting for him. She held out a slim hand which he found cool and surprisingly firm and strong. "Mr. Thompson, my name is Wang Li-fa, and I will be interpreter this evening. Please come in."

A man and a woman were seated in large, square overstuffed chairs in the dim light of the far corner of the room. The familiar-looking man stood, smiling a greeting. "This," the girl said with a graceful gesture, "is Premier Chou En-lai, who welcomes you."

"Welcome, Mr. Thompson," Chou said in Chinese, shaking Matt's hand. "I am glad you have made the long journey to be here." He wore a handsome gray Mao jacket and gray pants. Matt was drawn to his dark eyes under wide, bushy brows. Matt made an instinctive respectful bow in the Chinese fashion, as he would have to one of his father's friends. His mind was nearly overloaded with new emotions he had not begun to attempt to define. Later, he would call it a thrill, but it also involved a modest measure of calculation. Next to Chairman Mao Tse-tung himself, this man in the gray jacket was at the top of the Chinese hierarchy. So Teng was wired in at the highest level, as Matt had suspected! And he, a young and inexperienced American lawyer, had become the go-between for Richard Nixon and Chou En-lai. Face to face! God damn!

"The Premier welcomes you and is pleased you have made the long journey to be here," Wang Li-fa translated into English. "And Madame Soong, may I present Mr. Thompson from the United States? Madame Soong is your host in this house."

Sun Yat-sen's widow extended her large hand from her

deep chair in the corner. "How do you do, Mr. Thompson? I am very happy to have you in my house." Her pronounced features were different from the old pictures he remembered; her body was large and vague in the flowing caftan she wore, but she seemed dynamic and attractive, considering her age.

"Thank you, Madame Soong. I am very happy to be here," Matt replied. "I am honored to be in your home." Yang had called her Ching-ling in the car; at the time the name had stirred an old memory for Matt, but he hadn't been able to think about it clearly. Now, he knew. His father and mother had spoken of the Soong sisters more than once, because one had married General Chiang Kai-shek, while her sister, this woman, had become a Communist symbol of Chiang's deadly opposition. Chiang's wife was Soong Mei-ling. A third sister, Ai-ling, had married a banker. The old saying was:

> Ai-ling loves money,
> Mei-ling loves power,
> Ching-ling loves China.

"My father and mother have told me that you are the Soong daughter who loves China," Matt said, smiling, "and so I am very glad to meet you."

Soong Ching-ling laughed, a broad baritone laugh, deep and resonant. "I am also very fond of the United States, you know. I went to college in Macon, Georgia, many, many years ago. I would like to see it again; I am sure it has changed very much."

"Please sit here, Mr. Thompson," Chou said, gesturing to the large chair next to him. "Did you have an interesting journey?"

Matt grinned. Chou was speaking very good English. "Yes, sir. The entire trip has been very meaningful and important to me."

"Meaningful?" Chou turned to the young interpreter. She defined the word for him in Chinese, and he smiled and nodded. "Comrade Wang helps me with my very imperfect English, you see, so I keep her close by when I try to speak your language. I am glad you found the journey *meaningful*. There is much to be seen and understood in China these days."

"Yes, sir. I feel as though I could spend many years here, learning."

"Where do you live in America?" Madame Soong asked.

"I live in New York City, Madame, but my home was in California for many years."

"You once lived in Tientsin, did you not?" Chou added.

"Yes, as a small child. My parents taught there in a mission school. I feel as though I'm coming home when I walk the streets of Hong Kong or drive through Peking; it's very strange, because I was so very young when I lived here. But many memories of old sights and sounds are awakened."

"Smells, too." Madame Soong laughed. "When I went to America for school I noticed how different our cities smell."

"I'm sure that's a big part of it."

"Did your father live in China long?" Chou asked.

"Yes, Premier. He was a student here because his parents were missionaries. Then he went to the United States for college and divinity school, got married, and came back. Finally, the Japanese drove us out."

"And he knew our comrade Teng Shan-li?"

"Yes, sir. Mr. Teng and my father were students in Tientsin together. Mr. Teng is his good friend."

"Are you hungry, Mr. Thompson?" Madame Soong asked abruptly. "Have they fed you on your trip?"

"We had very good fish in Wuhan, but that was at noon. I am getting hungry, yes."

"Shall we eat, Comrade?" she asked Chou in Chinese. "I intend to retire after dinner and to leave you alone, but I will eat a little something with you. We can go in at any time; I am sure it is ready."

Madame Soong's dining room looked as if it had been furnished from a Sears, Roebuck catalogue many years before, but the blond dining table offered the best of

Chinese food. Chou En-lai acted as the host, putting some of each new course on Matt's plate with his own long chopsticks, explaining the origins and identities of the different foods with the help of Madame Soong and Wang Li-fa.

At dinner Matt truly noticed the interpreter for the first time. In the living room her manner had seemed pale, formal, even brittle, perhaps because she was following everyone's words carefully in case she was called upon to give the Premier a translation. Her translator's voice had the high, harsh tones of Chinese women which Matt subjectively recalled from his childhood. His amah had always been harsh of voice.

But at dinner she seemed to be slightly more relaxed, her own girlish personality breaking through her professional facade as she talked about the Cantonese food with which she was the most familiar. When she spoke English her vocal tones softened and lowered.

The girl has an interesting face, Matt thought; it combines the best of Chinese features with a vaguely Western facial physique. Her padded jacket required some speculation about her body, but her hands and wrists were strong and graceful. Wang Li-fa's gleaming black hair was gathered back above her ears and tied in a short ponytail with a piece of blue yarn that was the same color as her jacket. Her eyes expressively dominated her face, at once conveying an impression of everything she was and all that she secretly felt. She could not ever hide her likes and dislikes, he thought; unless she closed those big brown eyes. Everyone always will know what this girl thinks.

After the soup course, which signaled the end of the relay of courses, Madame Soong summoned her houseboy to help her upstairs to her bedroom-study.

"I have profound optimism that China and the United States can resume good relations, Mr. Thompson," she said. She had shuffled to his side as he stood, and she now laid a hand on his arm. "It will not be easy, but it is very important. Your honorable father is correct; I do love China. I love my country more than my sisters do, perhaps more than anyone alive today. Like China, I was once in the world, but for nearly twenty years I have been out of world affairs. Oh, I've gone to India and Moscow and Ceylon, but I have not been to the Western Hemisphere or those exciting European countries my husband and I loved. It is not good for a person—or for a nation—to live in isolation from the world's ideas, which are so stimulating. It is time we moved back into the world."

"It is a great honor to have been a guest at your table, Madame Soong."

The large, ungainly woman said formal good-nights to Chou and Wang Li-fa in Chinese and left the room on the arm of her servant.

"Comrade Soong is Vice Chairman of the Communist Party of China," Chou said. "She is a great and remarkable world figure."

Matt nodded.

"For my part, I am not sure whether all those stimulating Western ideas are precisely what China needs at this moment," Chou said wryly, "but we do need the friendship of your country and we need commerical exchange to supplement our own invention and production."

"I'm sure it's a two-way street," Matt said. Chou looked at Wang Li-fa and raised his thick eyebrows. Her eyes, amused, met Matt's. She translated the idiom for Chou, and he said to the young woman: "Send for Teng, then join us. Tell Yang I do not wish to be interrupted." The girl said, "Yes, Comrade Premier."

Chou led Matt back to the corner of the living room and pointed to Madame Soong's chair. "Please sit here and tell me about the American election. I read about it and it seems very confusing."

Matt shrugged. "I'm no political expert, Premier, but I will tell you what I can. Of course, Lyndon Johnson is still considered by most people to be the likely winner, but Johnson may be in serious trouble in his own party. He could lose some primary elections."

"It would be a vote of no-confidence in Johnson's war policy, wouldn't it?" Chou suggested.

"Yes, sir, I guess you could say so."

"Does Mr. Nixon favor the war?"

"No, but he feels that America must emerge from the war in a strong position. He is for a 'just and lasting peace' in Viet Nam."

Chou laughed derisively. "That is what everyone wants, of course. But what is 'just'? Your ally in Saigon is a very bad, reactionary regime which oppresses the people. It is not 'just' to perpetuate oppression." Chou opened a cigarette box on the low table beside him and lit a cigarette. "What Mr. Nixon seeks is not a just peace, and I do not think it will be a lasting peace even if America causes Saigon to prevail. I think Mr. Nixon is wrong about that."

"I understand," Matt said without expression. He felt as if he had been bawled out by an elder uncle.

Teng Shan-li and Wang Li-fa came into the room and took chairs facing the Premier about fifteen feet away.

"Mr. Thompson says Nixon believes Saigon must win the war; otherwise the peace will not be just or lasting," Chou told Teng in English. "I told him I believe the opposite."

Teng smiled. "One cannot pretend that China and the United States have the same interests on all subjects. Many difficult issues exist, and the war is one of them. Taiwan is another."

Chou turned to Matt. "What does Nixon say about the reunification of Taiwan? Would he oppose the return of our island province to us?"

"I believe not. We talked about it when we were in England, just before the New Hampshire primary, and he told me then that he was very flexible on Taiwan, so long as the people there are not persecuted by your government."

Chou nodded. "We have some old enemies there who deserve to be punished, but the important goal for us is reunification. So I could give him assurances about the safety of the people. But to go back to my first question: Who will be your next President? Will it be Johnson again?"

"I think the people who wager money would bet that it will," Matt replied, "but I haven't yet mentioned the other

Democratic candidate, George Wallace, who is out trying to form a third party. If he does, he may take votes from both Johnson and Nixon."

"The American blockade is very serious," Chou said, abruptly changing the subject. "If Chinese ships are stopped and boarded by Americans, we will fight. There will be shooting."

"Will you try to sail supplies to North Viet Nam through the blockade, Premier?"

"Try? Of course we will try!" Chou said forcefully. "China is a sovereign nation, entitled to the free use of the open seas. Our Vietnamese friends are entitled to our support. How would the United States react if China stopped your ships going to Saigon? I would have your protests within the hour, wouldn't I?"

"Yes, I'm sure you would."

"Yet the United States is in exactly the same position as China: Neither has declared war, each supports a Vietnamese ally, each has the same legal right to use the open seas. It is precisely the same position, is it not? Why is China treated differently?"

"Perhaps," Matt said tentatively, "President Johnson believes he has a right or duty to blockade because American soldiers are being killed with the arms the ships bring into Hanoi's harbor."

"China's ships? We send them food and medical supplies and clothing. Do you think we can send guns and airplanes?"

"I don't know."

In Chinese Chou asked Teng: "Can we show the lists of goods on the ships? Am I correct about armaments?"

Teng replied, "Comrade Yang will have to find out tomorrow. I am willing to guess that we have sent ammunition and light arms, but I do not know for certain."

Chou turned to Matt and asked in English: "Are you tired? I know you have had a long journey, and yet there is much I would like to learn from you. The evenings are my time for learning."

"I am fine, Premier. I feel fine."

"As Comrade Wang Li-fa will attest—is that the word? Attest?"

The girl nodded and said an equivalent Chinese word, smiling.

"As she will attest," Chou continued, "the daylight hours are hectic. That is why I asked that you meet me in the evening. Perhaps some tea?" He looked at Li-fa, who rose and went to find the houseboy.

"Does Richard Nixon work at night?" Chou continued. "What are his work habits?"

"He works alone most of the time," Matt replied. "The issues I deal with are presented to him in writing, without much face-to-face conversation. He prefers it that way. He sometimes works at night."

"Does he read much?"

"Yes, he reads the daily press in detail. Most of the books he reads, I think, are history or biography. I don't know of any fiction. I know he has been reading Disraeli's biography recently."

Chou nodded. "Worthwhile. Perhaps some interesting parallels. Who advises him on foreign affairs?"

"At present it is George Bothwell, a young professor, but I think Mr. Nixon draws largely on his own knowledge and experience. And he is in touch with many leaders in other countries."

"You do not have a high regard for Professor Bothwell?"

"I don't think he has much to offer Mr. Nixon."

Chou smiled. "Perhaps I should lend him Comrade Teng."

Teng looked surprised, then smiled broadly.

Matt nodded. "That would be a great advantage to Mr. Nixon, but he wouldn't want to send him back. He would want to keep Mr. Teng."

Everyone laughed.

"Now," Chou continued, "I would like to ask you about several other areas of Richard Nixon's thinking. How does he regard the United Nations?"

*   *   *

At 2 A.M., while their conversation continued, the houseboy silently entered the living room, emptied Premier Chou's ashtray, and removed the teacups.

"It is getting late," Chou said, "and I can see that you are—what is the word?" He said a Chinese word to Li-fa, who responded: "Flagging."

"Perhaps I am wilting a little," Matt said. "But I am fine. I can continue."

"No, you have answered my questions and I will let you sleep now. When I have more than six hours of conversation it becomes of no value, I think. I wish to ponder what you have told us. I believe I will have other questions about the United Nations and also Japan. Foreign trade is a difficult problem for every government. You sleep here and perhaps there will be time tomorrow for a further unfolding of those subjects. Comrade Teng will see to your needs." Chou reached across to Matt without standing, and they shook hands.

"When he is in bed, please return here," Chou said to Teng Shan-li in Chinese.

Matt was led across the courtyard garden to the west wing. His suitcase had been taken to a guest room furnished with a Western bed. Teng showed him the adjoining bathroom which also appeared to have come straight from the Sears catalogue, even to the toilet-bowl brush in its white plastic holder.

"We will awaken you for breakfast, Matthew," Teng said. "I do not know the Premier's schedule for tomorrow, so I cannot predict. Perhaps we will have time to ride around and see the Temple of Heaven and the Forbidden City, eh? Sleep well."

Matt lay deep in the oversoft bed, his eyes open, the coarse sheets against his naked body reminding him of the foreignness of his situation. His mind skipped back over the hours with Chou En-lai, replaying parts randomly, stopping to wonder why the Premier had raised a certain question, recasting some answers, seeing Wang Li-fa smiling, bending to retrieve her pen, touching her ear.

All of Chou's arguments were based on the premise that China, the Middle Kingdom, is and always was the center of the universe. Non-Chinese are barbarians. The locus of all right and morality is Peking. Matt's father had often spoken of the difficulty the Chinese had in seeing other peoples as anything but inferiors.

Repeatedly, Chou had expressed dismay that other nations did not see and accept the correctness of China's position on a given issue. There seemed to be no place in the Chinese cosmos for two views.

The girl kept coming back to him as a mystery, unreached and therefore unsolved, open to him when their eyes met, but totally remote and closed in what she said and how she said it. They had not spoken ten sentences to each other all evening, but he felt there was a strong mutual attraction between them. He had felt it from the moment they shook hands, and it was reinforced whenever their eyes met. Realistically, they had no future. He would see her only when he saw Chou, perhaps once more, tomorrow. But he very much wanted to get her to open up to him; he needed to understand the mystery.

Teng Shan-li shook Matthew Thompson awake about 8 A.M. The lack of fresh air in the room had congested Matt's breathing and made him logy; it was hard to wake up. When he was dressed he crossed the courtyard to the main house, where Teng waited for him. Together they ate a breakfast of meat and vegetables in Madame Soong's Americanized dining room while Teng disclosed the plan for the day.

"The Premier may call for us this morning, Matthew. If he does not, then we will depart for the airfield immediately after lunch and you will return to Canton. Madame Soong invites you to be at home in her house; she has already gone to her Party duties and will be away all day. She told me to suggest that you read in her library, down the hall. She has many books in English."

After breakfast Matt took several books from the library; one of them was an atlas of Asia and another a contemporary Chinese history. Crossing the courtyard, he walked around the stela in the center, touching its rough carving, feeling the deep cold of that ancient stone. The stela was a link to the unreachable past; touching it seemed to be important.

A few minutes with the atlas restored a large measure of Matthew Thompson's inner sense of place. He noted carefully Peking's proximity to Tientsin, the Yellow Sea, and Korea beyond. He roughly measured the Russian border to be as close to Peking as Los Angeles is to San Francisco. He saw that China's Grand Canal joins Shanghai to Peking, passing through most of China's major cities in the eastern half of the country. The city map of Peking in the atlas showed two lakes, one longer than the other, north of the Forbidden City, which coincided with his rough estimate of the location of Ching-ling's estate.

Before he could turn to the history book, the door opened softly and Wang Li-fa stood in the doorway. She wore a different jacket and slacks, the light gray wool jacket open at the collar to reveal a white blouse. She smiled.

"Good morning, Mr. Thompson. Am I disturbing you?" she said. Her voice seemed more animated than it had been the night before.

"Please call me Matt. May I call you Li-fa?"

The young woman blushed. "My close friends call me Li."

"Li." He stood up and put the atlas aside.

"Is your suitcase packed, Matt?"

"Yes. Are we going somewhere?"

"The Premier has sent Comrade Yang and me to get you. We are to bring you to a meeting place. He wishes to discuss with you some news from the United States."

"Fine. Do we go now?"

"Comrade Yang will come to tell us. We can wait in the living room. Leave your bag here for now."

Without the lamps on, the living room was dark and uncomfortable, like a private hotel banquet room the morning after an unsuccessful party. It tasted of old cigarette smoke and stale air.

"Can we go out in the courtyard to wait?" Matt asked. "It's sheltered from the wind, and the sun feels good today."

"Of course."

They sat on the white concrete base that held the stela in place, facing the thin early-spring sunlight.

"Have you ever been to the United States?" he asked. The base they were sitting on was circular, requiring them both to turn a little to see each other full face.

"Oh, no. I lived in Hong Kong until my father died, but otherwise I have not been away from China."

"You speak English very well," he said. "Are you married?"

She blushed. "Oh, no. I am not even promised, as you say, except to my job. Is your work exciting? I have read books about American lawyers. Have you read *To Kill a Mockingbird*?"

"I have read it; but I'm working in international law, so it's very different from small-town trial work. This trip is the most exciting thing I've ever done."

She looked at him intently, her eyes asking him to tell her precisely what—or whom—he found exciting. Or at least, that was what he told himself he saw there.

"Is China what you expected it would be?"

"I haven't really seen China except from a car window last night. But the people are wonderful, you—and the others."

She blushed again, her pale skin flushing as if it had tanned. "Do you think you will come back to China?"

Matt nodded. "I'd like to come back very soon. I'm sure I will. When I do, how will I find you?"

"Find me?"

"Yes. I will come back to spend time with you. How do I locate you? Where do you live?"

Li-fa blushed deeply. "I do not understand. We do not know each other." It was more of a question than a statement.

"I think we both know we are not strangers," he said. "But we need time together. I want to know everything about you, but this visit is too hurried. So I will come back to see you, soon.''

"How will you do that?''

"I don't know exactly, but I will. When I look into your eyes I know that I will. Where will you be?''

The woman laughed nervously. "Are all Americans so impetuous and unrealistic?''

He smiled. He liked to look at her face. "Can I call you on the telephone, Li?''

"Oh, no, there is no telephone where I live; I live in a dormitory, you know.''

"Well, maybe I can call you at the Premier's office?''

"Gracious! You must never do that, Matt. How could I explain to my colleagues?'' Her eyes widened. "You really would not call me there. Please! Promise me you will not do that.''

"Well, then, how do I find you?''

"I don't know. My family is in Canton, you see.''

"Will they always know where you are?''

"My sister in Canton will always know where I am, even if I am changed to a different assignment. Sometimes people are sent to the embassies overseas as interpreters. My sister's Hong Kong name was Nancy.''

"Nancy Wang? Can you write her name and telephone number for me?''

"Oh, she has no telephone, but I will write her name and address.'' Li-fa gave him a page from her small notebook. "That is Nancy's name in Chinese,'' she said, pointing. "It is Wang Pa-cho. You can show this paper to someone in Canton if you go there. This address is the house that was my grandmother's. It is not far from the memorial to the Canton Uprising Martyrs.''

"Where do you live in Peking?''

"In a dormitory for those who work for the State Central Committee.''

"How can I write to you?''

"I think you can't.'' Her eyes were suddenly clouded with realism. "It would not be good for me to receive mail from America. I'm sorry.''

"Can I write to Nancy?"

Li-fa's eyes opened wide. "You mean send me a letter that begins 'Dear Nancy'?"

"Sure."

She laughed. "Nancy works for the Canton International Trade Corporation." Li-fa wrote on her pad. "Here's her company's address. Write her there about how you are a Frenchman who wants to come and buy Chinese fans."

"I will write her that I lie awake at night and think about Chinese bicycles and I cannot sleep. My wish is to come to Canton to meet a representative of the bicycle industry to discuss many things." Their eyes locked and they smiled. "If I could get there, would you be able to visit your sister at the same time?"

"I think that would be very doubtful. I may visit my family only when the Premier is away on a trip for which my languages are not needed. Americans are very romantic, I have read. Do all Americans attempt to arrange a rendezvous on brief acquaintance?"

"No. I certainly don't. But our time is so short, and I feel something very unusual has happened between you and me. Do you feel it?"

"The sun is very pleasant in this beautfiul courtyard, is it not?" she said pointedly.

Matt turned to see Yang Te-chong standing in the doorway of the garden room. "Is he ready?" Yang asked Li-fa in abrupt Chinese. Matt put the two small, folded pages into his coat pocket.

"Yes, Comrade Yang. His suitcase is in the guest room. Are we summoned?"

"Yes. We will go to the Fishing Pavilion, where the Premier meets with the Africans. He will come to talk to the American boy as soon as we get there. Where is Teng?"

"I do not know."

"Find him. Tell him to come to the car at the side door." Yang pointed beyond the guest wing. "Tell the boy to follow me."

Li-fa turned to Matt. "We will go in the car now. Please

follow Comrade Yang; soon Comrade Teng and I will join you. Just get in the car." She had once again become the tense, dutiful interpreter. There was no sign of the laughing, forthcoming woman who had sat beside him in the sunshine talking about romantic Americans.

"My bag?" Matt reminded her.

"It will be in the car, I am sure," she said. "Please go quickly."

They had driven back past that florid Russian wedding cake of an exhibition building and the zoological gardens in the same Red Flag limousine with the black gauze curtains. Wang Li-fa sat in the middle of the back seat with Teng Shan-li on her left and Matt Thompson on her right. Yang was in the front seat with the driver, as before.

Beyond the zoo, the driver turned left into a broad avenue from which a planetarium dome could be seen behind a thick border of trees. During the turn Li-fa's legs had shifted just enough that Matt could feel her thigh against his.

"That is a center for the study of astronomy," Teng said. "We will soon be at our destination."

Li-fa sat demurely, her hands folded on her lap, looking straight ahead.

"Mr. Teng," Matt said, "can you send me some material on China's international trade policy? I was very interested in the Premier's long-range predictions about Japan and I'd like to tell Mr. Nixon the substance of his views, without saying how I learned them." As he spoke, Matt turned to his left to look at Teng, putting slight pressure into his leg contact with Li-fa. Matt thought he felt Li-fa return the pressure without perceptible movement.

"Of course, Matthew," Teng said. "I will have Mr. Hung send you something which I will prepare."

"Where are we going?" Matt asked.

"This place is a compound of guesthouses for high-ranking official visitors. Sometimes substantive meetings are held here with our state visitors, for everyone's convenience. Today the Premier is holding talks with the Prime Minister of Angola. During a recess he will complete his talks with you." Teng seemed to be more animated than usual. "He has a matter of some importance to discuss."

"Oh? What's that?" Matt leaned forward to have a better view of Teng's face. Li-fa's thigh pressed harder against Matt's leg, he was sure.

Teng smiled with embarrassment. "I cannot say. I'm sorry. The Premier will tell you."

"Sure. Does the guesthouse have a name?" Matt wanted to ask why Yang Te-chong had called it "the Fishing Pavilion" in Chinese.

Teng looked a little confused about Matt's question. "We call it *Tiao Yu Tai* in Chinese."

"That means a fishing stand or a fishing pavilion," Wang Li-fa supplied, turning to look at Matt. "It was once a place where members of the Imperial Court came to fish in the lake. Sometimes the Emperor fished, too. There was a nobleman's villa there. Now there is a very beautiful old home on the grounds which belonged to some landlord or warlord in the old days."

Li-fa's voice was high and tight. Matthew wondered if Teng or Yang had noticed the change.

The gate to the guesthouse grounds was guarded by sentries with bayoneted rifles. Two uniformed soldiers stood by widely separated guardhouses on either side of a broad, landscaped driveway. The design and landscaping gave the entrance a feeling of openness in spite of the strong iron gates that were swung back against the shrubs behind the walls. There was an Occidental quality to the entry which made the Chinese soldiers seem out of place.

The sentries in the heavily starched tunics knew the Premier's limousine and popped to attention as the driver slowed. An officer emerged from the building on the right and waved the Red Flag through as he shouted an order to the guards. The driver accelerated, wheeled into a paved, curving road to the left, and followed the shore of a good-sized lake.

On both sides of the road Matt saw massive, two-storied

houses which might have been more comfortable in Bavaria than in Peking, their Chinese tile roofs notwithstanding. All of them were faced with light-hued brick and every one appeared to be constructed of tons of reinforced concrete.

The Red Flag pulled into the massive porte cochere of the third guesthouse. A large black numeral 8 on a white signboard had been posted on the narrow lawn beside the driveway.

"Please come in," Teng said. "We will wait for the Premier here. He is just next door there." Teng nodded at the even larger *Gasthaus* beyond, before which a flagpole bore the national colors of Angola.

Four middle-aged Chinese men in gray Mao jackets stood waiting in a parlor to the left of the entry hall. They watched Matt and his escorts move along the hall toward the back of the house. A young man, similarly dressed, stood by the door at the end of the hall. He was a local secret-service man, Matt guessed.

"He is already here," Yang said in Chinese. He nodded and the bodyguard opened the door for them.

"Go in," Teng said.

Chou En-lai was standing, a cigarette in one hand, a telephone held to his ear, saying in Chinese: "Do you have the text yet? No, don't read me all of it; just the last part where he says . . ."

Chou's cigarette motioned for Matt to sit in a chair near the window. Lace curtains obscured any view of the grounds."

"Yes," Chou said, "that's the part. From there to the end." He nodded as he listened.

The room had been furnished in Munich classic, with heavy wooden side tables, old-fashioned overstuffed chairs, and ugly but serviceable table lamps. Matt looked at the nondescript sepia landscape photographs in gold frames that dotted the walls at random. The Chinese, he thought, should have stayed with their classic Oriental style. When they try to emulate Western design they invariably fall short. The room wasn't really terrible; in fact, it was functionally comfortable. But this is supposed to be their best effort. This is where they put the visiting kings.

"That is all?" Chou asked the telephone. "He has issued no eleboration? Very well." Chou hung up and turned to Matt. "Big news," he said, arching his eyebrows. "I must ask you what it means. Three hours ago President Lyndon Johnson announced he will not seek a second term as President. What do you think of that?"

Matthew Thompson's flight from Peking to New York involved stops in Wuhan, Canton, Hong Kong, Tokyo, Anchorage, and Minneapolis. Once he was out of China he bought newspapers at each stop to read about L.B.J.'s announced retirement and about the forthcoming Wisconsin primary. In the papers the syndicated columnists seemed to gather around Lyndon Johnson's political corpse like hyenas, each tearing at the cadaver for whatever journalistic nourishment might remain on its bones.

All the writers speculated on the new lineup of Democratic candidates: Eugene McCarthy, Vice President Hubert Humphrey, and the former Attorney General, Robert F. Kennedy. Matt Thompson measured the writers' predictions against his own instinctive reaction to the dramatic announcement of Johnson's withdrawal, and he was certain he had not added much to Chou En-lai's knowledge of American politics.

"My God!" Matt had first exclaimed. "Did he *quit,* too? Is Humphrey President?" After brief reflection he had offered Chou En-lai several off-the-cuff judgments that his subsequent reading showed were thoughts shared by most of the commentators:

—Eugene McCarthy would now be touted as the giant-killer. The New Hampshire primary vote would be recorded as a repudiation of Johnson's Viet Nam policy.
—Vice President Hubert Humphrey would soon enter the race.

—Kennedy and McCarthy would run against the war; and it would be very hard for Humphrey to become anything but Johnson's surrogate.

—Among the three, Humphrey would have most of the establishment vote at the Democratic convention, and that might be enough to win the nomination. But Bobby Kennedy was a strong dark horse.

Chou En-lai had said he knew the idiom "dark-horse candidate" very well and asked what effect the Johnson news would have on Richard Nixon's candidacy. Matt had replied that with Nelson Rockefeller also out, Nixon should have an easy time taking the Republican nomination from the very conservative Ronald Reagan. Then it would be Nixon versus Humphrey. Nixon would beat Humphrey because Lyndon Johnson would be an albatross around his Vice President's neck. But if Robert Kennedy could somehow get the Democrats' nomination, he would probably defeat Richard Nixon.

"Humphrey I understand a little," Chou said. "But Robert Kennedy I do not know. Will you please send Comrade Teng whatever I might read about Mr. Kennedy's foreign policy views?"

Matt promised that he would send the material via Mr. Hung in Hong Kong.

Wang Li-fa handed the Premier a small wooden box which Chou, in turn, gave to Matt Thompson. "I would like you to have this as a small remembrance of your visit to China. It comes to you with the personal gratitude of Chou En-lai."

Matt expressed his thanks along with a correct Chinese bow. Then he realized that something more was expected of him by Chou and his people.

"Open it, Matt," Li-fa said impulsively. Her tone was tolerant, a bit familiar, and unmistakably affectionate. As he pried the tight-fitted lid from the box Matt did not notice that both Yang Te-chong and Teng Shan-li had turned to look quizzically at the young woman. But Matt had not missed the nuance entirely. Looking up, he saw that she was blushing deeply.

The box held a cut jewel of the deepest green about one and a half inches long. To cover Li-fa's embarrassment Matt offered extravagant thanks to Chou, showing the stone to everyone. Li-fa stared at her feet, saying nothing.

"You must go now," Chou said. "These gentlemen will look after you."

Matt and Chou shook hands. "I believe," Matt said, "that you and Richard Nixon would come away from a negotiation with great admiration for each other."

"Perhaps, if you get him elected, we shall see," Chou replied, laughing.

"This has been a great honor for me, Premier. The greatest of my life."

Chou replied in Chinese.

"The Premier says," Wang Li-fa began in her high, taut professional voice, "that you do his house great honor by your august presence. He bids you a safe journey."

Chou nodded in confirmation, smiling.

"Thank you, and goodbye, Miss Wang," Matt said blandly. "You have been very helpful."

"You are too generous," she said.

As Matt passed through Hong Kong's teeming airport, transferring from Mr. Hung's Jet Star to the commercial transport that would take him to Japan, he was twice processed by the Hong Kong Crown Colony's efficient immigration service. Within twenty-four hours, photocopies of his passport, its visa pages, and his entrance and exit documents were on their way to London.

Matt was scheduled to spend three hours in the Tokyo airport. He walked in from the loading area to the vast shopping arcade which offered a traveler all the world's goods in clusters of small stores. An elaborate jewelry store displayed strands of pearls of all sizes and grades, many watches, and some conventional rings and brooches. Matt walked to the back counter and asked an older clerk if he could advise him about a precious stone. The Japanese nodded confidently. Matt took Chou's green stone from his pocket handkerchief and placed it on a velvet counter tray. The jeweler picked it up, turned it, and examined it with a jeweler's loupe. He turned to a young woman behind the counter and summoned her.

"He says," she explained to Matt, "that he does not understand why you wish him to see this stone."

"I want to know what kind of stone it is."

The girl talked to the older man and nodded her understanding of his answer. "He says it is a very fine emerald of a very unusual, old-fashioned cut. He asks if you wish to sell it."

"No, I don't think so. What is its value?"

"He says he will pay you one hundred forty thousand dollars in American currency," she said.

Matt was astonished. "No, thank you. It has great sentimental value," he improvised. "Thank you."

Between Tokyo and Anchorage, Matt Thompson tried to sleep. Wang Li-fa, Chou En-lai, and their emerald had so energized his thoughts that his mind churned hyperactively, parading images, spinning scenarios, asking questions beyond his capacity to answer.

For a man who preferred his women tall, blond, and Nordic, he reflected, Li-fa had made an extraordinary impression on him. He had heard about romance based on personality or charisma or intelligence, and he was willing to acknowledge that such a phenomenon was possible. He had friends who were in love with women who were not fashion models. Some were downright ugly. But it had never happened to him. All of his personal forecasting had involved beautiful, blond women.

Now here was this woman with jet-black hair consuming his attention as he lay back, his eyes closed, trying to sleep. He liked her face, especially her smile, but she was far from beautiful by conventional New York standards. She had a good body, but nothing like Glenna's, he reminded himself invidiously.

Anchorage, Alaska, was Matthew Thompson's port of entry to the United States. An hour and a half out over the North Pacific a stewardess brought him a customs declaration form and an immigration entry to be filled out. Matt's seatmate, a Korean man in an expensive suede suit, asked the stewardess several questions about the forms and then industriously attacked them, muttering unintelligibly to himself. Matt closed his eyes and briefly debated how he should now describe his trip to other Americans, official and unofficial. In the blank provided on the government immigration form he informed the United States of America that he had spent the past several days vacationing in Hong Kong. On the other form he assured his countrymen in the U.S. Customs Service that, unlike every other American who had ever visited Hong Kong on holiday, he had purchased absolutely nothing while there.

Chou's emerald lay swaddled in his pocket, as dangerous as an asp. That, Matt told himself, is a bit of glass given him by an old Chinese man as a charm against evil spirits. It was surely worthless. Unlike Mr. Hung's five new thousand-dollar bills, there was no way that this bit of mineral could become a Chinese hold on him. Who could prove he even had it? But was it really different from the money? Should he return it, for the same reasons he had given Murphy the money?

One hundred and forty thousand dollars!

Was it simply the difference between a small temptation and a huge one?

The immigration inspector in the glass booth scrutinized his passport and the immigration card and accepted, without question, Matt's assertion that he had been in Hong Kong all five days he'd been away.

The customs agent at the next in-bound hurdle found it possible to believe that he had nothing to declare beyond the allowable exemption, but he clearly doubted that Matt had bought nothing. So Matt's suitcase and attaché case were opened and vigorously searched.

Chou's little wooden box was discovered under his dirty shirts.

"I totally forgot about that, sir," Matt said. "It was a gift. I didn't think of it as a purchase."

The agent scrutinized it. "What was in it?" he asked.

"It was empty when it was given to me. I figured I could use it for paper clips."

The customs agent fingered the box as he turned it. He squinted at the bottom of the box, then looked up and around the crowded Customs area.

"I'd like someone else to look at this; just stay right here," the agent said gruffly.

"Sure," Matt replied.

The burly officer walked to an open door beyond the last inspection counter. Another uniformed agent came to the door and looked at Matt, then went back into the room beyond the door.

Matt stood looking around the room. He shrugged at the two women in the line behind him. They smiled their sympathy for his plight. Matt wiped his damp hands on his trousers. He had very nearly reached for his handkerchief. He flushed at the thought of the emerald falling to the floor where everyone could see it.

After about five torturous minutes the agent returned and handed the little box to Matt. "You can close up your stuff. Want to know what it says on the bottom?" the officer asked.

"Sure," Matt said.

"Those Chinese characters are the insignia of an emperor named Chian Long who lived about two hundred years ago. So your little box is probably that old. We can call it an antique, I guess."

"No kidding? I had no idea. Thanks for telling me."

"Okay," the agent said, "put your bag on that rack

over there. It will go back on the plane. Welcome back.''

"Thank you," Matthew Thompson replied. He felt a trickle of perspiration leave his armpit and start down his side. "It's always good to come back home."

PART

FOUR

Twenty-three

Richard Nixon's election-night pantheon was a mansion of many rooms and many levels. The gilded Waldorf-Astoria Hotel on Park Avenue perfectly accommodated Nixon's widely various supporters. It afforded large ground-level rooms for the unwashed masses, intermediate suites for the putative insiders and big givers, and a few high-level suites in the Waldorf Towers for the truly favored. The candidate, with only H. R. Haldeman and two or three others, occupied the uppermost chambers where they sat in half-shadows watching a huge, silent television set. Nixon hungered for the quick state-by-state vote counts the networks were showing on their elaborate tally boards, but he could not tolerate the comments of the television news personalities, so on his set there was a picture but no sound. In the interest of practicality, however, Haldeman posted several junior campaign aides in the cramped maids' quarters of Nixon's Towers suite to both watch and listen to the networks—all of them—on three small TV sets. If anything of importance was audibly communicated, a note was sent to Haldeman and he relayed the information to the dour man who was in fact the President-elect but

237

wouldn't know it until his long vigil ended at about three o'clock in the morning.

Matt Thompson and Glenna Harrison had been told that nothing much would happen until the California polls closed, so they didn't arrive at the Waldorf until about ten o'clock, New York time. For a moment they looked into the big ballroom that was open to the public; a middle-aged collection of American Federation of Musicians members in good standing were playing old Glenn Miller arrangements for several hundred nondescript onlookers and five television cameras. Balloons and streamers and leftover campaign posters (NIXON'S THE ONE) gave the room a distractedly festive aspect. But the most uninformed viewer could see that the real action was elsewhere.

On election eve Matt and Glenna had been issued badges which allowed them passage past uniformed security guards posted at the doors to other rooms at the Waldorf. Badge wearers could enter the big pressroom, where they saw a few benighted journalists watching television sets amidst countless rows of empty tables and chairs which would never be used. A hand-lettered blackboard notice said the next press briefing would be at midnight.

"Most of them," said Glenna, "are out at the bar, you can be sure. I've learned that much about the guys who cover this campaign."

"Or they're at home watching on TV," Matt said. "They'll see as much there as they will here. I doubt that Nixon is even here; he's probably home too."

"No. Rose said he has a suite up in the Towers, which is like a separate little hotel here. It's where President Hoover and General MacArthur and the U.N. Ambassador live."

"Hoover and MacArthur are dead."

"Well, Nixon's up there tonight, anyway."

On the fourth floor they visited a noisy party hosted by the candidate's advance men and the tour personnel. The crews of the chartered airplanes, the public-address-system expert, and the baggage manager were trading war stories with the schedulers, headquarters secretaries, and the advance men who put the campaign trips together and made the schedule work, day to day.

Rose Mary Woods was holding court in a suite on the fourteenth floor, attended by some old Nixon friends, former Nixon staff people from Vice Presidential days, and a couple of Rose's perennial bachelor escorts. Glenna knew many of the prosperous people in Rose's room and introduced Matt around until they came to the food. Miss Woods's buffet was the best Matt had seen all evening, and by midnight he had become very hungry.

The returns from Ohio, California, and Illinois were critically important and persistently ambiguous. Rose Woods's brother, a former FBI official, was in Chicago in charge of making sure no one stole Illinois for Hubert Humphrey, and from time to time Miss Woods called him from her bedroom to try to find out who had won Illinois.

"It's looking better," she confided to Glenna and Matt at 12:30 A.M. "But The Boss won't go downstairs until Hubert concedes, and the Secret Service says Hubert has gone to sleep for the night. Their detail told our detail."

"So we might as well go home," Matt concluded. "We won't know anything for sure until morning."

"We could stay and party, couldn't we?" Glenna asked. "We're invited upstairs to the fat cats' party, and that should be really fancy."

Matt made another roast-beef sandwich at Rose Woods's buffet and turned to look around the room. "If you don't mind, I'd just as soon go back to your place. We can watch the results there."

Glenna turned on the television set in her bedroom and they watched ABC award Ohio and Illinois to Nixon.

"That means we win," Glenna said. "Because we'll carry California for sure. It was Nixon's home state, after all. That means we're going to the White House!" She squeezed Matt's upper left arm with both her hands. "Aren't you really excited?"

"I guess. It's good that the whole thing is a success. But I'm not so sure about the White House."

"What do you mean? What aren't you sure about?"

"Well, in the first place, I'm not so sure anyone is going to ask me to work there. I don't think George Bothwell is all that crazy about me. By the way, we didn't see him tonight. Was he there?"

"Rose says he probably didn't show up because Mitchell wouldn't let him up on the thirty-fifth floor with Haldeman and the others. He figured he'd lose face if he had to hang out at one of the other rooms downstairs. But of course they are going to ask you to work in the White House! Rose has already asked me to work there. I'm going to be her secretary."

"Even if they do, I'm not so sure I will accept."

"My God, Matt!" Glenna faced him. "Of course you'll accept! Are you crazy?"

"I don't have the background to be on the National Security Council staff, Glenna, and there's nothing else I'd want to do. I don't see myself working for Haldeman as a flunky. I'm better off going back to the law firm."

"Matthew Thompson, that's really just dumb," she said with unusual heat. "Any young lawyer would be crazy—"

"Listen," he interrupted, pointing to the television set. "ABC is giving California to Nixon. They are declaring him elected. How about that?" They embraced and fell sideways onto the bed, kissing.

"Promise you won't turn down any job offers until we talk," she demanded, wriggling away from him. He reached out for her arm and pulled her back on top of him. "Matt, you can write your own ticket as a lawyer if you've worked in the White House. It sets you up for life."

"Okay—we'll talk about it again if I get an offer. But I probably won't."

"I've got some champagne in the icebox," Glenna said. She jumped off the bed and looked for her slippers. "We should drink a little toast now that The Boss is elected, don't you think? To him and to our new lives?'' She gave up the search and padded barefoot down the lighted hall-way toward the kitchen.

Matt lay on his side and watched her walk away from him. The girl-who-has-everything goes to the White House, the nation's favorite lighthouse. Rich, beautiful, and at the center of power.

And then there is Wang Li-fa. What a contrast! She is living in a Communist dormitory, eating plain food, wear-ing plain clothes, and living a spartan life, even though she is at a power center too. Li, bright as hell, wise, calm and insightful: she would understand his reluctance to work in the White House as some kind of stooge, Matt reflected. But if he didn't work in the White House, how would he get back into China to see her again and be with her? How could he hope to persuade Nixon to make the first moves in the game with China? Thompson rolled onto his back and closed his eyes.

They will be rejoicing in Peking tomorrow, he thought with amusement. Teng Shan-li's dark horse has come in a winner, and he will be the local hero. They will be counting on Matthew Thompson to follow Nixon into the White House, of course. They probably will expect their friend Matt to go right into the Cabinet, at the very least.

''I don't know whether this stuff is any good or not,'' Glenna said. She was carrying a bottle and two glasses; a wisp of frosty vapor came from the uncorked bottle. ''It's not French. Somebody gave me two bottles and I just stuck them in the refrigerator without really looking at them. Now I see it's Spanish sparkling wine; it's not even champagne.''

''That's okay. Let's try it.'' Matt sat up and propped the pillows against the headboards.

''What's happening on TV?'' she asked.

''I don't know; I haven't been listening. I've been thinking about what you said. I guess you're right about working at the White House.'' He moved up on the pillows and took one of the tulips from Glenna. ''It is a chance of a lifetime. But do you think there is any way I can get a job in foreign policy work? In spite of Bothwell?''

Glenna frowned. ''First we have to make a toast, before we drink. What shall we toast—the new President?''

''The President,'' he said solemnly, and they touched their glasses and drank. ''May he bring the world peace,'' Matt added.

''Don't worry about Bothwell,'' she said earnestly. ''I don't think Nixon will choose him to run foreign policy. From what Rose says, Nixon doesn't like him too much.''

''You think they will dump him now?''

''Could be. And The Boss really likes you, don't forget. Want more wine? Do you like this?''

''It's sharp, isn't it?'' He put the tulip on the floor beside the bed, folded his hands behind his head, and looked at the television screen.

''There's Herb Klein,'' Glenna said. ''He's out too.''

''Out?''

''He wants to be press secretary, but Nixon told Rose last week that if he was elected President he would choose someone else. He thinks Klein panders to the press too much.''

''So the White House staff will have a lot of new faces?''

''Some, anyway. Haldeman will be the head of things, I guess. He likes you too.''

''I've only met him those two times. That's not much for him to go on. All the same, I don't want to work for Haldeman, I don't think. He looks harsh.''

Glenna nodded. ''I'll help if I can. I'll ask Rose who is going to be in charge of the foreign policy department in the White House. What do you call it?''

''The National Security Council.''

''I'll try to help. Do you want more wine?''

''I want to sleep. It's almost three o'clock. What do we do tomorrow? There's no campaign; do we go to the office anyway?''

"I suppose I'll go in about noon and help Rose. Don't you have anything to do?"

"I guess the files all need to be boxed up. Bothwell will be telling the press how we won the election for Nixon. I can help him get ready for that."

Glenna turned off the television set and the light. Matt lay on his back and held her in his right arm, but he suddenly realized he was thinking about Wang Li-fa. I am some kind of a rat, he thought, taking Glenna's body and her help with the job in the White House, and all the time I'm thinking about another woman.

"Good night, Matt," Glenna murmured. "I'm glad you'll be in Washington."

"Good night," he replied.

He wondered how it would be to live with Wang Li-fa—to go to bed with her every night, to see her brush her teeth and to take showers with her. He dimly suspected that he was foolishly idealizing the Chinese woman. There was no way they could ever be together, and he knew that rationally, but her very inaccessibility made her more attractive to him. She was bright and good-looking, and she was also an unsolved puzzle. He didn't know much about what she was really like. He had marshaled random scraps of evidence which tended to establish that she had a sense of humor. She was physical; she had pressed her leg against his in the car. At least, he hoped that she had. Her part in the episode of the emerald meant that she liked him, and was even affectionate toward him, he told himself.

If he got back to China he intended to try to get her to open up to him. He would just ask her flatly how she felt about him. If she loved him, would she come to America with him? Or could he stay there with her? Of course not. So where was all of this going? Wasn't he better off with this rich, gorgeous blonde who loved him? Of course he was.

As he fell asleep, Matt thought about Li's strong wrists. He wondered if she knew how to play tennis.

Twenty-four

"I'm damned sorry, Matt, but I'm afraid I just can't tell you what is going on," George Bothwell said, standing at Matt's window and looking down on the Park Avenue traffic. "I'll probably be going to Key Biscayne in a few hours by Air Force jet, and when I get there I'm going to urge the Old Man to make some quick decisions. It's just not fair to people like you to be left dangling. They should tell you if you're hired or not."

Matt suppressed a smile. The President-elect, Richard Nixon, had flown off to Florida with six of his campaign staff in an Air Force jet within minutes of Hubert Humphrey's televised concession speech. But no one had called George Bothwell to tell him that he was invited; worse, no one had called him to tell him anything.

Angie confided to Matt with some amusement that Dr. Bothwell had tried to telephone John Mitchell and then Bob Haldeman at Key Biscayne all Wednesday afternoon without success. Both men were closeted with the President-elect and were not to be disturbed, Bothwell had been told.

"As I've told you, Matt," Bothwell went on importantly, "I've given you a very favorable recommendation. I've proposed that our whole National Security Council apparatus be modeled after Eisenhower's, and that will mean that I head up a staff of about two hundred and twenty. There's a place in there for you, Matt, I assure you. The only thing that might hurt you is your inexperience. If Mitchell and Nixon decide to go with a smaller operation, then I'd be compelled to prioritize, you understand.'' Bothwell looked at Matt quickly from the window, then turned back. ''The more experienced and qualified people would have to be brought aboard ahead of some campaign workers. You understand that, of course.''

''Of course.'' Matt nodded. ''What should we be doing here in the meantime?''

''Doing? Well, I don't know. Until I've met with them down there I'd say that things can just stay as they are. Before too long we'll be moving to temporary quarters in the District, of course, and I'll arrange for all of that when I'm in Florida. I'd say you can just sit tight until then. I'm lunching with Don Oberdorfer Friday, you know, and I'd like you to put together a little talking paper for me, if you will. I might lift up the corner of the tent for *The Washington Post,* just a bit. How we'll work with Johnson's outgoing people, keep the policy work going, drop no stitches, pass the torch, effect an orderly transition. Something that will reassure our allies and let the Russians know that nothing will slip by us.''

''I get it.''

''I should be getting briefings from the Agency and State every day starting very soon. Then I'll be summarizing for the President-elect. I'll need a daily meeting with him of an hour or so.'' Bothwell moved toward the door. ''I'm going to make a call or two and then I'll be at home. If there are calls from the President-elect, that is where I will be.''

''Fine,'' Matt said.

Thursday morning, as he was spinning the fluffy cotton candy which was the Oberdorfer talking paper, Matt's telephone rang twice. The first call was the first he'd had from Mary Finn in many months.

''So, your man won,'' she said with a note of surprise. ''Are you gloating?''

''Nope. I'm sitting here waiting to be told what happens next. It all seems sort of unreal. How are you? I haven't talked to you for a long time.''

"Well, you've been busy, boy. Are you going to work in the White House?"

"I really don't know. I guess I will if they ask me to. But no one has asked me except George Bothwell, and I don't think he himself has been hired yet."

"Sounds confused."

"Very. Did you catch D'Amico?"

"Not yet. The FBI says they are getting closer, but I think they always say that."

"Did you know I went to Hong Kong for the firm?"

"Someone told me. I forgot who. Did you like it?"

"Loved it."

"It's odd, but I have no desire to see the Orient. Europe, yes. Especially Greece. But not anything from India to Japan. It all smells bad, I think."

"That's because you've never been there. It's really a beautiful, fascinating part of the world, and an important part of civilization."

"All right, if you insist. Just between us, I may be leaving the dear old Justice Department, but I haven't told anyone yet."

"Really? Where will you go? Do you have an offer?"

"Oh, you know me, Thompson. I get offers all the time."

"I mean job offers."

"So do I, you turkey. I may go with Baker and McKenzie; it's an offer that is nearly impossible to turn down."

"Good for you. They do a lot of international work, don't they?"

"Right. I'd be going to Washington too. It's a job in their D.C. office. I'm getting a lot of pressure to stay in New York, but the Baker job is wonderful."

"Is the boyfriend pressuring you?"

"A different one; not the doctor. I'm getting incredible pressure."

"Tall, beard, dapper dresser?"

"Yeah. How did you know?"

"I saw you one time."

"Why didn't you say hello?"

"I was in a cab. If you do come to Washington, don't worry about him. I'll buy you a humburger now and then."

"Hamburger, hell. I'll settle for nothing less than state dinners at the White House."

"It's a date, subject to a few loose ends like the fact that I'm not at all sure I'm going to be there."

But a few minutes after he'd talked to Mary Finn he was certain that he was going to Washington.

"Matt, this is Larry Higby," the high-pitched voice on the telephone said. "Bob Haldeman asked me to call you."

"Yes." Matt knew Higby, Haldeman's young, super-efficient aide. "He'd like you to answer to a couple of questions and then perhaps do some things for him," Higby piped.

"Okay."

"First, are you available to help out with the transition?"

"I'm not sure just what that means. Is that a job? Does it pay money?"

"Right. It pays at the rate of thirty-four thousand a year, lasts from now until January twentieth, and is a Government job."

"Doing what?"

"National Security work. We don't have the head of the White House department, but things need doing right now. Bob and the President-elect want you to come on board and do them."

"What about George Bothwell? He's wandering around here like a sleepwalker. Does he have a job?"

"Why do you ask? Will you only work for him?"

"Oh, God, no. I'm just curious."

"When I can tell you about Bothwell I will, but not now. Do you want the job?"

"Sure, if the law firm doesn't object."

"They don't."

"Is that in Washington?"

"Nope. Everything important will be in New York. The office will be at the Pierre Hotel."

Matt laughed. "That'll be the most expensive office space in the world."

"Your tax dollars at work," Higby intoned. "Second question: Are you interested in a White House job?"

"Probably, but it depends on what job it is."

"How about the NSC staff? Interested in that?"

"Definitely."

"Okay. I'll tell Bob. Here's what he'd like you to do: First, box up all the foreign policy files, all the files the Bothwell operation created, and get ready to move them to the Pierre. Then take Friday, Saturday, and Sunday off. Monday is moving day. Be at the campaign office at seven-thirty A.M. and supervise your stuff getting to the Pierre. Wait a second and I'll tell you your room number there." Higby clattered clipboards and flipped pages. "It's 2410."

"Okay."

"Do you have a good secretary?"

"I use Bothwell's. And she is excellent."

"Okay, tell her she's hired until January twentieth, will you? She can move with you. She works for you, not Bothwell. What's her name?"

"Angie. Angela Cruz."

"Last question: Do you know Henry Kissinger?"

"Personally? No."

"Have you read his books?"

"I tried to read one for a Dartmouth course, but I could never finish it. He writes thickets and swamps. What do I say to Dr. George Bothwell?"

"Just tell him Haldeman instructed you to pack it all and move it."

"Okay. Thanks."

George Bothwell came to Matt's office the next morning, Friday, for the talking paper that would prepare him for his Oberdorfer lunch conversation. Matt was piling files into handsome government packing boxes which the General Services Administration had eagerly provided for the President-elect and his staff. Bothwell was dressed up in his professor's suit, dark blue, matching vest, white shirt, striped tie. Matt was in blue jeans and a wool checked shirt. Matt handed him the typed Oberdorfer memorandum he'd come for and returned to the half-empty file drawer.

"Where will this stuff be?" Bothwell asked, pointing to the boxed files. "How do I find it if I want it?"

"It's all going to the Pierre," Matt said, looking intently at a file.

"Pierre? What do you mean?"

"The Hotel Pierre."

"You're storing stuff at the Pierre? That would cost like hell. What are you talking about? This stuff should all go to D.C. in case I need it," Bothwell said dogmatically.

"The transition office will be at the Pierre, George," Matt said softly.

"It will? At the Pierre?" Bothwell tried not to show the pain he was feeling. "Did someone call when I was out?"

"I heard from Haldeman. I'm to report to work at the Pierre on Monday. Angie too."

"Well. Well, that's fine. They are starting to move on personnel decisions, as I wanted them to do. I'd better go check my calls."

"I gave Angie a few days off," Matt said. "Mrs. Tuohy is taking her place today."

"What the hell?" Bothwell protested. "By what right? Who the hell are you to send *my* secretary away without checking with me?"

"George, she's working for me now. They have shifted some of the secretaries and other people around."

"Who shifted them? Who's operating behind my back?" Bothwell bellowed. "What is going on here?"

"Haldeman and Mitchell shifted them, George. Why don't you talk to Haldeman or Larry Higby about all of this?"

"Higby? Higby! By God, I refuse to talk to Higby. I'll talk to Haldeman or I won't talk to anyone! I'm going to find out who is trying to undercut me!" Bothwell turned toward Matt's telephone, obviously intending to place his call to Florida in Matt's presence.

"George, I'm sorry, but I'm expecting a call. Could you phone from your office?"

"What?" Bothwell wheeled. "What the hell!" He charged out Matt's door flapping the Oberdorfer memo in his left hand.

The Hotel Pierre did not willingly lend itself to the President-elect's whim. The Pierre was only two blocks from Richard Nixon's apartment home on Fifth Avenue. That aside, the hotel's management and guests and most of Nixon's staff agreed there was no other good reason for the Presidential transition's offices to be located in the Pierre's small upper floors. The elevators, adequate for the occasional comings and goings of wealthy guests—even princes and sheiks—could not begin to meet the needs of Nixon's large staff and security force. The hotel's old furnaces so overheated the bedrooms-become-offices that wilting clerks and secretaries opened the Pierre's casement windows to admit the moist winter winds that swirled about the Pierre tower.

The hotel's small yellow-and-cream lobby was jammed with security guards and a throng of people who had been invited to the Nixon floors. Others loitered about the lobby hoping for an invitation. Elegant guests of the Pierre gave up and moved elsewhere.

But Richard Nixon was oblivious to such practical problems. His transition staff would have offices at the Hotel Pierre and he, the President-elect, would conduct his business there. It was, after all, his home neighborhood.

Angie Cruz and Matt Thompson moved into room 2410 on the Monday after the election and began to tell people that they were sharing a bedroom at the Pierre. Bright, unfaded rectangles of carpet evidenced that room 2410 had offered twin beds before the General Services Administration had replaced them with the two desks, two file cabinets, four chairs, aluminum water carafe and tray, and American flag (and stand) that were allotted to each "office." Against one wall, on either side of the bathroom door, the paper boxes of campaign files were stacked to the ceiling. Matt's used metal desk had been placed near the window, in front of the radiator. A thick telephone cord was nailed to the wall beside it. Matt soon discovered that the Pierre's old radiators could not be adjusted; they radiated heat constantly and excessively. But when the window behind his chair was opened to moderate the heat, the cold outside wind blew everything off his desk. Monday and Tuesday, Angie spent most of her time trying to get the desk and its telephone cable moved away from the window. Telephone technicians were in great demand and short supply on the Nixon floors.

With great foresight Angie had boxed up the office supplies and equipment she and Matt had foraged during the campaign. For several days it was impossible to find a government-issue pencil with an eraser at the Pierre, but Angie had her hoard. Most of the pencils read NIXON'S THE ONE, but they did the job.

Richard Nixon returned from a week at Key Biscayne with the six-man nucleus of his government gathered about him. They had paid a call on Lyndon Johnson and had toured the White House en route back to New York, but they had not been persuaded to change the White House plan that had been made in crude sketches on the campaign airplane weeks before. There would be a chief of staff—H. R. Haldeman—and some principal assistants for National Security, domestic affairs, and economics, but the strength of the Executive Branch would lie in the President's Cabinet. For a month and a half—until Christmas, 1968—Nixon's principal work would be to recruit about twenty good men to become his Cabinet and staff. It had been agreed in Florida that John Mitchell would be Attorney General. Bob Finch would become something in the Cabinet, but no one was quite sure what. William Rogers was to be Secretary of State.

Beyond that, there were lists which always ended with question marks. Nixon's own list began with the question of a National Security assistant. Nixon would run foreign policy from the White House, by God, and he needed a strong staff at the National Security Council to keep State, Defense, and the CIA in line. Who would head that staff? Robert Murphy, perhaps? Rockefeller's Henry Kissinger? Maybe Andy Goodpaster from the Eisenhower staff?

Angie Cruz held her hand over the telephone mouthpiece and said to Matthew Thompson, "Matt, do you know a William F. Buckley, Junior?"

"No, but I know who he is."

"He's calling for either George Bothwell or Frank Shakespeare. Do you want to take it?"

"I guess. He's an old friend of Nixon's." Matt picked up the phone and cleared his throat.

"Mr. Buckley, this is Matthew Thompson. Can I help you? Neither George Bothwell nor Frank Shakespeare works here, but I am handling some of the President-elect's calls."

"Well, Mr. Thompson, actually I am trying to get word to President Nixon about the situation in Viet Nam that seems very urgent." Buckley's stilted drawl was unmistakable.

"Yes, sir. Can you tell me what it is about?"

"As a matter of fact, Henry Kissinger called me with it. It has to do with a *presidential assassination*, you see, and I think the President ought to be talking to Henry directly about it. That's my, ah, my recommendation. He should call Henry."

"I'll sure pass this along right away," Matt promised. "Thank you for calling."

When he'd hung up, Matt organized his scattered notes of the call and headed for the door. "I guess I'd better give this to someone upstairs," he said.

"Don't forget your badge," Angie reminded. "You'd better wear it or they're liable to shoot you up there."

In Bob Haldeman's outer office, once the sitting room of a small bedroom suite, two secretaries talked on telephones. Matt stood, waiting, since no chairs were provided. Probably that is a Haldeman efficiency technique, Matt reflected. People will keep moving if you don't give them a place to sit.

"Yes?" A secretary nodded to him. She was middle-aged, expensively dressed, sophisticated.

"I need to speak to Bob or Larry. I'm Matt Thompson."

"About?"

"I don't think you really want to know."

"Yes, I need to know," she said firmly. He didn't doubt it.

"Okay," he shrugged. "It's about *assassination*. It comes from William Buckley."

The secretary looked at him for a few seconds, got up, and went into the adjoining room, reclosing the door behind her. Heavy green-and-gray damask draperies swayed in the window behind the other secretary. It was snowing lightly outside, but Matt noted with satisfaction that Haldeman's secretaries had opened their window too. The Pierre's radiator clanked and hissed defiantly.

Bob Haldeman followed his secretary into the room, smiling broadly. His front teeth were large, square, and very white. Matt wondered if they were real. Haldeman carried seven or eight file folders in his left hand.

"Who's getting killed today, Matt?" he asked genially.

"I'm not sure. I talked to Buckley and he says the President should call Henry Kissinger about it."

"Oh?" Haldeman's smile broadened. "Why don't you come in and tell him about it?" Haldeman nodded west, toward Nixon's suite, then led the way out into the hall and past the elevator and a security desk to a door at the end where a Secret Service agent stood.

The Nixon suite was furnished in Pierre antique, with gray walls, heavy gray draperies, wooden cabinets, and silk-covered furniture. Haldeman led Matt into a living room arranged with couches and overstuffed chairs, low tables, and silk-shaded lamps. The coffee table was covered with tablets and files.

"The view from in here is spectacular," Haldeman said. "Too bad it's always snowing."

A door near the foyer opened and Richard Nixon emerged shaking water from his hands. "Bob," he said, "there are no towels in there. Could I have some towels?"

"Certainly," Haldeman snapped.

Someone will hear about that, harshly, Matt reflected. Some poor housekeeper, probably.

"Matt Thompson just had a very interesting call from Buckley," Haldeman said as Nixon sat deeply in the chair nearest the windows. Haldeman nodded at Matt.

"How are you, Matt?" Nixon asked. "Are you getting along all right?"

"Yes, sir. Mr. William Buckley called about twenty minutes ago for Dr. Bothwell or Frank Shakespeare. I took the call. He said Henry Kissinger had phoned him about a possible presidential assassination in Viet Nam. Mr. Buckley urged that Mr.—ah, the President-elect—call Dr. Kissinger right away."

Both Nixon and Haldeman smiled.

"Kissinger called Buckley?" Nixon asked.

Matt looked at his notes. "Yes, sir. That's what he said."

"*Good,*" Nixon declared. "Very good. He's sending us a signal that he wants the job. Bob, you call Kissinger and say I want to see him. Has Mitchell talked to Rockefeller yet?"

"Yes." Haldeman nodded once. "That's undoubtedly why Kissinger is campaigning. I'd say no more brokering is necessary. He's ripe for the plucking."

Nixon nodded. "But before he comes in you need to cover a few things with him. Be sure he agrees to keep George Bothwell and Dick Allen. And also Matt, here. Matt is doing a special project for me." Nixon's voice dropped to a conspiratorial tone. "Henry Kissinger should not know that. Okay, Matt?"

"Yes, sir."

"You see, Matt, we are going to offer him the NSC job," Nixon confided. "That is what the Buckley call is really all about. I'm glad you told me about it right away. When he comes in I want you to meet him. When will he come, Bob?"

Haldeman opened a folder and ran his finger over a

calendar. "I think the twenty-seventh is best. I'll call him, then let Matt know."

"Good," said Nixon. "The sooner the better. We need to get going right away."

Matthew Thompson first met Dr. Henry Alfred Kissinger in Bob Haldeman's office at 10:45 A.M. the morning of November 27. It appeared that Kissinger had less idea of why they were meeting than Matt did, even after Haldeman explained that Matt was the housekeeper of the embryonic Nixon NSC operation.

"Do you come from the State Department?" Kissinger asked.

"No, I'm a lawyer with Mr. Nixon's law firm," Matt said. "I've been working for Dr. Bothwell during the campaign."

"Oh, yes," Kissinger said without enthusiasm. "I'm sure you must have learned a great deal from him."

"No, not really."

Kissinger looked at Matt as if appraising a six-foot stack of salted ling cod. "Did you attend U.C.L.A.?" he asked evenly.

Matt smiled. "No, Dartmouth College and Harvard Law."

Kissinger pursed his lips and nodded. It was evidently a pleasant surprise to find a Nixon person who was not from a cow college Out West.

"Did you have courses from Jenkins at Dartmouth?" Dr. Kissinger asked.

"Yes, several. He was my adviser."

"We were in the Army together," Kissinger said.

"I know," Matt replied.

Kissinger shot back a look which asked: How much do you know?

The door opened and Haldeman's secretary nodded.

"We've got to go," Haldeman said to Kissinger. "The people's choice is waiting."

Matt and Kissinger said goodbye to each other, and Matt

returned to his pile of pink telephone-call slips on the twenty-fourth floor. The next day Larry Higby called to report that the job had been offered to Dr. Kissinger and he had asked for time to think about the offer.

"I could work for Kissinger," Matt told Glenna Harrison, "but he is going to want Foreign Service experts and Harvard professors working for him, I think."

"He's going to need someone like you," she assured him. "You have the confidence of the Nixon people, and he's going to need that, don't you think?"

Matt and Glenna were sitting on the floor in his apartment on a thick carpet of sheepskins she had given him for his birthday. The Sunday *Times* had been pulled apart, selectively browsed, and set aside near the debris of a Continental breakfast Glenna had laid out on the coffee table.

Glenna wore a short, loose-fitting robe of heavy white terry cloth which rode her bare thighs above their equators.

Matt had tied his long blue wool robe at his waist, but it had fallen open revealingly as he read the first section of the *Times*.

"You're always so pessimistic about people wanting you," Glenna said, looking at his lower body. "You'd better not doubt that *I* want you."

He smiled and looked up. "So?"

She stretched her arms along the couch she was leaning against. Her fingers wiggled lazily. "So come on over here, why don't you?"

"In a second. I want to finish this story about Kissinger. Do you think he inspired it? How could the *Times* find out he'd been offered the job?"

"Who cares? I'm all full of croissants and coffee and I'm feeling lazy and cuddly. Why aren't you over here?"

"I have decided to serve the President," Kissinger told H. R. Haldeman. His telephone voice was deeper than it had been in person. "You know, it is impossible to decline a President's call for help, however personally difficult it might be. This assignment will not be without personal sacrifice for me."

"He'll be very glad to hear that you accept, Doctor," Haldeman said briskly. "I'll arrange for you to see him tomorrow."

"Thank you. You spoke to me about Dr. Bothwell and Dick Allen and the young lawyer."

"Thompson."

"Yes. Of course, if it is the President's desire that they have places on my staff, I will arrange to employ them. That goes without saying. But I wish you would tell the President that I have some reservations about George Bothwell, after talking to some of his colleagues at Virginia. I would have to say that I intend to separate politics from the substance of the work the National Security Council will do for the President. I am concerned that Dr. Bothwell puts politics first sometimes."

"What about Thompson?" Haldeman asked noncommittally.

"I simply know very little about him. I have talked to Dr. Jenkins at Dartmouth, who says Thompson was an adequate student of unexceptional attainment. It is my intention to hire remarkably talented people."

"Well, Doctor, the President-elect made a particular point of this. He definitely wants these two and Dick Allen at the NSC because he knows them and has confidence in them. He *insists* upon having them there."

"Then they shall be hired, Mr. Haldeman, and I shall be happy to have them. No more will be said on the subject. In view of the President's wishes, I assume there is no need to run the usual security checks on them?"

"Right. Have them go through the conflict-of-interest review with the Counsel, but none of the rest of that FBI stuff is necessary."

Kissinger was surprised at the collapse of his security-check gambit and quickly changed the subject. "Will I have an office there?" he asked.

"We are holding Room 2411 for you. You can move in any time."

"A secretary?"

"Do you want to bring one?"

"I think not."

"Then we'll get you one."

"Henry," Nixon said, "I've asked Matt and Bob to come in to hear this too. Matt is my China expert—he helped me write the *Foreign Affairs* article, you know—and Bob needs to know what Johnson had to say."

"Fine, Mr. President," Kissinger said approvingly.

"President Johnson called this morning to talk about several things," Nixon continued. "He seems to be very decent about making the transition work well. Anyway, he has a message from the Chinese and they propose that our ambassadors in Warsaw resume the bilateral talks. They were primarily talking about a Korean peace treaty before the talks were suspended—right, Matt?"

"Yes, sir, primarily."

"Johnson thinks they might eventually broaden into something more important," Nixon continued. "He didn't want to commit the United States unless I agreed, however. What do you think, Henry?"

"As I recall," Kissinger hedged, "the talks broke off because of Viet Nam."

"Because of Johnson's blockade of the Northern ports," Matt supplied.

"Has the blockade succeeded?" Kissinger asked Matt.

"No."

"Then why not authorize our ambassador to meet with them?" Kissinger asked.

"Henry"—Nixon stood and walked to the window to look at the swirling snow—"I want a new relationship with mainland China. We can talk more about it when you are ready. Matt has prepared a paper on China you should read. Right, Matt?"

"Yes, sir, the memorandum is ready."

"Good. We'll all talk about China later. Meanwhile, I am inclined to tell Johnson to go ahead in Warsaw."

"Perhaps," Kissinger cautioned, "you will be changing your ambassador in Warsaw. Why not say that no talks should be scheduled until February, to give you a chance to instruct a new man and get him over there?"

"Good thought." Nixon nodded. "Bob, you can let Rostow know we agree, as long as talks begin after February fifteenth. You'd better go call him now. And Matt, I have some things I need to talk to Henry about."

Matt and Haldeman stood and started for the door.

"Don't say anything about this to anyone," Nixon called after them. "It will be better to let Johnson announce it and explain it. I don't want Goldwater on my back quite so soon. Let it look like it's Johnson's decision."

"Yes, sir," Matt replied, closing the door behind him.

"I quite agree about China, Mr. President," Kissinger said. "It is time for a new arrangement. We can use the China card in our hand. I am not sure whether the Chinese are ready to open up to us, but we can try."

"I have reason to believe that they will deal with me," Nixon said conspiratorially, "where they wouldn't talk to L.B.J."

"I will read Thompson's paper with great interest," Kissinger said. "I have decided to employ him and, of course, Doctors Bothwell and Allen, as you directed. I will have Thompson focus on the Orient."

"Good."

"Apparently Thompson has some contacts in the Far East. I'm told he has recently been to Hong Kong."

"Yes, I know about his trip," Nixon said impatiently. "What is more, his father and mother—who are friends of mine—once lived in China and taught there. I think Matt was born there, or at least lived there when he was young. Does someone see something sinister in all of that?"

Kissinger held up his hand in reassurance. "Oh, no, Mr. President; in fact, old China contacts may prove to be helpful."

Nixon nodded. "Make sure no one harasses Thompson

on account of his family's background with the Chinese. I don't want Hoover or Helms mucking around in questions of China; is that clear?"

"Yes, Mr. President," Kissinger said solemnly. "You can be certain that they will let Thompson alone. I will see to that.

"Mr. President," Henry Kissinger continued deferentially, "I am making some progress, but the clearance procedures involve delays. Some of the people I have selected already work for the government, but your attorneys insist on new financial investigations before a person can come to work here, even during the transition."

Nixon nodded. "I am particularly concerned that everyone avoid an appearance of a conflict of interest. We can't afford to have that. They tell me even you may have a little problem; right, Henry?"

Kissinger opened his hands. "No, I don't think so, Mr. President; not that I know of. I have very little in stocks or that sort of thing."

"Who have you hired?" Nixon asked.

"A career Foreign Service officer named Eagleburger, whom I think you will like. He is young, tough, and bright. Very hard-line with the Russians. I am going to be able to bring in other people from RAND and from Defense. It is shaping up."

"What about George Bothwell and Dick Allen? What will they be doing?"

"I haven't decided what to do with Bothwell. I think Allen would be best working on the European and Russian issues."

"Fine. He will be very helpful, I think. Tell him I want to see him from time to time. He may feel as though he's being demoted—which, in a sense, perhaps he is—but he shouldn't feel that way. After all, he is going to work in the White House, on some very substantial issues. Tell him he will have the President's ear."

"I'll do that, Mr. President. I'm sure Dr. Allen's morale will improve once we are down in Washington."

Twenty-five

"Bob," Nixon said, "I'm concerned about Kissinger's staff. He tells me he is hiring people who are career Foreign Service."

"One. Eagleburger. He's given me a list of some others, but they aren't hired and won't be until we check them out."

"I told him to move ahead with Bothwell, Allen, and young Thompson quickly. I think he's dragging his feet."

"I know. I've told him they are positively to be hired, and I'm sure he understands that."

"Without all that FBI crap, I told him. My God, those people have been working for us for months. I think he is just using the need for investigations as an excuse to delay."

"Right. Investigations aren't at all necessary. You can swear them in today if you want to."

"No, I want the ceremonies to be in the White House, where it will mean something to them. We will wait on that."

"Okay."

"Now, Bob, I want you to be damn sure that Kissinger doesn't shunt Bothwell and Allen aside. They are my men in that NSC staff, and if they are going to be at all useful, they've got to be included in everything. You make sure of that."

"Yes, sir, I'll try."

"It is very important."

"I understand."

"Let me explain: If Kissinger loads up that staff with a lot of State Department pantywaists it is going to be impossible to run foreign policy out of the White House. They will all go running back over there and tell their boyfriends everything we are doing. And it is very important for State to be kept out of some of these things. China, for instance. The traditional State Department reaction will be to confide in the Japs and Chiang Kai-shek and the Koreans and every other son-of-a-bitch in the Far East. They think they have to spill everything they know or the others will get mad at us. So we will have to do it without telling State. And Henry Kissinger's staff must be loyal to the President, not to the Foreign Service. Clear?''

"Sure."

"All right."

The inauguration of Richard Nixon was a four-hour respite in Matthew Thompson's work schedule, but it was not the great, emotional experience he had anticipated it would be. Matt's seat at the swearing-in at the Capitol facade had been in a section reserved for Kissinger's staff, off to the side, behind the Marine Band. The upper echelons of the staff—Kissinger, Haldeman, and Moynihan— had seats up on the platform, behind the Presidents, Johnson and Nixon. Even better, the senior staff and their families moved about the congested city in military sedans escorted by Army colonels who found seating for the wives and children and produced extra blankets. It was late January and the wind off the Potomac was cold.

Matt went to the ceremony in a shared taxi from the Executive Office Building, where he was helping with the move-in. Kissinger's belongings had arrived at the White House in dozens of odd-sized crates and boxes, a mix of Harvard paperwork, books, soiled laundry, a manuscript in progress, and 227 highly organized files on foreign policy. The professor's possessions were to be stored in the basement of the West Wing of the White House until they could be sorted. A crew of General Service Administration roustabouts was supervised in this work by Matt Thompson

and the indispensable Larry Eagleburger, who had become
Kissinger amanuensis, body servant, punching bag, and
executive assistant.

Matthew was also assigned to oversee the unloading of
the Hotel Pierre files, which were to be kept in a suite of
rooms on the third floor of the old building next to the
White House. There an administrator would soon begin to
manage the vast flow of paper that inevitably would pour
through the offices of the National Security Council every
twenty-four hours. Every sheet would be logged, routed,
classified, or filed by clerks recruited from the Department
of Defense and the Central Intelligence Agency.

At precisely 11 A.M. on Inauguration Day all work there
ceased. The open file drawers were left half-filled, the
massive wooden office doors were locked, and everyone
made his way to an Inaugural vantage point. Many preferred to watch the whole thing on television, warm and
comfortable at home. Those with tickets scrambled for
cabs which took them to the foot of Capitol Hill, and from
there they hiked to the east facade of the Capitol itself to
find their folding chairs.

Nixon, Spiro Agnew, the new Vice President, the Cabinet, and the senior White House staff ate lunch with senior
congressmen after the brief swearing-in ceremony while
the throng scrambled for a place to stand or sit along
Pennsylvania Avenue for the Inaugural Parade.

Glenna Harrison's father had paid a stiff price for parade
seats in a box built in front of the White House, not far
from the President's bulletproof, heated reviewing stand.
Matt met Glenna and her parents at Glenna's new apartment in Columbia Plaza, near the Kennedy Center. Joe
Harrison provided a rented limousine which was purring
warmly at the curb outside, and they rode comfortably to
Seventeenth and K streets. Matt expected that Mr. Harrison
might have hired someone to carry them the rest of the
way, but the Harrisons walked to their seats like almost
everyone else.

The Harrisons' seats were among other Nixon fat cats'
with whom Joe Harrison felt at home, and he moved along

the rows shaking hands and chatting while they waited for
the parade to begin.

Once the President and Vice President had passed by in
their limousines, Matt began to make his excuses to
Glenna and her mother. Before three bands had marched by,
eyes left, saluting the new President in his glass box, Matt
had worked his way behind the reviewing stand, showing
his new plastic White House pass to policemen, Secret
Service agents, and soldiers at countless checkpoints. Someone had constructed a duckboard sidewalk across the
White House lawn from the back of the stand to the front
of the West Wing, and from there Matt walked down a few
steps to the narrow street that separated the West Wing
from the Executive Office Building, where Matt's office
was. An elevator just inside the basement door took him to
the high-ceilinged third floor. He turned left and walked to
the south hallway, where a huge old curving stairway
occupied the corner of the building.

The Haldeman staff, young men who were caricatures of
efficiency experts, had assigned the offices in the Executive Office Building to the new Presidential employees
with jealous precision. At precisely noon on Inauguration
Day new nameplates were posted beside each office door
and the appointed occupants were permitted to take possession. Furniture and accessories had been allocated by a
formula based on the rank of the tenant. Certain people,
notably women appointees—there were not many—were
given living plants. High-ranking staff members were allocated three television sets so all network news programs
could be watched simultaneously.

Telephones were also formularized. Top staff had
"Call Directors" with sixteen buttons. Their deputies
had eight buttons. Matthew's phone had four buttons for
two inside lines, one private outside number, and an
intercom line on which he talked to Angie Cruz. Angie
had arranged for a sister to care for her elderly parent in
Brooklyn so she could come to work at the White House
with Matthew Thompson.

Room 321 in the Executive Office Building consisted of

Angie's room, which doubled as a reception area and her workroom, and Matt's large adjoining office. He had been granted a desk, big desk chair, two side chairs, and a small striped couch, with assorted small tables. The wainscoted walls were bare of decoration. Before long, framed pictures of Richard Nixon would abound all over the building, like small toads after a rain.

Matt sat at his desk, looking south out the very tall windows toward the Washington Monument, which rose above the trees near the Ellipse.

"Angie," he called, "do you know how to get long distance on this?"

"Hit 88 on one of the inside lines. Wait for the dial tone, then dial your number, okay?"

"Okay."

In a moment Matt's father, Ezra Thompson, answered his telephone.

"I should have had the operator announce the call," Matt said. "The White House calling."

"Son! Are you there?"

"I'm in my office. I look out over the mall—Lincoln to the right, Washington to the left. The parade is still going on, I guess."

"Yes, I've been watching. I think I saw you at the swearing-in this morning, you know. Were you seated by the band?"

"Right."

"The TV showed them playing, and so I saw you. You looked cold."

"Freezing. But now I'm at work and it's fine in here. This is some office. The ceiling must be sixteen feet high, with fancy plasterwork. I have a fireplace, great tall doors and windows, and parquet wood floors."

"It sounds very grand."

"The doorknobs have the seal of the Treasury on them. The Treasury, State, and Defense—the War Department— were all in this building at the same time in the late 1800s. Imagine that!"

"Is Kissinger nearby?"

"No, he's in the basement next door, in the little West Wing where the Oval Office is. All his peons are over here."

"The Whittier paper has a story about you in last night's edition. I've cut it out."

"How come?"

"Local boy makes good. It's a special edition mostly about Nixon, of course, but there's nearly a page about you and your mother and me. Quite a few pictures."

"How did they get the pictures?"

"Oh, I loaned them some."

"How's the story?"

"Very generous, I'd say. It's written by a young woman who took a few of my courses at the college, so we had an unfair advantage. She wrote up some flattering things your colleagues at the law office in New York said about you."

"That's nice. The partners and some of the others from the firm are down here with bells on this week. They are all going to the Inaugural Ball tonight. Even Eldon Carnahay's wife is going all dressed up, and she hates Nixon to the marrow of her bones. All the ladies have new dresses."

"Are you going?"

"Oh, yeah. Glenna Harrison and her folks are taking me with them. It's going to be very crowded and confused and sort of a mess, but I guess everyone should do it once. At least the tickets were free. Are you sorry you decided not to come?"

"Not really. You were kind to have them send me the invitation and all, but I'm not one for all that social stuff. Perhaps when you are settled into your routine I'll come back for a visit and a look around."

"Good. The President is going to Europe next month and it will be frantic until that is over, but late March or in the spring I'd love to have you come."

"Are you going to Europe?"

"I think so. I'm working on the briefing materials right now, especially the stuff on the European Economic Community and NATO. I may be dropped if he decides not to visit them, but that's pretty unlikely."

"I find it remarkable that you are there, doing all of that. Aren't you fortunate?"

"I sure am. Dad, I have got to get going. We aren't really moved in yet and there's a lot to do."

"Fine, son. You were good to call."

"Watch the parade for me."

"I'll do that. You run the world and I'll watch the parade."

"I love you, Pop."

Inaugural festivities went on all through the week of January 20; a few receptions and White House parties for Nixon supporters were even held the following weekend. But Matthew returned his rented tuxedo on Wednesday and quickly settled into his new office and staff routine.

The new Kissinger staff was predominantly male, white, vintage 1928–1938, and perhaps 65 percent former Foreign Service officers from the State Department. Most of them knew one another from Harvard, State, or work at one foundation or another, and it was evident to Matt that a good many preferred to view themselves as working for Dr. Henry Kissinger and not Richard Nixon. Dick Allen and George Bothwell were there, as promised, at desks in the crowded basement room just outside Kissinger's door, but Matt seldom saw them. Bothwell hinted that he was often away working on some special Presidential project.

Matt's work assignments usually came from Kissinger via Larry Eagleburger or in memoranda from the NSC Staff Secretary, a woman who operated a kind of press-room city desk in the midst of the NSC paper mill on the west side of the third floor. The first assignment memo that came to Matt in his new office asked for suggestions for what the President ought to say about the resumption of the Warsaw talks with the Chinese if he was asked at a press conference at the end of January. The China Lobby was raising hell about that decision. Nixon and the boys in the West Wing needed a statement that would mollify the Lobby's pro-Taiwan conservatives, but would keep the door open for broader negotiations with the Chinese later.

Matt drafted a page for the President's press-conference briefing book:

> Q: Mr. President, you were consulted by President Johnson before he agreed to a resumption of negotiations with Communist China, were you not? Did you concur in Mr. Johnson's decision to authorize our ambassador to Warsaw to resume talks with the People's Republic of China?
>
> A: Yes, I did. As you know, for years those talks have been related to settling the old questions— the very old questions—which have prevented a formal end to the Korean War. I see no reason to abandon that effort.
>
> But neither President Johnson nor I contemplated a major change in policy toward mainland China at this time. Such a change will have to wait until there are some changes on their side.

Matt attached a note to the Q-and-A:

> Mr. President:
>   This response should mollify the China Lobby, but I doubt that it is a helpful signal to the leaders of the People's Republic of China.
>   Their offer to President Johnson was extraordinary, considering that troops, ships and aircraft of our country are ranged close to China's southeastern border, in active combat with China's client, North Viet Nam.
>   Some top leaders of the P.R.C. oppose any overtures to the United States. Chou En-lai and others have gone out on a limb in offering

resumed talks in Warsaw. If they are rebuffed or
ignored by you, the Lin Piao element may be
able to convince Mao that he appears to the
world to be a rejected suitor and he will back
away.
   I would recommend this answer:
   The proposal to resume the Warsaw talks is
an important one, not to be ignored or rejected.
By agreeing to talk, President Johnson reaffirmed
a long-standing policy of this country, and I joined
with him. Talking about our areas of agreement
and disagreement with any other nation can only
bring the world closer to peace. My administration
is always going to be for such talks.
                                        Matthew Thompson

Matt's route to the President was always through the
National Security Council apparatus. His question-and-
answer briefing paper and memorandum went by messenger to the NSC paper mill, and because it was intended to
be seen by the President, it was routed to Lawrence
Eagleburger to be included in Henry Kissinger's evening
reading.
   The next morning Eagleburger went through Kissinger's
briefcase, culling the pile of papers the professor had
looked at the night before. Matt's original press-conference
answer was endorsed in Kissinger's cryptic scrawl: *OK for
PC briefing book.* The memorandum was marked only
with a question mark, so Eagleburger carried it into
Kissinger's office.
   "Is this memo to go to the President?" he asked Kissinger.
   "What's that?"
   "The memo Matthew Thompson wrote about the
Warsaw-talks question. You put a question mark on it last
night."
   "Yes, I remember the problem with it. That will hopelessly
confuse our fearless leader. We can't send that in. Nixon
wants to get the right wing off his back, and the Thompson
boy's original answer does that. All that guesswork

about Chou En-lai will only lead to a lot of hand
wringing upstairs. Where does Thompson get that stuff,
anyway?''

Eagleburger shrugged.

''Find out what he reads about China. Perhaps you had
better select some China reading for me now, anyway. If
we do anything with China, I'm going to have to master
the subject. Maybe Professor Fairbanks will give you a
reading list. Throw away Thompson's memo. It is more
than Richard Nixon can handle.''

That same day, an NSC paper-mill messenger delivered
to Matt a copy of a State Department cable from the U.S.
Embassy in The Netherlands:

1243 24 JAN 69 AVBIM 1739344 WIP
SEC STATE ROGERS
WASHINGTON
URGENT
MORRELL, CHARGÉ
THE HAGUE
   UNIMPEACHABLE DUTCH GOVERNMENT SOURCE
ADVISES PEOPLE'S REPUBLIC OF CHINA CHARGÉ
D'AFFAIRES (NAME TO FOLLOW) THIS MORNING
DEFECTED AND WILL SEEK POLITICAL ASYLUM IN
USA.
   DEFECTOR IN DUTCH CUSTODY. NO DIRECT
USA CONTACT HAS TAKEN PLACE.
   DUTCH INQUIRING FOR USA POSITION.
   URGENTLY REQUIRE INSTRUCTIONS.
                                        MORRELL

Almost at once Matt was summoned to Kissinger's
inelegant basement office. As he waited for Kissinger to
return from a meeting, Matt wondered why the professor
preferred this austere underground room to the spacious
suites in the old Executive Office Building. The basement
was like a busy Western Union office, cable machines
clattering, people coming and going in a hurry. Food

smells seeped from the kitchen of the White House Mess next door. Desks were arranged for staff workers in rows in the open bay, so close together that privacy was impossible.

A tall, thin young man in a gray suit came in from the basement hallway and held the door open. As he waited he grimaced at his colleagues at the desks, arching his eyebrows and rolling his eyes. In a moment Henry Kissinger stumped through the doorway and into the narrow aisle that led to his office door at the west side of the NSC room. As he passed Matt Thompson's chair Kissinger muttered, "Come on" in a deep voice. Matt looked at the thin man in the gray suit for verification of the mumbled invitation and was nodded toward Kissinger's door. "Better you than me," the thin man said laconically.

Matt stood inside Kissinger's door while the professor leafed through a stack of telephone slips and cables. Finally, Kissinger looked at him impatiently. "So, close the door and sit down. We need to talk about China. What do we do about the defector at The Hague?"

"Get him asylum somewhere else? Give him back? I don't know." Matt shrugged. "If we take him, the Chinese are going to be bitterly unhappy."

"If we turn him away, we are cruel and heartless at best. At worst we are soft on Communism. Do you think that tower of jelly upstairs—the President—can take that kind of press reaction?" Kissinger blushed and looked out his high window at the sky.

He's reminding himself that he can't talk about Nixon derisively because he thinks I'm a Nixon loyalist, Matt realized. "Would the President be willing to take some heat if it led to fruitful negotiations?" Matt asked.

"Everything you say is a question, Mr. Thompson." Kissinger turned back to look at him. "Could I just have your advice, as succinctly as possible?"

"Sure. I favor negotiating a refuge for the defector with some other country."

"And if that can't be done?"

"Then inform the Dutch that we decline. Let them take responsibility for him. At the same time, send word to

China through Warsaw or some other channel that we denied the man asylum because we desire improved relations."

Kissinger nodded slowly. "Very neat. But it may be too late for all of that. Look what that ninny Rogers has done!" Kissinger tossed a short cable at Matt's edge of the desk.

1621 Z 24 JAN 69 AARU 1739344 BB
MORRELL, CHARGÉ
THE HAGUE
URGENT
ROGERS, SEC. STATE
INFORM DUTCH ASYLUM DECISION FORTHCOMING SOONEST. CONTACT WITH DEFECTOR AUTHORIZED. CABLE NAME, RANK, BIOGRAPHY AND CONTENT OF CONTACT.

                                              ROGERS

"He is quickly painting us into a corner. The fool has no talent for this kind of thing, of course. That is obvious. And your friend upstairs is only worried about what Barry Goldwater will say. I will make your suggestion to him and we will see."

That day Matt Thompson's work assignments left him little time to think about the Chinese defector. The President was determined to rejuvenate NATO during his February trip to Europe, and Matt had responsibility for soliciting policy proposals from Defense, State, and the CIA, circulating the best of them for comment, proposing new NATO policy to Kissinger, and preparing a briefing book for the President to get him ready for his day at NATO.

When he went home that evening, however, Matt found a long letter at his apartment, postmarked Houston, Texas, and signed by the Hong Kong industrialist, Hung Wailang. Matt tossed his coat and briefcase on the couch and immediately read the letter through; by the end of the first page it was evident that it had been written by Teng Shan-li, and perhaps had been reviewed word for word by Premier Chou himself, although the language was guarded. It read:

My dear Matthew Thompson,

All who value your friendship rejoice that President Richard M. Nixon has seen fit to include you among his trusted advisers. Many of my friends have heard this good news and feel it can only be an omen of warmer relations between the United States and Asian people. We feel your keen love for our part of the world.

May I presume to mention several facts to you?

Not everyone sees the United States as a potential friend. Within my own circle of acquaintances there are two views of where China's best interests lie. One view is that America is coming to recognize the futility of the war in Viet Nam. Your President Nixon has said many things recently which confirm this view. You seem to have a good, peaceful intent toward China.

The other faction, however, has long seen Russia as its best potential friend, in spite of her past mistakes. The people in this group, however, have been less persuasive recently because of Russia's invasion of Czechoslovakia last August.

In October, as a result, America's friends were able to be convincing that some overture should be made, and you know about that. Warsaw is a good place to begin, next month.

But the differences of view persist, and it would be very desirable for the United States to support its friends with tangible gestures between now and mid-February. Matters now rest in a very delicate equilibrium.

All of your friends here join me in congratulations and best wishes for a successful experience as an adviser to the President of the United States, Mr. Richard M. Nixon.

With regards,
Hung

Matthew put the letter in his desk and locked the drawer. It seemed clear to him that the problem of asylum for the defector was of critical importance.

In the morning, as he was drafting a memorandum for Kissinger about the defector, Matt was summoned to the President's informal office on the second floor of the Executive Office Building. A Secret Service agent sitting at a bare desk outside the door waved Matt in. The first room, a conference room sparsely furnished with a table and six chairs, was empty. Matt could hear the rumble of voices beyond a large door in the far wall so he walked to it and knocked. In a moment William Rogers, the Secretary of State, opened the door.

"Yes?" Rogers said.

"I'm Matt Thompson. I was sent for."

Rogers turned and said, "Mr. Thompson."

"Have him come in," Nixon said from deep in the room.

Rogers smiled and held the door open.

Nixon was seated in the far left corner of the long room in a deep easy chair. Matt recognized it as the chair that had been in Nixon's room at the law office. Kissinger sat on the long couch against the right wall.

"Come in, Matt," Nixon called. "We are talking about that damn Chinaman in Holland."

"Yes, sir."

"Bill Rogers has just received a protest note from the P.R.C., by way of the Pakistanis. The Chinese say they will view asylum as an unfriendly act. It's a very blunt note," Nixon said. "Sit there by Henry."

"Do the Dutch still have him?" Matt asked.

"Yes," William Rogers said. He sat in a spindly wooden chair by a small table along the end wall, his legs crossed.

"The Dutch have hidden the fellow in a safe house and he's under heavy guard. They are asking us for a yes-or-no answer by tomorrow," Rogers added. Rogers' suit cost him $500, Matt reflected, and the shoes another $200; even his haircut looked expensive.

"I was just writing you a background memorandum about what the China watchers are saying," Matt said to Nixon. "It may bear on this."

"What is the point of it?" Kissinger said unpleasantly.

"That the Chinese leadership is deeply divided between an anti-American element led by Lin Piao and the military on the one hand, and a pragmatic group led by Chou En-lai which favors better relations with the United States and the West. Since the Russian invasion of Czechoslovakia last fall the rabid anti-Americans have lost Mao's ear. I don't think it was mere coincidence that President Johnson was offered a renewal of the Warsaw talks sixty days later. But the struggle goes on and Mao still plays the factions off against each other. This defector could be the cause of real trouble for Chou En-lai."

Rogers was shaking his head. "Mr. President, I have to disagree. The experts think that there is very little division in China. Mao runs things, and it's a monolith. My experts think the Warsaw-talk invitation was only a gambit to mask the bad publicity they were getting from the Red Guards right then. My concern is that we might send a wrong signal to the free world if we turn this fellow away. What will political asylum mean if we turn him back to the Communists?"

"Turn him back?" Kissinger challenged. "I thought the Dutch had him."

"They do," Rogers replied curtly.

"The Chinese will certainly be offended if he's given asylum," Matt said. "His defection has cost them much face."

"If we turn him away," Nixon said reflectively, "what will Goldwater and Murphy and that bunch say? I'll be accused of selling out a human being to godless Chinese Communism, won't I?"

"Probably," Kissinger grunted. "There is some cost either way."

"If it comes down to a question of American domestic politics, perhaps that can be explained to the Chinese," Matt said.

"Who is going to explain it?" Rogers said skeptically. "We have virtually no means of communicating with them."

"What about Edgar Snow?" Matt asked. "He is friendly with the hierarchy there, isn't he?"

Rogers and Nixon both shook their heads. "We can't use him," Nixon said flatly.

Matthew Thompson felt frustrated to the bursting point. He knew so much more than these men, yet how could he convince them? He had a channel—he was a channel—to communicate with Chou En-lai himself! But if he told them that now, it would all evaporate, he was sure. He would lose his place in the White House instantly. They were going to make a major mistake for purely domestic political reasons and he was going to have to let them make it. He could write to Teng and try to explain, but he sensed that Teng and even Chou himself might be in grave jeopardy if the defector were given American asylum.

"Henry," Nixon said finally, "I'm afraid we've got to take him in."

Rogers nodded. Kissinger shrugged.

"Mr. President," Matt began, "coupled with that press-conference answer last week—about no change in our policy—we will be telling the Chinese that there are no doors open here. I really wonder if that is what we want to be telling them."

"That press-conference answer was prepared by you," Nixon said defensively. "Isn't that correct, Henry?"

Kissinger looked uncomfortable. "Well, there were several draft answers of which that was the best, Mr. President."

"The one I preferred, Mr. President," Matt began, "was one—"

"All of that is behind us," Rogers interrupted. "There

was nothing wrong with that answer. It correctly restated our policy, and everyone is comfortable with it. The question is whether or not we grant asylum to the defector."

"He comes in," Nixon said with finality. "Does he have enough rank to know anything? Can the CIA get anything out of him?"

Rogers nodded. "The Dutch think he may have had an active espionage assignment. He says he's an officer in the PLA—in their army."

"So, have the CIA look after him," Nixon said to Rogers, "and be careful about how his defection is announced. There's no sense in offending the Chinese any more than is necessary. Henry, I want you to tell Murphy and Goldwater that this could have fallen either way, but I went along with them on this and I want some credit for it. You just put it to them."

"Very well," Kissinger growled.

"And," Nixon continued, "someone has to try to explain all of this to Mao. Who can do that?"

"What about the Pakistanis?" Matt asked. "That was their channel for the protest. And how about the French? The P.R.C. has an active embassy in Paris."

"Stoessel can do it when he meets with their ambassador in Warsaw next month," Rogers suggested.

"I'm not sure there will be a meeting there next month," Matt said.

"Why the hell not?" Nixon asked angrily. He glared at Matt.

"It's my guess that Mao will call it off to get your attention."

"Oh, I doubt that," Rogers said soothingly. "They would merely appear intransigent if they retaliated that way. I wouldn't worry about that."

"I suggest," said Kissinger, "that we have Stoessel explain that you had no alternative, given the realities of our domestic politics. They should understand that."

* * *

On February 18, 1969, the Chinese unilaterally cancelled the Warsaw talks. Five days later Nixon, Rogers, Kissinger, and their entourage left Washington for a tour of the Lowlands, France, Germany, Italy, and England. Along the way they were scheduled to meet with NATO, the European Economic Community, and the Pope.

For several days Matt thought Kissinger would drop him from the traveling staff. The cancellation of the Warsaw talks was seen by the Washington press as a failure of American foreign policy, and Matt knew that his sin was that his unpopular prediction had been correct. He was the messenger who bore bad news, and Kissinger was obviously displeased with him.

What other effect he'd had on Sino-American relations was unclear. He had sent a long handwritten letter to Teng via Hung, explaining the origin of the President's press-conference answer, along with the text of Matt's memo to Nixon urging the alternative answer. He also included a near-verbatim account of the meeting in Nixon's EOB office with Rogers and Kissinger as an explanation of why the defector had been granted asylum. Matt's last paragraph said:

> I cannot say whether the President fails to realize what is going on in China or whether he knows but fails to understand. Rogers is obviously misled by the State Department "experts" who are egregiously wrong. Kissinger is poorly informed. And I lack the credibility to persuade them. If the talks are cancelled, as I predicted, perhaps they will begin to believe me. Cancellation could take some of the pressure off my Chinese friends too, couldn't it? I will urge that General de Gaulle be enlised as a conduit between the two countries. The President will see him in Paris for several days. Let us see whether my advice is heeded.

On February 21, Larry Eagleburger called to ask a question about the NATO briefing book.

"Am I going to Europe?" Matt asked him.

"Are you going?" Eagleburger laughed. "Of course you're going. Why would you ask a question like that?"

Twenty-six

Colonel Alexander Haig had been sitting in a straight chair at his employer's desk listening to Henry Kissinger for thirty-five minutes, occasionally nodding in agreement, shaking his head in wonder and amazement, and providing a minimal vocal counterpoint. "Sure" and "Really" and "I agree" were all that was required to punctuate the Assistant for National Security Affairs' description of the State Department's mistakes in preparing the President's briefing books for Europe.

When Kissinger seemed to grow impatient and uninterested in what he was saying to Haig—he had, in fact, said it all before—Haig took a sheaf of papers from his attaché case and held them on his lap. "We may have a problem with our China expert, young Mr. Thompson," Haig said with an edge to his voice. "The British have a file on him and they tell our intelligence people that Thompson has close ties to a Chinaman who is a known P.R.C. sympathizer." Haig leafed through his pages. "Hung Wai-lang. An industrialist. Thompson has stayed at Lang's house in Hong Kong."

"Hung," Kissinger said.

Haig looked at him inquiringly.

"Hung," the professor repeated, "not Lang. Lang is his given name, Hung is his family name."

"Right. I knew that. It's the same in Viet Nam."

"No," said Kissinger, "it's the other way around in Viet Nam. Anyway, do they have anything specific about our Mr. Thompson?"

"This Hung is a client of Thompson's former law office, and the kid has done legal work for him. Last year he flew somewhere in Hung's plane; they aren't sure where. It may have been to China. He has phoned and cabled Hung."

"That is also Richard Nixon's law firm. Do they have anything recent?"

"No."

"Well, I'd like to know more about Mr. Hung and his connection to the P.R.C. And perhaps, while you're having Hoover do all that other listening, the FBI should listen in to Thompson too. Maybe he will phone this Hung. Maybe all of this is evidence that Richard Nixon has a back channel to Chou En-lai."

"Do you still want Thompson to go on the trip?" Haig asked.

"Yes. Put him somewhere that Nixon will see him, and Allen, too. We may as well get credit for being obedient to instructions."

The White House
February 20, 1969
Memorandum for the President
Re: A *new China conduit*
In your meetings with President Charles de Gaulle it may be possible to enlist his help in creating a reliable channel of communication with the People's Republic of China. France and the P.R.C. maintain active embassies with well-connected ambassadors. Huang Cheng, in Paris, is an old soldier who is close to Chou En-lai and other Chinese leaders.
Talking points might include:

(1) The United States would like the P.R.C. to
   know that we seek a new and normal
   relationship;

(2) Talks need not be limited to Warsaw, nor to
   the ambassador level. The President is
   prepared to designate a special emissary;

(3) The French would be an acceptable third party
   through which to communicate;

(4) The United States intends to withdraw
   substantial numbers of troops from Viet Nam.

France is due to send a new ambassador to
Peking shortly (to replace a man who has been
reassigned).

China-watchers indicate the likelihood that the
French conduit would be satisfactory to the P.R.C.

                              Matthew Thompson

It was nearly 10 P.M. when Matt Thompson was
summoned from the Hôtel Crillon room he shared with
Henry Kissinger's advance man. He was directed to Richard
Nixon's lavish corner suite, overlooking the Place de la
Concorde. The elevator and hallway approaches on the
sixth floor of the hotel were heavily guarded by the
French. But the doorway itself was the jurisdiction of the
U.S. Secret Service's tall, burly young men, who seemed
out of place in the hallway of a hotel in Paris.

Nixon wore a blue bathrobe over the trousers to his suit
and a white shirt. He had on highly polished leather
slippers instead of highly polished shoes, and he was
tieless, but otherwise he appeared to be as formal as
ever.

Nixon went to business at once, without greeting or
salutation. "I talked to De Gaulle today about China,"
Nixon said. He had eaten dinner from a room service table
which had been pushed against a wall. He motioned Matt
to the couch and slumped into a wingback nearby.

"I talked to him at the Petit Trianon without Henry for
nearly two hours, with only his interpreter there. I'm
convinced De Gaulle wants to be helpful. I ran through

your talking points and he said their new ambassador will
deliver the message.''

"Very good, sir.''

"Your memo was excellent. I want your China memos
direct from now on. Don't send them through Henry; just
hand them to Rose for me. I was glad Henry wasn't there
with De Gaulle, because he tends to throw cold water on
our China opening, as I'm sure you've noticed. The
problem is that China isn't his idea, you know. He's like
that with some other projects, too. The trick is to get him
to feel that it is his initiative and that history will record it
that way. You and I know that in this case our *Foreign
Affairs* article and your long memorandum on China will
establish for historians that the President intended to change
our policy toward China long before he ever met Henry
Kissinger. But if history writes it a different way, that's all
right too. Some will say we want the China card for our
game with the Russians. You know and I know that kind of
power politics is too simplistic in the real world, but they
will write it that way. The Russians will always be a
problem; the best we can hope for with them is equilibrium. But China is different. What is important is that we
put the new policy in place and have a new relationship
with China. Peace in the world is what is important, isn't
it?''

"Yes, sir.''

"If we restore peace and an equilibrium among the great
powers there will be credit enough for everyone, you see.
Henry doesn't seem to understand that; he is so damn petty
and jealous about such things; we may have to resort to a
certain amount of—artifice, shall we say?—to get him to
work balls-out on something like this. He's afraid of
failure, you know. It's a Jewish trait, I've noticed.
They would rather not try than try with a possibility of
failure.''

Matt nodded, but he wondered where this monologue
was headed.

"On the other hand, I relish the risk. In international
affairs there is never a sure thing. You must just take your

chances and press on. It takes courage. We are going to have to give Henry some backbone along with the feeling that he's going to get the credit; then he'll work like hell. You can help me with that. Tell him how the world is going to applaud his bold China initiative, why don't you?''

Is the professor that gullible? Matt wondered rhetorically. Nixon hunched forward in his chair, holding the fountain pen he had taken from his shirt pocket.

''You can tell him that the China watchers in the great universities have confidence in him. They probably wonder about the President, but Henry is a fellow academic and they are sure he will do the right thing. Tell him that. Maybe you can leak a story to Joe Alsop or someone about how Henry is courageously undertaking a secret, profoundly important project that can rock the world. No. No, you'd better not. Then the press will swarm around Henry and he'll tell them about everything he is working on. He's terrible at keeping secrets. At times, I'm afraid, he shows very bad judgment. No, don't encourage the press. He loves to have them sucking around.''

Nixon shook his head in frustration. Matt thought: He knows I can't peddle this stuff to Kissinger. They are competitors for history's judgment already, and everyone on the staff will be a witness for one of them or the other. We're all going to be suborned to perjury by both of them before it's over, especially if the China project is a success.

Nixon flashed his instant smile and tipped his head from side to side a little. The smile disappeared as soon as he spoke again, but it had served to draw the dividing line. He had finished with talk of China and Henry. ''Well, are you enjoying Paris? Is this your first time here?'' the President asked paternally.

''Yes, sir, it's my first time. Actually, I haven't seen much except from the car in the motorcade coming in. I've been pretty busy.''

''Well, that motorcade went pretty fast; the French do that to screw up all the demonstrators. And it works. We can learn from them. Tomorrow, take some time off. I'll be with De Gaulle all day. There's no reason why you can't see the city. Take off and get a feel of it. The people are wonderful.''

"Thank you. I'd like that.''

"I envy you. Ah, to be young and in Paris for the first time. It's a very romantic place.''

"Yes, sir.''

The smile appeared and disappeared instantly. Nixon heaved himself awkwardly to his feet without warning; it was a kind of standing-broad-jump motion, his head lowered, then raised, his arms moving back, then forward one ahead of the other—all badly executed. For a moment Matt thought the President was going to fall back into the chair, but just before Matt could start to rescue him, Nixon pushed his right hand against the arm of his chair, swerved to his left, and broke the inertia. He searched Matt's face for a sign of a reaction to his ungainliness, saw none, and decided that nothing need be said about it.

Nixon gave a laughing bark, then another. "But don't get the French clap, now. I have had no personal experience, of course, but I hear that's no joke. I have friends who tell me about things like that.''

Matt smiled weakly and stood. "I'll see what I can do with Henry on China,'' he said to bring the talk to a close.

"We just can't have Henry dragging his feet,'' Nixon said. "Have a good day tomorrow. I envy you. I envy you.''

The concierge at the Crillon assured Matt that he could walk to the Louvre "without too much exertion.'' Three blocks from the hotel, Matt stopped on the rue de Rivoli to look in the window of a store that offered antique maps. He became aware of a sudden movement in a doorway halfway back down the block. A Secret Service man on the airplane had cautioned him that the French might be watching and listening to the President's staff, but Matt had assumed people like Kissinger and Haldeman would be their targets. Matt turned and walked ahead to the next corner. As he entered the intersecting street, he saw a middle-aged and balding man in a tan trench coat behind him. The man carried a rolled newspaper. Midway in the next block to the north, Matt moved quickly into a small arcade and entered the second shop. In a minute he watched the man with the newspaper urgently peering into the shop. When their eyes met, the man turned and hastily left the arcade.

These French aren't very good at this, Matt thought with some amusement. He left the arcade, turned right, and walked on, glancing back occasionally until he came to the Louvre.

Inside the main entrance of the Louvre, a Frenchwoman about sixty years of age came close behind him and said, "Monsieur Thompson, is it not?"

Her voice was firm, and her English was lightly accented with traces of French. Matt thought her cadences suggested an Oriental language, but her appearance was distinctly French. Matt was tempted to turn away and run; he immediately assumed that the woman had some connection with the man with the rolled newspaper. Instead, he looked at the woman's face closely for a moment; he wanted to be able to describe her to the Secret Service. He noted that her nose was long and fleshy, rising to a pale, flat forehead, black eyes a little sunken, dark pouches over sallow cheeks, a wide mouth, no makeup. Her most striking feature was her thick mass of hair, coarse, gray, streaked with black, gathered severely in a large bun.

She wore a heavy black coat with a worn brown fur collar, low black shoes, and brown knit gloves. She might have been a concierge or an office clerk or someone's middle-aged wife, out for an afternoon at the Louvre to see the paintings.

Before he decided what to do, she moved around in front of him, faced him, and laid her gloved hand lightly on his arm. The foyer was not empty. An aging conces-

sionaire in a blue uniform sat on a stool near the door, one
foot resting on the floor. Eight or nine people were putting
on coats and gloves, turning up collars, winding mufflers
around their necks.

"Monsieur Thompson, I am Madame DeLisle. I am a
friend of Hung Wai-lang in Hong Kong. He has told me so
much about you."

"I see," he said lamely. It was all wildly improbable. It
was inconceivable that this woman had anything at all in
common with Hung, he of the elegant ridge-top house and
the fabulous office. "How do I know you know him?"
Matt blurted.

The woman smiled. "He has told me about the emerald
in the little wooden box. Does that convince you?"

"The . . . my God! How do you know about . . . ? Who
told him?" Matt looked around to see if anyone had
overheard the woman.

"I have told you. Our mutual friend has told me. His
friends told him. Now, if you are satisfied, I would like
you to come with me for a short time. You will be quite
safe, I assure you." The hand on his arm increased its
pressure.

"We have a car and we will take a drive. That black
one, there."

A Citroën sedan waited at the curb near the bicycle
racks. Nearer, Matt saw that the driver was the balding
man in the tan trench coat. Matt slowed as the man turned
to look at him. He felt the woman's hand tighten on his
arm.

The woman's reference to the emerald had destroyed
Matt Thompson's defenses. No one knew about the emerald except Chou En-lai and Li-fa and Teng. When he'd
returned from China, Matt had wrapped the stone and its
wooden box and put them in an otherwise empty safe-
deposit box in the Bank of Manhattan, safe and forgotten.
No one could even trace the safe-deposit box to him. It
had been rented by a tall young man who gave his name as
Marco Harrison, his address a post-office box at the
Chelsea branch post office.

Matt had been of several minds about the jewel when he got home from the trip to Peking. No matter how he had turned the question in his mind he could not see how the valuable stone gave the Chinese a hold over him. So long as the stone remained in the bank box it was no threat to him. If he needed to sell it, there might be a second order of problems, but he could face those when it was necessary. Knowing he had a $140,000 nest egg hidden away had actually changed Matt's life more than a little. He thought of it as financial ballast. He no longer considered that he lived from paycheck to paycheck, even when he depleted his bank balance to $12.81, as he had in January. There was always the emerald if he needed it.

The Frenchwoman sat next to him in the backseat of the Citroën. The trench-coated driver constantly searched the rearview mirror as he zigzagged his way across Paris, generally moving east. Several times they crossed the River Seine; then at last they paralleled the river to the southeast. Before long Matt identified a village named Limeil Brevannes by a sign on a factory wall. There they took a back road through two tiny farm villages.

The woman broke the silence to say something to the driver in rapid French. He grunted and turned on his headlights. After a quarter of a mile he turned into a gravel lane which crossed poplar-bordered meadows toward a large brick house which was a red cube, as tall as it was wide, and flat-roofed. The second-story windows were hidden by heavy wooden shutters, but the first level was brightly lit. As the car pulled into a large and carefully raked gravel parking area, the front door of the house opened.

"Please alight and go into the house," the woman said calmly. "A gentleman there would like to speak with you. He is a very kind man." She sat relaxed, her gloved hands folded on her lap, evidently relieved that she had delivered Matt safely.

"What is this place?" he asked.

"I do not know what it is called. But you have friends here."

Matt instantly thought of Li-fa. Was it even remotely possible that she was inside? He opened the car door and walked briskly toward the house, without looking back, until he heard the car's engine start. The Citroën made a U-turn, passing between Matt and the house, and went back out the lane the way it had come. Matt noticed that the man had turned off his headlights. The woman still sat behind him looking straight ahead. It was about 4 P.M. and would be getting dark before long.

The front door of the house stood open, unattended. Inside, the floor of the foyer was carpeted with fine Oriental rugs and seemed bright and inviting. A carpeted stairway rose at the left side, beyond an archway which led to the living room.

"Come in, Mr. Thompson, come in," a man said from the living room. If Li-fa were there, he thought, she would have greeted him at the door. He wondered briefly how she might have acted; would she have kissed him or allowed him to embrace her? No, he decided, she would always bow and keep her distance in the presence of others.

Matt walked to the archway, from which he could see the entire living room. A stout old Chinese man in a gray Mao jacket and gray pants sat at the far end of a couch, his short legs levered out, his slippered feet barely touching the floor. He had thick gray hair which was carefully combed to the side, and evidently pomaded. The old man's facial features were all broad, his cheeks fat, his chins a cascade all the way to his high collar.

"Come in, sir. Please sit here in this chair. Will you have tea?" The old man's voice was deep and full.

Between the couch and the upholstered chair to which the man pointed, a small table held two covered teacups, a plate heaped with wrapped Chinese candy, and a plate holding a pyramid of tangerines.

"Thank you," Matt said, crossing to the chair. The room was distinctly European except for the tea table, which was pure Chinese. "I am glad that you know who I am, honored sir. May I know who you are?"

The old man waved a thick hand back and forth in front

of his smiling face. "That is of no importance, Mr. Thompson. If I must have a name, you may call me General Chiao." With his index finger he traced a complex Chinese character in the air. "Chiao—teacher. I am here to be your teacher. And once I was a general in the army, so that is a good enough name."

It was unusual to encounter an old military man who spoke English so well, Matt reflected; perhaps he had been educated in the mission school. "You speak English fluently," he said. "Did you learn English when you were young?"

"Yes. I have asked you to come here so that I may tell you of a serious situation that is developing in the north— along the border between China and Russia. It is vital that you know about this."

Matt nodded. There was to be no small talk about missionaries.

"The geography is fairly simple," the General continued. "The Amur River runs generally east and west and is the border. Then the border turns south where the Amur and Ussuri rivers join." He traced the rivers in the air with his finger. "The border then follows the Ussuri for some distance south, then crosses the middle of Lake Khanka at a place north of Vladivostok. The Ussuri is broad, shallow in places, and has many low islands. The islands are China's, and some are occupied by our soldiers. But also, some are claimed by the Russians."

Matt took a tangerine and peeled it; the skin came away from the fruit easily, and he ate the sections absentmindedly as he listened to the General.

"Since 1965, since shortly after Brezhnev came to power, there has been trouble along this border, especially along the Ussuri River. For about three years, the Russians have provoked nasty little battles between their border forces and ours. They have steadily built up the strength of their army and air force in the border area. They have gone from twenty divisions to nearly forty, along with rockets and even nuclear weapons."

"Have there been real battles?" Matt asked. He could not recall reading about border fighting.

"Thus far, no shooting. But patrols have engaged in hand-to-hand fighting, and on their side there is much maneuvering, with loudspeakers and insults and feints with troop movements, attempting to provoke the People's Liberation Army. Much of this action is at Chen Pao Island, which the Russians falsely claim; they call it Damansky Island."

"What do you believe the Russians are trying to do?" Matt wiped his hands on a napkin from the tea table.

"Several years ago Chairman Mao said plainly that the Russian claims to territory along this border are false. Recently he has told the Russians that there can be no settlement of any disputed border claims unless and until the Soviet military withdraws from all the disputed areas."

"What area was he talking about—those river islands?"

"Oh, no. Chairman Mao said five or six years ago that the old Tsars and the Soviets have been grabbing our territory for years. He said there was an 'unsettled account' between China and Russia which involved all the area east of Lake Baikal, including Khabarovsk, Vladivostok, and the Kamchatka Peninsula. It is a large area that is at issue. There were some negotiations after he said that, but the Russians held to the old, unfair land-grab treaties, so the talks collapsed."

"So Russia sees those Chinese claims as a threat and they are building up their border forces?"

"The Russians become ever stronger and more belligerent. It is only a matter of a few days before things may escalate into a serious shooting conflict. The People's Republic of China takes a very serious view of the Russian border aggressions."

"What is to be done, General?"

"Why, the Russians must withdraw! There is no alternative."

"Otherwise, there will be fighting?"

"Yes. There has been fighting. There will be shooting."

"Do you think the United States should do anything?"

"Perhaps someone should warn the Russians that China will fight."

"Perhaps, but that can hardly be the role of the United States, can it? We have no official contact with China, do we?"

"Perhaps the United States can say to Russia what a serious view the United States would take of any border war by the Russians against China. That would surely be helpful in many ways."

"Yes, I see. Perhaps that could be said."

It was evident that the General had finished his lecture. He sat quietly, his hands folded in his lap, for a count of ten. Matt said nothing, waiting.

"Will you have more tea, Mr. Thompson?" the General said. "Another fruit?"

"No, thank you. The fruit and tea were delicious."

The General unfolded his hands and smiled. "I am very glad you were able to come for this visit, Mr. Thompson," he said abruptly. "Your many friends in China send you their sincere regards."

Matt stood. The General did not. "Thank you, General Chiao. It has been very worthwhile."

"Yes, I hope so. Now there is a car waiting for you outside to take you to the Hôtel Crillon. You should be there in time for your supper."

Twenty-seven

• MARCH, 1969 •

At 2 A.M. on the morning of March 2, Matt Thompson was awakened by a telephone call from the duty officer in the White House situation room. Matt had been deeply asleep when the telephone rang, and he had trouble finding the light switch that controlled the hotel lamp; at last he located a push button just off the night table, a foot down the cord. Matt reached for the black telephone and instantly was connected to the national security nerve center.

"Mr. Thompson, I'm sorry to wake you," the voice on the black Signal Corps phone said routinely. "This is Scott Davis in the situation room."

"You sound close by," Matt said thickly. "Where are you? Washington?"

"Yes, sir. Something has just come in that Mr. Eagleburger said I should give you."

"Okay. Wait a minute." Matt retrieved the note pad and pen he'd left on the other twin bed with his NATO files. Since he'd been at the White House, he had taken only one other call from a night duty officer in the situation room, and he was more than a little excited by the urgency of the event. At home he did not have a White House phone, as many staff people did, and duty officers would be chary of conveying secret information on his ordinary Chesapeake and Potomac telephone line.

"All right," he said. "I think I'm awake now."

"Mr. Thompson, the Russians are saying that units of the Chinese People's Liberation Army have crossed into Soviet territory at a place called Damansky Island in the Ussuri River north of Vladivostok. Russian troops have engaged the Chinese."

"Huh? Okay. Does it say if they are actually shooting at each other?"

"It says there are casualties on both sides."

"So, I guess they are shooting. Anything else?"

"The CIA will have satellite photos of the Damansky area at eleven hundred hours your time. I can give you the number of their interpretation people if you will want to call for that information then. NSA has the layout of the battle communications on both sides, and we have transcripts in translation."

Matt wondered if a picture of Chinese and Russian soldiers shooting at each other on a sandbar would really add anything. "No, I don't need any of that. Thanks," he said.

After he'd hung up and turned out the light, Matt wondered what to do with this information. If Eagleburger knew about it, then Kissinger did, or he surely would when he woke up. The Professor could decide whether the President needed to know. Nixon would see an account of it in his daily intelligence briefing anyway, for sure. So why had Eagleburger, who was in a room a hundred feet from Matt's room in Claridge's Hotel, told the duty officer in the situation room in Washington to call him?

The Chinese were clearly worried about those forty Russian divisions. That was the only possible explanation for their elaborate charade in Paris with the DeLisles and the little General. The Chinese were probably sorry now that they had chilled things with the United States; they needed someone to scare the Russians off for them. Matt wondered if the Russian report was true; had the Chinese attacked first, escalating the shoving match into a shooting war? General Chiao had strongly hinted that the Chinese planned to attack. Why?

In the face of a larger, better-equipped Russian force, why would Mao and Chou authorize the PLA to attack? Surely, if General Chiao knew of the plan, it had been approved at the highest levels. Was Lin Piao calling the shots? Had he supplanted Chou En-lai at Mao's ear? Why would he want to attack the Russians? It made more sense that the Russians had done the attacking. He would write Henry a memo about the border conflict in the morning, he decided. Perhaps it was an opportunity for Richard Nixon.

Matthew Thompson discovered he could not sleep. England was the last stop on a trip that had taken the President and his retinue across Europe from Brussels to West Berlin, down to Rome, and into and out of eight countries in two weeks. The pace and stimulation of the trip had been exhausting for the President and his people, and the quick series of hotels and government guesthouses had afforded little restful sleep.

Matt arose and put on a sweater and pants, sat at the narrow hotel desk, and composed a memorandum.

For the President:

In the past twelve hours the Russians and the People's Republic of China have fought a military engagement of some kind about 100 miles north of Vladivostok on the Sino-Soviet border.

For years this border has been in dispute, each side claiming the islands in the Ussuri River— even though most of the area is uninhabited and unused.

In the past 3 or 4 years the Russians have increased their army along the border from 20 to about 40 divisions. The Chinese PLA may have as many as a million men in the border area.

China watchers report that the Chinese are *very* concerned about the Russian threat along this northern and northeastern border. The Russians are believed to be better equipped and trained than the Chinese Army opposite them. The Chinese are known to be open to help from the United States or others in deterring the Russians from pressing their military advantage in the region.

The Chinese leaders, especially Chairman Mao Tse-tung, have imposed impossible conditions on any negotiation of a peaceful settlement of the border dispute. They have invested much "face" in making territorial claims in the area. If it develops that the Chinese have attacked the Russians today, "face" is the only rational explanation for their decision to do so, and it is reliably believed that the decision would have been taken at the highest Chinese leadership levels some time ago.

On the other hand, if the Russians attacked, it may represent a major change in their policy with respect to this disputed area. Until now, there have been some fistfights and taunting, pushing and shoving, but both sides have been under orders not to shoot.

The point of all of this is that the Chinese will be looking for help.

If this fight announces a more aggressive Russian policy, the Chinese will resist, and they will be looking for allies within the Communist bloc and outside as well.

There is nothing for the United States to do or say for the moment; we need more information about the extent of the fighting, how it began, etc.

But we should be getting prepared for Chinese overtures. I expect that within 30 days or so we will be hearing from them. Meanwhile, your French-carried message will arrive in Peking.

All parts of our government—especially the State Department—should avoid saying anything about the border dispute or the fighting that would hint

—that we favor the Russians
—that we hope they'll destroy each other
—that we anticipate the Chinese will come to us for help
—that we are indifferent.

Perhaps the White House should say substantially: "We are always concerned about armed conflict, anywhere, anytime, because in the modern world everyone is affected by any war. For that reason, we intend to stay informed about what is taking place on the Sino-Russian border."

Matthew Thompson

On the President's instructions, a Policy Guidance Memorandum was sent from the elaborate communications console on his airplane telling State, Defense, and the rest of the government how to deal with the press concerning the Sino-Soviet border clash.

Jerry Warren, the President's Deputy Press Secretary, issued a mimeographed White House statement on the chartered press plane exactly as Matt had drafted it.

Among her other duties, Glenna Harrison was the keeper of the tickets for the President's box at the Kennedy Center for the Performing Arts. She kept them safe in a locked drawer and served them up only upon written instructions from H. R. Haldeman or the President himself. They were doled out with profound calculation to the people who could do the President the most good. At a given moment they might be bestowed upon a senator whose vote was critical to the success of some piece of Presidential legislation. Such a senator and his lady would be invited to use the box by the President's senatorial lobbyist and his wife, who would act as host and hostess, serve champagne from the President's refrigerator during intermission, and make sure the senator knew why he was there. The box was backed by an anteroom (where the refrigerator was located) which held the White House telephones, coatracks, and extra chairs. There the President's lobbyist and the senator could sit and talk undisturbed while their wives enjoyed the performance. The lobbyist might even use the direct White House telephone to permit the senator to talk personally with the President if that was necessary to gain the senator's commitment of support for the President's position on any upcoming vote in the Senate.

Occasionally, especially when the Congress was in recess, or when the artist or performance did not appeal to the catholic tastes of those with a right of priority to the tickets, Glenna Harrison could claim seats in the President's box for herself.

Shortly after Matt returned from Europe, Glenna arranged what she called a theater party. She bestowed Presidential tickets on Lewis Puller, a young lawyer who worked for the Counsel to the President, and Martin Weinstein, one of Bob Haldeman's efficient minions, both of whom had wives Glenna liked. According to Glenna's agenda, she and Matt Thompson would meet the Pullers and Weinsteins in the President's box, and after the Supremes had performed, everyone would meet at Rive Gauche for dessert and drinks.

Matt drove Glenna's car from her apartment, as he often did. The Chinese border fights continued, at several places along the lines, but there had been no signal from the Chinese to Nixon. As Matt drove he only half-heard Glenna's description of Nixon's unpleasant encounter that day with a Cabinet Room full of black leaders and welfare mothers.

"And there's something new in our place," she continued. "Just yesterday we began to get special FBI reports from J. Edgar Hoover himself for the President. They come in through Colonel Haig."

Haig's name took Matt's total attention. The maneuvers of that ambitious and jittery Army officer had been widely noticed and commented upon, with some humor, by everyone on the Kissinger staff. The man's grim intensity and the obviousness of his effort to become Kissinger's right-hand man had made Haig the butt of the considerable wit of Kissinger's people.

"What FBI stuff does Haig get?" Matt asked skeptically.

"Well, the FBI is tapping some people's telephones— some of them on the White House staff," Glenna said with a tone of confidentiality, "and these are logs that tell who called whom and what they said."

"Huh?" Matt was surprised. "Like who?"

"The names are all coded, you know, but one of them is that smart-aleck writer I can't stand."

"Who, Buchanan?"

"Oh, no, he's nice. William Safire, I mean; I'm sure it's him they're listening to. You can tell from what he says. He's always wisecracking about the President and everyone."

"Are there several taps?"

"Oh, there must be twenty or more. The code names of the staff people are all trees. Some of the others are

reporters with animal code names. One fellow called
Redwood actually telephones Communist China! Imagine!''

"He does?''

"Well, they think he does, but they haven't caught him
at it yet. Another one, Elm, is taking out stewardesses
while his wife and kids are at her mother's. The FBI has
caught him calling up for dates and talking about their
night before and everything.''

"Who is he?'' Matt wheeled into the line waiting to
park in the basement of the Kennedy Center.

"I don't know who Elm is, but I'll bet that pretty soon
I'll be able to figure out who it is from the logs.''

"Why are they doing this?'' Matt wondered out loud.
His mouth tasted leaden. They were tapping his phone! He
tried to think of whom he had called and what he had said.

"I think they are trying to catch people who betray
secrets.''

"When a tree calls an animal, do they talk about
military secrets?'' he asked.

"One of them told about the SALT talks, but most of it
is pretty dull. Even Safire isn't very interesting. He calls
his agent a lot, though. He plans to write a book about the
White House and make a lot of money.''

"Ha! You'd better watch what you say to him. You'll
end up in a book.''

They parked in the basement of the Kennedy Center and
walked toward the elevators. "I wonder why they are
doing that,'' Matt said.

"I told you what I think. It's secrets.''

"There must be more to it than that. Maybe there is
more than one reason.''

"Maybe,'' Glenna conceded.

Matt was trying to remember if he had called Mr. Hung
from his apartment. He wondered when the taps had been
installed. He would have to warn Hung not to call him.
He'd have to do that tonight, somehow. "How long has
this been going on?'' he asked.

"I don't know. There's a big pile of them.''

They had worked their way through the crowd in the

broad concourse that led to the entrance of the concert hall. Most of the audience would be young that night. As they started up the staircase to the mezzanine, Matt noticed three public telephones under the opposite stairway.

When everyone had greeted everyone else and all six were seated in the box, Matt excused himself. In the anteroom he looked at the three White House telephones arrayed on a long table. The White House switchboard could reach Hung Wai-lang in two minutes, but in the morning ten people would know Matt had called Hong Kong.

He walked down to the public telephones and waited until some latecomers had hurried through the lobby area between the staircases.

Matt placed his call to Hung and instructed the operator to charge the call to his father's telephone number in California. As he waited, he could hear the band music and singing seeping through the main doors of the concert hall. The Supremes were singing a medley of old standards which made him think of Whittier High School. It took about ten minutes for his father loyally to agree to pay for the call and for the operator to persuade Hung's secretary to let her employer talk to Matt.

"Hello, Matthew?" Hung's voice was faint and quizzical.

"Mr. Hung, I am calling from a public telephone. Can you hear me?"

"Yes, Matt, I hear you. Are you well?"

"Fine, thank you. Please listen. I must tell you something important. The Federal Bureau of Investigation is listening to my telephone at home." A loud, rolling thunder of applause filled the lobby when someone opened a door at the end of the medley. "Could you hear what I said? It's very noisy here."

"Yes, I hear you. They are listening to your telephone?"

"Yes. You must not call or cable me there. Do you have that?"

"Yes," Hung said. "Are you under suspicion?"

"I don't know; I guess so. I just learned of this an hour ago."

"Very well, I will be careful."
"Goodbye, Mr. Hung."
"Goodbye, Matthew."

When he dropped her at her apartment that night, Glenna Harrison asked, "Is something wrong, Matt?"

"No, I'm fine; just a little tired."

"Weren't those people fun?" she asked.

"Great. I had a good time with them."

"I wonder if you did. You were so glum all evening."

"I'm sorry. I'll go get a night's sleep."

But at his apartment, Matt's eyes were continually drawn to his telephones, one in the kitchen, the other in his bedroom. He felt sure someone in the FBI could hear him as he undressed and brushed his teeth.

The next morning he realized clearly that he had no choice. He could not disconnect the phones, as he was tempted to do. That would be a sure signal that he knew they were tapping him. He wondered, suddenly, if they were also following him. If so, they had seen him phone Hung last night and could trace the call. Glenna hadn't said anyone was being followed, but he must ask her. He would have breakfast at the office; he couldn't eat with that telephone in the kitchen.

At noon in the junior mess, Matt saw a man Angie Cruz had told him about, an Army major who helped run the White House Communications Agency. Matt took his tray to the major's table and sat down.

"Okay if I sit here?" he asked.

"Sure," the major said. He had a folded *Post* next to his tray.

"Major Dienneker, I'm Matt Thompson. You know my secretary, Angie Cruz."

"Yes, she's a fine young woman."

"I should say. You have an interesting job. It's always a mystery to me how you keep everything going so well. Even during foreign trips."

Major Dienneker smiled. "Did you go with him to Europe?"

"Yes, all the way."

"We moved two complete telephone units, leapfrogging ahead of him, you know. They are in containers and fit into a C-130. We just truck them to the hotel and we're in business."

"Remarkable. Do you do all the other stuff too? Tapping and surveillance and all that?"

The major laughed and shook his head. "Oh, no, thank God. The FBI and the NSA do all of that."

"I've always wondered: when they tap a phone, is there a bug in the phone or what?"

"It depends. Here in Washington, if the phone is here in town, the FBI can just go to the phone company and hook up there. They have some special auditing rooms at Chesapeake and Potomac Telephone for that."

"Is it like in England? Do phones pick up everything in the room?"

Major Dienneker looked at Matt closely. The questions had moved from Gee whiz! to some pretty specific information.

"Well, that's a different rig. The FBI has to have a special instrument or they have to go in and put a bug right in the phone. Why? Are you planning to have someone listened to?"

"No. But this is all such mysterious stuff that it's interesting to the layman."

"Well, I've got to get back to the shop," the major said, picking up his tray. "Say hello to Angie for me, will you? She's a fine lady."

"Sure." Matt smiled. "I'll do that."

He wondered if they had gone in and bugged his apartment, too. From now on he'd have to keep Glenna out of it, for her sake. This thing was going to change his life, he could see. He'd be tiptoeing around his house, afraid to make a sound. The bastards! He'd love to screw them up.

For a moment he thought of warning Bill Safire that he was being tapped. Safire had been with Nixon for a long time and was thought of as a White House insider. Why would they tap him? Maybe he was making calls to the Israelis. Or worse. He shouldn't warn Safire unless he was sure the writer was innocent of wrongdoing, Matt decided. Moreover, Safire would ask a lot of questions about how he knew and why *he* was being tapped. If the FBI found out he'd told Safire, what could they do to him? He was better off just looking out for himself, he decided.

Had the President ordered this? Or Kissinger? Glenna had mentioned Haig, which probably meant Kissinger had done it. Was Henry looking for a reason to go to Nixon and insist that Matt be fired? Matt wondered whom else he was after. Probably George Bothwell. Was he Elm? Was Bothwell's wife away? That would be easy to find out. Bothwell hardly seemed like the type who dated stewardesses.

The bastards, Matt thought. The pluperfect bastards. He put his tray of dishes on the rack and walked out of the basement of the EOB into the spring sunshine. It was a gorgeous Southern spring day. But, he reflected, the bastards had even spoiled the sunny day.

Twenty-eight

In the first weeks of April, 1969, Matthew Thompson suffered. His apartment had become a hostile place in which he could no longer live naturally. Someone listened to everything he did in there! He played his radio louder than usual, but he had no confidence that the vaunted technology of the FBI wouldn't just filter out the music so they could hear him brush his teeth or fold the newspaper or flush the toilet.

He couldn't sleep. He lay in bed self-consciously, constantly aware that someone was listening to every breath he drew. He began watching late movies on television in the hope that he would fall asleep from boredom, but it didn't work. There was someone there, always listening. The ubiquitous, unseen FBI agent was as intrusive and disrupting as he would have been overtly standing in the middle of the bedroom watching Matt's every move.

One night Matt did calisthenic exercises, hoping to exhaust himself to the point that he could fall into a deep sleep. He did push-ups, knee bends, and sit-ups until he was panting. He wondered what the listener thought he was doing. What was the bastard writing in the official FBI logbook for the 12:42 A.M. entry? They probably called it 0042. "Subject *Redwood* engaged in physical activity causing heavy breathing. No other person heard in the apartment. Probable activity: autosexual stimulation."

On Sunday he began looking at the classified ads in the *Post* for apartment rentals. If he moved, he wondered, would they bother to follow him? Of course they would. Haig had probably told them that the President considered this surveillance to be a top-priority operation. God *damn* Al Haig! How could one work with people like Henry and Haig in an ordinary, everyday manner, knowing that they had done this? They had destroyed his house—his only home, even if it was only a rented apartment—and his normal way of life. He couldn't be there alone, but he couldn't have company there either. The FBI, and ultimately Haig and Henry, would know every word he and his guest said and everything they did. He could imagine Haig bent over the log, titillated by Glenna's bureaucratically described exertions. Matt found he hated to answer his phone when it rang. He couldn't talk to people on the phone in a normal way.

He had become a butterfly mounted on a long pin for Haig and Henry to look at and push about with their blunt fingers each morning when the FBI logs came in.

The worst of it was how he was made to feel; by putting their superinvestigators on him, they had cast a vote of no-confidence in him and made him feel guilty of some wrong. In their eyes he was disgraceful. If he were not, why would they have invaded his house (and his office, no doubt) with their listening machines? He felt dirty.

Did he deserve to lose their confidence? What had he done? What did they—Kissinger and Haig—want of him?

Since the days when he was a child he'd always tried to do right—to please his parents and teachers and the scoutmaster and others. It had been relatively easy to figure out what they wanted of him; each one wanted something different, but he was able to tailor his actions to their desires and be thought by each to be a "good boy."

But this was a game of blindman's buff played out over a complex new terrain full of unseen holes; everyone playing for himself, each piously covering himself with the flag, or national security, or "the President's best interest," to justify what he was doing. How could a person know what they expected of him?

So, why would they listen to everything Matthew Thompson said? Glenna had said it was because he phoned China. Of course, he hadn't phoned China; but he had called Mr. Hung in Hong Kong, and probably the CIA knew that Hung was a P.R.C. supporter. But Hung had been his law client; surely they knew that. Wasn't that a good reason to talk to him? What did they fear?

Everyone wanted better relations with China. Nixon had decided on that, and Haig and Kissinger and everyone—including Matt Thompson—should be moving in that direction together. So, if I'm working on that with Hung, he rationalized, why should anyone object? Because they aren't in control, of course, and they can't be sure they will be given full credit for any good results. Control seemed to mean everything to Haig. And Henry wanted to be sure of the applause.

It was now obvious that neither Haig nor Henry knew anything about China or the Chinese. The problem of the defector in Holland had been badly handled, and the

Sino-Soviet border wars would have been ignored if he hadn't forced them to pay attention to them. For the President's sake China couldn't be left to Henry and Haig. Perhaps Nixon doesn't realize how badly they serve him, Matt reasoned. Perhaps he should be told. That would be one way to get even with the bastards, Matt fantasized. Probably Nixon doesn't even know that they have been bugging his staff. He surely would be outraged if he knew.

Matt felt better. He would arrange with Glenna to get a letter to Nixon exposing what Henry and Haig were doing. And he'd tell Nixon, too, how incompetent they were to handle Nixon's China initiative, and he would catalogue their mistakes.

But first he had to get some sleep; when he didn't sleep enough he became jittery. He could feel the jangles, and he knew he had to go somewhere to get some rest.

That night he rented a room for the night in a motel in Prince Georges County, Maryland, and slept soundly for the first time in three weeks. The room cost $46; he really couldn't afford it. But it had a direct-dial telephone, and before he slept he spent two hours calling his father, Mary Finn, Glenna, and other friends. He left all of them with the impression that he was calling from his apartment.

He also called Eldon Carnahay in New York. Matt had asked Carnahay to go to the Chelsea branch post office occasionally to check Marco Harrison's mailbox. The redheaded lawyer told Matt he was holding several letters and some junk mail for Harrison. Matt had explained to Carnahay that Marco Harrison was Glenna's cousin who was serving abroad in the Peace Corps; he was someone Matt had befriended. Carnahay promised to send Matt the mail from Marco's box at once.

Mary Finn was glad to hear from him. She said she had been in Paris the week after Matt had been there, but she had seen museums, galleries, the Parc Monceau, and other good things in her free time. He did not tell her about his tour of the Parisian suburbs, but he described some of his impressions of his late-night talk with Nixon at the Crillon. He knew how Mary Finn felt about Kissinger.

"Nixon may be okay," Mary offered, "but that Kissinger gives me the creeps. He comes across as devious and crafty and secretive. Don't your instincts tell you anything? How can you work for such a person?"

"Maybe I can't," Matt conceded. Perhaps she was his only ally in his fight with Kissinger. He instinctively opened up to her; she was on his side. "The work is what holds me there, in spite of Kissinger. I have absolutely no use for him now; he's worse than you suspect. But I'm involved in really interesting stuff that you wouldn't believe; I wish I could tell you. I'd hate to give up that work."

"I think you ought to get out before they really hurt you." There was concern in Mary's voice. "Those two— Kissinger and Haig—and all those White House people look awfully ruthless in their newspaper pictures."

"You may win two prizes before the pageant is over: Miss Congeniality and Miss Perspicacity."

"But not the swimsuit event? I plan to recite 'The Boy Stood on the Burning Deck' for the talent contest."

"You're a shoo-in. I'll bet the other girls are jealous."

"It's the mothers that are the worst."

"But seriously, folks, who resigns from the White House after four months? What do I put on my résumé?"

"How about 'January to April, 1969: fell among evil companions'? Do yourself a favor, Matthew. Do *me* a favor. Check out now. Or else I'll worry about you."

"Listen, Mary, there is this one thing that I'm very close to accomplishing. Would you believe me if I told you that it's important for the country—for the world—and I'm probably the only person who can pull it off?"

"That's what my father calls a 'fatal sense of indispensability.' I hope *you* don't really believe that."

"I do; I think it's true. And it's the reason that I feel that I have to stay for a while. I've got to try to make it happen. If I do, and then I tell you everything that has been happening, I think you'll agree that I've made the correct decision."

"Well, obviously, you're the only one who can decide

what to do, Matt. But I'm going to be awfully afraid for you. Meanwhile, how are you getting along with the beautiful blonde? I saw your picture in the *Post* a couple of weeks ago. How does that dress of hers stay up with no visible means of support?''

''It's an engineering marvel. Actually, it's sort of a cantilever design.''

''I don't have the boobs for it.''

''Few do. That's Glenna. She works at the White House as a secretary. She's nice, and she likes Henry Kissinger—''

''With an endowment like that, who cares?''

''How about you? What do you do for fun in the Nation's Capital?''

''Well, the other day a cabdriver made what I was pleased to construe as a suggestive remark when I undertipped him. And I went to the Smithsonian last Saturday. But otherwise, you might say that I'm between engagements. Why? What did you have in mind?''

''Oh, maybe dinner and a walk along the river, drinks at your place, something like that. Tomorrow?'' He wasn't sure why he had asked her, but it was pleasant to have a conversation with an intelligent woman who was sympathetic to him after three weeks of isolation.

''I'd like that. Can you pick me up at seven?''

''Sure. Where?''

''Thirty-one oh eight N Street Northwest, in Georgetown.''

''Stylish. Have you been to La Niçoise?''

''No.''

''The waiters are on roller skates. The food is only fair, but the show put on by the cooks and waiters and busboys around ten o'clock is rude, lewd, and funny. And it's all in French. The place is mostly financed by some U.S. Senators, and you'll probably see some famous faces in the crowd. Maybe we'll meet someone who knows one of the bathing-suit judges.''

All evening Mary Finn made clear that she liked Matt more than she had ever indicated to him up in New York.

She was lonely in Washington, and she was feeling afraid
and sorry for him. The veal was not as tender as it should
have been at a stylish restaurant like La Niçoise, but the
wine was excellent and the show was funny.

She asked questions about Kissinger and held Matt's
hand, and when the liqueurs were gone she became very
serious and advised him again to resign from Kissinger's
staff at once. Her mouth drew down at the corners and her
lower lip protruded and a vertical worry line appeared
between her widened eyes. "You've just got to get out of
there, darlin'," she said intensely.

He leaned toward her on the banquette, sliding his left
hand along the top of the leather back behind her head,
and kissed her softly. He was going to say something
reassuring like "Don't worry about me," but he felt her
tongue flip his lips, and his tongue met hers and moved
into her mouth. She drew back and laughed.

"I've wanted you to kiss me ever since your client ran
away with all that money," she said, smiling. "It's about
time."

"Well, you had that boyfriend, so I stayed away."

"That whole thing was a mess," she said seriously. The
worry line reappeared above her nose. "He still calls all
the time, but I'm clear about him now. I was some kind of
a zombie, I guess. He would tell me what to do and I
would do it! Can you picture me being some man's little
slave?"

"Not really."

"I hated every minute of it, but I didn't want it to stop.
It was really sick. And a lot of the time I knew you were
out there and that we'd be good together if I could just get
us together. I am very attracted to you, and I have been for
a long time."

"So." He smiled and took her hand, gently caressing
her wrist and arm with his other hand. "So, what do we
do now? It's certainly not too late to start things right, is
it?" He briefly realized he was crossing a line, leaving
Glenna and changing his life, but he told himself that it
didn't matter.

"Nope. The only question is my place or your place, I guess." She turned her hand over and returned his grip. "What's the matter—did I say something wrong?"

"Of course not," he said quietly.

"You got an awful look of realization. What are you thinking about?"

"I'd like to have you come to my place, but I just remembered I can't. I'm expecting a guy from New York. I left a key out for him."

"So come to Georgetown."

"I'd like that."

"But kiss me again right now."

He did.

Mary Finn had rented half of a divided Georgetown brownstone: half its front steps, half a basement, and half a narrow yard in the back. At the rear of her long, thin living room, steep stairs led to two bedrooms and an antique bathroom, all of which was set precariously atop the kitchen and a sun porch that banded the rest of the house. One of the bedrooms was large, the other too small for anything but a single cot and boxes, odd pieces of furniture, and an ironing board. Matt wandered through the house, opening doors, turning on lights, and casually peeking into rooms, while Mary Finn made drinks in the kitchen. Her living room was crowded with furniture obviously acquired for a different house. It had an intramural unity, the pieces doing well among themselves, but they did not really work in the narrow brick-and-wood room with the two-story ceiling and tall windows.

Matt took off his jacket and tie and sat for a moment deep in a wicker easy chair, then decided to build a fire in the brick fireplace. There were some small split pine logs in a brass washtub with newspapers and a box of kitchen matches, and before long he had laid the wood on Mary's brass andirons, stuffed the paper under it, and slid open the matchbox.

"What are you doing?" she asked him from the kitchen door.

"We're going to have a fire," he said proudly.

"Oh, God! That's a fake! Don't light it, whatever you do. We'll have smoke everywhere. The place will burn down!" She handed him a goblet and led him to the couch, which faced the tall, uncovered windows fronting on N Street. The brownstone across the street had been painted white and glowed softly in the streetlights. He could see a dimly lighted chandelier in one of the upstairs windows over there.

Mary sat with her bare feet tucked under her, turned toward Matt, her right arm along the cane that topped the couch back. "This is a summer drink called a 'peachy,' and I can't think of anybody I'd rather try it on. It's guaranteed to zap you in two drinks. I had a Southern roommate who used to make it." Her hand lazed against the back of his neck. "Sorry about the fire, but the wood is just a stage prop that I brought down from New York. I've had it for years. It's too warm for a fire, anyway, isn't it?"

"I had visions of us stretched out on the rug in front of the fire. I'll bet your hair is beautiful in firelight." He reached to hold her hair in his fingers, then cradled her head in his hand, drawing her toward him.

"The other problem is that I always feel like my across-the-street neighbors are behind their shutters watching everything that goes on in this room. They can look right down into here."

"So, let's turn out the lights."

"How about if we go to another room?"

"Okay."

"Come on, then, and bring your drink." She led him by the hand to the stairs, turning out the lights as she passed the switch. "The other room I have in mind is up here. Will your friend be sad if you don't get home tonight? The fellow from New York?"

"No. He'll probably be glad I'm not there. He'll never miss me."

* * *

A few days later, in the first week of April, the National Security Agency reported that the Chinese Communist Party Congress had heard an important speech delivered by Defense Minister Lin Piao, Mao's shy and devious number two man. First indications were that the text was unusually bellicose and anti-America. It was not the encouraging Chinese signal the White House was looking for. Matt formally asked the several United States intelligence agencies to get for him the exact language of Lin's broadside. They reported that the text had not yet been released by the Chinese Government.

Two days later, when he returned to his apartment to change for a dinner date with Mary Finn, Matt found an envelope which had been pushed under his front door. In it was the text of Lin Piao's speech and a typewritten analysis of it, but there was no indication of who had sent the material, or how.

He sat in his one comfortable chair and read the speech. It was very tough, full of the usual anti-Western jargon the Chinese had used for years.

The accompanying analysis—by Teng Shan-li?—was essentially an effort to soften the impact of Lin's tough words. It made two basic points:

(1) Although the speech is belligerent in tone, the Defense Minister emphasized that China will not attack another country unless she is attacked first; and

(2) Lin clearly designated Russia and the United States as equal threats to China. Therefore, the U.S. is not seen as China's *primary* enemy, and from this it may be implied that some trilateral relationship may be possible.

Matt reread Lin's speech slowly. Teng Shan-li—or whoever had written the apologia—was correct on the first point. Lin specifically renounced any first attack. But Matt had trouble with that proposition because there was no mention of the border fighting with Russia, and after a month, it was clear that China had shot first on Damansky Island. Maybe, Matt mused, Lin claimed a Russian had shoved a Chinese first in the preliminary scuffles up there.

It was hard to take comfort from Lin's rabid attacks on Russia and the United States, but the analysis was useful and important. Once this Lin Piao speech text hit Washington, President Nixon would strongly react if it were presented to him cold. He needed to be forewarned and positioned. Some more conciliatory signal would surely come from Chou En-lai soon, Matt reasoned. If not, why produce this analysis and make the considerable effort it must have taken for the Chinese to put it under his door?

The next day Matt rewrote the analysis and sent the speech and his memorandum to Kissinger. That afternoon he received a note from Al Haig:

> Matthew:
>   Dr. Kissinger remarked that your intelligence sources are apparently better than his. So please expand your Lin Piao speech memo to analyze all that occurred at the Party Congress. Have it in my hands in 48 hours.
>
>   A.H.

The CIA's Hong Kong observers were able to telephone Matt a helpful summary of the other events at the Party Congress, although they apologetically admitted that they could not get the text of Lin's speech.

On April 29, Kissinger sent Nixon an account of the Chinese Party Congress which was a verbatim retype of Matt's lengthy analysis. The only change was the insertion of Kissinger's signature in place of Matt's. Thus it was that Richard Nixon read Teng Shan-li's explanation of Lin Piao's speech and believed it to be another of Henry Kissinger's hopeful statements.

"Henry is getting a little soft-headed about the Chinese," Nixon said to Bob Haldeman on May 1. "He's straining at gnats to find optimistic things to say about them while they are kicking us in the nuts. He wants relations with Chinese so badly that he's liable to give them anything they ask for to get it. We've got to watch out for him.''

Haldeman nodded and made a note on his yellow pad.

Matt had begun to write the confidential note to Richard Nixon exposing Henry Kissinger and Al Haig, but it was becoming impossible to find the time to work on it during the day. He dared not leave it anywhere that Haig's FBI minions might find it in a search of the apartment or Matt's office, so he carried it everywhere with him, folded, in his pocket.

Mary Finn was out of town on business more than she was in Washington, but she and Matt had begun to spend more and more of her in-town time together that spring. Unlike Glenna, Mary Finn took some of the initiative, calling Matt from Chicago or London, suggesting weekend trips, inviting him out to dinner. He was pleased and flattered, but not romantically serious about Mary Finn.

Matt's apartment was a problem. He would not invite Mary Finn there, and she outspokenly resented it. Finally, he went further than he had intended to in explanation.

"The perennial question now arises," she said one evening after dinner at Sans Souci. "My place or my place? Right?"

"I guess that's right."

"May I ask why? Do you throw your dirty socks around? Are there dishes in your sink? Or are you keeping dead maidens in your bathtub?"

"Not really. Look, I'm sorry, but I'm very uncomfortable about this. I wish I could explain, but I can't."

"Okay, Matt, then just tell me this: do you live alone?"

"Sure."

"Glenna the Blonde isn't your secret roommate?"

"Absolutely not."

"So we'd be alone if we went there?"

"Yeah. But it's not really private, like your place is."

"Oh? Thin walls?"

"Yeah. People can hear everything that goes on."

"Ever thought of moving?"

"I intend to. But I don't want to end up in a worse place. I have to look around."

"Okay. I accept this. So let's head for N Street. I have nice thick brick walls."

Glenna Harrison saw Matt walking with Mary Finn one spring evening on Wisconsin Avenue in Georgetown. The next day Glenna came to Matt's office for an explanation. She sat beside him on his couch, but refused to let him touch her.

"That was a lawyer friend from New York; her name is Mary Finn," he said matter-of-factly. "Why?"

"Why? What kind of question is *that*? Do we love each other or not? Are we going steady with each other or not?"

"Please keep your voice down. There's no need to include Angie in all of this, is there?"

"Oh, excuse me. You parade around in public with Mickey Finn but I shouldn't tell anyone. Excuse me! Are we all washed up? Is that it? I sure couldn't tell it Tuesday night, I must say. Or am I still for sex and she's to talk to? Is that it?"

"Glenna, there's nothing for you to get all upset about. Nothing has changed."

"Nothing except that you're dating someone else, that's all. Are you fucking her too?"

"Hey, slow down! She's just moved here and I've seen her a couple of times to show her around. Is that so terrible?"

"What's terrible is that you're seeing her behind my back. Why didn't you just tell me you had an old friend come to town and you'd be showing her around? I could understand that, really. What is mutual trust, anyway?"

"Glenna, trust is one thing and my being required to get your permission in advance is another. Is that the kind of relationship you want us to have?"

"It's not that at all."

"If the situation were reversed, would you want to come to me, hat in hand, and ask for a pass to go out with an old friend? It seems to me that would just destroy everything that's between us."

"Will you be seeing her again?"

"I imagine so. We're good friends. She travels a lot in her work, but when she is in town I expect I'll see her some."

"Matt, you know all of this would be easier on me if I knew where I stood with you." She put her hand on his on the couch between them. "We've talked about it, but nothing has changed."

"You mean engagement?"

"Sure. My folks are on me all the time; they keep asking questions about you and me and it's embarrassing. We've been going together for nearly two years and I've turned away a lot of boys my folks think are 'very suitable.' My father wants to know if you intend to marry me or not."

"And so do you?"

"Sure. I think we love each other and we're terrific together. I think we'd be very happy."

"Women want to settle down sooner than men do; they mature sooner."

"But you and I aren't teenagers in high school, for God's sake." Her voice became shrill. "I'm twenty-four years old and you are twenty-seven! That's pretty old!"

"Well, maybe I'm retarded. I've told you before: I'm just not ready to settle down with you. I love you a lot, but I just can't."

"You know, I wish you'd just said 'I love you.' That really means something. But 'I love you a lot' sounds like 'I like to get into your knickers.'" She stood and looked down at him. "So I guess I found out what I came over to the EOB to find out. So we'll keep fooling around and be great in bed, and that's it."

"Is that so terrible?" He stood and faced her. "Most of

the people I know would give anything for a relationship like that.''

"They must all be men.''

"No. Women too.''

"Even Mary Finn?''

"I think so.''

"Well, not me, Matthew Thompson. Not me.''

To her great credit, Glenna did not slam the huge old door with the Treasury knobs to punctuate her departure. Matt was grateful to her for that.

On July 21, on the eve of Nixon's departure for a trip around the world, the White House announced that the United States' embargo against shipments of goods to China would be substantially relaxed. The same day Matt Thompson mailed Hung Wai-lang a long letter explaining the announced action in detail. In conclusion he wrote:

> No response to our French message having been received, this should be understood as a further gesture of goodwill.
> At meetings in Bucharest a new message will be entrusted to the Romanians with the hope that a new channel will produce better results.

Sixteen letters and a parcel, all addressed to Hung Wai-lang, were carried by a young Chinese woman from the huge mail-sorting room of the Hong Kong post office to a glass-enclosed cubicle. She laid her canvas tray on a side table.

"Here is more for Hung Wai-lang, addressed to his house,'' she said to a young Englishman dressed in a white suit. "This is all for today.''

"Please hand it to me,'' he said. "Thank you very much.'' He sat at a battered metal desk which was covered with blue manila folders. He quickly sorted Hung's mail and kept out two letters. He leafed through the blue files until he found one labeled:

THOMPSON, MATTHEW 01190537
CROSS: HUNG WAI-LANG 0983122
UNITED STATES
P.R.C.

He opened it and examined a photocopy of a letter. "Handwriting appears to be the same," he noted quietly. He handed the two envelopes to the young woman. "Open these for me," he instructed.

When the young woman returned with the carefully steamed envelopes, he quickly browsed their contents.

"This one," he said, "you can reseal and return to the delivery stream. We really don't care whether Mr. Hung buys a new auto, do we? But I shall require four copies of this one, as soon as possible. Thank you ever so much. It would appear that our Mr. Hung has become something of a foreign affairs expert, eh? Very interesting, don't you agree? Very interesting indeed."

Miss Leong, the postal clerk, took the two letters to her desk, where she carefully resealed the letter from Mercedes-Benz of San Francisco. The second letter, from Matthew Thompson, was photocopied on the machine just outside the office of the Director of the Post Office.

Miss Leong made the four copies she had been instructed to make. Then she made one extra copy, which she slipped into her purse when she returned to her desk.

Twenty-nine

Matthew Thompson first met Emory Latham in Washington, D.C., while Richard Nixon, Henry Kissinger, and their dozens of attendants—among them Colonel Alexander Haig—were engaged in a stately circumnavigation of the world in July and August, 1969. Matt met Latham sometime after Nixon greeted the three astronauts' return to earth in the Pacific Ocean but before the absolute ruler of Pakistan lavishly hosted and wooed the American President and his retinue. That day, after work, Matt found a plain, typewritten note in his mailbox along with a few bills and circulars and a picture postcard from Mary Finn in Florence.

The typed note said only:

> Archives
> Declaration of Independence
> 4 p.m.
> Tomorrow

Mary Finn's card pictured Michelangelo's statue of *David* and said:

> Let's come to Florence together sometime—soon.
> It is the most romantic city! I'm horny, pinched
> and holding out for you (or David). Love, M.

Matthew smiled at Mary Finn's card, but in the pit of his stomach he felt uneasy. If Haig and Henry and the FBI could listen to him, surely they could have his mail read too. Would FBI agents be posted tomorrow to watch him make a rendezvous in the lobby of the National Archives building? Maybe it was some kind of trap. He had to know.

He folded the anonymous note carefully and put it in his pocket, walked to the Riggs Bank in the shopping district a few blocks from his apartment house, and bought three rolls of quarters. He hailed a cab which took him to the Washington Hilton Hotel, where he rode the escalator down to the cavernous convention level.

Matt Thompson walked seventy-five feet to the end of the curved hallway where a rank of six pay phones could be seen in the dim light of the unused passage. It took several minutes to reach the Hong Kong office of Hung

Wai-lang and then nearly a minute to deposit the stream of quarters the overseas operator demanded.

"Yes, Matthew?" Hung said faintly.

"I have a note from someone today. I am afraid to go to the place selected. I may be watched," Matt blurted. He realized he was talking too loud. But he could see to the escalator, and no one else was in the concourse. At least the FBI had not followed him there. They would not know which phone he had used, so they could not trace this call, he assured himself.

"The purpose of the note—are we talking safely?" Hung asked.

"Yes."

"Very well. Call this number and tell them your name: 202-555-4736. New arrangements for communication are being made."

"Fine. Goodbye."

Matthew had written the number Hung gave him on the stainless steel counter of the phone with a felt-tip pen. He memorized the number, wiped it out with a wet finger, and moved to one of the other telephones to dial 555-4736. It rang eight times before Matt hung up.

He dared not dial the number from his apartment. He walked back to the escalator and rode up to the lobby, walked to the coffee shop, and stood in line with several tourist families and two matrons in tennis clothes, complete with racquets and cans of balls.

After an indifferent salad and iced tea, Matt found six pay phones behind the elevators in the lobby. They were crowded into a narrow space, and all of them were being used. He would be overheard by other telephone users no matter how careful he was. He left the hotel, took off his jacket, and walked down the hill on Connecticut Avenue toward Dupont Circle. The sun had set, but the twilight hour had brought no relief from the humid heat of the day. The sidewalk and buildings he passed radiated multiples of the heat in palpable waves. In the first block Matt took off his necktie, opened two shirt buttons, and turned up his shirt cuffs. At the far corner of R Street he stopped at a pay phone to try the number again, awkwardly juggling his jacket and the coins with the receiver.

On the first ring of the number Hung had given him, a man answered. "Hello?" The voice was tenor, light, tentative, as if he did not belong there or was only answering the phone for someone else.

"Hello," Matt said. "My name is Matthew Thompson."

"Yes?"

"Yes. I was told to call this number and tell you my name."

"I see. What is your name again?"

"Matthew Thompson."

"Matthew Thompson?"

"Yes." Perhaps Hung had not had an opportunity to reach this man to say Matt would call, he thought.

"Is there a number where you can be called?" the man asked.

"Not really, no."

"Well, can you call here again this evening? In sixty minutes?"

"Sure." Matt heard the telephone abruptly disconnect. He hung up his receiver and looked around. There wasn't a pedestrian on his side of Connecticut Avenue for a block in either direction. A woman with a small dog was walking toward him on R Street, half a block away.

Either a bar or a movie would be a cool place to kill an hour, Matt decided. Not booze; he needed to be clearheaded. He remembered a theater just below Dupont Circle and walked unpurposefully toward it. He wouldn't be able to see the marquee until he had passed the Circle, but it didn't matter.

The movie beyond Dupont Circle offered something called *Albion Again*; Matt paid $4 and went in. Air conditioning had made it very cold in the lobby. He put his jacket on and buttoned his shirt. There were only ten or eleven other people in the theater, scattered among two hundred seats. Matt sat in the back of the theater, watching the boring film and who came and went. He felt sure no one was looking for him.

The theater lobby provided a pay phone beside an unattended refreshment counter. Matt dialed 555-4736 and the first ring was immediately answered.

"Hello." This time it was a different voice, less tentative if no deeper.

"This is Matthew Thompson. I called a while ago."

"Yes, Mr. Thompson. I am sorry I wasn't here before. I understand there is some problem with the Archives?" The speech cadence was firm and decisive.

"Well, I was afraid my mail had been read," Matt explained.

"I see. Are you at home now?" Matt could hear a radio playing classical music behind the man.

"No; a pay phone in a movie theater."

"Good. Where?"

"Connecticut near Dupont Circle."

"Fine. Do you know El Bodegón?"

"Sure."

"Walk over there and I'll meet you out front in a few minutes. I have a message for you from a friend of yours."

"Who?"

"I was told to mention Li-fa's name if you asked."

"Okay. I'll be there in a little while," Matt said.

The hot evening air was waiting for him like a heavy, moist quilt when he emerged from the refrigerated lobby. He felt the perspiration begin to gather on his face and under his arms, so he took his coat off again. He walked deliberately to Dupont Circle and partway around it, then northeast on New Hampshire Avenue for two blocks and east on R Street, through a black neighborhood that had always made him feel uneasy. This area was quintessential Washington-in-the-Summer, simmering, threatening, dirty, and nearly hopeless. There had been summer riots here a few years before. Sagging steel gates guarded the dark store fronts; black men in undershirts lounged on the stairs of deteriorating brownstones.

At the corner of Seventeenth and R streets, Matt saw three taxis idling, double-parked, in front of the two Hispanic restaurants located in the first two buildings of the next block on R Street. La Fonda and El Bodegón sat together, confusing their customers from out of town, sharing the salsa trade; the restaurant critic in *The Washingtonian* had correctly described them as a lively señora and her macho companion side by side in hostile surroundings.

Matt walked to the base of the tall front steps of El Bodegón and stood in the light of its facade, looking in all directions. He wiped his face with his handkerchief, refolded it, refolded his jacket, and slung it over his shoulder. A minute later the door of the first taxi opened and a man got out, looking at Matt.

He was as tall as Matt, but slimmer, and wore a loose-fitting short-sleeved white shirt, tight Levi's, brown moccasins, and white gym socks. Matt immediately noticed the man's arms, which were incongruously muscular; massive arms and shoulders on a frame that seemed otherwise almost delicate.

The man came close to Matt and spoke quietly. The accents and tone seemed Southern and a little less assertive than they had been on the telephone, trailing upward at the ends of sentences.

"Matthew Thompson?"

"Yes?"

"I am Emory Latham. I'm the one you've just spoken to on the telephone."

"Yes."

"I suggest we walk somewhere and talk. Bodegón is just too damn noisy with all that flamenco going on."

"Where?"

"Let's go down to Sixteenth. We can get a drink at the Statler, I expect." He began to move east along R Street into deep shadows.

"It sure is hot. I'll be ready for a drink. You have

a message from Li-fa?'' Matt asked, walking beside Latham.

"My message is not very elaborate, actually, but I guess it is quite important. Your former client sends you his regards. So does Miss Wang.''

"Is that all?''

"No. I'm to say that it is becoming harder and harder for you to communicate with your friends; that seems obvious. So from now on I am to be your conduit.''

"For everything?''

"Yes. You will find that I am very reliable and I'll be available to you on no more than an hour's notice. Your friends have found me to be very, very discreet, I assure you.''

"How do I work it? Suppose I have a letter I want to send?''

"You simply call me, leave the letter where we agree you will, and I pick it up.''

They moved into Sixteenth Street, where the new anticrime streetlights created a yellow-gray daylight. Matt looked at Emory Latham more closely. In another ten years he would be bald, Matt decided; his ash-colored hair was receding from his temples, thinning on top and at the back. By contrast, his eyebrows were dark, perhaps dark brown or even black, behind amber-rimmed glasses. His regular features were kept from being ordinary by his prominent nose and thin lips. He walked with a confident, masculine stride.

"You work for Kissinger, I am told,'' Latham said. He spoke softly so that street noises made it impossible to hear some of his words. "That must be very interesting.''

"Have you been to China?'' Matt asked.

"I don't think we should talk about me,'' Latham replied. "Just think of me as a delivery boy.''

"Well, naturally I'm curious about who you are and how our friends picked you to do this. You don't want to tell me anything?''

"No, it will be best for both of us if I don't. I gather you are under some kind of surveillance?''

"I've learned I'm being tapped or bugged. I don't think they are following me."

"I don't think so either. I watched from the cab as you came to El Bodegón. Why are they listening to you?"

"Because they learned I had made a phone call to Hong Kong. Do you know Mr. Hung?"

"Hung Wai-lang? Did you call him?"

"Yes. And he has called me."

"Well, the British may have him tapped on that end, or the NSA may have overheard you from here. Either way, Kissinger could have found out."

"The NSA? National Security Agency? It's the FBI—"

"No, the NSA routinely monitors all overseas calls. Its computers select out those going from or to certain people, to particular numbers or places, or they pick up discussions of various subjects they are interested in. They may have all the White House staff programmed into their machines so they can keep track of what all of you are up to overseas."

"Right. What about tonight? I called Hung from a pay phone and he gave me your number. Will they get that?"

"Where was the phone?"

"In the Washington Hilton."

"They might. Did you use your full name in talking with his secretary or with him?"

"I may have. I'm not sure."

Emory Latham stopped under a streetlight and produced a pen and a small note pad. "Here," he said, "is another number to reach me. To be safe we'd better use it instead of the one you were given. I'll not be at that number any longer." He wrote 555-3303. "Please memorize this as we walk along and give me back the paper. And always call me from a pay phone—a different one each time."

"All right. I think I've got it." Matt closed his eyes, visualized the numbers and said, "555-3303, right?" He looked at the paper and handed it back to Latham. "This is getting to be real cloak-and-dagger stuff, isn't it? I wonder if it's all necessary."

"It depends. Is someone trying to stop you from doing something important for our friends?"

"Well," Matt said thoughtfully, "no, not really. But if it were known that I have Chinese friends I'd be knocked out of the White House, I suppose, and then I couldn't accomplish anything. Does that make sense?"

"Certainly. So there is a part of your life you need to keep secret."

"That's right. How do *you* make calls to the Orient without the computers picking up your conversations?"

"When we talk, usually we are merchants dealing in paper of all kinds. The computer isn't interested in paper."

"So it's like an oral code?"

"Sometimes. But I don't think you need to know too much about all of that. You can be sure that we take most of the risk out of it. That's all you need to know."

Matt wondered why Latham had put it in the plural. They passed the Soviet Embassy and turned into the Statler Hilton's side door.

"Nice and cool," Matt said. "If I run into anyone I know, how do I introduce you?"

"Just say I'm one of your father's former students. He asked you to look me up. That keeps it casual."

Matt shot him a questioning look. "Casual?" This fellow knows about my father and Hung and even used Li-fa's name, he realized.

"Yes. We should not appear to be close friends. That could create problems for both of us."

Latham led the way through the glass door into a dimly lit bar. Only one couple sat at a table, close to the bar.

"We can sit there in the far corner if you like," Latham said very quietly.

"Fine."

They ordered draft beer, and Matt began to eat popcorn

from a small bowl on the table. "I'm hungry," Matt said. "I've walked about twenty miles tonight, I think." Latham was looking at him intently. "I have a message that needs sending. Can I give it to you now?"

"Of course."

"Tell them the two yachtsmen should be released at once in return for loosening the embargo. It will be well received."

Latham nodded. "I will. Right away. Do you work out?" he asked.

"Not much these days. I did before I moved down from New York."

"I want you to enroll at a gym near here where you can use exercise machines and other equipment. I go there every day, and we can meet there to exchange messages. I'll give you the combination to my locker so you can leave things there for me."

"That sounds good. And I can use the gym work; I need it."

"Go here tomorrow"—Latham took out his note pad—"and give your name to Tommy in the locker room. Don't say that you know me. We'll be strangers there, at least for now. As time passes we can strike up a casual acquaintanceship, but let me decide when and how that will happen." He handed Matt the small note. "My locker number and combination are there at the bottom."

"Okay. Capitol Health Room. Fine."

Latham took a five-dollar bill from his pocket and laid it on the table. "I'm going now," he said. "Give me about ten minutes before you leave. See you later."

Matt nodded. Latham quietly thanked the barman as he threaded his way among the empty tables to the door. He did not look back at Matt, who was watching him leave.

Matt felt better about this new arrangement; it would take a lot of the pressure off. He wondered how Latham had begun working for the Chinese. Matt assumed that Latham was a spy for them. He certainly appeared to understand how the NSA worked and all of that. And he appeared to be a genuinely nice person, very quiet and well mannered, but with those arms and shoulders he could be tough to tangle with. Matt wondered how much the FBI knew about Emory Latham.

Three days before Richard Nixon returned to the United States to be greeted by a wildly enthusiastic crowd at Andrews Air Force Base in suburban Maryland, the People's Republic of China released the two American yachtsmen who had been arrested when their boat sank near Hong Kong.

Late in the afternoon of Nixon's arrival, Matt Thompson was among the two hundred and eleven members of the White House staff who were brought to Andrews AFB in chartered buses which had been paid for by the Republican National Committee. Several hundred other citizens had been brought from the solid-Republican precincts of northern Virginia to greet their returning President for the benefit of the television news networks and their millions of viewers. The President, Secretary of State Rogers, Dr. Kissinger, and the other travelers were received by the Vice President, members of the Cabinet, and assorted diplomats whose countries had been visited during the President's trip around the world. The Marine Band played stirring music, the President made a speech, and everyone clapped and cheered.

During the long bus ride back to the White House, Matt sat next to a young economist on the staff of the President's Council of Economic Advisers who was reading a paperback novel about someone's manipulation of the world money markets.

When the bus let everyone off at the southwest gate, between the Executive Office Building and the West Wing of the White House, Matt decided to go up to his office to clean up the day's paperwork before he ate a lonely dinner. Angie Cruz had gone for the day, but she'd left a note taped to his door.

* * *

Matt:
They called for you from the plane. The President
wants to see you *tonight*. Call Carol Phinney or
Tom James as soon as possible.

                                                        A.

The switchboard operator quickly found Carol Phinney,
who told Matt to come to her desk just outside the Oval
Office at 7:30 P.M. She would then tell him where to go for
his meeting with the President. No, she didn't know what
it was about, or what he should bring with him.

At 7:30 P.M. he was standing in the small suite of rooms
that constituted the passage between the President's office
and the Cabinet Room. Carol Phinney soon emerged from
the Oval Office carrying the President's attaché case and a
handful of papers and folders. She greeted Matt and
suggested he sit on the small couch. The French doors in
the east wall of the office offered a full view of the Rose
Garden with the Residence looming behind it. The National Park Service continually rotated the plantings in that
garden. Matt went to the windows to watch a floodlighted
crew of twenty men and women take up the hundreds of
massed annuals whose blooms had begun to fade a little.
They would be replaced that evening with plants from a
greenhouse so that the next day's Rose Garden ceremonies
would be backed by flawless blooms in the fullest flower.

In a few minutes, responding to a short signal on a
buzzer, Mrs. Phinney nodded toward the Oval Office door.
"Go on in," she said.

The Oval Office had been completely redecorated during
Nixon's long trip. Lyndon Johnson's faded green carpet
had been replaced by a vibrant gold-yellow and royal blue
monstrosity with a giant Presidential seal inlaid in yellow
carpet exactly in the center of the room. Bright yellow
stars marched around the border of the whole thing. New
draperies at the windows behind the President's desk
carried the same strong colors up the walls.

Almost anticlimactically, Richard Nixon sat at his bare
desk watching Matt approach him. No one was with him.

Walking across the new carpet gave Matt a flash of doubt:
Was it proper to step on the President's seal, or must he stay
on the blue field and detour all the yellow part? Chairs
blocked the blue path—surely he was not expected to jump
over the seal. He walked lightly on the eagle, but he
wished there had been a way around it.

"Come in," Nixon said jovially. "How's your father?"

"He's fine, thank you. Welcome home, Mr. President."

"Well, how was it here with all the cats away?"

Matt smiled. "Pretty quiet, sir. The Chinese did let the
yachtsmen loose, as I'm sure you know."

"Right. That's why I asked you to come over tonight:
China. I am going to work here for a while because my
sleep mechanism is so screwed up. I'll probably sleep for a
few hours around two A.M. I sent Bob and Henry and the
others home because I don't really need them, and maybe
they can sleep. Each person is different, of course. I
learned to get along on very little sleep when I was in the
Navy in the South Pacific in the war, so I can keep going
here. But Henry is very tired; it was an exhausting trip for
all of us. I'm told it was the first working trip around the
world by a sitting President. I'm having Costigan check
that. Too bad we couldn't have gone to China. But that
may be for another time, eh?"

The summer light was fading in the sky behind Nixon;
the thick, curved windows behind him had a green tint
which made the sunset muddy. Nixon played with a letter
opener as he talked.

"What about China, now?" the President continued.
"I've had some good talks with the Paks and the Romanians
and they are both optimistic that we are going to hear from
the Chinese very soon. What do you think?"

"I think we had a favorable signal when they let go
those two from the boat. I believe that was an unusually
quick response to your relaxation of the embargo."

"You do? Good. Both Yahya Khan and Ceauşescu have
offered to help, and Henry says the Pakistanis will be the
more helpful. They should be, by God, because we are
giving them a huge amount of aid right now. I have a

hunch Yahya is planning to go after the Indians pretty
soon, although he denies it. He's a tough bastard, and I
wouldn't mind it if he knocked Indira Gandhi's block off.''
Nixon wagged his head side to side in a small, jerky
movement. "In fact, we might even help him a little."
Nixon's smile flashed on and off instantly.

"You need to talk to Henry," Nixon continued. "He
had long talks with one of the Pakistanis who had just
come from a visit with Chou En-lai. This fellow goes
back and forth all the time, and he will carry our
letters."

Matt nodded. "I'll see Henry in the morning." Matt had
never finished writing the secret letter he had started to
write Nixon about Henry and Haig. This conversation, he
reasoned, might be the only one he would ever again have
with the President alone. He'd better tell Nixon how he felt
about Henry now, he decided.

"Mr. President," Matt blurted, "are you aware that
the FBI is bugging my apartment and tapping my telephone under instructions from Dr. Kissinger or Colonel
Haig?''

"What?" Nixon's eyebrows went up and he moved
forward in his chair. "My God, why?" He folded his
hands on his desk and listened earnestly. "I've been away,
of course. Are you sure?"

"Yes, I am. I believe they are suspicious of my loyalty
because I have friends in the Orient, especially Mr. Hung,
my former client in Hong Kong."

"Of course you have friends there!" Nixon exclaimed.
"So do I, for Christ's sake. You used to live there!"

"Once before, when we talked alone, you mentioned
Henry's motives with respect to China, and I know that's a
problem for you. But a bigger problem is that he is quite
unfamiliar with that part of the world. As a result, the
advice he has been giving you on some things has been
just plain wrong. He is not sensitive to Chinese tradition
and modes of thought."

"I see."

"I am very concerned that you succeed in your Chinese

policy and I'll do everything I can to help you, and that is why I am telling you these things."

"The FBI is doing this?" Nixon tapped his palm with the letter opener, then reached for his telephone. "J. Edgar Hoover, please," he said to the operator. He swung his chair to his left so he was not looking at Matt as he talked.

"Edgar? Edgar, some of your people have a surveillance on a man on Henry Kissinger's staff, I'm told. His name is Matthew Thompson."

Nixon paused to listen to Hoover. Matt could hear the old FBI man's high-pitched voice in the receiver.

"I think Henry or his man Haig made the request," Nixon said. "No, I haven't seen anything on it. In any case, Edgar, I want Thompson let alone. He's doing some very sensitive work for me, if you understand me. He should not be bugged."

Hoover talked for a long time.

"Why don't you come over and I'll get Bob in and we'll talk about this whole thing?" Nixon replied. "In the meanwhile, please take care of this one fellow."

Nixon hung up and swiveled back to face Matt. "He says he doesn't know about you, but he'll make some calls tonight and make sure no one is doing this. My God, I don't understand what gets into Henry sometimes. In any case, you won't be bothered anymore, but I wouldn't say anything to Henry or Haig about it. By the way, how did you find out about the bug?"

"Well, it's in the phone. You can hear funny sounds, so I asked someone I know about it and he admitted that it was on there."

"Lucky thing you caught it. I might have called you about China some night and they would have recorded the President, for God's sake! I really wonder what gets into Henry sometimes. It's that chronic paranoia you see in so many of them, I suppose. It infects him too." Nixon's eyes brightened as he rubbed his nose from side to side with two fingers. "But he is as rough on the Israelis as he is on the Arabs. I guess he's not accepted as a member of the real Jewish inner circles—Loeb and Lasker and Max Fisher and that crowd—so he feels free to work them over when it suits his purposes."

"He can be ruthless," Matt contributed.

"Ruthless? Oh, my, yes." Nixon barked a laugh. "You should have seen him with the poor Paks. He bargains like a lace peddler. It's always someone else's money he's spending, but you'd think it was his own last dime. I realize he knows very little about China, and I expect that Al Haig knows even less, but when the time comes we will need Henry and we'll be lucky to have him. You realize, I'm sure," Nixon said, turning to look at a painting on the wall to his right, "how much the President puts up with. Henry is in here all the time, bitching and whining, taking up valuable time, complaining about Rogers or some other damn thing. Now he wants a better office, but it has to be in the West Wing, he says. Even if I gave him this one he wouldn't stop bitching. Why does a President put up with all of that? Because we need him when the going gets rough. He's ruthless, as you say, and I need people like that when I need them."

"I understand."

"But all of that is no excuse for tapping your phone, for God's sake. I do not understand that! Be that as it may, it's taken care of now and you don't need to worry about it. If I were you I'd be cautious about what I said to Henry about all of this. Perhaps you should just let me handle it."

"That's fine with me."

"I want you to prepare a letter to send to Chou En-lai by way of Yahya Kahn's man in Pakistan—or do you think it should go to Mao? Something general to open up communication."

"Perhaps a formal letter to Mao and a more down-to-earth letter to Chou. I don't think you should ignore Mao, but the real business will have to be done with Chou."

"Good. You draft them and let me know when they're

ready. I'll hand them to Henry after Rose has typed them."

Matt sat for a moment, waiting for Nixon to go on, but he said nothing more. He sat in profile to Matt, looking down intently at the letter opener in his hands, turning it over and over. Matt stood. "I'll do that—I'll draft those letters," Matt said. "Good night, Mr. President."

Nixon did not look up at him. He shook his head slightly. "Don't worry about Hoover, now. I've taken care of that."

"Thank you," Matt said with finality. He turned to his left and walked to the curved door in the northeast quarter of the ellipse. When he looked back, Nixon was still deep in thought, toying with the letter opener, his feet propped on the desk. As Matt closed the door gently behind him he could hear the muted buzzer signal which informed the Secret Service man in the main hall that the President's door was no longer open.

"Hello, Tommy," Matt said with excessive cordiality.

The small man in white pants and white T-shirt handed Matt a towel that smelled strongly of disinfectant. "Afternoon, Mr. Thompson. Is it hot out there?"

"Boiling. You're lucky to be in this nice cool gym."

"It seems hot in here to me. We close at nine tonight, Mr. Thompson."

"I won't be that long; I'm sure of that."

Matt went to locker 303 and began to change into the shorts he'd brought to the gym several weeks before. He heard a door close behind him, but he didn't turn to look. A man sat on the bench next to him and put a small canvas bag between them on the bench.

"Good afternoon," Emory Latham said.

"Hi," Matt replied.

Latham opened locker 307 and took from his bag a pair of tennis shoes, shorts, and an athletic supporter, which he placed near the end of the bench. Matt looked around the small room. No one else was in sight. Matt took an

envelope from his coat pocket and stuffed it into Latham's
bag. Latham immediately put the bag in the bottom of his
locker, took off his street shoes, and placed them on top of
the bag.

As Latham undressed, Matt tied his tennis shoes, looking
sidelong at the courier as he stripped off his underwear
shorts and polo shirt. Latham dropped a letter into Matt's
locker, leaning in front of Matt as he did. Matt closed his
locker and snapped the combination lock as soon as
Latham had withdrawn to his end of the bench to begin
dressing in his gym clothes. Matt stood and walked to the
toilet. Latham did not follow him.

After his workout on the exercise machines Matt returned
to his locker. He had not seen Latham again. Other men
were dressing in another row of lockers, but Matt assumed
the courier had dressed and gone shortly after they had
silently exchanged letters. Latham had told him on the
telephone that midafternoon would be the quietest time in
the locker room, and they had made their appointment
for 2:50 P.M. to minimize the chance of being seen by
others.

Matt put his exercise clothes in his locker, took a
shower, dressed, and walked back to the Executive Office
Building. At his desk he opened Latham's envelope and
read the typed, unsigned letter it contained:

> The border situation has deteriorated to a critical
> phase. Soviet troops are massing behind their
> frontier in unprecedented numbers. Several wings
> of heavy bombers and over 100 fighter aircraft
> have been moved to airfields around Ulan Bator
> in Mongolia and Ulan-Ude near Lake Baikal.
>
> Russians agents in Eastern Europe speak open-
> ly of the possibility of an invasion of China and
> of air strikes against Lanchow and other Chinese
> cities.
>
> Armed acts of aggression by the U.S.S.R.
> along the border increase in number and severity.

Sixteen attacks occurred last month with loss of lives on both sides.

Urge that the strongest representations be made to the U.S.S.R. by the U.S.A. that any attack on China will be met with vigorous military measures by all affected nations.

Matt immediately wrote out a talking paper for the President. The National Security Council was scheduled to meet two days later, August 14.

For Dr. Kissinger
National Security Council Meeting
August 14, 1969

China-Russia Border
Talking points for the President:

(1) I am aware that the Sino-Soviet border clashes continue with increased frequency and severity.

(2) There are intelligence reports of a material buildup of Soviet strength in Mongolia and southeastern Russia, including heavy bombers and unusual numbers of MIGs.

(3) Russia is telling its allies it may attack China. One target identified is a nuclear production facility at Lanchow in central China, southwest of Peking.

(4) The Administration deplores this border conflict between two major powers as a serious threat to world peace.

(5) If Russia should attempt a preemptive air strike at China's nuclear facilities, the United States would view it as a serious act of war against China which potentially would affect the vital interests of the United States.

(6) Spokesmen will be designated to make these policy views known to the Russians and then to the general public.

Matt Thompson

Not long after Angie Cruz sent the talking paper to the NSC secretariat, Matt received a phone call from Lawrence Eagleburger.

"Matt, where do you get this information about Russians at the Chinese border? We haven't seen anything on that."

"I talk to the CIA folks who watch China," Matt answered. It was true; he did talk to the Chinese people at the Langley headquarters occasionally.

"Can you get something from them in writing? There should be a backup for these talking points, don't you think?"

"I can get something, I suppose."

"Ask them to send it directly to Henry, will you? He's a little upset that you're getting this stuff around him. He intends to talk to Helms about it."

"Why? I need the information, so I go get it. What's wrong with that?"

"Nothing, except that Henry's not included. You know how he hates to be left out of things." Eagleburger chuckled hollowly.

"What about the memo? Is he going to send it in?"

"Yes, he is. And he wants you at the NSC meeting tomorrow, prepared to talk about it, if necessary. Nine A.M."

"Okay."

At the NSC meeting the next day, Matt sat nervously at Eagleburger's left in the row of armchairs that lined the western wall of the Cabinet Room. He was not asked to speak by Nixon, who sat at the middle of the long table, facing Matt and Eagleburger. Henry Kissinger sat at the north end of the table. Haig was in a wall chair to Kissinger's right. Ranged around the table were the Secretaries of State (Rogers) and Defense (Laird); the Attorney General (Mitchell); Richard Helms, Director of Central Intelligence; the Chairman of the Joint Chiefs of Staff; and Vice President Agnew.

Matt was surprised that Nixon followed Henry Kissinger's agenda to the letter, all through the meeting. When the China border matter came up, Nixon delivered Matt's talking points almost word for word, from memory. He appointed the Undersecretary of State, Elliot Richardson, and Richard Helms to "go public" with statements of the President's "deep concern." Kissinger was instructed to tell the Russian Ambassador, Anatoly Dobrynin, that he was closely watching the Russian troop buildup along the Chinese border.

Richard Helms then contributed a bit of intelligence which occasioned Matt's next meeting with Emory Latham. "We have recently seen," Helms said in his laconic, aristocratic drawl, "clear pictures of some medium-range Soviet missiles being installed in Mongolia. I'd say either they could reach China's atomic works at Lanchow or they could hit Peking with them. The Russians have been preparing the sites for some time, but the missiles themselves just went on-site about a week ago."

About the time Elliot Richardson was warning the Soviets at a press conference the next morning, Matt Thompson was calling Latham from a pay phone in the Peoples Drug Store catercorner across Pennsylvania Avenue from the EOB.

"Hello." Latham's voice was familiar to Matt by then.

"This is Matt. I have something to give you."

"Today?"

"Yes."

"That is difficult; where are you?"

"Seventeenth and Pennsylvania."

"I'm just going out. Can you come to Georgetown?"

"I suppose so. Where?"

"Do you know the pre-Columbian museum in Dumbarton Oaks?"

"Yeah. I've been there."

"I'll be there in forty minutes, out in front of the museum building. We can walk in the park."

"Fine. See you then."

Latham was wearing the same short-sleeved shirt he had been wearing at the El Bodegón the first time they met. When he saw Matt approaching the museum on Thirty-second Street, he smiled broadly and held out his hand.

"Let's go to the lower garden," Latham said. They walked up to R Street and around the corner to the entrance to the Dumbarton Oaks estate.

"When you came here, were you followed?" Latham asked casually.

"God, I don't know. I hailed a cab in front of the drugstore and came directly here. But I hadn't even thought about being followed. I'm sorry."

Latham looked troubled. "I'm going to sit on this next bench and tie my shoe. You keep going. Meet me at the far side of the pool in the Ellipse garden down below in ten minutes. I'll see what's going on." Latham sat down and bent over. Matt walked on to a long flight of stairs which led down several terrace levels. At the bottom, tall trees surrounded a cement pond. Matt saw a vacant wooden bench in the shade on the far side, and walked to it.

In a few minutes Latham sat down on the bench next to Matt and folded his hands over his stomach.

"Everything all right?" Matt asked.

"Apparently. We will leave through different gates, though, in case someone is sitting outside waiting for you. Do you have something for me? Don't hand it to me. Just say yes or no."

"Yes."

"Okay. In a few minutes get up and walk over to that trash basket at the corner of the path. Drop it in there. I'll go where I can watch it for a while. First, though, I have a short message I've just received for you."

"Yes?"

"This is it: 'Pakistan or Romania? Pakistan is the preferred channel.' Do you understand that?"

"Yes, I do." Matt felt exhilarated. There was good communication with Chou En-lai at last. This conduit was working well. He was suddenly optimistic that they could do what had to be done to bring the countries together.

"All right, now," Latham said quietly. He hadn't moved. His eyes were still closed.

"Now?"

"Go." There was an urgent edge to Latham's soft voice.

Matt got to his feet and walked awkwardly toward the wastebasket, finding the thin envelope in his inside coat pocket, crumpling it in his fist and, without slowing, tossing it into the woven wire basket among other papers and a small yellow pillow. Why is there a pillow in there? he wondered. What kind of person would bring a little yellow pillow to Dumbarton Oaks? He climbed the long flight of stairs to the top, then turned as if to rest and admire the view. Latham was not on the bench, nor could Matt see him on the paths. The wastebasket was hidden from his view by trees.

PART

FIVE

In spite of messages sent via the USA, Romanians and the French, there has been no direct response from the P.R.C.

Thirty

The Defense Minister, Lin Piao, had not been well. Since early in 1968 the thin and balding old leader had been confined to his elaborate bedroom at his suburban home, under the care of Army physicians who were enjoined to keep their commander's deteriorating physical condition a deep secret.

Lin Piao found it necessary to husband his strength in his darkened room for the inescapable occasions that required his personal appearance. Then, with the help of the doctors' hypodermic syringes and large doses of stimulants, he was able to greet the vast crowds in Tien'anmen Square, attend meetings of the State Central Committee or preside at unavoidable military exercises or reviews. He handled routine Defense Ministry business from his bed with the help of a relay of aides.

Lin Piao was an old soldier, China's third Marshal and one of Mao's earliest adherents. He was a small, retiring, but intense man who had grown powerful as a result of his absolute loyalty to Mao, his cultivation of Mao's wife, Chiang Ch'ing, and the fact that he commanded the one remaining coherent force in China, the People's Liberation Army.

At Mao's insistence the People's Congress had named Lin Piao Vice Chairman of the Chinese Communist Party and had formally designated him Chairman Mao's successor. Since his elevation, however, Lin had seen the fates conspire to keep him from the chairmanship he so passionately coveted.

For one thing, Mao Tse-tung seemed to have perpetual life. His mind and body were deteriorating, but he had long periods of lucidity—even brilliance—and his physical health was relatively good for a man of his age. He held on to the chairmanship and China's ultimate power as if to frustrate Lin's growing ambition. At the same time, Lin Piao had been afflicted with one illness after another.

Lin and his wife, Ye Chun, realized that Chairman Mao wanted an heir who was in good health; they had heard him say so on several occasions. So Lin's frailties must be kept a secret from Mao and his wife at all costs. Twice Lin sent Mao false reports of physical examinations which declared Lin to be in the best of condition.

Not everyone believed the stories Lin encouraged about his robust physical condition. Chou En-lai had received secret reports of Lin's illnesses almost from their inception. Some high-ranking military commanders were well aware of their Minister's long absence from the Defense Ministry, and a few knew the specific nature of Lin's sicknesses. Chiang Ch'ing suspected Lin's two medical reports were false, but she said nothing to Mao. Mao's wife was a prime mover of the Cultural Revolution, and she needed her alliance with Lin Piao and his army. She would do nothing to cause Lin's downfall until it suited her purpose.

When Lin Piao received Premier Chou En-lai's request for a private meeting in mid-September of 1969, he had just suffered a particularly debilitating attack of stomach cramps. Lin's aide and secretary tried to negotiate a postponement, but was told by Yang Te-chong that the need for the meeting was urgent.

When Yang told him of the call from Lin Piao's man,

Chou En-lai sent Lin a second note proposing that as a convenience to the Defense Minister, they meet at Lin's home in the Northwest Hills. As Chou had anticipated, that offer gave Lin no choice. To mask his illness, he had to rouse himself and travel across the noisome breadth of summertime Peking to Chou's house at Chungnanhai, in the compound of the State Central Committee. He must demonstrate his vigor.

Lin arrived punctually at the arranged hour, freshly bathed and marginally invigorated by an injection of a medicine for which his new Army doctor held out considerable hope.

Chou En-lai greeted Lin, who came into the small library closely escorted by his tall son, an Air Force officer about thirty years old. The round-faced son glanced around Chou's den nervously, as if he expected his father to be ambushed by the Premier's guards.

"You know my son, Li-kuo," Lin began. "He serves as my aide some of the time these days."

"Yes, he is welcome," Chou replied. "This is my secretary, Comrade Yang Te-chong. I suggest that Comrade Yang serve your son some tea in the anteroom while we talk. He will be more comfortable there."

"Very well," Lin said reluctantly.

When they were alone, Chou sat facing Lin across a low table. The small room would have seemed crowded with four men in it; Lin Piao could hardly have refused to send his son out.

"I felt we needed to talk, Comrade Vice Chairman, about Russia."

Lin Piao reached for his teacup and sipped noisily. "Russia," he repeated.

Chou En-lai took a sheaf of papers from the low table beside his chair. "I am sure you are aware that the Russians have sent secret letters to Party leaders in Bulgaria, Poland, and East Germany this summer cautioning them that Russia might find it necessary to mount a preemptive strike at China's nuclear manufacturing and testing facilities."

Lin nodded. "I find it hard to take such letters seriously."

"On August eighteenth," Chou continued, "an official of the Soviet Embassy in Washington, who was lunching with an official of the State Department of the United States, asked what the United States' reaction would be if there were a Soviet attack on Chinese nuclear installations."

"That I did not know," Lin said. "Evidently you have better sources in America than I do. I would be interested in knowing what the American official replied. Perhaps he agreed to a joint military operation against us?"

"No, he was noncommittal. But the President's adviser, Kissinger, later cautioned Dobrynin that the United States would view such an attack as a very serious matter. The director of the CIA told some reporters the same thing."

"Is that what you wish to discuss?" Lin asked derisively.

"There is more. " Chou shuffled his papers. "This week a known Russian agent wrote an article for the *London Evening News* which was probably composed in the Kremlin. It says that 'well-informed sources in Moscow' say that Russian nuclear weapons are aimed at Chinese nuclear facilities and that the Soviets have a plan"—Chou held up a clipping and translated from it—"'a plan to launch an air attack on Lop Nor.' And he says that whether or not they will attack us is 'a question of strategy, and so the world would only learn about it afterward.'"

"Propaganda," Lin said dismissively. "Why would anyone hit Lop Nor? It's a test site; we don't make anything there."

"Let us assume there is some flame in all of this smoke," Chou replied. "It is a fact that Russian missiles in Mongolia can hit Peking and Lanchow, is it not?"

"If there are missiles there. We are not certain."

"I have sources which affirm that American spy satellites have pinpointed many such missiles there. Assume, as I do, that they are there; assume further that the Russians use them to wipe out Lanchow. Then assume that Chairman Mao summons the Defense Minister and instructs him to retaliate quickly, before Peking is also destroyed. What will occur?"

"Comrade Premier, we are not without resources, as you well know. If you can tell me where these missiles are that your American friends have found, we can aim our nuclear missiles at them immediately."

Chou shook his head. "You do not yet have a missile which can travel fifteen hundred nautical miles and accurately hit such a target, do you? We have poured a vast fortune into missiles for five years and you still don't have one as good as the Russians' intermediate-range ballistic missile, do you?"

"That is true, for many good reasons." Lin nodded. "But we can reach Mongolia with some accuracy with what we have."

Chou put his papers back on the table. "I must make certain recommendations to Chairman Mao concerning these Russian threats. They are directly connected to the fighting along the northern border, of course, which has manifested Russia's increased belligerence."

Lin shifted in his chair and reached for his teacup. "Are you telling me that the Army will be withdrawn from protecting the border, Comrade Premier? Have you made a secret agreement with the Russians?"

"There are no secrets. Everyone knows I met Kosygin at the airport the other day. As I told the State Central Committee, I kept him out there and did not bring him into the city for two reasons. I wanted it to appear that he was being given no courtesies beyond a cup of tea. But also, I was afraid to bring him in. Some crazy Red Guards might have burned his car with him in it."

"The Army could have protected him."

"He initiated the meeting on very short notice. He was flying from Indonesia to Russia. You would not have had time to take adequate precautions for his safety. Be that as it may, Kosygin proposed that both armies be pulled back from the border an equal distance. He suggested thirty kilometers."

Lin snorted. "I'll bet he did. They have rocket artillery up there that reaches well beyond that. So, did you agree to that?"

"No, Comrade, I did not agree to anything. I said I would give him our position in due course. Now I must make recommendations, first to Chairman Mao, then to the State Central Committee."

"It appears, Comrade Premier, that the Russians are frightening you. What will you recommend?"

"A wise man counts his arrows before he enters battle, Comrade. I have no doubt that we could eventually defeat a Russian invasion with our in-depth defense strategy. But if they chose to use their missiles to destroy our industrial production, the Russians might force us to our knees without coming a meter across the border. We might find ourselves redrawing borders and giving them warm-water ports as the price of peace. We have almost no counterattack capability, and we have no allies on whom to call. So, I will recommend we recognize our weakness and enter talks with the Russians to cool off the border fighting."

"And what do you want from me?" Lin asked. "Do you expect me to agree to all of that?"

"I think you should, but I will not be surprised if you do not. If you can show me that our forces are capable of deterring the Russians, I will certainly listen. But I believe you must admit that we lack the logistical capability to invade Russia and win; we lack the missiles to assault Russia or the economic strength to sustain a counterattack. Our internal affairs are in a shambles. Food production is off badly. Local government just does not exist in many regions. If the Army were to leave the localities now to fight a war, they would leave only anarchy behind. You and I both know we are in no condition to enter battle, Comrade."

"I do not concede that for a moment," Lin Piao said, bristling. "Our forces are well equipped and well trained. In most cases the leadership is good, and it's getting better. Deadwood is being rigorously cleaned out of the officer ranks. New ideological training is resulting in heightened morale among the rank and file. The People's Liberation Army is ready, I assure you. And I will assure Chairman Mao and the others of that fact."

Lin struggled weakly to get out of the deep overstuffed chair.

"Shall I help you, Comrade?" Chou asked.

"No! I am quite well and I am able to stand without assistance, thank you." Lin turned in the big chair so he could push his back against one arm of the chair with his feet, balancing with a hand on the other arm. With great effort he levered himself to a standing position, rearranged his tunic, and bowed slightly to Chou. "I am quite well, thank you," he repeated.

"I am, of course, very glad to hear that you are in good health, Comrade," Chou said blandly. "Let me show you where your son is waiting."

Thirty-one

December 20, 1969

Dear Mr. President:

This letter is about what I see taking place with respect to Communist China.

First, let me congratulate you on an extraordinarily successful first year in office. Your foreign trips have invigorated America's alliances everywhere and the Russians have been put on the defensive for the first time in years. I had serious doubts about Henry Kissinger when you hired him—as I told you then. It appears that you have held him in check, for the most part, while making him useful in carrying out your policies.

But in the matter of Communist China I fear

he and his staff—notably young Matthew Thompson—have gotten away from you and are pursuing a course of action that is antithetical to everything your Administration stands for. When recent events are examined, I submit, an ominous pattern emerges:

— In February Kissinger and Thompson initiated a reexamination of long-standing U.S. policy toward Communist China. After a preliminary set of reports, a meeting was held and the Departments were given further assignments. That work continues at State and the CIA.

— The embargo on trade with the P.R.C. has been partially lifted, travel restrictions have been relaxed and trade has begun between the U.S. and the P.R.C.

— Kissinger has actually interposed this country between Russia and Communist China, warning the U.S.S.R not to attack the P.R.C.

— Three weeks ago the Communist Chinese released two Americans they had held prisoner for ten months.

— Two weeks ago the U.S. Ambassador to Poland was invited to tea at the Red Chinese Embassy in Warsaw—and he went!

It seems clear that Dr. Kissinger and Thompson have been quietly and effectively turning this country's policy in a direction I am sure you would not approve. Nor, if they knew of it, would a majority of the American people approve of a policy of friendship with the Communist Chinese who ruthlessly killed Americans by the thousands a few years ago in Korea. The same Chinese are arming and supplying North Vietnamese soldiers today, with the expectation that their bullets, which were made in China, will kill Americans in South Viet Nam next week or next month.

All patriotic Americans will deeply resent Kissinger's new "friendship" with a godless,

Communist country which has made a foreign policy out of killing Americans.

If some new relationship with Communist China is openly sought by Kissinger, what must our allies think of us? The Republic of China relies upon us to prevent Mainland hordes from invading Formosa. Will we repudiate our solemn undertakings in Taipei? The South Vietnamese can only wonder if Dr. Kissinger might sell them out to their enemies in the North. Burma, Thailand, Indonesia, Malaysia and, certainly, Japan would feel less secure. Are we prepared to give Communist China a free hand to overrun those countries too?

I hope I am wrong about what Dr. Kissinger is up to, but the signs seem very plain.

Patrick J. Buchanan

To: H. R. Haldeman
From: The President

Here is a note from Pat Buchanan. Rose says he has talked to her about China and seems very upset. He has not gone to Buckley or Murphy yet, but indicates to Rose that he feels he should "go public" if Kissinger persists.

Bob, we cannot have this. The President must be able to set foreign policy without everyone on the White House Staff running all over Washington making it more difficult. Please see Pat and make it clear to him that the President is doing the best he can to bring peace to a troubled world. No one likes godless Communism, least of all the President.

Do what you can to make sure Pat does not go further with this.

R.N.

Outside the glossy black White House fence, all of the United States was celebrating Christmas, and occasionally

352   John Ehrlichman

slivers of the holiday squeezed between the sleek vertical
iron bars, to arrive, within the center of power, oddly
misshapen. The staff in the EOB and in the West Wing
knew that over in the residence, the First Family had
decorated a big Christmas tree for the Blue Room; that was
known because the *Post* carried a picture of the First Lady
hanging a bauble on it.

In part from necessity, in part from a desire to gain
control over the far frontiers of foreign policy, Henry
Kissinger drove his staff harder during the holidays of
1969 than ever before. Deadlines were advanced, not
relaxed. Near-perfect work was returned for reworking. A
staff Christmas Party was cancelled in favor of a second
meeting on a subject which had been exhausted at the first
meeting. The married employees suffered grumbling at
home; the bachelors cancelled their pre-Christmas dates as
Kissinger increased the pressure on them to produce. Staff
morale languished.

Neither Colonel Haig nor Kissinger had said anything to
Matthew Thompson about the President's intervention with
the FBI, nor had Kissinger spoken to the President about it.
But both Haig and Kissinger had been made well aware of
the removal by J. Edgar Hoover of the *Redwood* tap.

After Nixon called him about Matt Thompson, J. Edgar
Hoover had had elaborate memoranda inserted into the
file, recounting exactly what the President had instructed,
for Hoover was a survivor. Having been a Washington
bureaucrat for decades, he knew better than to be caught
between someone like Richard Nixon and someone like
Henry Kissinger. Hoover sent Kissinger a short memorandum, too:

   Dr. Henry A. Kissinger
   Assistant to the President
   for National Security Affairs

   At the President's specific direction the surveillance
   of Matthew (nmi) Thompson (Redwood) of your
   staff was discontinued.
                                      J.E.H.

No oracle ever scrutinized the entrails of a sacrifice more closely than Haig and Kissinger looked at, around, and beyond that Hoover memorandum the morning it arrived.

"We knew he was Nixon's man when he came!" Kissinger recalled excitedly. "Haldeman insisted that we hire him, along with Dick Allen, remember. Did you ever tell Nixon we had Thompson tapped?"

"No, but the President was getting the coded logs for a while," Haig reminded him.

Kissinger nodded. "He might have figured out who Redwood was, or he might have asked Hoover. Or maybe someone who knew leaked it to Thompson or Nixon. Or maybe this is Haldeman trying again to wound me. We've got to know how this has happened!"

"Only you and I knew, outside the FBI," Haig said suggestively.

"Nixon has said nothing to you," Kissinger affirmed.

"Not a word."

"Nor to me. Are we certain that it is legal to do these taps?"

"Mitchell says they are okay if there is a national security threat."

Kissinger nodded. "Then Nixon has nothing hanging over our heads on that score. But it may turn out that our President is playing a double game with Peking through Thompson, you know? I wouldn't put it past him. I want to be sure that the NSA watches closely for Thompson's overseas phone calls from now on. Give them the name of that Chinaman in Hong Kong and ask the British to keep a closer eye on him. There is more to all of this than we know, I think."

"Do we share China information with Thompson from now on?" Haig asked. "We should be getting word through the Pakistan pipe. Does he see it?"

Kissinger looked at his desk top, deep in thought. "Yes, I think he must. I don't want trouble from Nixon about this, and he will surely object if we cut his man out. Be

sure Thompson sees everything. Tell people he is our
China expert. But be careful of him.''

Matt Thompson never doubted that the FBI had removed
the listening device from his apartment when the President
ordered J. Edgar Hoover to remove it. Matt began to sleep
well again, to talk freely on his telephone, and to invite
Mary Finn and others to come to his house. But as long as
he worked at the White House, Matt could not forgive
Henry Kissinger and Alexander Haig for having invaded
his existence with their surveillance.

The President and Dr. Kissinger met with their Ambassador to Warsaw, Walter J. Stoessel, Jr., and instructed
him to meet secretly with China's ambassador there. The
President wanted the Warsaw talks resumed; he was getting impatient since there had been no Chinese messages
coming through the French, Romanians, or Pakistanis.

But it was not until the first week of December that
Stoessel cabled Kissinger that he had finally been able to
talk privately with China's chargé d'affaires, Lei Yang.
(The Chinese Ambassador had been removed during the
Cultural Revolution.) On December 5, Stoessel reported,
the Chinese had telephoned and invited him to come to tea
in a few days. By Christmas the Ambassador could report
that on January 20 he would meet with the Chinese to plan
the resumed ambassadorial talks in Warsaw.

Haig made certain that Matt Thompson had copies of all
the cable traffic with Stoessel. The State Department also
received the Stoessel cable traffic. And the China experts
in the State Department immediately began to prepare
State's instructions to Stoessel for his January meeting.
Matt Thompson was thereupon summoned to Kissinger's
office.

"This Warsaw connection may be the wrong way to
go," Kissinger declared in his most solemn and guttural
voice when everyone was seated. Haig, Matt, and John
Holdridge sat to Henry's right. Winston Lord took a chair
to his left.

"Even now, the geniuses at State have decided that they
are the ones who are going to tell Stoessel what to do and

say." Henry Kissinger waved his hand at his desk. "Here are State Department draft guidelines already, about which embassy the talks should be in and questions concerning the Korean truce line which should and should not be raised! What they do not consider is that Stoessel is the *President's* ambassador and takes his instructions from here—and only from here!" He slapped his desk top heavily. "So, how does the President control these talks?"

"Well"—Winston Lord, a young man with a vest and a heavy manner, spoke deeply and slowly—"surely we can reject their guidelines and prepare our own."

"Of course," added John Holdridge, "they cannot prevent the President from instructing his ambassador."

"The problem," Haig began in his high, whirring voice, "is that State has run these Warsaw talks since the fifties. It would be hot news, and they would surely leak it, if we shorted them out of the Warsaw talks now. It would put a bright light on U.S.-Sino relations." Haig stubbed out a cigarette and fished in his coat pocket for another. "I don't think we want to call that much attention to what we are trying to do."

"We don't," said Kissinger flatly. "So the problem is to make sure the talks go well, in spite of the State Department."

"Why don't you go over to Warsaw—secretly, of course—and sit in with Stoessel, Henry?" Winston Lord asked.

"It is not out of the question," Kissinger said, nodding slowly. "But one can't be sure the Poles will cooperate to keep the secret. And there are other things to be done here. At this stage someone must make certain that State instructs only with our prior approval. Al, that is your job. You must make sure Elliot Richardson understands. I want someone to review every word they propose to send Stoessel before it goes. Thompson, that is you. Go over and sleep there if you have to. Nothing goes unless I see it first. Understood?"

"Yes," Matt said.

"Work with Winston on the substance if I am not here. But I must personally see everything before it is sent. There must be no slip-ups. Understood?"

Everyone nodded except Matt. "How is this to be enforced at State?" he asked. "If they want to send Stoessel a cable from the Secretary and you haven't approved it, how do I stop it from going?"

"I'll talk to the Undersecretary," Haig said patiently—too patiently—"and he will issue procedural instructions. You can show them to any troublemakers. And you can always call me."

"Thanks."

"Other questions?" Haig asked. There were none. "Okay, back to work."

Matt went to his office and began to draft a list of topics for Stoessel to be instructed upon:

1. Taiwan—U.S. prepared to concede—what?
2. Exchange envoys
3. Presidential visit
4. Viet Nam, Korea, other mutual impediments
5. Future Warsaw talks

That afternoon Haig sent Matt a copy of the State Department's first draft guidelines, prepared by a China expert on Assistant Secretary William Huntoon's East Asian staff. It was clear from its modest content that the State Department did not understand Richard Nixon's wide-ranging intentions. Matt called the man who had prepared the guidelines, Barton Kleinfeldt, and asked him to come to Matt's office the next day to talk about them.

Kleinfeldt was a small, middle-aged China expert. He had worked for two years in the consular section of the embassy in Tokyo, then had been a junior political officer in the embassy at Taipei for a year and a half. Barton Kleinfeldt spoke Mandarin fluently and had become a keen student of Chinese history. He was William Huntoon's protégé at State, and Huntoon, with some foresight, had encouraged him to read everything he could find about China. Now, as a matter of routine, China matters went to Kleinfeldt's desk for handling.

"I've never been over here at the White House before,"

Kleinfeldt confessed, looking around Matt's office. "Does the President have an office in this building?"

"Down one flight on the east side," Matt pointed. "It's an informal place for him to work. The Oval Office is over there in that little west wing of the Residence. The bushes hide his window."

"I see."

"Sit there, Mr. Kleinfeldt. We need to talk about Stoessel's instructions and the Warsaw talks with China. I've seen your draft and so has Henry Kissinger. He and the President have asked me to work with you to introduce several new topics in the second draft." By this time, Matt had learned to invoke the President without shame.

"Fine. I'll just take some notes." Kleinfeldt produced a reporter's note pad from his coat pocket.

"First," Matt continued, "you should know that the President has talked with Stoessel and told him that he is to try to open things up. Nixon wants to move fast. The long-range goal is normal relations with China; the short-run goal is an exchange of representatives for talks, leading to normalization."

"I see. Very helpful. Does Bill—Assistant Secretary Huntoon—have all of this?"

"I doubt it. The President sees three stumbling blocks to normal relations. The big ones are Taiwan and Viet Nam. Korea may be raised by them, but we don't need to bring it up. Let's try this formula in the next draft: Stoessel opens by saying the President hopes—repeat, *hopes*—to materially reduce the number of American troops in Asia very soon. He hopes to bring down the numbers in the garrisons in Taiwan and South Viet Nam, specifically.

"His objective is peace in the Far East. To that end he proposes talks at a high level in the near future. He is willing that those talks take place in Peking or elsewhere in China."

"If I may say so," Kleinfeldt said after he had finished with his notes, "that will be seen by the Chinese as moving very fast, perhaps too fast. They have not talked to

us since 1949. Now, all at once, we are proposing high-
level talks. Don't be surprised if they run away.''

"The President has to decide the pace and timing of
this, and he intends to move it along. That's all I can tell
you.'' I'm not about to tell you how ready the Chinese
really are, Matt thought, nor tell you anything about the
other messages we've sent them.

Kleinfeldt went away promising to have his second draft
on its way to Rogers within twenty-four hours. But several
days, if not a week, he reminded Matt, must be allowed
for a departmental review before something could show up
at Kissinger's door.

Mao Tse-tung's library was the warmest room in the
house, sheltered from the insistent north winds by the high
walls of the State Central Committee Compound, and
cocooned from the rest of the big house by walls of
shelves stuffed with Chinese books, manuscripts, and scrolls.
At Mao's insistence the cotton summer slipcovers remained
on the massive furniture in this one room even in the
winter.

Mao slumped in his favorite chair with a cashmere robe
over his knees. His hands and arms lay heavily inert on the
high arms of the old chair. He was at rest, a mountain of a
man, held together by the residue of his waning strength.
He said a few loosely formed words to the young woman
assigned to care for him and she knelt to rewrap his right
foot in the folds of his blanket. She stood, took the cover
from Mao's teacup, and held it to his mouth. He noisily
drank a little, then drew back from the cup.

Premier Chou En-lai came into the library without
prelude and sat in the big chair next to Mao. "Thank you,
Comrade,'' Chou said to the attendant. "I will look after
things for a time. You will be called when you are
needed.'' The girl bowed and carefully closed the door as
she left.

"What is happening in the streets, old Comrade?" Mao
asked.

"It is bitterly cold. The wind has driven everyone indoors. The streets are nearly empty."

"So the Red Guards are not rampaging," Mao assured himself. He spoke through open teeth, his round face immobile.

Chou saw Mao often and was accustomed to the difficulty of understanding the old Chairman. Mao often sat in this chair, a woman reading to him, his round head bowed forward, his body massively heavy, cascading, his stomach a great, soft boulder above his legs.

"Comrade Chairman," Chou said loudly, half to get Mao's attention, half because the old man was gradually going deaf, "there are developments with the Americans."

"Yes?"

"The man in charge of our Warsaw embassy has talked with their ambassador. And the young man in the White House in Washington has sent us a message. It appears that the American leader, Nixon, would like to come here for talks with you. They wish to talk soon."

"Well, that is one good thing. Neither you nor I could possibly leave Peking now, eh?" Mao turned slowly to look at Chou. "Do you agree?"

Chou smiled. "We might not be let back in? I'm not sure it's that bad."

"I think it is. Our exalted Defense Minister and my dear wife would be running the country, with the help of the Army, ten minutes after we left."

Chou leaned forward in his chair. "As you suggested, I am having Lin Piao and his family watched closely. Some occurrences confirm your suspicion that he is very ill. It is perhaps a blood cancer. He spends almost all of his time in bed in his house in the Fragrant Hills. He arises only for those occasions which are important and unavoidable."

"What would he do if we had an American come here for talks, Comrade?" Mao asked.

"That might trigger him to move against us with the Air Force and part of the Army," Chou said matter-of-factly.

Mao was surprised; he turned with great effort to look at Chou. "Do you believe that?"

"I think it is possible. First, he is very much against our moving toward the Americans. He would prefer the Russians, I think, if he were forced to choose. Second, I'm convinced he will try to take over whenever he thinks he can successfully do it. His eldest son eggs him on. They may move under the pretext that the Cultural Revolution has created anarchy and he must stabilize the situation in China with his troops."

Mao nodded slightly, his jowls quivering. "He has been here this week to complain about your American adventurism. He has a thick dossier which identifies several American agents and a Hong Kong businessman as your cat's-paws, and his file is full of their secret messages to your agents here. He charges that you have recruited agents from those who were banished in the Great Proletarian Cultural Revolution as elitists."

"There is very little truth in some of that, Comrade Chairman, and I will be happy to tell you everything I am doing. It is not a secret from you."

Mao raised his left hand an inch or two above the chair arm and moved the hand slowly from side to side. "No, you need not tell me."

"I am genuinely concerned," Chou continued, "with our economic problems. It is possible that we will have another famine because so many communes have been disrupted. We must have some foreign sources of rice and grains."

"Yes, you have told me before. I do not regret the disruption, Comrade. It may be necessary to shrink China's stomach to save her soul, and that is all right."

"The Russians know we are in trouble," Chou went on. "When we met out at the airport, that bandit Kosygin made that clear. He offered to help us, but in the next breath he said they wanted us to cede some of the northern lands which they claim. I think the Americans will send food at a much better price."

"What is their price?"

"We do not fully know," Chou admitted, "but I think they hope we will mediate for them in Viet Nam. Their

Viet Nam war is a serious political liability for their leaders. I believe they will ask us to create a peace there which both sides can accept.''

"And will they give us Taiwan?"

"No, but I think they will turn their heads and let us take it. Perhaps that is just as good."

"So what is to be decided?" Mao asked. He was visibly tired and wanted the conversation to end.

"Shall we agree to an American envoy's coming to China?" Chou asked.

"I say yes, but they must agree to our demands on Taiwan first. They must do more than avert their gaze."

"Perhaps their President is prohibited from that by their Congress and existing laws."

"Then he must agree secretly. I must be able to tell Lin Piao that we have won back Taiwan. The Army must have a reason to tolerate the Americans. Nixon must make a secret promise."

"Anything more?"

"You must be prepared to counter Lin Piao and his family. You must beware. I think the Air Force is disloyal to us. We must change the leadership of the Air Force."

"If we were to try, Lin Piao would strike at once, I believe. If he remains Defense Minister, you cannot stir up the Air Force, Comrade Chairman. We must bide our time."

"Very well, but beware. Tell the man in Warsaw to say their envoy may come here but he must come in absolute secrecy. There are two reasons for secrecy: First, the world, and especially the Russians, might read this as a move which is born of China's weakness or desperation, and we cannot have that. Second, our military leaders should not know of it until we are ready to tell them. Finally—a third reason I had not thought of: our friends the accursed Vietnamese must not know of it. They might misunderstand. The envoy can be kept at a secret place. Bring him here at night and I will talk to him. Let him fly into a remote airfield. Nixon must promise that it will be secret, too. Do you trust him?"

"Not entirely. But my men in their government are in positions to know if he engages in treachery. We can be warned."

"Comrade Premier, one more question. My successor opposes all of this with the Americans. I can prevail on Lin Piao to accept the idea that an envoy is coming and in return we will have Taiwan and the Americans will send us grains. But he will continue to oppose a long-range relationship with the hated Americans. How is he to be neutralized?"

"Perhaps, Comrade Chairman, he must be removed from his leadership of the military. Perhaps our comrades in the People's Liberation Army who so deeply dislike him can be persuaded to act."

"It is not just Comrade Lin, of course," Mao said, reflectively. A small smile twitched at the corner of his mouth. "Never kill the male tiger only, they say in India. You must find his mate and their cubs and kill them too. It is that son of his who looks bad to me."

Chou nodded. "And the wife. If the military commanders neutralize Comrade Lin, the Army must be convinced that their commanders have done the proper thing. We cannot afford a backlash; the Army still gives us some stability in the provinces."

"It must be a careful plan, and my wife, Chiang Ch'ing, must not know. Lin and his wife have flattered her too much; she has become a daughter in their house and a spy in my house."

"We must talk again about all of this, old Comrade," Chou said. "I will go now and send word to the American President that you require a secret pledge that Taiwan will be restored. We will soon know what his price is. Thank you for your gracious hospitality, Comrade Chairman."

Mao closed his eyes and made an almost imperceptible gesture with his left hand. "You honor my house . . ." he slurred. Before the Premier had left the room, Mao was asleep.

* * *

Angie Cruz opened the door and came to Matt's desk with a quizzical look on her face. "There's a fellow on the phone who says he was a student of your father's. He wants to talk to you."

"Angie," Matt said with annoyance, "I have all of this to finish up today." He prodded a pile of memoranda. "Who is he?"

"Somebody named Jack Emory."

"Emory? Yeah, I've heard Dad talk about him. I'll take the call." He reached for the phone without waiting for Angie to close the door.

"Mr. Thompson?" It was Emory Latham's voice, beyond question. "I'm sorry to bother you, but your father said it would be okay."

"That's all right, Mr. . . . ."

"Emory."

"Emory. How can I help you, Mr. Emory?"

"There is an important envelope for you in your locker. You had better pick it up right away."

The envelope in Matt's locker held a typed letter without salutation or signature, but its origin was clear to Matt:

In the matter of an envoy, this is a subject which must remain absolutely secret on both sides. Absolutely secret, with no breach.

In the matter of timing, it will not be possible to receive an envoy until your leader secretly assures the other leader that the problem of Taiwan will be removed satisfactorily. When the secret assurance is given, an envoy's reception can be scheduled immediately.

Matt reread the letter as the taxi swerved around a corner into Connecticut Avenue. By the time he'd arrived at the northwest gate across West Executive Avenue, between the White House and the Executive Office Building, Matt had replaced the letter in its envelope and shoved it deep into his inside coat pocket. He paid the cabdriver and walked past the guard with a wave. A young man he knew was in the process of taking off his coat and tie beside his Volkswagen in one of the coveted parking spaces in West Executive Avenue.

"Hi, Matt," Bill Jameson called. "It's time to go home." Jameson worked for Patrick Moynihan on urban problems.

Matt shook his head. "How's the new baby?"

"Great. Want to see some pictures?"

"Can't right now."

"Are you and Glenna still going together?" Jameson asked. He was leaning on the top of his little car, his collar open.

"No, not really. Big fight," Matt said cryptically.

"We wondered. We were going to invite you to a little party, but we'd seen her out with that Iranian so I figured I'd better ask you."

"What Iranian?"

"That Ranjani, the chargé at their embassy. They were at the British garden party together."

"Oh, yeah. Well, we agreed to go our separate ways. She got very upset with me."

"Too bad. Maybe we can just invite you and you can bring a different date. How about that?"

"Sure. When is it?"

"In about a month. Martha likes to plan ahead. I'll let you know."

"Sure." Matt went up to his office, thinking about Taiwan and Glenna and the Iranian. He closed his door, put the letter on his desk, and hung up his coat. When he sat down he reread the letter, then dialed Glenna's telephone number. She answered on the second ring.

"Hi," he said. "It's me."

"It's who?"

"Matt. It's me." Silence. "What are you doing?" Matt asked.

"Well, as a matter of fact, I'm reading a book."

"Really? Which book?"

"I guess you'd say it's a travel book."

"Going somewhere?"

"Not right away, but I get a vacation in a few months. I haven't really decided."

"So you're reading *Iran on Five Dollars a Day*, right?"

"Close, but no cigar."

"Right country, wrong book title?"

"Something like that."

"Have you had dinner?"

"Hours ago. You?"

"Not yet. Want to come out with me while I eat?"

"No. We are all finished. Remember?"

"I never really believed that."

"Well, I believe it. You have a new girlfriend and I have other interests and we are finished. That's what I believe."

"Jim and Martha want to invite both of us to their party, but they're afraid we'll have a big fight and damage their house. They think I might kill that Iranian in their kitchen."

"Will you?"

"Probably. I guess I'm very jealous." It pleased him to say that. She had been jealous of Mary Finn and he had criticized her for it. Now he could admit to the same base emotion graciously and compliment her at the same time. And emotionally, it seemed to cost him nothing. He wondered why.

"Are you? Is that an apology?"

"I guess. I really miss you."

"What about your new girlfriend?"

"Mary is not a romantic girlfriend, if that's what you mean. Besides, I haven't seen her. She's out on the Coast. She's been gone a long time. She has a big case out there or something."

"Poor boy. Where are you?"

"At the office. I'm nearly finished here, though, and I'm hungry."

"I'll just bet you are."

"So, how about some dinner? I'll eat and look at you and you can have dessert and coffee?"

"Are you going to ask me to marry you?"

"What? You mean at dinner?"

"Or after. Sometime tonight?"

"Well, I hadn't planned to, but we could just sort of let the evening unfold. Who knows what might happen?"

"That's too indefinite."

"What do you mean?"

"I need to know for sure. Either you are or you aren't. Are you?"

"Going to propose, you mean? Are you teasing me? Kidding?"

"No, I am definitely not kidding. I want to know." There was steel in her voice. "Just tell me, yes or no."

"Hey, I didn't call up to argue with you. I really miss you, so I thought we could have a date tonight. We can eat and talk and everything. I wouldn't propose to you over the telephone, I'll tell you that. And I don't think it's much different to answer your question on the phone, either. It just amounts to the same thing."

"But Matt, if I go out with you we'll end up going to bed after dinner and you'll just start taking me for granted again, and I can't stand that. Either we get engaged first or I'm not going to see you anymore."

"But if you love me and want to get married, how can you not see me?"

"I don't know."

"You don't know?"

"No."

"But Glenna—"

"Good night, Matt. If you decide to propose, call me up. Otherwise, don't."

"Are you kidding?"

She hung up softly. He looked at his telephone, shook his head, and hung it up less gently.

For: Dr. Kissinger
From: Matthew Thompson
Re: P.R.C. responses

In spite of messages sent via the Paks, Romanians and the French, there has been no direct response from the P.R.C.

I have tried to analyze what else might be done
to elicit a response to the President's messages.

I have one suggestion which might break the
logjam. The one single and greatest remaining
impediment is Taiwan. The President has made
clear his intentions with respect to troop levels
in Viet Nam and has said he hopes to reduce
troop levels in Taiwan. But P.R.C. leaders may
still doubt America's intentions with respect to
the reunification of Taiwan with China.

I suggest that the President secretly message
Premier Chou En-lai that the Taiwan problem will
be negotiated away satisfactorily when the
President or his envoy meets with the Premier.

No specific formula need be spelled out in such
a message. But it may be urgent that some firm
assurance of good faith is given at this time on
this centrally important issue.

Matthew Thompson

Thirty-two

"Come in, Matthew, come in." Henry Kissinger smiled
a great, hemispheric grin.

Not "Thompson," but "*Matthew*," noted the object of
the Teutonic jocundity. That is probably the first time he
has ever used my given name, Matt realized.

Kissinger was in his new upstairs office, a suite of rooms
where there had been a pressroom before. The White
House pressroom had been on the northwest corner of the

West Wing since the days of William Howard Taft, but now the press was removed to space that had once been stables, had then become storerooms, and had then been used as Franklin Roosevelt's swimming pool. Richard Nixon had been in favor of moving the press two hundred feet west, into some cavern in or under the old Executive Office Building, but representatives of the press corps had objected so violently and vigorously that he had reconsidered. The swimming-pool location was an expensive compromise.

In the new Kissinger suite there was a large corner office with tall windows in the north and west walls, cubbyhole offices for Haig and two other assistants, and room for three secretaries. It was all very near the West Wing's lobby, on the same floor level as the Oval Office. Nelson Rockefeller had lent Kissinger a large, monochromatic modern painting in blue for his south wall; the General Services Administration had supplied a Williamsburg Reproduction desk, table, and chairs; and when all was in perfect readiness Kissinger had moved into the "better space" he had been demanding for a year.   .

"It has come!" Kissinger exulted. "A message from the Chinese! Stoessel has just cabled from Warsaw to say their chargé d'affaires has given him a message. They agree that an American envoy should come to Peking!" Kissinger was flushed with excitement.

"That's wonderful news," Matt replied. Hardly news, he thought. Teng Shan-li had forecast this development eight days before in a message Matt received in his gym locker.

Pak and other conduits are proving awkward. Warsaw chargé will tell Stoessel an envoy may be sent. Utmost secrecy is an absolute condition. The Taiwan message is satisfactory. Good work.

"I have not yet told Nixon, but I must do so soon," Kissinger continued. "In a few minutes Stoessel's message will be all over the State Department and that damn Rogers will be calling to be congratulated on his vast managerial and diplomatic skill in bringing the Chinese to agreement."

"If it's known at State, how can you keep it secret?" Matt asked.

"Maybe we must tell them lies," said Kissinger. "Perhaps Nixon tells Rogers he's decided not to send anyone."

"Who will go?" Matt asked.

Kissinger flushed. "We will be preparing a list right away. I expect Nixon to come up with three or four names as soon as I tell him. None of them will be suitable, of course, but the list will look good in his memoirs." The National Security Adviser looked out the window at a limousine that was slowly approaching the West Wing from the Pennsylvania Avenue gate. "Is that Rogers coming?" Kissinger demanded. He jumped up and went to his door. "Al!" he yelled. "That is Rogers coming! He's driving up. Don't let him in! Have them keep him in the lobby for at least ten minutes!"

Kissinger came back to his desk and looked at Matt distractedly. "I've got to go. Where is that Stoessel cable? I want you to begin a briefing book for whoever goes to China. Get everything on Chou En-lai and Mao. Get CIA psychological profiles on them. Prepare a big section on Taiwan. Put in all the numbers on U.S. troops in Asia. Prepare an issues forecast. But this must be done in absolute secrecy! Keep State out. It's top secret!" He moved to the door, a pad in one hand, a sheaf of cables in the other.

As Kissinger rushed through his anteroom, he bellowed at the secretary who sat just outside his door, "Tell Tom James I'm coming! I have to get in ahead of Rogers. Don't let him out of the lobby until I say so!"

Matt sat in Kissinger's office for several minutes making notes of what Kissinger wanted included in the briefing book. A secretary came into the doorway and Matt recognized her. She had worked for Dick Allen when he first came to the White House.

"Are you working up here now?" he asked.

She nodded. "It's more interesting. Mr. Allen is away so much, there wasn't too much to do for him. Matt, they want you at the President's office right away."

He was surprised. He quickly decided to go by way of the inside corridor, although it would have been faster to cross the lobby. He didn't want to be waylaid by the Secretary of State, who was doubtless being restrained there. Matt walked past the congressional liaison office to the Haldeman corner, then went left. As he passed Rose Mary Woods's suite Matt looked into the open door. Glenna was sitting at a desk, typing. She wore a light brown cashmere sweater over a white blouse, and he was glad to see her. She did not look up, and he decided she had not heard him say hello as he passed her doorway. A Secret Service man stood down the hall outside the President's northwest door. He watched Matt approach with only moderate interest. Across the hall there was a meeting going on in the Roosevelt Room. Matt recognized Senator Jennings Randolph of West Virginia on the far side of the table as he hurried by the open door. The Roosevelt Room seemed to be full of people.

"Good morning," Matt said to the agent as he passed him. The man nodded. In the Cabinet Room corridor Matt turned right into the small office where Carol Phinney had her desk. Another secretary was typing there. She looked up and nodded. "Go on in."

Nixon was behind his desk. Haldeman sat in one side chair at the right and Kissinger occupied the other, on the opposite side, his cables piled on the President's otherwise clean desk top beside him. They continued to talk as Matt approached.

"Pull up that chair, Matthew," Nixon said. "We have good news here at last."

"So I hear," Matt replied. He moved a wooden chair nearer the desk and sat down.

"Rogers is waiting outside, and we need to agree on several things before he comes in," Nixon explained. "First, there is the question of who should go to China. Bob, here, thinks the President ought to go himself right away to seize the opportunity. Henry disagrees. What do you think? You understand the Chinese better than any of us; how would they react?"

"Mr. President, they have profound internal problems," Matt began. "I don't think you can go yet; they won't be ready for you. This first, exploratory visit must be a total secret from some of the political elements inside China who are strongly opposed to all of this. How can a Presidential visit be kept secret?"

Kissinger nodded in vigorous agreement. Haldeman shrugged.

"How can all of this be kept secret?" Nixon echoed. "The little shits in the State Department will all know about it soon and they'll leak it all over hell. How do we stop that?"

"Are you asking me?" Matt asked with some surprise. Nixon nodded.

"Well," Matt began, "I would guess that William Huntoon, over there, will oppose sending an envoy to Peking right away. The State Department's China man has told me that Huntoon favors first working out the Peking agenda between the ambassadors in Warsaw. Then, he thinks, Stoessel should sound them out on each point and report their position on each one. Then State ought to prepare position papers on each point."

"My God! All of that will take a year!" Nixon said impatiently.

"We could appear to be playing along with that, though," Haldeman suggested.

Matt nodded. "Perhaps you can put Bill Huntoon in charge and tell him that it is a very secret project. Meanwhile, appoint your envoy and we can get him ready over here in the White House and send him as soon as possible."

"If some of Huntoon's work leaks," Kissinger added, "everyone can deny it with a good conscience. I can have the Paks tell Chou En-lai what we are doing so he isn't confused."

Nixon nodded. "That's fine. Let's get Rogers in here and tell him. Henry, you and Matthew go into the Cabinet Room. I'll call you in when Rogers gets in here."

Kissinger gathered up his loops of cable copy and led the way to the northeast door, stumping reluctantly, his whole body showing that he resented the President's order. As they crossed Carol Phinney's room, when the President's door had closed behind him, Kissinger grumbled: "Childish. All to save Rogers' vanity and pride. Someday his vanity will cost this country a high price! Why shouldn't he be told that the President knows about China already?"

In the vacant Cabinet Room Kissinger sat in the chair to the right of the President's larger chair, his back to the windows, reading the long rolls of cable copy. Matt stood at the windows looking at the Rose Garden. A man in a Park Service uniform was trimming the edge of the grass with a hand clipper. Two women stood in the portico to Matt's left pointing at the garden and talking. A black butler in a suit of tails walked toward them from the Residence carrying a tray covered with two starched linen napkins. The President's lunch? Matt wondered. About the time the butler disappeared to Matt's left, Carol Phinney came in to say, "You can go in now, Dr. Kissinger."

While Matt and Henry Kissinger were waiting in the Cabinet Room, Nixon, Matt deduced, had constructed an elaborate charade for William Rogers. The President evidently had explained Rogers' long wait, received Rogers' report of Stoessel's cable, then sent Haldeman out, ostensibly to summon Kissinger and Matt.

Rogers was seated where Kissinger had been, and Haldeman had pulled up two wooden chairs for the latecomers. When they were seated and had been greeted, Nixon said: "Bill has just been telling me that China has agreed to receive my representative in Peking."

"Congratulations, Mr. President," Kissinger said solemnly. "This can be a historic breakthrough. It may change the world."

"We need to know who you want to send," Rogers said. "It occurs to me that Alex Johnson has the background for such an assignment."

"What I'd like you to do, Bill, is to put together a list of your recommendations along with their résumés. I know Alex, and I know he's your undersecretary and spent time in Japan, but some of the others I might not know."

"I'll do that," Rogers agreed. "The other question is substantive. What are we willing to discuss and what won't we talk about?"

"I'm willing to talk about anything," Nixon said. "Why not everything?"

"Well," Rogers continued, "William Huntoon feels that it would be dangerous to broach Taiwan, for example, until Stoessel can find out what it is that they want. A number of trade questions are very, very touchy too. When the Japanese hear we are talking to the Chinese, they will want to be consulted about textiles, coal, and oil."

"Must we tell the Japanese that we're in touch with China, Mr. Secretary?" Matt asked.

"Oh, I think so," Rogers said with a hint of condescension. "After all, they are our allies, and they have a big stake in Sino-American relations. We have an obligation to keep them informed; don't you agree, Henry?"

"Well, they are certainly allies with a strong interest," Kissinger replied, "but the President must also look at these negotiations from the Chinese standpoint. The internal Chinese situation has many crosscurrents today. We are probably dealing with less than all of the leadership factions. Stoessel says they have demanded secrecy, and I think that precludes consultation with Japan and the other allies."

"Well, Huntoon and I construe Stoessel to be saying that the talks—their content—must be secret, but one could hardly hope to keep the fact of the talks secret," Rogers countered.

"I want everything secret," Nixon said heavily. "There is no reason why we should tolerate a single leak. I think Henry is right. The leak of the fact that there will be talks could compromise Chou En-lai or someone else in China, and we can't have that happen. Is Wiliam Huntoon telling us that no one over there can keep a secret, Bill?"

"Not at all," Rogers replied defensively. "The Department keeps a great many secrets, and does it very well."

"I would like it kept secret," Nixon said. "All of it. Perhaps State can begin to prepare an agenda and the necessary backup material. When does Stoessel meet the Chinese again?"

"In mid-April. In about eight weeks."

"That should be time enough," Nixon said wryly. "Can't this move any faster?"

"There's a lot of work to be done," Rogers replied. "But if there's to be no consultation with Japan and South Korea and the others, perhaps the next meeting can be moved up a little. I'll see what can be done."

"Please do, Bill," Nixon said. "And for God's sake, keep it a secret. Tell Bill Huntoon to work with Matthew, here. He will keep Henry and me informed. I intend to be personally involved as this thing progresses."

Matt was kept fully informed. Huntoon found the requirement of secrecy inhibiting; consultations with China experts and allies were indicated, he insisted. He called several times to urge a relaxation of the classification. Matt assured him that the President was adamant on the matter of secrecy.

Huntoon then erected a network of preconditions to any Peking negotiations, each of which should be met by the Chinese in the Warsaw talks before a Peking date could be set.

At Kissinger's direction, Matt approved all of Huntoon's preconditions and in a few days Stoessel informed State that the Chinese had postponed the April Warsaw meeting until May.

Meanwhile, the Pakistani Ambassador to Washington was given a note for Chou En-lai from Richard Nixon explaining the two-track process the U.S. Government was engaging in.

Matthew dropped his own explanation into Emory Latham's gym locker:

For reasons which I do not wholly understand, Richard Nixon will not tell the State Department to stay out of his negotiations with China. I assume he fears that the professional diplomats might oppose what he is doing and build Congressional or popular opposition.

Nixon has told me that his strategy is to build up such a powerful *fait accompli* in secret that no effective opposition could be mobilized after it is announced. So he wants secrecy as much as China does.

The State Department has run the Warsaw talks for years. To cut it out of the talks now would be impossible without endangering the President's objectives. Strong press reaction would surely result.

So State's people are being encouraged to "run" the Warsaw talks, and they are demonstrating bureaucracy at its worst. While State is delaying, complicating and confusing matters in Warsaw, the President intends to agree with the Premier on who should come to Peking, when he should come, and under what circumstances. Messages will be sent via the Pakistani Ambassador in Washington and can be received by the same route.

I remain optimistic. The President seems committed, even impatient.

— Matthew Thompson

Thirty-three

In mid-April, 1970, Washington, D.C., was in full bloom. The magnolia, dogwood, and redbud were rivaled by the vast beds of tulips, daffodils, and other flowering bulbs massed in the Ellipse and the parks and gardens around the White House.

Matt had bought a bicycle in March, intending to get some weekend outdoor exercise. But on April 17 he decided also to ride his bicycle to work. It was a glorious morning, and as he effortlessly glided past the crowds at bus stops along Connecticut Avenue, he wanted to sing. Great drifts of deep red azaleas bordered Connecticut Avenue near Saint Alban's. The morning air was thin and cool. He arrived at the Executive Office Building in high spirits.

"Sure," said Angie Cruz, "it's all downhill this way. But you have to pump uphill all the way home this afternoon, when it's hot. You must be crazy."

"Not at all. I'm going to sell my bike here and buy another one to ride to work tomorrow. As long as I don't run out of buyers I'm okay. Want to buy a bike?"

"Sure—I'll give you a dollar and ten cents for it. Do you know Haig has called a meeting for ten A.M.?"

"No. What does General Jerry Jitters want?"

"He didn't say. Shall I cancel that reporter from Mutual Radio?"

"I guess you'll have to."

"Gentlemen," Brigadier General Alexander Haig began, "this briefing is Top Secret. You are here at the direction of the Commander in Chief on a need-to-know basis. I will brief you on a military operation. Lives depend on your maintaining strict security. Are there any questions, so far?"

There were seven people with Haig in the small conference room; all but one were male, Caucasian, and under forty-five. One was a Navy officer in full uniform who was standing by an easel covered with a white cloth. Winston Lord, Anthony Lake, and John Holdridge were there. Matt didn't recognize the other men.

"Very well, Admiral," Haig said portentously.

The Navy man slowly lifted the cloth off the map and folded it neatly as Haig lectured.

"This is a map of Viet Nam and Cambodia," Haig said. He reached into an inside pocket of his suit coat and produced a penlike silver device which turned out to be a telescoping pointer. Haig extended it and tapped the map at several places. "To orient you, here is Saigon, Hanoi, Danang, the Mekong River. The Ho Chi Minh Trail runs so. Our intelligence informs us that the Viet Cong operating in the south"—he described a circle with the red tip of his pointer—"are supplied from the Trail. Goods come down from the north by truck and bicycle, and a certain amount comes from the Gulf of Thailand, with goods coming up by boat and by trucks over these Cambodian roads. The supplies are stockpiled on the Cambodian side of the border. Admiral."

The Navy officer reached behind the map and brought forward an acetate overlay which was fastened to the top of the map. It shaded a part of eastern Cambodia in red.

"Not only are supplies cached in this shaded area, but VC troops go into these border refuges, across in Cambodia. They rest and resupply there in perfect safety because neither our troops nor the ARVN can go after them there in Cambodia. They have sanctuary, and it is costing us heavily. Any questions, so far?"

No one said anything.

"Admiral," Haig said again, and another overlay was brought over, this one consisting of blue and green arrows.

"The President has ordered a limited incursion, a joint U.S. and ARVN operation, to clean out the sanctuaries and destroy the VC command center which is known to be in operation there. Once the stated objectives have been achieved, all troops will be withdrawn from Cambodia. On this overlay U.S. forces are in blue, ARVN in green. The operation will jump off at oh five hundred hours on twenty-six April, three days from now."

Several of the men in the room looked at each other with surprise. Haig saw the exchange and asked, "Do you have some problem with the President's decision?"

A man Matt did not recognize asked Haig: "What about Cambodia? Are we invited in?"

"Yes," Haig answered.

"Won't the Viet Cong be pushed west by this action?" the man asked. "Isn't the Cambodian capital going to be in danger?"

"That has all been considered," Haig said impatiently, "and the decision has been made."

"Then why are you telling us about it?" the man asked. "Clearly, you don't want our reaction. What *do* you want?"

"Henry wanted you briefed. Some of you have responsibilities in areas which may be affected by this operation. He wants you to think about it and anticipate any problems that may arise. Do you think you can do that, Watts?" Haig asked the man.

That's Bill Watts, Matt realized. They had met at several other meetings, months before, but this time Matt had not recognized him.

"I'm not sure I can, Al," Watts said. "I'll talk to Henry about it."

"That is the second thing I intend to tell you about," Haig said to the group. "While this operation is under way, both Henry and the President intend to give it full-time attention. They ask that you route everything through me until further notice. I will attempt to get you fast answers to your priority questions, but I can't promise anything. It will be wartime conditions around here for a while."

"Are you telling me I can't see Henry?" Watts challenged.

"Procedure will be for you to request time. I will do my best to arrange it. It will help if requests are in memorandum form."

"How many copies?" Watts asked sarcastically.

"One will do."

"Are other governments being informed of this—what did you call it?" Matt asked.

"The correct term is *incursion*, I believe," Haig said. "It has been quite some time since we've asked another government how we should run the war there. No consultation is planned.''

"Well," Matt followed, "I would expect Thailand, Burma, and China to be pretty upset if we invade Cambodia without warning. Has any thought been given to that?"

"Larry Lynn has critiqued the entire plan and I am sure such questions have been raised. Any other questions here?"

"If we have forecasts of secondary problems, to whom shall we give them?" Winston Lord asked.

"To me," Haig replied. "For the time being, I am in charge."

For the President
(via Dr. Kissinger/Gen'l. Haig)
From Matthew Thompson
    It is predictable that the People's Republic of
China will have a strong negative reaction to the
planned "incursion" into Cambodia.
    First, Cambodia is a longtime ally of China
and is within the area which China conceives of
as its sphere of influence. Even with the recent
change of Cambodian governments, China still
recognizes Prince Sihanouk as the legitimate head
of government of Cambodia and has given him
refuge in Peking.
    Second, the U.S. has been reassuring China
that it intended to *reduce* its military strength in
southeast Asia. If the incursion were undertaken
only by South Vietnamese forces the Chinese
would probably not have a great problem with
it. But American involvement in Cambodia is
certain to be seen as an expansion of the
American role in southeast Asia.
    To lessen the negative impact in Peking I
suggest an urgent message be sent via Pakistan
explaining the military justification for the
Cambodian operation and its very limited scope.
The message should reaffirm your intention to

reduce forces in the improved climate which you
expect the operation will help create.

Matthew Thompson

"Mr. Thompson?" a woman's cool voice asked. "General Haig is calling."

"Fine." After several clicks and a long wait Haig came on the line.

"About this memo, Thompson," Haig purred, "the answer is 'No.'"

"No what, Al? No message to China?"

"No memo to the President. He's far too busy. I can't get it in."

"Bullshit. I hear he's been off on the Presidential yacht every evening. If he can go sailing he can read a short memo."

"Those are working meetings on the yacht. Anyway, the bottom line is that the memo isn't going in."

"You may not know what he's trying to do with China, Al. If you don't, you shouldn't keep that memo away from him. It's vitally important."

"I'm fully advised, you may be sure," Haig said importantly.

"Let Henry see it, then," Matt asked.

"Henry has his hands full. Among other things, we have a lot of bleeding-hearts around here who are submitting resignations."

"So I hear. Is it true that Tony Lake and Watts and Larry Lynn are all leaving?"

"You don't need to know that now," Haig said curtly. "I'd advise you to just keep out of all of that."

"So you are willing to take the responsibility for screwing up the China project by suppressing my memo; right, Al?"

Haig said softly: "Matt, I have a lot of respect for you and as much as anything I want to save you from trouble. It's best to do it my way." He hung up abruptly.

Matt got out a lined pad and began to write a longhand letter.

Dear Mr. Teng:

By the time you read this, the "incursion" into Cambodia will be well under way.

I fully anticipate that China must make some response to demonstrate your disapproval. I only hope that it can be some moderate action such as a cancellation of the next-scheduled Warsaw conference.

The President is convinced that this limited operation—limited both in duration and in geographic scope—will materially contribute to a climate in which he can withdraw substantial numbers of troops before long. The North Vietnamese have enjoyed "sanctuary" across the Cambodian border, stockpiling material there, maintaining camps for troops and even operating a command center there. This has resulted in high casualties for our troops.

I hope your leadership will not be diverted from the path of reconciliation by this one, relatively subsidiary, military operation.

Matthew Thompson

The summer of 1970 was hot and unpleasant. And from the last day of April, when the Chinese curtly cancelled the Warsaw talks, there were no encouraging signs from Peking.

The Cambodia incursion met widespread opposition, fueled by reaction to the shooting deaths of four Kent State University students by National Guardsmen in early May. Young people found their way to the White House—delegations, carloads, and even one at a time—to tell Nixon, Kissinger, or anyone else who would listen that the war must stop. They came to the gates, camped in the parks, and marched in the streets in great numbers.

Matt Thompson was put to work preparing briefing books and talking papers for the Administration's counter-attackers, the beleaguered President's surrogates who were sent out to justify his policy in Southeast Asia. These

spokesmen were booked on television in the ten major
media markets to stress Nixon's arguments. Their audience
would be Nixon's core constituents, that great mass of
middle-class, middle-aged Americans who liked to be
called the Silent Majority.

Mary Finn was in Washington for the summer, she
announced to Matt, and she had decided to undertake her
own campaign to pry Matthew Thompson out of the White
House. She began with an elaborately fashioned dinner in
her backyard one June evening.

"Did you cook all this?" he asked with surprise.

"Not any of it. There's a great gourmet take-out place
that has opened up on the other side of M Street. Try those
shrimp while I get the wine."

Matt was the only guest. When he'd eaten all he could
and had finished his coffee, Mary Finn blew out the
candles and brought him into the house for a liqueur.

"What about the dishes, lady?"

"You want to do dishes?"

"I'll help. You wash, I'll dry."

"I try not to do dishes. Evelyn comes tomorrow and
she'll do them. We have an understanding. She does
dishes, and I lawyer. She doesn't draw wills, and I don't
do pots and pans."

"Pretty soft life you lead."

"And when I'm not lawyering I worry about my friends."

"Sounds like you need a hobby."

"That *is* my hobby. Mostly I worry about you." She
rubbed the back of his neck lightly with her fingers. They
were sitting on the floor in her living room, their backs
against her couch, with legs straight out. She shifted,
gathered her legs under her, and looked at him. "How
much longer are you going to stay there, Matt? How much
more can you take?"

"Mary, I can't leave now. I really can't. Remember that
project I told you about?"

"You mean the one you didn't tell me about, but you
wished you could and someday you might? Yeah, I
remember."

"It's so very close. If I walked out now it would just fall apart. I can't do that."

"Are you involved in this Cambodian disaster?"

"No. If they'd asked me, I would have begged them not to do it."

"Is there any explanation for it, other than the garbage in Nixon's speech?"

"Do you want a little amateur psychiatry? I think the explanation lies in the makeup of both Nixon and Kissinger. Nixon needs to be macho and Kissinger needs to be thought to be adequate by his peers. So they can't just sit there and negotiate and administer a withdrawal from Viet Nam. The North Vietnamese are poking their finger in Nixon's eye there, so he has to hit back."

"How is the North doing that?" Mary pressed.

"I think I've said too much. Anyway, Nixon decided to get active on short notice, so Cambodia is what they put together. The hell with the secondary consequences."

"What a zoo you work in. Are you ever going to take some time off?"

"In September. Henry is going off on a speaking tour around the United States and that will be a good time for me to go away."

"What are you going to do?"

"Go fishing, I think."

"Can I go?"

"Have you ever fished?"

"A few times off a dock at Kitty Hawk. I caught some fish, too."

He kissed her gently. "How about trout, with a fly?"

"No, but that doesn't look so hard."

He kissed her again.

"I suppose," Mary said when they had finally drawn back, flushed and excited, "that all of this necking is by way of not saying you don't want to take me trout fishing. Right?" She put her hand on his chest to fend off another kiss. "Right?"

"The place I'm thinking of going is in the backcountry in Alaska, and it's so rough there that they don't take women."

"You're kidding! I don't believe that there is such a place."

"There is," he nodded. "I'll show you the brochure."

"Chauvinist Chalet in Scenic Alaska! They should be sued!"

At breakfast he said: "I'm sorry about the fishing. I'd really like to go somewhere with you when we can. I liked your idea of going to Italy."

"I had no business inviting myself fishing. Besides, I've got to work. How about Florence in the spring?"

"I'm for that. Meanwhile, do you want to learn to fish for trout? We could go up to New Hampshire some weekend and I'll teach you."

"I'd like that. Shall I buy a rod?"

"No. Not until you know you like it."

"God, look at the time! I've got to run real fast, boy. I've got an early meeting. Just toss the dishes in the sink."

After she left it seemed to Matt strange to be in Mary's house without her. The quiet house, full of Mary's clothes and Mary's furnishings, was an odd place in which to sit alone and think. He had almost brought up the subject of marriage while they were eating breakfast, and he wondered how the colloquy would have gone:

"Have you ever thought of getting married?"

"Sure. All the time. Do you think about it?"

"I'm thinking about it now."

"Shall we? Do you want to?"

"I'm not positive. I think maybe I do. But there are some things I need to think through."

"Glenna?"

"No. The job. You would need for me to quit first."

"Not necessarily."

"There's also a Chinese woman."

"You want to make love to her too?"

"That makes me a miscegenist, right?"

"It sounds to me like you're not quite ready for marriage."

Mary Finn's telephone rang, stridently breaking the

thick silence. The repeated ringing demanded that Matt do something, but he could not answer her telephone. He realized he had been postponing his departure; he wasn't eager to expose himself to the neighbors as he left her house in daylight; but the telephone would not stop ringing. He gathered his jacket and opened the front door. If anyone was watching, the scene would seem strange in the extreme: not only was he leaving a young woman's house, but he was walking away from a loud and insistent telephone—suspicious conduct by anyone's standards.

At the office, Angie Cruz looked at him oddly. "Growing a beard?" she asked. Mary Finn's razor was impossibly dull, and she had been out of blades.

"No, indeed. I was out of blades, so I figured I'd shave here, or at the gym."

"The gym called. This guy wants you to call." She handed him a phone slip: *Call L. Ham at the gym.* "They found something of yours."

"Okay," Matt said. "Take my calls for a while, will you?"

Thirty-four

Latham was sitting on the bench in front of his open locker, his back to the door. He was naked, his hair was wet, and a spot in the middle of his broad back was also wet where he had missed with the towel. Matt sat on the bench three feet from Latham and nodded to him when Latham turned his head.

"In your locker," Latham said softly. "I'm to wait for an answer. Go read it in the toilet."

Matt opened the locker and saw an envelope on its floor. He took off his clothes rapidly, carefully putting his shoes on top of the envelope. Latham continued to sit looking at Matt. Matt bent over and reached for the envelope and stood. "I'll be right back," he said.

In the toilet stall Matt carefully wiped the seat, sat down, and opened the envelope. The closely typed message said:

> Internal affairs, the invasion of Cambodia and various uncertainties have contributed to the delay of negotiations.
> We consider it essential that you come here for consultation at once. Ambiguities must be dispelled.
> We are confident you can do so secretly.
> Our civilian airline service is now good from Tokyo. Advise route and arrival time by return messenger.
>
> > > > T

Matt reread the text, then folded it carefully and returned it to its crisp envelope. He walked back slowly, taking a towel from the reception counter and wrapping it around his waist.

Latham was fully dressed when Matt returned.

"Lend me your pen, please," Matt said, sitting in front of his locker. "I have to give you a reply." He wrote quickly on the envelope.

> Will leave via Anchorage September 16. Cover is fishing trip to Alaska. Please arrange itinerary from Tokyo for me. Can only be away 10 days.

There was too much to do. He emerged from the gym into the sunlight and crossed the street slowly to a sports shop.

"I'm going to Alaska after silvers—silver salmon—and I need a lot of stuff," he told the clerk. In thirty minutes he had assembled a credible selection of fishing paraphernalia on the glass counter. The Chinese are going to have to pay for this, he reflected; and they will have the airline fare to pay for, too. He would speak to Teng Shan-li about money for the trip. Surely they did not expect him to sell the emerald to finance these trips.

"Look here." He had invited Angie and her friend Tina, the secretary from across the hall. "I'll show you something beautiful." He opened his package and spread his purchases on his desk. There were brightly colored flat lures, large bucktail flies, and an assortment of dry flies in three sizes. He had bought spools of heavy leader, bottles of salmon eggs, a dozen cherry bobbers, lead wire and rubber tubing, and large, bright salmon hooks.

"I'm going fishing and it won't be long now," he explained. "I just couldn't stay out of that store today."

Angie smiled. "What's this tubing for—transfusions?"

"The lead wire fits in that. It weights the leader down, and if you get snagged it pops out and you don't break your line."

"Pretty flies," Tina enthused. "They would look good on a hat. When are you going?"

"The sixteenth of September. The silvers—silver salmon—should be running then. They are wonderful!"

"Meanwhile," Angie said, "crass reality intrudes. Haig has called twice. Mary Finn called. Eagleburger wants you to talk to a delegation of angry students from Dartmouth at four P.M. You are invited to the Turkish Embassy for cocktails next Tuesday. And your friend in New York—Mr. Carnahay—called. He's sending you some mail."

Matt carefully deposited his fishing gear, piece by piece, in his top left-hand drawer.

"All right, Miss Legree, we'll do all your scut work for another nine days, four hours, and ten minutes, and then I'm out of here. I need plane reservations, by the way. To

Anchorage early on the sixteenth and back here late on the twenty-sixth, loaded with salmon. See what can be done, will you?"

"Of course, Mr. Walton. Right away."

PART

SIX

Thirty-five

Memorandum

September 9, 1970

To: Matthew Thompson
From: Alexander Haig
   Deputy Assistant to the President
   for National Security Affairs
Subject: *China*

Dr. Kissinger notes that we have now invested eighteen months of effort in seeking a *rapprochement* with the People's Republic of China and we have had *no* results:

China continues to supply North Viet Nam.

Our messages via several third parties remain unanswered.

The early and encouraging Chinese responses in the Warsaw talks have proved ephemeral and now the talks themselves are postponed indefinitely.

In June, General Walters' attempts to make contact with Chinese diplomats in Paris were rebuffed.

In July, the P.R.C. scrambled its MIGs to

intercept one of our C-130s over international waters east of China.

When Dr. Kissinger returns from his trip in September he wishes to convene the Review Group once again to chart our strategy with regard to the P.R.C. The President does not favor an indefinite effort.

Please prepare a historical review of our attempted negotiations from January, 1969, to date and an agenda of possible options available to the President, for review at that time.

                                                A.H.

                                        August 10, 1970

For: Dr. Kissinger
From: Matt Thompson
Re: China

I agree that a review of our China strategy in late September will be timely.

In context, the progress to date has been considerable.

The Chinese response to the Cambodian invasion by U.S. troops was in fact quite restrained. Only one bellicose statement was issued in Mao's name. A few official warnings were published in the Peking papers, and the Warsaw talks were once again temporarily derailed. North Viet Nam asked China for help, but China didn't send troops or even send more supplies than usual.

I continue to believe the correct conduit is via Pakistan, not France, and General Walters' efforts in Paris will continue to be fruitless.

I would guess that the MIG episode in July is symptomatic of the serious internal problems in China. The Chinese Air Force is the least stable element of the Chinese armed forces today. While the Air Force may not be characterized as "out of control," its actions are less likely to be representative of Mao's policies than other military elements' are. The CIA post in Hong Kong has been asked to explain that MIG–C-130 episode. They are reviewing radio transmissions and quizzing their informants. We should know more by the time the review group meets.

I plan to take a short vacation while you are gone, but a China review will be ready when we both return.

Matthew Thompson

Everyone wanted to celebrate Matt's first real vacation. Mary Finn cooked him a fish dinner, on the premise that he'd be eating only moose meat all the time he was in Alaska.

And this repast, her formal, written invitation read, *will be complete, beginning with fishhead chowder and ending with a Piece of the Finn.*

Angie Cruz baked dozens of molasses cookies for Matt to take along in small packages "which will just tuck in odd corners of your suitcase."

Glenna Harrison sent Matt a canvas Dopp Kit with a note:

The man at Abercrombie in New York says you can send this back if you'd rather have hooks or flies or something. But he says this is very practical for camping in Alaska.

I was in N.Y.C. because my mother is sick, and you know she is almost never sick. My father is very worried about her and so am I.

I confess I continue to miss you very much.

Have a wonderful trip.

Glenna

On September 16, 1970, as Dr. Henry Kissinger was addressing a luncheon of the Detroit Economic Club, Matt Thompson was stretched out in a first-class seat on Northwest Orient Airlines' Flight 003, scheduled to fly from

Dulles International at Washington, D.C., to Tokyo by way of Anchorage, Alaska. Matt had successfully persuaded all of his friends to stay away from the airport, principally with the argument that a 2 P.M. weekday departure from Dulles was just not a respectable social occasion. In the absence of witnesses he was able to check his luggage through to Tokyo, but if anyone he knew had shown up to see him off, he was prepared to act out the Anchorage fishing-trip charade. He could get off there, claim his bags, and check in again during the ample refueling layover; but with no one watching, he offered his ticket and passport—complete with Japanese visa—and declared himself to the ticket agent to be a Tokyo passenger.

When Matt came out of the jetway at Tokyo's teeming airport, about thirty people were waiting for arriving passengers, but none of them seemed to be interested in him. He followed the plastic signs and arrows and yellow lines which brought him to the Customs and Immigration area, where he expected a Chinese agent to tap him on the arm and lead him to another airplane. But when no one spoke to him and his bags arrived on the conveyor, he claimed his luggage, offered his passport for scrutiny, and emerged into the public lobby, still without a contact. The concourse was chrome and plastic and bright neon, even at ten o'clock in the morning. Hordes of Westernized Japanese hurried in all directions, with not a Japanese kimono to be seen. Matt stood to the side of the exit from Customs, trying to appear nondescript, wondering how long they would keep him waiting. He knew the Chinese were there somewhere; they were never late. They were watching him, and watching for other people who might also be watching him.

After twenty minutes Matt began to wonder if they had received the message he'd sent by Emory Latham giving his arrival time. When thirty minutes had elapsed, during which fresh rivers of arriving passengers had poured from the swinging doors beside him, Matt noticed a young Japanese man standing just opposite him, across the concourse. He wore a very dark blue suit, a thin black tie, and black oxfords which needed a shine. He dropped a short cigarette on the floor and stepped on it, took a pack of Lucky Strikes from his pocket, and walked directly to Matt, smiling broadly.

"Welcome to Tokyo, Mr. Thompson; would you care for an American cigarette?"

Matt declined politely. "What is your name, please?" he asked.

"You should call me Minoru, if you wish. Are you ready to go?"

"Yes. Where are we going, Minoru?"

"You have a flight leaving in one hour and ten minutes." He reached into his coat pocket and smiled. "I must wear my button." He pinned a large badge over his breast pocket:

RISING SUN TOURS
MINORU MIHARA

"Do you have my ticket to Peking?" Matt asked.

Minoru looked puzzled, then embarrassed. "Not Peking. You are going to Hong Kong today. Is that all right? A Rising Sun representative will meet you there too. He will take care of everything. Very efficient. Here are tickets, but I will check you in. You have other baggage?"

"No." The Chinese had written that he was to fly direct from Tokyo to Peking. A detour through Hong Kong sent him two thousand miles south to go a thousand miles north and would add two days to his trip. It didn't make sense. It made him suspicious. "How do I know you are supposed to send me to Hong Kong?" he demanded.

Minoru Mihara looked puzzled. "How do I know? What is the question?"

"I want to know who changed my itinerary," Matt said.

The Japanese man smiled. "Have teletype." He reached into his jacket pocket and handed Matt a folded printout. "I will take your bags; you follow me while you read."

"This doesn't say who ordered the change," Matt pointed out.

"Your company, maybe?"

"Maybe. Is it far to Japan Air Lines?"

"Very close. I get you VIP treatment."

"That's a long trip, to Hong Kong. Am I booked first class?"

Mihara stopped and set down the bag and Matt's attaché case, took the airline ticket from his pocket, and peered at the top coupon. "Tokyo to Hong Kong, economy class. Not first class."

"Well, I want it changed, Mr. Mihara. I need to sleep, so it must be in first class."

"Will you pay?"

"Sure. Put it on my credit card."

"It is very late. Not sure any space can be found. I will take bags and see."

"Here, check this one. I'll keep the attaché case. I'll wait in that seat over there."

Mihara nodded and scuttled off with the bag and Matt's credit card. Ten minutes later he returned with a broad smile.

"All fixed," Mihara said. "First class to Hong Kong. Come with me now to pay exit tax, go through Immigration, and wait in VIP lounge. Very nice."

The flight to Hong Kong was five hours of fancy food and fitful sleep. Matt's seat companion spoke only Japanese, so there were no social intrusions. But the Japanese stewards and stewardesses were relentlessly attentive, offering drinks, washcloths, pillows, newspapers, courses and courses of food, slippers, toilet kits, and more food until the lights of Hong Kong finally appeared, blurred by sheets of wind-driven rain.

Once again, Matt's airport greeting delegation was not readily apparent. He stood by his bags outside the Customs area for twenty minutes, looking as unobtrusive as it was possible for a tall American in a wrinkled jacket to look.

Three men watched Matt closely as he waited. One, dressed as a porter, was employed by the Special Section of the Ministry of Defense of the People's Republic of China. The second, a young Chinese man sitting on a bench reading a newspaper, was an agent for the Hong Kong police. He also did chores for the Secret Service of the Republic of China on Taiwan. The third, an Englishman who had been sent to meet Matt by Hung Wai-lang, had spotted the Taiwan agent but had not identified the other observer. The police agent had seen both the others and knew who they were, and he recognized Matt Thompson from the picture in his dossier. The Englishman went to a telephone where he could watch Matt as he stood waiting.

"Let me speak to Mr. Hung, please. This is Carr. Mr. Hung?"

"Yes," said Hung Wai-lang.

"Thompson has arrived. A Taiwan agent, that Kim, is here watching him too. Perhaps we need more backup."

"Very well. Don't make contact until more men get there."

Twenty minutes later Stephen Carr walked up to Matt and held out his hand. "Frightfully sorry, Mr. Thompson. An accident in the tunnel. Hope you haven't been waiting too long out of Customs. I'm Carr. I work for Mr. Hung."

"Hello, Mr. Carr. I wondered what had become of you."

"Are these all your bags? I'll help you. We are going up to Mr. Hung's house."

"For how long?"

"I really don't know your schedule. I'm sorry." He said "shedyule."

The Oriental chauffeur drove Hung's Mercedes limousine through the heavy rain and up the twisting mountain road with an obvious contempt for the laws of physics. At the third hairpin turn he handled his steering wheel with one hand and buzzed the passenger telephone with the other. Matt could see the driver through the glass partition saying something to Stephen Carr on the telephone. Carr turned slightly, the phone still at his ear, as the Mercedes came out of the curve. Headlights were rapidly coming up the hill behind them, and Carr watched them for a few moments.

"Are we being followed?" Matt asked as Carr hung up the telephone.

"Perhaps. It's hard to say. We have a second car back there somewhere and I wanted to see what had become of him. That is our man behind us, I feel sure."

Hung Wai-lang was waiting for Matt, standing in the middle of his glass box of a den, above the dark hillside and the harbor. All the white, red, and yellow lights of Hong Kong blazed around the water below them, fading in and out as low clouds and rain moved across the scene. Hung grinned broadly and held out both his hands. He wore a loose white shirt over his black cotton pants, and plain black slippers; he called them his relaxation clothes, but he was obviously very tense.

"Matthew, my boy. Welcome to my house!" he said.

"Thank you, Mr. Hung. It is an honor to be in your home once again."

"I am sorry that you will not be here very long this time, but you have a fast schedule tonight. Come, sit down and have some tea and I will tell you about it."

Hung poured tea from a large carafe and offered Matt sweet cakes and fruit from a low table beside their chairs. Matt sipped his tea.

"It appears that you are having a difficult trip." Hung was serious and apologetic.

"Not so far," Matt said, "except that I didn't fly direct from Japan. Why did I detour down here to Hong Kong?"

"There was information," Hung replied. "The direct CAAC flight from Tokyo to Peking was not appropriate. It seems that several people are not happy that you are going to China this time."

"What do you mean? Who is that?"

"One can only conjecture. Perhaps they are Taiwanese. In any case, the route from Hong Kong, although it is longer, will be more—ah—will be of greater comfort for you. I had planned for you to fly in my airplane to Canton, but my pilot says the weather will not permit, so we are making other arrangements now. It is a pity that your trip is to be so hurried. You could await better weather here at my house.''

Hung reached for a black telephone and pushed a button at its base. "Have you arranged for the boat?" he asked in Mandarin. Matt stood and looked out at the blurred lights of Hong Kong; he understood Hung's Chinese perfectly. "No, I do not want a charter," Hung said. "It must be a vessel that is doing nothing out of the ordinary. I explained that to Stephen Carr. What have you found out?"

Hung listened impatiently. "Are there private staterooms on that one? All right. One hour after midnight? I want Sun to go with him. Yes. Certainly.''

Hung turned to Matt and smiled reassuringly. He looked at his wristwatch and said: "It is all arranged. You can rest now for two hours; then my man Sun will take you to the steamer. You must go to Canton on a boat because of the bad weather. It is a very nice boat and an interesting trip, and you will be there tomorrow morning. It is only one hundred eighty kilometers away. Then perhaps the weather will allow you to fly the rest of the way. Before you go, however, I should like to know how and why the FBI has been watching you." Hung's smile disappeared. "What do they accuse you of doing?"

"I am told that my phone calls to you were considered very suspicious. But no one has really charged me with anything. I spoke to the President about what the FBI was doing and he immediately told them to stop.''

"Are you sure they have discontinued?''

"No, Mr. Latham feels that the NSA or the CIA might still be listening to us.''

"Quite so." Hung nodded. "It appears that the CIA's Hong Kong agents have also brought along their British and Taiwanese friends into this watching. It is known that all three work very closely when it suits their convenience, and other times they spy on each other. They are such whores!''

"Are you being tapped?" Matt asked.

"Oh, yes. And followed. I have only a few secrets left." Hung laughed. "But I take precautions, and so must you. If we are to be successful in forging peace among the great powers we must be careful, but we must not let them deter us. Now it is time for you to rest before your journey. I have asked them to put a sandwich and some milk in your room in case you are hungry. Rest well, and I will see you just before you go."

When Hung's houseman came to rouse him, Matt washed his hands and face, put on his jacket, and met Hung and another man in the foyer at the back of the house.

"This is Sun," Hung said. "He will go with you on your boat ride."

Matt guessed Sun was about thirty, but his age was difficult to judge. He was a head shorter than Matt, well muscled for a Chinese, and made a stunning contrast in black and ivory. His black hair, heavy black glasses, and dark suit made his skin seem luminescent and lighter than it was.

"How do you do, Mr. Thompson?" Sun said. His English was deeply accented.

"Hello, Mr. Sun." Matt shook his broad hand.

"We will need our coats," Sun said. "It has been raining very hard. We are getting the edge of a typhoon, I think."

Hung, in a black robe over his pajamas, said goodbye to Matt at his door. In spite of the wide overhang beyond the door the heavy rain splashed them as they stood at his threshold. "Sun is a good man. You will be all right," Hung said seriously. "But please be careful, Matthew."

Matt shook Hung's hand and said a polite goodbye, then ran to the open door of the Mercedes.

Stephen Carr was waiting in the back seat. Sun sat next to the chauffeur. They drove down the mountain without incident, closely followed by a black sedan.

"That's our escort," Stephen Carr explained. "Mr. Hung wants to be sure you are safe."

"Very nice," Matt murmured.

The riverboat appeared tall, green, and quite old in the

uncertain and wavering lights that were tied along its top railing. The small wallawalla lurched and rolled in the rising wind as Matt and Sun approached the vessel, which—like many other riverboats—bore the name *The East Is Red*.

Mr. Sun and Matthew Thompson huddled under the arched canvas shelter at the stern of the small motorized sampan, but the wind-driven rain slanted in at the wide openings at both ends. Matt's clothes were wet against his skin before the wallawalla's two crewmen brought their boat to the accommodation ladder in the lee of the anchored riverboat. Matt carefully watched for the right instant to jump from the moving sampan to the shadowed and narrow platform at the bottom of the ship's steep steps. That dark wooden landing was moving too, at some other rhythm. The sampan crewman held Matt's arm tightly, then shoved him forward with a shout as the two careening universes briefly and approximately coincided. Matt lunged for the end of the wooden railing at the lowest step of the ladder and felt his forward foot slide across the wet open wooden squares of the grilled platform, followed by his other foot. When his feet were suddenly stopped by the solid steel wall of the ship's plates, he sprawled awkwardly on his side, holding desperately to the railing. He cursed the indifferent ship's captain who had not sent a crewman to the bottom of the ladder to help passengers board.

Someone at the railing fifteen feet above him shouted "Look out!" in Cantonese as Matt carefully brought his feet under him and stood on the rolling platform, his right hand against the wet steel side of the ship and his left desperately gripping the railing. Looking back over his left shoulder, Matt saw Sun and a wallawalla crewman in the half-light, rising and falling, Sun holding out one hand to Matt. Matt transferred his right hand to the stair railing and turned slightly to his left to extend his left arm toward his bodyguard.

Suddenly, Sun was moving toward him, an arm extended. Their hands missed. Sun crashed into Matt's left side, lost his footing, and seized Matt's left shoulder roughly.

Matt tried to climb off the platform, which he thought to be too small for both of them, but Sun's weight held him back. For a moment Matt was sure Sun would pull them both into the heaving black canyon between the ship and the wallawalla. Instinctively, he bent his knees and half-crouched, pulling Sun toward him, and he felt Sun's hand take the railing beside his hand.

"Son-a-bitch," Sun shouted, "that was close! Go on up the steps. Look out, they are wet." Sun released his hold on Matt's shoulder and pushed Matt toward the stairs. "I'll get your bag," Sun yelled.

A Chinese in a blue overcoat and blue Mao cap stood at the top of the stairs, pointing to a doorway across the deck, his hunched back turned to the wind. "Go there," he shouted in Chinese. Matt made the doorway in three strides and turned to watch Sun top the stairs with Matt's Valpak and his own small overnight bag under his right arm. Sun stopped and talked to the pointing man, who insistently waved his index finger toward Matt as he replied. The wind made it impossible for Matt to hear their argument. Three crewmen went behind Sun to hoist the accommodation ladder and close the opening in the railing.

"It's all right," Sun said as he joined Matt in the companionway inside the open door. "It's not going to be luxurious, but this thing will get us there. We are up on the next deck." He led the way inside to the center of the ship, found a stairway, and went up to a landing on the deck above.

"You are in Cabin 3 in Second Class. I am in Cabin 4. They are just ahead here, I think. That idiot wanted us both in number 3, but I arranged it."

"Let me take that bag," Matt said.

"Of course." Sun found number 4, then number 3; their doors were across from each other off the central companionway.

Cabin 3 was a small and inelegant steel-walled, pale green space which offered a pair of bunk beds, one above the other, a chair, and two portholes. Matt hung his soaked raincoat on a wall hook, took off his jacket and spread it on the back of the chair, and removed his wet shoes.

When the ship's engines began to throb purposefully, Matt looked out his forward porthole at the lights of Kowloon. *The East Is Red #38* slowly moved northwest, past Stonecutters Island, toward the narrow channel between the islands of Ma Wan and Tsing Yi. As the engines' tempo picked up, the ship began to overtake junks and small freighters in the driving rain.

When Sun knocked on the door a few minutes later, Matt had moved away from the porthole glass to put on his plastic airline slippers.

"Is everything okay?" Sun asked.

"Sure, come in. I was going to find the toilet."

"It is next door to my cabin. Just across. Then will you sleep?"

"If I can get warm I will. God, it is cold."

"I'll see if I can find you some hot tea," Sun promised. "Then you sleep if you can. Because of the wind the ship will go west, around Lantau Island, and the trip will take longer. So you sleep."

Sun left and soon a boy in a filthy white jacket delivered a big vacuum bottle of tea and a white mug. Matt sat on the narrow lower bunk, warming his hands on the cup and sipping the steaming tea. The regular beat of the engines and *The East Is Red #38*'s steady roll were hypnotic. Before long Matt was under all the blankets from both bunks, and his still-damp coat was spread out on top for whatever warmth it might add. Some light outside the ship reflected obliquely and faintly on the light green ceiling plates of the stateroom, but it was not bright enough to keep Matthew Thompson awake.

During the night *The East Is Red #38* stopped at a dock. Matt swung his feet to the cold steel floor and stumbled to the porthole to see dark-clad Chinese shuffling back and forth in the quarter-light of the pier's few shaded bulbs. The scene was partially gauzed by the continuing rain. He could see very little, so he felt his way back to the bunk and then decided to revisit the grimy toilet across the hall. When he had found the slippers and opened his door, he saw Sun sitting on a chair in his open doorway, his bare feet on a towel spread on the steel deck in front of him.

"Everything okay?" Sun asked.

"Sure."

"They stop along the way for passengers. We won't be here long."

Matt nodded and shuffled to the toilet in the plastic slippers. The deck felt cold through the thin plastic and his cotton gym socks.

When he had returned to bed and rearranged his damp coat on top of the thin blankets, his feet were so cold that they hurt. Matt tried rubbing them through his thick socks but with only a little improvement. As he was drifting back to sleep he wondered, momentarily, if he had thrown the sliding-bar lock on the door. He could not remember, but it didn't matter; Sun was keeping watch across the passageway.

If the weather had been cloudless, perhaps some dawn light would have come through Matt's portholes, but the typhoon's spawn persisted, and when he woke about 5 A.M., it was still very dark outside. *The East Is Red #38* was stopped again, and its engines were idling at such a low rate that they were barely perceptible. The change in vibration and the lack of roll had awakened him, Matt supposed. People were calling out somewhere outside. As he lay, half awake, Matt was aware of some activity in the hallway too. Two men were talking purposefully, and the sound of their voices came in under his door. He was lying on his side, his face toward the outside bulkhead and away from that door, but when the men's voices stopped Matt sensed that his door was open, even though he had heard nothing. Perhaps there was more light against his eyelids. And the room somehow felt different against his back and shoulders. Matt rolled onto his back, turned his head toward the door, and looked. A man was silhouetted in the open doorframe.

Instantly he knew the man was not Sun, and his mind photographed and tabulated several facts. The fellow's raincoat was glistening with water. His right hand extended into the shadows of the room, but Matt saw that he was holding something heavy. The Chinese man was not alone; there were others in the hall. His wet hat was a uniform cap and it was gray. In the center above the bill was a red star in a medallion. Matt had seen a hat like that somewhere before, but he couldn't recall where.

"Get up!" the man demanded. He spoke Chinese with a harsh regional dialect.

Matt grunted and shoved his covers back. As his eyes grew accustomed to the light he could see that the man held an automatic pistol.

"What's wrong?" Matt asked in English. "Where's Mr. Sun?"

"Put on your shoes; you are coming with us," the Chinese said harshly.

"Speak English," Matt demanded. He could not afford to reveal that he understood some of the Chinese, particularly if he was in some kind of trouble. "What did you say?"

"The foreign pig is saying something," the man called to his companions. "Mong, you come."

A second man appeared in the doorway in the same uniform as the first, equally wet. He pointed to Matt's shoes beside the bunk. "Shoes," he demanded loudly. "Coat."

Afraid of the gun the first soldier had leveled at him, Matt put up his left hand palm toward the gun, as he reached for his shoes with the other hand. "Okay," he said quietly, "I'll get my shoes. You don't need that gun."

The shoes were still wet and he had difficulty putting them on over his thick gym socks.

"Hurry!" the first man shouted in Chinese.

"Quick," the second man said in English.

"Okay, okay. I'm just getting my jacket and coat."

"Should we not search him, Comrade?" asked the second man.

"Of course. Turn on the light while I watch him. Then feel him for a weapon."

As he was being vigorously frisked, Matt looked beyond the soldiers. The chair in Sun's doorway was tipped backward into Sun's dark stateroom, and Matt could see bare feet and black-clad legs on the floor behind it.

Matt was terrified. They had killed Sun and were taking him prisoner. He didn't know what to do. "I am an American," he said to the one who was searching him. "You understand that? American?" he repeated slowly. "I demand to speak to the captain of this ship."

"No weapon," the searcher said in Chinese. "He says he's an American."

The man with the gun grinned. "A fornicating pig American. Let's get off this smelly tub before it sinks."

There were four more soldiers in the small lobby at the head of the stairs. Two of them carried submachine guns with polished wooden stocks and handles. All wore the same gray caps with the red star and wings above the bill. The machine gunners walked behind Matt as he was led down the stairs and out the door to the head of the accommodation ladder. Four more soldiers on the deck kept six or seven gawking passengers away from the procession.

On deck, Matt saw an unlighted wooden pier which widened about fifty feet from the riverbank into a broad concrete platform on concrete pilings. A few distant lights could be seen through the rain, but there appeared to be no nearby town or village. At the base of the pier a Chinese-made jeep and a large military truck were waiting, both with headlights turned on and engines idling.

Matt looked back at *The East Is Red #38* as he walked toward the vehicles. Already the ladder had been pulled up and the ship was backing away from the pier. The red star on its smokestack was illuminated with a small spotlight. There were no other people on the pier.

At the back of the truck four of the armed men debated whether to tie Matt's hands and feet. Matt stood in the warm, drenching rain, water streaming across his face, being held by one arm by the largest of the riflemen.

"It is unwise to leave him loose," Mong, the English speaker, said to his companions. "He is larger than any of us."

"If the fornicator moves we will kill him," said another. "Let us stop talking and get into the truck, where it is dry."

"There are ropes in the jeep. I say tie up the pig lover."

The handgun man, evidently an officer, came around the truck. "Load him aboard," he demanded. "We must go quickly. What is the delay?"

"We discuss whether or not to tie the American," Mong said. "I say tie him to be safe."

"I say let's get out of the rain," another man said. "All of us are armed and the fornicator of farm animals is not. Let's get in and go."

"Yes, let us go quickly," the officer said. "If you must shoot him, then so be it. Watch him carefully and take no chances. Put him in the truck."

There was no way for Matt to know where they were taking him. He reckoned they had been driving roughly northeast from the river, and the Pearl River ran north to south, he recalled. He had been shoved into the back of the truck and canvas curtains immediately had been dropped over the opening. The road had been very rough for part of the way; then the truck turned onto a paved road. Twice the truck stopped, and during those stops he heard distant voices. The two submachine gunners and four other soldiers with Chinese rifles rode in the truck with him on the side benches.

In an hour it was daylight, and Matt felt hungry, but the truck kept rolling. After they had ridden for about two hours, Matt deduced that they were driving through an urban area of some kind. He could smell coal smoke and cooking food. When the truck slowed, he heard people's voices. The smells reminded Matt that he was hungry.

At a street corner the truck turned and drove slowly for a few blocks. Matt could hear men and women talking; they were in some kind of street market. He estimated they had driven about fifty miles by then. In what he guessed to be another five miles, the truck turned off pavement onto a dirt road, took a left turn and bounced over ruts for a short distance, then slowed to a stop.

"It's the farm," the man at the curtains said to the others. In a moment the rear curtains were rolled up, and Matt saw bright gray light, a low farm building made of stone and adobe, and many trees. The sky was full of low, round clouds which were moving fast. The truck started up, jostled ahead a few yards, and stopped again. The soldiers dropped off the back of the truck and motioned for him to follow them.

None of it made sense. Unquestionably, these were soldiers of the People's Republic of China. If the Taiwanese wanted to prevent him from reaching Peking, Chou might have sent these soldiers to protect him; but a bodyguard sent by the Premier would not have killed Sun. Who were they, and why did they want him? Had the military revolted against Chou En-lai? Did they have orders to kidnap the American? Why would they take him to some farm in the countryside? To kill him and hide his body?

It was late summer at this latitude, and big trees still carried their full foliage. He wondered where the farm's fields were. From where he stood, this farmyard seemed surrounded by uncleared woods.

Suddenly, breathtakingly, Matt was overcome by a noise so loud that it seemed likely to knock him down. At once a silver airplane came looming over the nearest big trees in a takeoff attitude and moved across the low sky at enormous speed. It was immediately followed by a second roaring jet and then a third. The soldiers of his guard paid barely any notice to the shining MIGs with the bright red stars on their tails. Matt followed the fighters until they disappeared behind the truck with a hollow roar.

The platoon of soldiers began to talk to each other as soon as the noise of the jets faded. No order had been given by the officer—Matt assumed the one with the handgun was still in charge—but with the passage of the planes, the men seemed to be more at ease.

"How long must we wait?" one asked.

"Who can tell?" the officer said. "This is the correct place, so we will wait. I think we must put the American pig lover inside one of these buildings. You go and find a room with one door and no windows."

The man he pointed at nodded and turned away from the group to walk toward the low adobe building nearest them. Matt took off his damp coat and turned to face away from the blustering wind. The air was warm and carried every farm odor ever known, especially the smell of night soil along with those of rotting vegetation, standing water, and manure. Matt hoped the air would dry him off a little and help him get warm; he had been cold all night, and his feet were numb.

The soldier returned to the officer and said, "There is a room at the end of that one." He hooked his thumb at a low adobe-and-stone building with an earth roof. "We can put him in there."

Matt shook his head. "I am hungry," he said slowly to the officer. "Food." He pointed to his mouth.

The leader looked at the man next to him for translation. "I think he is demanding food."

"He is. I am hungry too. Will rice come from the base?"

"I don't know. I will go in the jeep and bring some food from the base. You put him in that room and post guards so he cannot escape. If the fornicator tries to get away, shoot him."

Matt looked at the speakers but made no sign that he understood them. When the second man tried to hold his arm, Matt shook loose and said, "Food. I am hungry."

"Go quick," the soldier said to Matt in English. "No food. Shoot."

Matt shrugged. They marched him across the littered farmyard toward the long shed. Matt was led to a storeroom at the far end of the long building. As he walked, he heard the jeep drive out of the farmyard but did not turn to watch it go. At the last doorway the English-speaking soldier pointed and said, "In," motioning vigorously with his hand.

When Matt bent to enter the low doorway he had a quick impression that the room was fairly deep—perhaps twelve feet—and half that wide. Immediately, the heavy door was closed behind him and he was in complete darkness. Behind him he heard them fumbling with a metal latch of some kind on the other side of the door. Feeling hesitantly with his feet, Matt made his way to his left to what was the end wall of the building. There he sat on his still-damp coat with his back to the wall. He was aware then that his throat was very sore and his head ached.

As his eyes gradually became accustomed to the darkness, he realized that considerable light was admitted around the old doorframe and through cracks where the roof joined the three outside walls. Before long he could make out the shape of some objects at the back of the room. He stood and groped his way along the left wall.

Suddenly, the wall upon which his hand rested shook with the vibration of a MIG's jet, and the engine noise blasted into the closed room. Before the shaking stopped, its intensity was renewed as a second plane passed over. It was, Matt realized, less a noise than a *feeling* which took over his body. No wonder the farm had been abandoned. Nothing living could survive in the takeoff pattern of a military air base. Cows and pigs would go crazy.

Several times, as he prowled the storeroom, Matt was jarred by the sudden onslaught of MIG engines which shook and blasted the little building.

By differentiating shades of darkness, he was able to discern pieces of wood thrown haphazardly against the back wall. He had begun to explore them cautiously when he heard a vehicle drive up and stop somewhere near his door. He quickly felt his way back along the side wall to where he had left his coat spread out to dry. He sat down on the dirt, his knees up, his back against the mud wall, arms resting on his knees. He could hear voices at the door but he could not understand what they were saying. He expected someone to open the door and bring him some food and drink, but nothing happened.

Minutes passed. When the door finally opened, the bright light was painful for a moment. Matt instinctively turned away from it and saw a pile of vegetation and the jumble of boards at the back of the room.

"Rice," the English-speaking soldier at the door said. "Come quick."

Matt rose slowly and braced himself with a hand against the outside wall. Adobe dust stuck to his damp fingers. He realized he was perspiring profusely.

"Quick," the soldier demanded, stepping back out of the door.

Matt stooped to go through the low door, then stood erect and dusted his hands, rubbing them on his trousers. The English speaker stood by the front right fender of the oversized Chinese jeep, holding out a small white enameled bowl full of white rice. They had moved the truck to the compound of stone houses; Matt could see it a hundred feet away. "Water," Matt said to him, making a drinking gesture. "Water."

"Rice, quick." The soldier shook the bowl, and Matt took it out of his hand. Two men with submachine guns watched him from near his doorway a few yards from the end of the building. The others must be eating, Matt surmised.

"Thirsty," Matt said. "Need water." It would be so easy just to tell this fellow what I want in Mandarin, he thought, but that would be very foolish. "Water," he repeated.

The guard nodded and went to the jeep. He returned with a mug of hot tea and put it on the front fender. "Tea," he said.

Matt ate the rice with his fingers and drank the tea standing at the fender. His throat was very painful as he swallowed the lumps of rice. While eating he fixed the locations of the buildings in his mind.

A descending MIG fighter flew over the farm from the north in a landing attitude as Matt was finishing his tea. It was because of the shriek of the wind through the MIG's flaps, Matt realized later, that he had not heard the rifle shots. He was eating a cluster of rice off his fingers when the jet screamed over, and he watched it until the extraordinary flight of the guards' bodies caught his eye. Within a heartbeat of each other the two men at the corner of the building seemed to fly up and backward. Their heavy submachine guns took different trajectories, but both bodies and both guns landed at the same moment in the damp earth near Matt's door. He continued to look at their crumpled bodies until the corpse of the English-speaking guard slid slowly along the jeep fender and nudged Matt's thigh. Involuntarily, Matt moved away from the nudge as the body slowly folded over its legs and fell to the ground beside the jeep's tire. He saw three small, bloody holes in the man's back, each within about two inches of the others.

"My God!" Matt croaked. He dropped his rice bowl. He crouched and quickly looked around the farmyard, but he saw no one.

With the disappearance of the landing MIG behind the tree line, there was complete silence again. There were no voices, no motor noises, not even any birdcalls. Matt did not doubt for a moment that the gunshots which killed the three guards had been intended for him. Perhaps the other Air Force soldiers had been ordered to execute him. He crouched behind the jeep fender, but the nearby corpses made it difficult and distasteful to find shelter there. He glanced behind him and saw the open door to his storeroom about seven or eight feet away. Still crouching, he ran awkwardly toward the door, expecting to hear shots. Once inside the dark room, Matt pressed himself against the wall next to the open door, his breath rasping. As soon as he was at rest, his back firmly against the wall, he drew a deep breath and realized that without any possibility of postponement, he urgently needed to urinate right then and there. And so he did, toward the corner of the room. Had he been less occupied with the necessity of the moment, he might have realized sooner that men were approaching the room.

When he was finished, he put on his coat and tried to arrange his disheveled clothing. Then he became aware of a soldier in the doorway, watching him. The Air Force uniforms of Matt's captors were gray-green, but this man wore an olive-green coat with red tabs on the collars. He held a rifle exactly like the one the soldiers on the truck had carried. It was pointed at Matt; the soldier took an alert, bent-knee stance, and Matt noticed that the man's finger was firmly on the trigger.

"Ho la!" the soldier shouted in Chinese. "I have found someone alive!"

Matt heard an answering shout from outside.

"I think it is the foreigner, but it is dark in here."

"Bring him out," a second man shouted. "Do not kill him until we are certain."

"Out!" the soldier screamed in Chinese, waving the tip of his rifle side to side.

"Don't shoot," Matt said as loud as his sore throat permitted, in English. "I am an American." He pushed off the wall and bent forward to walk through the doorway as the soldier backed out, still pointing his gun at Matt.

The three Air Force corpses had been arranged in a neat line, side by side in front of the jeep, face up, by two soldiers of the People's Liberation Army. They were dragging a machine gunner's body into position as Matt emerged. Each man held a foot and they were pulling vigorously. The corpse made a shallow mark across the muddy farmyard as it was dragged.

On the driver's side of the jeep two riflemen pointed their weapons at Matt from the shelter of the vehicle. To his left Matt saw more green-uniformed soldiers searching the other rooms of the farm building.

After Matt had stood outside with his hands entwined on top of his aching head for a few moments, a beautifully uniformed Chinese man stepped from behind the jeep, smiling and gesturing for Matt to put his hands down. His

jacket fitted him perfectly, and it had the extra pockets
which were the only symbol of rank permitted in the
People's Army. There was no mud on his shoes, Matt
noted as he put his arms to his side.

The officer walked up to Matt and offered his right
hand. They shook hands and Matt asked, "Have you
come to rescue me? I am an American."

"American," the officer repeated. "American."

"That's right. Matthew Thompson. I'm on my way to
Peking."

The officer shook his head and gestured for Matt to get
into the jeep. He said something to the soldiers which
began, "Guard us; we will drive . . ." but then he used
Chinese words in a dialect which Matt did not understand.

Stiffly, Matt climbed into the back of the jeep and waited
for the soldiers to form a skirmish line in front of and beside
it. The officer backed it away from the three corpses and
made a large circle which took them near the truck. A group
of PLA soldiers were loading other Air Force corpses into the
back of it. They were dragging the bodies from the stone
houses where the Air Force men had been eating their rice.

Three helicopters were on the ground in a clearing just east
of the tall trees and willow-choked stream, but it was a drive
of about a half-mile to reach them on a winding dirt road. A
platoon of PLA riflemen was deployed along the creek, and
other men guarded the margin of the clearing. Matt noticed a
helicopter aloft about a mile away to the east.

Apparently, none of the PLA soldiers spoke English.
Matt was motioned aboard the Russian-built version of the
Huey helicopter, pointed into a window seat on the left
side, gestured to fasten the peculiar Chinese seat-belt
latch, and reassured with broad smiles from the officer
every step of the way. But it was evident to Matt that the
PLA man thought they were in serious danger. Everyone
with a gun kept his finger on his trigger all the time, and
the soldiers were extremely vigilant.

Just before their helicopter took off, two MIGs were
heard, then seen, taking off from the air base nearby, and
the officer became very agitated. He was wearing a head-

set by then, and he did a lot of shouting into a microphone.
Matt couldn't hear him well over the noise of the MIGs
and the added racket of the helicopter engine and moving
rotor.

The helicopter rose slowly and flew across the clearing—
an area that had been a cultivated farm field not too long
before—barely clearing the tall trees. In the near distance
was a good-sized town. Matt looked back as the helicopter
banked and glimpsed a large airfield with many buildings
which apparently bordered the farm on the west. He could
see a long line of bright silver fighters ranged along one
side of the runway area.

The officer pointed to the town and shouted into Matt's
ear, "Dong Guan!"

"Dong Guan?" Matt rasped. The name meant nothing
to him.

The officer nodded and pointed ahead of them to the
northwest. "Canton," he shouted.

Matt repeated, "Canton?"

The officer nodded.

Matt noticed that two helicopters had moved into formation with theirs. The pocketa-pocketa vibration of the rotor
engine was authoritative and reassuring to him. For the
first time since he'd left Hung Wai-lang's house in Hong
Kong, he began to feel that everything was all right again.
He began to relax.

Thirty-six

Matt twice believed their helicopter was crossing the
main channel of the Pearl River. They flew northwest, just

above the surface of the water, so low, in fact, that the pilot had to gain altitude to go over a huge barge piled high with silver container boxes which was being towed north by a tugboat. The muddy gray waters were heavily traveled; Matt found it fascinating to look out at the big junks, loaded with goods; family laundry flapped from the lines as their great ocher sails caught the strong wind from the south.

Matt thought they had reached the main river channel, but then they flew across low grass islands to yet a wider waterway with even more boat traffic, and he had to amend his geographic assumptions. It was an estuary; the sea tide met the river flow there, and the currents swirled and boiled, making herringbone patterns in the luminous channel.

They passed over a small steamship flying a blue-and-white flag; Matt saw sailors leaning on the aft rail pointing up at them. As the helicopter neared the next island of grass, Matt noticed that the water beyond the steamer, between the helicopter and the shore, seemed suddenly to spout hundreds of small gouts of water, as if the sailors on the ship had all thrown handfuls of gravel into the river. Matt heard gravel hit the side of the helicopter, too. The helicopter pilot frantically tried to gain altitude as the aircraft tipped forward and to the left. The roll leftward went so far that Matt seemed suspended on his seat belt directly above the gray water. The safety belt sharply dug into his legs, and he grabbed for a handhold above the window. With a frightening lurch the rear of the helicopter went down, then swung violently to its left, then back right, throwing Matt into the bulkhead to his left. At the top of the windows Matt saw the belly of a shiny silver MIG as it flared up out of its gunnery pass and pulled to its left for another run.

My God, we are being attacked! Matt realized.

He turned to warn his Chinese rescuers of the MIG's attack. The PLA officer was half-standing on the other side of the helicopter shouting into his microphone. Matt smelled something burning. The pilots could be seen over the top of the dividing bulkhead, reaching for controls, frantically trying to correct for whatever damage the MIG had done to their frail bird. They abruptly pulled the helicopter's nose up, cut off the engine, and half-floated, half-fell about twenty feet into the tall grass of an island. The impact heaved everyone heavily to the right. Matt was violently smashed into the soldier next to him. There was the clash of metal, the fracture of glass, and a liquid sound Matt could not identify.

"Get out! Get out!" the officer yelled in Chinese.

Matt fumbled with the door handle next to him and finally figured out that it worked exactly the opposite from the way he'd assumed it did; it was necessary to push it forward, not pull it back. He rolled the side door open and then realized that his seat belt was preventing him from moving. He snapped the latch up and open and sprawled out over the doorsill, still holding on by the handle and the top of the doorjamb. Someone pushed him violently. His damp coat hem flapped over his shoulders, and he fell onto the round steel helicopter skid. He felt a shock of pain in his left knee. His hands sank into mud on either side of the skid. Chinese soldiers came out of the door behind him and scrambled away from the helicopter. He thought: The damn MIG is coming back, and I've broken my knee and I can't get away. I'll be shot right here in the damn mud, with my coat up over my head.

The officer hooked his arm under Matt's left armpit and hoisted him to his feet. "Run and hide," the man shouted in Mandarin. "Lie flat and hide."

Without looking back, Matt frantically hobbled away from the helicopter, sinking to his ankles in the marsh. His knee stabbed with pain at each movement, but body pain had become subordinate to the overriding fear of dying which had taken hold when his hands had first sunk into the mud beside the helicopter skid. He was mired in a swamp, and a man flying one of the most deadly killing machines in the world was trying to take his life. On the ship and at the farm he had caught a cold so severe that had he been at home, the symptoms would have sent him to bed with medicines and self-pity. But now he gave those manifestations no thought whatever.

He didn't hear the MIG approach, but behind him he heard the impact of its steel bullets on the metal and plastic of the downed helicopter, and there was a sound like someone repeatedly hitting a pillow with a stick.

Then the gasoline in the helicopter's tanks exploded with a sound like "whoomp" and Matt was violently thrown forward. The MIG thundered over him, seeming close enough to touch. When it had passed, Matt found himself on the side of a low hummock of grass and mud, his back so hot that he was afraid his coat was on fire. He could only lie on his face, gasping for the breath that had been knocked out of his lungs by the impact with the ground. The taste of burning fuel was sharp in his mouth and throat. The marsh under his nose strongly smelled like rotting grass, but the fire odor overrode it. Matt felt sick.

That bastard will be back looking for me, Matt realized; I've got to get somewhere out of sight. Painfully, he rolled onto his back. He could see the MIG far to the northeast, banking into a turn.

Matt laboriously scrambled to his feet and looked around. The helicopter was about seventy-five feet away to the east, blazing furiously, its ammunition exploding occasionally when it got hot enough, like popcorn. The hummock he'd been thrown onto was the highest place in the marsh grass, perhaps three feet higher than the rest. Matt saw the MIG swing out of its turn low in the east, and he mesmerically watched it begin its run straight for the bright fire. He shook off his fascination with the airplane, crouched and scrambled into the tall grass on the west side of the hummock, and pressed into the wet earth where he was sheltered from the heat of the fire. The soft mud closed around his elbows and knees, and he felt the water seep against his chest and thighs. Through the grass he watched the MIG coming toward him, drifting a little to his left; he kept his eyes on the plane's frontal silhouette until he saw its guns winking a pale white fire. He's shooting and he's coming directly for me, Matt realized;

I'm exactly in his line of fire. Matt turned his head to his right and pressed his left ear into the ground. He closed his eyes and held his breath.

This is when my whole life is supposed to flash before my eyes, isn't it? he thought. Where is the kaleidoscope? Death, where is thy full-color production?

He felt the MIG blast the air around him and heard the roar of its engine a fraction of a second before he felt the vibration shock of the powerful jet. Matt wondered what the bullets had hit. He rolled onto his back and shielded his eyes to watch the MIG bank low over the river toward the south. He expected it to stay in its turn and come at him from the east again. The wind was chilling him wherever water had soaked through his clothes. He wiped the mud from his ear with a less-muddy finger and rubbed the left side of his face with his sleeve. The marsh mud was slick with rotted vegetation.

The MIG made a diminishing hollow, vibrating roar in the distance. Once, when the jet tube was straight on, Matt saw the fire in its engine. The silver plane curved slowly to its left toward the east, but did not return to its attack pattern. As Matt watched, it turned right and climbed almost due south, growing smaller and smaller as it rose.

"Who is here?" someone shouted in Chinese. "Come this way."

Matt crawled to the high point of his hummock and looked north toward the voice. He felt the wind on his back. It was cold against the wet places, yet it was quite warm on his face and hands. His knee burned even when he didn't move it.

"All come here," the officer shouted. "It is safe. All come here."

Matt watched the Chinese soldiers slowly emerge, mud-smeared, from their hiding places. The officer had evidently run at a right angle to Matt's route toward a place where the grass was taller. Two soldiers had run south, nearly to the river's edge. One pilot was between Matt and the officer. There was no sign of the second helicopter pilot.

The officer began walking toward the pilot shouting,

"Everyone come here." He gestured to Matt that he should come. But Matt could not make his legs work. His left knee wobbled and threatened to buckle if he put any weight on it. It shot pain into his thigh when he moved it. His right shoe was stuck deep in the wet, soft earth, and he simply lacked the physical strength to pull it out. He half-turned away from the constant wind toward the burned-out helicopter and sank down. With that motion his buried foot levered out of the mud with a suction sound, and he was able to slowly and painfully draw up his knees and wrap his arms around his legs. He laid his right cheek on his dirt-covered knees and closed his eyes. His eyes were sore too, along with his throat. His head hurt, especially above and behind his eyes. Involuntarily, his shoulders and upper arms began to shake.

If I could get warm and dry, he thought, I wouldn't shiver like this. But it's hopeless. I'm out here in a swamp in southern China someplace, in a goddamned river swamp in wet clothes, so how am I going to get warm? The sun is low and cool and it is going to set in a little while, and these four soldiers have no way to get us rescued, so I'll be out here all night, wet and cold.

There was no doubt in his mind that the MIG pilot had been sent to kill *him*; the fellow didn't care about those PLA soldiers. He had been sent to shoot down the helicopter and strafe the survivors to kill the *American* and no one else. Perhaps there are more Chinese Air Force ground soldiers on their way out to this island to mop up and make sure that everyone is dead. When the Air Force men were holding him at the farm he had thought about escaping from the adobe building, perhaps by chipping out some of the earthen wall at the back of his prison room with the boards he had found. But the urge to escape had left him now. He was cold and sick, and his knee hurt. He would sit in the mud and they could just come and bayonet him if they wanted to. He was thirsty and bone-tired; he just didn't care anymore.

The Chinese officer had slogged across the marsh to Matt's hummock and stood beside him. Matt didn't know he was there until the man said, "Are you all right?" in Mandarin. Matt raised his head slowly and opened his eyes. It had felt good to sleep for a moment.

"I am sick," Matt said in English. "Ping"—he risked the Mandarin word for disease or illness. "Ping."

"Ah, you are sick! Do you speak Chinese?" he asked in Mandarin.

Matt pointed at his throat. "Very sick and cold," he said in English. He pointed to his left leg. "And my knee is hurt, too."

"Come, we must go away from the flying machine." The officer pointed. He put a hand under Matt's arm and lifted gently. "It is not safe here."

The officer put his palm on Matt's forehead. He walked three steps to the top of the hummock and summoned his two nearest men, the rifle soldiers. It took them several minutes to traverse the soft and wet ground for fifty yards.

"Comrades," the officer said to them, "this American has a fever and is sick. Perhaps his leg is damaged, too. That is very bad. It is getting dark, and we cannot stay here, because those disloyal Air Force vermin may come here in boats to find any survivors. So we will have to move out, and you must help the American. One of you will walk on each side of him. Put his arms over your shoulders. I will lead the way and carry your weapons."

"Comrade Major, where are we going?" asked the taller of the soldiers.

"The pilot says the village of Chin Tang is north of us, on the mainland. We will go this way across the island until we get to the water and then one of us will swim across to the village for a boat. That is my plan."

"It seems a good plan," the tall soldier said.

"I do not swim well, Comrade," the shorter man said apologetically.

"All of Unit 8341 should be proficient swimmers," the officer said. "When we return to Peking I expect you to attain a good ability to swim, Comrade, without fail. We are the Experts Unit—Comrade Chou calls us that—and we are expected to do many things with proficiency. Now let us go.''

Matt was helped to his feet and found that he could walk as long as he didn't have to put much weight on his left leg. He leaned heavily on the two soldiers. As they lurched across the marsh, Matt's fever caused his mind to run at top speed, in random directions. He briefly wondered what time it was in Washington and what day it was, but he couldn't bring his mind to do whatever calculation was required to figure it out.

When the men stopped to rest they could hear engine noises borne on the wind from far to the south, and the soldiers told each other that it was heavy river traffic on the Pearl River that they heard. Matt vaguely recalled that he must not react to their conversation. He knew he was losing control of himself, but he reverted to his early determination to be an ignorant American who did not speak Chinese. When they stopped for a rest he lay on his back, his eyes closed, the water in the damp earth seeping into the back of his coat and jacket. When they raised him to his feet to walk again, the wind chilled his back and he shivered uncontrollably.

At dusk the officer pointed to a few scattered lights several miles ahead of them. No one tried to talk to Matt; he alternated between frantic episodes of hyperthought and short periods of near-sleep. At their frequent rest stops the officer felt Matt's forehead and announced to the others that their ward continued to be very feverish, so they must hurry to get him to a doctor.

It took them nearly four hours to walk from the helicopter wreckage to the water's edge across from the fishing village. It was very dark, and at their backs the south wind continued to blow unceasingly.

Across the narrow waterway, on the mainland, most of the lights in the fishing village had been extinguished for the night, but a few remained. Matt's escorts let him sit down in the muddy marsh grass while they discussed what to do. One village fisherman seemed to be working on his boat by kerosene lamplight, and the dim glow was reflected in the wind-created waves of the waterway. Matt's luminous watch showed it was ten minutes after nine o'clock. He was very hungry and thirsty. The river smelled of salt and he knew they would not let him drink it. He could hear the soldiers' deliberations even though they were trying to talk quietly and their circle was twenty feet from where Matt was slumped on the marsh grass, lying on his right side to favor his injured knee.

"I swim well, Comrade Major," the pilot was saying, "and I come from a fishing village such as that. I am the logical one to go. I will know some of the ways of the people, and I speak some Cantonese."

"And you are needed with the American, Comrade Major," the taller soldier agreed. "You should send the pilot or one of us while you stay with him."

Matt fell asleep, his head on his arm, before the debate ended. He awoke when the major felt his forehead and buttoned the top button of Matt's still-damp coat.

"I'm really thirsty," Matt said in English.

The major smiled and said in Chinese, "A boat will come soon. The pilot has successfully swum across; already he has called to us from over in the village."

Matt closed his eyes and dozed off again without saying anything.

When they put him in the small, open rowboat he knew what they were doing, but he was not fully conscious. At the village they took him to the home of a cadre of the fishing commune where everyone was given hot tea, flat coarse biscuits, and fish soup. The tea revived Matt, dissolving some of the mental barriers which had masked the pain. His knee had stiffened and seemed seriously injured. His throat was so sore that, as hungry as he was, he could barely manage to swallow bits of the biscuits, soaked in the soup.

In about an hour the officer roused Matt and led him outside. Two men helped him into the cab of an old truck which, from its smell, apparently carried the commune's fish to market. The young driver from the commune, the

officer, and Matt were silent until they drove into the
eastern reaches of Canton.

"I must go to the first police station, Comrade," the
officer said. "Do you know where a police station is?"

"Yes, I think so, sir," the fisherman said. "Canton has
a very large police force, and there is a headquarters not
far ahead."

Matt dozed as the big truck lumbered through the
crowded outskirts of the city. When it stopped at a brightly
lighted police barracks, he barely stirred. He was only
distantly aware that the driver and officer got out of the
truck. Soon they returned for him and walked him through
the station to a small room where they helped him out of
his coat and onto a cot. Someone produced coarse, brown
blankets which Matt gathered close around his shoulders
and neck.

Later, someone washed his face with a warm cloth. At
the same time they put a rod in his mouth and then made
him drink, but he wasn't really awake for all of that. He
slept all through the ambulance ride, too.

At the hospital, two male nurses efficiently undressed
him and gave him a sponge bath. Then someone washed
his face and torso with alcohol, and the chill of its
evaporation woke him up.

"I'm freezing," he said.

"Good morning, Mr. Thompson," a woman said in
English. "How do you feel now?"

He was lying on a high iron bed, completely naked.
Two Chinese men in white T-shirts and white pants were
vigorously rubbing his arms and legs with rough towels.
The Chinese woman stood near his head, smiling.

He was in a room made of poured concrete which had
been roughly finished and whitewashed. Pipes were supported
by metal straps near the ceiling, and to Matt's left, under
double windows, a hot-water pipe clattered. Even stronger
than the smell of alcohol from his body was the odor of a
strong disinfectant which permeated the room. Everything
looked unfinished and worn. The paint trim around the
windows covered only three of the four margins. A metal

lampshade was chipped. Paint was flaking from around the edge of the only door.

"These guys are killing me, and I'm cold." he answered. "My head hurts like hell, too. Where am I?"

"You are in People's Hospital Number One, the Hospital of the Martyrs of the Revolution. You are quite sick, but you will get well." Her English was without a trace of accent.

"Are you . . ."

"I am Dr. Yu." She was short and round-faced, with close-cropped black hair.

"This is Canton?"

"Yes, of course."

"I need to get to Peking." He let the nurses put a hospital gown over his arms and tie it in the back.

"I think you need to sleep right now," Dr. Yu replied. "Just relax and let me connect you. When you wake up, your friends from Peking will be here to see you, I think."

"Good," Matt said softly. He barely felt the doctor prepare his arm and put the intravenous tube in place.

Thirty-seven

When Matt Thompson awoke he felt better. In the order of their appearance he saw a bouquet of zinnias on his bedside table, Teng Shan-li sitting on a straight metal chair near the window reading a newspaper, and Wang Li-fa sitting next to him, reading the same newspaper over Teng's shoulder. When Matt recognized Li-fa he smiled broadly, and she returned his smile.

She was more attractive than he had remembered. Her

nose was a little thinner than he had pictured it, and her mouth softer and more sensuous. Her eyes were incredible; they were wide open and sending him all the messages he had hoped to get from her. She was worried about his injuries, they said, and she wanted to spend time with him and she had so much to tell him.

"He is awake," a man said in Chinese from the other side of the room.

Matt turned his head to see a handsomely uniformed officer of the People's Liberation Army leaning against the wall near the door. Matt turned back to look at Li-fa, and he smiled again.

"Li-fa," he croaked.

"Hello, Matthew," she said. "How are you feeling?"

Teng Shan-li folded his newspaper and stood, smiling. "He looks as if he is feeling better."

"Did you come all the way from Peking?" Matt asked them.

"Yes, of course, Matthew," Li-fa said. "When the Premier was told of what had happened to you he sent us in his airplane at once, to make sure you are well cared for. As soon as you feel better we will all fly back to Peking together. How do you feel?"

"I'm not sure. Let's see: I guess my head feels a lot better. My throat is still very sore." He flexed his left leg and winced. "And my left knee hurts like hell. I hit it when I got out of the helicopter. Is it broken?"

"I don't think so," Teng said. "The doctor didn't say that it was. Is it bandaged?"

Matt nodded. "They have a big wrap on it."

Teng spoke in Chinese to the military officer: "Will you ask Dr. Yu to come in, please, Captain?" The man nodded and went out.

"Who is he?" Matt asked.

Teng Shan-li sat down by the window. "You are being guarded by a detail from the 8341 Guards Unit. The Premier had them sent here to look after you when it was known that you would come by way of Hong Kong rather than Tokyo. The captain is one of the leaders of that squadron."

"It was 8341 men who rescued you," Li-fa added. "They had been waiting at the ship dock for you."

"How did they ever find me?" Matt asked.

"We had a friend on the ship," Teng said. "He had the captain notify the shipping company in Canton as soon as you were taken away. The Guards got Army helicopters and began looking for you as soon as it was light."

"What happened?" Matt asked. "Who took me, and why? Was it Air Force?"

Teng held up his hand to quiet Matt as the door opened and Dr. Yu came in with the captain. Matt could see another soldier outside his door carrying some kind of weapon.

"Your patient is asking about his knee," Li-fa explained in English. "Comrade Teng sent for you with the hope that you could describe for him the nature of his injury."

Dr. Yu nodded and walked around to the window side of Matt's bed. She pulled down his covering sheet and put her palm on Matt's left kneecap. "The patella has been cracked from side to side, according to the X-rays." She traced the line of the fracture on the thick bandage. "It is necessary to keep the knee immobile for a week or so, until the crack heals, and so it is wrapped heavily to impede motion. It is not serious, but Mr. Thompson must be careful not to break it again. It will always be vulnerable from now on." She turned to the foot of the bed and looked at Matt's chart. Then she walked between Matt and the soldier, raised Matt's eyelids to look at his eyes, and felt his forehead. The captain closely watched everything the doctor did.

Dr. Yu said to Matt, "You are rapidly improving. You have slept for nearly twenty hours, and that is very healing. You are a good patient."

"When you are a little more rested, Matthew," Teng said, "we will return here to talk some business. The captain—who, incidentally, speaks only Chinese—will be here with you at all times. Another officer will take his place briefly when it is necessary."

Dr. Yu wrote instructions on the patient's chart and excused herself.

"To answer your questions," Teng continued when she was gone, "you were taken off the ship by an Air Force unit which is assigned to an airfield near the Pearl River estuary. Your helicopters were shot down by planes from that same base."

"But why were they after *me*?"

"It is complicated and not completely clear—" Li-fa began.

"There are problems," Teng interjected. "As you know, the Defense Minister, Lin Piao, is Chairman Mao's designated successor, and he is strongly opposed to any accommodation with the United States. We believe the Air Force was assigned to kill you to embarrass Premier Chou En-lai's efforts in that direction. What do you think the effect would have been if the body of a White House Assistant to the President were produced for the international press in Peking?"

"Sensational. Everything would be blown sky high."

"Exactly."

"How did they know I was coming?"

"We are not certain. Perhaps our messages were intercepted. We believe someone has followed you all the way from Tokyo, however, reporting on your movements."

"How in the world did your Guards ever find me in that barn on that farm?" Matt asked.

"Some of the men who kidnapped you got hungry," Teng Shan-li explained, "and they came back to the air base for food."

"I was hollering for food too. I demanded that they feed me."

Teng smiled. "To begin with, our Guards were very suspicious of the personnel at that base. They knew you had been taken by men wearing Air Force uniforms; our man on the boat told us that. This was the nearest base. So the Guards were there, searching for you on that base, when these men came back for food. When they took away their rations and enough for more men too, the Guards followed them. When they were led to the farm the Guards went back and pretended to leave the air base in their helicopters, but they flew only a short distance, to the farmer's field. Three of those four helicopters were destroyed by the MIGs, you know, and yours was the only one of the three that did not crash in the river. You were very lucky, I think."

Matt nodded his head. "Do you know how wonderful it is to see you both? I am very grateful to be alive. I really thought I'd never make it out of that swamp. I figured that MIG would eventually get us."

"He might have, but the Premier interceded when he received a message about the Air Force holding you, and he ordered all Air Force planes grounded in the Canton area," Li-fa said.

"You look wonderful, Li." Matt rasped. "That reminds me, Mr. Teng: do you know if anyone found my suitcase on the boat? There is something in it for Li-fa."

Li-fa blushed. "Your suitcase is here somewhere. I will go and find it."

"No," Teng Shan-li said to her. "I shall find it. I expect Matthew could use his razor, too. While I am gone, please find out when Matthew must be back in Washington, so we can make appropriate arrangements." And in Chinese he spoke to the guard: "Captain? Will you please step into the hall with me for a moment?"

When Teng and the soldier left it seemed very quiet in the room. Wang Li-fa stood up and looked at Matt. "Why did you bring me a present?" she asked. "Did you think I needed something?"

"No. I had missed you and I knew that when I was with you again in Peking I would be very glad to see you. I wanted to give you something beautiful so you would be glad too."

"Didn't you know that it would make me glad merely to be with you again? No other present is necessary."

"Well, sure, I hoped that." He smiled with pleasure.

"But I wasn't sure. It is very hard for me to know what you are thinking."

"The inscrutable Oriental, eh?"

"Really. I missed you very much."

She stepped to the bed so that her hip rested against the mattress; she put her hand on his forehead. Her hand seemed very cold to Matt.

"Do you realize that we have only been alone together once before?" Matt asked. He took her upper arm gently with his left hand, holding her hand in place on his forehead.

She slowly ran her index finger down the bridge of his nose, to his lips. He kissed her finger and she quickly withdrew it.

"I've been thinking about us all the time," he said. He circled her waist with his left arm and drew her gently toward him. He felt her warmth under her blouse, and it aroused him. He ran his hand up her back toward her shoulder and drew her down. "I think I love you, Li-fa," he said quietly. Their faces were very close. He wondered to himself that he had said that to her. Perhaps he did love her. It seemed extraordinarily good to be with her.

She put her hands on his arms and pushed herself away. "Matt, you are a very beautiful man, even with your awful stubble beard. But you must not love me, and I must not be attracted to you. I have thought about it very much since you were in China before, and I know that we have no future together. You must understand that!"

"Maybe it's something we just have no control over, Li."

She shook her head. "I am the Premier's secretary and I owe him my total loyalty. There is no place in my life for a tall American with beautiful brown eyes." She blinked away the beginning of tears.

"Come here, Li, and let me take care of those tears." He reached toward her again and took her right arm, which was thinner than he remembered. He pulled her toward him as he sat up and took her shoulder in his right hand. He felt the intravenous tube pull taut, then slacken as he pulled her. She smelled of sandalwood. He kissed her salty cheeks with small kisses, then kissed her mouth. She pressed against him and returned his kiss. Without thinking he opened his mouth as he kissed her and drove his tongue between her lips. Her eyes opened wide and she drew back.

"What is that?" she exclaimed. "Do you always do that with your tongue?"

"I've never kissed a girl before," he said, smiling, moving back against his pillows. "Isn't that how you're supposed to do it?"

"Never kissed any girl? I don't believe that for a minute! You could be married for all I know."

"I'm not. I don't even have a steady girlfriend. So, will you marry me?" He had the feeling that he had just passed a point of no return, without really intending to do so.

Li-fa had straightened up and was smoothing her sleek hair. "You are a crazy man, Matt Thompson. You don't mean that, so don't say it."

"I do mean it," he said somewhat defensively. "I think we would be a very good married couple. You are beautiful and smart and hardworking and have a good sense of humor, and I think we are in love with each other. If you took off all your clothes and climbed into this bed with me, we would undoubtedly make beautiful love together."

"Oh, Matthew!" Li-fa blushed and covered her face with her hands. "You must not talk that way to a Chinese woman. You are terrible! You must be more careful. What if the soldier came in and heard you?"

"He doesn't understand English, remember?"

"Where do you plan for us to live in this ideal marriage, Mr. Thompson? Are you planning to move to China?"

"I would do that," he said slowly, "or there's Hong Kong or even America. You would love my country as much as I love yours." He folded his hands behind his head. "I would be happy anywhere, as long as I am with you."

She shook her head. "You say that now, but I don't think so. I'm not at all sure I would like America. There are too many problems in all of this that you are forgetting. I think you hit your head on that helicopter and it has made you crazy. When you are well you will forget you ever said such a thing. I hope you forget it."

"I won't. I've been thinking about you all the time. It's funny, you know; I hadn't intended to ask you to marry me. But I've been out there by the river with people trying to kill me. I think it made me realize just how important you are to me."

"We hardly know each other, Matthew," she said. She had sat down in Teng's chair, her hands folded on her lap. "You have not been to my home or met my mother. You have only seen me at work with the Premier. As you said, we have not really been alone. How can one know about a person without a longer acquaintance?"

"Why don't you bring your mother and sister to the hospital? I would like to meet them."

"What would I tell them?" she wailed, her hands over her ears. " 'Mother, I want you to come to the hospital to meet an American man who is such a big secret that you must never tell anyone you saw him'?"

"Just tell her you are in love and you want her to meet the man you intend to marry."

Li-fa shook her head. "You really do not understand how things work in China, do you? I could not bring my family here unless they had a visiting pass."

"Teng could arrange that."

"They would be recorded by the hospital staff as visitors to an American. That could be trouble for them."

"Can't Teng make sure they will be okay?"

"It is not that easy. Mr. Teng is not a powerful official. He is from Peking, not Canton. And I would not wish to ask the Premier to intervene."

"So we'll get a cab and go to your mother's house. I'll be up and around pretty soon."

"You want their street committee to record that they have had an American visitor?"

"So we'll meet them at a hotel."

Li-fa shook her head.

"A restaurant? The park? The zoo?"

She thought a moment and suddenly smiled. "We could meet them at a place I know just up the street from here in the park. There is an orchid garden there."

"When I'm better you could take me for a walk, right?"

"We will see. But even so, if you meet my mother and my sister, you cannot then say that you adequately know me."

"I really know you, Li-fa. Don't worry about that. I have been running away from making a commitment to any woman all of my life. I don't really go around proposing marriage to all the girls, believe me."

She stood and stepped to the bed.

"You have a wonderful mouth, my love," he said.

The door swung open and Teng Shan-li held up Matt's Valpak. "We have found your bag!" he announced triumphantly. "It was in a closet in the administrator's office."

Li-fa blushed, embarrassed to be found so near the American man.

"Let me have it, please, Mr. Teng," Matt said. "I have something for you that I think you'll like."

Teng laid the suitcase on the bed beside Matt, and the American unzipped an outside pocket of the bag and searched the contents with his hand.

"Hell! They aren't here. Those villains stole your cookies, Mr. Teng. Wait. I had some inside, too." He opened two straps and a catch and folded the bag flat. Matt unzipped an inner pocket, searched, and smiled. He extracted a plastic bag tied with a piece of red yarn. "My secretary, Angie Cruz, made these. They are for you, sir."

Teng took the cookies and mumbled his thanks, with some embarrassment.

"Mr. Teng regrets that he has nothing to give you as a welcoming gift," Li-fa explained. "You embarrass him."

"Is that right? Look, you don't need to feel that way. It's only a few cookies."

The 8341 captain entered the room and stood by the door. "His lunch is prepared," he said in Chinese.

"Are you hungry?" Li-fa asked Matt. "They have lunch for you. We will go downstairs and eat, and you must sleep. We will return this afternoon. You did say you must return to Washington in ten days, did you not?"

"Yes. I can only be away ten days and I've been gone four days, I think. Is that right?" He shook his head. "I can't figure it out, with the time change and everything."

"We will assume six days remain," Teng said. "Is there anything you need?"

"The stuff in this bag is awfully wrinkled," Matt said, pointing. "Do you think someone could press the pants and jacket and could clean that awful stuff I wore in the swamp?"

"Of course," Teng said. "I will see to it. You eat now, and then sleep."

"Sleep well." Li-fa was smiling.

In forty-eight hours Li-fa had efficiently organized Matt's excursion to the park, and he read her determined stage management as a sign that she very much wanted him to be presented to her mother with propriety.

Somehow Li-fa had convinced Dr. Yu that fresh air was just what her patient required. The doctor arranged for a metal-and-leather wheelchair to be brought to Matt's room at 11 A.M. on the appointed day. The chair came with a leg prop which was arranged under Matt's left knee and under his foot so that his leg could not bend. Cotton pants and a shirt were produced.

"What do the letters say on this shirt?" Matt asked Li-fa. She was exceedingly nervous that morning, and he was devising diversions to ease her tension.

"It says you are the property of People's Hospital Number One."

"But I'm not. I belong to you," he said.

"Stop that and be serious! I need to explain something to you. The 8341 Guards are determined to go with us.

They would be severely punished if anything happened to you. The captain would like for you to stay in your room all the time. I've persuaded him to let you go, and he agrees not to smother you with guards. I explained that you wish to go into the park and have conversations with average Chinese people, and I am your interpreter. He and his men will allow you to do this, but they will be watching everything closely. That is the best I can do with him."

"So I'll meet your mother with soldiers standing all around?"

"A few. I suggest we talk to some other people both before and after we meet my honored mother. Perhaps we will find several families in the park."

"Okay, but it's weird."

The orchid garden was actually located several long and congested blocks north of the hospital. Matt thought they were a strange procession as they made their way up the sidewalk off Renmin Bei Road. The captain led, his right hand on his holster, followed by a soldier with his automatic rifle at the ready. Five or six yards back, Wang Li-fa pushed the wheelchair in which Matt rode with the bare toes of his left foot sticking up like a radiator cap on an old Pierce Arrow. Close behind came two more riflemen. As they passed the Dongfang Hotel several Europeans stopped on the steps to watch them parade by. This is very foolish, Matt reflected. If some smart foreign reporter recognized me rolling along here, there would be hell to pay.

At the park, Li-fa stopped twice to explain to mothers and fathers sitting on benches, watching their playing children, that her patient was an Englishman who had been injured in an unfortunate traffic mishap. Would they like to speak to him and offer their wishes for his speedy recovery? Li-fa dutifully translated the coerced condolences from the poor people who wanted no trouble from the Englishman's armed escort.

At the entrance to the orchid garden, Li-fa greeted a young woman in English. "Matt, this is my sister, Nancy," Li-fa said seriously. "I am overjoyed to see her, but I do

not want the captain to wonder too much about all of
this."

"Hello, Nancy," Matt said, taking the older woman's
hand. Nancy Wang had a wide, pleasant face with bright
black eyes. Her body was broad, her arms large.

"It's good to meet you, Matt. Our mother is here, just
inside the garden gate on a bench. She is waiting to meet
you." Then in Chinese she said to Li-fa: "My God, he's
beautiful. Does he really love you?"

Li-fa blushed. The captain watched Matt's encounter
with Nancy from a distance without interest. But when
Li-fa began to wheel Matt into the orchid garden, the
captain walked rapidly to the gate, signaling a soldier to go
in ahead of the wheelchair. "Wait, please!" he called to
Li-fa. "Let us go into the garden first."

"There is our mother," Li-fa said.

Chu Lin was a thin woman, taller than her daughters,
her gray hair pulled back into a large bun. Her strong nose
and wide mouth gave her a severe look until she smiled,
but when she saw Li-fa she grinned broadly and her dark
eyes were alight.

"Madame Chu Lin, may I present my friend Matthew
Thompson?" Li-fa said to her mother in English.

"I am very happy to meet you, Mr. Thompson," Chu
Lin said. "Is your injury healing?" Her accent was very
British.

"Yes, it's much better, thank you. I am sorry that our
first meeting is under these awkward circumstances—the
soldiers and everything. You are very kind to come here."

"I am happy to come. Will you return to your home
soon?" She sat with her hands folded, looking at Matt
intently.

"Yes, in less than five days I must be back at work. It's
much too short a time." Matt looked at Li-fa, who stood
beside his chair with one hand on the push bar.

The captain watched this conversation with obvious
curiosity. When he began to walk slowly toward Matt's
chair, Li-fa turned and said to him: "We have come upon

two old friends of mine! I knew these ladies when I lived here in Canton.''

''Ah,'' said the captain. He turned back and took his station near the gate to the garden.

''What work is it that you do, Mr. Thompson?'' Chu Lin asked.

Matt looked at Li-fa, who shook her head almost imperceptibly.

''I am a lawyer,'' Matt replied.

''That must be very interesting. My late husband was a teacher, you know.''

It was warm and very humid within the high walls of the orchid garden. Orchids grew everywhere; they had been engrafted on the large trees and on logs, and they grew as plants and bushes in lush profusion. A system of sprays kept the humidity very high within the garden walls. Matt found the enclosed and wet heat to be oppressive.

Madame Chu defied the heat. She wore a brown shawl over her silk blouse, and her woven skirt appeared to be made of a dark brown wool. Nancy and Li-fa both wore the usual short-sleeved white blouse and dark cotton skirt that were the summer uniform of most Chinese women. Madame Chu was adorned with strings of amber beads, accessories seldom seen since the Cultural Revolution began.

''My husband taught in Hong Kong,'' she said.

''Yes, Li-fa has told me a little about her honored parents. She respects you very deeply.''

Madame Chu shot Li-fa an inquiring look. Matt had assumed that Li-fa would tell her mother that he was a suitor, but evidently she hadn't found the courage.

''Is there anything you would like to tell us?'' Nancy asked Li-fa with a grin.

''Tell you?'' Li-fa repeated.

''As a matter of fact,'' Matt interrupted, ''there is.''

''No, there isn't,'' Li-fa said. ''And we really must return Matthew to the hospital now.''

''Madame Chu,'' Matt continued, ''I asked to meet you because of my deep feeling for your daughter.''

"We hardly know each other," Li-fa said, shaking her head in protest.

Madame Chu smiled thinly. "There seems to be a difference of opinion."

"I don't think so," Matt replied. "I think we love each other, but Li-fa can't bring herself to admit it."

"Is that true, daughter?" Chu Lin asked. "Are you serious about this man? Is that why you asked us to come to meet him today?"

"Americans are often brash and pushy when they should be patient and discreet, honored mother," Li-fa replied. "I don't think I could love a brash, pushy American."

"What about *this* American?" Madame Chu insisted, smiling at her daughter's evasion.

Li-fa turned to the captain and said in Chinese: "It is time for us to return, is it not? Are you ready?"

And in English she said to her mother and sister, "We really must go."

Madame Chu was amused. She looked at Matt, raised her eyebrows, and shook her head. "Well, Mr. Thompson, I guess you are going to be taken away before we really have an opportunity to become well acquainted. But I think I like you. Sometime I will tell you about the time my husband told my father that he wanted to marry me." She shook her head slowly. "What a time that was!"

"I look forward to our next time together, honored— Madame Chu. There are many things I wish to know from you."

"Goodbye, honored Mother," Li-fa said quietly. She spoke in English so the army captain would not understand her. "Thank you for coming. I am very much embarrassed that Matthew has spoken to you of his emotions, but he does not understand China very well."

"Goodbye, Matthew," Nancy said. "Are there any more at home like you?"

Matt laughed. "It sounds like your sister has no use for me, Nancy. How about you and me? Do you want to give me your phone number? I'll call you?"

"That's enough, Matthew," Li-fa said with mock seriousness. "This little family meeting has turned into a disaster; I can see that. Come along now and I will put you back in the hospital, where you belong. They should put you in the crazy ward!"

Madame Chu and Nancy laughed. Matt waved goodbye to them as his entourage formed around him to leave the orchid garden.

Li-fa said almost nothing on the long walk back to the hospital. She wheeled Matt along busy Tsi Fang Road to its intersection with Hai Tzu Road, where the white-jacketed policeman left his kiosk and personally escorted Matt and his soldiers through the congested, five-legged crossing. The policeman's white-gloved hand stopped all traffic on the west side of the intersection as Matt and his wheelchair paraded across the broad intersection.

"Just another block now," Li-fa said. "I had no idea this was going to become an imperial parade."

Matt was exhausted, he realized. The combination of Li-fa's tension, and the awkward procession, and meeting Li-fa's family had badly tired him. He knew that he should try to say something reassuring to Li-fa, but he was just too weary, and his knee hurt like hell. He relaxed with his eyes closed as the soldiers lifted his chair up the hospital steps and Li-fa wheeled him to the elevator.

"He is very tired," the captain said to Li-fa in Chinese.

"Yes," she replied, "I think the trip to the park was a bad idea."

At the fourth floor Teng Shan-li was waiting in the hallway. Matt nodded in greeting. "Did you enjoy your outing?" Teng asked.

"Very much," Matt said, "but I'm ready for a long nap now. I would like to speak to Miss Wang for a moment, to give her the little gift I mentioned, but then I will rest. Is that all right?"

"Of course," Teng said. "Comrade Wang, I will wait for you in the dining room downstairs."

The soldiers took the wheelchair away and left Li-fa alone with Matt. She brought him his attaché case and he took the small, gift-wrapped package from it.

"This is for you," he said. "Thank you for taking me to meet your mother and sister."

She took the small square box and looked at it. "I should not even open this," she said sternly. "You make me very angry sometimes, you know." She was standing between the bed and the windows, where she would see the door open if anyone came.

"Go ahead and open it. You have to open it."

"You were terrible to tell my mother those things. They are not true. I do not love you."

"I think you do. And if you don't I will marry Nancy. She likes me. And then I will be your brother-in-law and maybe we can live together."

Li-fa smiled and began to untie the ribbon, holding the box against her belly. She looked up at Matt and said: "What makes you such an awful fool?"

"It's love that does that—didn't you know?"

"What is this now in this little box?" She dropped the wrappings on the bed and held the box up for him to see her open it.

"What is it?" he asked.

"Oh, my God, it's the most beautiful ring," she whispered. "What is the stone?"

"It's a sapphire; do you like it?"

She looked at him. "It's too much. I cannot accept it."

"Why not?"

"It's too much! What does it mean? Does it have a particular message?" She took it out of the box and slipped it on her left ring finger and admired it.

"It means we are friends and I like you. It could mean we are engaged to be married, if we want it to, but it doesn't need to mean that if you don't want it to."

"When could I ever wear it? It is much too grand and expensive for a Chinese woman to wear. No, I cannot take it from you!"

"It looks wonderful on your finger. Does it fit?"

"Oh, yes, it is perfect. Isn't it a wonderful deep blue color?"

"Wonderful. I'm glad you like it."

The door opened and Dr. Yu bustled in, her long white coat open. "It's a hot day, isn't it?" she announced.

Li-fa blushed, folding her right hand over her left to conceal the ring.

"It's hot and I'm tired," Matt said. "But my throat feels much better."

"I must go," said Li-fa, quickly gathering up the ribbon and paper with her right hand. "I will return to finish the letter when you awaken, Mr. Thompson."

"Fine, you do that, Miss Wang," he said, smiling. "Doctor, my knee hurts like hell. How long is it going to feel like this?"

Thirty-eight

"We must talk, Matthew, if you are feeling well enough," Teng Shan-li said. He had opened Matt Thompson's hospital-room door a crack to be certain that Matt was awake. Matt had slept soundly for two hours after his extraordinary excursion to the park, and Teng had waited impatiently in the hall for him to awaken.

Matt had been given his midday meal of rice, green beans, onions, and bits of deep-fried fish about twenty minutes after Li-fa had left him to rest. He'd had very little appetite, but the hot tea made him feel better. He seemed so weak! His cold and fever were much improved, but after the least exertion he seemed to have soft noodles for bones.

When Teng looked in to find Matt awake the American was open-eyed, but he remained flat on his back, relaxed.

"I'm awake, Mr. Teng," Matt said softly. "Come in."

"I should let you sleep, I know, but we will be leaving here tomorrow and we may not have a good chance to talk on the airplane. There are some things you should understand before you get to Peking."

"Okay," Matt said. "Will you help me sit up?"

"Of course. Let us take the cushion from this chair to put behind your pillow."

Matt laboriously worked his hips back toward the head of the bed and rested against the pillow. "Thanks. I would drink some of that tea from the vacuum bottle there if you'll pour it. Please have some yourself."

"Thank you. I wish to tell you about Minister Lin Piao, the Defense Minister, Matthew." Teng poured two mugs of tea and handed one to the American. Teng walked to the windows and brought back a metal chair which he placed near Matt on the side of the bed nearest the door.

"The Vice Chairman, Minister Lin, is a very important person in China," Teng continued, sitting down. "Do you know about him?"

"I've read a little. He was a famous general, wasn't he?" Matt felt invigorated by the hot tea.

"Yes. During the Revolution he won important battles when he was still a young man. However, he did not become such a very powerful official until the Cultural Revolution. He was one of the Ten Marshals of China and a member of the Politburo, but it was only when the armed forces became so vital during the anarchy of the Cultural Revolution that Comrade Lin came into his present prominence. Now our constitution designates him to be Chairman Mao's successor."

Matt nodded. Several days before he left Washington he had sent across the Potomac River for the CIA's dossiers on Mao, Chou, and the other Chinese leaders, which he had studied carefully. He might know more about Lin Piao than Mr. Teng did, Matt guessed. He put down the empty tea mug and nodded again.

"The Vice Chairman," Teng went on, "has been extremely loyal to Chairman Mao. Every copy of the Little Red Book of the Chairman's sayings begins with an introduction by Lin Piao. And in his speeches and writings Minister Lin has been very praising of Chairman Mao's intellect and courage."

"Yes," Matt said. He wondered why he was having this lecture; was Lin responsible for his kidnapping?

"Last month, however, a schism appeared about which I think you must know in order to understand why you were taken prisoner and shot down in the helicopter."

"A schism?"

"Yes. In August the State Central Committee met at a resort called Lushan. It is in Henan Province, about halfway from here to Peking. The purpose of the meeting was to plan the next Party Congress, but Lin Piao also decided to propose there that Chairman Mao now be designated Chairman of the State. That is an office which has been left vacant for several years. I guess Lin Piao thought it would please Chairman Mao to be given that additional honor."

"But he guessed wrong?"

Teng grinned and nodded. "Very wrong. To understand the background, it is helpful to know that there are at least two major, conflicting views of the Chinese Revolution which are contended for among Chinese intellectuals. One, which rests on the early writings of Chairman Mao, holds that the masses—the peasants—are the genius and driving force of the Revolution. The opposing intellectual view is that once in dozens of generations a genius-leader appears and he causes vast changes in China."

"And this time it is Mao?"

"Yes, that is the point. For whatever his reason, Lin Piao stood up and made a speech at Lushan extolling Chairman Mao as the genius-leader of this age. He argued that without Mao there could have been no Chinese Revolution and no victory. Then, because he thought Chairman Mao desired to be designated Chairman of the State, the Vice Chairman proposed that action and sat down."

"Was all this in the newspaper?" Matt asked. United States intelligence agencies hadn't reported any of this.

"Oh, no," Teng replied. "I am told all of this by my

friend who was there. But my friend is a very reliable man; I am sure this is true. He says that Chairman Mao waited half a day before criticizing Lin Piao, and then the Chairman never mentioned his name. But he made a speech and he took swift action to show his displeasure. In his speech he said that anyone who called him a genius was guilty of betrayal of the Revolution; he said that such a person was a false revolutionary. The Chairman ordered the arrest of a prominent political theoretician, Chen Boda. Everyone knows that Comrade Chen and the Vice Chairman, Lin Piao, are very close. Chairman Mao also dismissed and arrested several high-ranking military officers in the capital, and he ordered the commander of the Air Force, the chief of staff of the People's Liberation Army, his deputy, and others close to the Defense Minister to undergo self-criticism. Do you know what that means?''

''Yes, I do.''

''The Chairman deliberately picked out only Lin Piao's men as guilty of Mao-idolatry. And of course, there are many others equally guilty of that, as you might imagine. The Chairman might have chosen many people for criticism, but he aimed his thunderbolts only at the Lin Piao faction.''

''I see. What has been the effect of all this?''

''It is difficult to say,'' Teng shrugged. ''It throws into question the matter of the succession, you see. If Chairman Mao Tse-tung has decided that Minister Lin is unworthy, then what will Lin Piao do? Perhaps he will resign, perhaps not.''

''Where is Chou En-lai in all of this?''

''Well, it is true that several of Chairman Mao's chosen successors have fallen by the wayside over the years, but Premier Chou En-lai has continued to serve China in the same way for a long time.''

''Maybe it is safer to be number three than number two?''

''It may be. Premier Chou has always been very loyal to Chairman Mao, and in a situation where a minister is in disfavor with the Chairman, you must expect that such a minister will be in disfavor with Chou En-lai also."

"And vice versa? Are you saying that the Premier and his people are in danger from Lin Piao?"

"It may be, Matthew. There is a well-known story that once Lin Piao ordered the Premier's plane shot down, but Comrade Chou avoided the ambush and came back to Peking with a copy of Lin Piao's written instructions in his hand to show to Chairman Mao. I don't know the truth of the story, but just now all of us are being very cautious." Teng stood and walked to the window. "Tomorrow we will take you to Peking. We will fly in a civilian aircraft rather than trust our fate to the Air Force. The Premier has arranged for us to use one of the CAAC transports."

"How much of the military does Lin Piao control?" Matt asked.

"It is difficult to say. The commanders of the Air Force and Navy are his very close friends and allies. But the People's Liberation Army consists of many more units led by very strong commanders."

"Can Lin Piao overthrow Chairman Mao and the Premier?"

Teng walked back to his chair and sat down. "It will not come to that, I think. The Chinese Government is much broader than two or three people, and it is very stable. And my friends say that Lin Piao is sick. In his youth he was a tiger and he won all his battles, but now he is old and less vigorous."

"Can Lin Piao prevent the Premier from making peace with the United States?" Matt asked.

"That is why we are having this conversation, Matthew. The Premier's strategy gives the Vice Chairman an ideological rallying point, you see. If an Army commander cannot be won to Lin Piao's side in some other way, he might be won with the information that Chou En-lai is conducting secret negotiations with the hated Americans. The Premier has been having problems from the very beginning of his United States project, and we suspect the Lin Piao clique has caused them. People have followed me

and spied on my activities, for example; someone wants to
know what I am doing for the Premier. Now the Air Force
has rather openly kidnapped you, and I am quite sure they
would have killed you to embarrass the Premier's efforts.
Perhaps your kidnapping was the idea of Air Force commander Wu Fa Ch'an, without the knowledge of Defense
Minister Lin, but that seems unlikely.''

"That sounds bad.''

"Well, it is told to you to explain why the Premier has
moved slowly in responding to the many messages of your
President. And it also explains why Chinese Air Force
fighter airplanes threatened an American plane right at the
time that the Premier was seeking a more peaceful atmosphere with the United States.''

"How will the schism be resolved, Mr. Teng?''

"One cannot say. If no one dies of old age perhaps the
Premier can mediate between the Chairman and the Vice
Chairman. Chou En-lai has successfully mediated between
Party factions since the birth of the Revolution, you know.
When I was a young man Chou En-lai was at school in
Tientsin too, a few years ahead of your dear father and
me. He went to Japan before I did and then he went on to
Paris, where he was in the Chinese Communist Youth
Corps with Teng Hsiao-ping and other Chinese leaders you
have heard of. He was in Shanghai in 1927 when Chiang
Kai-shek massacred so many Communists, and after that,
in Wuhan, Chou En-lai became a leader of the Communist
Party in China. He has held the Party together ever since;
for over forty years.''

"He's a remarkable man,'' Matt said. "You think he
can heal it, then? And why would Chairman Mao make so
much trouble for himself by deposing Lin Piao right now?
It seems that the military is awfully important to him, with
things as unsettled as they are.''

"Of course, I do not know,'' Teng said, "but I believe
that Chairman Mao cares more for ideological purity of
thought than for the transient political problems which
might arise from hewing faithfully to the proper line. I
think he decided that Lin Piao and his supporters were

veering too far from correct thought, by reason of their ambitions or for some other reason."

"Does all of this have anything to do with why I was asked to come to Peking, Mr. Teng?"

"The Premier asked that you come for several reasons, Matthew. He was concerned that his delay in responding to President Nixon should be exactly understood, and we all felt that this subject could not be well conveyed by a letter. Second, he is concerned over the reports that you are being put under surveillance by your own government. And, of course, he wishes your counsel. There are important substantive questions to be answered in future talks between the United States and China."

Matt nodded his understanding. He rubbed his eyes and blinked.

"You should rest again, Matthew," Teng said. "But before I leave you, may I ask one question?"

"Of course."

"It relates to Comrade Wang Li-fa and Matthew Thompson."

"Oh?" Matt felt his adrenaline surge.

"Comrade Wang is in a very privileged position for a Chinese woman; you understand?"

"Sure."

"She has the respect and confidence of Premier Chou En-lai and performs many important functions for him."

"Yes, I know."

"If her reliability were open to any question, Matthew, she could not stay in the Premier's household, you see. She would be reassigned quickly."

"What is the point, Mr. Teng?" Matt asked sharply.

"Given all that I have told you about the Premier's relationship with other high officials, I am sure you understand how awkward it might be for the Premier if it became suspected that his interpreter and assistant had a close liaison with an American. Do you understand?"

"Are you telling me to lose interest in her?"

"There can be no place for any romantic interest, certainly. I cannot tell you what to do, of course, but I can warn you that her career will come to an end immediately if anyone is given the least ground for suspecting that you and she are romantically interested in each other."

"That seems very unfair. Our relationship is certainly harmless."

"It is a matter of how things might appear to the Premier's enemies, you see. I am sure you understand this."

"I guess I do."

"Moreover, there is the question of what would become of Comrade Wang. Marriage between you—if you were to think about that—is out of the question. I cannot conceive that she could obtain the necessary permissions to marry an American. Nor could you enter or live in China; there is no chance for that."

"It sounds hopeless," Matt said. "Have you talked to Li-fa?"

"No. That is not my place. She knows all of this very well, and her superiors will remind her of her obligations in an appropriate way."

"That sounds rough."

"No, in China a correction of erroneous thought or conduct is understood to be often necessary for social growth. You need not be concerned. I have taxed your strength, I fear. It is important that you recuperate, because we will travel north tomorrow." Teng stood and went to the door. "Please rest now."

"Are you interested in my reaction to what you have said about Li-fa?" Matt challenged.

"Yes, of course, Matthew. But whatever your response is, the immutable realities remain."

"I have broken my back for China, Mr. Teng. For no good reason except that I love the Chinese people, I have worked very hard, long hours, for no pay. I've been kidnapped, shot at, and my knee is severely injured. I've gotten sick as hell running around in the rain and dragging across that swamp. I've given you and the Premier information and the best advice I could. But what you're telling me is that none of that counts for anything. In spite of all of that, I'm to stay away from Li-fa so I don't make problems for Chou En-lai. Right?''

Teng walked back to the bed and put his hand lightly on Matt's right forearm. ''Matthew, all of China will be eternally grateful for what you are doing. There is no question about that. But I have explained what must happen to Comrade Wang if you persist. I have told you this because I do not wish harm to come to either one of you. I am trying to persuade you to be realistic. In different circumstances you would have my heartfelt blessing. In these present circumstances I can only warn you and trust you will employ very good judgment. Now please take your rest, because there is nothing more to be said about Comrade Wang. It is not a subject for discussion or debate, you see.''

I need to talk to Li-fa before they jump on her, Matt thought. We should agree on what she will say to them if they ask her about us. Probably she will want to say that she doesn't love me and maybe that's the best thing for her to tell them. But they probably know that she took me out of here to meet her family, and that will look bad for her. She could say that I insisted. Is it all worth the struggle? She doesn't want trouble, and Chou's people don't want us to get together. They could send me home tomorrow, of course. They could send her to Outer Mongolia tomorrow and I would never see her again. I don't need to play out the last act of *Madame Butterfly* to satisfy my own ego. I think I know how to put the problem behind us.

Matt raised himself on one elbow and pointed at his attaché case, which was against the wall nearest the closet alcove. ''Will you hand me the case?'' he said to the uniformed 8341 Unit Guard who had entered the room.

The man stood up when Matt spoke to him. *''Wo bu dong,''* he said, shrugging his shoulders.

''Case,'' Matt repeated, pointing to it and then to himself.

The soldier smiled broadly in understanding, nodded, and brought Matt the case.

On a White House memorandum pad, selected from
several choices of paper in his case, Matt wrote a note:

> Dear Li-fa—
> Teng Shan-li has just explained to me the
> problems I may have created for you by asking
> to meet your family in the park the other day. I
> have evidently given Mr. Teng the impression that
> I am romantically interested in you and by asking
> to meet your family I have made it appear that
> I was contemplating marriage with you.
> Mr. Teng has pointed out that you would be
> compromised in your work if your superiors
> gained the false impression that there was some
> serious romantic attachment between you and me,
> and I can see how such a thing might occur.
> Of course, you and I both know that there is
> no reason for anyone to think there is such an
> attachment between us. I think you are an
> admirable woman and I like you as a person,
> but I would not presume to suggest that the quality
> of our acquaintanceship is in any way romantic.
> I am in China on a mission of importance, as
> you are aware. I know that you would not
> intentionally do anything to jeopardize its success.
> May I suggest that we both make all our future
> contacts so completely businesslike that there is
> no possibility that anyone could imply that you
> and I are other than business associates who
> mutually seek the favorable outcome of the
> endeavor in which we are engaged?
>   Sincerely,
>   Matthew Thompson

He folded the paper once and wrote Wang Li-fa's name
on the outside. Matt pointed to the door and said to the
soldier, "Dr. Yu come here?" The man stood again and
pointed at the door quizzically. Matt pointed and gestured
that someone should come. The soldier opened the door

and spoke to the guard outside. In a little while Dr. Yu bustled in, her long white coat open and flying behind her.

"Are you all right?" she asked.

"Sure. About the same. Can you get this note to Miss Wang for me, please?"

"Yes, of course. Is that all you wanted?"

"Yes, thanks. It's important that she gets the note today, if possible."

"I'll take care of it." Dr. Yu could hardly restrain her urge to unfold the note and read it, but she successfully carried it away unopened.

About eight o'clock that night one of the 8341 Guards brought Matt a piece of paper, folded once, with his name written on the outside:

> I am grateful for your note of clarification and reason. I too would deeply regret any misunderstanding which might jeopardize the important work each of us is doing. Please rest assured that I will do everything in my power to avoid misunderstanding. There is a saying which I find helpful:
>
> The foolish maid
> looks through a blue jewel
> and thinks that night has fallen.
> Sincerely,
> Wang Li-fa

Matt wondered how many people had read and copied their two notes. He reread Li-fa's message and smiled. What in the world did the reference to the blue jewel mean? Was she recalling for them both what they had said when she'd opened the box and tried on the blue sapphire ring? Clearly, she didn't read his note as meaning what it said. She saw it as an effort to repair the damage already done to her position with Chou En-lai and his staff. The tone of her note showed him that. She intended hers to be a billboard too; no envelope, no intimacy. A private note would have said something about Nancy or Madame Chu, he guessed.

It rankled that he'd had to appear to disown Li-fa. Teng and his master controlled him, it seemed, and Matt resented it. Perhaps he should just go home and give up this whole Chinese game.

He fell asleep, knowing that he was going to stay.

Thirty-nine

"Welcome to this house which is called T'ai Chi Chang, Matthew Thompson. Please do not get up." Chou En-lai held out his right hand as he quickly crossed the room to the chair in which Matt was propped, with his straightened left leg resting on a leather hassock. "I am so sorry that all of this has happened to you and that you were injured,"

Matt shook the Premier's hand, smiling. "It's fine now, Your Excellency. It's only a cracked kneecap."

"I feel very much embarrassed that this occurred, but" —Chou opened his hands, palms up—"these are difficult times in China, as you know. Comrade Teng has told you how all this happened?"

"Yes, sir."

"I assure you that those Air Force soldiers will be seriously dealt with, if that is of any satisfaction to you."

"Your 8341 Guards were wonderful, Premier Chou. Especially Captain Fan, who picked me up and led me across that island and out of the swamp. He is a fine leader and a man of spirit and courage."

"Captain Fan, yes? Thank you for telling me this. It is always important to know which people can be relied upon to perform their duties well. Comrade Yang Te-chong should know about Captain Fan, I think. Comrade Wang, will you be sure to tell him?"

"Certainly, Comrade Premier," Wang Li-fa said. She had followed Chou into the room and stood discreetly in the doorway, awaiting Chou's signal to stay or leave. She wore a lightly quilted gray jacket over her white blouse. Her hair was caught back in a style Matt had never seen her wear before. It accented her cheekbones and made her big dark eyes seem even larger and more beautiful.

Matt and Li-fa had not exchanged a dozen words during the long flight to Peking from Canton on the near-empty Ilyushin commercial jet. Now she avoided his eyes as she stood behind Chou.

"We have much to discuss," the Premier said as he eased into the big chair next to Matt's. "Are you sufficiently rested?"

"Yes, sir, I slept very well last night. This house is surprisingly quiet considering that it is right downtown."

Chou looked pleased. "I am very fond of this compound, and especially of its garden. Have you been shown the garden?"

"No, sir."

"You must have a wheelchair so you can get about. A former owner of the T'ai Chi Chang compound collected many rare trees and bushes which now have grown quite dense in front and along the sides. I notice that their leaves have turned color and they are at their best now. You must see them."

"Thank you, I will."

"As I say, this place is a favorite of mine. You wouldn't guess you were only a short distance from the Great Hall of the People here, eh? It is just outside the old Emperor's gate, and parts of the house are very old, I am told."

Matt heard a door open and close beyond the arched entry to the living room. Wang Li-fa turned to look into the foyer, and Matt saw her smile and make a little bow toward someone there.

"I have invited an important person to come here to

meet you," the Premier said. "This lady is one of China's leaders, an official of the Federation of Women and, not incidentally, my wife." Chou smiled. "Come in, Little Ch'ao," he called.

Teng Ying-ch'ao was a short, blocky woman with straight graying hair, dressed in a shapeless blue Mao jacket and blue trousers.

"How do you do?" Madame Teng said in heavily accented English. "I am sorry that you are injured." Her toothy smile corroborated her concern. Her hand was a warm muffin.

Chou's wife spoke to Wang Li-fa in rapid Chinese, only part of which Matt understood.

"Madame Teng Ying-ch'ao says that she is sorry her English is poor and asks me to express her regret that some bad Chinese soldiers injured you. She hopes you will not think badly of the Chinese people on account of this—this—incident," Wang Li-fa translated.

"I am feeling much better, thank you," Matt said to the diminutive lady. She smiled broadly and walked to a chair beyond her husband's.

Chou signaled Li-fa to come in. He sat down and turned to Matt. "I must ask you again about Viet Nam and your President Nixon."

Wang Li-fa had moved a straight chair next to Chou's wife and began quietly translating for her.

"Are his intentions different now?" Chou asked.

"No, I think his goals remain the same. He and Kissinger want to reduce the number of American troops there as soon as they can."

"But we see Americans expanding into Cambodia and Laos even now. How am I to interpret such adventures? These operations, so close to China's borders, can hardly be ignored."

"It is the difference between strategy and tactics, I believe, sir. Mr. Nixon does not intend to expand American operations in Southeast Asia. But the Cambodian incursion was required by the tactical situation at the time."

Chou turned to Li-fa, who translated what Matt had said. Chou nodded. "When can I expect to see American troops begin to fly home?" Chou asked.

"I don't know that," Matt replied.

"Can you find out that information for me?" Chou pressed.

"I don't know," Matt said. "I can try."

"It is very important that I know," the Premier added. "We have said we will receive an envoy here."

"Yes, I know that."

"Whom will Mr. Nixon send?"

"I am not sure, but I believe it will be Henry Kissinger."

"Why will Nixon select him?"

"There are several reasons. First, Nixon wants to keep this negotiation very close to himself, so he won't pick someone from outside the White House. Second, Kissinger very much wants to come. It is a historic event, and Kissinger always seeks to become a part of history. He will put great pressure on the President."

"Does Kissinger speak or understand Chinese?"

"No."

"Is he a student of China?"

"No. He has begun to learn, but he begins with very little knowledge. He is reading and talking with university experts on China."

"I understand he is very intelligent."

"Yes."

"Is he a man you would entrust with your life?"

Matt paused to think, then smiled. "In a way, I have done so, but as I think about your question I'm compelled to say that I ought not to do so. Dr. Kissinger is largely motivated by his own self-interest, I think. If it came down to a choice I suppose he would save his own life and let mine go hang."

Chou nodded as if Matt had confirmed something he had suspected. "Is his word good?" Chou asked.

"Yes, but you must listen very carefully to what he says. He is artful. . . ."

Chou looked at Wang Li-fa quizzically.

"He is skillful," Matt supplied, "at saying things ambiguously—with an unclear meaning, or with two or more meanings. I think with him it is a kind of game to truthfully mislead people. It's a game of skill."

"That is the diplomat's game," Chou said. "The world would be a better place if the nations' leaders spoke plainly to each other. If Dr. Kissinger comes here, will he bring you with him?"

"I doubt it; he does not trust me. I am Richard Nixon's man, not his. Kissinger was having me watched by the FBI, and it may be that some of my communications to and from Mr. Hung have been intercepted. Kissinger gets good work out of me, so I have not been fired, but I am suspect."

"Does President Nixon suspect you?"

"No, he still seeks my advice and is usually willing to heed it."

"I have read that Dr. Kissinger has very cordial relations with the Russian Ambassador; is this so?"

"I have not personally observed it, but I know he sees Dobrynin often. I believe Kissinger tries to use Dobrynin as a channel to the North Vietnamese, among other things."

"If you were Chairman Mao, what would you do next to improve relations with the United States?"

Matt rubbed his eyes with his thumb and forefinger wearily. "Well, sir, I would try to establish a conduit between us, a reliable mechanism for the exchange of ideas, one not dependent on third parties. For example, we both have trusted people in Paris. Why can't they meet and talk, face to face?"

"Who is your man there?"

"He is the military attaché, General Vernon Walters, a person Mr. Nixon has known for many years. He is a linguist and an intelligence expert."

"A spy."

"Yes, a spy and a very able one. He's a strange duck, but he's a good spy."

"That may be an excellent suggestion, Matthew. I will discuss Paris with my colleagues and let you know."

"It would be better to let the President know by way of Pakistan, I think. It would be very unwise to turn me into a go-between."

"Yes, I understand, of course. Do you realize why it is advisable for me to consult before taking any steps, Matthew?"

"Yes, I think so. Mr. Teng has explained to me some of the inner workings of your government. It is all clearer to me now."

"Good."

"Mr. Nixon has similar problems, as you might imagine. One of his trusted aides, Patrick Buchanan, is extremely upset that small steps are being taken toward China. He is bombarding the President with his objections. And several powerful members of the Congress are, too. And Mr. Nixon is very sensitive to the opposition of the so-called China Lobby."

"Yes, it is good that you have mentioned that," Chou said enthusiastically, hunching forward in his chair. "Does Henry Kissinger worry about the China Lobby?"

"No. I would say that he and the President have divided up their universe of worries. Nixon worries about the domestic politics of what they do, while Henry is the executor of the policy. Nixon thinks a lot about public opinion and Henry does too, to some extent, but I think Henry cares more for what people think of him personally than for what they think of the President or his policies."

"Does that cause friction between them?"

"Yes, some. But they are like a tiger and a jackal. Henry knows the President can hurt him, so he avoids friction as much as he can."

"Does Dr. Kissinger admire President Nixon?"

"He thinks Nixon was brilliant to have chosen Kissinger for his staff, of course, but otherwise he does not admire him."

"Whom does Kissinger admire?"

"I'm not sure. He is attracted to celebrities. How much he respects Nelson Rockefeller the man, apart from his money and power, I can't be certain. He has written favorably about Bismarck, Frederick the Great, and Metternich. I don't know who his hero is. Henry Kissinger, I guess."

"I believe the young man is very tired," Teng Ying-ch'ao said to her husband in Mandarin.

"I have nearly finished," Chou replied. To Matt he asked in English: "How shall I evaluate the opposition and resistance President Nixon is experiencing? Here, of course, the People's Liberation Army and the other military tend to be very slow to respond to a new initiative, but they will be obedient to China's leaders. Will Mr. Nixon's followers be obedient to his new policies?"

"He intends to give them no choice, sir. A new relationship with China must hit them as a *fait accompli*. Complete secrecy, no preliminary debate, just a huge, televised announcement to the nation—and everyone will be led along, Nixon figures."

"Do you believe that will work?"

"I think so. The makers of public opinion are largely internationalist, so the television and newspapers will support Nixon in this. He must worry more about his right-wing supporters than his usual adversaries, and by springing it on them he gives them a narrow set of choices. Most of them won't want to break openly with him on a matter of foreign policy."

"Sometimes"—Chou smiled—"the worth of a proposal can be measured by the identity of its opponents. In this case I am led to believe that is true. This has been very helpful to me. I hope I have not exhausted you?" He emphasized the word "exhausted" as he glanced at Wang Li-fa for verification that he had chosen the correct English word. Li-fa nodded slightly.

"I'm a little tired, but I'm fine," Matt said. "My knee has been bothering me some today; perhaps it is going to rain."

"It would be very convenient to have a reliable weather forecaster," Chou said, smiling. He stood and helped his wife from her deep chair. Matt noticed that Chou could not fully extend his right arm. Perhaps, Matt thought, I was so dazzled at my previous meeting with Chou that I'd simply not noticed the Premier's arm. He shook hands with the Premier and his wife and watched them leave the room. Other people in Mao jackets were waiting for them in the foyer, and Matt heard snatches of conversation as they walked out the side door of the villa.

Li-fa returned to the living room and said, "You look tired, Matthew."

"I am. Can we talk? We haven't been alone since the hospital."

"We aren't alone now. Comrade Yang Te-chong is bringing you a wheelchair now, and he will take you to your room. But I must ask you about arrangements for your trip home. Do you have tickets?"

"I really need to talk to you. The hell with tickets."

"Impossible," she said flatly. "Tickets?" She stood by the doorway, her hands demurely folded in front of her, one hand holding her small interpreter's notebook.

Matt sighed. "The tickets are in my attaché case in my room. Help yourself. I have a return ticket from Tokyo, but I'd better go by way of Hong Kong because every spy in town saw me get off there. They are going to know I was here if I don't leave from Hong Kong too."

Yes, it is very complicated. Comrade Teng suggests that you go from here to Bangkok and from there to Hong Kong, Tokyo, and Anchorage."

"God, that's a long time on an airplane."

"You could fly partway to Bangkok the first day, perhaps to Chungking, stay there one night, and rest. Then stay another night in Bangkok and perhaps overnight in Tokyo or Anchorage. Take four days to make the trip."

"What day would we get home?"

"*You* would be home on the last day of September, I believe."

Matt tried to stand; he swung his stiff leg off the hassock and raised himself off the chair with his arms.

Li-fa took two steps toward him. "Wait for the wheelchair," she said. "Wait for help."

He lowered himself into the chair again and felt sweat

on his forehead. "That is hard work," he admitted. "When you get the tickets, please notice that I've paid out about four thousand dollars for this trip. How do I get reimbursed?"

"No problem. I will get money for you before you go."

"Why are we talking business across an empty room, Li-fa? Do you understand why I wrote that note in Canton?"

"Of course. I believe I hear your wheelchair coming." She walked to the doorway and looked down the hall. "Yes, it is Comrade Yang."

Yang appeared in the door wheeling a brand-new leather-and-chrome wheelchair. He looked around the room and said in harsh Chinese, "You should not be in here alone with him."

"I was leaving, but he tried to get out of his chair. I feared he would harm himself, so I told him to wait for you," she replied in Chinese.

She's afraid of him, Matt noted. I guess I am too. He's a killer if I ever saw one.

"So, will you return via Bangkok, Mr. Thompson?" Wang Li-fa asked.

"I don't think there is time, and I'm not sure I'm up to a four-day trip. Could someone accompany me?"

"Perhaps we can arrange that. A person could join you in Bangkok and make sure you depart Tokyo safely. Is that what you mean?"

"Or come all the way home with me."

Li-fa suddenly understood. "No. I am quite sure that would be impossible, Mr. Thompson. But perhaps a reliable Siamese person could help as far as Tokyo. I will see. Now Comrade Yang will return you to your bed."

She said to Yang: "You must help him into the chair."

Yang took Matt's hands and hoisted him, half-turning Matt into the chair. Yang's hands were callused and heavily muscled. He smelled like hair lotion.

"Have a good rest," Li-fa said.

* * *

Chou En-lai and his wife, Teng Ying-ch'ao, sat alone in the deep cushions of the Red Flag limousine. The glass partition separated them from the chauffeur and the two bodyguards in the front seat.

"What do you think of the American?" Chou asked.

"He seems genuinely cooperative. I feel he was saying what he believed to be true."

"His government suspects him."

"That is too bad. He might otherwise be very, very helpful to China."

"I think our Comrade Wang Li-fa is in love with him," Chou said matter-of-factly.

"I can see why." Madame Teng smiled. "He is physically beautiful."

"And I think he loves her. He has given her a jeweled ring as a token."

"Poor children. How hopeless! Perhaps Comrade Wang Li-fa should spend some time in further education and in the reinforcement of her revolutionary values. If she is serious about this boy, she cannot be sufficiently reliable."

"No, I think she is all right. She has not really encouraged him, and she has managed to overcome her romantic feelings—with a little difficulty."

"We are invited to Lin Piao's house for a banquet in seven days. His wife called me this morning."

Chou scowled. His dark eyebrows nearly came together over his brow. "Can we avoid it? Who will be there?"

"The honored guest will be Chiang Ch'ing."

"I don't understand. Is the Chairman not to be there?"

"Ye Chun says the Chairman will be away but his wife will be here, so the banquet is for her."

"I had forgotten that Chairman Mao plans to be away just then. But how does Chiang Ch'ing dare to attend dinner at Lin's house when her husband has so strongly denounced Lin Piao? It is the same as a defiance of the Chairman, it seems to me."

"Chiang Ch'ing has defied him before, you know. We should not be surprised to see her playing with fire."

"I am not going to be comfortable attending that ban-quiet, nor will I be comfortable staying away; it is an impossible choice. I do not wish to rupture relations with Comrade Lin at this time, nor do I wish to offend the Chairman's wife. I think I will talk with Chairman Mao about it before we accept the invitation. Can it wait?'' Chou asked his wife.

"Perhaps a day or so. But not too long, please. For my part, I would just as soon stay away, as you have guessed. Chiang Ch'ing is not a woman I can sincerely honor. But I can do whatever you deem necessary, of course. We will go if you think we should.''

"I will leave it up to the Chairman. I predict that he won't be able to contain his curiosity; he will want us to attend and listen to what everyone says.''

The Red Flag had driven north, across Tien'anmen Square and through the gates of the State Council compound, Chungnanhai. They approached Chou's lakeside house along blacktop flecked with red and yellow leaves that had fallen from the overhanging trees.

"The car can take you on to the University,'' Chou said. "I will have no need of it until tonight. Will we go to the dinner at the Great Hall together?''

"Yes,'' his wife said. "Don't forget what I said about Wang Li-fa, husband. I think she has become unreliable.''

Chou nodded with annoyance. A soldier opened the door and he stood for a moment waving his hand as his wife drove away. Yang Te-chong walked toward Chou from the house, a sheaf of papers in his hand.

"Comrade Yang,'' Chou said, "you and I must discuss the American, Matthew Thompson. I fear he is of waning usefulness to China, but I would like your opinion. And we must talk about Comrade Wang Li-fa. I must know what you know about our young woman and I must decide whether she will remain here with us. Please, come in and let us talk, Comrade.''

Forty

The Federal Bureau of Investigation
Washington, D.C.
September 26, 1970
General Alexander Haig
The Western White House (by courier)
San Clemente, California
Subject: Redwood
Dear General:

By Bureau facilities in Hong Kong the
following very reliable information has just come
to hand:

Redwood arrived in Hong Kong at 2000 hours
18 September 1970 on Japan Air Lines Flight
321, from Tokyo. A photocopy of his passport
and Hong Kong immigration entry card has been
furnished by H.K. authorities, and positive
identification has been made.

Discreet inquiry of a reliable source reveals
Redwood told his secretary, Angela Cruz, and other
workplace colleagues he would be on vacation in
Alaska from 17 September through 30 September.

In Hong Kong, sources known to be reliable
confirm that subject was met by an Englishman
known to be an employee of HUNG WAI-LANG,
a resident of Hong Kong and a British citizen.
Redwood was taken by car to Number 3, Marine
View Way, a residence owned by Hung Wai-lang.

Surveillance of that residence was involuntarily discontinued during the night of 18 September. Two Hong Kong police detectives were kidnapped from their observation post (and later released). During the night *Redwood* presumably left that house and has not been seen since.

Hung Wai-lang is a wealthy industrialist and shipper who is known to have close ties to the People's Republic of China.

British authorities cooperative with the FBI have been alerted to maintain a watch for *Redwood*.

                                        J. Edgar Hoover
                                        Director

"You see what is happening, don't you?" Henry Kissinger shouted, waving J. Edgar Hoover's letter. "It's very plain, isn't it? It's a double game, and you know who is the victim, don't you?" He nodded his head vigorously as he slumped into the webbed lounge chair.

Haig put his finger across his lips.

"It is very clear," Kissinger repeated softly. "Al, why is Nixon treating me this way? Why can he not be straight and level with me?"

The fall sunshine was warm, with only a hint of September in the light ocean breeze that ruffled the elaborate landscaping. They sat at a glass table on the terrace just outside the door to Kissinger's San Clemente office. Beyond the lawn there were oceanside cliffs, and the Pacific surf could be heard if one listened carefully. A tall wooden fence divided Kissinger's patio from the patio of the adjoining office. Haig stood and went to the edge of the lawn from which he could see into the patio next door. He came back to his chair shaking his head.

"There is no one over there," he said, "but you'd better keep your voice down."

Haig was dapper in a tweed sport coat and creased gray pants. Kissinger had left his coat in his office and sat, facing the morning sun in rumpled shirt sleeves, his collar open.

"You think the President sent Thompson to China?"

Haig asked earnestly. He held an unlighted cigarette in his mouth, and as he talked it wobbled eccentrically. Kissinger watched, distracted, as Haig tried to strike a flame on a gold Zippo lighter, without success. Kissinger reached to a telephone table near the door and tossed Haig a book of matches from Sans Souci.

"Thompson is a back channel," Kissinger yelled dispiritedly. "He's a disloyal backstabber, that's what he is!"

"What do you want to do?" Haig asked.

"Do? Do? What can we do? We smile and bow and say 'Yes, sir' and let that weird man heap indignities upon us! That's what we do!" Kissinger had gestured north toward Richard Nixon's office, several patios away.

"Thompson is due back in Washington in a couple of days. Do you want me to have him in for a chat?"

Kissinger ponderously shook his head.

"You want me to let him get away with this?" Haig was surprised.

"Absolutely. Nothing will be said. Nothing will be done. As before, the President must not suspect that we know. What perfidy! How can a man treat his colleagues in this fashion? How does he communicate with the Chinese?"

Haig shrugged and looked closely at his cigarette. "If he used the CIA or State Department we would know about it at once. He hasn't sent messages via the Pakistanis, has he?"

"Probably not." Kissinger rubbed his chin, then pointed a finger at Haig. "Probably he has Thompson send word by that Chinaman in Hong Kong. Thompson probably just telephones him!"

"Then the NSA should have tapes of the calls. I'll send for them."

"You can do that, but it will do no good. This is another vote of no-confidence, you see. It's clear that I must leave here, if for no other reason than to preserve my sanity. I will write a letter. I will return to Harvard."

Haig could not suppress a grin.

"Why are you laughing, General?"

"That's not the first time you have decided to resign, is it, Henry?"

"But this time is the end. This secret Chinese back channel is the clear signal that I am no longer useful, no longer needed or wanted here!"

"We don't know for certain that Thompson is a back channel, do we? Maybe he has a girl in Hong Kong."

"That, I think, is not likely," Kissinger said drily. "Have you seen that young blond woman who sits in Rose's office? That is what Thompson has going for him. Why would anyone go to Hong Kong with that just down the hall? Tell me!"

"All I'm saying is that his being in Hong Kong is ambiguous," Haig explained.

"It's not ambiguous to me. It is crystal-clear! Richard Nixon is dealing with the Chinese behind my back, and it is time I faced some realities. It is time for me to go back to Cambridge, where I am so deeply loved and admired by students and faculty alike. Leave me now, Al; I must write a letter. I deeply appreciate your loyalty and devotion, I assure you. I shall recommend that the President appoint you my successor, and I hope I do not blight your career by doing so. Now leave me to my disappointments and sorrows."

Kissinger reached for a blank pad and took a pen from his shirt pocket. Haig rose and walked through the door into Kissinger's office and closed it behind him.

Dear Mr. President, Kissinger wrote. *For reasons which you know even better than I, it has become time for me to leave my post and return to Harvard University.* Squinting in the bright sunlight, he read what he had written, put down the pen, and crumpled the paper into a ball. He replaced the top of his pen and put it back in his shirt pocket. On the lawn west of the President's office he could see a television film crew setting up a camera. Kissinger reached for his telephone and said to his secretary: "Please get me Abe Rosenthal at *The New York Times* and Joe Kraft at his home. And have someone let me know as soon as Matthew Thompson returns from his vacation."

Forty-one

San Clemente was warm, that late-September day. But at the western margin of the Pacific Ocean, in the gulf called Bo Hai, the north winds had begun. Only a few hardy vacationers strolled the firm sand beach at Pei Ta Ho, bundled against the wind. The most energetic of them could walk for twelve miles if they chose, from the lighthouse point at the south to the outcroppings of Jin Shan Hill, which marked the northeast end of the great crescent beach. The ocean stretched unbroken to the horizon.

Heavily timbered hills rose away from the beach to the north. The eastern third of that beach, reserved for model workers and People's Liberation Army personnel on furlough, was deserted. West End Beach showed some signs of life around its half-dozen tourist guesthouses. In the center of the crescent, Middle Beach, the exclusive preserve of Party officials and guests of the State, a squadron of Air Force soldiers had been moved into position. They prevented beach walkers from straying off the sand onto the narrow black-topped road that rose north through the woods into Lotus Rock Park.

At the margin of the park, above and behind the Old West Hill Hotel, loomed Number Sixty-nine Building, a two-story gray stone house heavily guarded by more Air Force soldiers. They stood at guard posts and patrolled the wooded grounds with their submachine guns and automatic rifles at the ready. It was an elite guard force with standing orders to kill any intruder they found near the forbidding old house on the hill.

In the east courtyard of the H-shaped structure, four highly polished Air Force staff cars, a Navy jeep, and a Red Flag limousine were lined up with precision, attended by uniformed drivers who sat behind their wheels waiting. The drivers did not talk, smoke, or wander about as they waited for the adjournment of the meeting within.

The windows on the ground floor of the Sixty-nine Building were heavily shuttered with hinged, gray-painted steel panels, every one of which was closed. Heavy damask draperies concealed the triple-pane, soundproof glass windows from the seven men who sat around the conference table, situated at the center of a large, brightly lighted office at the northeast corner of the house.

The tall young man at the head of the table was attired in a tailored Air Force uniform. He held the rank of colonel in the Air Force, but the others around the table—generals and one admiral—noticeably deferred to him.

"I have asked you all to meet me here, in my father's house, to discuss several questions," the round-faced colonel said. "Some of you are from Shanghai and others from Peking. Some are Air Force, some Army, some Navy. But all of us are united. I propose that the groups represented here be consolidated today into a Joint Fleet."

"Ah"—the short, fat general with the bristle-short haircut smiled—"you have been watching Japanese war movies again, Lin Li-kuo. Joint Fleet, indeed!"

The others all smiled or laughed cautiously, their hesitation dictated by a continuing uncertainty. One never knew how Lin Piao's volatile son might react to teasing.

The younger Lin smiled at the Air Force commander's gibe, and the other men around the table relaxed.

"Yes, the Joint Fleet," Lin said. "That is who we are. We are several elements of the armed forces. We are come together out of love and fear for our beloved homeland, as you all know." He stood up suddenly and moved to the end of the table. As he walked, he pulled his tunic straight.

"A senile tyrant rules the land," he said loudly, "and the fates have dealt us a hand that must be played out to the end. It is no accident that we meet in this house. It is no accident that I am the leader of the Joint Fleet and that I am my revered father's son. It is no accident that you, my father's closest friends and allies, are the commanders of the Joint Fleet. There is no accident or chance in my honored father's destiny. The time will soon come when he must step forward and step up to the parapet of the gate, and all others must step down and pledge their fidelity to him."

As he orated, Lin gestured with both hands, carefully straightening his tunic after each movement. "Are you ready to hear my plan?" he asked.

The officers nodded.

"We feel," Lin said, "that any attempt to persuade Chairman Mao Tse-tung to resign would only end in failure. And there is no value in attempting a useless act, everyone agrees. It is clear that Mao Tse-tung must be killed. I have discussed this with each of you individually, and I know each of you accepts the necessity of Mao's death. The remaining questions are where, how, and when."

Two older officers at the table sat impassively, but the others nodded in agreement. Agitated by what he was saying, young Lin walked three paces to his right, wheeled, and returned to the table. He rested one hand on the table and waved the other back and forth as he spoke.

"We cannot reach Mao in Peking without a major battle, which would be fought out before a million onlookers. And we must think responsibly about how a new Chairman can govern once Mao is gone. No, we do not want an open civil war in the capital because we must immediately pick up the reins of government as effectively as possible."

"I totally agree," the small, fat man said.

"We must devise a plan to be put into operation when Mao is far away from Peking," a younger general said.

"Yes." Lin nodded. "We missed our first opportunity. We should have been ready for him a month ago at Lushan. When he treated everyone so despicably we should have been ready with a plan to remove him right then."

The heavy door behind Lin opened and a young woman

came in with two large teapots. She wore a sheer blouse and a tight Air Force uniform skirt which revealed an unusually full figure and shapely legs.

"Another one," the fat Air Force general whispered to the officer next to him. "Where do they all come from?" His neighbor smiled tolerantly.

While the young woman poured tea, no one talked. Every man in the room watched her.

"I will make assignments for the preparation of several specific plans," Lin began again. He had sat down at his place as the girl went around the table. When she came to his side Lin put his arm familiarly around her hips, but he let her go when she had poured his tea. "We will have a plan if the Chairman makes a flying trip. There will be another plan if he goes by train. One group must plan for what is to be said to the people and how the government will continue. Li, that is the matter I want you to work on. As First Political Commissar of the Navy, you are particularly well qualified to plan the governmental aspect of the operation."

Li Chuo-peng, tall and fleshy, nodded in acknowledgment of his assignment. He was a large young man; his round face, full cheeks, and heavy lips contrasted with a pug nose; his small eyes were obscured by dark glasses which he wore outdoors and in. "I will begin a plan at once, Comrade Lin," he said tightly.

Lin Li-kuo read a list of planning assignments from a paper on the table. "We will meet again in two weeks," he said, "at the Air Force Academy. We will use the strategic-planning room in Building Four, next to the principal's house." Lin looked at General Wu, the Air Force commander, who nodded his consent.

Lin stood, and the others rose; as they gathered in groups of two or three to talk, Lin strode to the door and hurried to a bedroom on the second floor which overlooked the beach. At the window, the young tea server was watching the play of small ocean waves in the last daylight. She had combed out her black hair and wore only a heavy blue terry-cloth robe. Her legs and feet were bare.

She turned to look at Lin as he locked the door and came to the center of the large room.

"Come away from the window, please, Jun, and let me look at you. When you poured the tea you made me very excited."

She moved gracefully, holding out her hand to Lin.

"It was a very important meeting, I think," she said. "I recognized several of those men from the headquarters in Shanghai. They are generals, I believe."

"You were very beautiful when you served tea, little soldier. The eyes of all those important men could not leave you." Lin untied Jun's belt and ran his hands around her body inside her robe.

"I think you were the most important of all those men, so I looked only at you as I served the tea," she said. "Will we have some time together now? May I make you more comfortable?"

"No. I will return to you in an hour or so."

"I looked in the big bedroom downstairs—your father's room—while they were making the tea in the kitchen," she said. "Why is that room full of the climbing bars? They are like the playground equipment we had at school. Are they your father's?"

"That is the Vice Chairman's room."

"It is otherwise so plain! I would have thought he would have an elaborate room, beautifully decorated, but it is not so. He must be a plain and frugal man."

"He cares very little for fine comforts. He used to climb on those bars like a monkey, and that was his favorite form of exercise."

When she unbuttoned one of his coat buttons, he backed away from her and rebuttoned it. "I must go," he said sternly. "If we start I will stay."

"I hope you stay."

"I cannot. I must talk with the commander. He waits for me."

"He will wait, you dear boy." She moved close to Lin and put her arms around his neck. The large sleeves of her open robe slid up her arms so that her skin pressed against the back of his neck. He groaned and backed out of her embrace.

"Do not move," he ordered. "I will return as soon as I can."

"I will be waiting," she said.

"General, I am sorry. There was an urgent message to deal with." Lin hurried into his father's large office, where General Wu Fa-ch'an sat deep in an overstuffed chair. All the other officers had gone. Wu's face was broad, nearly square, underlain with double chins. His wide mouth perpetually smiled, and his eyes were banded with smile wrinkles. Even when Wu was deeply worried—as he was that day—he smiled.

"I have been sitting here thinking, Comrade Colonel," Wu said in his deep, resonant voice. "Your father can be proud of you tonight, and I shall tell him so. He has given China a leader of men."

"Thank you, Comrade Commander."

"Some of those at the meeting attended because they wish to aid your father, of course, but all left the meeting as your followers. Everyone has deep confidence in you. And all of us are committed to the success of the Joint Fleet and its operations."

"Good."

"What has your father heard since the failed capture of the American near Canton?" Wu asked.

"He says nothing. Nothing has come from the Chairman or the Premier about that episode."

"The Premier has ordered the arrest of the Air Force people involved; did you know that?"

"No." Lin laughed. "How can he find out who they are?"

Wu smiled even more broadly. "He has asked me for their names and numbers."

"What will you do?"

"I will give him ten inmates from one of our disciplinary prisons. They will deny everything, of course, and

Chou's man will torture them until he kills them, I suppose. Too bad."

"That is a good plan," Lin said.

"But what of the American now? Is it still your father's wish that he be killed and exposed to the world? Or shall I ask your father about that?"

"No, Comrade, do not ask my father." Lin sat down next to Wu and put his hand on the arm of Wu's chair. "He would be very upset if someone raised the matter of the American with him. Always talk to me about that particular operation."

"Very well, Lin Li-kuo," Wu said reassuringly.

"If the American can be killed while he is still in China, then it should be done. If he can be killed in public, so much the better. Where is he now?"

"At last report he is in Peking in a house near Quianmen Street, outside the gate. It is a house the Premier uses. There is a heavy guard and a high wall. The Premier comes and goes there."

"Do we know why the American is there?" Lin asked.

"It is believed that he is an envoy of the American President, Nixon. This American is known to be an adviser to Nixon."

"All right." Lin stood. "The Joint Fleet is launched and planning has begun. Continue to watch the American, Comrade Commander, and kill him before he leaves China. His body must be seen by many people, and your Air Force newspaper must tell everyone who he was."

Wu nodded slowly. "We will try."

"Just now I must leave you for other business," Lin Li-kuo said. "Please forgive me."

"Of course," Wu said, struggling to his feet. "I too must be going."

At the T'ai Chi Chang compound the next day, Yang Te-chong sat erect at the desk in the basement room he'd commandeered to be his command post. Two uniformed officers of the 8341 Guard stood side by side at rigid attention about four feet from the desk, waiting for Yang's orders.

"Comrade Major, what is the situation?" Yang demanded.

"Sir, there are hostile forces arrayed against this house. We have seen their watchers in the upper floors of the apartment house across the street, and we believe some of them are snipers. At the ends of the street there are cars with men in them, watching."

"Air Force?" Yang asked.

"We are not sure, but the snipers have the finest equipment."

"Can you eliminate the danger, Major?" Yang asked.

"Yes, sir, but it might be bloody. It will surely be noisy."

"Time is running out. It is necessary that the American leave Peking on an airplane in about seven hours. Can he be driven to the airport safely, as matters now stand?"

"If they are determined to kill him, they probably will, Comrade Yang. He must run from the house to the car, and he will be a target for the snipers for a time. In the street there may be a blockade. We must either eliminate the hazard or avoid it. Captain Fan Ch'ing has a plan which may work, however."

Yang looked at the younger man. "Comrade Captain, tell me your plan."

"It is to take the American away from this house through the shelter tunnels. As you know, there are steps behind a door at the other end of this basement. The tunnel system here runs north and south, and we could put decoy cars in several places along the route. You could decide at the last minute where to bring him out."

Yang turned away from the officers and said nothing for a few moments. "This is a plan I cannot approve without discussing it with the Premier. But I will recommend it. Please return to your posts now; I will send for you shortly." Yang watched the officers leave, then dialed a telephone number.

"Comrade, this is Yang Te-chong," he said. "I must talk to the Premier at once. Is he still there?"

* * *

"You will be leaving in a little while, Matthew," Teng Shan-li reported. "Are you all dressed and packed?"

"I'm all set. The doctor took off my knee bandage a while ago, and it feels very strange to be able to move my leg back and forth, but I'll get used to having it work like that again. Will I see Li-fa before I go?"

"She is with Premier Chou now, I believe. I don't know if they are coming to see you tonight; perhaps so."

"I don't want to leave without speaking with her. Will you find her for me?"

"That may be very difficult to do, but I will go and see. Excuse me, please." Teng left Matt's bedroom.

Matt walked to the window and looked out at the garden at the back of the house. The last dusk light was nearly gone, but he could see a pair of soldiers walking the gravel path that paralleled the high wall. They had automatic rifles, which they carried in both hands. The soldiers on patrol somehow made him feel less secure. They reminded him that someone wanted him dead, his head on a pike pole in the square, his name in outraged headlines. Peking was a dangerous place for him to be, and he keenly felt the danger.

His bedroom door opened quietly and he turned quickly. Teng Shan-li said, "It is only I. I am sorry if I have startled you."

"I was just watching the guards patrolling around."

"Yes, they are very capable. I am sorry to tell you that Comrade Wang is very busy at the Great Hall of the People this evening. She asked me to tell you goodbye for her. She wishes you a safe and speedy journey."

"I really wanted to talk to her, damn it. Is there no way? Could we go by there on the trip to the airport?"

"When I tell you the plan, you will see that it is quite impossible." Teng smiled.

"What plan?" Matt was very much annoyed. There were things he had to say to Li-fa in private before he left, and they were not going to let him see her.

"Has anyone told you about Peking's shelters?" Teng asked.

"You mean the bomb shelters?"

"Yes."

"I read something about them. They are all over the city, right?"

"Actually, they consist of rooms and many, many miles of tunnels which connect all neighborhoods and districts. The people dug them for many years. They were finished in 1959. The Premier has given his permission for you to be taken from this house in the shelter tunnel. You will emerge at a place that is completely safe and you will then be taken to an airplane—Hung Wailang's jet airplane—which will fly you to Hong Kong. Your passport markings will demonstrate that you have spent your vacation touring the southern Orient—Bangkok, Singapore, and Hong Kong."

"How come?"

"An expert has marked your passport appropriately."

"I see. Where is my passport?"

"I have it here." Teng patted his coat pocket.

"When do we leave?"

"Right now. Comrade Yang is waiting for us in the basement."

Matt's knee complained about the two flights of stairs to the basement, but he forgot about the knee when he saw Yang, unsmiling, a pistol in his hand.

"I have sent guards into the tunnel," Yang said to Teng in Chinese. "We will wait here until I receive a report."

"We must wait a few minutes," Teng told Matt. "Do you want to sit down?"

Matt nodded. Teng found him a straight chair and Matt gingerly bent his left knee to sit.

"Is he able to run?" Yang asked Teng.

"I doubt it. This is the first day his leg has been without bandages," Teng replied.

"Well, if bullets fly down there, I wager he'll find a way to run."

"Yes, and so will I. You think it may come to that?"

"I don't know. I'll be surprised if they haven't thought of the tunnel by now."

Captain Fan appeared and saluted Yang. "Sir, it is safe for you to proceed." Fan smiled at Matt, who recognized him as the officer who had led him and the others across the Pearl River island. "Hello, Captain," Matt said warmly. "I'm glad to see you." Teng Shan-li translated.

"No sign of them?" Yang asked with annoyance. He wanted the Captain's undivided attention.

"No, sir. There were a few people from the neighborhood in the north tunnel, but we have sent them home. Otherwise it is vacant."

"Very well, please lead us. I wish to go to the exit in the store of the Textile Workers' Commune north of the hotel."

"Yes, Comrade Yang. I will take you there."

"Come, Matthew," Teng said. "I will carry your bag; you bring your coat and attaché case. Follow Comrade Yang."

Yang and the Guards captain led them to a corner of the concrete basement where a door and iron grille gate opened to a long flight of concrete stairs which went down about fifty feet. The stairway was well lighted by a string of electric light bulbs. Matt put on his coat so he would have a hand free to push against the concrete wall for balance. His knee cracked a little each time he stepped down on his left foot, but it was not painful. At the bottom of the steps Matt was aware that the descent had tired him. He wondered when he would get his strength back.

The Captain slid open a metal-sheathed door on tracks as they entered an arched tunnel about seven feet high and four feet wide, illuminated by bare bulbs spaced at ten-foot intervals. The walls and ceiling were plastered or painted a light brown color. The concrete passage ahead of them ended at another large metal door, where an 8341 Guard was standing. There seemed to be good ventilation down there; cool air circulated, although Matt saw no vents or pipes.

Yang walked ahead rapidly, setting the pace. Their footsteps echoed in the vault. Halfway to the second door they passed an intersecting passage, similarly constructed and lighted. It appeared to lead to another major tunnel which paralleled theirs.

The soldier opened the sliding door and saluted Yang and the Captain as they led Matt and Teng into the next section of the shelter. On either side of this tunnel segment Matt saw rooms, some dark and others brightly lighted, one of which was a clinic or hospital. Beds were arranged in one of the others. A few rooms held stacks of boxes.

After they had traversed four separate sections, the captain turned into a lateral tunnel and to a short flight of stairs which brought them up into a second tunnel system. Evidently there are several levels, Matt realized, at various depths. He pictured men and women digging all of this with picks and shovels.

After a short walk in the upper tunnel they came to a longer flight of stairs, at the top of which a soldier saluted Yang and pressed one of two buttons on a wall panel. Rumbling loudly, the rounded ceiling slid back to reveal a final stairway above them. The soldier preceded them and pressed another button near the top of the stairs. A second ceiling panel slid back and they emerged into a long, narrow area separated from an unlighted room by a counter. Two guards stood in the middle of the wooden floor facing a glass door which let out onto a busy street. By the stairway light and streetlights Matt could see sample clothing stapled to the walls of the store. One area displayed Mao jackets, their arms straight out. To his left Matt saw trousers of different colors, splayed on the walls above the service area.

"All is calm outside, Comrade Captain," a soldier called out.

"Let us go quickly," Yang said. "Go and get into that car in front."

"Come, Matthew," Teng said in English.

Matt followed Teng. At the car someone took his attaché case, as someone had taken his bag from Teng.

"Get in quickly," Teng called from inside the car.

Matt saw 8341 Guards at the ends of the sidewalk. The

street was not empty. The crowd of curious bicyclists slowed as they came to the knot of soldiers, but they were waved on impatiently by a young officer who underlined his capacity with a drawn pistol. Occasionally, cars and trucks passed in the inner lanes of the street.

The car was driven by a middle-aged man in a leather coat like Yang's. Matt, Teng, and Yang sat in the back. The car was a Toyota, Matt decided; one of the mid-sized models. As soon as two guards squeezed into the front with their rifles, the driver flashed his lights and eased away from the curb, through the flow of bicycles, and made a U-turn. Matt noticed an unlighted jeep pull away from the curb to lead them north. A small military truck was right behind them.

At a wider intersection bordered by one of the ancient city gates the convoy turned left and sped west, down the middle of a six-lane street past dark apartment houses and stores. The Toyota cornered with a squeal of tires at a broad intersection several miles west of the old city moat.

"It is very quiet behind us," the driver said to Yang. Yang turned to look out the back window. His shoulders crowded Matt.

"We are not followed," Teng said in English. "All is well."

"Those tunnels are remarkable," Matt said. "Are they all over the city?"

"In most places," Teng said, nodding. "Each neighborhood has dug its own, according to a master plan, and each connects exactly to the next one. From where I live, I could walk all the way out of the city to Feng Tai District in the southern suburbs without coming to the surface."

"Are they all equipped like that—with lights and blast doors and clinics and all?"

"Yes, all fully equipped. They were begun when the Russians left in the late 1950s, and it took years to finish them."

"What is all this talk?" Yang demanded in Chinese.

"He asked about the bomb-shelter tunnels," Teng replied. "He is very curious about them."

"Do they not have shelters in his country?" Yang asked.

"I don't know," Teng replied. He switched to English. "Do you have such shelters in the United States?"

"Nothing like that. A few people have them at home. The government has a few here and there, but there is no city-wide system of tunnels and shelters anywhere that I know of."

Teng leaned forward a little and said to Yang: "He says they have none like ours."

"They are fools if they do not," Yang said quietly.

At last the Toyota swung left through the guarded gates of the Western Suburbs Airport. As he stopped so the sentries could look into the car, the Toyota driver turned on his headlights for the first time. The 8341 Guards' jeep and truck turned on their headlights too. When the sentries waved them on, the small convoy rolled through the quiet air base to the ramp.

Under floodlights, Hung Wai-lang's Jetstar was being serviced by the crew of a large, unmarked tank truck, under the close supervision of Hung's pilot. Stephen Carr was standing beside the jet, swinging his arms to keep warm. The late-September night had turned cold with the onset of a steady north breeze.

It had been an hour's drive north and west from the clothing store to the airport. Matt had difficulty getting out of the small automobile because his left knee had stiffened and it pained him to move it. He limped slowly around the back of the car until the stiffness eased, but the ache persisted.

"Are you all right, Mr. Thompson?" Carr asked, walking over from the airplane. He wore a light cashmere topcoat which was not heavy enough for autumn in Peking.

"My knee was hurt a little," Matt said. "I hope there is room to stretch it out."

Carr nodded. "Look at your soldiers. Most remarkable. Are we expecting a fight?"

The 8341 Guards had parked the three vehicles in a broad V, to shield the Jetstar from the buildings around the control tower and the rest of the ramp. Six men had taken up firing positions behind the jeep, the truck, and the Toyota. Their automatic rifles pointed toward the control tower and the operations building.

The other four uniformed men were gathered in conversation with Yang Te-chong. Teng Shan-li stood next to Yang listening, occasionally looking back toward the tower. Yang pointed at the floodlights that were mounted on top of the operations building, and two of the four men trotted in that direction, their rifles at port-arms position. In a few minutes the floodlights were extinguished, leaving Matt and Stephen Carr blinking and groping for the plane's short stairway, toward which Matt had been limping.

"Damn me, that makes it dark!" Carr exclaimed. "Is someone chasing you?"

"I think they are worried about the Air Force," Matt said. "The sentries at the gate have probably told everyone that we are here. Can we go pretty soon?"

"Are you ready, Captain?" Carr asked his pilot.

"Nearly full," the Chinese pilot replied.

"We want to leave quickly," Carr said. "Very quickly."

"How much more?" the pilot asked the tank-truck crew leader in Mandarin.

"All finished, Comrade," the cadre said. "You come in the office and pay, please."

"Here, I'll pay you right here," the chunky pilot said.

"Sorry, Comrade. Must come in. Must make paper records."

The pilot turned to Carr and shrugged.

"Perhaps Mr. Teng can help," Matt said to Carr.

Carr looked at Matt sharply, then seemed to relax. "Yes, I'll ask him," Carr said. He walked over to Teng, Yang, and the soldiers and gestured toward the pilot as he explained.

Yang walked briskly toward the tank-truck cadre, calling out to him, "Please move your truck at once, Comrade, so this plane can leave immediately."

"We have rules and regulations at this aircraft service facility," the foreman said. "The proper documentation must be maintained at all times and it is my function—''

''Silence!'' Yang shouted, moving up close to the man.
''You move your truck instantly or I shall have these
soldiers place you under arrest. Do not trifle with me!''

The cadre wilted, intimidated by Yang. He weakly
gestured to the truck driver, and the ponderous vehicle
moved slowly away from the jet's wing.

''Goodbye, Matthew,'' Teng shouted as the small plane's
four jets began to roar. ''Here is your passport. Hurry and
leave now while it is safe.''

''Goodbye, Teng Shan-li.'' Matt climbed the steps with
some difficulty and turned to wave to Yang Te-chong.
Yang returned the wave with his pistol, smiling broadly.
Then he turned to look in the direction of the control
tower, where a military truck had rolled to a stop and
put out its headlights.

Matt shoved his way past a crewman who was standing
by to pull up the jet's boarding steps, even as the pilot
began to taxi rapidly to the end of the runway.

The jet turned in a narrow arc, the door latch clicked
shut, and the pilot gave all his engines full power. The
crewman fell into the seat across from Matt and looked out
his window toward the tower. Suddenly, the floodlights
came back on, and Matt felt the jet swerve a little as if
blown aside by the blazing lights.

''I say,'' Carr shouted, ''I believe we're going to make it!
Hang on, fellows! Hang on.''

The jet's wheels came up with a clang and the pilot
banked steeply, climbing up and away from the lights.
Matt could see nothing but darkness outside his window.

''There is an airplane on fire down there!'' the crewman
yelled. ''On the runway!'' He pointed down outside his
window. ''By the gods! It exploded!''

Matt Thompson realized that his face was coated with
perspiration, and his knee hurt like hell. He laboriously
took off his overcoat and wiped his face with his handkerchief.

If the Chinese Air Force were any good, he told himself, this plane would be shot down before dawn. And he
wouldn't ever need the elaborate Alaskan alibi he had

begun to construct to explain his absence, his injured knee, and his lack of fish.

Forty-two

• OCTOBER, 1970 •

The Washington sky was crowded with rounded, gray smudges of clouds, merged and indistinct; they seemed to keep the sidewalks moist without really raining. The city was cold, damp, and quiet in the calm of its biennial temporary peace. Congress was in adjournment and the members were at home striving for reelection; their staff people were in the home districts too, exerting every effort to keep their derivative and lucrative jobs. The attention of the press was drawn away from Washington to the individual contests out in the states. The rest of the government, the part not traveling the hustings for the congressional elections, was enjoying the unusual Washington atmosphere. It was possible to do a day's work in the White House without congressional phone calls. There were no hearings to disrupt the bureaucrats in the departments and agencies. The handful of decent restaurants had luncheon tables available for the asking.

Matt arrived at his office at 7 A.M., leaning heavily on the carved Alaskan cane he'd bought during the layover in Anchorage.

"What happened?" everyone asked.

"Broke my knee."

"What happened?"

"Fell down on a wet dock."

"Too bad."

The papers on his desk were neatly piled. Angie's

system prescribed that white notes were the most important; a pile of pink slips was marked #2; #3 was for
urgent memos and letters. Angie had stuffed everything
else into sequentially numbered file folders.

The number one pile included four inquiries from Dr.
Kissinger's secretary. The President had called for him
twice, too.

The best stuff was in folder number five. There Angie
had collected the letters from old friends, an invitation to
speak at Dartmouth, an L. L. Bean catalogue, and invitations to three parties that looked pretty good.

There was a note from his father who delighted in
sending mail to him addressed *The White House*, instead
of to his son's apartment:

September 25, 1970

Dear Matthew:

    I hope your vacation was a good one, and only
the first of many. You are wise to take time off,
especially when your work is stressful.

    Can you come here for Christmas? I find it
impossible to leave school for more than a few
days, and that would hardly justify the air fare.
So I hope you can come here.

    It has been too long since we have been
together.

Love,
Father

When Matt was summoned across the street, Henry
Kissinger, his secretary, and a new aide, William Peck, all
greeted Matt Thompson like an old and dear friend.

If that surprised Matt, Al Haig's overt and continued
hostility did not. As Matt entered Kissinger's office, Haig
left it, nodding curtly with obvious disapproval.

"No fish!" Kissinger said loudly with a broad smile.
"Come in and rest your leg! How is it?"

"It's better. It still hurts some, but it's better."

"Bill," Kissinger said to the young man by his desk,

"this is Matthew Thompson, at last. Please give him that file." Kissinger and Peck had been at work, it appeared, on stacks of papers.

Bill Peck handed Matt a thick red manila envelope. "How do you do?" Peck said. "Henry has told me a lot about you."

"Bill Peck," Kissinger explained, "comes to us from the Chase Bank to take Eagleburger's place. Bill, here, is a lawyer, a graduate of Miami University in Ohio."

Peck was robust, slightly overweight, with a good smile.

"That file," Kissinger continued, "is the President's annual Foreign Policy Report. He wants it written in the White House this year, not at State, and he wants you to do it. It must go to the printer in ninety days, so you must give it your full attention."

"Fine," Matt said, hefting the file.

"Please put aside other work until it is finished," Kissinger added.

"Everything?"

"Yes. It will require your full attention."

"Okay." Matt waited for Kissinger to open the subject of China.

"So, you caught no fish at all?" Kissinger asked.

"Not a one."

"In your absence William Huntoon has formulated four more reasons to delay talks with the Chinese. You will find them on your desk."

Matt nodded. He noticed that Bill Peck was taking notes of the conversation. Occasionally Larry Eagleburger had been the note taker at staff meetings, but only when the group was large and the subject was sensitive and substantive. Perhaps Peck was merely eager to appear useful.

"I've seen what Huntoon sent over," Matt said, watching Peck, thinking carefully of what he was saying.

"There has been no other progress via the channels," Kissinger said. "When the report is finished, if we have not heard from the Chinese, I will want your recommendations."

Matt nodded. He wondered if Peck recorded his nods.

"I'm sure we'll hear from them before that. You've set up so many back channels to them that one or another is sure to work soon."

"One can never have too many back channels, eh?" Kissinger said flatly. "Your top priority now is the Report. China is no longer as urgent as it was three weeks ago."

Matt waited for an explanation of Kissinger's change of mind, but the professor stood, indicating the conversation had ended.

As Matt was leaving Kissinger's office, the young woman outside his door smiled and greeted him by name. She had not been sitting there when he'd come to keep his appointment with Kissinger. The older woman at that desk had been uncharacteristically friendly when he came in, and he'd wondered a little at that. It seemed that everyone had been given orders to be nice to him. Even Kissinger. Maybe they all felt sorry for him because he'd hurt his knee.

There was a flurry of China work in the second week of December. Kissinger, in spite of his contrary resolution, had pulled Matt off the Report project for a week to help him. On December 9, the Pakistani Ambassador had come to Kissinger with the long-awaited message from Chou En-lai. An envoy from the President of the United States will be "most welcome" in Peking, it said, "in order to discuss the subject of the evacuation of Chinese territories called Taiwan." The Pak Ambassador reported that his President, Yahya Khan, had been in Peking in mid-November for long meetings with Mao and Chou, during which he had delivered a letter from President Nixon proposing that he send an envoy such as Henry Kissinger to discuss the Taiwan question. Yahya Khan had been given this written message for Nixon before he departed from Peking.

For a week thereafter Richard Nixon and Henry Kissinger fought a veiled and always deniable battle over the text of the reply to the Chinese, and they used Matt Thompson as their go-between.

"What is this?" Kissinger asked mildly when Matt

brought him the draft reply to Chou's note that Nixon had dictated to him.

"The President called me in to talk about the reply," Matt explained. "After a lot of conversation he told me to write this down and show it to you."

"When was this?" Kissinger demanded.

"This morning."

"I was here this morning. Why didn't he talk to me?"

"He didn't say."

"I'll tell you why he didn't; he didn't talk to me because he is trying to move this meeting out of Peking. He doesn't want me to be the first American to meet the Chinese in Peking. But he doesn't have the guts to say that to my face."

"I see."

"There is no way that old Mao and Chou and the others will travel to Shanghai or somewhere to meet me, is there?"

"Well, Chou might, but surely Chairman Mao won't."

"It's impossible!" Kissinger exclaimed. "When our President does things like this, I wonder why I am here. I am wasting my time! I am working for an ego-starved idiot who cares more about breaking some record than about world peace!"

"The Historic First syndrome," Matt offered.

"Exactly. Well, we won't let him get away with it. Here, take this back and redraft it without any reference to the venue. Then send it in to him with a memo that says I have approved it in that form."

"You're putting me in the middle," Matt objected.

"You put yourself in the middle. When he tries to pull something outrageous like this, don't let him get away with it next time."

"I assumed you and he had already discussed a venue other than Peking."

"Don't assume. It will get you in trouble."

Richard Nixon spotted Kissinger's change at once. He had telephoned Matt the next day to ask if Kissinger had approved the draft reply. When Matt told him that the

Professor had made some changes, Nixon summoned Matt to the Oval Office.

"Why, this won't do at all," Nixon said with surprise. He had greeted Matt with a give-it-to-me-quick outstretched hand and had read Kissinger's draft of the short message before saying a word to Matt. "Let me explain, Henry— ah, I mean Matt—why this change is not satisfactory. Oh, sit down.... Most experts will agree, I think, that a host country derives an advantage—some would say a very substantial advantage—when it holds such talks in its own capital. I never go to Williamsburg or New York to negotiate with a foreign envoy. I have him come right here, on my own turf. Why? Very simple. All of my resources are here: my staff, my files, the whole State Department if I want them. I eat better here and I sleep better. They go to a strange bed in their embassy or in a hotel and they aren't so well rested. Oh, no, I would never give up that advantage."

"I see."

"You'll understand when I say that Henry thinks in quite different terms about venue. He is concerned about what history is going to say about this trip and his part in it. He lusts to be the first American into Peking, you see. He is focusing less on results and more on cosmetics."

"Are you at all worried about how the Chinese might react to a proposal for a venue different from Peking, sir?" Matt asked. "It might rule out Mao's personal participation. He is somewhat feeble."

"Henry doesn't need to see Mao. He can work out the arrangements and agenda, subject to Mao's approval and mine. He won't have my *carte blanche*, and I would assume their man won't have Mao's, either. Everything is referred back when subordinates are in negotiations like this, anyway."

"I see."

"Do you have that draft I dictated to you?"

"Yes sir, right here."

"Good. I'll tell Rose to retype it and you can deliver it to the Pakistan Ambassador tomorrow morning."

When Matt returned to his office, he telephoned Kissinger to report that the President was going to back-channel his own draft message, rather than Henry's.

"You had better talk to him yourself," Matt said to Kissinger. "Otherwise, the message is going to say 'elsewhere than in Peking,' and he's going to tell me to give it to the Paks tomorrow."

"I don't feel I can do that," Kissinger said solemnly. "I must be careful not to reduce a procedural issue to a personal level, however important the issue may be. It will be better if you continue to represent our point of view."

"Well, he doesn't care much for my advice," Matt said.

"Do what you can," Kissinger said with a tone of sadness.

Matt immediately dispatched a message to Teng Shan-li via Emory Latham's gym locker:

> Mr. Teng:
>   The reply which is coming to the Premier via the Paks raises an issue of venue which is purely the product of a personal competition between Nixon and Kissinger. Each man wishes to be the first American to be received in Peking. Nixon also reasons that Kissinger will necessarily deal with persons of lower rank if the meetings are held away from Peking,
>   I recommend that your officials decide where *you* wish to have the meetings with Kissinger and simply insist on your venue. Neither principal here will insist to the contrary, I am sure.
>   Matthew Thompson

Ezra Thompson's old white frame house on Euclid Avenue in Whittier, California, was the place where Matt Thompson had celebrated Christmas for an unbroken twenty years. This time, when Matt settled in for his visit, the house seemed unusually dark and unused. The white paint outside was checked and peeling in places, and there was a smell of old upholstery and stale air inside. Ezra Thompson rarely used the living room, dining room, or sun porch anymore. He read or watched television in his bedroom, cooked for himself in the old-fashioned kitchen, and went in and out of the house through the back door. It had become less than half a house.

For Matt, this Christmas with his father was a disturbing series of departures from the old customs. For six years Ezra Thompson had been closing off the rooms of the mansion of his life, abandoning people, appetites, and vanities, narrowing his interests and enthusiasms. Matt realized for the first time during the holiday visit that his father had become some fraction of the man he had known. Ezra was not interested in going to a Christmas church service as the Thompson family had traditionally done. He declined invitations from relatives and fellow teachers. At restaurants—where he and Matt ate most of their meals—he ordered the plainest food.

One evening Ezra and Matt ate dinner at the Tick Tock Family Restaurant in Whittier, where the waitresses all called Ezra "Professor."

"You don't eat much," Matt said.

"I don't need it," his father said defensively. "I find I need less and less of the things I once thought so important."

"I guess that's good. The simpler the better, eh?"

"Something like that. Do you still live alone back there?"

Matt nodded, scowling at the bones in his fish. "I live in the same apartment, out Connecticut Avenue. It's what I can afford right now."

"Thinking of getting married?" Ezra asked casually.

"I've thought about it, but I'm just not ready."

"You're not so young anymore. At your age most men are married."

"I suppose. But the work I'm doing is pretty demanding, you know, and marriage is a big commitment."

"Is that Glenna still on your dance card?"

"Not right now. She gave me an ultimatum just before I went to—ah, just before I went fishing and got hurt."

"Ultimatum?"

"Get married or get lost."

"Well, that sounds serious. And you decided what?"

"That I'm not ready."

"Too bad. Has she some hidden defect of character that eliminates her from serious consideration?"

Matt smiled. "Glenna is a thoroughly fine young woman. I'm just not sure how she'll wear over the years. She is anything but intellectual."

Ezra nodded. "Some of the happiest men I know are married to women who don't read Aristotle in the original or own their own telescopes. It all depends on what is most important to a man. Some men want beauty. Others need mental stimulation and challenge, I suppose. Your mother's most sterling attributes were her abilities at the stove and her warm feet."

"Warm feet?"

"Take my advice, son: Never sleep with a woman with chronically cold feet. It can destroy a marriage faster than anything else I know. That's Thompson's Law of Domestic Tranquility. . . . Are you going to have pie? They make a good custard pie here."

"Sure. Berry pie too?"

Ezra Thompson shook his head. "Not like Mother's," he said. "Lord, I miss that girl!"

When the galley proofs of the President's Foreign Policy Report were read and finally approved in early February, Matt Thompson was ready for a rest. The White House had been a place of tension since the President's return from the West Coast in early January. Almost at once, Nixon had received another message from the Chinese, this one a near-duplicate of the December message, except that it was delivered by the Romanian Ambassador. The disputed issue of the venue of the first meeting with the Chinese was not resurrected by Nixon or Kissinger, and the agreed-upon reply message simply said the President looked "forward to productive meetings in China on the

widest range of subjects." But the President made clear to
Matt Thompson that he wanted Kissinger to stay out of
Peking, lest the drama of Nixon's eventual arrival there be
diluted.

Henry Kissinger began his China studies in earnest that
month, and he demanded Matt's help in organizing his
curriculum. Matt invited a cohort of aging and professional
China scholars from East Coast universities to come to the
White House to answer Kissinger's questions, and he
gathered news clips, essays, and books on China for
Kissinger to take to his cluttered apartment for weekend
reading.

Matt Thompson had several reasons for his mental and
physical exhaustion. First, his knee continued to cost him
sleep. And the overlong Foreign Policy Report was a
prodigious project which demanded late hours of detailed
work.

Matt's social life suffered all through January. When
Matt finessed Mary Finn's dinner invitations, she bluntly
objected: "What have you got going, Thompson?"

"I told you," he replied. "I've had this damn report
to get out."

"Well, you've got to eat dinner. I'll bring you dinner
and we can dine on your desk."

"It won't work. I have other people staying nights to
help me."

"Man people or beautiful-lady people?"

"Man people." There was a Chinese lady on his mind,
he told himself, but she was only part of the reason he
wasn't spending time with Mary Finn.

"This is twice you've put me off, Mister. One more and
you're out at the plate," she said.

"Come on, Mary. How about a little less pressure? Do I
do this to you?"

"You know you do. When I was so tied up with RCA's
French problem, you wanted me to go to the German
Embassy party with you—right? And you kept after me
unmercifully."

"Entirely different. You didn't have a printer's deadline like I do."

"Bullshit. I had deadlines too. Well, go ahead and be a drudge. I think I'll go up to the Georgetown Safeway and see if that cute new bag boy wants to go out to dinner."

"Now you've got me worried. How about lunch tomorrow, and we'll do something special on the tenth? When I get this thing done, how about celebrating?"

"Well, lunch is fine, and I'll pencil you in for the tenth, but if the bag boy is off that night I may have to cancel."

"Just make sure you're in town on the tenth, will you? We might even start with lunch and take the afternoon off."

"Okay. I'll keep things open. How about the Georgetown Club at one tomorrow? And you'd better not stand me up or I'll send someone around to break your other knee."

"Goodbye, gentle maiden," he said, laughing.

PART

SEVEN

Forty-three

February 8, 1971

Mr. Teng:

I have just learned, to my dismay, that Nixon and Kissinger decided to go ahead in Laos in spite of the warning I conveyed to them. No one told me they would do so.

By the time you receive this, the ARVN attack already will be under way.

I am convinced that this operation is in no way directed at China. I must stress the importance which is placed upon avoiding any successful Hanoi offensive in 1972, which is the election year here.

The President is fully as desirous of early talks with your leaders as before. Your message via Norway was received February 4.

The goal we mutually seek is very near; I trust this ignored warning about Laos will not divert either side from its attainment.

Matthew Thompson

To: The President
From: Matthew Thompson (via Rose Mary Woods)
Re: Laos and China

Leaders of the People's Republic of China have been assured by your several earlier messages that it is U.S. policy to deescalate military involvement in Taiwan and Viet Nam.

Since the current Laotian initiative gives the appearance of U.S. (and ARVN) military operations into yet another country which is a neighbor of China, some reassurance to China seems necessary.

Either via the press or in a message, the President should make clear that the new Laos operation is solely directed at the North Vietnamese supply line and not, in any way, at China or other Asian countries.

If it is possible to say that it will be of limited scope or duration, that too would be helpful.

Matthew Thompson

There had been another paragraph in his memorandum to the President, but Matt took it out. It expressed dismay and disgust that the United States would deliberately send ARVN soldiers into an area of Laos where the North Vietnamese must be waiting for them, forewarned and forearmed.

Matthew Thompson took that paragraph out because he wasn't ready to leave the White House staff. He had decided to hang on until the door to China was finally, irrevocably open. And so he would bite his tongue and say nothing more about Laos.

"I appreciate your giving me this time, Dr. Kissinger," said the old reporter in the brown suit. "I'm working on a particular story and it appears that you are the only one who can fill in some of the gaps."

"Please make yourself comfortable, Mr. Osborne, and

we will have some refreshment," Kissinger said affably. "What can I give you? Coffee or tea? Something cold?"

"Coffee would be fine."

Kissinger pressed a button on his telephone console and ordered coffee for John Osborne and a diet cola for himself. "I am an admirer of yours, Mr. Osborne, and a regular reader," he said.

"Well, I'm flattered and surprised."

"In fact, I first knew of you when you were at *Time* magazine. You came to Harvard with Henry Anatole Gruenwald one time to talk to me."

"I remember, but I am surprised you do. That's been fifteen years."

"Now, at *The New Republic* I expect you have more freedom?"

"Well, I only do the White House column, you know." Osborne coughed deeply and wiped his mouth with his handkerchief. "Excuse me. Even so, the deadline at *The New Republic* is as tyrannical as those at *Time*." Osborne picked up his pad and fished in his pockets for a pen. "I came here to ask you a few questions about this South Vietnamese operation in Laos that has turned out to be such a disaster."

"I had hoped"—Kissinger smiled—"we were going to talk about the President's environmental initiatives."

"I have heard," Osborne pressed, "that the Laos attack was authorized by the President personally. Is that right?"

"As you said, it was an ARVN operation. We had no ground troops involved at all. So the command decisions on our side related only to American logistic and support people."

"Are you saying that's the only thing the President decided on?"

"Unlike some earlier activities in Viet Nam," Kissinger continued easily, "this one was pressed upon the American command by our allies. They persuaded General Abrams of the worth of the operation and he recommended it to Secretary Laird."

Osborne put down his pad and drank half his cup of

coffee, looking at Kissinger all the while. "What went wrong?" Osborne finally asked.

"I am not sure." Kissinger shrugged. "Since we had no people on the scene, it has been most difficult to get the facts. But we do know now that the North Vietnamese had moved many tanks into the area. That was a surprise. And their troop strength was three or four times what the prior intelligence had led the commanders to anticipate."

"It sounds like they were tipped off in advance." Osborne's laugh was truncated by his emphysema. He seemed to chuckle and snuffle simultaneously.

"That is a logical deduction," Kissinger agreed. "The ARVN sometimes has that problem."

"How bad are their losses?"

"Reports on television are very exaggerated, I believe. Casualties were significant on both sides, I am told, and the North suffered a material disruption of its supply system. But I don't think we will ever have highly reliable casualty reports."

"I have been told that the ARVN retreated in great disorder, fighting to get on helicopters, some of them pretending injury to be evacuated, and that kind of thing."

"There may have been a little of that, but General Abrams feels that by and large the ARVN units performed very well. They were all on their own this time, you know."

"So you would say that the Vietnamization of the war is a success?"

"I would say that the ARVN has responded well to its training and showed in this operation that it can stand on its own feet, even against a superior enemy force."

"I have a rumor I need to check, Doctor. It's no more than that, but it is serious in its implications. Otherwise, I wouldn't even bother you with it. It is being said—again, so far as I know, without foundation—that the North Vietnamese were in possession of all the details of this Laos invasion a number of days before it was begun. . . ."

"That may well be," Kissinger interjected. "Look, I'm sorry, but I must—"

"Just let me finish the question, please. That they knew the plan and that the American command was well aware that they knew, but it was decided to let the ARVN go in anyway."

"That is not the kind of information people in the White House hear very often. That implies a kind of 'Charge of the Light Brigade' mentality, doesn't it?"

"Or that someone wanted the ARVN to fail?"

"I assure you, it is very much to our interest as a nation that they should succeed, and on the best available information I would say that they did succeed. They interdicted the Ho Chi Minh Trail and inflicted heavy losses on their enemy. Now, I'm sorry, but I must leave in a minute." Kissinger stood. "I am glad we had this reunion, Mr. Osborne."

"Thank you, Dr. Kissinger," Osborne said, standing slowly. "Perhaps I can call and see you again sometime? These brief talks are enormously helpful."

Kissinger opened his door. "Of course. Call Julie and she will set it up for us."

When Osborne had gone, Alexander Haig emerged from his small office and looked a question at Kissinger.

"Come in," Kissinger said to him.

"How did it go with Osborne?" Haig asked with a smile. "Did he snuffle and snort?"

"A little, but he is a very clever man. He has the rumor that we knew the Laos operation was compromised. How could he know that?"

"Thompson?" Haig asked. "Or Thompson's Chinese friends?"

"Perhaps. You'd better alert Laird that Osborne is working on the Laos disaster and emphasize that I told him it was a victory for Vietnamization. Osborne also tried to get me to say Nixon had personally approved it. Warn Laird about that. Osborne will go to Rogers too, I suppose, and he will say he opposed the whole thing. But you might try to get Rogers in line. Perhaps Haldeman should call him. No one should admit that the ARVN were defeated. That is very important."

*   *   *

"It appears, Comrade Premier, that the Saigon army was decisively defeated at the Ho Chi Minh Trail," General Yan Chong-chuan said. "They left behind about seven thousand dead and wounded, according to Hanoi."

Yan and Chou En-lai sat side by side in two of the wide seats in the forward section of the Ilyushin-17, one of six well-appointed transports in the Central Committee's fleet of airplanes. The short, wiry old general, a veteran of the Long March and countless battles against the Nationalists and the Japanese, held his teacup in both gnarled hands, his elbows on the arms of the upholstered seat.

"Those casualty counts are always inflated by both sides, aren't they?" Chou En-lai said skeptically.

"Yes"—Yan shrugged—"but I have this in confidence from General Giap himself. The numbers should be fairly close. The recovery of arms, ammunition, and machines has been extremely heavy too, he says."

"The fates are kind to us today, Comrade Yan," Chou said. "What intelligence do you have that the Americans may seek to retaliate somehow for this defeat?"

"General Giap has been alert to that possibility, but he has seen nothing so far. He will keep me advised."

"I doubt there will be retaliation. The Americans are telling their press that the ARVN won the battle, and that implies they will take the position that there is no occasion for retaliation."

Chou's eyes darted about the plane, then returned to his teacup. He moved it an inch, to the exact center of the small table pulled down over his lap. "When we get to Hanoi, General, please make it clear to Giap that I want talks only about logistics and supplies. There is to be no conversation about sending Chinese troops into Laos or Viet Nam."

"Of course, Comrade Premier," Yan Chong-chuan said. As Deputy Chairman of the Central Committee's Military Commission, Yan well understood that Chou En-lai's journey to North Viet Nam was wholly symbolic. The other

officers Chou had brought with him were all "rear services" men; there was not a combat veteran among them.
General Yan had seen many battles, but he would fight
again only if Chou En-lai told him to. He considered
himself Premier Chou's soldier and none else's.

"Have you talked to the military commanders?" Chou
asked.

"With many of them, Comrade Premier, as you suggested.
I have been to the south and the west. The commanders
there are even more hostile to the Defense Minister than I
had predicted. One of the Peking unit commanders is Lin
Piao's close friend, so I did not attempt to talk with him.
The Air Force is entirely Minister Lin's, as is much of the
Navy. But I believe we can count on seventy-five to eighty
percent of the Army without doubt."

"Good. Before long I will go with you to the commanders in the south and east. What about the people along the
Russian border?"

"I have not been there, but I believe them to be the
most unhappy of all my colleagues."

"I think you should talk to them at once," Chou said.
"It is impossible for me to know accurately how much
time we have to prepare."

"I will go up there at once, Comrade Premier," Yan
said. "Before we land, there is one other matter. Have you
heard of a military organization composed of Air Force
officers and a few from the other services called the Joint
Fleet?"

"No, but let us ask Yang Te-chong if he knows of it."
Chou touched a button and the steward appeared at his
side. "Please ask Comrade Yang to join us," the Premier
said. Turning to General Yan, Chou asked, "Have you
reason to think this is a sinister group? This Joint Fleet?"

"I think it may be."

Yang Te-chong walked up the aisle, nodded to General
Yan, and bent his head to receive the Premier's instructions.

"The General has mentioned a group of military officers
which is called the Joint Fleet. Do you know of it?" Chou
asked him.

"No, Comrade Premier, I do not," Yang said.

"In my conversations with two Army commanders in the southeast I was told that they had been approached to join this group," Yan said. "The Defense Minister's son is said to be its organizer, and some commanders would find it difficult to decline such an invitation. I have asked others, but only the two in the regions between Canton and Shanghai have been approached."

"Perhaps you should look into the Joint Fleet's activities," Chou said to Yang. "If Lin Li-kuo is involved, it may be more than just a group of old comrades getting together for a drink."

"At once, Comrade Premier," Yang Te-chong said. "We will find out what we can."

At the same hour, as Chou En-lai flew to Hanoi to exemplify China's support for North Vietnam, two men walked side by side in the Fragrant Hills, just twelve miles northwest of the center of Peking. The two met with full confidence that they would not be overheard or interrupted, since the hilly forest that surrounded them was the private hunting preserve of the Chinese military command and was within a vast and heavily guarded Military Zone.

Both men carried rifles with telescopic sights. The short, fat man in a heavily quilted gray overcoat was Wu Fa-ch'an, the commander in chief of the Air Force. His companion, Chou Yu-ch'i, his protégé and Air Force subordinate, was tall and slim. Chou walked easily, swinging his rifle in his right hand.

"My breath makes steam," General Wu complained. "It is a bitter cold day for a stroll in these woods. Was it really necessary to stage this hunting expedition in order to have a talk, Comrade Chou? And must you walk so fast?"

"I am sorry, Commander; I will slow down. But I think it is vital that you know what is going on. If you wish we can sit down up ahead."

"This is about Minister Lin Piao's son, I suppose?" Wu

asked. He was breathing heavily, and he had put his rifle over his shoulder because his arm was getting tired.

"Yes. Since you assigned me to be Lin Li-kuo's assistant he has come to trust me, I believe. As you know, he has created what is called his 'research and investigations group,' and he has now some one hundred Air Force men and women assigned to it. The day before yesterday he called me in to ask me to begin drafting certain plans with the designation *wu chi yi*, the numbers *five, seven*, and *one*. But the full name of the project is *wu chuang chi yi*."

"Armed uprising?" Wu exclaimed. "He has *openly* named the project this?"

"Exactly. Lin Li-kuo's plan is to kill Chairman Mao and overthrow his government, and young Lin assures me that the plan is actually the idea of Defense Minister Lin Piao, his father."

"I see." Wu stopped and sat heavily on a large tree trunk beside the trail. He bent over as far as his girth would permit to lay his rifle on the ground parallel with the log. "What did you respond to that?" he asked Chou levelly.

"At first, I did not know what to say. Then I remembered your instruction that in all cases, I should comply with the boy's requests but should keep you informed. So I told him I would begin to prepare the plans at once."

"Good," Wu said. "It happens that I know of this plan, and rather reluctantly, I also have become involved in it. In truth, I do not yet know if it is Lin Piao's idea or merely that of his son, but there are several signs that old Lin himself is running it. Therefore, we must cooperate fully with his son. If I see any evidence that the Minister is not fully behind it, I will warn you at once."

"Thank you," Chou Yu-ch'i said. "The plan had progressed through several refinements, evidently, before the son spoke to me."

"Can you tell me the details of the plan? But make it brief! In a few minutes I will freeze to death," General Wu said.

"Well, as you may know, Chairman Mao intends to go

south on an inspection trip this summer, probably in ninety or one hundred days.''

"No, I was not aware of that."

"No one seems to know if he will fly or go by train, but his ultimate destination is Canton. So the plan has several branches. The first is to recruit and train the needed personnel. The second is a plan, if the Chairman flies, for disposing of his craft."

"That should not be too difficult." Wu laughed. "Almost all of the Air Force can be expected to help."

"And the third leg of the plan, if he chooses to go by train, involves destroying his armored train and its guards so that Mao himself can be killed."

"When he travels by train there is the most complicated central control of all the railroad system," General Wu said. "Can you find someone who knows how that works?"

"We are looking for a man who used to be in charge of such things. I am told this person is in prison somewhere now."

Wu heaved to his feet, laboriously. "Will you hand me my hunting rifle, please? I lack the will to bend over to get it."

"Of course, Comrade Commander. I would carry it for you, but it may be worthwhile for you to appear to be hunting today."

"Anyone who knows me would think that an incredible phenomenon," Wu complained. "It would be more believable that you had forced me into this frozen forest at gunpoint." He walked stiffly, cradling the heavy rifle in both arms. "When you have completed the 571 plan I would like to see it."

"Of course, Commander," Chou said. "I should have a draft ready in a few days. Timing depends on how soon we can find the railroad expert we need."

"And whether he will talk to you?"

"I am told not to worry about that."

Wu laughed, his breath condensing into a small cloud of steam which held the thin afternoon light briefly, then disappeared.

*   *   *

"Well, Henry, it looks like we'd better decide who goes to China. We've had three messages in sixty days, and they are all favorable, eh?"

"Yes, Mr. President," Kissinger said somberly.

"What's the matter?" Nixon demanded. He was sitting low in his easy chair, his feet propped on its hassock. Kissinger was perched uncomfortably on one of the wooden chairs at the Chippendale table near Nixon's hassock.

"Mr. President, it is this Laotian operation. It is not enough that we are compelled to fight an unpopular war with an ally that cannot fight or even keep a secret. But now, along with all of that, the idiots at Defense and State have been working full time to disown any responsibility for the outcome."

"Typical," Nixon snorted.

"In the first place, they should be claiming some kind of a victory over there. Second, they could have a little backbone and accept responsibility for their part in it, instead of dumping it all over here. From the rumors one would think that you had personally decided where each helicopter should land and at what time. When something goes a little wrong it becomes a White House operation."

"Looking back now, Henry, was it a mistake to go in there? Knowing what we knew?"

"Mr. President," Kissinger said slowly, "we had other options, as you will recall. And we knew the risks. I think when you weigh the risks and the alternatives, you conclude that we made the best choice we could have made. There were really very few surprises, as it turned out. No one expected the ARVN to perform perfectly, and there were some command failures, I understand. But they chewed up some of the enemy's men and supplies, and the next time they will perform better for the experience. In summary, I would have to say that if I had known before it started that it was going to come out exactly the way it did, I would still have gone ahead with it."

"And what about the Chinese? Matt Thompson thought

we needed to reassure them, so I worked that message into one press-conference answer the other day. Do you think we need to do more?''

Kissinger smiled thinly. "Perhaps we would need to if the ARVN had won the battle. But since they retreated in such disorganization I can't believe that China feels at all threatened. I think you should just proceed to select your envoy and tell the Chinese who it will be and what day he will arrive.''

"I've been thinking about Tom Dewey," Nixon said earnestly. "He is an excellent negotiator. And they will know that he ran for President. That adds to his stature.''

Kissinger did not rise to the bait.

"Give some thought to George Bush, too," Nixon continued. "He's been an awfully good soldier, and such a trip would be a nice bonus for him. He's loyal, and he follows his instructions, doesn't he?''

"Mr. President, I really don't think you—''

"Premature is it? Well, we can talk later about who it will be. No reason to deal with all that now, right?''

"Fine," Kissinger said grimly, "but I feel you must settle on a person within the next week so that he has some opportunity to prepare.''

"Bill Rogers says Alexis Johnson would need almost no preparation," Nixon said.

"Alexis Johnson would be a deadly mistake, Mr. President. He is too close to the Japanese, and the Chinese would know that.'' Kissinger was not certain whether Nixon was teasing him or not. He gathered his papers from the table, stood as if to leave, then sat down again.

"All right," Nixon said dismissively. "I'll decide soon. If you have other names to suggest, other than Dewey or Bush, get them to me right away.'' It was evident that he was ready for the professor to leave.

"Of course," Kissinger said curtly. "None occur to me at the moment.''

It was seventeen hours before Henry Kissinger recalled that Thomas Dewey had been dead for several months. He deduced that Richard Nixon had been cruelly teasing his

National Security assistant. Only then did Kissinger dare to believe that he would really be the first American into Peking.

Forty-four

• MARCH AND APRIL, 1971 •

Chou En-lai appeared worn. The trip to Hanoi had been brief but tiring; he had returned to Peking at once, on March 8, but the next ten days had denied him any opportunity for relaxation. At age seventy-three, he had finally learned that one needed to rest. But Lin Piao's military revolt threatened. On his return from Hanoi, Chou had immediately gone to Shanghai and Foochow for a series of meetings with the regional commanders of the People's Liberation Army in the southeastern region.

The acting Foreign Minister, Chi Peng-fei, urgently requested the Premier to return to Peking from the southeast to consider intelligence reports that Yahya Khan's Pakistan Army was preparing to assault dissident factions in East Pakistan in open defiance of India's warnings.

Back in Peking, Chou also received a file from Teng Shan-li which contained a letter from Matthew Thompson:

March 15, 1971

Dear Mr. Teng:

In preparing a review of Sino-American negotiations for an impatient President of the United States and his impatient National Security assistant, it occurred to me that it may be time for some highly visible symbolism to move our relationship to fruition.

Without some overt acts on both sides, I fear, the issues that can crop up to divide us may prevail over our very good intentions.

A symbol of near-reconciliation is needed, and it needs to be somewhat innocuous and ambiguous, lest it cause the China Lobby or the Taiwanese or the Russians to become aroused. Therefore, it should be nongovernmental on its face. At the same time symbolism can go a long way toward encouraging our two peoples to open their thought to an improved relationship.

One idea: The United States Ping-Pong team—ten or twelve players and a few officials—will be in Nagoya, Japan, for the world championship tournament in a couple of weeks. I saw a news report that China will also be participating, for the first time since 1965. What if these young American players were invited to China (perhaps with one or two other Western teams, for the sake of ambiguity) and were generously received by your leaders? A few U.S. reporters should be there. A U.S. network television news crew should be there to send home pictures of the Americans playing, touring and visiting amidst smiling Chinese people.

Or vice versa, your team might be invited to the United States. But I'd guess a Chinese visit here would have less impact (and would be less certain of success).

I have not mentioned this to anyone here. It is merely my brainstorm. But I feel sure the U.S. Government would welcome such an invitation from China.

Regards,
Matt

In the margin of Matthew Thompson's letter Chou En-lai wrote:

> This is a superb idea. Please implement it.
> Invite the U.S.A., the U.K., Canada, an African
> and a Latin country. Made the welcome lavish—
> as it would be for an Italian Communist.

So it was that J. Rufford Harrison, an American table-tennis official who was finding it impossible to hail a taxi outside his Nagoya hotel, met Comrade Sung Ching, a Chinese table-tennis official. Harrison happened to be the first American Mr. Sung encountered after receiving an urgent cable from his superior, the Director of the China Sports Federation.

After many fruitless minutes spent waving at Toyota taxicabs, Harrison saw a gray cab slowing as it approached the door of his hotel. Harrison walked quickly to the point of probable interception and stood, expectantly, as Sung Ching and his interpreter emerged from the cab. Before he could take possession of the cab, Harrison was blocked by the thin young interpreter, who greeted him by name in flawless English: "Mr. J. Harrison, sir, please wait! Mr. Sung Ching, the Deputy President of the team of the People's Republic of China, wishes to talk with you! Mr. Sung says he is authorized to ask if the esteemed officials of the United States delegation would welcome an invitation for your delegation to come to the People's Republic of China for a short exhibition tour?"

J. Rufford Harrison was profoundly surprised. He opened his hands as he asked, "When would this be? We are scheduled to go home Easter Sunday. But I should think everyone would want to go to your country if we can!"

The interpreter translated briefly for Sung. Sung replied.

"Mr. Sung says that your delegation would be the guests of the Chinese people. You are invited to come this Saturday, directly from Nagoya. All arrangements will be made."

"That's very nice," Harrison replied. "I will see if I can find Graham Steenhoven, our leader, and give you an answer right away. This is terribly exciting. Thank you, very much." Harrison stood, shook hands with Sung

Ching and the young interpreter, then loped toward the elevators.

"I will guess," Sung said, watching Harrison cross the lobby, "that there will be Americans in Tien'anmen Square next week. Let us go and find the Canadians now."

"Thank you, Bill," Henry Kissinger said softly, hanging the receiver on the large telephone console. He looked up at Alexander Haig and Matthew Thompson and shook his head slowly. "Bill Huntoon says our colleagues at the State Department feel strongly that we should finesse the Chinese Ping-Pong invitation," he reported. "If our Ping-Pong team goes to China, they reason, that would be a cultural exchange. And, of course, Ambassador Stoessel in Warsaw has not yet achieved an agreement with the Chinese on cultural exchanges. So, it follows, we must refer the question of a Ping-Pong tour to the Warsaw ambassadors for endless discussion and a few dozen cables back and forth."

"So it will never happen," Matt Thompson added. He looked out the window at the Pacific Ocean.

"Huntoon's career will never be blemished by undue recklessness," Kissinger said. "He suggests we have our team officials thank the Chinese politely and refer them to him."

"Pitiful," Al Haig said.

"I am inclined to tell the team officials to accept the invitation," Kissinger began, "but I think I had better talk to the President first. If this Ping-Pong team goes to Peking, Richard Nixon is not going to be the first American to enter the Forbidden City, so he'd better know it in advance."

Kissinger rushed away trailing the long cable from the Tokyo Embassy about the Chinese invitation to the American table-tennis team.

"Comrade Wang Li-fa," Chou En-lai instructed crisply, "I have decided to speak Chinese to the table-tennis players, so you must translate for me. I will go downstairs in a few minutes."

"Of course, Comrade Premier," Li-fa said.

"Their visit has been a big success, I think," Chou continued. "Let me read you what *The New York Times* said yesterday. It quotes one of the American players, a young man named John Tannehill from Ohio." Chou pronounced it "Oh-hee-oh."

"Ohio," Li-fa corrected.

"Ohio. He says 'Mao Tse-tung is the greatest moral and intellectual leader in the world today.' What do you think of that?"

"It surprises me, Comrade Premier. I did not realize that Americans were so aware of Chairman Mao's qualities."

"It surprises me that this Tannehill would be so outspoken. I fear that other Americans reading this dispatch might believe that all the people on the American table-tennis team were Mao adherents before we invited them. I really hope that some of the other Americans here are less enthusiastic. I must give some thought to my remarks now."

"Yes, Comrade. Do you wish private talks with any of their leaders after your remarks?"

"No. I will answer all their questions while they are seated, but there is no advantage in talking with them away from the reporters. I see that one of these reporters has been in China before, during the Revolution. That is good. Go along now; I shall be down in about thirty minutes."

The players and officials from Great Britain, Canada, Colombia, Nigeria, and the United States were seated at small desk-chairs arranged in curved rows in one of the medium-sized rooms in the Great Hall of the People. There was a stir and all talking stopped when Premier Chou En-lai entered with Yang Te-chong and several bodyguards. Yang and the others stayed near the door as Chou walked to the center of the room and stood at a microphone, looking intently at the young people seated in front of him. Among the Americans was a man with hair to his shoulders who wore purple bell-bottomed trousers and a faded red shirt. As Chou stared at him, the young man gave him a nod and smiled. I hope that is not Tannehill of Ohio, Chou thought.

Premier Chou En-lai spoke rapidly in Chinese, spreading his arms wide.

Wang Li-fa, at another microphone at the side, said: "The Premier of China, Comrade Chou En-lai, says, 'What joy it is to bring friends from afar.' "

Kissinger, in his customary chair at the side of the President's great, carved desk, had prepared for this meeting with care. Matthew Thompson had been busy for four days assembling a briefing book on China, summarizing the course of Sino-American negotiations, analyzing China's position on Taiwan, trade embargoes, Russia, and Viet Nam.

"Mr. President." Kissinger cleared his throat and rearranged his notes on the desk beside him. "It is now the end of April. If you are to visit China by March of 1972, we must act quickly. You must soon decide whom you will send for the preliminary talks. That person must get fully prepared to go there this summer. An advance team of communications, security, and logistics people must then go in the fall. We must give the technicians adequate time to build the communication links required both for your needs and for good press coverage. Ziegler estimates they need a minimum of four months—one hundred and twenty days—for that work. So if we cannot send an envoy soon— in sixty days—you will find that the only time you can go is in the spring of 1972."

"That is too late. We'll be into the important primaries by then," Nixon objected. "And we may have a Russian summit then. So, who do you propose that I send?"

"I think," Kissinger began, "that George Bush is not suitable. He is seen as a political figure."

"Alex Johnson?"

"No. For the reasons I explained before. Too close to the Japanese, and—"

"You're telling me who not to send."

"Well, I think . . ." Kissinger nodded slowly and moved his notes close to the edge of the desk. "I think . . . that I should go."

"You?" Nixon feigned surprise.

"Yes, Mr. President," Kissinger said doggedly.

"You think you could do it with absolute secrecy? Every housewife in America knows the color of your pajamas."

Kissinger smiled. "Some of them not firsthand, only from wire-service stories. . . . Yes, I have a plan that will work. I could become ill and be sequestered in Pakistan. The press would be told my temperature three times a day. I can slip from sight and have two or three days in China without anyone knowing."

Nixon nodded. "Have you talked to the Paks about it?"

"Not yet, of course. I was afraid you would decide to send Thomas Dewey."

Nixon barked a two-note laugh. "Well, why don't you see if Yahya will help you disappear? I guess you are the only one I can send."

"Thank you, Mr. President. I am grateful for your confidence. I have amassed some preparatory materials, and I will contact the Paks at once. The Chinese response to your relaxation of the trade embargo the other day has been very favorable."

"It was a good move. After Chou was so gracious to the Ping-Pong team, it seemed to be just the right reciprocation, didn't it? What does Matt Thompson say about your going?"

"I have not discussed it with him, pending your decision, but now, of course, I will. I will ask him to help me prepare. I will ask him to write the message you must now send to Chou En-lai proposing the details of my trip."

Forty-five

When the triumphant Henry Kissinger secretly entered Peking on July 9, 1971, Matthew Thompson was already there. Matt had been in the Chinese capital for two days, living at Chou En-lai's downtown guesthouse and working there with Teng Shan-li and, occasionally, with Chou himself.

The Chinese were frank to say that they were determined to know everything they could about Kissinger, the three staff men who would accompany him, and the messages from Richard Nixon they would bring with them. Matt agreed to answer their questions, confident that the more the Chinese knew, the more likely there would be quick agreement.

"At the top of the list," Teng Shan-li said, in beginning his first intensive session with Matt, "is the matter of Taiwan. Will Kissinger resist our fundamental claim to regain our offshore province?"

"I think not," Matt replied.

They were at the octagonal table in Chou's small brown study, the cones of light defining sharp circles on the dark baize tabletop.

"Here is a part of the draft communiqué, the part on Taiwan. Will Kissinger agree to it?"

Matt read the paragraph drafted by the Chinese and looked up at Teng. "Henry is bringing a draft prepared by Winston Lord which is not far from this. It says, basically, that there is only one China, on both sides of the Formosa

Strait, and it's up to the Chinese to work out their problems with each other.''

"Did you bring a copy of that language?"

"I brought no documents, Mr. Teng. With your Air Force in mind, I was careful about what someone might find in my luggage if something happened to me.''

"Very prudent, I am sure, although you were in no danger, you may be certain. You have been closely guarded since last night when you arrived in Tokyo. Our men flew with you from Japan on the airliner.''

"I could tell. I appreciate the care the Premier and you have taken.''

"The Kissinger formula on the Taiwan issue says nothing about U.S. troops' being withdrawn?'' Teng asked.

"The draft the Premier will be given has nothing in it about troops. But Henry is prepared to give you that language if you ask for it. He will commit to a formula for phased withdrawal as tensions in Asia subside, if the Premier insists.''

Teng made notes. "What about the United Nations seat? Will the United States oppose the resolution to remove the KMT from China's rightful seat?''

"All of these matters are for negotiation, Mr. Teng. If Kissinger feels the Premier is being forthcoming, he is prepared to offer ways to resolve the U.N. problem too. But not if the Premier seeks to send him home empty-handed.''

"The President wants to come here and we will consent to that; what more must the Premier agree to?''

"Well, just on that one item, there are any number of details to be settled on.''

Teng nodded and looked up to realize that Premier Chou En-lai was standing in the doorway listening. Teng put his hand on Matt's arm and stood. Matt turned to see the Premier and exclaimed, "Excuse me!''

"Please stay seated,'' Chou said. "I will sit with you for a few minutes but then I must go. I do not wish to interrupt. Is your knee better, Matt?''

"Yes, sir. Much better.''

"I am sorry for the last-minute planning for your trip,

but recently it seemed advisable to have your help in making our preparations. Was your trip safe and comfortable?"

"Yes, fine. I didn't know until the day before Kissinger left that he was going to leave me behind. So I was practically all packed, anyway."

"Why did he decide to leave you at home?" Chou asked.

"I suspect he has been told that I was in the Orient in September when I was supposed to be in Alaska. He thinks I'm either working for the President behind his back or for you, and either way he doesn't trust me. I have been very well treated by all his people, so I guess they think I'm the President's secret agent."

Chou nodded. "I interrupted. You were telling Comrade Teng about Kissinger's demands?"

"Right. I was saying the timing of the President's visit becomes very important because of the 1972 election campaign."

"And his probable spring summit with the Russians?" Chou added.

"Yes, but as between the two, the election is a more important consideration."

Chou smiled. "Popular democracy leads to strange priorities," he said to Teng. Teng nodded, smiling.

"With the election in mind, the White House wants to be sure the press is well represented in the President's entourage," Matt continued.

"Of course," Chou said. "How many journalists are you talking about? I had guessed Nixon would bring about fifty."

"No, sir. This is a major historic event in our country. I would guess a thousand journalists will ask permission to come, and we will select about half of them."

Chou looked shocked. "Five hundred? Where can we bed them all?"

"Plus our own technicians, security people, and staff. I have heard the number seven hundred fifty being used as a working hypothesis."

Teng shook his head. "It is not possible, Matt. Not even in the Peking Hotel."

Chou smiled broadly and found a pack of cigarettes in his jacket pocket. "I think Kissinger will negotiate on this question of the size of the entourage as a very, very important matter. Won't he be prepared to pay a considerable price for each added camera or microphone?"

"Perhaps. It bears directly on the election, as you imply."

"Well," said Chou, "he and I will discuss it. I think I will begin at a very low number and see how he reacts. There is one issue that may not be on your list, Comrade Teng. Be certain to discuss Japan's rearmament with Matt, please. . . . Now, do not allow me to interrupt you again. Do not get up; I must go. I have many visitors in Peking just now, but I will return tomorrow so that we may talk more, Matt. I am grateful that you came."

"It's good to see you again, sir," Matt replied. "I hope I can help to bring about a successful result for both sides."

"I am certain you can," Chou said. "That is why I sent for you."

"Let us return to my list," Teng said when the Premier had gone. "Are there other issues in connection with the President's visit?"

"Kissinger and Nixon are also very concerned that other American political figures might be allowed into China ahead of the President. Henry will ask for specific assurances that they will be kept out."

"What about journalists?" Teng asked.

"As few as possible."

"Are you aware that Mr. James Reston of *The New York Times* is entering China today from Hong Kong?"

"My God, no. Is he coming to Peking?"

"Yes."

"He knows both Henry and me by sight, of course. If he sees either one of us, there could be big trouble."

"When he arrives in Canton," Teng said with a smile, "he will see many communes and factories. Then he will come north on a very slow train. We do not expect to see him until next week.''

"Good. By the time he gets here he'll be a self-proclaimed China expert.''

Teng nodded. "Can you tell me anything about Japan?''

"Kissinger argues that the closer Japan is to us, the less China has to worry about. They don't need to have nuclear weapons if we are committed to protect them.''

"Yes. Will Kissinger agree to maintain the status quo—a non-nuclear Japan?''

"I don't know, but I would be surprised if he didn't. Mr. Teng, there is a personal matter I must talk to you about,'' Matt said earnestly.

"Personal? About Comrade Wang? I advise you two to maintain an aloof separation while you are here.''

"No. Mr. Teng, I very much need to talk to her in private for a few minutes. Will you ask her to come to my room when it is safe for her?''

"No time would be safe, Matthew. That is what I am telling you. So you will believe me, you should know that the Premier's wife feels very strongly that Li-fa should be sent away for correction and rehabilitation right now. Yang Te-chong is watching Li-fa closely. The girl must be extremely careful. I cannot ask her to meet you.''

"Please, Mr. Teng.''

"I am sorry. It is impossible. Will Kissinger bring with him the full text of a proposed communiqué?''

Matt looked at his folded hands and did not reply. He looked up at Teng and said: "I'm feeling some jet lag. I believe I should go upstairs and sleep for a time.''

Teng's expression did not change. "Of course, Matthew. I will wait downstairs until you are refreshed.''

Teng flipped the pages of his notebook and was reading his notes as Matt left the small conference room. When enough time had passed for Matt to have climbed the old staircase to the second floor, Teng went to find Yang Te-chong.

Yang was in a room behind the parlor on the opposite side of the house, talking with two officers of the 8341

Guard. He motioned Teng into a chair near the leaded glass window.

"You will not find it necessary to leave through the tunnels this time, Comrade," Yang said to Teng. "We have the whole street so well covered that even the neighborhood birds are inspected before they return to their nests."

Teng nodded. When Yang had dismissed the Guard officers, Teng said, "Matthew Thompson is again asking for a short private meeting with Wang Li-fa, Comrade Yang. I told him it was impossible and he immediately terminated his cooperation. He has gone up to his room to sleep."

Yang shook his head vigorously. "He will ruin the girl! Doesn't he understand that?"

"I have tried to explain that to him, but he doesn't seem to believe me. I have said I will not be a messenger between them and he is very angry with me."

"The Premier needs the information you are to get from him?"

"Yes. Some of it can be very important. But it must be obtained without coercion. He must remain useful and friendly."

"Then we must give him what he wants, eh?" Yang said slowly.

"At the cost of Wang Li-fa's career?"

"Everything must be purchased at some price; is it not so?" Yang shrugged.

"Are you saying I should send her to him?"

"If you must have the information, is there another way to get it?"

Teng shook his head. "Will you speak to the Premier first? If I send her up to his room, she must leave Chou En-lai's service, I assume. He will wish to decide that, will he not?"

"He has decided," Yang said.

Teng's shoulders sagged. "I am sorry," he said. "I will miss her."

"She will be kept here to ensure the American's continued cooperation," Yang explained. "Neither he nor she should be given any reason to believe that the Premier has lost confidence in her. She will be given routine tasks, as before."

"But when the American has given us everything . . . ?"

"Then she must be given another assignment, of course. But that is no concern of yours, Comrade Teng, is it?" Yang Te-chong looked sharply at Teng.

"No, it is no concern of mine," Teng acquiesced. "No concern at all. When shall I give her his message, Comrade?"

"I will send her to you at once."

After Matt left Teng, he stretched out on the bed in his room. He slept at once and so deeply that he did not hear his door open and close, nor did he hear Wang Li-fa turn the thumb latch to lock it.

Li-fa stood beside the bed looking at Matt for a long time. Teng Shan-li had obviously hoped that she would not come here; he had given her Matt's message with great reluctance.

"If I have a talk with him it will be to convince him to leave me alone," she had assured Teng. "But some might misunderstand why I am there. Can I trust you to say nothing to anyone?"

Teng was upset, she could see.

"I will say nothing," he had promised.

If Matt had been awake she would have immediately lectured him, sharply, as she was determined to do. But her intentions eroded as she stood beside him. She could feel how it would be to lie upon his outstretched arm and rest her head on his shoulder. She had never before had the opportunity to look at his body deliberately. She ran her eyes down his frame to his thighs. She held her hand over his right thigh and could feel the warmth of his body; it was impossible for her to resist him. She gently rested her hand on his thigh and felt the curve of his muscle under her hand. She looked at his face and realized that his eyes were open and he was smiling at her. She quickly withdrew her scalded hand and folded it under her left hand in front of her belly.

"Sit beside me, Li," he whispered.

"I don't know why I came here," she breathed. "I should not have come."

"I can't hear you. Sit down. We have to talk."

"I can't. I don't dare. I am so ashamed that I touched you."

"Why? It felt wonderful. We should always touch each other. Sit here." He patted the bed beside his hip.

"I am forbidden to be with you, Matthew—did you know that?" She sat tentatively, lightly, her hands still folded primly on her lap, her eyes searching his face.

"Mr. Teng told me. So why did you come?" He smiled.

"Your message sounded urgent."

"It was. I needed you to come and touch my body like that."

She covered her face with her hands and felt him take her forearms gently and draw her toward him. He still exuded a sleeper's warmth, and she liked the way he smelled. She was in his arms on a bed. She rested the palms of her hands on his chest and pushed him gently. "We have to talk," she whispered.

He kissed her softly, and after a time she pulled her head away from his. "I said talk," she insisted.

"So you talk and I'll listen." He kissed her again and felt her tongue explore his lips. "What was that?" he said softly. "It felt like a little tongue. Is that what you always do with boys?"

"Matthew, what will become of us?" She pushed away from him and lay on her back, her arms crossed in front of her breasts. Her breath came in gasps. She was trying not to cry.

"I think we will run away together and live happily ever after," he said.

"We *can't* run away. *I* can't. Don't you *understand* that? I can't go anywhere. And you can't stay here." She shook her head side to side. "It is hopeless."

"What if I could figure out a way for you to leave?

Would you come with me?'' His arms tightened around her.

"There is no way. They watch me all the time. How can you—"

"I'll be back, either in eight months, when the President comes, or sooner with the technical people. I'll get you out when I come back."

She raised herself onto her left elbow and looked down at his face. "Matt, where could I go? America?"

He nodded.

"I would be very frightened to go there. I think you would be tired of me very soon, and then I would be all alone in a country that is unfriendly to a Chinese woman."

He pulled her down and kissed her eyes. "Don't be afraid, Li-fa. I wouldn't be going through all of this if I weren't sure about us. I'm not going to abandon you. You'll get used to America and you'll love it and everyone there will love you. Believe me."

She struggled out of his arms and sat at the edge of the bed, straightening her hair with her fingers. "I must go, quickly," she whispered urgently. "I am going to tell Comrade Teng that I have told you to leave me alone. Please, please do not say anything to the contrary. Now I will go. You remain here."

Matt sat up, his back against the headboard. "Will you leave with me when I come back? What are you telling me? Yes or no?" He stretched out his hand to her as she stood, but she did not reach for him.

"I'm telling you that it is insane to think I can come with you. I am the Premier's aide." Her whispers grew harsh and rapid and she clenched her fists at her sides. "I am Chinese, a member of the Party, dedicated to my work. My family is here. If I went to America with you— flagrantly, disloyally—what would become of my family?"

"I don't know. Look, you have to decide—for both of us. I love you. But I don't want to ruin your life, Li-fa. If it is impossible, then we won't do it, that's all."

Her hands opened and she flattened them against her thighs. "I love you too, Matthew," she barely whispered.

"But it is impossible and we both know it. We must leave each other alone now. We must be strong and sensible." She went to the door and unlocked it. She looked back at him, tears in her eyes. "Above all, we must be sensible, Matthew," she said.

After she had gone he went into the bathroom and washed his face. As he held her an idea had come to him, and for the first time he felt certain he could smuggle her out of the country. But, he realized as he dried his hands, if he got her out when the technicians left in December, the Chinese might retaliate by cancelling Nixon's visit. Li-fa and Matthew would go down in history as the star-crossed lovers who blew up the Sino-American *rapprochement*. They might become legendary figures in a tragic opera or an Ingmar Bergman movie, but the geopolitical cost would be enormous. Nixon would probably have him thrown into jail!

If he was going to smuggle Li-fa out, obviously she would have to want to go. She was a long way from that frame of mind when she left his room. And he could try it only after Nixon's mission was complete. Then she could be hidden on one of the backup planes or one of the press planes when they left China.

He returned to the bedroom and looked at the bed. He had been surprised when she'd rested her hand on his leg. Li-fa was reticent about physical contact. She must have been impelled by strong feelings to do that. He wondered if she loved him enough to try to escape. She was right to be afraid of a life in America, he admitted. She would be required to make profound changes if she came out with him; she would be giving up nearly everything she had come to value or believe in.

Five minutes later, he returned to the small conference room and sat at the octagonal table, alone. He knew that Teng Shan-li would appear at the doorway within moments. They always seemed to know where he was. For the first time he noticed the sepia photographs of landscapes on the walls of the small room. They were framed in the same blond wood of which the table and chairs were made, and he wondered why he had not seen them before.

"Did you rest well, Matt?" Teng Shan-li asked from the doorway. "Do you feel like answering more questions?"

"Of course, and thank you for delivering my message."

"It is forgotten. May I urge caution and discretion? Young men and women are sometimes impetuous. In a society like China's there is no place for impetuosity. It is most usually the occasion for severe punishment, even in these unsettled times. . . . Now, may I ask again about Japan?"

Forty-six

Matthew Thompson and Henry Kissinger both left Peking on July 11, 1971. Kissinger flew to Paris for a secret meeting with North Vietnamese negotiators. Two days later Richard Nixon received him at the Western White House in San Clemente, California.

Matt flew from Peking to Tokyo on CAAC, the civil air-transport line operated by the People's Republic. He was back in his office in the Executive Office Building the day before Kissinger and his aides arrived in California.

Alexander Haig and most of the rest of the senior members of the National Security Council staff had gone west to welcome Kissinger back from his "inspection trip" around the world. It appeared that Matt's absence had been overlooked or misunderstood by his colleagues. The few who had noticed that he was not there assumed that he was in the large group of staff people who had gone as far as Pakistan with Kissinger. Haig, in San Clemente, was unaware that Thompson had ever been gone.

During the long flight back from Peking to Washington, Matt had thought about Wang Li-fa in spite of his decision not to. He had last seen her in the foyer of the guesthouse when he had said goodbye to Teng Shan-li. Li-fa had come into the hallway behind the foyer and stood against the wall of the narrow passage watching Matt and Teng shake hands. Matt saw her as he turned to leave the house, and he turned back.

"Li-fa," he said insistently.

An 8341 Guard stood inside the front door and another walked between Matt and Li-fa, carrying Matt's suitcase. Teng Shan-li put his hand on Matt's forearm and said, "The cars are waiting. You must go."

Matt took several steps toward Li-fa, shaking off Teng's hand. The young woman turned and ran into the shadows of the hallway. Matt saw her dart into the dining room; he did not see her again.

"It is best," Teng Shan-li said. "You must hurry to catch your flight."

But on Pan American's flight from Tokyo to Washington, Wang Li-fa filled his consciousness; his thoughts of her would not be diverted or denied. He rehearsed her visit to his room, her hand on his leg and the brief time she lay in his arms.

"They are watching me," she had whispered. Was she so suspect now that Chou En-lai would give in to his wife and send Li-fa to a rehabilitation camp? Surely Teng would intervene for her. Perhaps he lacked the clout to save her. Was her escape from China the only way to protect her?

Is it "helping" to uproot a young woman and bring her to America? Perhaps the best life for Li-fa is in China and nowhere else. She has status and important work and she'll marry someone with privileges and live happily ever after. Had he done anything to destroy her prospects? Could she forget him and go on with her life?

It was all so damn impossible. It would be best for both

of them if he cut her loose. He'd try to put her out of his thoughts, he decided. He'd live his life without Li-fa, if he could. But could he? Perhaps, after all, his life lay with Mary Finn; he resolved to find out.

Mary wanted him out of the White House. He'd decided not to leave until after Nixon had been to Peking, hadn't he? In fending off Mary's demands that he quit, he had silently told himself that it was for that reason—Nixon must go to Peking for talks with Chou—that he would refuse to leave . . . yet. Sooner or later he would have to leave, he knew, because of Kissinger and Haig.

He asked Mary Finn to come to his apartment, promising her "an important announcement."

When he had served her a wine spritzer, he confided that Richard Nixon himself would make the announcement.

"Are you serious, Matthew Thompson?" Mary Finn demanded. "You have gotten me here to watch Richard Nixon on television? I got all dressed up for that?"

Matt gestured toward his couch. "I'm told it will be a very short announcement, and then we'll go on and have a drink someplace. You look wonderful, you know. I've got reservations at the Blue Room, and you'll be the best-looking girl in the place."

"Bullshit, Thompson, you're up to something." She sat on the couch and he sat next to her, his arm resting on her shoulders. "What is the reason? Why are we watching your fearless leader?"

"He's going to talk about China, Mary, and it's something I've been working on for a long time."

"It's the reason you won't leave?"

"Let's talk about it when he's done."

Nixon was on all the networks promptly at 10:30 P.M., sitting at a desk in a television studio in Los Angeles. He was tanner than when Matt had last seen him.

"Good evening," Nixon began. "I have requested this

television time to announce a major development in our efforts to build a lasting peace in the world.''

"God, isn't he ugly?" Mary Finn interjected.

Matt had just been thinking that Nixon looked better than he usually did.

"As I have pointed out on a number of occasions over the past three years, there can be no stable and enduring peace without the participation of the People's Republic of China and its eight hundred million people. That is why I have undertaken initiatives in several areas to open the door for more normal relations between our two countries.

"In pursuance of that goal, I sent Dr. Kissinger, my Assistant for National Security Affairs, to Peking during his recent world tour for the purpose of having talks with Premier Chou En-lai.

"The announcement I shall now read is being issued simultaneously in Peking and in the United States:

"Premier Chou En-lai and Dr. Henry Kissinger, President Nixon's Assistant for National Security Affairs, held talks in Peking from July 9 to 11, 1971. Knowing of President Nixon's expressed desire to visit the People's Republic of China, Premier Chou En-lai, on behalf of the Government of the People's Republic of China, has extended an invitation to President Nixon to visit China at an appropriate date before May 1972. President Nixon has accepted the invitation with pleasure.

"The meeting between the leaders of China and the United States is to seek the normalization of relations between the two countries and also to exchange views on questions of concern to the two sides.

"In anticipation of the inevitable speculation which will follow this announcement, I want to put our policy in the clearest possible context.

"Our action in seeking a new relationship with the People's Republic of China will not be at the expense of our old friends. It is not directed against any other nation. We seek friendly relations with all nations. Any nation can be our friend without being any other nation's enemy.

"I have taken this action because of my profound

conviction that all nations will gain from a reduction of tensions and a better relationship between the United States and the People's Republic of China.

"It is in this spirit that I will undertake what I deeply hope will become a journey for peace, peace not just for our generation but for future generations on this earth we share together.

"Thank you and good night."

Mary Finn put down her drink and turned toward Matt. "So you hurt your knee in China, not Alaska, and you've just been there again with Kissinger, right? You're Nixon's China expert and you stitched this whole thing together— that's why you couldn't leave?"

He smiled at her intuition.

"There are still things I can't talk about, Mary, but in general, that's why I wouldn't leave."

"Congratulations, Thompson. It's pretty impressive. I don't blame you; I wouldn't have left either."

"Even if your friend asked you to?"

"Am I your friend?"

He kissed her. "Aren't you?"

"Well, I guess I am at that. Shall we skip the Blue Room and give me a chance to prove it? Richard Nixon's speeches always put me in such a romantic mood."

Forty-seven

• SEPTEMBER, 1971 •

Kang Sheng sat in his office, halfway down the long table, hunched like a spider at the center of its web. At Kang's right the Premier's secretary, Yang Te-chong, sat erect, impassively watching the young physician walk toward them.

"Sit there, across from me, Comrade Doctor," Kang said genially. "It was kind of you to come. Do you know why we wish to talk with you?"

"No, Comrade," answered the tall, bespectacled man. Yang Ding-chun had a deep voice and a robust build. He gave the appearance of vigor and more self-confidence than Kang Sheng usually saw in the people who were summoned to his office.

"It is my duty to oversee investigations for the Politburo and the State Central Committee," Kang Sheng said, "and to report my findings to Premier Chou En-lai through his confidante, Comrade Yang Te-chong here. Now that you are betrothed to Lin Li-heng, it is required that I complete a dossier on Vice Chairman Lin Piao's future son-in-law. As a member of your future wife's family, you will find yourself rubbing shoulders with Chairman Mao himself before long, and it is a routine task for us to learn everything about you, Yang Ding-chun."

The physician nodded. "Before I became one of Minister Lin Piao's medical staff I underwent a similar examination. I will cooperate, of course."

"Thank you," Kang said. He opened a gray file and looked at the top page. "Before we begin, let us have some tea," he said, smiling. In a moment an attendant responded to Kang's signal and brought three large, covered teacups.

"You were born in Henan, I believe?" Kang asked. Yang Te-chong sipped his tea, glancing at the other Yang only when the doctor responded.

"Yes, Comrade. I am twenty-nine years of age, a graduate of the People's Military Medical Academy and a resident of Peking. My father is Yang Ji-da. He was an officer in the People's Liberation Army. My mother died when I was about ten years of age."

"So Yang Ji-da raised you?"

"Yes, sir."

"Who"—Kang squinted at his notes, pointing at the paper—"who is Chen Shou?"

"Which Chen is that?" The young man looked exceedingly uncomfortable, Yang Te-chong thought.

"The Chen who served the Chiang Kai-shek clique loyally. That is the Chen Shou I ask about," Kang said crisply.

"He . . . it is obvious that you know that he was my natural father, Comrade," Yang Ding-chun said in a low voice. "I know nothing about him, honestly; I know nothing except what my revered father—stepfather—has told me."

"Tell us, then, what Yang Ji-da has told you."

"He told me that my natural father was a landlord and KMT soldier. He was an officer in the Nationalist Army. He was also the head of a prefecture and the chief of a police bureau under Chiang Kai-shek's regime."

"So he was," Kang Sheng affirmed, pointing at the page of notes. "Did you confide your father's sordid career to Minister Lin Piao when you became his physician?"

"No, sir. I have never told this fact to anyone. I am deeply ashamed of it. My mother left Chen when I was a baby and I have always considered Yang Ji-da to be my father. He is a courageous and loyal soldier of whom I am very proud."

"Very convenient," Yang Te-chong said sarcastically. "You have a different father for every occasion."

The doctor began to answer, then thought better of it and slumped back into his chair.

"Why have you not openly denounced this Chen Shou to your colleagues, Dr. Yang—or have you done so?" Kang asked briskly.

"No, I have not, Comrade." Yang Ding-chun looked down at his hands, which were interlocked tightly on his lap. "I wished to forget Chen Shou. He has not ever been a part of my life. I hoped to avoid any connection with him; even the connection that would be implied from my renunciation. I hoped no one would ever think of us as in any way connected to each other."

Yang Te-chong put one hand flat on the table and said harshly, "Look up at me, Yang Ding-chun. I am of the opinion that you have deliberately concealed your background, in order to get into the medical academy and so that you would be selected for Minister Lin Piao's medical staff. What you did was base and antisocial. You should be given a military trial by your Army unit. It seems very clear."

The physician clasped his hands together and pressed them against his forehead. "What can I do, Comrades?" he asked. His voice quavered.

"To begin, you can stand up at attention like a man and a soldier!" Kang shouted.

Yang Ding-chun reflexively jumped to his feet and braced his shoulders. His eyes glistened with tears, but he seemed grateful to be treated to a measure of discipline.

"Do you renounce Chen Shou, your father?" Keng said evenly. "Do you now renounce him?"

"Yes, Comrade," Dr. Yang half-shouted. "Chen Shou was an enemy of China and the enemy oppressor of the people."

Kang Sheng turned to Yang Te-chong and said in a half-whisper: "I am favorably impressed with the doctor's contrition, Comrade. I am inclined to try to help him."

Yang Ding-chun looked at Yang Te-chong and a mixture of hope and suspicion briefly flashed across his face. Yang Te-chong shook his head and grimaced sternly.

"Anyone can mouth platitudes of regret," the Premier's secretary said. "This man has exhibited tendencies so harmful to the well-being of the people that I could not consider helping him. His military unit should try him. His betrothed, Lin Li-heng, should be given an opportunity to publicly denounce him, and her father, Marshal Lin Piao, should mete out his punishment. If Premier Chou En-lai asks my advice, that is what I will tell him."

Yang Ding-chun looked at Kang Sheng.

"I suggest you step out into my anteroom, Yang Ding-chun," Kang Sheng said softly. "Comrade Yang and I will discuss your case further. You will be notified."

Yang Ding-chun stood, made a crisp about-face, and left the room. Kang smiled at Yang Te-chong and pushed his desk button for hot tea.

"The Premier wants to see our young physician at two P.M. Do you think we will have him ready by then?" Yang asked.

"Oh, I think so," Kang said, smiling. "I would say that he is ready to help us even now. Do you agree?"

Yang nodded. "Lin's daughter is at the Air Force Academy, where she works. I will have the doctor meet her at once and enlist her. It would be wise to bring her to the Premier at the same time, do you not agree, Comrade?"

"If there is time, yes. Let us call him back now and make the bargain."

Chou En-lai and Kang Sheng stood as Yang Te-chong ushered Lin Li-heng and her fiancé, Dr. Yang, into the private dining room. Chou smiled broadly and said, "Come in, come in. I hope you have not yet had lunch. Please sit here." He gestured his guests to seats at a round table in the center of the large room.

"I am Kang Sheng, Comrade Lin," Kang said to the woman.

"How do you do?" Li-heng said. "It is a great honor to be included at your luncheon table, honored sirs. But I am wondering why we are here. Ding-chun says it is concerning a gift. What gift?"

"The gift of life," Chou En-lai said quietly. "As we eat I will tell you. It concerns your father and mother, I regret to say, and I must call upon you to help me understand what is taking place."

Lin Li-heng nodded. "Ding-chun has told me. He says that we must answer your questions. I do not wish to harm my father, Comrade Premier, but I will tell you the truth because I wish no harm to come to Ding-chun."

"Let me begin," said Chou, "by explaining that I have reason to believe that Lin Piao is in close contact with the Russians. A conspiracy with the Russians at this stage of our Revolution can only be harmful to the people of China. Have you heard of the Joint Fleet, Comrade Lin?''

''Yes, sir,'' the woman replied earnestly. ''My brother is its leader, he told me.''

''Do you understand its objective?''

''Lin Li-kuo told me that if it is successful our family will become world-famous and very powerful. He implied that its purpose is to depose Chairman Mao and install my father as Chairman. As you know, my brother is a boastful fool, but our mother is deeply involved with him in this plot and I have heard them talking about the planning of the Joint Fleet. My mother's ambitions are very plain to see.'' Li-heng looked over at Dr. Yang for support, and he nodded encouragement. ''She hoped to found a new dynasty.''

''What are their plans?'' Kang asked.

''They plan an attack on the Chairman's train while he is in the south,'' she said. ''I don't know any details, but that much was spoken of.''

''Is your father participating in the planning?'' Chou asked casually.

''No, Comrade Premier,'' Li-heng said flatly.

''How is his health? Perhaps you can tell me better, Doctor?''

''He is ill, sir. He suffers from arteriosclerosis, an endocrine infection, and a bone-marrow disease we have been unable to diagnose and treat successfully. In addition, he has an infected urinary tract just now. All considered, he must rest most of the day under medication.''

''How many hours is he able to work?'' Chou asked.

''A maximum of three hours in any period of twenty-four hours, sir.''

''Can Lin Piao be unaware of what his wife and son are doing in his name?'' Kang asked.

''I believe he must know,'' Dr. Yang replied. ''They keep no secrets in that household, as you see.'' He nodded toward his fiancée.

''Let me ask you about Huang Yong-sheng,'' Chou continued.

Dr. Yang shook his head. Lin Li-heng said: ''I have met

him, I believe, at my parents' home. He is a member of the Politburo, isn't he? And he runs the army? He is a friend of my father's. He has come to the house to talk with my brother.''

"Did your brother take Huang in to see your father?"

"I think so."

"Was your mother there too?'

"No. She was angry with my brother then. She had discovered that he had wired her telephone."

"Wired? To hear her conversations? His own mother?"

"Yes."

"And what did he hear?"

"He had others listen. They heard her talking to her confederates. She was plotting against Chairman Mao."

"A plot different from the plan to kill Mao on the train?''

"Yes. The train plan is my brother's."

"What is your mother's plan?"

"I don't know."

"Comrade Premier," Dr. Yang interjected, "I have heard Ye Chun speak to Minister Lin about a Fragrant Hills plan. I do not know what it is; it was never explained in my presence."

"My father has a house at the Fragrant Hills military zone," Li-heng volunteered.

"Several of the State Central Committee do," Chou affirmed. "Chairman Mao does, too. That is also an important military installation."

"Are you telling me, Comrade Lin, that Lin Li-kuo and Ye Chun have separately plotted against Chairman Mao, independently of each other?"

"Yes, sir."

"And your father, the Vice Chairman, knows nothing of either one?"

"To my knowledge, he does not. He is very ill, sir."

"Ill or not," Chou En-lai said levelly, "I suggest to you that he is the mastermind at the center of all this."

"I cannot believe that, sir," Li-heng said quietly. "He is very ill."

"Dr. Yang, is he too ill to spin two webs, as I have guessed?" Chou demanded.

The physician shook his head. "I suppose he could do it all from his bed, if need be. He can muster his strength to do what he wishes. He flies to the beach when he desires to be in that house, for example. He flies back to Peking when he wills it. He has even visited the Russian frontier."

"Recently?" Kang Sheng asked the doctor.

"Five weeks ago. We were able to keep him going on stimulants for four days up there. He toured the fortifications, inspected troops, and even flew over some Russian positions."

Chou rubbed his chin. "Interesting; I didn't know that," he muttered.

"I need not tell you"—Kang nodded toward Li-heng and the doctor—"that a plot against Chairman Mao is a most serious matter. It is a severe crime against the people of China, and it is every person's duty to come forward with knowledge of any such crime. Can you tell me why neither of you informed the authorities of these plots?"

"Comrade, Dr. Yang did not know of them," Li-heng said sharply. "I never told him. And I did not denounce my family because . . . because they are my family. That is all that I can say to you."

"I have decided that you two must go away from Peking now," Chou En-lai said. "You will go to Tientsin and wait in a comfortable house there until I send for you. Comrade Lin, when you arrive there you must telephone your mother to explain that you and Dr. Yang are there to buy furnishings—carpets and things—for your new home. Do not tell her when you expect to return to Peking. Do you understand?"

"Yes, of course, Comrade Premier. We will do as you instruct us."

The doctor nodded his agreement.

"Yang, please take them to the car now. I will talk with Comrade Kang for a time."

Yang Te-chong took the couple away, leaving Chou and

Kang looking at each other across the plates and cups of the lunch.

"What is your impression, Comrade?" Chou asked.

"I believe her. I believe there are plots and her mother and brother are pushing them. I'm not convinced that her father is innocent, however."

Chou nodded. "I must send word to Chairman Mao at once. He must not stay on that accursed train of his."

"Beware of the telephone and telegraph, Comrade. I don't know how you can be certain that your message will arrive safely."

"I will send Yang Te-chong to the Chairman," Chou said forcefully. "He can fly south today. He can deliver my message in person."

"What shall we do with the family Lin?" Kang Sheng asked. "They may be difficult tigers to cage."

"I think," said Chou, smiling, "we must lure them with a bait they cannot resist."

"When?"

"When Mao returns. Nothing should be done until I can talk with him face to face."

"As you wish," Kang Sheng said, pushing his chair back a few inches. "I think we must move quickly to quarantine the Joint Fleet military leaders who are involved."

"I do not know how to neutralize them without warning Lin Piao," Chou said, stubbing out his cigarette. "And in the case of Huang Yong-sheng, the Army chief of staff, and General Wu, commander of the Air Force, we may be better off watching them closely for a few days. Monitor their communications. Trace their movements. Gather the evidence."

"I will do that," Kang nodded.

"About the Lin girl," Chou began, lighting a cigarette, "I would like her held very securely. Someone should interrogate her every day about her father—his living habits; the identity of his secretaries, interpreters, and other aides; how he dresses; where he sits in cars and airplanes; how he communicates with his office and with military units; what he eats and drinks; his expressed opinions of you, me, Chairman Mao, and other members of the Politburo and Central Committee.''

"I think this is a job for Yu Feng. He is both clever and persistent. As he gathers information I will have it sent to you at once.''

"Yes, fine. I would like to have our Vice Chairman and his family taken care of before the Americans come back in about sixty days.''

"We will be prepared to move quickly," Kang Sheng said. He stood, pulled down his tunic, and picked up his notebook.

"Have your men take the couple, Comrade," Chou instructed. "Send Yang Te-chong back up to me. I will write a message to Mao while I am waiting here.''

Yang knocked on the glass dining-room door and walked across the empty expanse to the single table in the center of the room. Chou was seated at the far side, writing on a white pad. Chou looked up at Yang and nodded.

"I have a message for you to take to Chairman Mao at once," Chou said. "I am not sure exactly where his train is today; are you?''

"He is in Hangchow today, Comrade Premier.''

"I have two messages for you to give him, Yang. The first is this letter." Chou handed Yang the writing he had been composing in the dining room. "You are to exercise great caution, Comrade Yang." Chou gestured toward the letter. "Take with you a sufficient force of men to ensure your safe arrival in Hangchow. Perhaps you should fly into Shanghai and helicopter from there.''

"I will be careful, Comrade Premier, you may be sure.''

"Take with you the investigative data I refer to. Especially point out the telephone call where that intelligence officer says, 'Lin Piao is getting impatient for results.' Take the entire package.''

"Yes, sir.''

"Then, when you are with Chairman Mao I want you to say: 'Sir, the Premier says that your life is in great danger.

He asks that you return to Peking at once. Your arrival must be in secret. Use the code I will give you to tell Chou En-lai how and when you will arrive.' ''

"I will remember that, sir."

"Take him the new code Kang Sheng will give you. And tell the leader of his bodyguard that I believe there will be an attack on the train. They should move it out of Hangchow at once."

"Yes, sir."

"I doubt that he would be willing to fly"—Chou smiled—"even to save his life. So they must conceal the movement of his train. Perhaps they can run decoys to draw off the attackers."

"I will suggest that."

"Then you must return here at once. Fly back no later than tomorrow. When you return, please arrange for Lin Li-heng to enjoy the services of our Comrade Wang Li-fa. Send Li-fa to Tientsin tomorrow to supervise the household of Li-heng and her doctor; Li-fa is to send you reports every day. And you must inform the captain of the 8341 Guards that none of them—Li-fa, Li-heng, or the doctor— is to have any other contact. They can talk to you and Kang's interrogator, but no one else."

"I understand."

"Li-fa should be told that she is there to worm out all of Li-heng's secrets. She is to make friends with her and win her confidence. Impress upon Li-fa that this is an assignment of great secrecy and importance. This is why she may contact only you. She will not talk to Teng Shan-li or members of her family; only you."

"I understand, Comrade Premier."

"While you are gone I will rely on Kang Sheng to help me, but I do not want you to be away for long."

"I will return tomorrow; you may be sure of that," Yang Te-chong said with absolute certainty.

At midmorning on September 11, Lin Piao summoned his son, Lin Li-kuo, to his bedroom overlooking Pei Ta Ho

Beach. Li-kuo was surprised to see his father fully dressed and in his cap and greatcoat.

"We will not leave Pei Ta Ho until after lunch, honored father," Li-kuo said gently. "You could rest for another few minutes."

"Rest? Did you know that your target has left Hangchow and is headed for Peking?"

"Yes, sir."

"Do you still think you can blow him up north of Shanghai?"

"I am certain of it, Father."

"Well, I am not," the old man snarled. "I have decided to abandon that plan. You will disband the military units you have assembled down there; let them return to their bases. Tell them it was all an exercise."

"But Father—"

"That is final." Lin Piao teetered forward, then back. His son took his left arm to steady him.

"Take off your coat, please, Father. Sit in this chair."

"Your Joint Fleet is no more," Lin said without expression. "I have decided to disband it. We will act in the Fragrant Hills instead, but I intend that it be a carefully planned and professional operation. Preparation for attack is everything! When we arrive in Peking I want Huang Yong-sheng and Wu and Li and the others to gather at the house at Maojaiwan. You can tell them that the border attack on Russia will begin at dawn September twenty-fifth. That is a firm decision."

"I'll take care of it, Father," Lin Li-kuo said. "Don't you want to take off your cap until it is time to go?"

"No," the Vice Chairman snapped. "I will sit here. You go and carry out my orders."

The door opened and Lin's wife, Ye Chun, announced, "Lunch is ready. Is anyone going to eat?" Lin Li-kuo passed her at the door, shaking his head in dismay.

"I have told him," Lin said to his wife, "that the Joint Fleet is disbanded; the Fragrant Hills plan begins on the twenty-fifth. I hope you are satisfied." The frail old man leaned back in his chair and closed his eyes. His stocky wife walked to him and put her hand on his forehead. With her other hand she gently removed his cap.

"It is time for your medicine," she said. "The nurse will bring it. I will bring you some rice and soup. You must eat."

Lin grunted.

"Li-heng called," Ye Chun continued, unbuttoning her husband's overcoat. "She and Dr. Yang are in Tientsin shopping for furniture. She couldn't find anything she wanted in Peking."

"She had better come home," Lin whispered. "She must be home before the twenty-fifth."

"Of course. She is there for only a few days. How did our son react to the cancellation of his plan? He looked unhappy."

Lin grunted. "He is surly."

"We must give him responsibilities in the other plan to keep him faithful, I think," Ye Chun said. "Lean forward so I can get this coat off."

Lin opened his eyes. "A son is required to be loyal. Why must I buy his loyalty?"

"He is young and impatient. We must make allowances."

"I make no allowances," Lin whispered. "Hurry the lunch, wife. I wish to go to Peking at once."

Lin Piao arrived at his walled house in the Maojaiwan area of Peking surrounded by his co-conspirators: Huang Yong-sheng, the Army chief of staff; Wu Fa-ch'an, the rotund commander of the Air Force; Lin Li-kuo, Lin's son; Ye Chun, his wife; and Li Show-peng, the Navy political commissar. Huang offered the news that Chairman Mao would arrive in Peking at any moment. Li Show-peng disclosed that unknown elements of the State Central Committee had been transmitting and receiving telegraph messages by a new code which was unknown to his cryptographers. As Lin Piao sat silent, absorbing this information, a secretary whispered to Ye Chun that Premier Chou En-lai was calling the Vice Chairman.

"Chou is on the telephone; he wants to talk with you. You had better go into your office," Ye Chun said. She helped Lin out of his chair and supported him, balancing him, as he shuffled into the next room.

"Comrade Vice Chairman," Chou said with animation, "welcome back."

"Thank you," Lin said softly.

"Are you well?"

"Oh, yes. Very vigorous. I worked on my gymnasium bars this morning. I feel wonderful."

"I'm glad to hear that, Comrade. I am calling you with an invitation. I have a message from Chairman Mao this afternoon. He will arrive here sometime tonight. Since it may be late, he suggests no one come to the train to greet him. But he would like you and your wife to come to his house at the Jade Mountain for dinner tomorrow at seven."

"Very well. We will come," Lin said, "but I really should greet him at the train. I always do, you know."

"Comrade, his message is very firm on that point. No one is to be there."

"I see. All right. I have some fine seafood from the beach; I will send that to his house."

"I will look forward to seeing you tomorrow evening, Comrade," Chou said.

"Good night." Lin turned to his wife and put his hand out for support. She eased him into a chair beside the cluttered desk.

"What is it?" she asked with concern.

"Mao will be back tonight. Or, I suspect, he's already secretly back. We are summoned to dinner at Jade Mountain at seven tomorrow."

"Is everything all right?"

"I can't tell, but I fear this may be a trap. I said we will be there, but I am not at all sure it is wise to put our heads into the mouth of the tiger."

"Can we refuse?"

"I can say you are sick."

"He will expect you to come without me. We must say *you* are sick."

"I do not care to admit that. Let us sleep on the question overnight and decide in the morning." Lin closed his eyes and leaned back. "I am very tired. Send the others away; I will meet them again in the morning. Now I must sleep."

The next morning Ye Chun took two large boxes of shellfish to Mao's house in the State Central Committee compound at Chungnanhai, but she did not see the Chairman. Aides told her that Mao was asleep, recovering from his arduous trip.

"That may have been true," the Army chief of staff said when Ye Chun reported the rebuff to her husband and his confederates.

"There were several Red Flag limousines at the back of the house," she added. "I sensed there was a meeting going on somewhere in the Chairman's house. I think that evil old mountain of suet is plotting against my husband. I say we should not go to Jade Mountain tonight."

"I don't see how you can refuse to go without raising his suspicions," the Navy commissar said. "We do not know that he has any information about us, do we?"

Lin Piao raised one frail hand to stop the conversation. "I am convinced of two things," he said. "First, that we must go to Jade Mountain. If there are risks, let us evaluate them and take measures to ensure our safety. Second, we must begin the Fragrant Hills operation at once, tomorrow or within forty-eight hours. How soon can we assault the Russians and provoke their counterattack?"

"Oh, Comrade," the Army chief of staff said, "I cannot put the required troops in place in two days. I must move elements of forty divisions and we must mobilize trucks and railroad trains to make the movement."

"Why not attack with the troops we have up there?" Lin asked. "We need only enough noise, remember, to prevail on old Mao to go into the Fragrant Hills command center."

"If the Russians counterattack they will commit all the manpower they have up there. They'll come all the way to Peking if we don't have forty divisions to hold them,"

Huang explained. "It will take five days to move the necessary units into position."

"Will we be ready to destroy the people in the Fragrant Hills command center in five days?" Lin asked.

The Air Force commander nodded. "Our training can be done by then. The necessary gas is at hand."

"We must dispose of Mao's devoted helpers at once," Lin said. "Is there a list?"

"Yes, Husband," Ye Chun replied. "Your son and I have prepared the list."

"Is Chiang Ch'ing on it?"

"Of course. She is the tiger's mate, eh?"

Lin smiled. "Huang needs the list. In five days, as soon as Mao is deep within the Fragrant Hills, details of soldiers must dispatch the people on the list. I do not want Chou En-lai killed. Arrest him, but don't harm him."

"His watchdog, Yang Te-chong, is on the list, however," Lin Li-kuo said to his father.

"Fine. Chou and his wife may be important in the future government, but the rest of them are not. Now, what can be done to ensure my safety tonight at Jade Mountain?"

"I have been thinking about it, Father," Lin Li-kuo said importantly. "We can provide a signal in a wristwatch. If there is trouble, you can summon help. We will be nearby in a helicopter with a rescue force."

Lin nodded without evident conviction that such measures might help him. "And where might you take me to safety?"

"We could have your airplane standing by at the military airfield. It's not far."

"To fly where?"

"To Russia?" Lin Li-kuo offered.

"No," Lin said in barely more than a whisper. "No, to Hanoi. We will be safe in Hanoi."

"Very well, I'll arrange it," Lin Li-kuo said. "We can land in that courtyard of Mao's house and whisk you away if there is any trouble. The next thing you'll know, you'll be in Hanoi."

"Let us hope it does not come to that," said Wu apprehensively. "Perhaps it is unwise for you to go at all."

"I will go," Lin said flatly.

Mao's summer house at Jade Mountain, deep in the trees on the shoulder of the hill, was a series of interlocking squares built around flowered courtyards. When Lin Piao and Ye Chun arrived, promptly at 7 P.M., they were separated from their security men and the others in their train of automobiles. An 8341 officer directed all the others to a parking lot some fifty feet up the narrow black-topped road, out of sight of Mao's house. Only Lin's car was directed through the entrance gate into the outer courtyard. There the two bodyguards in the front seat of the Red Flag were motioned to wait behind as Lin and his wife were ushered into the house by a smiling chamberlain.

It was an evening of elaborate dining—tiger tendon, sea cucumber, and exotic seafood and fruits—and innocuous conversation. Lin Piao had gone to this small dinner in the hope that he could gauge Mao's mood during the evening. And Lin's confederates needed some information about Mao's future schedule. Yet when Lin raised the question of the Chairman's plans, Mao and Premier Chou En-lai adroitly turned aside the subject and moved the conversation to classical literature, the longevity of Orientals compared with other races, the harvesting of sea cucumbers, and similar banalities. There were no hidden nods or signals; Lin was watching the others closely for covert signs of conspiracy. Either there was no plot against him here or it was already so carefully set that Mao and Chou needed give it no further thought.

The room to which they retired after dinner was hung with brocaded tapestries which Lin had often seen before. They were very old, and one, a hunt scene, took his eye every time he was in this room. It will not be long now, Lin thought, until that weaving will be mine. But I shall not hang it in a room full of lacquered furniture and other tapestries. It shall hang alone, in a gray room, properly lighted. I shall place one chair before it and I shall come there to sit and contemplate China's future. Someone was talking to him, Lin realized, and he looked quickly from Mao and his wife to Chou and his spouse, trying to figure out who it had been.

"We must not tire the Chairman after his long journey, Husband," Ye Chun repeated. "We should make an early departure this evening."

Lin nodded, glancing back at the tapestry as if to say a reluctant farewell. This evening had been a waste of time. Mao seemed to be in a good enough mood, but one could never be certain about Mao. Perhaps it was important, Lin told himself, that no one would tell him about Mao's future schedule; that could be the telltale indication he was looking for.

Ye Chun began to say her goodnights to the other guests. Mao's two attendants materialized to balance him as he shuffled around the room, chatting with each person.

"We must have a long talk very soon," Mao said to Lin Piao. "Do you plan to stay in Peking after the National Day?"

"Yes, Comrade, I shall be here," Lin replied. "I should like a long talk very much. When will you leave again?"

"Not soon," Mao said elliptically.

They left Mao on the stone terrace of the tapestry room, waving his hand almost imperceptibly. Chou and his wife walked with them to the end of the terrace and Chiang Ch'ing saw them to their car at the broad front steps.

"I am so pleased to see the Chairman looking so well," Ye Chun said to Chiang Ch'ing.

"I think travel agrees with him," Mao's wife said. "A safe journey home, dear Comrades."

As Ye Chun and Lin Piao settled into the soft cushions of the back seat, their driver wheeled the limousine around the walled courtyard and rapidly drove through the opening between the tall steel grillwork gates onto the narrow blacktop.

"Where are the others?" Ye Chun asked. "The other cars? My secretary and the Vice Chairman's men?"

"They have gone on ahead," said one of the two men beside the driver. "We will meet them at the bottom of the hill."

"Who is that?" Ye Chun whispered urgently to her husband. "That is not Kim up in the front seat!"

The man turned and they saw that it was Yang Te-chong.

"Please sit still," Yang said.

"What is the meaning of this?" Lin demanded feebly. "Where is Kim?"

"He is waiting for you at the airfield," Yang replied reassuringly.

"Airfield? What airfield?" Ye Chun asked.

"We are going to a nearby airport. You are asked to sit quietly until we get there."

The car went through the military checkpoint at the bottom of the hill and turned onto the two-lane country road. It picked up speed, and Lin noticed military jeeps at every crossroads they came to. The soldiers were keeping all traffic off their road.

Yang Te-chong half-turned in his seat, then turned all the way and knelt on the front seat facing to the rear. The two passengers watched him with a premonition of death. Yang drew his pistol and shot them cleanly in the center of their foreheads, first Lin Piao and then his protesting spouse.

PART
EIGHT

Forty-eight

October 1, 1971

To: Dr. Kissinger
From: Matthew Thompson
Re: China; strange goings-on

As noted in the News Summary, the big
National Day celebration in Peking, scheduled for
today, was cancelled ten days ago. The Chinese
say a gathering of millions of people in
Tien'anmen Square would have offered the
Russians a juicy target.

The CIA says, however, that the Russians have
been quiet for several weeks along their border
with China.

Something else is going on.

All Chinese military commanders have been
alerted to prepare for an ''emergency'' and many
have been summoned to Peking, the CIA reports.

The CIA notes that the entire Chinese hierarchy
disappeared from public view for about a week.
Mao, Chou, Lin Piao and all the others made
no reported appearances in late September.

It is my guess that the internal schism between

Chou's moderates and Lin's conservatives has reached the breaking point and they are slugging it out behind the scenery.

By the time you are due to depart for China again on October 16th, we should have a clearer picture of who has won and lost. If Chou loses, your invitation will probably be withdrawn.

Matthew Thompson

October 4, 1971

From: General Haig
To: Matthew Thompson

You will accompany Dr. Kissinger to Peking October 16–26, 1971.

Please deliver your old passport to me at once for processing. New passports will be issued to all personnel. All required inoculations must be completed by October 10.

You must be at Andrews AFB no later than 4 p.m. October 16. Your baggage limit is 30 pounds. Your aircraft seat assignment is Row 17, Seat A on *Air Force One*.

"Row 17? That doesn't look very important." Mary Finn handed the memorandum back to Matt. "Where does Henry sit?"

"He has the President's private rooms, up front. He even gets a bed."

"How many people are going?"

"Quite a bunch. He's taking some Secret Service and some communications experts along with his staff."

"Why is he taking you?"

"Well, for one thing, I've been working on the joint communiqué Nixon and the Chinese will issue after he's been there. I'm there as a resource to Henry. I probably won't have any contact with the Chinese."

Mary Finn made a face. "That's not very glamorous."

"These things never are. It's small rooms and late

hours and hard work, with a certain amount of window dressing—banquets and toasts and pretty music.''

"And after Nixon has been there next spring, what are you going to do?''

Matt smiled. Mary seldom failed to raise the question of his future plans when they were together, and he had always finessed this until tonight. "Well"—he took her hand—"that's a long time off, but I expect some big changes in my life next year.''

"Double-talk. Be specific. What changes, Mr. Thompson?''

He smiled again, shaking his head. "Oh, a change of employment, perhaps. And big personal life changes.''

"Like what—a courageous move from black shoes to brown?''

"No, I'm serious. It's too soon to talk about it, but when it's time I'll tell you. I'll tell you first.''

"Why not now?''

"I have to go to China first.''

"Very well, but I'm no good at waiting. Go ahead and go, but hurry on back. And I do think little Henry should give you a better seat on the airplane. I think I'll speak to him about it.''

Henry Kissinger had already given his personal attention to the allocation of the seats aboard *Air Force One*. In the annals of diplomatic history only a few episodes—perhaps Marco Polo's journey to China and the opening of Japan by Perry and Alexander the Great's entry into India—rivaled these China trips for color, drama, and geopolitical significance. Kissinger was determined that every detail should be recorded in picture and words, so space must be reserved on the airplane for a photographer and a journalist.

Kissinger had pored over the list of reporters who had covered him in the past, diplomatic specialists who were assigned to write about the State Department, and men who had written books on international relations. One by one he crossed names off the list. This one had written an unfair article about Kissinger; another was too close to

William Rogers and the people at State; several others
were unacceptable to Nixon and his staff.

Near the end of the process Kissinger added a new name
to the list: John Osborne. The old reporter had been
remarkably fair in writing about the disastrous Laos invasion, allocating the blame, perceptively assigning culpabil-
ity in the fiasco, treating Henry Kissinger with a whiff of
deference which hinted at Osborne's hope that the professor might become a regular source of information in the
future. The more Kissinger thought about Osborne, the
more he liked the idea of taking him along. There would
be no other journalist on the trip. He would demand that
Osborne agree to write nothing until after Nixon's trip was
over. That would avoid the unfortunate consequences of
Nixon's jealousy. And still, Osborne's afterview would be
totally credible with the rest of the press who had to stay at
home.

Kissinger wrote a memorandum allocating one seat on
Air Force One to John Osborne of *The New Republic*. He
must, Kissinger wrote, be housed apart from the Kissinger
staff. His presence in China must be a secret from Haldeman
and the rest of Nixon's staff. The Chinese must be informed and must provide for his transportation in Peking,
access to the banquets and other "public" events, and
interviews with Foreign Ministry officials. Kissinger would
personally invite Osborne and brief him on the background
of the negotiations. Every effort must be made to provide
the reporter with the correct names of participants in talks,
ceremonies, and so on. One staff person should have
responsibility for preparing materials for Osborne, perhaps
Matthew Thompson.

Henry Kissinger was welcomed back to China with
spare correctness. An aging and obscure Marshal of the
Armies led a small Chinese delegation at the Peking
airport, but the welcoming speeches were perfunctory.
Upon the utterance of Henry's speechwriter's last formal
phrase, the Kissinger party was hurried into cars and vans

for the drive to the large Fishing Terrace guesthouse that was assigned to the American visitors.

As the motorcade sped across Tien'anmen Square, Matt noted several doubtful omens. All of the usual tourists, Red Guards, and local pedestrians who ordinarily would have been in the Square were missing. Small knots of People's Liberation Army soldiers were posted at intersecting streets and near the buildings that fronted on the Square. Matt noted that the soldiers appeared to be heavily armed. He saw large anti-American posters on several buildings and at a major intersection. They were the kind with big black symbols on a red background. They were not home-made signs put up by some Red Guard faction. OVER-THROW THE AMERICAN IMPERIALISTS AND THEIR RUNNING DOGS, said one. STAMP OUT AMERICAN IMPERIALISM IN ALL ITS FORMS, said a second. Matt read them out loud for the three American technicians he was riding with. Then he realized that their Chinese driver would certainly report his sign reading to his superior after he'd dropped his passengers. Matt wondered if the driver could distinguish one of his passengers from the others.

At the guesthouse compound Matt was told he would share a second-floor bedroom with a Secret Service agent, Ben McDermott. As they unpacked, Matt was surprised to see that McDermott's luggage contained one of the little square Uzi submachine guns and its ammunition clips, along with his shirts and socks. The agent moved the deadly little gun to an attaché case as Matt watched.

"Expecting trouble?" Matt asked.

"Not really, but some of us are here to protect Kissinger and that's one of the tools of the trade. Some of the other boys are here to do advance work, so they have different equipment." McDermott fitted a plastic earpiece into his ear and plugged its cord into a small walkie-talkie which he clipped to his belt. He adjusted its volume and spoke softly into a small microphone clipped to his coat cuff near his left hand.

"I've got to go," McDermott announced. He left, carrying his attaché case.

Matt finished unpacking and organized the files from his briefcase into neat piles on the dresser. His room was on the second floor in the rear wing of the guesthouse, and the window overlooked the good-sized lake that wandered among the villas. As Matt looked out the window, someone tapped softly on the door and a folded note was slid under it. When Matt opened the door there was no one to be seen in the long hallway. Matt closed the door and turned on the ceiling light to read the note.

"Dear Matt," he read,

> Welcome to Peking. Since you were last here there have been events taken from Shakespeare or Greek tragedy: murder, betrayal, plots and counterplots.
> I believe that you, Wang Li-fa, and I may be in some danger. Li-fa is at a place of safety now. I must talk with you. It is very urgent. Do not fail me.
> Please meet me at 4 p.m. tomorrow at the base of the transmitter tower which you can see from the front gate of the Fishing Terrace compound. It is about two miles southeast. Come alone.
>   Teng Shan-li

Matt reread the letter twice, then folded it, tore it into tiny pieces, and flushed it down the toilet in his bathroom. His mind spun. Why should they be in any danger? Were they targets because he had romanced Li-fa and Teng had arranged for them to meet? Danger for whom? How could he arrange to get away to meet Teng alone?

Matt heard voices in the hall; his American companions were heading downstairs for their scheduled ride to the Great Hall of the People for Chou En-lai's welcoming banquet. Matt's mind was wholly engaged with Teng's note as he moved automatically to the bus in front of the guesthouse. So, there had been a battle and murders before National Day. Chou, obviously, had survived. Matt wondered who the losers were. If Chou had survived, why were his people—Teng and Li-fa—in danger?

Chou En-lai gave a virtuoso performance at his reception for the Americans in the Hunan Room of the Great Hall of the People. He welcomed the delegation with a warm speech and mentioned each American from Kissinger to the three secretaries, saying something personal about each one.

"Winston Lord has been here before, of course, and we welcome him back. His wife is a Chinese woman, you know. Therefore we expected him to have a very deep understanding of the Chinese people, and he has not disappointed us. We all learn from our wives, do we not? And Mr. Matthew Thompson has also been to China before, as a very young boy. His father was a teacher in Tientsin and is still remembered there as a good and kind man." Although Chou had a list of the Americans' names before him, it was evident that he was drawing upon his memory for the personal remarks he made about each.

After the banquet that followed the reception, Chou moved to each American in the room, touching glasses and saying a few words of welcome in Chinese. When he came to Matt, smiling, there was no indication that Chou had ever seen him before.

Chou En-lai had taken Henry Kissinger into a sitting room away from the small dining room where their respective staffs were finishing their first "working lunch." They had worked that morning in one of the smaller Fishing Terrace guesthouses, about two hundred yards from the large villa in which the Americans were housed. Lunch had been a pleasant interlude for the eight participants, but during the soup course Yang Te-chong had called Chou En-lai aside for a whispered conversation and Chou had then asked Kissinger to step out.

"There is a matter I must tell you about," Chou began when they were seated in large chairs in the corner of the old-fashioned sitting room. "I had intended to talk with

you about it tomorrow, Dr. Kissinger, but I think this is a
more appropriate time, if you do not mind.''

Kissinger nodded. ''Of course.''

''I feel that our negotiations have shown great progress
this morning. I am confident that President Nixon will
come here soon and that our talks will be most productive.
I want nothing to stand in the way of that result.''

Kissinger pursed his lips and nodded again.

''To that end, I feel I must disclose that a member of
your party is an agent of the People's Republic of China.''

Kissinger's eyebrows shot up. ''An agent?'' he muttered.

''Yes. Your Matthew Thompson has been in our employ
for many months. He has visited Peking several times and
in fact, was here all during your first, secret trip to Peking
last July.''

''Matthew Thompson,'' Kissinger repeated, shaken and
off stride. ''I see. Why . . . why do you tell me this now?''

''As a gesture of good faith. Perhaps someday in the
future your security services might have reported this to
you as ancient history, long after we discontinued our
connection to Matthew. You would then have reason to
question China's sincerity as a friend. I do not want that to
occur. So I tell you now, so that there are no secrets
between us.''

''I see.'' Kissinger nodded slowly. ''I will need some
time to think about this. I am not certain how to deal with
him.''

''That, of course, is entirely up to you.''

''May I ask''—Kissinger leaned forward and entwined
his fingers—''how long you have been . . . ah . . . using
Thompson?''

''Since 1967. About four years.''

''Very farsighted of you, Premier. He was with Nixon
then?''

''Yes, at their law firm.''

''By any chance was the *Foreign Affairs* article on China
and the Far East written in Peking?'' Kissinger smiled.

''Only part of it.'' Chou smiled.

''It would seem that neither Chinese leaders nor Americans will find it in their interest for Matthew Thompson to publish his memoirs, eh?'' Kissinger's smile faded. "Surely you will not want it known that you manipulated Richard Nixon any more than Mr. Nixon will want it known that you did.''

Chou nodded once, conceding Kissinger's point.

''You know, the United States has a wonderful system of justice,'' Kissinger continued. "Everyone says so. But it has some evident disadvantages sometimes. The process is so open to the public that it is impossible to preserve state secrets once a prosecution has begun. If I take him back, the President may be forced to turn him free.''

''Or otherwise dispose of him?'' Chou offered, smiling thinly.

Kissinger quickly decided not to respond to that suggestion. "It may be to our mutual advantage if the young man stays in China,'' Kissinger mused.

''But what could I do with an American citizen?'' Chou opened his hands. "That would present some problems. Let us think about it and talk again. Meanwhile, I will ask that our people keep an eye on him so he does not write his memoirs quite yet.''

''Yes, fine,'' Kissinger said distractedly. He walked across the hall to the dining room and motioned for Winston Lord to come out.

''Where is Matthew Thompson?'' Kissinger asked.

''Standing by at the guesthouse,'' Lord replied. "Do you want him?''

''No. Chou En-lai just told me that he's a Chinese agent and has been for years.''

''My God! Shall I have him picked up?''

''There's a little jurisdictional problem, wouldn't you agree?'' Kissinger asked sarcastically.

''Why did Chou tell you?''

''I don't know. Perhaps he knows we would have found out something and he's hurrying to get credit for being a good fellow. This is a disaster! It is the sort of ruinous event that becomes a lethal weapon in the hands of someone like Bob Haldeman. It may well be the end of me. Why would Chou betray me like this?''

"Perhaps he wants to distract you from the negotiation."

"He's succeeded at that," Kissinger said flatly. "I keep thinking about everything that Thompson knows. Chou has probably been briefed on our entire bargaining strategy. He's been looking down my throat since the beginning. He knows what we're going to do at the United Nations! He knows the color of Nixon's pajamas!"

"Calm down, Henry. I'll have Thompson watched by the Secret Service."

Kissinger laid a hand on Lord's arm. "No, I'm not at all sure I want him. We may want the Chinese to detain him here. Let's let *them* watch him."

Lord shrugged. "Do you want to tell the others?"

"Absolutely not. Don't tell anyone. When we finish up this afternoon I'll give you a message for Nixon. Go out to the airplane and send it on that coded teletype. We'll see what suggestions he comes up with."

Forty-nine

When Matt Thompson came back to his room after lunch, McDermott was asleep in his bed, his face deep in the soft pillow, his right arm draped across his attaché case, which was on the floor between the beds. As Matt stretched out on his bed, McDermott turned onto his side, struggling to rearrange his covers around his bare shoulders. He withdrew his arm from the case, and Matt stared at it. If he was in danger, as Teng Shan-li had said in his note, should he borrow the Uzi for the meeting at the TV tower? He dismissed the idea at once as he thought about aiming such a gun; people had to train for months and years to become marksmen. It was foolish to think of an amateur shooting it out with the Chinese Air Force in the middle of Peking, for God's sake.

Matt dressed warmly. He'd brought thermal underwear and a heavy sweater, L. L. Bean's wool socks, and wool-lined gloves. At 3 P.M. he went down to the foyer of the guesthouse, buttoning his long blue canvas coat with the zip-in down-filled liner. He felt excessively warm, but he knew there was a cold Peking-in-October wind blowing outside. There was no one in the foyer. He walked back into the rear wing and went out a back door near the lake. He could see a soldier patrolling across the long bridge that carried the roadway south across the lake toward the old warlord's house.

As if intending to take a walk for exercise, Matt began to stride briskly south, across the grassy park between the row of guesthouses that followed the lake and those nearer the compound wall to Matt's left, along the eastern margin of the grounds. He passed behind four lakefront villas; to his right in the woods across the road he could see the low gate which guarded the traditionally designed old Chinese villa that had once belonged to a warlord of the nineteenth century. A small lagoon lay between the villa and the roadway. A classic arched bridge led to the gate.

Matt crossed the bridge and turned left into the woods between the villa and the lagoon. He heard a car on the road and crouched behind a large rock. A Chinese jeep carrying six guards approached on the blacktop and stopped at the far end of the arched bridge. Matt could hear their radio, but he couldn't understand the words. Two of the men got out of the jeep and took up sentry positions at the far end of the bridge.

Matt crawled carefully to the corner of the villa and looked back. There was no sign that the guards had seen him. He followed the old house wall back to its rear corner, where someone had haphazardly piled lumber out of sight. At the back of the pile was a homemade workman's stepladder constructed of weathered, dimensioned lumber.

The compound's rear wall was about thirty feet behind the villa. Most of the area was cluttered with discarded building materials and rocks unneeded in the shoreline riprap around the big lake.

The trees and underbrush had turned from green to autumnal yellows and browns, but most had not yet dropped all their leaves. Old leaf-mold piles around the lumber pile and rocks indicated that they had been discarded many seasons before. It would not be long before this autumn's leaves joined to bury the salvage more.

Matt calculated that the weather-beaten ladder would bring him within a few feet of the top of the wall. He awkwardly carried it through the bushes and around tree trunks to a place where the foliage concealed a part of the wall. There he hoisted the crude ladder and rested it on the wall above his head. The first thin rung complained at Matt's weight; he quickly moved up from one rung to another until he could rest his hands on top of the wall. He felt his right glove tear, and he withdrew his hands. He felt the parapet gingerly as he climbed to the top rung. Shards of glass had been embedded in the concrete; there were so many and they were so large that he could not risk rolling his body across the top of the wall. After looking down into the woods on the outside of the wall, Matt descended the ladder and went back to the scrap woodpile. He found a piece of gray concrete-coated plywood about three feet square, which he carried to the base of his ladder. There he took off his overcoat, carried it to the top, and threw it in a ball to the ground on the other side. Then he returned for his plywood, rested it on the top of the wall over the glass spikes, and sat upon it. He pulled the ladder up to the parapet and lowered its end on the outside, rung by rung, then carefully dropped it the remaining distance, so that it rested propped against the outside of the wall. Matt lowered himself to the top rung, pulled the plywood off the wall top, and dropped it near his coat. When he reached the ground he concealed the ladder and plywood in the undergrowth, dusted as much of the concrete dust from his clothes as he could, and put on his overcoat.

It took twenty minutes for him to reach the southwest corner of the Fishing Terrace wall in the thick underbrush. Matt expected to find a sentry post or watchtower at the corner, so he detoured some distance away from the wall to avoid bumping into soldiers there. He lay on his belly behind a fallen tree, where he could see the corner of the wall, but there was no sign of life there. Near the south wall the woods thinned, and he could see cyclists and a few motor vehicles going north and south on the broad avenue that ran by the gates to the Fishing Terrace compound. Knowing he would have to cross that thoroughfare, he angled southeast through the sparse woods to reach it as far south of the compound as was possible.

Before he left the cover of the trees he took from his coat pocket a blue Mao cap he had bought on his first trip to Hong Kong and settled it squarely on his head. It was about the same color as his coat. He put on thick, dark eyeglass frames from which he had forced sunglass lenses before he left his room. He reminded himself to take shorter strides than his Westerner's lope as he reached the street and looked both ways. There was very little traffic. A car—probably a Red Flag—was entering the compound gate five hundred yards to the north. Matt noticed a second gate in the wall closer to him which appeared to be solidly closed. A guard was posted outside it, but he appeared to pay no attention to Matt. Matt walked south to the first intersecting street and then east. Open, plowed fields soon gave way to three- and four-story apartment buildings which appeared quite modern. New trees were planted everywhere. As he walked, he encountered people from the neighborhood, walking, shopping, and tending their children. The pedestrians seemed not to notice him.

The television tower could be seen constantly as he approached it. Matt began alternating directions with each new street, walking a block south, then a block east, until he could see that he was still several blocks too far north. He noticed that the modern apartment development stopped

abruptly two blocks from the base of the tower. The steel
column was composed of crosshatched steel units of open
latticework bolted together, resting on a large one-story
concrete building without windows. The open field around
the building was surrounded by a chain-link fence topped
by barbed wire. A hard-surfaced street ran around the
fenced site. Immediately beyond it and pressing in on the
open area was the remnant of one of Peking's oldest
neighborhoods—low houses behind dingy walls, narrow
and winding lanes, coal smoke, heavily padded children
closely watched by sharp-eyed old women. The scene was
a mélange of browns, grays, and smudged black.

Where was Teng Shan-li? It was five minutes before 4
P.M. as Matt arrived at the pavement bordering the tower,
and he feared that he was as conspicuous as the tall silver
needle which was thrumming in the October wind. He
decided to walk all the way around the tower in the street,
keeping as close as he could to the houses along its
perimeter. If Teng didn't show up by the time he'd gone
around once, he would leave. He felt exposed and naked.

As he traversed the south side of the tower's square, an
old woman sitting on a stone block beside a compound
gate said to him: "You are a tall one, aren't you? Where is
your home? You do not belong in this neighborhood. We
have no ethnics here." He pretended he had not heard her.

Along the east side two elderly men watched him
closely as they smoked impossibly short cigarette stubs.
When he rounded the northeast corner and headed west,
Matt saw Teng Shan-li standing about fifteen feet back in a
small dirt-and-cobbled lane which came into the paved
street just beyond the next house. Teng nodded when he
saw that Matt had seen him, then turned and went deeper
into the lane. Matt followed him. Although midafternoon,
it was dusk between the close-packed houses. The cold
wind carried the odors of the congested life there, uniquely
Chinese, sweet, acrid, repellent, but completely natural.

Teng waited in the doorway of the fifth house, a small
tile-roofed building without windows on the west side of

the lane. Matt bent to enter the low opening, then stood to take Teng's outstretched hand.

"I am so grateful you have come," Teng said. "Do you think you were followed?"

"No. I came over the back wall at Taio Yu Tai."

"Then perhaps we are safe here for a time. This is the home of my brother's father-in-law. Come in."

The house was virtually bare of furniture; the beds and stove were built into the plaster walls. Four stools surrounded an old wood table near the stove. One bare electric bulb lit the room. A curtained doorway led to other space beyond. Matt sensed that someone was behind the curtain.

"Come sit here at the table," Teng said. "I cannot offer tea; I am sorry."

"No matter. What is going on, Mr. Teng?"

"There was a big showdown. Lin Piao and his family are dead and many of his followers are in jail. Chairman Mao has won again."

"But why are you in danger?"

"That is more complicated to explain, but I will try. You and I have become an embarrassment to Premier Chou En-lai, I am told. The Americans have become his friends now. He calls Dr. Kissinger by his first name. They sit by the hour telling each other secrets. Kissinger shows him satellite pictures of the Russians scratching their noses in Moscow and on the northern frontier. So how would it appear if the world discovered that you and I had brought all of this about?"

"Somebody had to do it."

"But history must record that it was done by Premier Chou and his dear friends Henry Kissinger and President Nixon, must it not? How can history say that two nobodies steered these two great powers into each other's arms?"

"Isn't there plenty of glory for everyone?"

"Perhaps, but there is also a sinister aspect to be realized. The Americans may believe that they had been manipulated all this time by a secret agent of the Chinese."

Matt looked at Teng intently. "Meaning who?"

"Meaning you, Matthew."

"Well, that's a crock! You know I've never been a secret agent, don't you, Mr. Teng?"

"But there is much circumstantial evidence, Matthew, which would argue that you have been. You see that, surely?"

"Like what?"

"Like your being recruited by Hung Wai-lang and me, and his payments to you. All our secret messages back and forth. Mr. Emory Latham and his methods. The payment to you of a valuable gem. Your love affair with a Chinese woman. Your disclosure of many White House secrets. Your secret trips to China with false papers. These are many bits of evidence which may be said to add up."

Matt sagged. "Where is Li-fa?"

"In a northern city, quite safe. As long as you don't try to contact her, I don't think she is in danger. But you must leave her alone."

Nodding, Matt said: "All right. So Chou is afraid Henry will find out about us. So what will he do?"

"Betray us, I think. He will imprison me and tell Kissinger about you. That way he appears to be wholly truthful with his American friends."

"What a mess!" Matt said helplessly.

"Yes. You can imagine how such explosive news will give Chou En-lai an advantage in the negotiations with Kissinger. My guess is that Premier Chou will tell him today in order to maximize the advantage. And they will go to my house in the Lane of the Crows to arrest me tonight." Tears welled in Teng's eyes and he pressed his lips together to control his mouth.

"What can we do?" There was a note of desperation in Matt's voice.

"There is very little I can do, I fear. Already the street committee of this miserable place is probably abuzz with news of the two strange men who are in Fong's house. By the way, your hat and glasses had me fooled for a few seconds. But the 8341 Guards are probably looking for you right now, and they will not be fooled. And I cannot hide in Peking; it is hopeless. I have only one idea."

"Yes?"

Teng stood and walked to the nearest bed. From under the quilt he took a package wrapped in white cotton cloth and twine and put it on the table in front of Matt.

"I am not sure how to use this, Matthew," Teng said, "but if properly employed it may be helpful. It is my daily journal."

"A diary?"

"An account of how I have served Chou En-lai from the time he brought me back from the pig farm until yesterday."

"Mr. Teng, how do you know Chou might betray us? Who told you?"

"Li-fa. Just before she went away, she was warned by Yang Te-chong. I believe he also has romantic intentions toward her. He warned her of how she must conduct herself to survive. She deduced that the Premier intended to disclose your role to Kissinger. She urged me to warn you."

"Bless her heart. What does your diary tell?"

"That Chou En-lai has manipulated Nixon from beginning to end. Nothing was left to chance. That China has schemed to seduce the United States for China's own ends. That there has been a carefully devised plan from the beginning and that it has been successfully followed for four years. That at least some of Richard Nixon's political success in 1968 was the result of China's money and intervention."

"My God!"

"I have written all of this in Chinese, of course, and today I have added an authentication in English and Chinese and put my chop on each page of the journal. It is my hope that you can use it to bargain for our safety."

"How in hell do I do that, Mr. Teng?"

Teng bent over his knees and locked the fingers of both his hands together, his arms around his legs. "I don't know, Matthew," he said tightly. "This time they will not merely send me to a pig farm, I fear. They will take my wife and my daughter, too. We will die in separate prisons

and will never see one another again. No grandchildren—
no quiet old years in a garden. Just oblivion.''

Matt put his hand on Teng's shoulder. "Can you hide
here for a while? Until I can try to figure out what to do?"

Teng shook his gray head. "My wife and I must get out
of Peking. We will try to go to Hong Kong. Hua Fan will
meet me near the train station in Tientsin tomorrow night.
I think we can get that far safely by rural buses, traveling
separately. Li-fa is there, and perhaps she will shelter us, if
need be. From there we can go by rail or canal as far as
Shanghai. One can go by boat from Shanghai to Hong
Kong. If we succeed, you can find us. I will tell the U.S.
Consulate in Hong Kong where I am. I will use the name
Hung. I will be Hung Shan.'' Teng was on the verge of
tears.

"That sounds pretty good, Mr. Teng," Matt said, but he
wondered how Teng and his wife could get passage on a
boat to Hong Kong if Chou's men were looking for them.
Surely every port of exit would be watched. "I'll take
your journal," Matt continued, "and maybe I can figure
some way to use it."

"We must leave here very soon. Someone from the
street committee will be coming in to find out who the
strangers are in this house."

"I should be getting back before they miss me," Matt
said. "I'll carry this journal under my belt and inside my
coat. The coat lining is bulky, so I don't think anyone will
notice. We have to be certain that it gets to a safe place."
Matt buttoned his coat and patted his bulging front. His
mind raced. He might smuggle the manuscript back to his
room at the guest compound, but then what? He had to
make a forward pass to someone who was immune from
suspicion. He suddenly smiled broadly and turned back to
look at Teng. "I think I know who can help us," Matt
said. "Do you know where the Minzu Hotel is?"

"Not far. It is beyond Yuetan Park."

"Can we walk there?"

"Of course, but the police are always on watch there. It
is an international hotel."

"There is an American reporter there who came to China with us. He is the only one I can think of who might be able to help us. Will you come with me to see him?"

"Of course, if you believe he is trustworthy." Teng stood slowly and called out toward the curtained doorway in Chinese: "We are going away now. If anyone asks, no one has been here. A thousand thanks for your shelter."

"Go in peace," a woman replied in a cracked voice.

Teng turned left when he came into the rough lane in front of the little house. A stout woman in a black padded coat stood in front of the fourth house, about thirty feet away, watching Teng.

"Come, Doctor," Teng said loudly in Mandarin. "The hospital car is this way."

"I come," Matt said in the same language. "We must hurry to return to the hospital." He stooped to clear the low doorframe and joined Teng in the lane.

Teng Shan-li could barely conceal his amazement at Matt's use of Mandarin. He nodded at the stout old woman and turned quickly to go deeper into the lane. "We must hurry, Doctor," he said loudly.

Teng Shan-li and Matthew Thompson followed the lane for about three hundred yards, dodging children, walking around piles of coal, stacks of baskets, and even a small mountain of cabbages which had been piled against the side of a shed. At last the lane intersected a thoroughfare, and Teng led first right, then left along secondary streets crowded with bicyclists and pedestrians who moved slowly between the small shops and walled houses.

"That's the hotel there." Teng pointed at a tall building that rose ahead of them.

"It looks old," Matt said.

"I think the Russians built it about twenty-five years ago. It is not a fancy place. See the police hut there by the driveway? They will stop me unless they believe my story; but they won't dare stop you, so you keep on going if they detain me. Take off your hat and glasses now."

"Well, let's not risk your getting caught," Matt said, stopping. He stuffed the hat and glasses in his coat pocket.

"Keep walking and let me do the talking. What is the reporter's name?"

"John Osborne."

Teng walked to the police kiosk and spoke to the two policemen in white tunics. "Good afternoon, Comrades. I am Teng Shan-li of the Foreign Ministry. This is a member of the American delegation. He is a guest of the Premier. He is on the staff of Dr. Henry Kissinger from the President of the United States. He is bringing me to meet the American journalist Mr. John Osborne at this hotel. I am to give this Osborne an interview concerning international affairs as a representative of the People's Republic of China. Do you know Mr. Osborne's whereabouts?"

"No, Comrade," one of the police said diffidently, "you must inquire inside. We do not keep track of the foreigners here."

"Very well," Teng said. And in English he said to Matt: "We must inquire at the desk inside for Mr. Osborne. Let us go there now."

Matt nodded, and they strode away from the police toward the main hotel entrance. Matt felt the police staring at his back, but no one called out after them.

The lobby was a barren area, darkly paneled and dimly lit. At the left of the door a pair of jacketed attendants manned a scarred wooden counter backed by plain, painted walls. Several Chinese waited for attention as the two men hunched over a long, handwritten paper looking for a guest's name. Teng went to the end of the counter and yelled, "Where is the American journalist John Osborne? This American official must see him at once."

One of the countermen looked at Teng resentfully. "Many are waiting," he mumbled.

"But this is an American guest of Premier Chou En-lai and he cannot be kept waiting!" Teng shouted. "John Osborne! His room!"

"Four level, room 31." The second man pointed at the list. "Ask the floor attendant if he is in."

"Thank you, Comrades," Teng said loudly. "Come,

sir; we will take the elevator to the fourth level," he said to Matt in English.

Matt looked toward the front door as he followed Teng to the old elevators. One of the white-coated police officers stood in the doorway looking around the lobby. Matt expected him to shout at them to stop, but the elevator door slowly opened and he and Teng boarded the paneled car.

The wooden doors rattled across the opening and Matt pushed the 4 button once more for emphasis. He realized he was perspiring heavily. He unbuttoned the heavy coat, momentarily exposing Teng's package, which was held to Matt's abdomen by his trouser band and his leather belt. Matt hastily rebuttoned the coat.

A young floor attendant stood behind a glass counter in the lobby of the fourth floor. "What room do you seek?" he asked in Chinese.

"We are to see the American journalist, John Osborne, in room 31," Teng said. "Which way is it?"

"Let me see if he is out," the hall porter said, turning to a board of key hooks. "He is one who forgets to leave his key sometimes. Perhaps he is not there."

"Which way?" Teng demanded.

"At the end." The porter waved his left hand. "But perhaps he is not there."

"We will see."

They hurried to the end of the north branch of the long, worn hall, where Matt knocked loudly on the scarred door marked 31. "John Osborne," he called, "it's Matt Thompson. Please let me in."

For a moment Matt heard nothing, and he began to wonder where they might hide. Perhaps there was a stairway or a laundry room where they would be safe until Osborne came back. Osborne might be downstairs eating. Teng could go look for him.

Matt heard a toilet flush, and Osborne's deep voice rumbled beyond the door. Matt knocked again and repeated, "It's Matt Thompson."

The door opened, and Osborne looked at Matt and Teng

with amusement. He coughed and put his fist over his mouth to mask the cough, then gestured them into the room with a sideways tilt of his head. He closed the door and waved them in. As Teng and Matt walked into the bare room Osborne, coughing, poured a glass of water from an aluminum carafe and drank it rapidly.

"Well," the reporter said, "I wasn't expecting company. Who is this?"

"John Osborne, let me introduce Teng Shan-li," Matt said. "Mr. Teng works for Chou En-lai. He is an expert on the United States."

Osborne nodded. "Sit down. I'll sit on this beast of a bed. Your Dr. Kissinger found me a hell of a room!" There were two straight chairs near the window. Matt took off his coat and pulled the cloth-covered package from inside his trousers.

"First, Mr. Osborne, here is a manuscript of enormous importance. I—we—are giving it to you for safekeeping. Please put it in your suitcase or somewhere safe. Then I will tell you about it."

Osborne looked surprised, then smiled. He tapped his cigarette on the nearly full ashtray and took the package to his closet. He opened a black typewriter case and laid the manuscript on top of the portable typewriter, then closed the case. "It's a tight fit, but it should work," Osborne snorted. "What do we have here? What is going on?"

Fifty

• OCTOBER, 1971 •

Matt Thompson approached the brightly lit sentry house at the gate of the Taio Yu Tai guesthouse compound with a heightened sense of fear and anticipation. He could see the two sentries stiffen when they became aware that he was walking toward them. One of them called out: "Officer of the Guard! A foreigner approaches."

A stout officer came out of the guardhouse at the right side of the driveway and peered at Matt, shading his eyes against the floodlight mounted on the pilaster at the far side of the gate opening. The trees along the wall threw long, exaggerated shadows like dark fingers across the roadway.

"Halt!" one of the sentries challenged in Chinese. Matt stopped walking. The guard pointed his rifle at Matt's head and the bayonet gleamed in the lights.

"I am an American," Matt called out in English. "I live here." His voice was not as steady as he had intended. He cleared his throat in case he had to do more talking.

The officer disappeared into the darkened guardhouse and stayed there for about two minutes, until a Chinese jeep drove up from inside the grounds at a high rate of speed. Then he emerged again and pointed at Matt. A radio crackled hollowly from inside the jeep.

A middle-aged civilian, hatless, wearing a long blue padded coat, nimbly climbed from the jeep and waved the sentry's rifle away from Matt. "Mr. Thompson?" he asked loudly. He was someone Matt had never seen before.

"Yes," Matt replied with relief. "I've been out for a walk." He cleared his throat again.

"Come along; we will give you a ride to your guesthouse. We were worried about you." The Chinese man's English was nearly without accent.

Matt climbed into the back of the jeep, where he joined two soldiers. The hatless man got in front, beside the driver, and turned to Matt. "I am Ling," he said. "I am from the Foreign Ministry."

"How do you do?" Matt replied.

"The gate officer had no record of your leaving the grounds and you have been listed as missing," Ling said earnestly. "How did you leave the compound?"

"Through the other gate." Matt pointed south. "It was open."

"Was there no sentry there?"

"Yes, but he was busy with a truck."

"I see. That explains it. Where did you go?"

"A few blocks that way and a few blocks over. I'm not sure where I was."

"At a hotel? Did you enter a hotel east of here?"

"Oh, yes. I thought I might have dinner there, but it was very complicated to buy dinner so I didn't stay."

"I see. Yes, sometimes it is difficult if you are not a guest of the hotel. Do you wish to eat there? I will be happy to arrange it."

"No, thank you. I hope I have not caused you inconvenience."

"Not at all. It was only that we were worried for your well-being."

The jeep pulled up in the porte cochere of Guesthouse 3, and Ling opened the rear door for Matt. "If you hurry you will get dinner in the dining room, Mr. Thompson," Ling said.

Matt went up to his room to shed his heavy coat. Agent McDermott was sitting on his bed cleaning a pistol.

"Well, where have you been?" McDermott greeted him. "The whole Chinese Army has been looking for you."

"I went for a short walk."

"The hell you say."

"I've got to go or I'll miss dinner," Matt said. "I'll be back shortly." He was not eager to have McDermott interrogate him.

The dining room was nearly empty. As Matt ate at a small table, Winston Lord looked into the room, hesitated, then came to Matt's table and sat on the other chair.

"Where the hell have you been, Thompson?" Lord said heavily. "Everyone's been looking for you."

"I went for a walk. What's up? Did Henry want me?"

"Well, he does now. When you're finished with dinner

you're to come to his room. He's in the suite beyond the library. Back that way." Lord pointed to the lake.

Matt knocked on Kissinger's door about 9 P.M. and was admitted by one of Henry's personal bodyguards. A meeting was under way in Kissinger's bedroom; Matt could hear several voices through the door. As he sat in the Doctor's living room under the agent's watchful observation, he heard the voices fade and another door close. The bedroom door opened and Kissinger, tieless, his shirt sleeves rolled up on his wrists, rushed into the living room.

"Thompson, where have you been?" Kissinger demanded loudly. As he entered, the bodyguard opened the hall door and left the room. Matt assumed he would stand sentry outside in the hall.

"I was out for a walk," Matt said quietly. "Were you looking for me?"

"Everyone has been looking for you. I think it is time for some explanations, don't you? What do you think you are doing to me?" Kissinger's hair, usually in neat waves, was disarranged. As Matt watched, the professor ran his fingers through it and scratched his scalp.

"I think I have been helping you to open China," Matt replied. "In fact, I don't think you could have done it without me."

"You call spying on me helping me?" Kissinger roared. "You come here secretly and you tell Chou everything we have prepared and you think that is helping me?" He sat in a chair opposite Matt and rubbed his face with the palm of his hand. "Help like this I don't need," he said softly. "What are you trying to do to me?"

"You think I am some kind of spy or a foreign agent or something? Is that what they have told you?"

Kissinger nodded slowly. "I am told you are paid by China. You have a back channel direct to Chou En-lai that works better than mine does. You come and go freely. You even have a Chinese girlfriend!"

"Most of that is incorrect, Doctor. Chou gave me a gift once. A jewel. They pay my travel expenses. Otherwise, I am not paid. That's all they've ever given me. I've been helping because I felt it was the right thing to do. I have come here twice, at Chou's specific invitation, and I came because, at the time, the two countries needed a push and I thought I could give it. I feel I've been serving the interest of the United States all the time."

Kissinger shook his head slowly. "I don't believe that, and Richard Nixon is not going to believe that. You must be crazy if you think that any American is going to praise you for coming here and giving the Chinese our secrets."

"What secrets? I didn't tell Chou anything he couldn't read in *The Washington Post*, for Christ's sake! I tried to explain our election system to Chou En-lai, and what Richard Nixon's motives were, and why you and Haig bugged my telephone."

Kissinger smiled, but it was obvious that he was embarrassed. "You can thank Richard Nixon for that," he said.

"He told me that *you* were responsible," Matt replied. "One of you is a liar."

Kissinger shrugged. "So what am I to do with a Chinese secret agent on my staff?" he asked. "It occurs to me that I should leave you to the tender mercies of the Chinese."

Matt felt a surge of adrenaline and his face flushed. "No, you're going to take me back to Washington with you," he said evenly. "And you are going to make sure that only good things happen to me. That's the way it's going to be."

Kissinger's eyebrows shot up. "You are hardly in a position to make demands, it seems to me."

"Well, as a matter of fact, I am. It turns out that a man on Chou En-lai's staff, Teng Shan-li, has kept a very detailed diary of this whole episode—including my part in it. I have that diary in a very safe place, and if I am not treated properly Teng's journal will be printed all over the world. You see, I have known for some time that Chou intended to tell you about me. I've known it because he has leaks on his staff too. I'm prepared for it."

"So what does this diary say?" Kissinger posed indifference, but Matt could see he had his undivided attention.

"It says that Chou conceived the reconciliation of China and the United States about five years ago. He has brought it about. He helped Nixon get elected President because Nixon offered Chou the best prospect for *rapprochement*. He manipulated and maneuvered you and Nixon for months. The diary says Chou En-lai thought it up and pulled it off. If Teng's diary is printed in the *Post*, you and Nixon will look like puppets."

"Where is this Teng?"

"I hope he's safe, but you are going to make sure. You are going to arrange safe passage for Teng Shan-li and his wife, Hua Fan. They must leave China, I'm afraid."

"I am going to do that?"

"Indeed you are," Matt said, standing. "And now, I am going to bed."

"Where is the diary?" Kissinger asked. "I should like to see a copy before I do all of these extraordinary things you say I am going to do."

"No. You will never see it unless Teng or I come to some harm. Then you will see it in *The Washington Post*."

"I must take your word?"

"Not at all. Ask Chou En-lai about it. Ask him what Teng Shan-li's diary would contain."

Kissinger nodded. "I will be meeting him shortly. We will talk about it."

"You do that," Matt said. He stood and tried to walk casually toward the door, but his legs were trembling.

Chou En-lai sat where Matt Thompson had been sitting forty minutes before. He had arrived at the guesthouse accompanied by Yang Te-chong and an interpreter.

"I have brought you a draft communiqué," Chou said after he was seated and tea had been served. "I hope we can agree on at least the general approach of the document this evening."

Kissinger cleared his throat several times and turned his

teacup slowly on the low table beside his chair. "Premier Chou, before I call in my assistants to work on the communiqué, I think we should talk again about the Matthew Thompson situation. Can we talk alone?" Kissinger nodded toward the interpreter, who had seated himself on a straight chair behind Chou's left shoulder.

Chou nodded. "Of course." The man stood and left the room.

"I am told that Thompson disappeared for a time and has returned," Chou began.

"He is here and I have just talked to him. He told me of a man named Teng who works for you."

"Yes, Teng Shan-li has been Thompson's principal contact here. He went to school with Thompson's father in Tientsin."

"I see. He has known of your plans and actions toward the United States right from the beginning?"

"Of course."

"Is he loyal to you?"

"He has reason to be. Do you imply that he is not, Henry?"

"Thompson threatened me with a diary kept by your Mr. Teng which is said to betray your confidence. Thompson alleges it would embarrass us all. Do you know of such a document, Premier?"

Chou nervously moved his teacup to the precise center of its table. "I do not know of it," he said, "but let us ask Yang. He would know." Chou walked to the hall door and summoned Yang Te-chong. In rapid Chinese sentences Chou described Teng's diary. Yang said a few words and left the room.

"My secretary, Yang, believes it possible that Teng kept a diary. He will make one or two calls and return with positive information. Did Thompson say where the diary is?"

"No. He claims that it is kept safe by someone who will give it to the American newspapers if he or Teng or his wife are harmed."

Chou smiled broadly. "How American! We are being—ah—*blackmailed*, are we not?"

Kissinger thinly copied the Premier's smile. "I fear that is the correct word for it. Is there someone on your staff who knew you were going to tell me about Thompson? He claims he was warned and had time to secrete the diary."

Chou En-lai lit a fresh cigarette. "Only Yang. But he is totally reliable. I am sure he would tell no one."

"Let me think out loud for a moment," Dr. Kissinger began. "Suppose we were to agree that the People's Republic of China should detain Thompson and this Teng until after the President has been here. Then, as a part of our new understanding, all Americans held in China would be released to return to the United States on the President's airplane, among them Thompson."

"But what about the diary?"

"Perhaps there is no diary. Perhaps, if there is, its custodian will not release it because he can't find out anything definite about what has happened to Thompson. I am proposing that we call the blackmailer's bluff—take the risk. Put Thompson where he can do no harm until after the visit."

"Let us wait to hear from Yang. Then we can more accurately calculate the risk. Did Thompson say where Teng is?"

"In a safe place, he said."

"No matter; Yang will find him. Shall we review the draft communiqué until Yang returns?" Chou handed Henry Kissinger a thick, typewritten sheaf of papers. Kissinger glanced at the top page briefly and put the document on the table in front of him.

"In candor, sir, I would prefer to delay our consideration of your draft until we decide what to do about Thompson. It is a very unsettling circumstance."

Chou stood and took a pack of cigarettes from his jacket pocket. "Is someone looking for the diary in Washington?" he asked casually.

"In Washington?"

"Yes, at Thompson's office or residence? With his friends? His father? His secretary?"

"No, I had not thought—"

"I am, of course, having people look here. Teng's home is being searched by now. His friends and relatives will be interrogated."

"Thompson said Teng had to leave China. Is it possible he has gone already? Perhaps he took the diary."

Chou shook his head. "I doubt that he could leave so easily, but we will find out." He stood and walked to the telephone on Kissinger's desk, where he stubbed out his cigarette. In a moment he was connected to Kang Sheng, with whom he talked for several minutes. During the conversation Yang Te-chong returned. He stood impassively, waiting for Chou En-lai's call to end. Then he spoke rapidly to the Premier for a long time.

Chou turned to Kissinger. "My secretary says Teng was known to keep a daily journal when he worked at the Foreign Ministry. One of my interpreters believes he has been following this practice since coming to work for me. It is likely that Thompson told you the truth. A search for Teng and his journal has begun. Yang does not believe Thompson has had contact with Teng Shan-li, unless they met today when Thompson disappeared. He went to a hotel not far from here, Yang has learned. Perhaps they met there. If so, Teng and his journal are still in China. If they are in China we will find them."

"Good," Kissinger said. "And if the diary is still here, our friend Thompson must remain here, too, until after the President's visit. Can we agree upon that?"

"Of course," the Premier said. "If there is no danger of publication of the Teng journal, Thompson can remain here as our guest and return home with President Nixon after the visit. And, of course, Comrade Teng is China's problem, to be dealt with when we find him. Now, shall we join our colleagues in the library and agree upon a joint communiqué?"

"Of course," said Henry Kissinger. "You have allayed my concerns."

* * *

The young secretary tapped on the library door before entering with the retyped draft revisions. She put them on the table in front of Dr. Kissinger along with a long yellow TWX tear sheet. "This just came in from the plane," she whispered to Kissinger. "It looked important."

Kissinger ignored the continuing discussion of Viet Nam that was going on across the table between Richard Smyser and one of Chou En-lai's advisers. Kissinger took the long cable in both his hands. It read:

129QRAF01139721z1420
TO: DR. KISSINGER
FROM: THE PRESIDENT
CLASSIFICATION: SYLINT/3—EYES ONLY—

MESSAGE RE MATTHEW THOMPSON RECEIVED WITH DISMAY. HAVE UNDERTAKEN COMPLETE REVIEW OF NSC SECURITY PROCEDURES WITH HAIG.

THOMPSON MUST RETURN HERE UNDER ARREST FOR VIGOROUS PROSECUTION. I CAN IMAGINE ALL CONTRARY ARGUMENTS FOR ALTERNATIVES BUT I HAVE CONSIDERED THEM AND MADE A FINAL DECISION. NATIONAL INTEREST REQUIRES HIS ARREST, PROSECUTION, CONVICTION AND SEVERE PUNISHMENT.

SUGGEST HE BE KEPT UNDER GUARD ABOARD YOUR AIRPLANE UNTIL YOUR DEPARTURE. ADVISE ME AT ONCE WHEN YOU HAVE HAD SECRET SERVICE ARREST HIM.

ATTORNEY GENERAL PROCEEDING AT ONCE TO GATHER EVIDENCE FOR PROSECUTION. ALL THOMPSON POSSESSIONS SEIZED, WITNESSES INTERROGATED, ACCOMPLICES SEARCHED OUT.

THOMPSON MATTER IS TOP PRIORITY. GIVE IT YOUR FULL ATTENTION. CASE MUST BE TOP SECRET. ADVISE CHINESE NOTHING MUST LEAK OR FUTURE TRIP IS OFF. REPEAT. TOP SECRET.

INCLUDING JOHN OSBORNE OF NEW REPUBLIC
ON YOUR TRIP NOW A DEMONSTRABLE MISTAKE.
HE MUST HEAR NOTHING OF THOMPSON. DO NOT
ALLOW HIM ACCESS TO YOUR STAFF. DO NOT
LET HIM ON AIRPLANE. HAVE CHINESE SEND HIM
HOME AT ONCE. NO APPEAL ON THIS. ADVISE
ME AT ONCE WHEN HE HAS DEPARTED CHINA.

                                                              RN

Chou En-lai watched Kissinger reread the cable, then asked: "The President?"

Kissinger nodded. "He raises several points I should discuss with you."

Kissinger and Chou En-lai returned to Kissinger's suite. The professor waved the yellow TWX and grimaced. "I must cable him about the diary," Kissinger said. "I am informed, however, that all of Thompson's possessions have been seized. President Nixon urges that the entire Thompson matter be kept very secret by both governments."

"Of course," Chou En-lai said. He lit a cigarette and drew a large ceramic ashtray to the corner of the table in front of his chair, then shifted the dish to a far corner, and finally to the center of the table.

"There is another request," Kissinger continued. "I brought one American journalist with me, an older man named John Osborne."

"Yes, he has been requesting an appointment to see me," Chou said.

"The President is very unhappy that I brought him along and he is now afraid that Osborne might get wind of the Thompson affair. I should have known that the President would be upset when he learned that Osborne was here. Now I am faced with a dilemma. I dare not take him back on my airplane. He might see or hear something. In fact, it will be better if he is simply bundled up and put on the first commercial flight out of here. Is that possible?"

"Very possible. I assure you that if you wish it, he will be on the early flight to Tokyo. It goes in about five hours."

"Perfect," said Kissinger. "I will try to make it up to him when I get back, but we cannot afford to have him nosing about over here."

"I will take care of it now." Chou walked to the telephone and called Kang Sheng. Then he sent for Yang Te-chong, who came to the suite at once. His report was long and detailed.

"Yang says they have not found Teng Shan-li, nor have they found his diary," Chou told Kissinger. "Both Teng and his wife have disappeared. He asks for permission to interrogate Matthew Thompson."

Kissinger looked surprised, then smiled. "Frankly, I had not thought of that alternative. Can it wait until I cable the President and have his reply?"

Chou shrugged and lit another cigarette. "As you like. Tell him that Yang gets very good results. I must go now. Please send for me when you have your instructions. Good night."

Kissinger went to his desk and wrote out a cable for the President:

To the President
From Henry A. Kissinger
Classification Sylint/1
    The Thompson matter is complicated by his claim that he has safely hidden the diary of one of Chou En-lai's aides which would embarrass Chou, you and the rest of us. Thompson demands virtual immunity or he will cause it to be widely published. The author is Teng Shan-li; it covers four or more years, and no one but Thompson knows where it is. Teng has vanished with his wife. Chinese diligently searching for diary here without success.
    Chinese request opportunity to quote interrogate unquote Thompson re whereabouts of Teng, his diary, confederates, other details. Do not believe we can agree to this.

Osborne will be on plane leaving Peking at 7 a.m. local time as *persona non grata* here.

Prosecution of Thompson could be very embarrassing. Example. He will testify you were Chou En-lai's candidate for President and that Chou helped finance your campaign.

Please advise at once re: interrogation of Thompson by Chinese.

HAK

It was 4 A.M. by the time the *Air Force One* radio operator transmitted the message to the White House and another three hours before he received the President's reply:

122WNBT3026z0035

TO DR. KISSINGER
FROM H. R. HALDEMAN
  ATTORNEY GENERAL STRONGLY WARNS
AGAINST CHINESE INTERROGATION. USGOV
CANNOT BE IN POSITION OF CONDONING CHINESE
METHODS OF GETTING ANSWERS. YOU MUST NOT
BE A PARTY TO CHINESE INTERROGATION OF U.S.
CITIZEN.
  URGENT YOU FIND DIARY. EXHORT CHINESE
TO GREATER EFFORTS. EMPLOY SECRET SERVICE
IF NEEDED.
  RECONSIDERING PROSECUTION OF THOMPSON
HERE. DO NOT ARREST HIM UNLESS DIARY
RECOVERED.
  CANNOT STRESS ENOUGH THE NEED FOR
ABSOLUTE SECRECY. WHAT EXPLANATION WAS
GIVEN TO JOHN OSBORNE?

HRH

At 8 A.M. Matt awoke with a start and quickly washed, dressed, and went downstairs to the dining room for breakfast. Across the dining room Winston Lord was breakfasting with General Don Hughes, the President's military aide. Lord looked as if he'd worked all night. Both of the men carefully avoided looking at Matt.

The fried eggs were hard-cooked, but the rice porridge was excellent. Matt realized he had a huge appetite. He larded the cold toast with peach jam and asked for a second cup of the strong coffee. When he'd eaten his fill he returned to his room, where McDermott was still asleep.

Matt was waiting for something, but he wasn't sure what it was. He was worried about Teng Shan-li and Li-fa. The next move was Kissinger's. As long as the manuscript was safe, what could he do?

If Osborne was caught with the diary, or if the Chinese captured Teng, he and Teng were both doomed. He had no doubt that Chou En-lai would order either of them killed without a qualm. And he wondered what Henry Kissinger would do to save a fellow American.

But what about Li-fa? Matt felt a pang of anxiety that made him sit bolt upright, as if the dentist had touched a raw nerve.

"Dr. Kissinger," the Chinese man said, "Comrade Chou En-lai directed me to deliver this envelope to you at once." The man held out a long brown envelope. Kissinger took it, thanked the messenger, and went back into his living room. Richard Smyser and Winston Lord watched him drop into a chair and open the message.

"Henry," Smyser said, "you had better get some sleep."

Kissinger did not hear him. He reread the cable he was holding and handed it Winston Lord. Lord read it out loud.

MATTHEW THOMPSON
USA DELEGATION
GOVERNMENT GUESTHOUSE
PEKING, CHINA
   ARRIVED SAFELY TOKYO EN ROUTE DC. WAS
EXPELLED BY PLAINCLOTHES POLICE AT DAWN.

ASSUME KISSINGER RESPONSIBLE. I INTEND TO
HELP YOU ANY WAY I CAN.

JOHN OSBORNE

"So, he has the diary," Winston Lord said.

"What diary?" Smyser asked.

"Will you leave us, please, Dick?" Kissinger ordered.
"You don't want to know about this."

Smyser looked at his colleagues, shrugged, and stood.
"I'd suggest you both get some sleep," he said.

"Sleep!" Kissinger shouted. "How can I sleep? Time is
running through my fingers and I am spending it dealing
with this Thompson when I should be in serious negotiations with Chou En-lai. We are not getting the communiqué
we should have. Chou is running me back and forth
between his Taiwan demands and this accursed diary,
dropping in here at all hours with new demands, distracting
me with news bulletins like this!" He waved at the cable
Lord was holding. "Do me a favor, Smyser. Don't tell me
to sleep! Don't tell me anything! Just leave me alone to try
to think my way through this! . . . No, there is something I
want you to do right away. Find out if anyone searched
Osborne and his luggage before they kicked him out this
morning. Find out fast and report back to me."

"Okay, Henry," Smyser said. He left the room without
looking back.

"Osborne won't get to the States until tonight," Lord
said. "He can still be intercepted at Customs and the
Agency can take the diary away from him."

"Good." Kissinger pointed at Lord. "Call Helms from
the plane and arrange that."

"I can't phone. I'll have to TWX."

"All right, do that. I'll write a note for Nixon, too.
Hand me that pad."

Kissinger wrote:

To the President
From HAK
    Strongly believe John Osborne may have the

missing diary. Asking Helms to intercept him en route to DC and retrieve it.

Running out of time here due to Thompson distraction. Departure now scheduled tomorrow morning.

Request recommendation for treatment of Thompson. Alternatives are Chinese incarceration, return to DC under arrest or return to DC as he demands.

                                                HAK

At 4:30 P.M. that day, October 25, just before the Chinese handed Henry Kissinger their "final" proposal for a joint communiqué to be issued by Richard Nixon and Chou En-lai at the conclusion of their February, 1972, meeting, Winston Lord returned from the airport with a TWX from the President.

129wwPAFo1139217z0710
TO HENRY KISSINGER
FROM H.R. HALDEMAN
CLASSIFICATION: SYLINT/3
HELMS HAS BEEN ORDERED TO LET JOHN OSBORNE ALONE. THIS ADMINISTRATION DOES NOT SEIZE THE PERSONAL BELONGINGS OF PROMINENT JOURNALISTS UPON THEIR RETURN TO THE UNITED STATES.

OPTION 3 IS APPROVED FOR RETURN OF THOMPSON ON HIS TERMS UNLESS CHINESE GAIN POSSESSION OF DIARY BEFORE YOUR DEPARTURE TOMORROW.

IF OSBORNE HAS DIARY WILL SEEK POSSESSION BY METHODS NOT INVOLVING FRONT PAGE STORY AND ENDLESS EDITORIALS.

                                                HRH

Henry Kissinger and his staff negotiated with Chou En-lai all night long. Finally, at 8:30 A.M. on October 27,

1971, they agreed upon a text. About one hundred days later it would become known as the Shanghai Communiqué.

At 10 P.M., during the crucial meeting, a secretary had handed Richard Smyser a note which he read and passed to Henry Kissinger.

> Mr. Symser:
>   The Premier's secretary advises that Osborne was *not* searched before departure because they were afraid an incident might have been created.
>   They had no reason to believe he possessed any contraband.
>   Agent Thos. Mulkey, USSS

At 4:30 A.M., during a brief break in the negotiations, Kissinger's secretary had handed him another TWX from the White House:

> 210CLXAF01139431z2010
> TO HENRY KISSINGER
> FROM H. R. HALDEMAN
> CLASSIFICATION: SYLINT/3
>   JOHN OSBORNE POSSESSIONS UPON REENTRY DID NOT REPEAT NOT INCLUDE ANY KIND OF DIARY OR JOURNAL.
>   OPTION 3 OBVIOUSLY REMAINS ONLY POSSIBLE ALTERNATIVE. HANDLE THOMPSON AS YOU WOULD THE PRESIDENT'S VERY BEST FRIEND.
>   HRH

At 6:05 A.M. Agent Mulkey woke Matthew Thompson and waited while he shaved and dressed. Mulkey escorted Matt to the living room of Kissinger's suite, where Premier Chou En-lai and Henry Kissinger were waiting for him.

"Come in, Matthew," Chou En-lai said cordially. "We are just having some tea and cakes. Please come and join us."

Kissinger's smile was forced. "Come in, come in," he said.

"Thank you," Matt said. He sat opposite Kissinger, to Chou's right, and picked up the teacup at his place.

"Are you all packed?" Kissinger asked.

"Yes," Matt said.

"You will be interested to know," Kissinger continued, "that your friend John Osborne was detained when he returned to the United States this morning."

"I didn't know he'd gone back," Matt said. "I assumed he'd return on *Air Force One*."

"No, he went twenty-four hours ago. And when the Customs agents went through his luggage they found Mr. Teng's diary."

"Well," said Matt calmly, "I wonder how Osborne got it."

"I believe," Chou En-lai said, "that you and Teng delivered it to him at his hotel."

"And did the Customs agents take it away from him?" Matt asked. "If they did, I'll bet Osborne's protests are in all the papers by now."

"Yes, it is in government custody," Kissinger said solemnly.

"Good," said Matt. "Then you are in a position to read it and realize that you cannot afford to have the original copy delivered to the press, aren't you?" Matt felt his thigh muscle quiver and he forced his body to relax.

"You think Osborne did not have the original?" Kissinger asked.

"Oh, I know he could not have had the original," Matt said confidently. "If Mr. Teng gave him anything, it had to be one of the copies."

"I was not aware there were copies," Chou said to Kissinger.

Kissinger leaned back in his chair. "Matthew, you will be returning on *Air Force One* with me. Only Winston Lord knows anything about the diary. I will trust you to say nothing to anyone about it. You are free to go home when we arrive in Washington."

"Fine. What about Teng Shan-li and his wife?" Matt asked Chou En-lai.

Chou waved his hand vaguely, tracing a pattern with the smoke of the cigarette he held between his thumb and forefinger. "We cannot find them," he said.

"I must have some assurances that they and their family will not be harmed," Matt said.

"Of course," Chou said easily. "You have my word."

"If I do not hear from Teng in a week that they are all safe in Hong Kong, I will release the diary," Matt said.

"They are hiding," Chou urged. "If they stay hidden, a week will not be enough time."

"You can find them. But I'll give you two weeks. Until noon November tenth, Washington time."

"And I suppose you want Wang Li-fa?" Chou asked.

"She wants to remain in China. But you must tell Yang to leave her alone. He's convinced her that you will punish her unless he protects her. I want you to tell her that she is safe without giving in to Yang."

Chou nodded. "So Yang is my 'leak,' as you say. Yang told Comrade Wang and she told Teng and Teng told you. Is that it?"

Matt nodded. "That's it, Premier. And as far as I am concerned, you can do anything to Yang Te-chong that you want to do. I never did like him."

Chou smiled. "You and Yang are rivals, so that is understandable. No, I will not discipline Yang, you may be sure. One's right hand sometimes drops a valuable cup, but one does not cut off his own hand."

"Get your breakfast now and be ready to go," Kissinger said to Matt. "The Premier and I have some last-minute details to discuss. I will see you on the plane."

Matt stood. "Goodbye, Premier Chou. I'm sorry it has ended this way. I suppose you thought you had to tell everyone that I had helped China. I wish you hadn't done it, of course. Now I'm expecting you to protect Teng and his family, and Li-fa. If you do, you'll have no trouble with me. If you don't, I'll be ruthless. I'll tell the whole

world about you. Goodbye." Matt held out his hand to
Chou En-lai, but the Premier did not take it.

Kissinger and Chou En-lai stared at Matt until he withdrew his extended hand and walked to the door. He turned
and looked at them. "I've learned a lot from you two," he
said loudly. "I think it's ironic that one of the great
international developments of the century will have been
accomplished by two people who are totally unworthy of
the respect of the people of China and the United States.
You use people without regard for the value of the individual. To you two, the ends justify any means at all, don't
they?"

"Listen to yourself, young man," Chou En-lai said
harshly, "and think. You have just described yourself! You
may be right about Dr. Kissinger and me, but you must
recognize that in fact you are one of us. We could not have
accomplished this reunion of our nations if you, Matthew
Thompson, were not as ruthless as we are. I congratulate
you on your pragmatism."

Matt fled from the room, slamming the door behind him
as if Chou En-lai had afflicted him with a curse.

As he climbed the stairs to his room he realized he was
forming the words "Not true, not true" over and over. He
forced his mouth to be still.

He had agreed—so long ago, in Hong Kong—to help
Teng Shan-li because he loved the Chinese people. He
loved his own country, too. He had done what he had done
to help them both. How could Chou En-lai say he was
ruthless?

He shouldn't have kept the emerald. That was a mistake. It made him look like a mercenary. But he knew
what his motives had been. He wasn't out to hurt anyone
or get some big reward for himself. He had always
intended to stay out of the limelight and let Nixon take all
the credit. How could they say he was ruthless?

Teng Shan-li and he had tried to make sure that Nixon
and Chou found their way to each other in spite of
Cambodia and C-130s and Laos and supplies to Haiphong

harbor. They had exchanged information, sure, but not precious state secrets.

Now he was a blackmailer and maybe that made him ruthless. But what else could he do? What else?

Fifty-one

• OCTOBER AND NOVEMBER, 1971 •

Henry Kissinger's return to United States territory was less than glorious. No sooner had the wheels of *Air Force One* left the Chinese runway than a steward brought Kissinger a teletype informing him that at that moment the United Nations was voting on preliminary motions to expel Taiwan from its U.N. seat. The United States' strategy had involved a proposed formula for the People's Republic to have a seat on the Security Council while Taiwan kept its membership in the General Assembly. But it appeared that Albania had outmaneuvered the United States and there might never be a vote on that compromise formula.

Richard Nixon took the advice of his Secretary of State and ordered that *Air Force One* delay in Alaska so that Dr. Kissinger, the President's personal envoy to Communist China, would not arrive in Washington just as the U.N. was voting upon the ultimate Taiwan issue.

Kissinger had been the first person off the plane at Elmendorf Air Force Base, near Anchorage. There he had brooded alone in elaborate guest quarters, apart from his aides. Kissinger spent much of the time he was grounded in Alaska talking on the telephone with General Haig about Matthew Thompson.

As Kissinger's aircraft sat on the ramp like a tethered bird and his entourage loafed in a visitors' lounge and lined up at the telephones to call home, Taiwan and the United States were resoundingly defeated in New York by Albania and a cohort of small nations most Americans had never heard of. Taiwan was expelled from the United Nations over American objections by a two-to-one ratio. Some Africans and other Third World delegates did a victory dance in the aisles of the U.N. as the Taiwanese left the chamber.

Matt Thompson and the others aboard *Air Force One* saw nothing of Kissinger during the long flight from Anchorage to Washington. The professor sequestered himself in the President's suite at the front of the airplane; the bodyguards had orders to keep all his people away from him.

In Anchorage, Matt had called Mary Finn. During the following hours in the air he had rehearsed that conversation, wondering what had gone wrong with it. He had been very happy to hear her voice; he was certain of that. But somehow, she had seemed remote, *disengaged* from him. She had talked about her haircut, for God's sake! At twelve dollars a minute, when he'd been off in China for a week fighting for his life, when he still wasn't sure he was safe, she told him all about her new short haircut.

"Your what?" he'd responded with disbelief.

"Haircut. Haircut; I had it all cut off short. I hope you like it. It's awfully short."

"Okay. Sure I will. Will you come and meet me?"

"Yes, darling. Of course. Where and when?"

"Andrews Air Force Base. I'm not sure when; you'll have to ask Angie Cruz to find out and let you know. We are being held here until the U.N. voting is over."

"Why?"

"I'll explain when I get there."

"Are you okay? You sound subdued. Was China hard?"

"Very. I'll tell you about it."

"We're invited to the Burleys' for dinner Saturday. Will you feel like going?"

"I doubt it; can we get out of it?"

"Well, he is my boss. I'd like to do it if you feel up to it."

"Can we decide when I get there?"

"Of course, Matt. I'll call Angie."

Kissinger had made sure that Matt wouldn't infect the National Security Council staff during the flight home. By tradition, *Air Force One*'s compartmentation allowed only one-way traffic, from front to back. The people seated in the rear spaces were not allowed to invade a seating area forward of their assigned compartment. Thus, Kissinger could walk back among any of the six compartments. Those in the area just behind his could visit any to the rear, but they were not allowed free access to the President's rooms where Kissinger lurked alone.

Matt was seated with nine men of the Secret Service detail in the second area from the rear. Behind them was a twelve-seat room normally occupied by the President's press pool. On this trip the communications experts and other technicians had been assigned the pool room. Forward of Matt, in ascending order, Richard Smyser, Winston Lord, and the rest of Kissinger's China team tried to catch up on their lost sleep. Matt could not have walked forward to talk with them without risking expulsion. He had nothing to say to his Secret Service companions, nor did they talk to him, so the long flight to Washington was without conversational distraction.

During the stop in Anchorage, Winston Lord and the other "professionals" shunned him. Their ostracism made him face the fact that his White House career had ended. He wondered if he should resign before Kissinger could fire him. Perhaps his pension rights were affected, he speculated. He'd better get some advice.

He couldn't go back to the old law firm; Nixon and Mitchell would make sure of that. Nor would he want to go to Baker and McKenzie, where Mary practiced.

Would Nixon & Company go after him? Not if the diary was safe, they wouldn't. He wondered if Teng Shan-li had made it safely to Hong Kong. He thought of Wang Li-fa and knew he must get word to her about his demands for her safety. Matt decided to try to write to her via her sister, Nancy Wang, in Canton.

Henry Kissinger deplaned in the dark of the hours before Washington's dawn. At the President's direction, *Air Force One* parked far from the floodlighted VIP ramp where Kissinger was accustomed to chat with reporters when he returned from foreign trips.

His limousine held a passenger, Alexander Haig, who greeted the professor with a set of grim instructions. As they sped toward the White House, Haig described the President's mood with unusual drama.

"Henry, he is boiling over," Haig warned. "The U.N. vote was the last straw, but he has been furious ever since he heard about Matthew Thompson. He blames you for the security lapse, and he keeps talking about cleaning out the whole NSC staff."

Kissinger nodded slowly. "What am I supposed to do about Thompson?"

"He won't say. He keeps saying that Thompson is your problem."

"Very convenient."

"And one other thing: John Osborne. He is more worked up about you taking John Osborne to Peking than any other aspect of the problem. 'Now, I want Osborne out of Peking by the close of business today, and there is no appeal. That is final.' He went on and on about Osborne. 'How could Kissinger choose someone who is not our friend? What was he thinking about?' He wants you embargoed from the press until after the February trip to China. You are to talk to no reporters at all until then."

Kissinger laughed. "At least I must call Osborne to apologize for having him kicked out of the country. Can I get a dispensation to do that?"

"Nixon is as wild as I've ever seen him," Haig warned. "Is there any sign of the Chinese diary?"

"It's not in Thompson's luggage. I had it all ripped apart while we were waiting in Anchorage. John Osborne didn't have it. The Chinaman who wrote it has disappeared. I'm out of ideas. Chou En-lai said he would let me know if they find it, but I am beginning to suspect that it does not really exist. Any word from China?''

Haig shook his head. ''What are you going to recommend to the President?''

''That we let Thompson resign, peacefully. Until we know one way or the other about the diary we must wait and do nothing.''

''Doing nothing is not going to appeal to Richard Nixon this morning,'' Haig said forlornly.

''That is too bad.'' Kissinger shrugged. ''I do not know what else to do.''

''Do you like my hair?'' Mary Finn asked. ''Is it too short?''

''It's short, all right. You look like a boy. But I like it. I'll get used to it.''

''I was afraid of that. Too short, eh? Do you want to drive? This is Carl Clark's Toyota and it has a stick shift.''

''You drive and I'll talk. I have something pretty important to explain to you.''

They had kissed chastely under the wing of *Air Force One* when he'd deplaned. He had found her among the handful of wives who had come out to Andrews at four in the morning to pick up their husbands. Matt had claimed his bag where it lay in the row of luggage beside the airplane, and they'd walked briskly to the little car she pointed to.

''Do you want to go home to your place?'' she asked as she started the engine.

''No. Let's go to your house. I'm not going to work today. Are you?''

''I have to take some depositions, but not until ten. How are you?'' She looked at him and put the palm of her right hand on his near cheek.

''Really beat. I'm glad to be back. You look good to

me." He put his hand on her coated shoulder and squeezed. She drove the car.

"So what's the matter? Jet lag?"

"No. I'm in a big fight with Henry Kissinger, Richard Nixon, and Chou En-lai, and—"

"What the hell do you mean, darling? Those are rough people to have a fight with."

As they drove through Washington toward Mary Finn's Georgetown house, Matt told her about Teng Shan-li and what Chou En-lai had disclosed to Henry Kissinger. He was explaining Teng's diary and what it said as they cruised N Street looking for a place to park. When they turned onto Thirtieth Street, Mary Finn looked into her mirror twice.

"I hate having a car in Georgetown; I want to live here sometime when I can have a double garage and my own Mercedes, but . . . Matt, can you imagine that Henry has bad guys in a black car following us already?"

"Could be. He figures that sometime I'll get the diary and he'll grab it, I suppose. Have they been behind us all the way?"

"I think so. There's a place to park by the church. I get a creepy feeling having those guys behind us."

"Get used to it. Have they searched your house?"

"No! *My* house? Well, not that I know of. I was gone yesterday, all day. I'll fix breakfast and you can tell me the rest." She needed three tries to get the Toyota near the curb. The headlights down the block waited patiently for her to park. As she turned and backed the car Mary grunted: "Were you really a Chinese spy, Matt? Is that true?"

"Hell, no," he said flatly. "I was a go-between to both countries. Wait till I tell you how I was kidnapped by some Chinese. I've busted my ass to get these countries together, and now they are both after me. When I've told you everything, I'll leave it up to you to tell me if I was a spy. God knows I wasn't a spy!"

He decided not to tell her about the emerald; at least, not yet.

It was nearly 8 A.M. when Matt's narrative ended. They
were still at Mary Finn's breakfast table at the back of her
living room, hunched over their coffee cups.

"Okay," Mary said. "I've really restrained myself for
about two hours. I've hardly interrupted at all, have I?
Now, how about some questions?"

"Sure." Matt sensed a defensive tone in his voice. He
would watch that. He didn't intend to be defensive with
Mary.

"Did the Chinese pay you? What did you get out of all
this?"

"Well, Hung paid fees and expenses for my legal
services, of course. After I left the Nixon, Mudge firm,
the Chinese paid my expenses for trips to China."

"No big packages of cash?"

"Absolutely not."

"*Did* you manipulate Nixon?"

"I influenced him to be open-minded about China, sure.
He got a lot of pressure from the other side, too. I drafted
articles and speeches for him that were open to China.
When we got there—to the White House—I sent him
memos explaining what was going on in China."

"How did you know?"

"Well, I went there, and Mr. Teng wrote me often."

"Did you write to Teng?"

"Sure. I was trying to keep communication going both
ways."

"How did you do that? Did you just drop a letter in the
mailbox at the corner?"

"No, it got complicated." Matt told Mary Finn something about Emory Latham and the lockers at the gym and
their method of passing messages.

"That sounds pretty clandestine," Mary said. "Why all
the secrecy?"

"Because Kissinger and Haig bugged my apartment.
That was the reason I would never bring you to my place.
They were listening to everything. I figured if they found

out I was communicating with China, they would fire me. Then I wouldn't be able to accomplish anything."

"Why did they bug you?"

"I don't know. Kissinger told me the other night that Nixon had ordered it. When I told Nixon about it he immediately ordered J. Edgar Hoover to take it off and Nixon said, 'That damn Henry,' implying that Kissinger had done it."

"All of that is about who did it. My question is *why* it was done."

"I don't know; you'd have to ask them."

"What did you send the Chinese?"

"Mostly explanations of why our government was doing what it was doing."

"Secrets?"

"No satellite pictures or aircraft plans. But I suppose some of it was secret in a technical sense. Kissinger's negotiating strategy was in classified documents, I guess. I never sent the documents, but I told Chou En-lai what was in them."

"That's serious, Matt," Mary said solemnly. "I'm sure your motives were the best—the purest—but a judge would look right past them to the technical violations of the law."

"As long as I have the diary, though, they won't dare prosecute."

"Have you actually read this diary?" she asked.

"No. There wasn't time. But Teng told me what was in it as we walked around in Peking. Nixon and Kissinger don't dare to let it get out."

"Where is it now?" Mary asked. She stood and began to gather the dishes and silverware.

Matt opened his mouth to answer, then closed it again. He had promised himself that he would never answer that question. But now the interrogator was Mary Finn, his friend. If he could trust anyone in Washington, it was Mary Finn.

"Do you think," he began, "that there is the remotest possibility that they might have come in here yesterday and planted a listening device in your house, hoping to hear me answer that question?''

Mary put the dishes down and looked around the room slowly. Her eyes widened as she nodded affirmatively. "Shit," she whispered. She walked into the kitchen and returned with a white plastic board on which she had written *Hellman's* and *pintos* the day before. She wiped the shopping list off the board with a paper napkin and used a black grease pencil to write:

LET'S GET OUT OF HERE. I HATE THIS.

He took the pencil and wrote:

OK, BUT THEY'LL FOLLOW. THEY HAVE MIKES THAT CAN HEAR US EVEN IN THE PARK.

She wiped the slate again and took her heavy coat from a peg near the front door. He followed, carrying the slate and pencil.

"Can they hear us in here?" Mary asked as they sat in the little Toyota, letting its engine warm up.

"They've had three hours to work on it," he said. "If they are any good, they can."

"Where can we go?" she asked.

He pulled the slate onto his lap and wrote:

JUST DRIVE. HEAD FOR VIRGINIA.

She pulled away from the curb, looking intently at the rearview mirror. As she turned left on P Street, Matt looked out the back window.

"I don't see anyone," she said.

"Wait."

She turned left on Wisconsin Avenue and started downhill in the heavy morning traffic.

"There," Matt said. "A blue Chevrolet van. It was at the corner. Turn right and go across the bridge, then get on the Parkway. I'll bet that's them."

"But if they can hear us, they'll know we've spotted them."

I DON'T THINK THEY CARE, he wrote.

The blue van stayed a hundred yards behind them as Mary maneuvered through traffic at the Virginia end of Key Bridge. A ramp led them onto the George Washington

Parkway, which was jammed with rush-hour traffic headed toward the District. Only a few cars were going upriver as Mary and Matt were; she increased their speed and moved into the inside lane to pass slower-moving traffic.

In about five minutes Matt said, "Get in the right lane." At a road sign that read NATIONAL HIGHWAY STANDARDS FACILITY, he pointed and said, "Take that ramp, then turn left on the overpass."

"They are right behind us," she said as she wheeled left over the Parkway on the bridge. They drove uphill through dense woods.

"Take the first right," Matt said. He rolled onto his left hip to extract his wallet from his back pocket. At once the trees opened and a broad roadway intersected from the right. As Mary turned they could see a large office building ahead, set back in the woods. She stopped at a gatehouse in obedience to a large STOP sign. Heavy double fences ran into the woods on either side of the gateway.

Matt leaned across Mary to hand the uniformed guard a plastic pass.

"My driver is Mary Finn, F-I-N-N," he told the officer. The policeman put Matt's card on his clipboard and made several entries on the form it held.

"Who are you seeing, Mr. Thompson?" the guard asked.

"The Director," he replied.

"Is Miss Finn going in?"

"No."

"Very well. Thank you." The guard returned Matt's White House pass along with two plastic badges. He touched his cap and waved them toward the buildings.

Mary pulled forward slowly. "The van is still back at the corner," she said. "This is the CIA, isn't it? Are you really going to see the director of this place?"

"Nope. We are going to sit in the parking lot and talk."

"But what about them?" Mary hooked her thumb back over her shoulder.

"They are going to have big problems here. They are way back there because they know their radios won't work in here, inside the fence. Neither will their little bugs transmit. There are wires buried all over this property which transmit jamming signals to keep anyone from overhearing what goes on in the CIA's buildings. As long as we're in here they can't eavesdrop on us.''

Mary pulled into a space in a large parking lot far from the buildings. When she turned off the engine she slumped back into her seat and closed her eyes. "Matt," she said softly, "how long will this go on? I really hate this.''

"They'll follow me until I can deliver a copy of the diary to Kissinger. Once I do that, they'll give up, I think. They will see how damaging the contents are and they will agree to my terms. I'll make them leave us alone.''

"Do you really believe they'll give up?''

"They will have to.''

"Won't they keep trying to find and destroy the original of the diary?''

"Maybe, but I can think of some safe places to put it.''

"Places where a custodian can't be bribed or threatened or even killed? These people are ruthless, Matt. You've got to assume that they will stop at nothing.''

"I know. But what are my alternatives? If they do get all the copies, they'll have me thrown in jail or killed. I've got to hold it over their heads.''

"What becomes of the quality of life, darling? Can you really go on all the rest of your life being followed and bugged and fighting back with blackmail schemes? What kind of existence is that?''

"They will have to quit it. I'll demand it. Or I'll destroy them.''

"Listen to you!" she said shrilly. "Listen to what you are becoming! You sound like someone I don't know.''

"Mary, help me with this. Don't make me out to be some ruthless foreign agent, because that's not what I am.'' He took her hand and held it tightly. She opened her eyes and looked at his face as he continued: "They have driven me into a corner, don't you see? What other chance do I have right now? But it will be over very soon, and then we can get back to normal.''

She shook her head. "Look at me; I'm shaking. I'm looking in the mirror for that blue van. When I go home tonight they'll be listening to me. I've got to take a deposition in forty minutes and here I am in the CIA's magnetic parking lot, hiding out from the cops. Matt, how can I live like this?"

"I guess you can't," he said flatly. After a long silence he said: "Let's go. You need to get to the office. Can you drop me at the Marriott at Key Bridge, where I can get a cab?"

"Where will you go?" she asked. "Where is it safe?"

"I need to go home. I'll clean up and read mail and all of that. I'll be there."

She started the engine and drove toward the gate.

"Before we leave here, will you tell me where the diary is? In case something happens to you?"

A small, clear warning bell sounded somewhere in Matt's consciousness. "If something happens, you'll read the whole thing in the Sunday paper," he said.

"You won't tell me?"

"I won't tell anyone, Mary," he said. "I hope you understand."

"I guess I've got to," she said with annoyance.

At the Marriott Hotel he took his bags from the car and walked around to her window.

"When will I see you?" she asked.

"I don't know. As you say, I don't have much to offer you right now. Maybe it will be when and if I can get out of all of this."

"What about the Burleys' party? We haven't talked about Saturday."

"You don't want me to take you to that. They'll still be following me, I expect. You can't want an evening of evasive action."

"But darling—"

"I'm in a jam and you can't abide it, so that's it. When it's all over, I'll call you. Have your firm send an expert to sweep your house and I'll stay away. They'll leave you alone, I think. Be happy, Mary."

Mary Finn looked at him for a moment, then quickly rolled up her window, put the car in gear, and drove away. Matt looked around to see if anyone was looking at him. The blue van was parked near the entrance to the parking lot. Matt felt embarrassed that they had heard him. He flushed and felt his hands begin to perspire.

As he rode in the taxicab through Georgetown toward his apartment, he reflected on his feeling of embarrassment. Once again he'd better get used to their hearing everything he said and did. They would be all over him until they saw the diary. His apartment, his friends' homes, his office—all would be listened to. They would be waiting until he made his move toward the diary. Then they would take it, and finally they would take him.

Among fourteen letters waiting for him at his apartment was a plain white sheet of paper on which was typed:

> Welcome home. At times like this a fellow needs
> a friend, and I'll help if I can.
> Ralph Waldo Emerson

Emory Latham, Matt told himself. But Latham works for the Chinese. Was there a chance that Em would turn on them and help him? Matt wondered how to contact him and how to test him. He needed a dependable messenger to get the diary and copy it, then secrete the original where they could not find it. Who would help him? Who was there who was not under surveillance?

Matt looked at Latham's note. They have already seen this, he realized with a surge of bile. They have been through my mail, my files, everything in this place. There are microphones here. There may be a camera somewhere, in a vent, in a little hole in the ceiling, behind a mirror, recording everything I do. They are watching me, right this instant.

He crumpled the note and threw it into the wastebasket beside his chair. For a moment he could not stand up. He knew they were watching and he was afraid to move. At last he overcame this transient terror and stood, walked to his bedroom, and began to unpack. It was obvious that they had ransacked his luggage, too. He wondered if they had taken it out of the Toyota to go through it. Carefully, he made piles of laundry and dry cleaning beside the bed, mindful that someone was observing how he did it. He opened a dresser drawer and at once could see that it had been disarranged.

He turned the shower to hot. Perhaps enough steam would obscure their camera lenses. They were making no secret of their surveillance, he told himself, and there could be several reasons for that. Obviously, they were looking for Teng's journal. But they had tossed the contents of his luggage and drawer so openly that perhaps they were also trying to terrorize him. If he let himself be rattled he might become careless. He might say or do something by accident that would lead them to the treasure. He would have to be very, very careful.

He wondered about Mary Finn's question. It was natural for her to ask where the diary was. Right? Could they have suborned her? She used to work for them, of course. Was there some argument—some *blackmail*—that might induce her to turn against him and work for them? Was there something she had done wrong when she worked for the government? Did they still blame her because Ron D'Amico got away with all of that money?

He smiled as he thought of D'Amico going around with his suitcase emptying all those bank accounts. He wondered if his little client was enjoying the money. He turned the shower a little hotter and began to shampoo his hair.

It had been a long time since he'd thought of Ron D'Amico. Matt wondered if he could find him. Maybe, with all of his disguises, D'Amico could be the invisible messenger.

When he had dressed in fresh clothing, Matt retrieved a cardboard box from the top shelf of his hall closet. The masking tape had been torn off and roughly replaced with a different kind of strapping tape. That, he thought, is going to be par for the course from here on. I can't let it bother me. They had read his copy of the D'Amico file and all the others in the box, beyond question. There was a folder with copies of his pleadings in a Swiss-bank-account case. The box also held a copy of a securities registration he'd worked on at Nixon, Mudge. Two folders contained miscellaneous letters he'd written and received. Perhaps a hundred different individuals' names were to be found in the box. Would they track down every one? How would they ever find Ron D'Amico, who had probably changed his name, identity, and birth certificate many times since he'd walked away from Allenwood Federal Prison?

Matt tore the bottom half from the first page of the indictment in the D'Amico file, folded the scrap of paper, and put it in his shirt pocket. When the box was back on the shelf Matt gathered up his laundry and dry cleaning and put on his down parka.

It took him fifteen minutes to walk to the shopping area on Wisconsin Avenue. At One-Hour Martinizing he chatted easily with the countergirl as she made out the claim slips.

"Is Mr. Mustian here today?" Matt asked.

"Back in his goldfish bowl"—the girl gestured—"as usual."

Matt walked behind the counter, past the long racks of hanging clothes, to a bay in which giant machines noisily revolved drums like great washing machines. At one side big commercial dryers rumbled. Across the area nine women operated steam presses which hissed and roared. In the middle of the noise and confusion was a glass cube, fifteen feet on a side, in which the graying proprietor of the place sat at his littered desk, watching Matt approach.

"Come in, Thompson, and close the door!" Mustian roared. "How are things at the White House?"

With the door closed there was virtually no sound from the machinery.

"Amazing how quiet it is in here," Matt said. "I got back from China this morning. I haven't seen the office for nearly ten days. I don't know how things are going there. How are you?"

"Fine. Can't complain. It's triple glass, you know. Special soundproofing. Vacuum in between."

"Mr. Mustian, I need a favor."

"Sure. Did we lose your shirt?"

"No. Nothing like that. I need to use your phone. I'll pay you for the calls. But I'd appreciate it if I could be alone in here and if you would say nothing about it."

"That all? Of course. Government business, I'll bet." Mustian stood and waved Matt to the phone on his desk. "I'll just go on out to lunch," he said. "You can leave the charges with the girl. Don't worry; my lips are sealed." He took his coat from a coat tree in the corner and opened the door. The cacophony of vibration and noise was violent but brief.

Let them try to overhear this with their mikes, Matt thought triumphantly. He punched out the phone number written on the scrap of D'Amico's indictment.

On the second ring a male voice answered by repeating the telephone number.

"My name is Matthew Thompson, and I was given this number by Mr. Ron D'Amico," Matt began.

"Spell it," said the voice.

"R-O-N, D-apostrophe-A-M-I-C-O."

"So?"

"I need help. I will tell you what needs to be done. If you can reach D'Amico and if he can do it, fine. If not, someone else will have to do it. When the job is done someone must call this number—area code 202, 555-4148—and say, 'Teng is safe.'"

"Dung?" the man said quizzically. "D-U-N-G?"

"Right."

"Okay. I'm going to repeat the number and message, and then you tell me what you want done. Then I'll repeat that. Don't hang up until I tell you."

"I'm hanging on," Matt said.

"As I cabled, Mr. President," Kissinger began cautiously, "Chou En-lai has agreed to the February date for your trip. You will be there in just over one hundred days from now.''

"Fine," Nixon said tersely. "What about the communiqué text?''

"We agreed, subject to your approval, that each side will set out its position on the issues that remain, without trying to resolve them. I will leave with you the tentative texts, and we can discuss them after you have had a chance to read them over.''

"Did it take two extra days to settle on a text, or did you need that additional time to have your picture taken at the Great Wall and in the Imperial Palace? You were front page in every paper in the country.'' Venom dripped from his every syllable.

"The extra time was required because of the Thompson problem," Kissinger said. He shifted position on the stiff couch to which Nixon had directed him. Kissinger hated the uncomfortable furniture in Nixon's "hideaway" office in the Executive Office Building. "I decided to postpone the substantive talks while the Chinese verified the existence of the diary and tried to find it. Work was impossible. That's when I took the sight-seeing tours.''

"Well, your press secretary must have been working overtime," Nixon said wryly. "I guess we'll never know how many votes we lost in the U.N. on account of the picture of you on the Great Wall. There you were palling around with the Chinese Communists just when we were all back here fighting to save the Taiwanese. But you have a great image now, eh, Henry? The great statesman! So what are we going to do about Thompson, now?''

"Nothing, now," Kissinger flushed as he replied, doggedly ignoring Nixon's fury. "There is no sign of the diary yet. Thompson says he has it. Chou En-lai says there probably is a diary and it will say they have been manipulating us—successfully—for nearly five years. It can be very dangerous for you if we move against Thompson right now.''

"I am thinking seriously"—Nixon looked at Kissinger

sharply—"of cutting off all contact with the People's Republic of China, right now. They don't deserve our help. They planted a spy, for God's sake, right here in my office! That damn kid has sat right there where you are sitting! Why should I do business with a country like that?"

"We are doing more than helping China, of course," Kissinger said. "We must never forget the Russian side of the equation. Who knows when we may have to play the China card? And we also gain China's elimination from Viet Nam. As I see it, those Great Wall pictures send a message to North Viet Nam which can only be helpful to us in the peace talks with them. I hope you will consider very carefully before derailing your trip to China."

"How can I sit and be friendly with bastards like that?"

"Well, of course, we do spy on them too." Kissinger smiled.

"I don't put spies in Chou En-lai's household," Nixon shot back. "U-2 flights are one thing; a spy in the house is quite another. Thompson has actually been in my bedroom when I was asleep. He could have killed the President!"

"I understand. With your permission I will fire him when he comes in tomorrow. I sent him home today. We will make a routine announcement of his resignation. We already are having him closely watched. Sooner or later he will move toward the diary, and when he does we will seize it."

"If there is a diary."

"Yes. That remains a question, but before long we will know; then we can decide what to do."

"John, did I wake you up?"

"Yes," Osborne coughed. "Who is this?"

"Satterfield. Lester Satterfield. What the hell is this stuff you sent me from Japan? This manuscript in the middle of the cardboard box of dirty shirts and socks?"

"I'm glad you got it, Les. Just put it away for me,

someplace safe, will you? I'll pick it up in a couple of days.''

"How was China?"

"Awful. Terrible hotel and I caught a cold. And I got almost nothing to write about."

"Is this a Chinese manuscript?"

"Right. A fellow hopes it's a book, but I doubt it. I sent it to you for safekeeping."

"Why me?"

"I was in a hurry and I happened to have your address. I hope you don't mind." Osborne was racked with a chain of deep coughs.

"When you sing like that it reminds me to quit smoking," Lester Satterfield said.

"Good idea. Chou En-lai smokes like I do. But he doesn't cough."

"How was Henry in China?"

"As usual. He and Chou got along like a couple of burglars. I think Nixon's going to have an easy time— excuse me." Coughs overtook Osborne's words.

"I'll put this in my safe until you're feeling better, John. You take it easy."

"Thanks, Les. Please say nothing to anyone about that Chinese book. I've promised it will be a secret for a while."

"Dissidents?"

"In a way. I'd hate to get anyone hurt by having its whereabouts known."

"I understand. Nothing will be said. How long were you in Japan?"

"About three hours, between planes. Just long enough to buy that laundry box and get it mailed."

"Sorry I woke you up, John."

"No matter. I'm going back to bed until I shake this damn cold."

"Take your phone off the hook. Get some sleep."

"I'll do that. Thanks, Les."

* * *

Matt had always liked the Columbia Plaza apartment complex. It was near Kennedy Center and the parks along the river, yet handy to the White House. Perhaps if Glenna had not decided to live there, Matt would have, but when they first came to Washington he had thought it a very bad idea for them to live in the same place.

He had been to her apartment many times and it seemed natural to bypass the lobby and go directly to her door. He could see light fanning onto the hall rug as he waited for her to respond to the doorbell. He hadn't seen her for about two weeks. When she opened the door, there was a moment like a stab of static electricity as they looked at each other.

"Hello, Glenna," he said, subdued.

"Well, Matt. This is a surprise."

"Is this a convenient time?"

"For what?"

"Talk; can I come in?"

"I suppose so. I have to go out about eight, but I can talk for a while. How was China?" She swung the door open to let him in.

"It was okay. A lot of work. Have you heard anything about it?"

"No. I didn't go to work today. Sit over there. What's so important?"

"I wanted to warn you that the FBI or someone is surveilling me, and I have reason to think they have planted bugs in the homes of some of my friends."

"Me? You think they are listening to me?"

"Could be. They followed me here tonight; I saw them."

"But why, Matt?"

"It's a long story. Kissinger is doing this to try to find out where a very important Chinese document is."

"You have it?"

"Yes."

"Why won't you give it to him?"

"I will, when it's safe. Many people want to get their hands on it."

"It sounds like a mystery story."

"It is. But how are you? How is your mother?"

"Dad has her in a nursing home, and I'm just sort of waiting for the call to be by her bedside when she dies. Isn't that awful? She isn't very old, you know. She's going to die and she will never see my children or have a good old age . . . there is so much left for her to do that she has never done." Glenna began to cry softly.

Matt walked to her and sat on the arm of her chair. He put his hand on her shoulder and patted it gently. She was wearing a thin silk housecoat through which he felt the warmth and contour of her back and upper arm. Her familiar physicality stirred him; his throat tightened.

"I'm sorry," he said. He cleared his throat. "How's your dad holding up?"

"He is peculiar about this. He is not good at expressing his emotions, you know, but I think he's very afraid of death. He wants to comfort her, but his fear gets in the way. He goes to the nursing home and just sits. He doesn't talk to her or read to her. He just sits there."

"Where is she?"

"It's a place in Manhattan, on Ninety-sixth. It's very nice, but it's full of old people who are dying. It's very depressing."

"Do you go up on weekends?"

"I was there today. I just got back. I'm so sad when I've been there."

He rubbed her arm familiarly. She looked up at him and wiped her eyes with the back of her hand. He gave her his handkerchief.

"Who's your date?" he asked.

"When? Oh, tonight? I don't have a date. I just said that."

"Trying to make me jealous?"

She smiled.

"Do you want to go to Howard Johnson's for a hamburger?"

"Why don't I fix something here? I don't feel like

getting dressed. Dressed up! . . . God, if they are listening I have to be careful how I say things, don't I?''

He laughed. "Maybe if we put on some music they can listen to that instead. Do you have anything new?"

"Not much. There was this fellow who used to bring me records, but he quit coming around.''

"Why did he do that?"

"Well, I didn't handle him very well. I told him he had to make an honest woman of me and he got pissed.''

"He sounds dumb.''

She stood and put her arms around his neck. "When I look at my mom,'' she said, "and realize how short life is, I think I'd better go after what I want on whatever terms I can get. You are who I want to be with, Matt Thompson, and if you don't want to get married, then why don't you just tell me what I have to be to be with you?''

"Wait, Glenna; please listen. I need to talk to someone.'' He reached back and took her arms from his neck. "I think we'd better not touch each other. I'll sit over here and you sit there.''

Glenna pulled her robe around her legs as she sat down again. She was flushed, and a strand of hair had fallen over her right eye. Matt pulled a straight chair close so their feet nearly touched when he sat down.

"I don't know who else to talk to,'' he began, "and I think maybe I have no right to ask you for advice. But I know you care for me enough that you'll tell me exactly what you think.''

Glenna nodded. "Are you in trouble?'' she asked.

"Maybe, but that's not what I want to ask you about. It's about a woman.''

"Your lawyer friend?''

"No, a Chinese woman who lives in Peking. It's complicated. We're attracted to each other, but it makes all kinds of trouble for her to be interested in me. She has a job in the government and they would distrust her and punish her. So she told them that she wanted nothing to do with me.''

"How do you feel about her, Matt?" Glenna asked tentatively.

"I've been asking myself that for weeks. I was convinced that it was impossible. I couldn't be with her in China and she would hate it here, even assuming I could get her out of China safely. So I decided to end it. Not that it really began. But I miss her so much! I just feel like I need to be with her all the time. There are huge problems to be overcome, but—I know that I love her."

Glenna smiled thinly. "What are you going to do about it?"

"I don't know. Maybe she would be better off if I just disappeared from her life."

"Does she love you?"

"I'm sure she does. She tries to deny it, but it shows."

"Will she come to America if you ask her?"

"I don't think they will let her out. And she is scared of living here. All her life she's been told terrible things about the United States."

"So what is the question? What advice do you want?"

Matt stood and walked to the window. He raised his shoulders and dropped them. "I guess the question is: What shall I do? Shall I just try to forget her? Is it fair to her to try to get her out?"

Glenna stood and ran the fingers of both hands through her hair. "Matt, this is a mistake." She shook her head. "I think they call it a conflict of interest, don't they? I'm in love with you. Remember? How can you come here and ask me what to do about some other woman?"

"I said—"

"I don't believe you, Matthew Thompson! You make me furious! Why can't you just do something without analyzing and getting advice and thinking about it and talking until you've squeezed all the real life and love out of it? Why don't you just do what your heart—your instincts, your feelings—are telling you to do?"

Matt turned to the window. He could see the west end of the Lincoln Memorial, softly floodlit.

Glenna wouldn't stop. "Here I tell you I love you and

you ask me what to do about some Chinese woman! How
the hell do I know what to do about her? I don't even
know what to do about me! You are a heartless slob,
Thompson. You have no right to come here and do this to
me!"

"I felt like I needed help . . ."

"So get help from somebody else. I have a mother
dying and I love you. Go get Henry Kissinger to tell you
what to do."

Matt stood. "Listen, Glenna, if I've hurt you I'm very
sorry. I don't want to hurt you. I shouldn't have come
here. I'm very sorry. I just thought you were the one
person who would tell me what was best for me. I guess I
didn't think . . ."

"Your problem is that you think too much," she said.
She had folded her arms to hold the robe around her as if
she were cold.

Matt thought it was oppressively hot in her apartment.
He picked up his coat and walked to the door. "I'm truly
sorry if I've upset you," he said, turning to look at her.
She hadn't moved.

"Go on, leave," she said. "Go somewhere and listen to
your heart."

Fifty-two

• NOVEMBER, 1971 •

"It is obvious that you cannot stay here," Henry
Kissinger said. "I must ask you to be out of your office by
five P.M. today. Turn in your White House pass and other
credentials and do not come back. There is no place here
for a foreign agent. That is all I have to say."

Matt Thompson had expected some such ritual when he'd been summoned to Kissinger's office at 10 A.M. his first day back at work. As he'd anticipated, Al Haig sat in a side chair nodding encouragement as Kissinger delivered his speech.

"I really have no desire to work for you, or even work near you," Matt said. "When the press ask you why I've left, you can just tell them that it turns my stomach to work for you."

"Go on, get out of here," Haig said sharply.

Matt stood. "There's one other thing: I've decided to let you see Teng's journal. I never believed that you captured Osborne's copy. You never did, did you? I'll have a copy sent to you, Henry, so you can estimate the damage it will do to you and Nixon if it is published around the world. It's in Chinese, of course; I hope you can find a translator who will keep your confidence." Matt smiled and took the doorknob in his hand.

"How do we know *you'll* keep it a secret?" Haig demanded.

"You'll just have to trust me, Al," Matt said. "I know that if it is published the Chinese will probably go after poor Mr. Teng, so I won't let it be released unless you force me. If you call off the FBI, or whoever that is following me and tapping me and my friends, and if I stay healthy and happy, you don't have a thing to worry about. I'll have every incentive to be quiet and let you alone." Matt wondered at his own bravado. He pressed his hands against his legs to keep them from shaking.

"When will I receive the copy?" Kissinger asked slowly, his deep voice solemn.

"In a few days, perhaps. It will come when it comes."

"Meanwhile, then, you give me no choice; I must continue to have you watched," Kissinger said. "If there is a chance to recover the manuscript before you make copies of it, we must not miss that opportunity."

Matt laughed. "Henry, you are living in a dream world. I'm not going to tell you how many copies exist, but you can be sure there are several. It's too late for all this tailing, and it is making me unhappy. You people need to keep me happy. I suggest you call the FBI and Helms and end all this surveillance.''

"I must talk with the President," Kissinger said.

"You do that. Be sure to let him read the diary. He probably wonders how he got elected in 1968, and the diary will answer all his questions. Goodbye, Henry. Goodbye, Al. It's been interesting.''

Matt closed the door behind him. The Williamsburg Reproduction antique brass door latch engaged with a satisfying click. Matt nodded to the three secretaries in the outer office and decided to walk out the front door of the West Wing rather than take the basement route back to his office. Through his window Kissinger would be able to see the U.S. Marine pop into a brace and salute as Matt came out the front door.

The telephone rang just as Matt opened the front door of his apartment to leave. He was late for a farewell lunch with Angie Cruz and he decided to let it ring. But some instinct—some imagined nuance in the ringing—caused him to turn back, drop his coat on a chair, and pick up the phone.

The voice was smooth: "I have a message about dung?" the man said, a question in his voice. "Is dung right?''

"Yes," Matt replied, "but be careful. This phone is probably being overheard.''

"Okay. The dung is safe and both loads have been delivered. Do you understand that?''

"Yes. Did you locate my friend? Did he do it?''

"He is fine. He said to tell you he is a very happy man. He handled the big part of the job.''

"Good. Thanks very, very much." Matt meant every word of it.

"You're welcome," the voice said.

Matt picked up his coat and left his apartment smiling. The message meant that the Teng journal had been picked up from John Osborne and one copy had been made. The

original was in the competent and confidential hands of an
attorney in Switzerland who had been recommended to Matt
by Eldon Carnahay. The Swiss lawyer had received instructions for the safe deposit of the manuscript and for its
release to the press under certain circumstances. The single
copy had been left at the White House, addressed to Henry
Kissinger.

The man was telling Matt that D'Amico himself had
delivered the original abroad. With the original locked
away in Switzerland, Matt reflected, Kissinger's chance to
get his hands on it was almost reduced to zero. He smiled
broadly. Now, when Kissinger had his copy translated,
they will call off the surveillance and life can be normal
again.

"Mr. President," Kissinger said, "I came as soon as I
could when I got your call. I was at the Bradens'."

"I'm sorry to pull you out of your fancy party, Henry,
but I've just read that damn Chinaman's diary, and I must
say, it is not as bad as I thought it was going to be. Sit. Go
ahead; sit over there." Nixon waved at a plush chair at one
side of the small Lincoln sitting room on the second floor
of the White House residence.

Kissinger took off his overcoat. He was splendid in a
tailored dinner jacket and black tie.

"It may seem warm in here, with the fire going,"
Nixon continued. "Take off your jacket if you want to."
Nixon sat deep in an easy chair, his feet on a hassock on
which someone had spread a handkerchief. He wore a
deep blue smoking jacket and dark trousers with a knife
crease. "Have you read this whole thing?"

"Yes, Mr. President." Kissinger sat stiffly, on the edge
of the horsehair chair.

"It's long; I've spent all the damn evening reading it.
The fellow's style is rather difficult—or do you think it's
the translation?"

"Perhaps both. The translator is someone I got from the
military language school and I am not sure how competent

he is. But he is discreet and reliable and completely under control, and that was my primary consideration.''

"How many copies of this thing are there?" Nixon riffled the pages of the thick manuscript in his lap.

"We have made only two copies in English, and one of the Chinese copy I received."

"Do we know yet who delivered it to you?"

"The FBI has found the messenger, but the trail is a dead end. Some man paid cash in advance for the delivery."

"Thompson?"

"No. He has been watched around the clock. He didn't go anywhere near the delivery service."

"Has it occurred to you that this whole thing may be a clever forgery?" Nixon asked.

"A forgery? No. I don't understand. By whom? For what purpose?" Kissinger looked bewildered.

"To try to embarrass you and me," Nixon said.

"No, sir. It looks and sounds authentic to me, I must say."

"I wonder if the Agency could authenticate it."

"Do you really want to let the CIA see it?" Kissinger asked.

"Perhaps not. You have to admit that this fellow who wrote it was clever in the way he put you and me in the role of mere pawns of the Chinese. Do you agree?"

"Well, actually—"

"Or do you? Perhaps you feel that he's right. Do you think we were manipulated by the Chinese?"

Kissinger nodded slowly. "Mr. President, the diary is convincing, I have to say. Take his account of the genesis of your *Foreign Affairs* article, for example. This Teng Shan-li quotes the early drafts and traces his own influence on the final text. You would find it difficult to deny Matthew Thompson's part in the drafting, and it seems evident that Thompson was taking his orders from this Teng in Peking."

"Deny it? Of course I will deny it! That damn big woman—what was her name?—she worked on that article with me. Thompson had very little to do with it. The

China section was my own language, as I recall. You're damn right I will deny it!''

"What about the campaign contributions which Mr. Teng documents?''

"Maury Stans was the treasurer of that campaign. I guess you would have to ask him about that. How should I know if someone named O'Reilly gave a million dollars?''

"I was not aware," Kissinger continued, "that the Chinese had substantive contact with Thompson during your De Gaulle talks in Paris. And the account of Thompson being kidnapped and rescued in China lends an authenticity to the document. His knee was injured; everyone here will recall that."

"Oh, I am sure it has been salted with all kinds of provable facts in order to make the rest of it believable. But Henry, you know and I know that we undertook the China opening without any Chinese manipulation. I conceived the idea and you carried it out. That is the central fact."

"The diary makes the contrary case very convincingly," Kissinger said soberly. "Thompson was bombarding us both with arguments for relations with China up at the Pierre Hotel during the transition and when we first got here in the White House. Now we see where his arguments and information came from. This fellow Teng makes the record in the diary that Matthew Thompson was working on us at the very time that you made the decision."

"I see what you are saying," Nixon tapped the pile of papers. "So what do you suggest we do? Are we just going to let him blackmail us with this thing?''

"Yes, sir. I don't see that we have any choice. I suggest that we burn the second copy of the translation and keep only one copy in English and one copy in Chinese."

"Where can we keep them where others won't see them?''

"I have begun a small archive, away from the White House," Kissinger replied. "I could keep them there."

"How could I get access to it?" Nixon asked.

"That would be difficult. Perhaps we should use the vault in the rooms under Aspen Lodge at Camp David?"

Nixon nodded. "That would be better. Leave them with me and I will put them in that vault when I go up to Camp David this weekend. Then what do we do about Thompson?"

"I have fired him. He is out of his office and out on the street."

"Do you think that was wise, Henry? To let him get away from us?"

Kissinger nodded. "Of course, we are having him watched closely. His apartment is under constant surveillance—his telephone and all of that. I still hope that he will lead us to the original Teng Shan-li document. But he is useless to me here and I cannot stand to have him around."

"How did he take it when you fired him?" Nixon lowered his feet to the floor and sat back in the deep chair.

"He is bitter. He does not understand why we do not give him a medal." Kissinger smiled ironically.

"Suppose we offer him a trade? Would he take it?"

"What trade?"

"He gives us all copies of the diary and we give him a nice job. And even a little medal, if that's what he wants. He's a lawyer; we could find him all kinds of good jobs."

"He wants vindication. He wants you to say he acted in the nation's best interest. He might be willing to trade for that."

"We could put on a secret ceremony for him, like they do for CIA agents." Nixon rubbed his nose enthusiastically. "I'll give him the Medal of Freedom and read a citation about his profound contribution to world peace. Put in all that about the Chinese kidnapping him and his escape. Make it very dramatic. But the whole thing has to remain highly classified. Then I give him the medal and he gives us the diary. Will Thompson settle for a trade?"

"I don't know, Mr. President. I can certainly find out."

"You put it to him, Henry. Offer him some damn good job, away from the White House. Make him an Assistant Secretary of State—how's that? Rogers will shit!"

Kissinger smiled. "Not Assistant Secretary for Far Eastern Affairs, I hope."

"Oh, hell, no. Something harmless. Give him the international narcotics problem. Or this Law of the Sea I was reading about."

"I'll talk to Rogers. Perhaps there is something in AID."

"Invite his father to the secret ceremony. Who else—the people from the law office?"

"No, I think it should be very small. Perhaps Rogers and me."

"Of course. Well, you make the deal with him. I'll leave it up to you."

"Very well, Mr. President. I'll try, but I have no confidence that he will accept."

"Why wouldn't he? My God, there are people in this country who would give both nuts for a Medal of Freedom. You would, wouldn't you, Henry?"

Kissinger laughed. "I think that is too expensive, Mr. President. Perhaps I will wait and secure my just reward in heaven."

"You'd better take what you can get on earth, Doctor. I'm not so sure you can count on getting to heaven."

"Well, I am sure we will be together, sir, wherever we are, and I take some consolation in that."

"So we make the bargain and we get the diary and destroy it. Then what?"

"You mean: What becomes of Matt Thompson?"

"We're free to punish him then, aren't we?" Nixon waggled his head deviously.

"I would be surprised if he didn't obtain some ironclad guarantee against retaliation. Perhaps a presidential pardon?"

"Well, don't suggest it to him, Henry. Tell him I want to consider any demands he makes, then we'll see."

"Very well, Mr. President."

"Imagine a pipsqueak like Thompson making demands to the President of the United States, Henry. What a paradox! You and I have sweat blood to make peace between China and the United States, and look at the problems we have! You know, Henry, my father was a tough man. He'd had some hard knocks during the Depression but he always fought back. I can remember him saying to us, 'Boys, sometimes it is going to seem as if bad people come out ahead. But you can have faith that their victories will have short lives. Just keep watching,' he said. 'You'll see their victories turn to dust because that's the way God has built the world. Sooner or later the good will triumph.' And Henry, he was right, you know. Thompson seems to have a whip hand over us right now, but sooner or later the good people will triumph. My dad was wrong about a few things, but he was right about that.''

"Yes, Mr. President," said Henry Kissinger.

Fifty-three

• DECEMBER, 1971 •

The taxicab driver had trouble finding Henry Kissinger's small town house. The address that Kissinger had given Matthew Thompson on the telephone was on Rock Creek Parkway, but it turned out to be in a little cul-de-sac between the Parkway and Massachusetts Avenue. Above the park and hard behind the Japanese Embassy, four narrow brick town houses were perched above a small black-topped parking lot. They were painted white but someone had spent a lot of time scraping off the paint to make them look old. Kissinger lived in the second house. His street number was on his door in metal numerals which had been painted the same dark blue as the door and its trim.

A Secret Service agent greeted Matt at the front door,

then went upstairs, leaving him standing alone looking at
the stairway on the left side of the house. There was no
entry hall; the living room was just inside the front door.
Matt turned and looked around as he took off his coat and
muffler. The narrow room seemed dark and cold. One table
lamp beside a plaid couch provided enough light so the
room could be seen, but it was too dim to read by. The
couch's back was the division between the room and the
small area that served as the entry and the landing for the
narrow stairway.

Matt could hear men talking upstairs. As he looked
around he realized that every level surface in the living
room was covered with books, files, and sheafs of paper.
At the end of the couch a paper carton overflowed with
newspapers and copies of the White House news summary.
All the papers had the appearance of stage props. There
was dust on the books. Everything looked as if it had been
stacked there for a long time. Two modern paintings had
been hung on the back and side walls, but the light was too
dim for anyone to tell what they were. Matt hung his coat
on one of the brass hooks behind the door, beside two
other coats. A damp umbrella rested in the corner.

"Matthew," Kissinger shouted from upstairs, "sit down!
I will come down as soon as I can. I am on the phone." It
seemed odd to encounter Kissinger the bachelor house-
holder in these less-than-elegant surroundings. They were
a shabby contrast to his princely office. Which reflected
the real Henry? Matt mused.

"Fine," Matt answered. He looked for a telephone in
the living room. There wasn't one. He moved a pile of
files and sat in a reclining rocker near the kitchen door at
the back of the room. One other chair, a blue upholstered
wing chair, had no papers or books on it. Matt assumed
Henry would sit there when he came downstairs for their
talk. The professor said he wanted to talk when he had
telephoned Matt the night before. "I won't take much of
your time," he had said, "but I have a rather important
message from the President for you." Kissinger had insisted
that they meet at his home, rather than at the White House.

It was another five minutes before Matt heard him coming down the stairs. Kissinger was in a black tie and dinner jacket, smiling broadly. He held out his hand and pumped Matt's hand enthusiastically.

"As you see, I am on my way out for the evening, but I wanted to see you before you left town on a vacation or something. Do sit down and I will sit here."

"I thought you would," Matt said, looking around.

"I don't use this room much, as you can tell," Kissinger said with amusement. "This house is a place to sleep and change clothes. I never eat here. I wish to convey the President's best wishes."

Matt looked surprised. "Really?"

"Really. He has been thinking about you and has come to the realization that you made a considerable contribution to our new relationship with China."

"You don't say."

"It is true. Our first reaction to Chou En-lai's revelations was extreme, I confess. That was partly my fault, as I am sure you know. I was under great pressure in Peking. I hope you understand. There has been time for reflection and perspective now, and the President would like to arrange some suitable recognition of your unique role in bringing about this significant change in foreign relations. And he would like you to remain in his Administration."

"I'm surprised," Matt said. "Is that the whole message? No strings."

"Strings?" Kissinger repeated. *"Quid pro quo?"*

"Right."

Kissinger smiled. "Yes, of course. Everything has a price, doesn't it? The President would like the Teng diary, of course. The original and all copies."

"Of course," Matt said wryly. "Of course he would. Would he like to give me a pardon in advance and a letter of commendation too?"

Kissinger nodded. "He was thinking of the Medal of Freedom, actually."

Matt made a disbelieving face.

"No, really. And he would agree to some appropriate, blanket protection for you, I feel sure."

"What job?"

"That is open. Do you have something in mind?"

"I've decided to go abroad. I think I'll go to Scandinavia or Switzerland for a few years. Maybe Paris."

"That sounds lovely. I envy you your freedom."

"I figured I'd affiliate with an international law firm. How about a letter of recommendation instead of a government job? As you know, I'm not anxious to work for you people anymore."

Kissinger nodded again. "That is possible."

"Well, we can probably do business, Henry, but there is one other thing I am going to want you to do, as a part of the bargain."

"Yes?"

"I know that Teng Shan-li and his wife are in Hong Kong. I hope they are safe there. But Wang Li-fa is still in China."

"Wang Li-fa is who?"

"She is—or was—Chou En-lai's interpreter. He had her moved to Tientsin about four months ago."

"Yes, now I remember who she is."

"I want her delivered safely to this country or, better yet, to Europe. When she steps off the airplane in a city I'll designate, I'll hand your man everything you want. Right on the spot."

"Let's see if I understand. You get a pardon, a secret medal and commendation, and the Chinese woman. We get the diary in all its forms—all copies. Is that our bargain?"

"And recommendations to European law firms."

"Of course. You realize how difficult it may be to get the woman—Miss Wang?—out of China?"

"It must be done with Chou's blessing, of course. There can be no reprisals against her family."

"This may take time to arrange. Perhaps I will have to send Haig or someone to talk with Chou. The Premier is not going to like it."

"He may. It will save him the trouble of killing her."

Kissinger looked surprised. "Is she under a death sentence?"

"As far as Chou is concerned, I'm sure we all are. Once I turn over the diary, he'll destroy Teng and Li-fa and me too, if he can."

Kissinger held up one hand in protest. "Oh, I don't think Chou—"

"Don't kid me, Henry. You know that's true. So let's get her out of China and I'll figure out some way to keep her safe."

"Does she know about this?" Kissinger asked.

"No one does. We're just making it up here and now. I'll write a letter to her for Chou to give her. I can explain what is going on."

"It is nearly Christmas. I will need until the middle of January to put all this together," Kissinger said. "And it is all subject to the President's approval, of course."

"Call me tomorrow if he disapproves. Otherwise, I'll assume you have his okay and I'll begin to make my arrangements."

"Very well," Dr. Kissinger said. "Can I drop you anywhere? I am going to Kay Graham's Christmas party in Georgetown."

Matt wrote his letter to Wang Li-fa seven different times. At last he hurried a more or less final version to Kissinger so that it could be sent to Chou En-lai along with letters from Nixon and Kissinger in a diplomatic pouch which left Washington on December 27th.

"Dear Li-fa," Matt's letter read:

> I am sure you will be confused and worried
> because of the way this letter comes to you. The
> Premier will hand it to you as part of an
> agreement he, President Nixon, Henry Kissinger
> and I have made.
> Briefly, I agree to give them Teng Shan-li's

journal, which is very damaging to Chou, Nixon
and Kissinger. In return they will make it possible
for you to travel safely to a place I designate in
Europe. And they promise to absolve me of any
wrongdoing and make it possible for me to
practice law in Europe.

Li-fa, I have come to realize how deeply I love
you. If you are willing, I want to marry you and
live with you in some sheltered place in the world
where we can both live fulfilled lives. When we
are together we can agree on choosing such a
place.

I believe you are in serious danger in China,
Li-fa, and I could not live unless I knew that
you were safe. I do love you so!

You have the choice, of course. You may refuse
to come out of China and join me. Or you can
come out safely and then tell me that you have
no interest in marrying me. As long as I'm
satisfied that you have made a free and uncoerced
decision, I'll abide by it.

If you come to me, I will do everything
possible to make sure that you will never regret
it. I will cherish you, but I will also be respectful
of your individuality and independence.

Please come, Li-fa. *Please*.

                                                    I love you,
                                                            Matt

On January 21, 1972, which was the day Matt traveled
to Europe, Henry Kissinger claimed he still did not know
whether Wang Li-fa would agree to leave China.

"Chou delivered your letter to Miss Wang; I know
that," Kissinger told Matt. They were standing just inside
the door of the old Cabinet Room in the family quarters of
the White House residence. Matt had just been given his
pardon, his medal, and his citation by the President in the
yellow oval room on the third floor of the White House

residence. Only Matt's father, Secretary of State Rogers, and Kissinger were there to view the brief ceremony.

The President had stood in front of the marble fireplace, stiff and ill at ease, with a Marine Corps major at his side. The pale yellow room seemed too feminine for a military ceremony. The paintings on the curved walls were sitting-room subjects—a reclining woman in one, a Venetian seascape, a colonial portrait of a woman in a white collar and lace bonnet.

Ezra Thompson stood at his son's left. Matt wanted this symbolic vindication for his father more than for himself. When he'd told Ezra that Kissinger was going to fire him, the old professor had taken the news badly. He had barraged his son with recriminations about misplaced loyalty and a ruined career. Ezra had watched the medal ceremony with a half-smile. He had accepted Henry Kissinger's explanation that Matt's award must be kept totally secret lest the Chinese be offended.

After the President wordlessly shook Matt's hand, Ezra Thompson had embraced his son. "I'm very proud," he whispered.

When William Rogers had offered Matt perfunctory congratulations and left, Ezra and Nixon had begun to talk about Whittier College. Kissinger took Matt's arm and walked him to the hallway.

"So what do we do," Kissinger asked, "if the plane arrives and the lady is not on it?"

"You had just better be sure that she is," Matt said. "I leave tonight and I'll be prepared to deliver on my end. But if she doesn't arrive in Vienna on January twenty-fourth, you don't get Teng's journal—and that is all there is to it."

"I will notify you as soon as I know," Kissinger said. "Chou is willing to let her go."

"So he says."

"So he says," Kissinger agreed. "That leaves it up to her. If she has a boyfriend in Tientsin, perhaps she won't come."

"Perhaps. If she doesn't, the deal is off."

"My people will be at the Vienna airport on the twenty-fourth to meet her airplane, and I assume you will be there too—with the diary."

Matt laughed. "Not exactly. As soon as I know she is there I will have someone deliver it, but I'm not going to let you snatch it."

"We would never do that, Matthew," Kissinger said solemnly. "We have gone a long way to honor our commitments, have we not? You have your pardon and the other things, and so far we have nothing."

"You're doing fine, Henry. Just keep up the good work," Matt said, walking into the broad hallway.

Kissinger turned and walked beside him. Matt pushed the button for the small elevator. "If you and Chou were smart, you would roll her up in a rug and put her on that airplane regardless of what she decided."

Kissinger smiled. "Something like that occurred to me. But the statistical prediction for forced marriages is very poor. Here is your elevator. *Bon voyage*. Al Haig will meet you at the Vienna airport."

As he descended in the tiny elevator lined with mirrors and marquetry, Matthew opened the large leather box to look at his Medal of Freedom, lying on its ornate ribbon. Kissinger had done a good job. The citation the military aide had read at the ceremony included an account of Matt's kidnapping and knee injury, and it made him sound like an intrepid go-between.

It was coerced, of course. That mitigating thought flashed across Matt's mind but instantly he rejected it. The citation speaks the truth, he vigorously affirmed to himself. That is the central and controlling fact. They *owe* me the medal, on the facts. Never mind the means to that end.

Fifty-four

It was snowing lightly at Vienna's Flughafen Wien-Schwechat when Matt Thompson's Air France flight landed there, a few minutes late. He looked at his watch as he walked up the aisle toward the jetway. Allowing for Austrian Immigration and Customs, there was still plenty of time.

In the doorway of the airport restaurant Matt looked around uncertainly. A short man with close-cropped blond hair wiped his mouth with a napkin and stood at a table near the large windows. He smiled and gestured toward the vacant chair at his table. Matt walked toward him, looking at him intently; he smiled tentatively and then broadly.

"Ron?" Matt asked.

"Hello, Matthew. Care for some lunch?"

"God, I didn't know you. The blond hair and all that weight you've put on. And that baggy suit? Who are you supposed to be today?" Matt shucked his coat and sat across from Ron D'Amico.

"The name is Patricio Palanza, sir, from Milano. I deal in tile and brick, you know."

Matt looked around the dining room. "Do you have the—ah—the briefcase?"

"In a safe place and closely guarded. You too are closely guarded, as you have been since you got off your plane. The people I have here are very reliable Italian boys, very good at their profession."

"I'm grateful, Ron. I'm really suspicious of Kissinger

631

and Haig. I've been afraid that they would try to strong-arm me if I were unprotected.''

"No problem. Let's be sure I understand the message. A plane arrives here from Cairo in a little while. If a certain person gets off, you give me a signal and I hand over the package I picked up in Switzerland. Right?''

"You hand it to a man named Al Haig, who works for Kissinger.''

"Will he find us?''

"I'm sure he will. Is the private plane ready to go?'' Matt asked.

"Under guard. I flew in on it.''

"Okay. We go briskly from Customs to the plane and then leave.''

"The pilot needs to file a flight plan and you'll have to clear Immigration before we can leave.''

"Okay. Tell him you're returning to Switzerland. Ron, there is a remote chance that someone will try and hurt us between the time the lady gets off the plane and the time we take off. There's a Chinese fellow who may be harboring a grudge.''

D'Amico smiled. "As soon as your friend clears Customs we walk straight out to the curb. There's a car there with very thick walls. We will drive to the plane; it will be safe and very quick.''

Matt nodded. "I'm really impressed with the way you've set this up, Ron. Do you live in Europe?''

"No small talk, Counselor. And call me Palanza, please. The less you know about my personal life, the better, right?''

"Okay. But tell me this: Is that a wig or your real hair?''

"You want the name of my stylist—right? It's the real thing. I had him touch it up a little to match the picture on my passport, that's all.''

"Okay, Mr. Palanzo, let's go,'' Matt said, standing. "It won't be long now.''

"Palanza. Palanz-a. . . . We go out to the left. She comes in at one of the international gates. We can stand at the window and watch her go through Customs and Immigration. If you see her, just say 'There she is' to me. I'll send for the briefcase. Okay?''

"Okay," said Matt.

Matt had wiped his hands with his handkerchief. He was more nervous than he could ever remember being. His stomach was knotted. He had read novels about people whose stomachs were tied in knots, but he'd never experienced the feeling before.

If she wasn't on the plane, he would have to fly to Switzerland with Ron D'Amico; he would have Ron give the journal back to the Swiss lawyer for safekeeping.

Two minutes before the plane was due, Al Haig arrived, flanked by two tall young men in trench coats. He left them twenty feet away and walked up to Matt.

"Where's the manuscript, Thompson?" Haig said in a low voice, his jaw barely moving.

"Well, hello, General," Matt replied. "You don't get it unless Li-fa gets off the airplane. And"—Matt turned to look at Haig's bodyguards—"your hoods make me nervous. Please tell them to go away."

"Fuck you," Haig gritted.

"Okay. If they stay, you don't get the journal, even if she *is* on the plane. I don't deliver if I'm nervous."

"You prick." Haig walked to his men and spoke to them quietly. They disappeared.

The passengers from some flight had been trickling into the large, tiled Customs area as Haig walked back to the window, on Matt's right side.

"Here I am," D'Amico said as he came up to Matt's left side. "This is the Cairo flight coming in now."

Matt looked intently at every woman who came through the distant doors. The window was scratched and dirty. He wondered if he would recognize Li-fa if she came into Customs.

Suddenly, Matt touched D'Amico's arm, then grabbed

his wrist. Matt smiled and turned toward the exit doors. "There she is!" he said.

"General, you just stay right here," D'Amico said to Alexander Haig. D'Amico took a small radio from his pocket and pressed several buttons. "We'll have your package here for you in just a minute."

Fifty-five

It was not a large bar. The hotel that it served was small itself and catered to a year-round clientele of salesmen and other commercial travelers. The skiers could be found at the inns on the east side of the small Swiss town, near the ski lifts and the ice rink. As on most evenings, the barmaid was serving seven or eight beer-drinking Europeans in business suits. At one of the four tables a pair of Englishmen were finishing their gins. A young American and an Oriental girl, oblivious to the television sound and the noise from the bar, talked earnestly to each other at the table in the corner. Her hand lay on the table. His were in his lap.

The Swiss bartender looked at the television screen in response to a customer's pointed complaint. He reached up and changed channels, then shrugged. "It is on all of them," he said. "It is Nixon; he is arriving in China."

The young American looked up at the television set. The black-haired girl turned so that she could see it too.

A television newsman explained in German that the American President's plane had landed in Peking and had just rolled to a stop where a small honor guard of the

People's Liberation Army was ranked parallel to a red carpet.

As Richard Nixon walked down the stairway and began to shake Chou En-lai's outstretched hand, Matt Thompson covered Li-fa's hand with his own.

"What do you suppose they are saying to each other?" she asked.

Matt smiled and shrugged. "Nixon is asking why the crowd isn't bigger, I suppose."

"And the Premier?"

"He's asking why Nixon let us get away."

"He's wondering that anyway, I'm sure. What's the answer to that, darling?"

"Because we held the trumps, of course. Nixon gave up two losing tricks to get at the card he wanted so much."

"The Premier plays bridge; he will understand that," Li-fa said. "Why are they shaking hands so long?"

"This is called a photo opportunity at the White House. They don't want to disappoint a single photographer."

"I want to watch it all," the young woman said. "I feel that I have too much invested in this moment. Perhaps my whole life. I don't want to miss seeing any of it."

"Of course, darling. We both do. We'll sit here and watch it all."

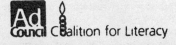